INFINITY KINGS

ALSO BY ADAM SILVERA

More Happy Than Not

History Is All You Left Me

They Both Die at the End

The First to Die at the End

The Infinity Cycle

Infinity Son

Infinity Reaper

With Becky Albertalli

What If It's Us

Here's to Us

INFINITY KINGS

ADAM SILVERA

Quill Tree Books
An Imprint of HarperCollinsPublishers

Quill Tree Books is an imprint of HarperCollins Publishers.

Infinity Kings
 For information address HarperCollins Children's Books, a division of HarperCollins Publishers, 195 Broadway, New York, NY 10007.
www.epicreads.com

Library of Congress Control Number: 2023948725
ISBN 978-0-06-288236-3 (trade bdg.) — ISBN 978-0-06-338256-5 (int.)

Typography by Erin Fitzsimmons
24 25 26 27 28 LBC 5 4 3 2 1
First Edition

For those who followed me to the end of infinity.

Shout-outs to Sabaa Tahir and Marie Lu, the first champions of this series, years before this lifelong fantasy became a reality.

THE WORLD OF GLEAMCRAFT

Gleamcrafters—practitioners with powers. Applicable to both celestials and specters.

Celestials—their true origins unknown, these people carry powers that have a connection to the stars and sky. Some powers are presented at birth, others surface later in life. The range of their abilities is wide. Celestials can be distinguished by the way their eyes glow like different corners of the universe as they use their gleam. Notable group: the Spell Walkers.

Specters—sixty years ago, alchemy was developed as a way to use the blood of creatures to give humans powers. People who receive their powers this way are known as specters, and the range of their abilities is limited to the blood of that creature's breed. Specters can be distinguished by the way their eyes burn like eclipses as they use their gleam. Notable group: the Blood Casters.

DRAMATIS PERSONAE

THE REY FAMILY

Emil Rey—a reincarnated specter with phoenix blood who can cast gray and gold fire, self-heal his mortal wounds, sense feelings from other phoenixes, fly, and resurrect. Known as Fire-Wing and Infinity Son.

Brighton Rey—a specter who drank Reaper's Blood for the powers of a phoenix, hydra, and ghost. Known as Infinity Savior and Infinity Reaper.

Carolina Rey—Emil and Brighton's mother. No powers of her own.

Leonardo Rey (Deceased)—Emil and Brighton's father. No powers of his own.

SPELL WALKERS AND ALLIES

Maribelle Lucero—a celestial-specter hybrid who can cast dark yellow fire, fly, self-heal her mortal wounds, retrocycle, and detect danger. Spell Walker heir.

Ness Arroyo—a specter with shifter blood who can change his appearance at will. Former Blood Caster. Recent ally to Spell Walkers.

Iris Simone-Chambers—a celestial with powerhouse strength and skin impervious to most gleam attacks. New leader of the Spell Walkers.

Atlas Haas (Deceased)—a celestial who could conjure winds.

Wesley Young—a celestial who runs at swift-speed.

Eva Nafisi—a celestial who can heal others but gets harmed in the process.

Prudencia Mendez—a celestial with the power of telekinesis.

Ruth Rodriquez—a celestial who can create clones of herself.

Bautista de León (Deceased)—a reincarnated specter with phoenix blood who could cast gray fire, self-heal his mortal wounds, resurrect, and remember details from his past life. Founder of the Spell Walkers.

Sera Córdova (Deceased)—an alchemist and celestial who had psychic visions. Founding member.

BLOOD CASTERS AND ALLIES

Luna Marnette—a supreme alchemist who created the Blood Casters. No powers of her own.

Dione Henri—a specter with hydra blood who can grow extra/regrow missing body parts and run in bursts of swift-speed.

Stanton (Deceased)—a specter with basilisk blood who had serpentine senses and venomous, acidic, petrifying, and paralytic abilities.

June—a specter with ghost blood who can phase through solid objects and possess people.

POLITICIANS

Senator Edward Iron—a presidential candidate who opposes gleamcraft. No powers of his own.

Barrett Bishop—a vice-presidential candidate and chief architect of the Bounds. No powers of his own.

Congresswoman Nicolette Sunstar—a celestial presidential candidate who can create burning hot dazzling lights.

Senator Shine Lu—a celestial vice-presidential candidate who can turn invisible.

HALO KNIGHTS AND PHOENIXES

Tala Castillo—a Halo Knight with no powers of her own.

Wyatt Warwick—a Halo Knight with no powers of his own.

Crest Calder—a Halo Knight with no powers of his own. Commander of the Bronze Wings.

Nox—an obsidian phoenix that excels at tracking. Wyatt's companion.

Roxana—a light howler phoenix with stormlike powers. Tala's companion.

Soleil—a breath spawn phoenix known for spontaneous combustion. Crest's companion.

OTHER NOTABLE CHARACTERS

Keon Máximo (Deceased)—an alchemist and specter with phoenix blood who could cast gold fire, self-heal his mortal wounds, and resurrect. He developed the alchemy to give normal people powers and became the first specter.

Darren Bowes—a celestial who can cast illusions.

Lore—a progressive influencer.

The Silver Star Slayer—a conservative YouTuber. Real name is Russell Robbins.

So long as you fight the darkness,
you stand in the light.

—SABAA TAHIR,

A TORCH AGAINST THE NIGHT

ONE
LIFETIMES

EMIL

My past lives will be the death of me.

No one was supposed to know about my resurrection power; that secret was supposed to die with me, but my brother straight outed that to over a million of his online followers to make me the villain and himself the hero. Brighton is a mess, but never in a billion lifetimes would I have bet he'd kick me out of a phoenix's nest like this. I'm shaking while holding the phone, right as Brighton exits out of his Instagram live. The one he ended by telling everyone that he would stop the Infinity Son even if that means becoming the Infinity Reaper to do so.

My brother has threatened my life.

And he's called for backup—an army.

Brighton has thrown an inferno of heat my way by revealing I'm the scion of the very first specter, Keon Máximo, as well as the founder of the Spell Walkers, Bautista de León. I'm going to be blamed for all their crimes even though I don't remember living those lives.

No one is going to care.

Except my crew.

I'm outside in the New Ember Sanctuary's courtyard with everyone—my mom, my best friend, the Spell Walkers, and both boys who get my heart going—and we haven't gone back inside the castle since we last saw Brighton speeding off across the bridge and into the forest. Everyone is freaking out and talking over each other about Brighton's live, but I can't focus. I'm stuck thinking about every last person who's dreaming about immortality now that they know resurrection is possible. Most heartbreakingly, how every single phoenix is now going to become targeted because they're the only creatures whose blood can turn a mortal human into an immortal specter.

Brighton has marked all phoenixkind for death.

Deaths even they won't be able to return from.

I flash back to the short life of Gravesend—the century phoenix who was both born and killed in my arms—and the memory of her being stabbed by the infinity-ender dagger haunts me. I'm swaying, like I might faint on the spot. I wanted to protect Gravesend, to give her the longest lives she deserved, and now her blood is running through my brother's veins and making him all-powerful.

I failed to protect one phoenix before. It'll be impossible to protect them all.

I look up to the night sky, where a cycle of phoenixes are flying under the stars, living their lives, unaware that everything is about to come crashing down. I can practically picture all the feathers that will be floating on rivers of blood.

All of this because Brighton got so damn pissed after I overpowered him in battle. There's been a lot of throwback moments where I didn't feel connected to Brighton, but nothing has felt more severing than watching him call a manhunt against his own brother. Maybe the problem is Brighton doesn't see me as his brother ever since we discovered that I wasn't his twin, like we'd spent our entire lives believing. Our father had found me out on the street, burning up like I had a fever, and he assumed I was just a baby abandoned under the sun. No one thought that I had been reborn in phoenix fire.

I wish I hadn't resurrected.

I wish I wasn't even alive.

I won't be much longer if my brother gets his way.

Life as the Infinity Son is not a life I want to live anyway.

These dark thoughts are digging deeper and deeper into me; I got to fight my way out of this. That starts with getting some space away from everyone cursing out Brighton over his betrayal like he can hear them.

I look up at the Sanctuary, a gorgeous two-story stone castle that a city boy like me still isn't used to. I want to summon my burning wings and fly up to the south-facing tower, which serves as a nest for baby phoenixes. On my first day here, I was taken up to that spot so I could chill out and catch my breath since I was so stressed. If I went up there now, there's no way I would ever come back down. Not when I know what showdown awaits me if I do.

Halo Knights are staring at me from their windows and the bridges that connect the towers. They already weren't about that Emil Rey life since they're the protectors of phoenixkind and I'm not just a specter with the blood of a gray sun phoenix running through my own, but they're now seeing me as the creator of specters everywhere. And now that I've turned these sacred grounds into a battlefield, I know they're going to want me out of here more than ever. I can't even get mad at them for that.

I turn, walking toward the open door with the brass knocker that's shaped like an egg. I hear Ma calling my name, but I keep going until I'm out by the moonlit stream. I take deep breaths as I run my fingers through the water, but my peace is about to be super short-lived because there are footsteps approaching. I get up and find my favorite shape-shifter, Ness Arroyo, and my favorite Halo Knight, Wyatt Warwick. Two of my favorite humans ever if I'm being straight up. Ness is limping after his own fight with Brighton, but that doesn't stop him from picking up speed to keep up with Wyatt. They both reach for my hand at the same time and exchange glares because they're not exactly each other's favorite humans. Probably because there's a lot of confusing romantic feelings flying around. But no one gets ahold of me because I back away like I might burn them if they touch me, and the fear of not being able to protect everyone is the only feeling I can afford to pay attention to right now.

"Everything is ending," I say, my voice cracking. "And I'm too powerless to do a damn thing about it."

"You're not powerless, firefly," Ness says.

He knows better than most. We're always finding ourselves in situations where we got to have each other's backs, like tonight when I helped bust him out of the Bounds with my phoenix fire—and a lot of help—before the other prisoners could tear him apart with their own powers. Ness also said it's as if we're stuck in our own infinity cycle where we keep saving each other's lives. That was before we kissed for the first time, something that surprised me because not only was he supposed to be dead, but because he's so out-of-my-league beautiful it's as if he's using his morphing power to make himself so perfect.

But he doesn't.

Everything in front of me is all Ness.

The amber eyes.

The dark curls.

The beautiful brown skin.

The lips that gave me the kiss of a lifetime.

But if I'm not careful, he'll actually get killed because of me. I would never be able to forgive myself if someone who has survived multiple assassination attempts from his father died because he got too close to me.

"I have powers, but I don't have the power to stop what's coming," I say.

"You're not expected to stop it alone," Wyatt says in his English accent. His broad shoulders are sinking, like he's unable to stand tall because the weight of everything is pinning him down too. "Before we map out the best way to lay into your brother, we need to prepare an evacuation of the Sanctuary. Brighton's unspeakable actions have now put every single phoenix at risk."

Wyatt stares at me dead-on with his blue eyes, which first reminded me of Brighton's flames and do so even more now. Except Wyatt would never hurt me. Unlike the other Halo Knights, Wyatt has never blamed me for being a walking violation of everything his movement stands for since he knows I didn't choose this life of being a specter and would never because I love phoenixes with my whole damn heart. He even thinks I could become a Halo Knight after all the work I've done re-creating the Starstifler, a potion that can bind the powers of any specter. But maybe I'm stupid to trust someone I haven't even known for a month when my own brother, who I grew up with, just tried forcing that very potion down my throat so he could kick my ass in battle.

There's no wrapping my head around being at war with Brighton.

But I can protect some lives now.

"What do we got to do to get the phoenixes out of here?" I ask.

"Unclear. I'll need to get in contact with my commander and the other higher-ups to alert them of the issue," Wyatt says.

"You got this, then?" Ness asks. "We've got bigger problems."

Wyatt's pale cheeks are flushed red as he bites his tongue. "Such as?"

Ness rises to the challenge. "I don't know if you're aware, but we have an election going on in this country. One where my dangerous father is this close to securing the presidency thanks to his insidious lies and new shape-shifting powers that the public doesn't know about. If he had no problem abducting his political rival and organizing a terrorist attack to have his own son killed, you think he won't sentence every last one of us to death once he has the full force of the government in the palm of his hand?"

Wyatt's jaw drop is very theatrical. "You know, I can't say that anyone had me aware of the election happening between Senator Edward Iron and Congresswoman Nicolette Sunstar, who happens to be the first ever celestial candidate pursuing presidency in the United States of America. This is all absolute news to me, and I thank you for that education." He takes a second to fluff his brown hair while peering over at Ness. "Perhaps my sarcasm got lost with my accent, but I'd like to make it very clear that I was being highly sarcastic just now."

"I don't have to be good at reading people to catch that," Ness says with a steely gaze. He adds, "And I'm *excellent* at reading people."

"I must cast a little doubt on that after the way you provoked Brighton."

"Emil needed to see that Brighton wouldn't let anyone get in his way. Not even his own brother. I'm sort of the poster boy for family betraying you."

"And as truly unfortunate as your father's treatment of you has been, perhaps your read on Brighton was missing the pages where he would turn on everyone if pushed away."

Ness is quiet, like he's thinking about the blood on his hands.

Before the power brawl, Ness tried convincing me to get Brighton to drink the Starstifler before he could grow out of control. I totally see where Ness was coming from, I do. He was raised by a manipulative man who molded him into a mouthpiece against celestials, painting them as nothing but dangerous individuals who had to be put in their place before they could rise above everyone else. Ness got smart, but it was too late. He doesn't want to see me get played by my brother like that. He proved himself right when he shape-shifted into me to get Brighton to take the potion and got attacked in return. There's some light bruising around his face from when Brighton was laying into him with super-fast punches—Brighton didn't even know that wasn't me until he looked up and saw me in the doorway. Ness took one for the team by showing me that my brother is willing to kick my ass if I get in his way, but the thing is, it's hard to feel like a team because Ness went and did that behind my back.

"I wish you hadn't done that," I say.

He sighs. "You needed to learn this lesson sooner rather than later. Brighton is not at the height of his strength yet. You can still beat him."

"Yeah, but I never wanted to get into a fight with him."

"It was inevitable."

"You say that like it's written in the stars," Wyatt says. "This isn't destiny. You made this happen by pushing Brighton."

Ness looks like he wants to clock Wyatt, but restrains himself. "Did I push Brighton to kill Stanton?"

I flash back to earlier tonight during the battle at the Bounds, where Brighton ripped out the heart of the Blood Caster with basilisk blood before setting it on fire. I get that Brighton had been terrorized and tortured by Stanton, but still . . . the way he showed no remorse. The way he smiled after taking a life. The life of a killer, but a life. However long I get before I die, that smile where my brother became a killer will haunt me. That should've been a one-off, but Brighton has already made it super clear that he will play judge, jury, and executioner if it means winning this war. I can't make him see reason. It's legit got me trying to see if I'm looking at this all wrong. It wouldn't be the first time I've been pushed to be a better soldier since my methods aren't as charged as everyone else's.

"Brighton only killed Stanton to save us," I say, hoping someone will back up this hollow lie.

"You know damn well that he doesn't care about me," Ness says, and he closes the space between us and rests his hands on my shoulders. "I don't care that he only cares about protecting you. That's fine. But you need to let it sink in that Brighton is Team Brighton above everyone else. Even you."

"He's only running his mouth when he talks about killing me."

"Is he? Do you think the world will believe me when I tell them that my father is behind my mother's murder? And how he organized the Blackout to pin my death on the Spell Walkers? They won't, but it's true." His amber eyes are tearing up. "I got lucky and survived. I won't let your final thought be how surprising it is that you've been killed at your brother's hands."

I shrug him off, as if that'll help me shake away these thoughts of Brighton using any number of means to murder me. Would he lay into me with swift-punches that come at me so fast I might not be able to think? Incinerate me with his fire-bolts? Reach into my chest and rip out my heart, or better yet, stab me in the heart with an infinity-ender dagger so I can't one day resurrect and rise to power to defeat him?

This is all nonsense.

Brighton's ego was wounded when he hopped on Instagram. I bet once he settles down and catches his breath he'll try and undo his call for war against me and the Spell Walkers.

"Brighton isn't going to kill me," I declare.

Ness shakes his head. "Emil, you can't possibly be this stubborn or naive—"

"Perhaps you should go for a walk," Wyatt suggests, stepping to Ness and pushing his chest. "Your father has inflicted unforgivable pain and grief on your life, but that doesn't mean everyone's family members are out for the blood of their own."

Ness shoves Wyatt so hard that he falls onto his back. "Don't ever touch me again," he says coolly. The threat is deeper than Wyatt probably recognizes. As a former Blood Caster, Ness has been forced to kill other people for his own survival. I see how it eats away at him, how he wakes up and finds himself morphed like his victims because he's so haunted that he can't stop thinking about them. And if Wyatt keeps trying him, there might be another corpse added to his body count.

"Cut it out!" I shout.

This is so stupid, everyone is acting out in this sanctuary.

"I'm afraid I must defend myself," Wyatt says as he gets up, wiping his palms. "Now, Ness, I make no claims of being the best fighter, but you should be warned that I hold my own in quarrels just fine."

"Just shut up and throw a punch," Ness says, his fists ready.

Wyatt charges Ness with a wide swing like a phoenix's wings in battle, and just as Ness is about to jump into an uppercut, they both go flying into the air as if swept up by gale-force winds. I turn to find Prudencia standing outside the Sanctuary's front doors, her eyes glowing like skipping stars as she telekinetically suspends Ness and Wyatt.

"Are you children for real?" Prudencia asks.

"Put me down," Ness says.

"I quite like it up here," Wyatt says. "Feels like flying."

"You're being restrained until someone tells me what the hell is going on," Prudencia says as she comes closer to me. Ness and Wyatt talk over each other, and if Prudencia wanted to fling them into the river that runs along the forest so they can cool off, I honestly wouldn't be mad. "Shut up!" And they do, almost as if she's used her power to suck the air out of them so they can't speak. "Emil, what happened?"

My head hangs low. I can't even meet my best friend's gaze. "They're fighting over what Brighton will or won't do."

She stares up at Wyatt and Ness. "You guys don't know Brighton like Emil does."

"Or like you do," I say.

Prudencia looks haunted as she stares into the distance.

Ever since Brighton and I met Prudencia in our freshman year of high school, they've been living this will-they, won't-they life. I've been rooting for them to get their act together because I've always thought Prudencia could keep Brighton in check, and I loved the idea of welcoming Prudencia into our family even more than we already have, especially since she was living with a pretty terrible aunt after her parents were killed. The timing was just never right for the Brighton-Prudencia love story until a few days after Brighton drank the Reaper's Blood, which gave him this deluxe set of powers sourced from a phoenix, hydra, and two ghosts. But before Brighton became the Infinity Reaper, he was dying. The doctor said he had weeks, maybe months to live. Nothing like death to make someone change their life. Brighton and Prudencia got close, and it was a dope shot of happiness with all the other heartbreaking things we had going on at the time, like when our mother had been taken captive by the Blood Casters, or when I was grieving Ness because I thought he was dead.

Then everything went wrong.

I should've known it was too good to be true—that Brighton wasn't going to love someone more than he loves himself. But Prudencia made it clear that this wasn't some plot twist that caught her off guard. Right when Brighton and I were beginning to battle, Prudencia used her power against him. Brighton was pissed she didn't take his side and she let him know that his side wasn't worth taking. He tried bad-mouthing her, but Prudencia was unfazed, as if she had built some telekinetic shield around herself to ward away anything that could hurt her. But I can tell she's as heartbroken and betrayed by Brighton as a lover as I am by Brighton as a brother.

Prudencia gracefully lowers Ness and Wyatt to the ground. "I won't be gentle next time."

Ness crosses his arms. "If I can't change your mind about Brighton, I'll stay out of your family affairs and go deal with my own."

He walks away, heading back into the Sanctuary even after I call his name.

"That simplifies things," Wyatt says.

"Look, you won, okay? You pissed him off."

"I wasn't seeking to piss him off. I was simply—"

"You're pissing me off too right now," I snap because I came out here for peace and haven't gotten it.

Wyatt is just as stunned that I've come at him like this as I am. "I'll give you a moment." He turns on his heel and returns to the Sanctuary's grounds.

Prudencia comes over and gives me a hug right as I feel like I'm about to collapse. It's like she's holding me up, as we've had to do for each other a lot in the four years we've been friends. I'm really missing that life I got to live before I was the Infinity Son or Fire-Wing or whatever people want to nickname me that makes me look more like some superhero than an eighteen-year-old kid who never wanted to fight in this war. I want to go back to the times when I was there for Prudencia when she was going through her breakup with this celestial Dominic instead of the heartbreak that comes with my brother's betrayal. Or even how Prudencia was there for me when I was grieving my dad instead of wondering how we're going to deal with my brother wanting me dead.

"Am I being a total idiot about Brighton?" I ask.

"If you are, then I am too," Prudencia says. "Brighton refusing to part with powers he should've never stolen in the first place is one thing. Threatening your life to keep them is another."

"Yeah, I wasn't betting on that either."

Memories pop up again, this time fully centered around Brighton. How he tried keeping a brave face when he found out he wasn't going to be valedictorian. How upset he got the morning of our birthday when he saw another YouTuber's video of a Spell Walker showdown go viral instead of his own. How let down he was when the meet-up he was hosting for his online fans was underattended. How defeated he was when we didn't get powers on our birthday. But nothing has eaten away at him more than my phoenix fire bursting to life for the first time, taking me down a path I would do anything to go back in time and reverse. Not Brighton, though. He pushed me into a world of Spell Walkers and Blood Casters, of Reaper's Blood and Starstiflers, and now he's going to rule if I . . .

If I can't stop him.

"Brighton isn't going to kill me," I declare again. "But that doesn't mean I won't have to fight him."

"I'm on your side. Us against whatever sad army he builds."

"I'm hoping it won't just be us. Come on."

We head back into the Sanctuary, where all my people are still in the courtyard. There's Ma sitting on a bench with Eva Nafisi, the team's healer. The two of them got really close when they were held captive inside Senator Iron's manor. Iris Simone-Chambers is on her phone. She's a legacy Spell Walker who took over as leader after her parents were killed in the Blackout. She's short, but I've always thought of her as small and mighty because of her powerhouse strength and power-proof skin that protects her against most spell-work. Wesley Young is holding Ruth Rodriquez close, rubbing her arms to keep her warm on this night, which is only getting chillier the longer it drags on. They've been dating for a minute, a power couple with lots of heart. Their baby, Esther, has got to be somewhere back inside the Sanctuary, probably being monitored by one—or even several—of Ruth's clones that she can conjure at will. If needed, Wesley can always go grab Esther in the blink of an eye with his swift-speed. And then there's Ness and Wyatt, keeping their distance like the sun and the moon.

The closer I get, the more eyes on me. I can't even look at Ma, who must be cycling through a thousand terrible thoughts of her own. The courtyard has gone quiet except for the overhead phoenix screeches that catch Iris's attention, and she hangs up her call.

"How you feeling, buddy?" Wesley asks.

"Heartbroken, anxious, terrified," I say.

"A day in the life," Iris says.

I've had it extraordinarily bad for a couple months, but this has been all Iris has known since childhood. I get how she's strong enough to lift a car over her own head, but even her power can't help her carry the weight of the world like she does. I'm in legit awe.

I feel this pressure to hype everyone up with some pep talk about how we're going to get through this together. But that's not what I got in me, so I keep it real because that's all I can do. "I got to apologize to all of you. I'm so sorry for how much harder your lives have been since I entered the picture." I fight back my tears and add, "If I could've done this all differently, trust that I would've."

They look at one another with confused gazes and then back at me.

"No one's mad at you, Emil," Eva says.

"And we like having you around," Ruth says, then turns to Ma. "Carolina too."

"Brighton is the pain in the ass," Wesley says. "But even he wasn't the biggest pain in the ass."

"Until now," Iris says. "Out of all the power that boy has, his platform is his biggest. I was on the phone with Ash Hyperion just now, and there are still no leads on Sunstar's disappearance . . ." She shoots a look over at Ness, whose head is hanging low since he was forced to aid his father in the abduction of the congresswoman. ". . . but finding Sunstar is probably useless for our cause anyway since Brighton's messaging has only further tanked our reputation. And I . . ." Iris sits on the bench beside Eva, holding her girlfriend's hand. "I think I'm ready to take the L. Put the Spell Walkers to rest."

Everyone's quiet.

In a world where my brother threatens to kill me, this is still shocking.

Ever since the Blackout earlier this year, the next generation of Spell Walkers has been risking their lives to keep the people of New York safe from all sorts of threats. They've protected celestials from the government enforcers who try to lock them up in the Bounds or kill them dead in the streets. They've gone up against celestials and specters who terrorize those without powers of their own—even saving the very people who hate them simply because they do have powers of their own. And out of this new wave of Spell Walkers, only two are legacies—Iris and Maribelle Lucero, a celestial-specter hybrid with a complicated past. Maribelle has always been the one who hates saving the people who hate her, but Iris has always remained a dutiful Spell Walker in honor of her fallen parents. That fire within seems to be extinguishing.

"But then they win," Wesley says. So this is news to him too. "We can't let that happen."

"My entire life has been about fighting," Iris says. "Yours hasn't."

Wesley got kicked out by his parents when he was fourteen years old. He was living on the streets and would dash in and out of supermarkets and restaurants for groceries and hot meals until he met his best friend, Atlas Haas, the Spell Walker who was killed last month. No matter how heavy all that is, it's not the same as the lifetime of hate Iris has experienced.

"You've been in this forever so you could create a better world, Iris," Wesley says. "It won't always be this way."

"When will the fighting end?" Iris asks.

I've asked myself that question a lot.

"I don't know," Wesley says. "But it's going to be impossible for us to get on with our lives if we don't fight."

"You're not in this like I am. You have literally started your own family in the time I've met you. Eva and I would love to have what you and Ruth do before everything comes crashing down on us."

"I understand that. Just know that it's no joyride leaving my girlfriend and daughter for weeks at a time for their own safety and wondering if I'll ever be able to get back to them."

Ruth offers Iris a small smile. "I'm so looking forward to watching you and Eva become mothers. Just know in the meantime you're our family too." She looks around at all of us and ends her gaze on me. "You all are."

"I'm delighted to be considered family," Wyatt says, both hands to his heart.

"Mostly all of you," Wesley corrects with a grin.

I step closer, like I'm about to form a huddle with everyone. "I can't force anyone to fight, but if we're all game, I think we've got to give this one last push before we tap out."

"Easy for you to say," Iris says. "You've been fighting for what, two months?"

"Not even," I admit. Almost, but not quite. "I don't envy the weight you've been carrying your entire life, Iris. Let me help."

"Let us all help," Ma says, wiping tears from her cheeks. "However we can."

Iris reaches over Eva to give Ma a gentle squeeze. Then her gaze is back on me. "Assuming Sunstar is even alive, if we can't find her and do everything in our power to convince everyone to vote her into office, then no more Spell Walkers. I won't give up the rest of my life fighting for people who don't want to be saved. Deal?"

"Deal," I say.

Election Day is our deadline.

No Sunstar means no Spell Walkers.

Other heroes can rise up, and they'll have to if we can't get it together.

Who knows, some new blood could be good, but for now, we're all going to fight.

"How do we do this?" Iris asks.

She's not coming in with ideas.

She's letting me help like I asked.

She's letting me lead.

In a fight against my brother, I got to become a leader.

"Um . . ." I look around at our team—four celestials, a specter, a Halo Knight, and a mother who is as ordinary as the life she used to lead. We have a lot of enemies to take down and not a lot of time to do so. "Okay, Wyatt, begin the evacuation process so we can get the phoenixes and Halo Knights to safety. Wesley, figure out our next hiding spot. Somewhere that's removed from everyone so we don't have to disturb anyone's lives any more than we have. Iris, take the lead on Sunstar since you're already in talks with her husband."

"I could help," Ness speaks up. "It's partly my fault."

"No one blames you," I say. "Your father practically had a wand to your head." And the heads of my mother and Eva if Ness didn't agree to shift into Sunstar and impersonate her during the last presidential debate to tank her support.

"I could have let him kill me," Ness says.

"I'm so damn glad you didn't."

Our eyes are locked, but I can't help but feel Wyatt's on me too.

"If finding Sunstar means defeating my father, I'm in," Ness says.

"So we've got that covered," Iris says. "It's safe to assume that if Luna wasn't killed in the Bounds that she was freed with the other prisoners. We need confirmation either way."

"I can do some research," Ruth says.

"Great. So that leaves one last obvious threat."

Ma is sobbing harder, like this is all her fault since she brought that threat into this world. It's killing me; I can't even look at her.

"I'm going to handle Brighton," I say.

"Me too," Prudencia says.

"How do you plan on doing that?" Iris asks.

"I'll get him to take the Starstifler potion."

Iris shakes her head. "That might not be good enough."

I know what she's asking of me, but it's not happening.

"I'll die before I kill my brother," I say.

Everyone's silence is practically screaming, *Then you'll die!*

Life won't be worth living if it's always going to be like this, but it doesn't have to be—it *won't* be if I can get my life together.

If I fight, surviving will be worth it for everyone, not just myself.

But not if I hold back like I have been.

I got to get stronger, just like a gray sun phoenix who resurrects more powerful than its previous lifetime.

Once I win the war, I can drink the Starstifler, bind my powers, and restart my life.

One last rebirth.

If I want to be reborn, I have to stop my brother from pursuing the life he's wanted since we were kids fanboying over the Spell Walkers and pretending we had powers.

I got to go to war with Brighton with very real powers.

The Infinity Son versus the Infinity Reaper.

To end infinity, I have to beat the brother who will kill to keep it.

If I can't, I'll see him in the next life.

TWO

THE BRIGHTSIDERS

BRIGHTON

I am on my own, but not for long.

My army is waiting for me.

Running away from the Sanctuary and returning to the city to reach my followers hasn't been easy. I've been traveling on foot thanks to the dashing abilities I received from the blood of the golden-strand hydra, but unlike Wesley's celestial swift-speed, which zips him non-stop from Point A to Point B, my power only allows me to move in short bursts. I'm still getting the hang of moving this quickly too, such as making sure that I wasn't running off cliffs back when I was still in the forests, or the close call with a truck once I made my way to a Bronx intersection. I made it through in one piece, but even if it had crushed me, I would've regrown my bones and regenerated any lost limbs, also thanks to that hydra who died so I could become the ultimate survivor.

Still, there's so much more to being powerful than just surviving.

For instance, instead of being slowed down by the nature of my superspeed, traveling would be a lot smoother if I could fade away like a ghost and teleport as I've seen June do, or fly like a phoenix as my brother—as Emil can.

It's fine. I trust I'll get there.

After all, I was supposed to die and now I'm the Infinity Reaper.

I've been tapping into more powers as the days pass.

I will be unstoppable, but tonight, I have to accept my limitations. I take a break, resting my sore legs curbside of a bodega that has seen better days. I'll pop in to grab water in a moment but not before I go online to check on my followers, just as I have every other time I've needed to stop and catch my breath.

Since exposing Emil's past lifetimes, I've been garnering a lot of support. People eager to help, both with and without powers of their own. Unlike the Spell Walkers, I'm not going to turn normal people away as if phoenix fire and powerhouse strength are the only ways to win wars. Battles, maybe. But wars are won by numbers and I intend on having a legion to call my own. That legion will include those who can't burn their opponents or crush skulls. They're just as valuable in the fight, if not more sometimes, which I proved multiple times back before I had ultimate power.

I was once a nobody who no one wanted, and now I'm the one everybody wants as their leader.

Their king.

My inbox on Instagram says as much too. The majority of my DMs are from people who believe in me. They're sharing so much. Stories of betrayals. Motivations for justice. Even sympathy and love for putting a world of strangers before someone I grew up with through any means necessary. It makes the sting of everything I've been through tonight a little easier. More than that, it makes me feel less lonely.

There are plenty of people dragging me online too for not keeping my family business between family and wanting to hear Emil's side of things, but I ignore them for now. If they become really obnoxious, I'll block them, but I do want to give them a chance to not only follow me online, but join me in person too. I focus on those who trust me first, and as I've done during multiple stops tonight, I glance at their profiles before privately replying to them with where I'm hoping to meet my army at dawn. There are plenty of ordinary people, many who seem to have a lot of admiration for celestials on their individual pages. I remind myself to not trust everything I see online. I certainly have held parts of my life secret from my followers, and I can't rule out someone masking their identity after a certain someone who almost became my girlfriend hid the fact that she was a celestial for years.

Prudencia had some absolute nerve suggesting that I'm an egomaniac when all I'm doing is making the world a fairer place for people like her. I rose to the challenge and—

Never mind.

She chose the wrong side, and one day she'll be forced to thank me for making her life easier.

I'm going to go meet up with those who've chosen the right side.

First, I desperately need to hydrate, but I didn't bring my wallet when vacating the Sanctuary. I peek into the bodega, eyeing the fridge from the doorway. I got to get my hands on a gallon of water, maybe two. I consider explaining the situation to the man behind the counter, but I already know how this is going to go. He'll say no and I'll have to just take the water anyway, so I just cut to the chase and dash inside the bodega, grab two gallons of water, and dash right back out and down the block until I can round a dark corner so I can drink in peace. The entire time I'm chugging I remind myself that I'm not doing anything that Wesley himself didn't do when he was nothing but a celestial trying to survive on the streets. If he got to become a Spell Walker after all his petty thefts, then I'm still primed to become a hero too.

The hero.

I look to the sky, refreshed, and dash and dash until I've arrived at the meeting spot.

Whisper Fields, the park where I hosted a pathetic meet-up on my birthday last month. I had thought it would be cool to finally meet some of my followers and subscribers, and even sell them some merch on site, but only six Brightsiders showed up that afternoon. It was humiliating, but more than that, it was infuriating. Society cares more about prankster videos than the important coverage I was providing about the highs and lows of celestials. I worked really hard on that and received gratitude from a handful of people—technically over a handful of people but just barely. This is going to be different. I wouldn't have returned here if I didn't believe that with my whole heart, but I have come back because Whisper Fields has always held sentimental value for me. The people of the Bronx named this park after our fellow native Gunnar Whisper, a celestial soldier who fought necromancers and ghosts in the Undying Battle of Fountain Stone, and I'm hoping my community provides me the same recognition after I save not only our borough, not only our city, not only our country, but the world itself; Brighton Park or Brighton Fields or Brighton Garden is the least they can do.

As I walk through the park, alone, I know I won't be soon.

Birdsong is rising with the sun, but I'm not paying that any real attention. How could I when there's real music playing through

Whisper Fields, like the soundtrack of a crowd cheering. They're so loud and absolutely disturbing the peace, and if the stars are finally merciful, this will all be for me. I step into view, and even though they aren't holding signs, I'm certain I've brought everyone together this morning. It becomes clearer when I'm spotted by a follower who begins chanting my name. Everyone else turns to me, and the chant builds and builds.

"Brighton! Brighton! Brighton!"

Six people could never be loud enough to have my name booming across the park like this. There might be sixty people here, at least. I'll admit, I was counting on more, but this is very impressive since I only offered very short notice. Most people have slept through my updates and my following will only grow and grow as everyone else wakes up to the news of Emil's past lives and my determination to protect them from Emil and the Spell Walkers as well as Blood Casters and enforcers and corrupt politicians.

If someone isn't with us, they are against us.

For the most part, the sea of Brightsiders is parting as I walk through them, but others are so eager to get their hands on me like I'm a god, squeezing my shoulders and arms and hands, and I let them. I'm in no danger. Even the most powerful in this crowd wouldn't be able to kill me. But I can certainly rip their hearts out of their chests if they move against me.

I reach Gunnar Whisper's bronze monument and stare up at this hero of the past. I realize the Brightsiders are taking pictures and filming me. Many of them have great instincts for social media; I noticed this while glimpsing their profiles. Some are big influencers whose content admittedly made me cringe a few times, like this power couple who post ad after ad, but if I play my cards right, their followers will become my own. I better put on a show if I want to build my empire. I kneel before Gunnar and rest my palm on his plaque, covering his dates of birth and death. They're no longer chanting my name, like they're respecting my need for privacy in this moment. I close my eyes and hear nothing but whispers as if I'm lost in thought about Gunnar. I am in a way, but I'm not reflecting on his life or his vulnerability to die, which I won't ever have to worry about. I just keep thinking about all the heroes that will one day bow before my own statue.

I rise to full height, wishing I could fly above everyone here. I'm tempted to try, but on the off chance I do manage to tap into this buried power and only hover ever so slightly, I don't want to embarrass myself in front of the people I'm winning over. I need to show strength and strength alone. Thankfully I have a better handle on my other powers. I dash vertically up Gunnar's bronze leg and chest and stand on his flat shoulder, fifteen feet above everyone else. Applause breaks the silence. A celestial doing this on any given day isn't exciting to most people, but I'm a specter, someone who wasn't privileged enough to be born with powers but strong enough to host them later in life. Some people actually die when they infuse creature blood into their own, and while it was touch and go with me after drinking the Reaper's Blood elixir made from the essences of ghosts and a hydra and a phoenix, I survived, infinitely more powerful than before.

Everyone is looking up at me.

Most are taking pictures or filming me.

Others are just watching me.

Whatever they are doing, they are here for me.

Me.

I now need to prove myself to them.

"Thank you all for this warm welcome!" I shout down at them with my hand to my heart. "I'm still recovering from my brother's betrayal. I probably will be forever. But I'm less alone because of you—all of you." There's some applause, but I settle them down. "I've been running for my life, but I'm feeling braver and stronger. I must rally—we all must rally. There's some serious action on the horizon. The Spell Walkers will come for me, but I'm more concerned for the rest of the country—for all of you. Powerful prisoners who were locked up in the Bounds have been set free because of a dangerous rescue mission to break out Ness Arroyo from his cell." I avoid looking any of them in the eye as I hang my head. "I participated in this. Emil made me use my powers to get everyone inside, and I'm sorry for all the harm I've caused in aiding him. But I can make this—I *will* make this right." No one needs to know that I was more than eager to prove my heroics and abilities in the Bounds. "This is where you come in. If you're unable to protect the city against these dangerous criminals, do not engage. Send me a message and I'll see to it. For those of you who can fight, let's coordinate. In a world where we cannot trust the enforcers or the Spell Walkers to take care of us, we must take charge and become the heroes."

Silver and blue flames snake around my forearm. "If you come across Emil, let me know. He caught me off guard before, but he won't be able to overpower me next time. I'm ready for him."

I cast the fire-bolt into the sky.

The Brightsiders roar with cheers.

My followers will become my eyes and ears, my soldiers.

It's far from a legion, but it's a start.

THREE
UNDO, RENEW

MARIBELLE

I can bring my boyfriend back to life.

This is all I've been able to think about since fleeing the Bounds on the back of a light howler phoenix, far away from the chaos of a mass breakout. My Halo Knight companion, Tala Castillo, steered Roxana through the skies to get us—including Luna Marnette, the leader of the Blood Casters, who is the heart of all my pain—to safety. The only reason I didn't kill Luna in her cell like planned or throw her off the phoenix's back while we soared across the river is because she knows how to bring Atlas Haas back to me.

It's possible Luna is lying; it's a language she's certainly fluent in to get her way. But I'm also good at reading people. I saw the surprise burst in her eyes when she discovered I'm her granddaughter—it was just as surprising to me when I retrocycled through my birth mother's life and made that same discovery. I'm not looking to have a familial relationship with this woman who is responsible for the deaths of my real parents who raised me, as well as the biological parents I only remember vividly after walking through their memories.

Everything with Luna is transactional.

A life for a life or a death for a death.

Deaths—so many deaths.

Every second that passes feels like I should be returning to reality since I've never witnessed a resurrection, but there's no grounding me. Instead, I feel like I'm floating higher and higher, like when I started coming into my powers of levitation as a young girl, or when I would glide alongside Atlas through the streets of New York, or when I unlocked my phoenix powers and could fully fly as high as the city's tallest skyscraper.

Hope is soaring within because resurrection is reality.

Back in her cell, Luna revealed that she once brought someone back to life—June, the specter with ghost blood who did all the dirty work for these assassinations.

Those words were shocking to hear, but it makes so much sense. We'd never seen specters with ghost blood before June, and there's always been something so mystifying about her. Only once has she shown fear for her existence, and that's when we both realized that she's not impervious to the effects of the oblivion dagger hanging from my belt, a bone blade that can kill ghosts, but beyond that, it's been as if she's living a half-life. And she has—she still is—thanks to a botched resurrection.

If this is how Atlas comes back to life, then he's better off dead.

Luna needs to make this right.

I'm watching Luna in the home of some phoenix activist; I never got the woman's name. After brawling with Tala at the Light Sky Tower, where we first met—the both of us there to investigate the whereabouts of the Blood Casters—she stabbed me with a No-Fly

Tranquilizer best known for sedating phoenixes. I could've been killed, but miraculously, I was only knocked out cold for thirty-some hours. I had awoken here in this living space, and it was that very night when Tala and I formed our partnership to avenge our loved ones.

And now maybe we can bring some of them back.

Luna is staring at the black-and-white photos on the wall of phoenix wildlife. Her hands are clasped behind her back as if she's in handcuffs, but I see no reason to bind her. She might be seen as the most powerful queenpin in this city, but she's actually powerless, especially since Brighton stole the Reaper's Blood from her like a true hero, preventing Luna from becoming unstoppable with the powers of a specter, hydra, and ghost. Still, I wish I could read her mind, or that my psychic power to sense danger could spell out whatever scheme Luna is plotting. But that's not how my power operates. It's for more immediate danger, like a dagger being swung or fire being thrown my way. It can't reveal someone's master plan.

All I can do is keep my eyes on the enemy.

Luna looks over her shoulder, blood smeared around her lips, which curve into a smile. "What an honor to be welcomed into this home," she says.

"You know the owner?" I ask.

"Of course. Bella Quinones hates me." Luna returns her gaze to the pictures, tapping her nails against a black-and-white photo of Bella Quinones smiling at some phoenix perched on her shoulder. "She doesn't approve of my work with blood alchemy. I can't claim to be her fan either given all her so-called activism to protect phoenixes prevents necessary work from being fulfilled."

"A lot of death in your line of work."

"Don't speak ill of my line of work when it's what you're seeking to undo death."

I want to jump into flight and tackle Luna, smashing her face against each and every framed photo, screaming at her so she understands that deaths wouldn't have to be undone if she didn't cause them in the first place. But I remain grounded, biding my time to get what I need, almost as if I inherited a calculating gene from this sadistic grandmother of mine.

What happens to Luna after Atlas is brought back to life is to be decided. I'm leaning toward execution, personally. It's the only way to assure these secrets of resurrection die with her, so the only living souls who know how to bring someone back to life are me and Tala, and us alone.

"The Halo Knight is taking forever," Luna says as she returns to the living space, sitting on an armchair, smelling the rosemary on the side table.

"She's tending to Roxana, who was wounded during a phoenix fight," I say. That brawl between the light howler and a cerulean tasked with guarding the Bounds was intense, and if I hadn't flown onto Roxana and commanded her to strike the other phoenix with lightning, she may have been the one who was destroyed into nothing but feathers and ashes.

"I haven't been successful converting any specters with the blood of a light howler, I admit. Perhaps we can put Roxana out of her misery and offer her powers to a deserving soul."

"Or I can kill you instead," Tala's voice declares from behind as she rounds the corner, stopping in front of the wall of pictures. She can't fly across the room, or cast lightning like her phoenix companion, but Tala is deadly. Fighting against her the night we met really had me questioning if she really was just a human or actually an undercover celestial.

Luna waves her off. "Hollow threats are boring, dear."

Tala goes straight for Luna, and I step in her path, gripping her shoulders.

"We need her," I say.

"*You* need her," Tala says.

"If she can bring back Atlas, she can bring back your parents too."

It's only recent deaths that can be undone as far as Luna is concerned, and she's hoping a trip to the past will provide solutions to not only bringing back people who have been gone far longer, such as her sister, but also returning them to this world as they were, and not stripped of humanity like June.

"She cannot bring my parents back," Tala says.

Luna scoffs. "You Halo Knights carry such faith in the unproven whereas I have produced living, breathing evidence of resurrection in the form of June. That's more than can be said for your beliefs on your fallen being reincarnated as phoenixes."

Tala shrugs me off. Her watering amber eyes glare at Luna, and tears slide down her sun-kissed cheeks. "You require the ashes of the deceased, don't you?"

"I certainly can't make someone snap back into existence on imagination alone."

"Then you can't bring my parents back," Tala spits. "They were set ablaze by their phoenixes, and we didn't collect their ashes. We never do."

"Ah, your remembrance ceremonies," Luna says. "Ashes scattered to the winds. A true pity. I'm afraid you're correct, then. I cannot bring your parents back to life."

This is unreal. It's a huge blow, like hearing that Atlas can't actually be resurrected. Except Tala has known all along that she wouldn't be able to cash in on Luna's offer. I've been so focused on bringing Atlas back that I hadn't reflected on Tala's story about watching her parents' corpses burning under the night sky. Maybe she was holding on to hope of some sort, but now that Luna has confirmed that there's nothing she can do, the fury is building in Tala again—her gaze narrowing, nostrils flaring, fists clenching.

I keep an arm outstretched to hold Tala at bay while I turn to Luna. "Find a way to alter the ritual. Maybe there are still bones back at the Sanctuary we can scavenge for."

"I am dying," Luna whispers, then rolls her eyes. "The greater part of my life has already been spent seeking to defy every dimension of death as we know it. Years and years of work, and you think I'm going to simply make some tweaks for effective resurrections, as if I'm swapping out star-root for its cousin ingredient in some everyday elixir? Be wiser than this, granddaughter." She then tightens her fist and stares at Tala with her tired green eyes. "As for you, dear, hold on to hope that your parents will swoop out of the sky as a pair of reincarnated phoenixes, coming to check up on you during your lonely nights."

Tala's faith being mocked is the last straw. She shoves me aside, and I grab Tala's wrist to hold her back, only for her to twist my arm behind me, snatch the oblivion dagger from my belt, and kick me so hard that I slam into an art print on the wall. Everything happens so quickly that I don't even get a chance to decide if I want to fight back or not. This is what it's like to go one-on-one with Tala, a match Luna is about to lose as swiftly. By the time I turn around, Tala has already reached Luna and is about to slide the bone dagger across her throat, just as I was ready to do back at the Bounds, except Luna's death will kill all my hopes of resurrection.

"Please don't!" I scream.

"This was our plan," Tala says.

"Before everything changed," Luna whispers with a strain. "Her love only lives if I do."

"It's not fair, I know," I say. "I wish we could bring back your parents, just as you have always known them, and maybe one day we can, but right now, I need Atlas."

"You've been living without him, and you still will," Tala says, pressing the dagger deeper against Luna's throat, ready to send her to oblivion, just as the weapon is named for.

"I've faced enough grief already," I say. "I'll do anything to get someone back."

"You'll let this murderer live? Even though we promised to end her forevermore?"

I'm aware that what I say next can destroy this alliance, but she deserves my honesty—even an honesty that she will not respect. I'm not a Halo Knight; I don't share in the beliefs that my loved ones will resurrect as phoenixes as some natural progression in the cycle of life. My parents and my boyfriend are dead, but Atlas doesn't have to stay that way. "It breaks my heart to ask you to let her live. But my heart can heal if you do." I'm so close to getting onto my knees and begging for the life of my greatest enemy. "Please, Tala . . ."

Tala's hand is shaky, so close to killing the queen of the Blood Casters, to getting her revenge, but instead she shoves Luna back into her chair and hurls the oblivion dagger into the wall behind me. She steps to my face with teary eyes. "I thought we were in this together," she whispers. "I was wrong about you." She bumps her shoulder into mine and heads back down the hall, stomping upstairs to the rooftop.

Maybe Tala will fly away, never to be seen again.

That hurts my heart too.

Luna clears her throat. "That outburst was not my fault. It's not as if I personally swept away the ashes of her parents."

"No, you only sentenced them to their deaths."

She nods. "That's a fair counter."

I rip the oblivion dagger out of the wall and hold it close as I sit across from Luna. "Tell me everything about how you resurrected June," I say, swinging the dagger like a metronome, fantasizing about how I'll end June's second life.

Luna looks out the window, the sun rising, as if it's another ordinary day, and not a dawn where undoing death is on the schedule. "It was inspired by a family secret. A secret that now belongs to you as much as it does me, granddaughter. Your grandfather Santiago Córdova was a quintuplet, one of five brothers who all possessed deathlike abilities. There was much debate between the brothers on whether these powers were gifts or curses. The youngest, Davian, had a deathly touch, so much so that he killed the mother upon entering the world, as well as many childhood friends and even a future lover before accepting his life would be spent alone, without ever knowing the warmth of a hug or a kiss that didn't result in one's lifeless eyes frozen open. Alvaro could smell your bones and blood and tell you how long you would live, and those around him did not live long unfortunately, especially since Mattias's piercing howls combusted brains whenever he found himself having a disturbing episode."

After losing Mama, Papa, and Atlas within nine months, I'd begun feeling like I was personally touched by Death.

This story about my lineage is proving that true.

"What about Santiago?" I ask. "What was his power?"

"He had visions of imminent deaths," Luna says. "Just like your mother."

Just like I should've.

I'm stunned, silent.

I don't know if my celestial power that I inherited from Sera got watered down because of the specter powers I received from Bautista, or because my ability to detect danger never got nurtured in the first place, but everything could have been different if I'd had the power to foresee Atlas's death. Maybe there isn't anything I could have done to prevent it, but I could have said goodbye, let him know how much I love him. . . . Instead, it all happened so quickly.

June used her ghostly powers to possess me.

I lost all control of my body.

I couldn't stop her as she aimed the wand at Atlas and shot him in the heart.

I couldn't catch him when he fell out of the air.

I couldn't say goodbye.

"You look haunted," Luna says.

"I had a dream before the Blackout," I say. "The stars were shining above as I said goodbye to my parents."

"Prophetic," Luna says.

There is no smirk on her face even though she's the one who successfully orchestrated that terrorist attack, using June to possess Mama as she blew up the Nightlocke Conservatory, a disaster that Senator Iron pinned on the Spell Walkers and used to elevate his campaign for presidency.

"It would've been helpful to know I could foresee death," I say.

"Don't blame that on me, dear. I didn't even know you were family."

"Just as Sera wanted. She didn't want you using me for my powers as you used her."

"Well, my daughter's dream came true, but that only birthed your nightmare, a life of loss."

I could never pretend my life has been handled well with all the family secrets and secret families. Still, I won't let Luna turn me against Sera, the mother I never knew was mine, but who, thanks to retrocycling, I got to know through experiencing all of her feelings as she lived them, such as the dread and terror as she witnessed the vision foretelling her and Bautista's deaths, as well as the heartbreak of not being around to watch me grow up. But it wasn't all grim. I got to feel her absolute love as she cradled me, her little sunflower, and hear her sing a lullaby about a girl with a garden crown.

What I'm holding in my heart are the last words Sera said to me.

"Be strong and be loved, Maribelle Córdova de León. Your father and I have constellations of love for you," my mother had said, right before kissing me on the forehead, and watching me fly away in Mama's arms, my history rewritten from that moment on so the world only knew me as Maribelle Lucero.

I only wish I had the power to protect my loves as Sera did.

"How did Santiago's visions help you bring June back to life?" I ask.

"They didn't," Luna says.

"Back at the Bounds, you said that Santiago—"

"I said that Santiago taught me how to bring ghosts back to life. But his visions did not serve him apart from showcasing deaths, including his own at my hand and—"

"I can't say I'm shocked that you killed your husband after watching you drag a dagger across your daughter's throat."

There is no smirk on Luna's face, no pride, but no grief either. "I did what had to be done."

I'll hold myself to that same vow when it's time to kill Luna.

"So how did Santiago know how to bring ghosts back?"

"As I was saying before you interrupted me to paint me as nothing but a storybook villain, Santiago's visions did not aid us in deciphering resurrection, but in pointing us in the right direction to discovering it. This is not Santiago's story, Maribelle. You have had your eye on the wrong brother. It was the eldest, Fabian, whom I wish I'd gotten close to, the Córdova I wish I married. But he sadly took his life before we could meet."

Given how tragic all the brothers' stories are, I'm scared to ask why but I do. "Was it because of his power? Could he bring back the dead?"

"Ah, you've missed the pattern. That's fine. Most do."

"What pattern?"

"Think of each Córdova brother as if they carried one of Death's senses."

Five brothers, five senses.

The youngest had a deathly touch.

The other could smell impending death.

Another's voice caused sweeping deaths.

And my grandfather could foresee death.

That must mean the eldest could hear the dead.

"Ghosts spoke to Fabian?" I ask.

"Indeed, but unlike every other living soul on the planet who can only hear a ghost's howls, Fabian understood what the dead were saying."

"What did they want? Messages passed on to loved ones? Closure?"

"The ghosts wanted their lives back," Luna says, and a chill runs up my spine. "The dead spent their afterlives telling Fabian how to bring them back to life, and Fabian, the one living person who could hear them, chose not to listen. Naturally, the restless ghosts never allowed him peace, so Fabian ran that very oblivion dagger into his heart to extinguish his soul and distance himself from the dead forever."

I stare at the oblivion dagger, wishing Fabian would have used it to kill each and every ghost that wouldn't let him live his life. He had the one weapon that could silence the dead, and instead he turned it on himself.

There has to be more to the story.

But one thing is for certain: "The Córdova powers were a curse."

"The Córdova curse is our gift," Luna says, coughing so violently that she spits blood into her palm and wipes it on the sleeve of her crimson robe. "A gift that will be restored from time thanks to your retrocycling talents. Between my mother's studies, my own research, and theories born out of fear and curiosity by the Halo Knights, I'll admit I'm still not a scholar on retrocycling since I've never known a specter who's successfully done it, and I'm unable to ask the phoenixes myself how it works. Tell me everything. How do you do it? How far back have you gone? How many times?"

This is where I have to watch my back around Luna. I hate to admit it, but she's a brilliant alchemist whose discoveries and formulas are on another level. I have to be careful with how much I say at the risk of her using it against me, but I also can't withhold too much since she has to know what I'm capable of if I'm going to resurrect Atlas. These are tricky grounds I'm walking on, but this is the territory that comes with siding with the enemy.

I tell Luna about my limited experiences retrocycling.

How a phoenix has two bloodlines, one familial, the other personal. That means I can travel back through the lives of my ancestors, and if I had past lives like Emil does, I could go to those too. How we set ourselves on fire just as hibernating phoenixes do when they're retrocycling. Then it was following our instincts from there, just as Tala had told us to honor during our first attempt into the past, and I found myself hearing Sera's voice even though I had sworn I had never heard it before, not knowing how she would speak and sing to me when I was two months old. The more I embraced Sera as my mother in our next session, the more she filled out as a human, as a family matriarch whose life I could travel through.

"And then I retrocycled to the day Sera died—the day you killed her," I say, glaring at Luna, who has been listening with full attention, her green eyes practically glowing in wonder. "That was the first and last time I retrocycled."

"It won't be the only time, my dear granddaughter. When you

were in the past, were you bound to Sera and seeing everything through her eyes? Were you inside her skin?"

"No, I could roam on my own. But there seems to be a limited radius for how far retrocyclers can be away from the person they're traveling to," I say, remembering how when Sera was fleeing down the hallway to rush baby Maribelle to Mama and Papa, I couldn't help but follow like a second shadow.

The gears are turning in Luna's brain; I can see it in her eyes. It feels dangerous and hopeful all at once. "This is marvelous news. So if I wanted to send you back to a certain moment in time—"

"Let's be clear, Luna," I interrupt. "*You're* not sending *me* anywhere. *I'm* in control."

She waves me off. "Of course, of course. But are you in control of where and when and who you go to?"

This is complicated. When Emil and I wanted to retrocycle to Bautista and Sera, we started at the end of their lives. It was the closest path in the timeline to reach them. "Retrocycling isn't some exact science we understand. It's just very . . . instinctive. The more I knew about Sera, the stronger the connection was in helping me travel to her. . . . It's sort of like listening out for an echo of a moment I never lived."

Luna shakily stands, and I rise as well with the oblivion dagger in one hand and a fire-arrow I've quickly summoned in the other. She's unbothered by both as she walks to the window, staring out into the city. She's not a threat, so I clasp my fist and the fire-arrow disperses.

"Minutes before Fabian took his life, Santiago had a vision of his brother's death. Fabian had been confining himself to a once-dragon-infested island off the coast of Colombia. He was performing experiment after experiment to kill his powers so he could live in peace from the dead. But nothing worked. It seemed he was beginning to give in to the demands from the ghosts of his family, among many others, preparing the resurrection ritual as if the only way he could ward away the dead was to bring them back to life. Then, in this vision, Santiago saw Fabian hovering over a book of scrolls that told of how to undo a death to renew a life. But instead of performing the ritual, Fabian snapped, setting the house on fire and driving the dagger into his heart. The evidence was burned, but Santiago's psychic periphery collected enough knowledge about the ritual. He hoped I would be able to use my talents to bring all his brothers back to life and maybe even create an elixir that would strip them of their powers."

"Did you try bringing them back?"

"Yes. The resurrection called for ashes and Fabian left behind many in that house."

"Why didn't it work?"

"Creations are born from trial and error, and it's rarely the first that sees the light of day."

"How many errors before you learned from your mistakes?"

"Many." Luna returns her gaze to me. "The mistakes will become history after you go back in time and collect all the information from the burned scrolls."

If I'm going to bring my boyfriend back to life, I have to retrocycle to the day my great-uncle killed himself in a burning home.

Luna has no idea what she's asking of me.

"When I . . . when I retrocycle, I feel everything that person is going through. When Bautista was killed, I lived through his death, and I felt Sera's heartbreak all at once. Then I felt everything as you killed her."

The grief, the defeat.

The dagger across Sera's throat.

Fabian's seems worse.

Tormented by ghosts.

The panic, the defeat.

The fire raging on.

The dagger through Fabian's heart.

"I don't want to kill myself like Fabian did," I say.

I'm a survivor, and no matter how defeated I have felt this past year, I don't want to take my own life.

"Then get in and get out."

"I don't know if I can control that. I've only ever been evicted, right after Sera's timeline ended."

Luna returns to her seat, pondering. "Unless you plan on walking through Fabian's entire life to stumble onto a moment in which he spoke about the resurrection ritual, I'm afraid you have no choice but to visit the day of his death."

I'm still standing, as if I'm frozen in fear. If there was ever a time for Luna to snatch my oblivion dagger and stab me, it's now. But she's preying on my desperation to bring Atlas back, that I would do anything. Even if that means burning alive and ending it all with a dagger to my heart.

She needs me, and I need her.

I grip the oblivion dagger, accepting my fate.

No matter how much death I have to face, I will bring my boyfriend back to life.

FOUR
CRISIS

NESS

No one will ever know the real me.

How could they when I don't even know who the hell I am.

I'm trying to center myself, but I feel like my soul is having an identity crisis, urging my power to shift into absolutely anyone else since being Ness Arroyo is a nightmare. I could turn into the fourteen-year-old celestial whose teeth I knocked out when I was a teenager supporting the wrong cause. Or one of the guards who had their necks telekinetically snapped after they failed to defend the Senator's manor last night, the latest crime that's been pinned on the Spell Walkers. I could even shift into that obnoxious Halo Knight. It doesn't have anything to do with the way Emil looks at him or the time they spent together when I was held hostage. There's just comfort in being someone who everyone trusts instead of reckoning with my history of double crosses for my own survival. But I don't want to hide behind another mask—I will face myself, flaws and all.

Except I could do all that work and it won't matter, anyway.

No one in this world will ever accept me as a hero after everything I've done.

It's hard enough getting anyone to trust me inside this sanctuary to let me help with the evacuation. Probably something to do with Wyatt being the one who is delegating duties. He either suspects I won't listen to him or he doesn't trust the criminal he helped break out of the Bounds in the middle of the night. I have no idea if he's actually in charge, but everyone seems to be listening to him like he's a leader: the Halo Knights are collecting young phoenixes, placing them inside cushioned baskets for transport as if they're the most majestic beings on the planet; Prudencia is up on the bridge, telekinetically lowering supplies down to the courtyard; Ruth and her clones have created an assembly line across the yard, passing down boxes of medicine, nesting hay, and clothes to the Halo Knights at the front entrance who will know what to do with them next; Iris is carrying crates of food that are stacked three times as high as her, which looks unrealistic if you're unaware of her powerhouse strength; Wesley is holding his daughter by the pond, pointing at a swimming phoenix as he's on the phone trying to find a new hideout for us; and Emil has returned to the potions lab to pack up Bautista's journal and the prepared Starstifler vials and the remaining ingredients to brew more. I knew better than to accompany him when he's been wanting space from everyone. Even me.

The only other people who aren't busy are Carolina and Eva. They're on a bench, their backdrop a trellis. Carolina is staring at the sky as Eva holds her hand, almost like she's trying to bring her back to earth. No words are being uttered, but it tells a story. I bet any film director would kill to get this on camera since it's so beautiful and tragic all at once. I'm tempted to keep my distance knowing how much harm I've caused them by being forced to impersonate them, and how I triggered Brighton's rage by posing as Emil, but if I'm serious about facing myself and every regretful thing I've done, it begins here.

Step by step, I walk toward Carolina and Eva, admittedly scared to reach them in the same way I would get nervous when I was infiltrating enemy bases on Luna's behalf. But Carolina is a loving woman with no powers of her own and Eva is a healer who has willingly put herself through hell to heal me. I stop a few feet away in case they need space, but Carolina doesn't turn my way. She continues staring up at the sky where a bunch of phoenixes are circling above.

"Pretty beautiful, right?" I ask, an icebreaker.

"She's not really looking," Eva says.

I crouch before Carolina. There's so much pain in her reddened eyes. "Carolina?"

Nothing.

Back when we were all prisoners in my childhood home, locked away together in the panic room, Carolina still found it in her heart to be a caretaker. Even after she'd been struck by the Senator's bodyguard and disrespected by everyone on his team. Now here she is, underneath a clear sky and breathing in fresh air and surrounded by some of the strongest heroes in the country, who would go to war for her, and she looks like she's behind prison bars. Her crime: creating Brighton Rey.

"I'm sorry for pissing off Brighton," I tell Carolina. I hold her hand. "I wanted to protect Emil and everyone, but I should have just minded my own business. It's not like I don't have tons of messes to begin cleaning up without creating another for your family. But this wasn't your fault. You raised two sons, and Emil is the kindest soul I know. Don't forget that."

My speech doesn't turn the light on in Carolina's eyes.

"She's in shock," Eva says.

"Her life has changed so much for the worse in weeks. And now again overnight."

"I wish I could heal souls," Eva says. "Take her pain away."

From what I remember, Eva used to serve as a therapist for celestials in the shut-down elementary school the Spell Walkers once used as a haven; Emil and Carolina even had a session with her. But therapy only works if the client will communicate.

"I guess we do the next best thing."

"Which is?" Eva asks.

I want to say that we have to cut the head off the snakes before they can strike again. But any talk about murdering our enemies—which now includes Brighton—isn't going to help Carolina. I find the PG version: "There won't be any pain to take away if we stop those causing it."

"As much pain, anyway. There's always going to be some."

Eva is talking about heartbreak. I take it she can't heal that either.

"I'm going to stop the Senator," I promise. "It's not going to be easy outsmarting him now that he has so much support and power of his own, but I will do whatever it takes to prevent him from winning the White House and ruining your lives any more than he has. More than I have too."

She shakes her head. "You didn't ruin my life, Ness."

"The Senator forced me to go public as you both and say things—"

"He threatened our lives if you didn't, and you saved us when you could." Eva gives me this sympathetic look that makes me believe she wants to heal my soul too. "Besides, everything you said as us doesn't hold any real consequence. Not to the people who matter. Iris knows I love her. And Emil and Brighton know Carolina loves them too."

Carolina stops looking at the sky and turns to us. "Does he? Does Brighton know?"

I hold her hand and stare into her eyes. "Take it from someone whose father has organized multiple assassination attempts on his life. Your sons know you hold nothing but love in your heart."

"I should try calling him again. Make him see reason," Carolina says.

"That's a good idea," I say, even though I don't believe that will be enough. But who am I to stomp out her hope.

A flash of wind blows back my hair, and Wesley appears with his fussy daughter, dirt almost getting in my eye as he skids to a halt. "I found a new hideout. Technically, my buddy Xyla found it, and while she wasn't in love with asking her ex-girlfriend for a favor, she is always happy to do one for me."

"Where's it located?" Eva asks.

"Mele's Melee in Greenpoint. It's a celestial gym."

"That the best we can do?" I ask.

"Open to other ideas if you got them," Wesley says, bouncing Esther.

I—well, the Senator, really, has a house upstate in Albany. The nearest neighbor is a few minutes' drive away, and there are four bedrooms and six bathrooms and a barn house that my mother adored and hoped to one day welcome many animals into for a simpler life away from all the politics. But the Senator insisted on keeping us in the city, where the action is, claiming his supporters wouldn't view him as an asset if he wasn't living among them. I think that was bullshit because he wanted to stay in the city himself and not upstate in the quiet, where his thoughts might grow loud enough to tell him what a monster he is. Still, I don't know if he has eyes on the house, especially after the manor invasion. Maybe we could go somewhere that—

Wesley imitates a buzzer sound. "Too slow. To Brooklyn we go, where the owner will welcome us with a tale of young love getting old fast and some equipment if you want to get a nice pump in before our many big fights."

"Looking forward to trading in this fresh air for a sweaty sock smell."

"Feel free to hop on a phoenix and ride back to your prison cell, my many-faced friend."

"Touché."

"Anyway, I got to keep passing on the word, so see you late—"

Wesley dashes away, his last word clipped.

Carolina sighs. "I want to know where Brighton is staying. You don't think he's out on the streets, do you?"

I shake my head. "If he's back in the city, he probably just went home."

Carolina shudders and breaks into tears. "We have no home," she cries.

Eva wraps her arms around Carolina's shoulders. "Brighton and Prudencia brawled some specter at the apartment. The entire building was destroyed."

"Shit, I had no idea. I'm sorry. I—" I stop talking because first I couldn't say anything to comfort Carolina and now I've just caused her more harm and who knows what I might say next to really triple down on her pain.

Maybe it's a good thing when Emil comes out of the Sanctuary with a drawstring bag over his shoulder that's adorned with colorful feathers. I step away to give Carolina a chance to breathe and to check in on Emil, who slows down when I approach. "I got everything," he says. "The potions, ingredients, Bautista's journal. I just—" He sees his crying mother. "What happened?"

"I stepped in it. I didn't know about your apartment. I'm so sorry."

Emil's head is shaking like he still can't believe that himself, when he forces a nod. "It's all good."

"You don't have to play at being brave, firefly."

"Telling everyone how much I've been freaking out doesn't seem to fly," Emil says.

"It does with me. Your vulnerability is what sets you apart."

"Yeah, well, I got to lead now. I don't get to be chill about this anymore."

"What's chill about going back in time so you can create a potion that will protect the world against specters who are abusing their stolen powers? Or how you busted into the Senator's house so you could rescue your mother and friend? Don't even get me started on how there is nothing chill about breaking into the Bounds and fighting guards and prisoners so you can save my life." I take hold of his hand, and I'm relieved he doesn't rip it away. "Find whatever fire you need to lead, but don't lose your light, firefly."

Emil nods, and this time he means it. "You're right, I got this."

I step in closer, our held hands pressed against each other's chests. "Don't forget that you may be leading, but you're not alone."

"You're definitely hanging around? It's fine if you want to run away. I get it."

Back when we were all camping out in that shuttered elementary school, I had abandoned Emil and the Spell Walkers. I wanted to get away from the Senator and Luna and the Blood Casters, but when I saw enforcers about to storm the school, I had to go back and help. That led to my capture. I get why Emil is giving me an out so I can run away and change my face and restart my life far away from all of this, but I'm not going to find any peace in that.

My mission is to expose the Senator as the fraud he is.

Once he's locked up—in the Bounds, where he now belongs as a specter—then I can live.

I stare directly into Emil's hazel eyes. "This war is made up of many battles, and I got to fight mine. I'm not going anywhere."

"I got your back too," Emil says.

We're living our own infinity cycle where we save each other's lives, just as I told him.

"I'm going to need it. Public enemy number one."

"Times two," he says, raising his hand.

"We're both being hunted for crimes we didn't commit."

"And the world will never believe us."

"Honestly, knowing you believe me means the world. We're not going to be able to change everyone's minds. Some people will never trust me since I'm the son of a politician who hates all gleamcrafters and I've been a Blood Caster and I've done terrible things with my powers. But I know the truth and I'm going to start there on this path of self-discovery." I pull Emil in closer, our gaze magnetized. "Not only will I find myself, but I'll make sure you don't lose yourself."

I'm settling into my skin, like Emil is my anchor.

He makes me want to be my best self—the kind of person I would fight for.

My lips want his.

I lean in, and Emil does the same.

I close my eyes and—

"Sweet Emil, did you accomplish your task?" Wyatt asks.

I turn to the Halo Knight, and he's not the least bit sheepish about breaking up our kiss.

Emil raises the feathered drawstring bag, vials clinking inside. "Got everything."

"Fantastic. We should be ready for takeoff in another twenty minutes. Half past seven."

"Okay. Is someone packing up cauldrons?" Emil asks. "Got to make more Starstiflers."

"Best I go check with Ruth," Wyatt says.

"Best you do," I say.

Wyatt's smug expression lives on; he's lucky Prudencia broke up our fight. He turns on his heel and jogs over to Ruth.

"We got enough fights going on," Emil says, turning my chin so I face him. "I can't start freaking out about you guys when we're all on the same side."

"Is this an order, King Emil?"

Emil smiles, which feels like a well-earned victory.

Right up until an explosion of spellwork blows apart the Sanctuary's entrance.

FIVE
CYCLE OF CHAOS

EMIL

The Sanctuary is about to become a war zone.

The screams and screeches send shivers down my spine, and I want to sit in a corner and cry, but I got to get it together. I bet Brighton is back already, this time with an army to finish our fight. It's a special kind of low to attack Halo Knights and phoenixes who are not only innocent in all this, but who hosted us even though we have phoenix blood coursing through us. Now Brighton is bringing danger to their home.

This is my fight to lead.

"Stay back," I tell Ness, even though there's this ache in my chest to kiss him.

"No. Where you go, I go. We just talked about this—"

My gold and gray wings of fire burst into life, and I head up into the sky, where Ness can't follow.

"Catch!" I shout, dropping the feathered bag into Ness's possession.

I fly across the courtyard, right as dark smoke begins rising into the air, clouding the Sanctuary's entrance. I can't tell what's on fire yet, but I'm betting it's the supplies everyone's been collecting for the relocation. This is all my fault; I never should have brought my business to this peaceful castle where reborn phoenixes are tended to as they adjust to their new lives. Instead they're going to be facing death—violent deaths way ahead of their time. Halo Knights bust through the smoke and retreat back into the courtyard, carrying young phoenixes against their chests like parents fleeing from a disaster with their children.

How deranged are Brighton's followers to willingly follow him into committing senseless violence?

More people come out of the smoke, but they're not Halo Knights. It's a dozen enforcers, dressed in their bronze helmets and sea-green power-proof vests and armed with the wands they've never been shy about using. It may not be Brighton leading the charge, but he definitely cast this storm over the Sanctuary. An enforcer fires a spell, striking a Halo Knight in the back. As he's falling, a young phoenix tries flying out of his arms, only to be failed by their small wings. An enforcer lifts his boot to stomp out the phoenix, when he's suddenly flung across the courtyard, like a puppet pulled by invisible strings. I already know the hero of that story is Prudencia before I even find her below, her hand raised as she prevents a different enforcer from striking down another Halo Knight.

Now that I know who we're up against, I got to get people out of here.

I glide down to Ma and Eva as they're retreating into the castle, calling Prudencia over. She comes running, looking over her shoulder and deflecting a well-aimed spell that's been cast her way, telekinetically bouncing it into a wall and blowing a hole through the brick; a spell with that force could have killed my best friend. The enforcers aren't here to stun and capture us—they're going for blood.

"What do we do?" Ma asks, clutching her chest.

"Take a deep breath," I say, guiding her into the hallway and leaning her against the wall. "You're going to get out of here safely."

"As are you," she says with wide eyes.

"I have too much power to fly away now, but I won't be far behind."

Endless spellwork explodes outside, and Prudencia peeks at all the action. "I'm guessing our ride out of here has been destroyed. How are we going to escape?"

"Um . . ." I take a deep breath. I can send them running into the woods, but Ma's heart wouldn't last long out there. "Okay, change of plan. We're not escaping. Pru, we're going to fight and hold them back as Ma and Eva hide."

"We'll be defenseless if they find us," Eva says.

"No, you won't. I'll send Iris your way. Head upstairs into the library and hide behind the farthest bookcase. Don't make any noise."

"My Emilio—"

"I love you, Ma." I kiss her forehead and charge back into the battlefield before she can waste her breath trying to get me to stay. I don't turn back because Ma wouldn't even need words to send me back to her side. One look would do the trick.

Prudencia catches up to me but splits away when she sees a bleeding Halo Knight on her knees, protecting a phoenix with her body as if she's nothing but a shell. The last thing I see before turning away is

Prudencia getting the Halo Knight to her feet and urging her to get inside the castle.

I scan the courtyard, trying to find Iris in all the chaos: Wesley hands Esther over to Ruth before he dash-tackles an enforcer into the pond, punching him repeatedly before hopping back to his feet and barreling straight into another enforcer, all in a matter of seconds; Ruth's clones have spread out, acting as decoys to give her enough time to get her daughter inside the castle safely; Wyatt wrenches open a crate of weapons that has been toppled over, passing out swords and axes and shields to Halo Knights; and I don't see Ness anywhere, but I hope he's found his way inside too. Still, no sign of Iris until an enforcer is thrown out of the dark smoke and she steps outside, coughing into her arm. I rush over, asking if she's okay.

"Their spells can't hurt me," Iris says, her eyes watering from the heat.

"But they can hurt everyone else. Get to the library and protect Eva and my mom."

"What about—" Iris punches a spell with her power-proof fist, and it fires back into the enforcer who cast it, shooting straight through the woman's arm. "What about all of this?"

"I'll hold it down, and once it's safe to leave, we'll bounce."

"I'm the strongest—"

"Which is why you're protecting the defenseless. Please, just go!"

Iris nods and takes off, accepting that her place in this war doesn't have to be on the front lines.

Six more enforcers clear through the smoke, riding quad bikes that are as metallic gold as the tanks I've seen in the streets of New York. But these vehicles aren't just for getting through rough terrain—they're killing machines mounted with turrets.

An enforcer drives straight at me, firing rapid spells that I'm only just dodging by soaring into the air, zigzagging until he accepts he won't hit me. He shifts focus, headed toward Wyatt, whose shield won't be able to protect him from an onslaught of spells or a speeding automobile. I zoom down as fast as I can and hurl a fire-orb into the front tire, and as the quad bike spins from momentum, the enforcer flips off and slams down on the ground.

"You good?" I ask.

"The start to this day is a bit more propulsive than I'd like," Wyatt says.

"Don't worry, we'll get you back to morning joyrides on Nox and reading books in the sun."

"And waking up next to cute chosen ones, I hope."

"I'm not chosen—"

"You may not be an official chosen one, but I do choose you."

I point at all the destruction happening around us. "We're not doing this now."

Wyatt nods, like there's only a light skirmish or two happening. "A respectable plan. But I will say being a leader is a good look on you. Like that perfect pair of pants that highlights everything worth highlighting. You know what I'm talking about?"

I grab his shoulders. "I'm going to set you on fire if you don't get your head in the game."

"You can burn me all day long—"

"Wyatt, for real."

"I apologize. Humor masks the fear."

That must be nice; I've just got fear on top of more fear. Works out since that triggers my power unlike any other emotion. "It's all good. I'm freaking out too—"

I shut up when I hear that familiar roar of helicopter blades.

"They want us bad," Wyatt says.

Two helicopters hover above the Sanctuary.

"What are they waiting for?" I ask.

"For us to try escaping," Wyatt says.

Ground and air, they're cornering us. I can't attack a helicopter without expecting the passengers to die in a crash. I'm not ending their lives. Same goes for the enforcer whose quad bike I flipped over. He's flat on the ground but still breathing. No matter how many lives Keon and Bautista took in their time, I won't be like them. Not even in self-defense.

No matter how much someone wants me dead, I won't turn into a killer.

This choice is probably why I'll die.

But for now, I strategize another way to get around this. "Can Nox outfly the helicopters?"

"That's as silly as asking me if I would hit on you in the middle of battle," Wyatt says, his grin barely lasting a second before concern melts his joy. He's staring upward and shouts, "No! Turn back!"

I look to the sky to find a Halo Knight riding a full-sized crimson phoenix toward the helicopters. The sun swallower breathes fire, setting one helicopter aflame, and it cycles through the air before it crashes just outside the Sanctuary, its explosion so powerful that it blows apart a wall, and the east tower comes tumbling down. It's suffocating how something that took ages to build, lives that took years to grow could all be gone in a matter of seconds. But the carnage isn't ending here. The Halo Knight guides the sun swallower toward the last helicopter, but before the phoenix can attack, the pilot aims their turret and unleashes an assault unlike any other. The phoenix that can withstand the heat of a thousand suns stands no chance against the barrage of spells, crying in agony with each hit before it explodes in nuclear fashion. The fight ends when the burning Halo Knight falls out of the sky, which is raining ashes, his charred corpse crashing into the courtyard, where life was once nurtured.

The nightmare lives on as a cycle of phoenixes take to the sky, a sight I've loved so much during my time here at the Sanctuary, but it's absolutely horrific watching the helicopter's turret rip into each phoenix.

Some explode in the air.

Others fall out of the sky.

All will be resurrected, but I'll never forget their deaths.

The shield crashes alongside Wyatt, clattering at his feet. Then he drops onto his knees with tears in his eyes. I have no idea how to console him after something so horrific. But I know I can't let him live in this grief right now.

"Wyatt, hey, Wy, you got to get it together," I say, crouching in front of him. He's staring at me, but he's not really looking. It's like he's reliving the horror we just witnessed on a loop. "I'm sorry, but I need you." The Wyatt I know wouldn't waste a single second hitting me with some suggestive response, but this Wyatt still isn't reacting.

I got to snap Wyatt out of this, and someone else would probably slap him in the face to break this trance, but I try something more loving to revive him. I kiss Wyatt, pressing my lips against his until they push back against mine. I'm about to pull away so an enforcer can't take us out, but Wyatt holds me close. I wonder if he's reliving our first kiss, while we were flying on Nox, or if he doesn't want to let go because he fears this might be our last time. I don't know what the future holds for us, if we'll even have one if we don't stop making out on a battlefield that is raining phoenixes and fire.

"Wyatt," I breathe.

Life flickers in his eyes, and he finally sees me.

"Hey, look, you can save more lives if you and Nox get that helicopter away from here. Then, once you've lost the enforcer, you come find me at Mele's Melee in Brooklyn. You have to get back to me, Wy."

"I'll come back to you," Wyatt promises.

"Go save the day."

"You too, sweet Emil."

Wyatt caresses my chin lovingly before he jumps to his feet, off to find Nox.

I return to the fray, where Wesley, Prudencia, and some Halo Knights have been holding it down. Prudencia braces herself for the enforcer that's speeding toward her on his quad bike, and she spreads out her arms, her hands clawing at the air as if she's personally ripping off the tires of the vehicle before telekinetically ejecting the enforcer. On the other side of the courtyard, an enforcer is casting spell after spell into the little pond to harm a sky swimmer until he suddenly finds his wand missing as if it's vanished into thin air. Wesley waves with the wand before blasting the enforcer in the center of his power-proof vest, knocking him off his feet; he blows the smoke from the tip of the wand like some old-school cowboy.

I keep busy with the enforcers, trading fire for spells, right up until

I see Wyatt and Nox soaring through the sky. My heart shoots up into my throat, and I'm desperate for Wyatt to get away safely and not crash against the ground like a comet. Nox darts around the helicopter at dizzying speeds until it slows down, stopping right underneath where the turret can't spin to fire. Wyatt seems to be staring at the helicopter's belly, and I'm praying to the skies that he doesn't exact revenge, no matter how many lives have been lost. I'm just about to fly up there myself, when Nox zooms out from underneath, and the helicopter follows, firing spells and missing every last one.

Once they're gone, I turn to see where I'm needed, when a spell clips me in the shoulder and I fall to the ground. The faintest phoenix song plays in my head as my healing power kicks into gear, closing the wound and cooling down the white-hot pain. But all I can think about is how if I hadn't turned right when I had, that spell would've shot straight into my heart and killed me. I wouldn't have come back to life, not as Brighton would have the world believe, at least. I'd resurrect as someone new, as a baby who has to grow up all over again, and I would be nothing but a past life.

The enforcer aims his wand again, but he must be out of ammo. Spells or no spells, this doesn't stop the enforcer from charging straight at me, unlatching the gauntlets from his belt so he can cuff me and render me as powerless as him. It would only be temporary, not like the Starstifler that binds the powers forever, but the enforcer would have more than enough time to finish me off with his fists. I could stop him now if I wanted to. I'm plotting to hook him with a flaming punch, but when another enforcer flanks him to join the fight, I got to think bigger. I charge up a fire-orb, bigger than usual, even though it sucks more energy out of me. Right before I can throw the fire-orb on the ground between them, counting on the explosion's seismic wave to blow them away, the second enforcer rocks the first's jaw with a killer punch. Why did he betray him?

The traitor enforcer stands over the other enforcer's body. "Surprise," he says as a gray light consumes him, transforming him back into Ness, who wasn't hiding in the castle after all.

"It's you," the enforcer says.

"It's me." Ness pins down the enforcer with his foot. "Did the Senator send you here?"

No answer.

"I'll take that as a yes." Ness kicks the enforcer in the face, knocking him out cold. "I'm going to kill him."

"He's laid out," I say.

"No, I'm going to kill the Senator." Ness stares out at the chaos. "Look at what he's done."

The sky is going dark with smoke as the courtyard's fire rages on. The grounds have become a colorful graveyard for bloodied phoenixes. I have no idea how many Halo Knights have been killed, but I can easily count ten. There are probably more buried under the rubble or out by the entrance, where the attack began. But there don't seem to be any more enforcers who are up and running, which is a win. Too bad this victory looks like an absolute horror show.

Prudencia and Wesley join us.

"We should've stolen that helicopter," Wesley says.

"Do you know how to operate one?" Prudencia asks.

"Technically no, but it can't be that different from the ones I've flown in arcades."

"Were you in the air at the arcade?" Ness asks.

"No."

"Then you weren't flying," I say.

"Wow, I'm telling Ruth and all her clones to gang up on you guys to see how you like it."

I still can't believe how catastrophic this all got. "Pru, do you think you can settle that fire?"

"I can try dousing it with the river water" Prudencia heads off to do her thing. This is a pretty big ask, but she's our best shot.

I want to lie down so badly, but I have to keep leading. "Some of those quad bikes might still work. Maybe we can use them to get into the city. Wes, can you go check on everyone and let them know the coast is clear?"

Wesley salutes and dashes away.

I'm left alone with Ness. "Keep an eye out for any phoenix that may be wounded and not dead. If you see one that's brown with emerald wings, let me know. Those are evergreen blazers and they literally eat fire and can help us out—"

"Slow down," Ness says.

"I can't. We don't know if more enforcers are on the way."

"The Senator wouldn't send them in waves."

"I wouldn't pretend to know what the hell your father is thinking."

Ness doesn't say anything.

I turn and find him staring at the enforcer he knocked unconscious. "Look, I'm sorry. I'm not trying to act like I don't have unpredictable family either. All this wouldn't have gone down if Brighton never outed where we were and—"

"Shut up for a second," Ness says as he crouches above the enforcer.

Did something bad happen? Did he accidentally kill the guy?

"Is he breathing?" I ask, getting down on my knees and feeling for a pulse. I find one immediately and release a deep breath. "What's up?"

Ness points at a small black device sticking out of the top pocket of the enforcer's vest. We both lean in and stare into the lens. "Body cams."

This violation sends goose bumps up and down my arms. "They attacked us and what, they've got footage of us fighting back?"

"They'll twist this against us," Ness says. "Consider this one of those times where I know what the Senator is thinking. Especially since he now has me on camera saying I'm going to kill him."

He rips out the body cam and crushes it under his boot.

I could set it on fire, but it wouldn't matter.

The damage is done.

SIX

THE FLOW OF LIFE AND DEATH

MARIBELLE

I'm praying to the stars Tala hasn't taken to the skies and abandoned me.

I lead the way to the rooftop garden, Luna slowly following me up and around the spiral staircase. I can't risk leaving her alone. What if June appears and rescues her? I have a key to the past now, but I've also taught Luna how to unlock those doors herself. I refuse to rule out Luna having another secret relative who can retrocycle to Fabian's life like I can—like I hope I can. Who knows what hell Luna can unleash with this intel. Where I go, she goes. Unless she's being watched by someone who also doesn't want Luna to make this world any worse than she already has.

And there she is.

Tala is standing knee-deep in the hot tub with Roxana, still tending to the phoenix's wound. She's wearing nothing but her black bra and compression shorts, her tanned skin basking in the sunlight. Roxana's head tilts, her lightning-blue eyes on me as we approach. Tala's gaze follows, and she gives me and Luna dirty looks.

Am I just as bad as Luna in Tala's eyes?

"Come any closer and Roxana will attack," Tala warns.

"That threat for both of us?" I ask.

Tala doesn't answer.

I get Luna to back off, but I'm not taking Tala seriously. I'll be able to sense any imminent attack from Roxana, not to mention I'm paying close attention to the phoenix to make sure she doesn't open her mouth to unleash a lightning storm on me.

"Not only do you not honor your word, you also do not listen," Tala says.

"You're pissed at me for not killing Luna."

"We vowed to do so."

"That was before I could bring Atlas back to life."

Tala steps out of the hot tub, water dripping from her tight six-pack and down to her toned legs. I've never seen this much . . . *Tala* before, and the sun must be targeting this rooftop like it's the only place in the world that needs light because I feel like I'm on fire. She's gorgeous; I've always known this. But seeing her stripped of her gear really helps me see her like . . . it just helps me see her. Tala doesn't seem to be paying me any mind like I am her. She glares across the garden and over at Luna, fury in her eyes.

"I would have done all of this alone if I had known you weren't capable of getting the job done," Tala says, dragging her pants up her soaked thighs.

"I won't lie. If our positions had been switched, I'd still want Luna dead too and I would be pissed off at you for trying to stop me. Please understand that I have only ever loved one person the way I loved Atlas, and everything in me that feels empty can be filled once again. If we could bring your parents back, I know you would feel the same way."

"My parents will come back," Tala snaps.

"As phoenixes," I say, trying to respect her beliefs even if I don't share them at all. "But your parents won't return as you knew them."

"And Atlas will come back as you knew him? Will he even remember you? If he does, will he return as some vengeful version of the boy you loved, packing the powers of a ghost to exact his revenge on you?"

I sink onto the stone bench, weighed down by those haunting thoughts. The saddest is Atlas not remembering me, but at least he would be alive. He could get to know me all over again. I just hope that I'm still the same girl he once fell for, and not someone with so much blood on her hands and desperation in her heart that he could never love someone like me. "This is why I have to travel into the past. Luna told me that I have an ancestor who could speak with ghosts, and the ghosts taught him how to bring people back to life. If I can return with that information, then I can resurrect Atlas as I knew him."

Tala kneels before me, like I'm her queen. "Maribelle, something could go wrong. Beyond anything we could even fathom because you're tampering with the unholiest of forces. There are natural ways for souls to return to this world, even if it's not what you're picturing. . . ." She looks up at the sky, as if her parents have already reincarnated as phoenixes and will be flying down upon her shoulders any moment now. Then her amber eyes zero in on me, and she rests her elbows on my knees, closing this space between us, as if she's about to let me in on a secret. "Life and death is a cycle, a flow that isn't to be disrupted. Do I want my parents back as I knew them, as I loved them? As the humans who shaped me? Yes. But I would never trust their killer to be the one who brings them back to life."

I glance over my shoulder at Luna, and she's staring out into the city she used to reign over. "This might be my only chance."

"Don't be so naive. Luna has cast clouds of grief over our lives. Even if this ritual is as foolproof as the ghosts claim it to be, that doesn't mean something can't go wrong along the way. Something a supreme alchemist like Luna won't even anticipate—or something she even twists to her advantage. She could weaponize Atlas against you, as she has June." Tala taps the oblivion dagger hanging from my belt. "If needed, could you kill Atlas? This time forevermore?"

I hang my head low, unable to meet Tala's eyes.

It doesn't matter. She knows the truth.

I would die before I kill Atlas again.

Especially if that means obliterating his soul.

"I didn't think so," Tala says, leaning back, the weight of her body off of mine, making me feel alone.

"This is love, Tala. I don't know what to say, or if you've ever known anything like it."

Tala rises to her feet and folds her arms like she's cold, or maybe something deeper, like she's guarding her heart. "Love is not foreign to anyone on a path for vengeance."

"Losing your parents is its own nightmare. I've been living it even longer than you. But I'm talking about the kind of love that burns so brightly that you feel like your light is extinguished when you lose it. A love that you would not only disrupt the flow of life and death for, but also break apart the cycle if it means fixing your heart. Have you ever felt that love, Tala?"

Any stranger would think Tala is cold with how she's folding her arms, but I know better. This girl is guarding her heart with everything she's got. "I have not. You also make love sound terrible."

"It is when it is and it's not when it's not."

"You understand that if you bring back Atlas, he won't be immortal. You could lose him again. Is love worth reliving all this pain?"

"I would bring Atlas back for the rest of my life if it meant feeling the way I do when he holds me."

Tala sighs. "It's clear I'm not talking you out of this."

"Atlas's own ghost couldn't stop me."

"And I'm assuming you need me for some reason."

"I can't do this without you. You can help me find my way back into the past and make sure Luna doesn't chop off my head while I'm busy retrocycling."

"And if she makes a wrong move while you're in another life?"

"Then I expect to find her dead at your hand, as she deserves."

It's our lives before hers—and Atlas's above my own.

SEVEN

INFLUENCERS

BRIGHTON

My speech at Whisper Fields was a hit, and instead of immediately going online to see if I was trending, I spent time getting to know some of my Brightsiders. Most of them admitted to only discovering who I am after my Spell Walkers of New York feature and Emil's training videos. Others started paying more attention after I did my Instagram Live with Emil, announcing my powers and introducing us as the Infinity Kings who were teaming up to take down the bad guys; the crown has fallen off Emil's head, but mine is still sitting high. But everyone has been following my every move since last night when we broke into Senator Iron's house and the Bounds. The life and times of Brighton Rey have become a reality show for many, but for others, it's a call to action—and my followers, new and old, are answering that call.

I can already tell these followers will become more than just soldiers in my army, but also friends—maybe even family that will always have my back in times of need.

The meet-up was winding down because I was starving and

exhausted. I was ready to go grab some breakfast and find shelter somewhere, like an empty hotel suite that I could've phased into so I could get a full day's rest. But a celestial named Alpha insisted I go and stay at his influencer house so I could make more friends (and then make content with those friends when I was rested). I was going to pass because Alpha is a stranger who I've never seen before in my life, which is odd since I live on the internet. Then I found out Alpha is big on TikTok, which feels awkward since he's in his late thirties and that app is more for my generation. But when I saw that he has nearly three million followers because of nonsense he performs with his water powers, I not only took him up on his offer, I'm also planning on doing some collabs to grow my own TikTok following; everything he's doing on TikTok I can do better.

If I'm going to be the world's leading voice, I need to stand on every stage.

Even the stages I've despised because they demand performances that aren't natural to me.

On the drive to the great foreign land known as Staten Island, I nap in the backseat, waking up to a house that warms me up to New York's bastard borough. It's a cliffside modern mansion with bronze terraces wrapping around the white stone walls. Two more cars pull in beside us in the massive garage, and more celestial influencers who attended my meet-up spill out, including this power couple that never even introduced themselves to me and instead just enjoyed the spotlight as my fans asked them for pictures at—once again—*my* meet-up. But it's impossible to pay any mind to that social violation when Alpha is touring me around the mansion and its six bedrooms with skylight windows so celestials can rest powerfully under the stars. He lets me know which rooms are up for grabs, and I choose the one that has a view of nothing but nature because that seems really nice. We continue on, going through the living room, where a shirtless man is posing in front of a backdrop while holding a piano above his head with one finger, and his muscles are well lit by the glow of electricity emanating from a woman's palm. We step out into the backyard to find what looks like octuplets dancing before a tripod until the song ends and the clones vanish, leaving behind this influencer I recognize, Reed Tyler, who seems disappointed as he reviews his content. Alpha then shows off his outdoor pool and runs across the surface—which is a lot more graceful than my own power will allow—before he dries himself off with a towel that's branded with his own face.

This place is a paradise.

Why hide in abandoned schools and tiny cabins and sanctuaries where I'm not even welcomed when I can be here, living openly and proudly as a gleamcrafter?

I will never spend another night of my life holed up somewhere I don't want to be.

"You got this place because of TikTok?" I ask Alpha as we enter this state-of-the-art kitchen that I would only ever expect to find in an A-list celebrity's home.

Alpha's laughter is deep. "I got this place because I'm always reinventing myself, man. I wanted to be an actor, but was only getting cast as lifeguards and divers, so I quit that noise. Then I wanted to be an Olympian, but no one wanted me to have an advantage as a celestial, so I had to keep moving with the tides of life. I started posting videos online of me creating water and giving it to homeless people this summer. The TikTok audience *drank* that up. Every video was hitting a million views, man."

"Wow," I say.

"I know, right?"

He thinks I'm wowed in an impressed way when I'm actually disgusted. Every time someone posts a video where they're performing a charitable act and recording the unhoused person's reaction, it honestly makes me sick. Viewers will often call the deed exploitative, and then the original poster will get very defensive about how they're being inspirational. It never fails. I would be impressed if Alpha used his money to provide some basic housing for others instead of living so grandly here.

But!

I can't fight every fight, and as someone who is technically houseless myself, I'm not about to vacate this palace to make a statement. When you think about it, I'm actually going to be making the streets a safer place to live with all my heroics.

"I could definitely take some tips from you," I say.

"Reinvention is the name of the game, man. Oh, and sponsorships and branding deals." Alpha opens his fridge, which is packed with water bottles. He tosses me one. "Enjoy that Alpha Aqua. I wouldn't be mad if you wanted to post a video of you drinking one after a big battle."

I will reach into my own chest and rip out my own heart before I do that.

"Totally, man."

Alpha has no idea that I'm mocking him.

That power couple walks into the kitchen. They both seem to be about my age. The girl is five feet tall with long red hair that falls down to her waist, flowing like a cape as she's on the phone, telling someone that she knows her worth and won't come down on the price for her work before hanging up. The boy is much taller with a widow's peak in his dark hair. He's glued to his tablet, sitting down beside one of the many charging stations throughout the house.

"Make yourself at home, man," Alpha says on his way outside. "I'm going to hit a swim."

I'm left alone with the power couple.

Neither of them are familiar to me, but that doesn't mean they don't have influence. I look around again at this house that's owned by someone I've never heard of before today. This power couple could have double Alpha's following; hopefully they don't have some joint account because that limits their reach. If I make friends with them, that could help me with my own legion.

As the boy idly plays with the girl's hair, I can't help but think about how this could have been me and Prudencia—how it was us for a bit. It's hard not to remember every incredible moment from the night when I told Pru she had always been too extraordinary for someone like me. I was near death back then, still suffering from Stanton's poison. But then things got amazing when Prudencia and I kissed for the first time, and got even more amazing when we had sex too. Then my hydra abilities kicked in and I got a second lease on life. Not long after that we found ourselves on a mission that may have resulted in a brawl against a specter that got my entire building blown apart, but we also got a glimpse of life as a power couple, having each other's backs and saving lives. Our work was a lot more meaningful than whatever these influencers get up to, but unfortunately, Prudencia doesn't actually have my back so I need to make do with the company I do have.

"Have you tried this?" I ask, holding up the Alpha Aqua bottle.

The boy looks away from his tablet. "Kind of hard not to."

"Is it good?"

His eyes return to the screen. "It's just water."

"I could make cooler water," the girl says.

"Literally, Zelda. But let Alpha have his thing."

She shrugs. "Maybe I want to make that my thing too. He's the one always going on about reinvention." She turns to me. "Have you gotten that speech yet?"

"Just now," I say.

"The whole reinvention thing started because his name is actually Al and he wanted to sound more badass, so he rebranded as Alpha." She rolls her eyes, openly mocking this guy in his own home. It's cutthroat. "Please tell me you're smart enough to not be influenced by him."

It's juvenile to bring up how I was salutatorian in my high school graduating class, so I don't. "I didn't let my own brother brainwash me. No one else is going to change me just like that."

The girl—Zelda—leans on the kitchen counter. "Pretty bold to see you turn on your own flesh and blood."

The world must still be piecing it together that Emil being resurrected means he's not actually my biological brother. He's as much my flesh and blood as anyone in this house. "I reacted when I should've acted. Emil turned on me first, but that's the last time I'll be stupid enough to let him."

"You've got fire," Zelda says.

"And so much more. What do you got?"

Zelda walks up, smelling like a flowery perfume, something that makes me want to lean in but could actually be poisonous. Her eyes glow like stars as she presses her finger on the Alpha Aqua bottle. The water not only freezes in seconds, but a rose forged in ice blossoms out of the cap. "I have the shadow to fire's light," Zelda says.

"Get a room already," her boyfriend says.

"Don't be jealous, Samuel. I'm just making a friend."

"Why didn't you say hi at my meet-up, then?" I ask, setting down the freezing cold bottle.

"It's not cute for us to fawn over other influencers," Zelda says.

"I'm more than some influencer."

Zelda hops up on the counter. "Come on, Brighton, you're not stupid enough to believe that."

I could set her on fire, but I don't need a bunch of keyboard warriors trying to cancel me. "I'm not trying to be offensive, but I fight against Spell Walkers and last night I ripped out the heart of a Blood Caster." At this, Samuel looks up from his tablet with wide eyes. "Don't group me with celestials who are dancing with their clones on TikTok."

"Wow, I didn't know I was in the presence of a murderer," Zelda says.

"I'm a savior first and a reaper when necessary."

She acts like she's shivering. "Ooh, chilling."

Maybe I don't want to be in this house after all.

"I don't need to prove myself to you," I say, turning to walk away.

"Freeze," she says with a little laugh. "I'm playing with you. Now, don't get bigheaded like you're the only constellation in the sky, but it's crystal clear you're bigger and badder than all of us. Just like it's crystal clear that you're also here because you know we build followings and you're aching to grow yours. A fun fact about me is I love me some beauty sleep, but even I woke up when we got your little notification of you going live. Thank every star in the galaxy that you weren't walking us through your nighttime routine."

I cross my arms. "Cut to the chase."

"You're going places, Infinity Reaper, and we want to help you get there."

"I'm not paying you for sponsored posts."

"Oh, please. I've made a cool million this year alone from commissioned ice sculptures that I make in minutes. And Samuel's revenue from all his viral videos of pranking people with his camouflage powers has us set. We don't need your money."

"Then what do you get in return?"

"We get to live in whatever world you're building for us," Zelda says. "We're doing just fine, but it's hard for celestials to live large in this country. True monsters like Senator Iron are only going to make things worse for us. You may not be a celestial yourself, but I've always admired the heart of a specter. They're scrappy with can-do attitudes that I wish more celestials had. Maybe if we did, we wouldn't need heroes like you to fight for us."

I think we're all finally starting to speak the same language. Emil is coming for my power, and I'll be damned if he succeeds.

"How can you help me?" I ask, understanding that they now have to impress me and not the other way around.

"I can give you so much needed PR help. I've been tracking your name online, and wow, you're getting some love but people are mostly bad-mouthing you. I wouldn't do a deep dive if you're still feeling vulnerable after the big betrayal because some haters think you're a bad brother, others think you're power-hungry, and tons think you're a criminal who should be locked up in the very prison you broke into last night."

"Don't forget about those who think he's all of the above," Samuel says.

"And then there's those who think you're all of the above," Zelda singsongs.

"Screw them," I say.

"No, don't screw—*woo.* Woo all of them. Go online and show them who you really are."

"Your strategy better not involve TikTok dances. That's not me."

Zelda laughs. "Ha, good one. Don't worry, we'll show everyone what an action hero you are and get the message out loud and clear that Brighton Rey is here to save the day. Then everything—and everyone—else will follow."

This is good company I'm keeping; I should've gone my own way sooner.

"Fine. You're hired under one condition."

Zelda's gray eyes narrow. "A complimentary ice sculpture?"

"It's actually your boyfriend's power I'm interested in."

Samuel seems on edge. "What about it?"

"Golden-strand hydras can camouflage too, but I haven't been able to tap into that ability yet. Give me some pointers so I can access it."

"Sure thing. Just don't go pranking people. That's my thing."

"That's not mine. Don't worry."

I'll never fully trust anyone ever again, and having a stealthy power like camouflage on my side will allow me to check in on my allies to make sure they aren't plotting against me. If someone is thinking about betraying me, then I'll have no choice but to reach into their head and rip out their brains so they can't think about anything ever again.

If word gets out that I'll do anything to survive, then maybe people will think twice about turning against me.

How's that for influence?

EIGHT

A BEAUTIFUL DAY

EMIL

There's no time to tend to the dead in the Sanctuary.

Once those evergreen blazers finish devouring the raging flames that were burning the castle and the surrounding woods, it's time to bounce. If that enforcer in the helicopter called for backup, an army could be rolling up any minute now with numbers we won't be able to beat this time. The surviving Halo Knights prioritize getting the young, living phoenixes to safety, praying to their holy fires for forgiveness since they're abandoning the corpses. These phoenixes deserve burials, like Gravesend; it's one of the few things I've gotten right in this life. Most Halo Knights vacate by foot through the forest while three others take to the sky on grown phoenixes, carrying the essentials that weren't blown to the heavens.

On our side, we pair up on the functioning quad bikes—me and Ness, Prudencia and Ma, Iris and Eva, Ruth and Wesley with their baby held tight—and we get the hell out of here even though none of us have experience with these vehicles. But when you're always on the run, you become an expert on keeping it moving. Ness, Prudencia,

Iris, and Ruth take a few minutes to test drive the bikes before going into the woods, following Wesley's lead as he regularly hops off his bike with Esther to dash ahead and scout the best path forward. My spirits on the way out are different from how I felt on the way in. We were rolling through these red, yellow, and orange trees with pure wonder, and I was admiring all the paintings of phoenixes on boulders and watching real ones fly around. They were so alive until . . .

Until I brought a massacre to the Sanctuary.

I'm not going to kill Brighton, but I'm definitely getting some punches in.

I hang on tight to Ness, my arms wrapped around his stomach and my chin resting on his shoulder as we move through the forest. He's the one bright spot that's following me away from the horrors we just survived. I feel like Ness and I are driving off into the sunset instead of fleeing for our lives. But that fantasy dies real fast because this is far from the end of our story—and I don't know if Ness is going to be by my side when this nightmare does end.

I look up at the clear sky, hoping to find a phoenix that's as black as night.

But Nox isn't flying above us, and I have no idea where Wyatt is.

Or if he's alive.

This is bringing me back to the days where I swore Ness was killed.

I don't know Wyatt's fate, but I hope that my gut instinct is wrong. Until I know what's up for sure, I hold on to Ness like I never want to let him go.

The ride is bumpy as we travel across rocky terrain, but eventually we glide onto this smooth path that brings us out into the Storm

King State Park. Prudencia shouts for everyone to pull over and we stop and chill by a trail that gives us a clear view of the mountains and clouds and the river.

"I have a headache," Ma says, getting off the quad bike and going straight toward a water fountain.

"I tried to stabilize us with my power as best as I could," Prudencia says. She looks really guilty as she watches my mother drink.

"It's not your fault, sweetheart," Ma says, drying her lips with her palm. "The ride itself and everything else has me feeling sick."

I rush to Ma's side, holding her hand. "How's your heart?"

The last thing I need right now is my mother having another heart attack.

"Broken," Ma whispers. "But I'm alive."

I can't believe everything Ma has been through this year: becoming a single parent after Dad died; confronting the family secret of my adoption after I threw that first fire-dart on the train; having to leave her home after I agreed to fight alongside the Spell Walkers; a heart attack after Brighton was held hostage; Brighton stealing the Reaper's Blood and almost dying before he became invincible; our family home being destroyed because of a specter who was hiding there to ambush us; and of course Brighton publicly threatening my life as if a mother wants to watch one son kill the other. And now Ma sits on a park bench after a rocky getaway on stolen enforcer bikes. This can't be what she thought her life would be.

"I'm sorry for everything, Ma. This is no way to live."

"It's not your fault either, my Emilio."

"It's our families' faults," Ness says. "Brighton for exposing our location and the Senator for siccing enforcers on us."

Iris keeps looking over her shoulder. "And to make sure more enforcers don't come our way, we can't stay out in broad daylight. We're not going to be able to park these bikes outside the gym either. Let's ditch them and find another way to Brooklyn. Any ideas?"

"We should've stolen the helicopter," Wesley says, bouncing Esther.

"Again, we're looking for something inconspicuous."

"I'm not saying we would have landed the helicopter on the street. Just parachuted out."

"I no longer trust you with our child," Ruth says. "Hand her over."

In seconds, Wesley has passed Esther to Ruth and returned to his original spot. "None of you are any fun. What do we do, then?"

Even faster than Wesley dashing, everyone turns to me.

I get it; I'm now the leader because I talked a big game and convinced our team to give it one last shot. But this doesn't instantly make me some master strategist. I'm trying to cook something up, but it's hard with all these eyes on me, like I'm walking a tightrope in front of a full stadium and desperately trying to not screw up my performance. Maybe there's a nearby train we can hop on, and I immediately realize that's stupid because Ness is the only one who could change his face and blend in with the crowd. What if everyone camps out here and I fly them out to Brooklyn one by one? Yeah, sure, maybe I'll not only suddenly regain the stamina to do that seven times, but I'll also discover that I have the powerhouse strength to carry everyone. (I can obviously carry the baby, I'm not that weak, but still, that trip would be exhausting.) Damn, more than ever I wish I had my own phoenix. I could load up our more passive crewmembers, like Ma and Eva and Esther, on my phoenix's back and they could all fly safely to

Brooklyn while our more active-powered gleamcrafters could find another way to the next haven. But that's also stupid because riding on phoenixback isn't exactly discreet, and I went ahead and ordered Wyatt to fly away with the stealthiest phoenix I know.

I look to the sky again, thinking about what a terrible leader I am.

Iris snaps her fingers. "Emil? Anything?"

"Yeah, sorry, we could . . ."

I swore speaking would make something happen, but I got nothing.

All I can think about as I stare up at the sky is how it's a beautiful day and how it's so strange that I watched a burning corpse and dead phoenixes fall out of the sky on a beautiful day. How the hell does that happen? For carnage like that, there should be lightning storms and floods. It should be raining fire. But that much death shouldn't happen on a beautiful day. That's got to be some law of nature moving forward or something because—

"Come walk with me, firefly," Ness says, snapping me out of my trance.

I take his hand, following him across the park.

"Not a great time for a hookup, fellas," Wesley calls after us. "Happy to book out the gym locker room once we settle on a getaway plan."

"Just back up and give us some space," Ness snaps.

"It was just a joke!"

No one else says anything. Myself included. I don't know what's got Ness heating up like this, but it could be a million things. We're all running on fumes, starving, and hating this cycle of life.

We sit at our own park bench, close enough that we can keep an eye on everyone, but far enough for some privacy.

"You keep staring at the sky," Ness says. "I take it you're not daydreaming. You're looking for Wyatt, aren't you?"

"I mean, yeah. I'm concerned about him. He's one of us."

"Absolutely. He's one of us, but the rest of us are here and we need your attention too."

"But I know you're alive—"

"Not for long if we don't get our act together."

My tears are coming in hot because I know where this is coming from, and I know where this is going. "Ness, let's not do this. I'm not trying to get into a fight about Wyatt."

"Me either. None of that is my business." Ness slides his hand out of mine. "You're not my boyfriend, Emil."

Those words hit like a swift punch to my gut. They seem to knock the air out of Ness too even though he's the one who swung at me.

I stare at Ness like he's a stranger, like he's wearing someone else's face, someone I have never seen before in my entire life and wouldn't ever think about again. But Ness isn't a stranger and I'll think about him until the day I die, no matter what goes down between us. And I guess he's making his choice pretty clear.

"I was up front about Wyatt," I say, my voice cracking. "I seriously wasn't trying to fall in love and—"

"So you're—"

"No, I'm not in love with Wyatt. I'm saying that I wasn't trying to catch feelings for anyone. I'm just trying to survive and keep my people alive. And that includes you, Ness. But when I swore you were dead, I had regrets about not acting on anything with you. Look at everyone around me." I point back to our group. "Wes and Ruth have their family. Iris and Eva have each other. Even Prudencia and Brighton were figuring things out before he ruined everything. I'm the one who thought I should wait until all the stars were aligned before I start living my life, and when I connected with Wyatt, I realized that was stupid. He could easily die too. I'm just trying to be real and find happiness, even in times of war."

Ness snickers, which is the last thing I expected from him.

"What's so funny?"

"You're definitely finding happiness in times of war all right." Ness's amber eyes stare at me dead-on as he says, "I saw you kissing the Halo Knight while everyone was fighting for their lives."

I'm shaking like it's so cold, but it's not, it's a beautiful day, and the ugliest things keep showing their faces on this beautiful day.

"Look, I'm sorry you saw that—"

"You can kiss whoever you want, Emil. I'm done thinking I actually matter to you that way even though you said things were different now that I'm alive. But I certainly don't see you risking your life to kiss me in the middle of a battlefield. You could have been killed."

"You're right, I got lucky—"

"You didn't get lucky," Ness says with tears in his own eyes. "An enforcer was about to blast a hole in your skull when I laid him out. You would've died in Wyatt's arms. But I saved your life because that's what I do."

I'm choking on my next words, an apology, maybe a thank-you.

"If you're just trying to survive, Emil, do a better job."

Ness gets up, and I practically fly to stop him.

"Wait, wait." I catch my breath and wipe my tears.

He's looking at me expectantly, like there's something that I could do or say that could diffuse all of this right now.

"I want to fall in love, have my own family. Everyone here has gotten that. The closest I've come to it was in a past life. But right now I'm the Infinity Son. I have people to save, a team to lead, and a war against my brother to win. The only thing I'll be doing on a battlefield is fighting." I pause, like I'm taking a moment of silence as I grieve the times of kissing Wyatt on Nox under the moonlight sky or that first kiss with Ness that finally changed things between us. "I'll do everything in my power to make sure you survive this, Ness. And if I get out of this alive too, I hope you'll want to see my face as much as I'll want to see yours."

I plant my lips on Ness's cheek, the last time I'll kiss anyone until the war is won.

Possibly the last kiss of my life.

NINE
CHANGING THE GAME

NESS

I understand why people hide behind masks.

Telling the truth isn't always a good look. Lies let people live in peace.

If I never said anything to Emil, he wouldn't be closing himself off to love. That's not what I was trying to do. I just need him to be more careful so he can live the life he's fighting for. But I have to take off my own mask and confront the greater truth: it hurt my heart way more than I thought it would to think about Emil fighting for a life with Wyatt. That kiss on the battlefield was reckless, it was idiotic . . . it was passionate.

I have to accept Emil isn't my boyfriend. That's why I said it out loud. Not only so Emil could hear it, but so I could too. That declaration hurt, but it's true. It was clear when we were driving away from the Sanctuary that I wasn't euphoric over having Emil's arms wrapped around me even though I've dreamed about sharing intimate spaces with him. But I couldn't get my mind off Emil kissing Wyatt and thinking about how often they've been wrapped around one another, and how far they've taken things when Emil and I have only had the one kiss.

Emil might be closing the door on love right now, but there's hope for us after everything.

That's assuming the country's most hunted specters get out of this alive.

After Emil kisses my cheek, he returns to our group. I follow. Judging by everyone's faces, they're picking up on the tension.

"I'm sensing you don't have a plan," Iris says.

Emil shakes his head.

"Then we go with mine," Iris says, turning to Wesley. "Go steal a van."

"Wait. What if someone sees him?" Emil asks.

"I'm pretty fast, bro," Wesley says.

"Still, if you get caught on camera, that's another strike against us."

"They already think we're criminals," Iris says.

"So we're going to commit crimes and prove them right?"

Iris approaches Emil, looking up into his eyes. "Just because we're heroes doesn't mean that we're going to get anything done by respecting the law. It's a sad reality, but to survive in a world where the government is doing everything they can to make our lives harder, to weaken us, we're going to have to get a little shady to protect our light. Food, housing, the essentials."

This isn't something I've had to think about throughout my life. I may have grown up with a tyrant for a father, but I did so in a three-story manor that was paid for with my grandfather's invention of the power-proof vests that all enforcers wear when combatting gleamcrafters. Blood money.

Emil's head is hanging low. "Okay, but can we not, I don't know, steal any vans that have car seats inside? Let's not screw over some parent."

"Deal." Iris turns to Wesley. "Go."

"Hey," I call out. Emil turns to me quickly, but I'm not talking to him. "I'll tag along, Wesley. No one needs evidence to make your life harder. I'll shift into someone else and the public can pin the theft on a person who doesn't exist."

"Hop on up," Wesley says, inviting me into his open arms.

"Absolutely not."

"Are you more of a piggyback rider?"

I shake my head. Both options are terrible, but I choose the first. I feel like some dude in distress in his arms, and Ruth is laughing while Wesley smiles down at me. "Make it fast," I say.

"Only way I know how."

The last thing I see clearly is Emil watching me like he's doubting I'll come back, and then everything becomes a sickening blur. Colors come and go as fast as lightning and my lungs are ready to explode from air when we find ourselves down the block from a gas station. Wesley sets me down, and I'm dizzy for a few seconds before all is right again. We scout for cameras, finding the obvious ones at the gas station but none around us. Still, I waste no time shifting, pulling from different features of the enforcers we battled at the Sanctuary—buzzed brown hair, white skin, six foot three, very muscular to intimidate whoever I'm going to rob, and I add a fresh black eye similar to the one that must be forming on the enforcer I punched before he could kill Emil during his battlefield make-out session.

"You have a perfectly forgettable face," Wesley says, observing my guise. "This fake face, obviously. I'm not gay, but I certainly get why Emil is into your real face."

I almost tell him to let Emil know that, but I keep my mouth shut.

If Emil is focusing on the mission, then so am I.

Once I get a sense of direction from where Wesley brought us, I head to the gas station alone so we don't even risk his blur getting caught on camera. It's tricky wanting to steal the first van I see so we can get everyone to safety while also wanting to respect the moral rules. These things didn't matter when I was a Blood Caster. If we needed something, we took it. Money, weapons, potions—even people.

But I'm no longer a Blood Caster.

I'm not a Spell Walker either.

I'm Ness Arroyo—whoever that is.

One thing I do know about myself is that I agree with Emil's heart when it comes to not stealing from the innocent. That's why even though there's a van that's big enough for everyone in our party, I don't hijack it when a woman comes out to fill up the tank since there are literal babies on board. Triplets. If anything, I'm tempted to go inside the station and fill up her trunk with milk and food and maybe even some alcohol since she deserves some grown-up time too. More cars come and go, but none big enough. I'm starting to think we should take whichever cars we can get and go in groups until a perfect black SUV pulls in, blasting music from some white rapper whose name I've forgotten, and the car and song come to a stop by the gas pumps. I casually walk by, studying the driver—he's as tall as my current shift height and he's wearing a real gold chain. I tour the car from the outside, peeking through the tinted windows to make sure there aren't any children inside I'd be evicting, or too many adults I wouldn't be able to fight off. It's completely empty. Then I see something that drives the nail into the coffin for why I will feel no remorse robbing this pathetic excuse for a human: bumper stickers that read *STRONG AS IRON!* and *THE IRON BISHOP*.

When the man finishes filling the gas and returns to the driver's door, I'm ready to pounce. But I should give him the benefit of the doubt. This might not even be his car.

"Excuse me, sir," I say in my best military voice. "You also voting for Iron and Bishop?"

"You know it, my guy!" The enthusiasm is not infectious. "Let's send these celestials—"

I'll never know where he wants to send celestials because he's knocked out with one punch. I snatch his gold chain to make it look more like a robbery and also because terrible people shouldn't have nice things. I hop in the car and keep the window down because it reeks of cologne and cigarettes. My time as a shifter has trained me to not be surprised by gorgeous exteriors not matching their insides. I slam my foot on the pedal and drive off, waving at Wesley out the window as I speed down the street so he can catch up. It's no surprise when I pull up to the park that Wesley is already there, lounging on the grass with our group.

"All good?" Emil asks sheepishly.

"I stole from one of the Senator's supporters," I say.

"I bet that was delicious soup for the soul," Wesley says.

"The first sip," I say.

We waste no time loading into the car, with Prudencia driving us into the city. I'm sitting up front with her so Emil and I aren't forced into each other's spaces. We quickly switch off the horrible rap track that the owner was listening to and turn the radio on. There's a news station covering the breakout from the Bounds and cautioning civilians to be mindful on the streets because of all the freed prisoners with an added warning about all of us. The radio stays off for the rest of the drive, and we all sit in silence.

Two hours later, we arrive in Brooklyn.

Prudencia pulls into an alley and telekinetically turns a shop's camera upward so it won't capture us exiting the car. Iris crushes the license plate, smashes the windows, rips out the steering wheel, and slashes the tires so it won't be recognizable to anyone who stumbles onto it. We're careful as we go down the street, not wanting to be spotted by a single soul. I wish I could extend my power to everyone or that Halloween was today so it wouldn't be suspicious if they walked around in masks. There's one close call when a kid turns the corner, but he's too absorbed in his fantasy book to notice the very real heroes sharing the sidewalk with him. Then again, who's to say that he would think we're heroes at all. The Senator winning in the polls means there are more people who hate us than support us.

We rush to the back door of Mele's Melee, and Wesley knocks seven times. We're greeted by a woman who appears to be in her thirties with brown hair that's pulled back into a tiny bun, muscles similar to the ones I sported with my disguise except very real, and a wide smile that makes me feel safe enough that my heartbeat slows down. She is helping, not hunting, us.

"Get on in, friends," the stranger I assume to be Mele says.

I'm the last one in.

The gym smells like a gym. Just because gleamcrafters have powers doesn't mean we can't work up a sweat just as much as anyone doing cardio or deadlifting.

Everyone in my group has already begun going down the stairs into the basement, where we're going to be living, but I can't help but peek through the ajar door to see where we'll be training whenever the gym is closed. There's an obstacle course that someone is literally flying through while hugging a punching bag, probably strengthening their chances of helping someone else escape a dangerous situation. Someone with swift-speed is on a treadmill with a belt that's moving faster than I've ever seen before, not even whenever Dione would train. A trainer wearing the same gym-branded shirt as Mele is coaching a young celestial who is casting fire at moving target boards, scorching the bull's-eye when she gets her first hit. A woman's arms stretch like elastic, and she begins using them to jump rope. There's a match in the boxing ring between two people with powerhouse strength, and I don't get to see the outcome because the door suddenly closes shut.

I turn, and Mele's eyes are glowing like stars.

I'm suddenly on edge again, my heart racing.

"Telekinetic?" I ask.

"Yes. And you can look like anyone?"

I'm bracing myself for some perverted follow-up. "Yeah."

"How much can I pay you to turn into your father? I'd love to punch that face of his."

I laugh a little. "I'd let you get a free hit if I wasn't scared of you breaking my skull."

Mele leads me down the stairs. "He sucks so bad I finally registered to vote. It feels pointless right about now, but progress is progress. That's what I always tell my clients, especially the ones who don't want to work out their powers until they've got some big job or showcase right around the corner. Stay ready so you don't have to get ready, you know."

I do know.

But we're not ready for the fights ahead of us. I can't think of a better place to get ready than this gym that we'll be using as a haven.

Downstairs in the basement are three cots, a couple air mattresses still boxed up, and pillows thrown onto rubber mats. None trump my bed back at the manor, but it will do. The smell of sweat has been replaced with pizza grease, and my stomach is tearing itself up as I find the four pizza boxes stacked on a table next to vitamin waters. Emil wastes no time opening the box, getting a slice for Carolina as she sits down on a cot. Everyone else is preparing plates and hydrating when I realize there's nothing here for Emil.

I quietly go up to Mele. "You got anything vegan-friendly?"

"I didn't know you were vegan," Mele says.

"I'm not, but he is."

Emil looks at us. "It's okay. I'm glad you all got something."

"Eating is part of survival," I say.

Mele gives me a thumbs-up. "It sure is. Emil, I'll order in the heartiest vegan meal of your life. Does anyone else need anything?

Something to feed your stomachs? Or your souls? Heroes need nice things too!"

Everyone puts in their requests: Carolina needs more medicine for her heart; Ruth requests some baby food and diapers for Esther; Iris wants some hair dye since her green has been fading; Eva asks for candles so she can meditate to serene smells; Prudencia is aching for something sweet; and Wesley wants the gossip on why Mele broke up with his tattooist friend Xyla.

"I need to watch the news," I say. Everyone else might be exhausted by what's being said about them, but I need to be up to date on whatever lies the Senator is spreading. "Do you have a computer or phone I can borrow?"

"You can use Brighton's laptop," Prudencia says, pulling it out of a duffel bag and handing it over. "I packed everything he left behind."

Holding this laptop feels like carrying a loaded wand. Anyone who thinks the internet can't ruin someone's life as much as—if not more than—a weapon has never been a victim the way I have.

"I don't know the password," Emil says.

I open up the laptop and stare into the camera. "No need," I say as gray light washes over me and my face shifts into the one that millions watched on social media out his brother's secret. Not only is my replica of Brighton effective enough to bypass his laptop's facial recognition, it draws a gasp out of Carolina and she stares at me like I'm the ghost of her son. Whenever I imitated someone for Luna's missions, it always impressed the other Blood Casters. But there's nothing but tension in this room and everyone seems to have lost their appetites. I drop the morph before they forget it's me behind a Brighton mask.

"Is anyone else thinking what I'm thinking?" Ruth whispers as she holds a sleeping Esther.

"How creepy that was?" Wesley asks.

"How realistic it was," Ruth says.

"That was a pretty easy job, to be honest," I say.

Ruth comes closer so she doesn't have to raise her voice. "I didn't mean to doubt your abilities. I'm only pointing out the special position we're in since we have your power and Brighton's possessions. Can't you film a video as him and post it on his channels?"

If only it were that easy. Even the Senator understood that impersonations are tricky when you're trying to cause harm on your enemy while not exposing yourself. His campaign manager, Roslyn Fox, wanted me to film propaganda as fake victims of the Spell Walkers, but the Senator prevented me from doing so because he knew that it could be traced back to him. It's hard enough thinking about how I'll outsmart the Senator without giving everyone more reasons to distrust anything they see online knowing they can blame it on me and my power.

"Any impersonation of Brighton would be pulled by the day, and our attempt at costing him followers will only help him gain some. No one will let us live that down," I say.

Ruth digests the information and doesn't fight me. "You're right, Ness."

"It was a good idea," Emil says, keeping her morale up.

I go online, and the obvious news stories are trending: the break-in at my family's manor; the reveal that I not only survived the Blackout, but have become a specter with shifter blood; the Senator sentencing me to the Bounds and the mass breakout that included me; Brighton telling the world that he'd been attacked by the Spell Walkers and how Emil can resurrect. Then there's a new story as I expected. It's about the Sanctuary and the headline is sickening: "Eduardo Iron Threatens to Kill Senator Iron."

"Shit."

Emil and Prudencia watch over my shoulder as I play the video in the article. It's the footage from the enforcer's body cam. He was on the ground at the time, so the camera is aimed on me with the sky thickening with smoke behind me.

"It's you," the enforcer says in the video.

"It's me," I say before pinning him down with my foot. Then it looks really bad as I ask, "Did the Senator send you here?" And it gets worse as I say, "I'll take that as a yes." Worse again when I kick the enforcer in the face. But nothing is as incriminating as when I say, "I'm going to kill him."

Then Emil's voice can be heard saying, "He's laid out."

But I wasn't talking about the enforcer. I make it very clear: "No, I'm going to kill the Senator."

The footage from that interaction ends there, but there are more clips from body cams that incriminate everyone else as well: Emil throwing fire; Wesley casting a spell with a stolen wand; Prudencia telekinetically destroying a quad bike; and other snatches from the fight.

"How do we beat people who keep turning us into the villains?" I ask.

This must be payback for everyone I've wronged in my time as a shifter.

"We don't stop being the heroes," Emil answers.

"That's nice in theory, but it's not a plan. We need an actionable step."

Emil picks up his brother's laptop. "We're going to take a page out of Brighton's book. We got tons of support when he was posting those Spell Walkers of New York interviews. All we did was tell the truth. So let's do a new feature, but this time . . ." He pauses, fighting to meet my eyes. ". . . this time it'll be the two of us."

Me and Emil, in front of a camera.

Together.

"Everyone is going to think we're lying our faces off," I say.

"You got me to trust you, even after you manipulated all of us."

"You have a better heart than most people," I say. I wonder if that's crossing a line.

"I'm not the last good person in the world. If someone's on the fence right now, it's up to us to get them on our side. You got this, Ness. I believe you."

I'm going to tell the truth.

No masks.

I pray to the stars that it's a good look that wins us some peace.

TEN

FABIAN CÓRDOVA

MARIBELLE

The stars are appearing in the night sky as I prepare for my trip to the past.

I first retrocycled at the New Ember Sanctuary's meditation space. Incense sticks were burning, smelling like rain, which felt odd because how could fire smell like rain; that could be why the incense failed to relax me. Or it was because I was too tense around Emil, who I will never forgive for not letting me kill June when I had the chance, or I was too annoyed by Wyatt, whose showmanship was slowing down the process. I couldn't settle in until Tala guided us retrocyclers through breathing exercises, asking us to focus on the lives we haven't lived, why we were visiting them in the first place, and what knowledge we hoped to return with. She encouraged us to follow our instincts, just like a phoenix who wasn't taught to use this power would.

It's Tala's voice that will usher me through this once again.

But it's Luna who speaks now: "Kindly set yourself on fire, granddaughter, so I may keep warm."

As unwelcome as her interruption may be, she's not wrong. The temperatures have dropped tonight; low forties, maybe even high thirties. I'd rather do this indoors instead of out here on the rooftop, but I'm hoping my celestial connection to the sky will aid me in this journey. It was hard enough retrocycling to Sera's final day, and she was my immediate predecessor. Fabian is an ancestor who died over forty years ago. I'm going to need every ounce of gleam to get me in.

"If all goes well, we won't be out here too long," I say.

"If all doesn't go well, you will become familiar with a crueler fire," Luna says.

She means I'll burn as Fabian and his secrets did in that house.

Tala steps toward Luna with the oblivion dagger. "Shut it."

"I apologize for requesting warmth as an elderly, dying woman," Luna says with absolutely no note of a sincere apology in her voice.

"I don't care about your comfort. Don't mess with Maribelle's head."

No one gets what they want if I can't do this.

Luna seems to realize this too as she tells me, "As you were."

Before I ignite my flames, I close my eyes, trying to find Fabian, and it's like trying to find a light switch in a pitch-black building. I don't know what floor or what wall the switch may be on, but I know it's somewhere in here. This time retrocycling is trickier than the last. I'd grown up familiar enough with Sera Córdova and had access to more pictures online to solidify her image in my head. All I'm working with for Fabian are Luna's stories and descriptions of photographs she abandoned long ago because she saw no value in holding on to them. Online searches about the Córdova brothers only resulted in stories about their mysterious powers, written like folklore instead of truth and illustrated like skeletal grim reapers instead of men. A clear look at Fabian's face would've been useful, like searching for a light switch in a building that is only dimmed instead of pitch black.

"I don't know enough about him," I say, opening my eyes. Maybe I can pull an all-nighter on the laptop and find some pictures of Fabian in some archive about the Córdova brothers.

"He was a quintuplet, correct?" Tala asks, turning to Luna. "You have no photographs of your ex-husband anywhere?"

Luna scoffs. "I'm not of your generation, gripping a device everywhere I go and capturing moments I won't ever return to."

"That's not how I fly either," Tala says, flicking open her empty, phone-less palm. "It's not stupid for me to assume you have pictures of the man you married."

"No, it's not stupid. But it is very wrong. Besides, I already conjured up descriptions of Santiago as best as I remembered."

"Then you'll describe him again. I'll draw him this time, and once we get it right, Maribelle can focus on bringing him to life."

"A Halo Knight and a sketch artist," Luna drawls. "Quite the talent, you are."

It's a miracle Luna hasn't found that bone blade between her eyes yet.

I'm getting restless. I'm tempted to go for a flight to think alone for a moment. But there's no way I'll return to a living Luna. "A better visual would be helpful, but it's Fabian himself I'm struggling with . . . I don't know who he is. I don't know when he saw his first ghost, or if he got along with his brothers, or if he's ever been in love."

"This is why you focus on the life you haven't lived," Tala says. "Recall what you do know."

"The ghosts, the family possessing Death's senses, the burning home."

"That's all surface, Maribelle. Dig deeper."

I close my eyes, trying to feel my way into Fabian's skin, no longer concerning myself with all the ways that skin took shape over his flesh and bones. "He didn't know peace," I say. "It's impossible to know peace when ghosts are begging for their lives back."

"Do you know what it's like to not know peace?" Tala asks, beautifully coaching me.

I channel the countless instances when I hated this world for hating me.

How I would bring them peace, but they didn't want me to have it myself.

How it's hard to walk around when I feel eyes on me at all times, glaring, judging, loathing.

How I don't deserve my own life unless it's spent saving theirs.

Fabian would know this feeling, this pain, this misery, this injustice.

I'm sympathizing with my great-uncle because even though I have not lived his life, I have lived mine without peace.

"Think about what you need from Fabian," Tala says.

I'm going to collect the resurrection ritual, but no, it's deeper than that.

I need my great-uncle to help me bring back my boyfriend.

I cannot retrocycle into Atlas's lifetime. He's not my blood or some ancestor, but he doesn't have to stay in the past. By collecting the resurrection ritual, I can return Atlas to the present, where he belongs. I can have the life Fabian was unable to have himself, a life that became so haunting that he couldn't stand to live it anymore.

"Ignite," Tala whispers.

Fire crawls all over me, like dark yellow flames are about to devour me whole. But I don't fear it. I embrace it, like I'm a candle whose entire existence revolves around me burning.

I am becoming my own portal to the past.

I'm reaching for the peaceless life Fabian lived so I can find peace in my own.

This is how our family's legacy will no longer be death and death alone.

It will be a legacy of rebirth.

The flow of life and death.

Accepting that I'm not simply a Lucero but also a Córdova and a de León was crucial in helping me find Sera through time and space. I picture my hand going through the earth, gripping the roots of my family tree. My grandfather and great-uncles are all flowers, wilted, flattened, nothing but stems with thorns so sharp that I feel like I'm being shredded apart. This isn't true, but it is, and it's a lie, but it's not. There's something psychedelic about retrocycling, where being one with yourself is one of the greatest impossibilities because you must connect to the greater world around you to walk it. Last time I remember smelling the color blue, and hearing pain. Right now, I can feel fire on my tongue, like the sun-hot moonberry pies Mama baked, a family recipe that once felt destined to be passed on to me but never was. Maybe Mama felt weird passing the family recipe on to a daughter that wasn't hers biologically. But I was her family, and I feel powerful declaring that, owning that. She welcomed and accepted me as I must now welcome and accept Fabian. My mouth goes dry, and I can't call up any spit, but I'm tasting words—some I know in

Spanish, others are completely unfamiliar to me—and every letter is like eating chalk.

I can hear Fabian's voice.

The ghosts too, but I can't make out what they're saying.

I feel everything—the fire on my tongue and chalk between my teeth, the thorns and roots crowning around my head.

Fabian's voice cries out in Spanish and English, begging to be left alone.

His life has been disturbed by the company of ghosts so much that he not only chose to live in solitude, but he also obliterated his soul so he wouldn't have to spend his death with the dead.

Suddenly, I'm glowing, I'm crackling, I'm burning.

Then everything goes out and I have become darkness.

No, I'm in the darkness and I'm not alone.

Fabian Córdova is standing before me.

My great-uncle has my brown complexion and dark hair, his also tied back in a ponytail. He reminds me of a gardener in his muddy rubber boots, overalls stained by the earth, and an apron with pockets full of vials, seeds, and the oblivion dagger. I close the distance between us and stare into his sad eyes, into his soul that will soon be obliterated.

The darkness shrinks away and the world around us finds color.

This house is tiny, and even without tapping into Fabian's feelings, I know this place isn't a home. There's no warmth here. No family pictures and no art apart from the letters and symbols that have been written in chalk on the walls. There are ingredients for the potion he must have been working on to get rid of his powers. A trunk sits in the corner, lid closed. The messiness of overflowing dishes and fruit flies buzzing around trash make it clear that Fabian has been staying here, but I would never say he's living here.

That might have something to do with the fact that the darkness peeling away hasn't only revealed color and life, but also the dead.

The ghosts are so humanlike it's as if they're alive already, which unfortunately they're not because otherwise they wouldn't be so damn pissed off. This house could comfortably host six, seven people, but there must be hundreds of ghosts packed in here, all crowding together and blending through one another. There are heads poking through the walls, and when I peek through the only open window, I'm chilled by the sight of thousands of ghosts across the island, some even standing in the ocean. It doesn't stop here. Shadows of black light keep popping up under the night sky, manifesting into even more ghosts who add to the howling chorus, begging Fabian to bring them all back to life.

I feel eyes on me even though no one can technically see me.

But I feel it because Fabian feels it and what Fabian feels I now feel.

Somehow, Fabian isn't cowering in a corner as I would. I detect some fear within him, but it's nowhere near close to how scared I am. He's more . . . sympathetic.

"No te ayudaré," Fabian gently says.

My Spanish is rusty since I only really used it with Mama and Papa, but I know what it's like to have Spanish-speaking civilians asking me for help in their language. But Fabian isn't asking for help or even offering it—he's rejecting the dead's cries for help.

All I hear are the howls, a thousandfold. I don't know if I'm channeling Fabian's suicidal feelings or if I truly want to die myself because of this hollowness in my heart. It's only been a few minutes of my life and I already want this to be over; I can't believe Fabian has lived with this for decades. Maybe it's different for Fabian since he can understand them. I thought I would become fluent in ghost by being here, but I guess it doesn't work that way since I'm not in his head, where his power is translating these howls into words. This tracks given my only other experience retrocycling, when I witnessed Sera receiving the vision that foretold her and Bautista's deaths but didn't get to actually see it for myself.

I'm miserable here. What I would give to hear Atlas sing, or to see him smile. Something good, anything good—it's a feeling that Fabian echoes.

Fabian walks through the ghosts as if they're not there, making his way to a counter where he begins grinding a ruby with a granite mortar and pestle. He wipes the sweat off his forehead before he continues pounding away at the gem. His lips are twitching, like he's about to respond to one of the many howling ghosts, but he keeps his words to himself. He knows better; he knows his words don't matter. I sympathize with that feeling after pleading with people to give me space to grieve the deaths of my family, to believe me when I told the world that Mama and Papa weren't terrorists, to not just see me as a girl with powers but a human being too. Instead of screaming into microphones and on telecasts and even on streets after saving the lives of others, giving the public a chance to see me as someone real, as someone hurting, as someone with a broken heart, I was better off keeping all my words inside, where no one could be faulted for not listening to me if I never spoke at all.

"No te maté," Fabian mutters, his shoulders tensing, like he can feel the dead gripping him even though they should leave him alone since he's just told the ghosts that he didn't kill them, that he's not responsible for their deaths.

My great-uncle pours the red dust onto a silver plate, the tiniest of pebbles clinking, and in its natural form, I realize this is gempowder—the very same substance used for explosives before some craftsmen created gem-grenades. Then my own tragic memory floats to the surface while I'm living inside Fabian's most tragic moment. I've seen the footage of the Blackout attack so many times that it's burned into my memory, it's as if I was there myself or witnessed it unfold while retrocycling, but everything is blown to the sky after Mama—while possessed by June—hurls ruby gem-grenades around the Nightlocke Conservatory, destroying everything and everyone. All the writing and symbols on the walls of Fabian's house will be lost to the world, completely indecipherable.

Along with the book of scrolls I've come back in time to find.

I have to move if I'm going to stand any chance of escaping Fabian's death.

I hesitate before stepping through the ghosts, as if I'll be risking possession, but I'm safe from them. It's still odd as I move through the dead, who mostly appear as living people, and I stop in my tracks as a black light sparks into existence, manifesting into an older woman who reminds me of myself in another life.

The woman howls, and Fabian freezes.

"Debes quedarte ahí, Madre," he says in Spanish.

This is his mother—my great-grandmother.

I don't know her name, only that she died in childbirth after delivering the youngest brother with the deadly touch. She's family, but in this timeline she's dead, and it looks like retrocycling has its limits since I can't tap into her ghostly emotions. I may not know what she's feeling, but I can take a stab at it. Ghosts are born out of violent deaths, and she must've had one of her own. I had assumed the only pain she faced was from childbirth, and that she died immediately after, but maybe her son's power was more nightmarish and traumatizing than a quick merciful kill. I'm guessing my great-grandmother wants to be brought back to live the life she lost after she died creating it, but her son is rejecting her, telling her she must stay in the afterlife. I would howl at the world too.

Three men—ghosts—appear before Fabian, all looking like him, but different enough for me to know that they are—that they were—their own people in life. I didn't know Fabian and Santiago's brothers had already died by this point, but here they are now, howling stars knows what.

"Lo siento, mis hermanos," Fabian says, an apology that doesn't quiet them. "No debo ayudar." He's saying he can't help. Then I realize my translation is off because of course he can help them. He's spent his life having the dead telling him how to help them. Fabian is saying that he *shouldn't* help them—any of them. His mother, his brothers. They're all looking at Fabian as if they hate him, and I wonder how long it took before the ghosts of his family turned on him like this—the mother who never got to raise him, the brothers who grew up alongside him—all of them looking murderous. All could be forgiven, all could be repaired if he just brings them back. "Lo siento," he apologizes again, and he means it with his entire heart—I can feel how much it's breaking.

The ghosts keep howling, and Fabian presses his palms against his ears and squeezes his eyes shut. It's pointless, and we both know it.

There's no shutting out these voices and there's no pretending that they aren't there. He drops his hands to his sides, defeated.

I'm hating this family I've never known and I don't know if they were as horrible in life as they are in death, but I want out of here. I'm searching for the scrolls, when Fabian sucks in a breath, and we both jump like scared felines. I turn to see if something or someone else has appeared, but Fabian is only staring at his family.

"No me amenaces," Fabian breathes, pointing at the ghosts of his mother and brothers one by one and staring at them dead-on.

His family's threatening him? With what? What can they possibly do that they haven't already done? That they aren't already doing? What could be worse than this vicious haunting?

Fabian howls, the kind that can only come from the throat of the living, one that sets his apart from the chorus of the dead. He flips around and goes to the trunk in the corner, flipping open the lid in a rage, and it bangs against the wall. Fabian retrieves what looks at first like a family album, but when he slams it down on the table, there aren't photographs of him and his brothers, but instead aged pages.

This is it.

The book of scrolls.

How I can bring Atlas back to life, how Fabian could have done the same for his family.

Fabian looks down at the book. I know what the future holds for this moment, but I can still feel the contemplation in his heart, like he's ready to just bring everyone back so he can move on. What I don't know is how long from this point Fabian will set everything on fire and drive the dagger into his heart. I look down at the scrolls, wanting to commit the ingredients and instructions to memory, but it's not in English or Spanish—it's in Latin.

A dead language.

How the hell am I—

Fabian turns the page and now it's in Italian.

Again, and now German.

French.

Portuguese.

As Fabian keeps turning, I'm realizing that he's taken down the instructions from ghosts in every possible language, many of which I'm sure he's not fully fluent in.

Or maybe he is.

I don't know what it's like to spend my life speaking to the dead.

Fabian arrives at the page in Spanish, and beside it is the one in English. I look between both pages, trusting the Spanish page more since it's his native language, but I consult the page in English since that's mine.

Undo a Death,

Renew a Life

To resurrect the deceased you must place their ashes inside a Phoenix Pit. What was once a grave will now become a resting place in which the dead will wake up. To hold the soul of the human, remove the corpse of the phoenix first. The unnatural death of an immortal is the heart of a natural resurrection for a mortal. Those essences will consecrate your grounds. Fill the hole of the earth with boiling water as you would a cauldron. Drop in the bones of a breath spawn phoenix, the heart of a gray sun phoenix, the feathers of a century phoenix, the eyes of an obsidian phoenix, and the eggshells from the hatching of a crowned elder phoenix. Underneath the stars, pour the ashes into the Pit and cast phoenix fire upon it all so you may welcome the dead back to life.

I inhale a deep breath like the time I was thrown into a freezing river during a power brawl, the iciness shocking my system. Goose bumps dot my body like stars in a night sky. My brain feels foggy, but everything soon clears because this resurrection ritual is going to change everything.

It's as if I can foresee the future like Sera, but unlike her visions of death, I'm able to glimpse Atlas coming back to life. He'll emerge from this Phoenix Pit and walk into my arms.

My heart is racing because this hasn't been some gigantic lie that Luna has fed me.

I reread the ritual again, eternally grateful for the translation. All these different breeds of phoenixes make it hard to commit everything to memory without also having to worry about if I'm getting the translations right. I'm sure someone like Emil would have an easier time if he'd been able to retrocycle here since he's always been a phoenix fanboy. Tala of course would have even more familiarity, but wouldn't want to bring this information back to the present. She's going to be pissed off at me for doing so, but I can't care about that right now. I have to remember everything. Breath spawn bones, gray sun heart, century feathers—

Fabian slams his hands down on the book, covering the ritual's instructions as he drags his nails down the pages, giving us both chills.

"Move your hand!" I shout, as if he can hear me.

I try grabbing at Fabian's hands, but I go through him. Same for the book of scrolls when I try to snatch it out from under him. I'm nothing but a visitor in a memory. All I can do is observe as he lived, and if he doesn't move his damn hand so I can get the hell out of here, I'll have to watch as he died too—and also feel it.

"No me vas a aterrorizar en la muerte como lo tienes en la vida," Fabian says to his family.

Fabian is telling his family that they won't terrorize him in death as they have in life. Was that the threat? Makes sense. If the ghosts have spent years haunting Fabian and he still hasn't given in to their demands after making his life a living hell, then maybe they're targeting his afterlife next. This is why Fabian not only kills himself, but why he destroys his soul too. It's the only way he'll know peace.

I'm crying over how tragic and devastating this is, over how cruel ghosts can become over lifetimes. I wish I could grab the oblivion dagger from his apron and kill each and every last one myself so Fabian can live his life. I don't know whether or not Fabian has already tried killing gangs of ghosts, but it doesn't matter. As long as there's life, there will be death, and as long as there's death, there will be dead missing their lives.

Fabian steps away from the book of scrolls and lights a match, hovering it over the mortar of gempowder. "Nadie te salvará," Fabian says, telling the ghosts that no one will save them. He's about to blow this place apart, along with the knowledge that I came back in time to collect.

I don't actually know whether or not I can retrocycle back to this moment or if it's a one-and-done situation. I need to memorize this ritual, fast.

Remove the phoenix corpse.

Boiling water in the grave.

Breath spawn bones.

Gray sun heart.

Century feathers.

Obsidian eyes.

Crowned elder eggshells.

Perform under the stars.

Scatter the ashes into the Pit.

Cast phoenix fire to bring Atlas back to life.

I'm staring at the page, committing it to memory, not wanting to get anything backward because I can't exactly summon more of Atlas's ashes if I confuse the ritual and use obsidian feathers instead of eyes or breath spawn heart instead of bones. Emil has the blood of a gray sun and the heart of someone who's not ready for war, so that will be easy to remember. Crowned elders are old at birth, and I think of their shells cracking like tired bones. No, I can't bring bones into this, not when I actually need the bones of a breath spawn. Crowned elder eggshell, breath spawn bones. I repeat it over and over until I'm sure I have it down.

I will not mess up Atlas's resurrection the way Luna screwed up June's.

My boyfriend will not become some soulless killing machine.

I'm overcome with my heart breaking when it should be strengthening because my life is about to change. But so is Fabian's. Everything is coming to an end and there's a shade of relief, but mostly he's mourning what could have been. What should have been.

Fabian holds the oblivion dagger in one hand and the lit match in the other. "Moriré en paz," he says.

He's vowed to die in peace.

I have to go, I have to return to my time before he strikes himself and blows this place up. I try to sever my connection to Fabian. I got here by comparing our lives and our pain, but the pain he's lived will no longer be mine since I'll use the tools he never did to change my life. I tell myself how he's technically my great-uncle but he's not actually my family because the family that raised me, that chose me is the one that matters the most to me, but nothing is ejecting me from this timeline.

Then I'm stuck with a horrible thought: What if Fabian destroying his soul destroys mine as well? If I can feel his death, can I die by it too?

I try cycling back to my life, thinking thoughts of moving forward, of my own childhood, of everything I have been through, a world of memories I can draw on to return me home.

But it's too late.

In one moment, Fabian drops the match and swings the oblivion dagger into his heart. Electric red light washes over us as the bone blade pierces his chest—my chest—and twists. Fire erupts, blowing everything apart except the ghosts who have lost their only chance to live again.

The pain is short-lived, as is the moment of relief and pain I'm channeling.

Darkness takes over and I'm alone with Fabian.

I'm the last person to see him alive, and then my own darkness lives on.

ELEVEN

PLOTTING FOR PHOENIXES

MARIBELLE

The darkness of oblivion fades away.

I'm finding my way back into my own body.

My yellow flames vanish.

I scream at the top of my lungs, as if the oblivion dagger is still twisting inside my heart or the fire is still melting my skin or that sadness of Fabian's life is still piercing my soul. I haven't screamed like this since Atlas died. Retrocycling is traumatic, and I'm zero for two with returning home peacefully. I first got killed with Sera and have died again with Fabian, but now I know how to resurrect Atlas. I would walk into a hundred burning homes and straight into a thousand daggers if it means stealing back the love that was stolen from me.

I fight for my next breath as if it's not going to come.

The ghosts are gone, but I'm not alone. Tala is kneeling before me and begins massaging circles into my wrists. Luna is sitting on the rooftop's bench, holding her robe close. It's freezing out here, but I welcome it more than ever after sitting in my tomb of fire for however long I was gone. My shirt is damp, and I feel the sweat dripping down my neck and onto my chest.

"Are you okay?" Tala asks.

"Better question," Luna says. "Were you successful?"

I'm still finding my breath, but I force out my new favorite words: "I know how to bring Atlas back to life."

Luna rises with a clap. "Brava. Tell me everything."

"Give her a break," Tala says.

"I have waited decades. I—"

"Then you can wait a few more minutes."

Luna's face is flushed by the garden's light and underneath the stars. She coughs, wiping the blood on her robe like usual. It's looking more and more like she might not have the time to wait.

Unfortunately, I need her.

"I'm going to be okay," I tell Tala. "I've been through greater hells."

"Understood. I'll still feel better if we get some water in your system."

I don't push back.

We return downstairs so I can hydrate and get refreshed. I walk into the half bath chugging a bottle of water, and I already feel like a human being who belongs in my body. It smells like rosemary in here, which seems to be a staple scent in this woman's loft. I'm about to wash my face when I stop.

The girl in the mirror has been through it. It's hard to believe anyone could ever think of her as beautiful in this moment, but I do. Especially as she begins crying and a smile cracks across her face. I can't remember the last time I've seen myself so happy. I'm loving this girl looking back at me because she's the most powerful person I know. She didn't give up even though she wanted to, and she now has the keys to unlock a better future.

This girl is the hero of her story, and she's going to save the day.

Gathered around the living room, Tala and Luna listen as I walk through my recent retrocycle.

They now know that Fabian may have tried secluding himself on that island, but he was never alone. Not then and probably not ever. Countless ghosts kept him company, and I'll never forget the sight of watching the dead pack that tiny house and stretch out across the field and beach and ocean. Then there were the ghosts of his mother and three brothers howling at him, and I can still never know the specifics of their threats to Fabian since I couldn't tap into his power to hear the ghosts myself, but I make it clear that's why he took his own life.

"That's tragic," Tala says, her head hanging low. "May his soul—"

"There is no soul," Luna interrupts.

Tala does not know this long-dead man who chose oblivion, but her heart seems to break for him. She's already been so furious and devastated losing her parents, but I can only imagine the rampage she would be on if their souls had been obliterated, preventing them from being reborn as phoenixes; not proven, obviously, but that faith is grounding her.

"Let's return to what matters most," Luna says.

"That man mattered," Tala says. "He had values and—"

"And he couldn't bring himself to kill the ghosts of his family and chose oblivion instead."

I think back to the night at the cemetery when Luna killed the ghosts of her parents so she could steal their blood for her immortality elixir.

"He wasn't only trying to escape his mother and brothers," I say, defending Fabian. "Every other soul would've terrorized him in the afterlife too."

Luna folds her hands together, as if she's about to beg. "Would we like to spend our time mourning this man or welcoming our loved ones back into this world?"

Tala glares. "Who will mourn you when you die?"

"Perhaps my sister, if she ever stands a chance at resurrection," Luna says. She turns to me, and there's a genuine concern in her green eyes. "Is there hope for Raine?"

I do not have any intention of letting Luna bring her sister back into this world; one Marnette villain is enough. But she has to believe there's something in this for herself if I'm going to be able to count on her support throughout this ritual.

"As long as you have her ashes, we should be able to bring back Raine."

Tala shoots me a look, questioning if I'm actually resurrecting Raine. I'll fill her in later.

"Tell me what you know of the Phoenix Pit," Luna says.

"I'm not loving the sound of this," Tala says.

"Prepare to hate this ritual with your whole heart, Halo Knight."

That's one of the most honest things to come out of Luna's mouth.

"The Phoenix Pit is how we undo a death and renew a life," I say.

"Consider it a stew in the earth, cooking phoenix parts," Luna says.

Before Tala can do anything, I create a fire-arrow and aim it straight at Luna's heart. "If you taunt her one more time, I will kill you."

"Then you will have a difficult road ahead," Luna says, her sunken features lit up by the dark yellow flames.

"But not an impossible one. Don't forget that I can retrocycle through your entire life to learn everything you do."

"Ah, I'm sure that will only take up an afternoon or two."

"I have time. You do not," I say, eyeing the blood she's been coughing up on her robe.

"My dear granddaughter, let's not pretend as if you are willing to spend your years walking through my entire lifetime. You do not want to be an old woman when you welcome your young lover back into your arms."

"And you don't want to die," I say.

Luna gives me the slightest nod, practically imperceptible. "If you'd like to withdraw your adorable arrow and continue on with your tale, I'd be most appreciative."

I reach for the burning arrow's tip and close it back into my palm. I then rest a hand on Tala's shoulder. "It's okay if you don't want to listen to this."

Tala takes a deep breath, her shoulders untensing. "I've seen my share of phoenix mistreatment over the years. I can handle a story."

She can't say I didn't warn her.

"The Pit is a grave for any phoenix who has been buried after an unnatural death. The book said this is the heart of a mortal's natural resurrection. You dump boiling water inside—"

"Did it state a desired temperature?" Luna asks, opening the side table's drawer and retrieving a pen and pad.

"No."

Luna takes note. "Next were the phoenix parts, correct?"

I remember my mnemonics for the ritual, beginning with Emil's clue. "The heart of a gray sun phoenix," I say, and Tala immediately winces. "The eggshells from a crowned elder phoenix. The bones of a breath spawn phoenix. The feathers of a century phoenix. The—"

"The eyes of an obsidian phoenix?" Luna asks.

I nod as Tala shudders. I wonder if she's thinking about how violating it would be for someone to take the eyes out of Wyatt's phoenix companion.

Luna taps the pen against the pad. "Were there any mentions on proportions? How many eyes? Quantity or weight of feathers? If the bones belonged to an infant or adult phoenix?"

"Nothing like that."

"Anything on the sequence in which to mix the ingredients? Santiago relayed it as breath spawn, gray sun, century, obsidian, and crowned elder. Is this what you saw?"

I didn't memorize the sequence because I honestly didn't think it mattered. But as I play it over in my head it seems right. "I think so."

"Then maybe Santiago wasn't as useless as I thought," Luna muses. "I tried many combinations, and none seemed to have more of an effect anyhow. Were there any other ingredients used?"

"No. It just said to pour the ashes into the Pit while standing under the stars and to set it all ablaze with phoenix fire."

"Did it say anything about a prime constellation?"

I tell her no again.

Luna flings the pad against the window. "You have returned with nothing new. I cannot help you."

It's as if I'm staring at the happy girl in the mirror again, but this time, the glass explodes. The shards are slicing into me and tearing me apart. The dreams of saving the day have been shattered.

"I played my part," I say. "It's your job to save Atlas now."

"If you want me to replicate my formula to bring back Atlas as I did June, very well, but when he returns without a light in his eyes or love in his heart, just kill me instead of threatening me for the thousandth time."

"Happily. If you can't bring him back to life as he was, then you don't get to keep yours," I say, jumping to my feet and getting in her face. I'm gripping the armrests of her chair, and I'm tempted to set it all on fire and watch her burn. "What good are you anyway? You had a chance to undo some of your pain, and you can't even do that right."

"I wish I could achieve true resurrection as much as immortality," Luna laments.

"Then do it! You know everything you need to! Remove the phoenix corpse, pour in the boiling water, then do the bones and eyes and feathers and heart and—"

Luna's eyes go wide. "Remove the phoenix corpse?"

"From the grave."

"Did the ritual say to do that?"

I ease back, hope rebuilding within me, like the shattered mirror piecing itself together. "I thought it was just ceremonial, but the ritual said that to hold on to the human's soul you have to remove the phoenix's corpse. Then something about those essences consecrating the grounds."

Luna smiles, and it reminds me of the girl in the mirror who knows she will save the day. "I believed that the corpse was to remain in the grave as sure as I was to scatter the ashes into the Pit while under the stars. Santiago spoke nothing of that line, perhaps dismissing it as nothing but poetry instead of instruction. Alchemists choose our words wisely and will go through great measures to conceal our truths with other words when necessary. But Fabian was not an alchemist. He was simply a man who could speak to the dead." She's beaming with pride as she adds, "These words would have remained buried in time without you."

I am proud of myself, but I'm uncomfortable receiving praise from this monster. "Why does it matter whether or not the corpse is in the grave?"

"Alchemy is delicate work where a universe of properties come together for grand transformations, and resurrection is the rarest transformation of them all," Luna says with so much life in her voice. It's almost like there isn't a sickness that's been inching her closer and closer to death. "Ordinary birds fully decompose within days, but phoenixes often take years. This is because everything about their essence is always actively working to bring them back to life."

"What does that have to do with resurrecting a human?" Tala asks.

"Just like humans, phoenixes seep grave wax, all from their tissue that allows them to fly for hours and days on end. That ferments the soil, and all those properties prepare the bed for resurrection. I suppose by removing the corpse of the phoenix and scattering in the ashes of a human among the body parts of select phoenix breeds, it will trigger one's revival . . . as they were. A shame for June, who could have been the true miracle I always believed her to be if only I'd removed that phoenix's corpse beforehand so she could have held on to her soul." She releases the deepest sigh. "Oh well. I won't repeat that mistake twice. We should go collect the supplies. In one of my underground vaults I should still have some leftover organs, feathers, and bones in stock."

"Where at?"

"The Li—"

"We won't be going to any base of yours," Tala snaps at Luna, then turns to me. "A word?" She walks down to the hallway, and I follow, keeping an eye on Luna over my shoulder. "You can't possibly be so reckless that you would walk into any territory of Luna's and give her home-field advantage. There could be Blood Casters or acolytes waiting for us."

I actually was about to be as reckless as Tala is accusing me. I'm so close to something that I never thought was possible, and it's clouding my senses. "You're right. Thanks for grounding me."

"I don't trust her. The longer you keep her around, the deeper she'll get into your head. I say we get rid of her now, quick and clean."

"She's a true alchemist. She understands the nuances of this ritual better than I ever will."

"You have the power to rise above her, Maribelle."

"What does flying have to do with that?"

Her eyes narrow. "Retrocycling . . ."

I blush at my idiocy. "Oh. It's been a long night."

"Long nights."

"You heard Luna yourself. It would take lifetimes to go through everything she's lived."

"Luna is manipulating you into believing she's valuable. You don't need everything she's lived through. You only need the one day where something went sort of right."

"Which is?"

"The day Luna brought June back to life. Retrocycle back to that moment and study everything she does. You now know her critical error. Correct that and—"

"I can bring Atlas back to life myself," I say. I won't owe any grace to the woman who's responsible for his death in the first place.

I've dreamed of that moment so much; I've had it within reach. But my dreams have grown bigger in the past twenty-four hours, in the past twenty seconds even.

I'm already imagining the greatest moment of my life:

Fire bursting.

Ashes swirling into flesh and bones.

A soul that was gone too soon coming back home.

Life returning to Atlas's eyes as he returns to me as the boy I loved.

The boy I get to love again.

Without looking into a mirror, I can practically see my smile all over again. "You're brilliant, Tala. Thank you, I can't believe how desperate I was to resurrect Atlas that I would've trusted Luna to handle it on my behalf. Now I can be the first person he sees when he's alive."

"Let's not forget about getting rid of the dead weight," Tala says with an eye on Luna.

"Don't whip out your crossbow just yet. I still need to learn everything I can about what went into June's resurrection, and I have to collect . . ." I can't look this defender of phoenixes in the eyes as I say this next part. "I have to collect the organs for the ritual. I'm sorry to disrespect the dead like this, but . . ."

Tala holds up a hand. "Let's skip your justifications, Maribelle. I already know what we have to do to get you what you want. But I can't stomach any speeches about how someone good can be born out of the deaths of phoenixes."

"You don't have to play any role in this. I can figure it out alone."

"No, because then you'll die and I'll have to get my hands dirty bringing you back or feel guilty for the rest of my life knowing I could've resurrected you but didn't," Tala says with an eye roll as if my resurrection would be a nuisance. "I'm helping you, but we won't go anywhere near Luna's bases."

"Then where do we go? Is there a vendor at the Shed or—"

"Not anymore. They've faced the wrath from Halo Knights too often."

"If we can't use Luna's supplies and no one at the Shed has anything, then how do we get what we need without more phoenixes getting harmed or killed?"

Tala's head hangs low. "Wyatt called when you were retrocycling. There was an attack at the Sanctuary."

The punch in my gut tells me that something horrible has happened, like Iris has been killed. We used to be friends who were so close we felt like sisters, and while I don't know how to keep her in my life after she withheld all my family secrets, I still don't want her dead. I'm also nervous for everyone else, like Eva and Wesley and

Ruth and the baby. They were practically my family too, and if only my power worked like Sera's or Santiago's, I could've been able to foresee their deaths.

"Is everyone okay?"

"The humans you know got out alive, but a few Halo Knights were killed," Tala says as angry tears begin surfacing.

"What the hell happened?"

"Enforcers stormed the Sanctuary to detain the Spell Walkers. Phoenixes were killed in the cross fire. Young phoenixes who'd only just come back to life . . ."

I don't need the empathic skills from retrocycling to know Tala's heart is breaking. I reach out with a hug in mind, but she steps away, pinning her back to the wall like my touch would set her on fire.

"The Sanctuary," she whispers. "That's where we'll go to get what you need."

"Okay. Than—"

"Don't thank me. Just never speak of this to anyone."

"I will take it to my grave."

"You will carry it across infinity," Tala says, a plea in her eyes.

This must betray her ethical Halo Knight codes, but she's breaking them for me. I'll have to remember this the next time I'm wanting to break any vows I make with her. Even though she doesn't owe me anything, Tala has pointed me in the direction of fallen phoenixes who will help Atlas rise, reborn from his ashes like the creatures she's sworn to protect.

I can start making things right now.

"I will carry this across infinity," I promise.

TWELVE
EXPOSE

EMIL

Starting to swear that I won't sleep until I'm dead.

I got a few hours of rest throughout yesterday afternoon and last night, but I was always in and out of it. There's a lot working against me. For starters, there's no real silence when you're sharing a gym basement with eight other people, especially Esther, who cries louder than any alarm clock I've ever set. And yeah, the mat I was sleeping on wasn't super comfortable, but I would've been tossing and turning even in my own bed because my anxiety kept—and keeps—spiking. I've convinced everyone that we stand a chance at winning this war, but we have too many enemies coming at us from all sides. Politicians, alchemists, law enforcement, Blood Casters, the public . . . and family.

Brighton hasn't posted anything since the video that outed my resurrection powers, but he's been seen by tons of people. He had some meet-up yesterday morning at Whisper Fields, the park in the Bronx where we spent our birthday with a few of his followers. This time he had a crowd that cheered him on. If I know my brother—who knows if I still do—I bet Brighton was still underwhelmed by the turnout. But I was overwhelmed by it. These are people lining up to help him in his war against me.

It made me want to cuddle up with Ness, who was a few feet away, thinking he would also appreciate someone close since he spent the night shifting into other people in his sleep, including Congresswoman Sunstar, who is still missing. But I laid down new rules and now I've got to play by them.

The same goes for Wyatt too, if he's even still alive. I searched for any sign of life online, like a video of a helicopter chasing an obsidian phoenix because surely someone would have recorded that and posted it, but there's nothing. Nox is a fast phoenix, so I'm holding on to hope that they got out alive.

But then why isn't Wyatt back?

Maybe he's finally caught on that I'm not worth the trouble.

I'm nothing but the flame that kills moths.

∞

It's nine in the morning, and we've all been forbidden from hanging out in the gym for three hours since the regulars have been exercising their powers since six. It's good that everyone is forced to rest for a bit even though Iris is aching to be in her body, especially since she didn't get to hurl any quad bikes or broken concrete at any enforcers yesterday; a blessing if you ask me so she's not caught on camera attacking anyone—in self-defense!—the way the rest of us were. Wesley is the only one who got to get some fresh air, hitting the streets to get us all new phones since we lost a lot of ours back at the Sanctuary.

While my new phone is charging, I'm on Brighton's laptop, emailing back and forth with the one person who is not only game to hear me and Ness out, but has a big enough platform to make sure others will listen too: Lore, the YouTuber whose following Brighton has always envied. Me, Brighton, and Prudencia got to see Lore onstage last month interviewing Sunstar at the Friday Dreamers Festival, an hour before my powers surfaced for the first time. Everything was hard but simpler then. Brighton was supposed to be leaving for college, and I was going to figure out what life looked like without my twin. Now I'm figuring out what life looks like without Brighton, who was never really my twin, and how he's going to be extra pissed that I'm turning to his internet role model for help.

Lore has been responding quickly, living on their phone like anyone else. They agree to meet in a couple hours, respecting the fact that I can't give them our location for security reasons, but that a Spell Walker will pick them up.

"I can't wait for you to meet them. They're amazing," Wesley says, getting dressed. "We did a video for my birthday last year where I got to talk about life and play with puppies. I wanted to bring home a golden retriever but someone"—he dashes behind Ruth, points at her, then back to his mat where he's putting on his shoes—"wouldn't let me."

"Someone and her many someones are all allergic," Ruth says.

"Excuses, excuses." Wesley kisses Ruth. "Be back in a sec." He dashes away and then dashes right back. "Not literally. That's just an expression. Sometimes it's true, but this time—"

"I love you, but hurry up," Ruth says, blowing a kiss.

Wesley catches it and leaves in a blur.

Everyone is going stir-crazy while we wait for Lore. Mele brings us magazines, playing cards, and even a board game. Ma tries reading the celebrity gossip but seems stuck on one page. Eva is playing with Esther as she wakes up from her nap. Iris, Ruth, and Prudencia are on another round of Uno.

Then I start going a different kind of crazy when Ness finishes his shower and comes out of the bathroom wearing nothing but sweatpants. I wish retrocycling wasn't just going back in time, but actually time-traveling so I could undo my stance on not pursuing any emotional—or physical—connection until the war has been fought and won. Ness is so toned that his outline feels very defined, even as the steam from his hot shower pours out of the bathroom. We're out of towels down here since everyone's used them up, but Ness dries his chest with the raggedy shirt that's been torn apart since getting shot outside Iron Manor, attacked in the Bounds, and every other skirmish.

Ness sees me looking at him.

I'm on fire.

He turns around, his back to me.

The fire has been put out, but this burns even more.

Ness throws the old shirt in the trash and puts on a long-sleeved shirt. He walks over. "You should get ready. There's still hot water."

A cold shower is a better idea.

I head into the bathroom. The mirror is still fogged up, and I'm dreading when it clears. I hop in the shower, so cold that it hurts because it forces me to think about anything else. In here, there's no war, there's no betrayal, there's no love. Only my body's survival. But when the water is switched off and I'm shivering in front of the mirror, it doesn't look like my body is surviving. I'm scrawnier than ever, the last thing people expect when they call someone a superhero. I've somehow lost more weight and the little muscle I had—or that's how it looks to me, at least, and I can't exactly ask Ness since he's only seen me shirtless once and I can't ask Wyatt either since he's missing. I'm alone and still feel so exposed, like my reflection is another person watching me.

I stare at the scars left over from when Ness carved into me with the infinity-ender dagger, lucky I didn't die on the spot.

I'm lit up inside as I realize something in this time of darkness.

My body is a hero's body because it's a body that's been surviving.

An hour later, Lore has arrived with their own camera and a smile for everyone. But they immediately rush to Ruth for a hug as if they're meeting the much-talked-about new girlfriend of a long-time friend even though Ruth has been in Wesley's life much longer—and more intimately—than Lore. I won't go so far to say Lore has got a parasocial vibe that needs to be checked, but I am on guard again, remembering they are a young influencer who I don't know any more than they know me. Yeah, I know the basics of Lore's origin story, like how they first made the local news when they became the first genderqueer Korean American to be elected as class president in their high school, and how Lore was savvy enough on social media to know how to make sure their fame ran way longer than fifteen minutes.

Lore greets everyone else, shaking their hands, lingering the longest with Iris, whose legacy as a Spell Walker runs deeper than

Wesley's. I can't get mad if Lore tries exploiting this opportunity to get more content out of this since I'm using them too; I was up front about it, though. As Lore walks my way, their billowy black sweat suit moves like ocean waves and their many bracelets clink like music. "Fire-Wing, the Infinity Son," they say, shaking my hand.

"You can call me Emil."

Lore nods and turns to Ness. "Eduardo Iron."

"Eduardo Iron is dead," Ness says.

"So we thought."

"My name is Ness."

"Welcome back to the land of the living, Ness."

"It's been a blast," Ness says dryly.

Lore's smiles have vanished, like they're really listening. "I hope I can help turn this around. I don't want to invite any more chaos into your lives."

We're going to be filming in the corner of the room, using the concrete wall as a backdrop so no one—Brighton, the Senator, Blood Casters, etc.—can identify our location. We've set up three foldout chairs, positioned so Ness and I will sit opposite of Lore as they interview us. Lore mics us up to ensure better quality, and once we're hooked up, we're ready to go. Prudencia monitors the camera, having done it enough times with me for Brighton.

"Quiet on the set," Wesley announces. Iris glares. "What? I've always wanted to say that."

"Pronoun check before we begin," Lore says.

"He and him," I say.

"Same," Ness says.

Lore puts a hand on their chest. "They and them. You both ready?"

Ness and I turn to each other. I wonder if his heart is racing as much as mine, and not just because of the pressure that comes with convincing the world that we're not the public threats that our families have made us out to be.

"Ready," we say together.

"Hello, my beauteous friends," Lore says into the camera, their energy dialed up but warm too. They gesture at me and Ness. "As you can see, I'm joined today by two very special, albeit controversial guests. Emil Rey is of course known to many of you as Fire-Wing and the Infinity Son and has been blazing our feeds for the past few weeks, ever since the viral video of him fighting a specter on the subway. And to his right is Edua—is Ness Iron, the son of presidential candidate Edward Iron, who was recently sent to the Bounds by his father and was immediately broken out by the Spell Walkers."

I'm glad they managed to correct themself on Ness's first name, but I'm bummed we didn't let them know that Ness's last name is now Arroyo like his mother.

"I understand politics can be divisive," Lore says. "You beauteous people certainly make that clear whenever I air my support for Nicolette Sunstar, especially after the final debate. But this upcoming election is crucial and it's important we collect as many facts as possible before casting our ballots."

Election Day is creeping up on us. The anxiety is choking me again.

Lore gestures at us. "You both have been making headlines everywhere the past forty-eight hours because of your apparent resurrections. Can you clear the air on what has been happening here?"

"I wasn't killed in the Blackout like Senator Iron would like you to believe," Ness says.

"Then what really happened?"

"I was saved by a Blood Caster."

"Why would they save you?"

"Leverage. Iron worked with Luna Marnette to stage the Blackout, pinning it on the Spell Walkers. His outrage against gleamcrafters, his grief for me . . . it was all engineered. That collaboration was to kill two enemies with one stone, allowing Luna's Blood Casters to be unbothered by law enforcement and the Senator to gain support for his campaign. But Luna isn't stupid. She expected Iron would betray her, and he did just that when he also banished her to the Bounds at the same time as me so we could be killed by the prisoners. So we could be silenced." Ness is clear, but I wonder how the rage in his eyes is going to play with the public. "You all thought I was dead, but I'm only alive because my power was useful to Luna and the Senator."

Lore is nodding, gripped by every word. "So you weren't resurrected, but would you say you want your life back?"

"No. I don't want that life I was living. It's always been dictated by someone." Ness looks my way, blinking away tears. "I want to decide what my life looks like."

Lore turns to me. "How about you, Emil? Your brother, Brighton, has claimed you can resurrect? Is this true?"

I'm tempted to lie, not even for my own sake, but for all phoenixkind. But I can't risk anything backfiring, especially when we're working to gain the trust of the public. "It's true that I can resurrect,"

I say through my teeth. I can't believe the words are coming out of my mouth. Brighton was there for every major discussion, where it was decided that it would remain a secret. "But if you're getting hyped about becoming a specter as if it's going to make you immortal, it's not. If I died, I wouldn't come back as myself. I would be reincarnated as someone new."

"Speaking of, Brighton said you're the reincarnations of the Spell Walker Bautista de León, and the first specter, Keon Máximo. Is this what happened? You were killed in those lives and returned as someone new?"

"Yeah, but I don't remember those lives," I say, not bringing up retrocycling. No one needs to know that I got to glimpse Bautista's life or find another reason to get excited about becoming a specter. "I discovered I was the scion to Bautista and Keon last month, the same day I was seen fighting that specter on the train. Before that, I was just living my life as someone who had no idea he was reborn with phoenix powers."

"What did that life look like for you? Is it something you miss?"

The question almost gets me crying. "Yeah, big-time. It's an honor saving lives as a Spell Walker, but I'm not cut out for this. I was working at a museum gift shop before this and daydreaming about phoenixes. Now I'm on the run all the time, and even if I wanted to go to the home where I was born and raised, I can't because it's been completely blown up. It wasn't always easy being there because there were all these memories of my dad, who passed a few months ago, but that's what was beautiful about it too. Especially when I got to grieve him with Brighton and our mother."

"I'm sorry for your loss," Lore says. "This might be too personal, so feel free to not answer, but can you explain to me and our viewers what your resurrection means for your connection to your family? What is that process?"

I almost look at Ma as I think back to the evening where she shared the big secret. "I was reborn in flames, and my dad found me on a street as a baby. Brighton had just been born, and our parents adopted me and raised us together."

"If Brighton is watching this, what would you want him to know?"

There's no doubt that Brighton is going to watch this video.

I stare into the camera. "Bright, I get it. You're pissed and you want to keep your powers. But we got to bind them before things really spiral out of control. You're out here threatening my life, like I'm not the first person who would jump in front of a spell and die for you. My powers were literally manifested because I was scared you were about to get killed. But these powers aren't ours, so let's fight together one last time as the Infinity Kings, as the Reys of Light." I crack and start crying, dreaming for this to become a reality. "Then we'll get rid of the powers, and our brotherhood can be reborn, stronger for infinity."

Lore brings the interview to a close, inviting all viewers to really sit on this discussion and consider the lives of the people behind the powers.

But all I can think about is how Brighton will react to this video that paints me as a hero.

Will he swallow his pride and rejoin us?

Or will he expose himself as the villain of my story?

THIRTEEN
UNSEEN AND SEEN

BRIGHTON

I woke up bright and early so I could spend the day mastering a new power.

I've been filming my training sessions with Samuel for my own personal records, but that footage is going into an archive. The point of learning how to camouflage is for stealth missions and evasion during fights. Nothing aids that discretion more than no one knowing I can hide among them in the first place. What's been most difficult about tapping into this new ability is how passive it is. All my other powers are so active—casting fire-bolts, running at swift-speed, phasing through solid objects. But camouflaging requires an uncomfortable stillness. Every time I stood against a wall, trying to blend in, I was itching to grab my phone and check in on my socials. This power requires mental resilience to only focus on the task at hand. It took two draining hours, but I finally got in touch with my body, with all the fibers of my clothes, and I vanished against an influencer's black backdrop.

The rest of the morning was spent turning my camo on and off, trusting Samuel when he says it will become second nature and won't require as much concentration. I moved from the black backdrop to a white wall and then to a green screen. The latter was tricky because of the nylon, but I altered my process to success. Then we leveled up to varied backgrounds like the tiled kitchen wall and the bushes by the pool. I have to be conscious of all patterns and textures, but the hope is that one day I will be able to switch on my camo and let my power do all the work for me; I have all the time in the world as an immortal to achieve this. My true goal is to reach Samuel's zenith, where he can stand in an open space and camouflage himself with the moving world so effectively he may as well be invisible. But whereas people will be able to bump into him, I could combo my camouflage with my phasing and allow them to walk through me, as if I'm not there at all, watching their every move.

Drinking that Reaper's Blood was the greatest decision of my life.

I'm back inside the house, blending in against this canvas painting of Alpha swimming with a cerulean phoenix, when Zelda rushes into the studio space with her phone in hand.

"Where's Brighton?" Zelda asks Samuel.

"He's—"

"Boo!" I shout, jumping out from this canvas and scaring Zelda. Her phone falls to the floor.

"Not cool," Samuel says. "I told you that's my thing."

Zelda picks up her phone. The screen is cracked. "Really not cool."

I apologize to both of them. "Someone will replace that for you, right?"

"You have bigger problems."

Zelda leans in, showing me some new video of Lore's. I would've seen their upload myself if I wasn't so busy becoming one with my environment as Samuel put it. But I'm ready to destroy the phone beyond repair when I see Lore sitting across from Emil and Ness in some room with concrete walls. This can't be the Sanctuary because I know from the news that there was a mass evacuation after some showdown with the enforcers. Everyone I know, including Emil and Ma, got out alive, which is a relief. But did Emil actually reach out to Lore for help—or was it the other way around? I don't get an answer by the video's end, but watching Emil play the martyr when I was the one who was outnumbered and overpowered has me blazing up so hot that Zelda might need to turn me into a block of ice to cool me down.

"This is why you have a pseudo publicist now," Zelda says. "Lore's new book club is meeting this evening. I'm going to go talk to them and—"

"Where's the book club?"

"I don't know, some bookstore's café."

"Find out. I'm going to go pay Lore a visit. It's time we finally meet."

I travel alone, like an alpha predator hunting prey.

Zelda and Samuel drove me out of Staten Island, but I wanted to make the rest of the journey through Brooklyn on foot, enjoying the fresh air as I run with swift-speed across the many streets to reach the bookstore in Greenpoint. I arrive within minutes, but I don't walk through the front doors of Cygnus Pages. I like the element of surprise. I go around the side of the building and phase my head through the brick wall, confirming the coast is clear before stepping into the bookstore's nonfiction aisle. My eyes immediately find the spine for *The First Spell Walker*, that bestselling biography about Bautista that was written by someone who didn't know him in life. I wonder if the author will release a revised edition because of Emil; he would be smart to see how this all ends before writing more.

I go through the romance and fiction aisles, following the sounds of Lore's voice to the café. There's a circle of twenty people, which is the intimate experience Lore has been advertising on their channels. Weeks ago I would have been jealous of these attendees. Now I'm above them all—including Lore, who actually had the nerve to take sides in a family affair they know nothing about. I could step out from behind this bookcase and this conversation would cease. But I'm not here to alarm anyone. I'm certainly not here to fight. Can something even be called a fight if you can win in seconds? I think annihilation is more appropriate. It doesn't matter. I'm only here to talk, but I'm not here to talk about this book, so I wait and listen, camouflaging against this wall with flyers for the store's upcoming events, like a predator watching their prey from the bushes.

Lore is gripping their book club pick, *Catch the Dark*. Their eye shadow is a glittery silver and matches their top, which feels like if someone turned a disco ball into a long-sleeved shirt. Maybe they have some party they're going to after this book club. If so, they're going to be late.

"I love whenever literature imagines a world without gleam. It's my favorite trope in a fantasy novel," Lore says. They hug the thin hardcover to their chest as they look between the other readers and the camera they have on a tripod for posting later. "But I've never read portal fiction of this quality. Do you think it's because it was written by an actual celestial?"

The club discusses the novel's strengths and weaknesses, but *discussion* may be too strong a word. Everyone is agreeing with Lore's takes. They're nothing but sheep, probably sucking up because they think Lore is going to follow them back on Instagram or something. Lore is not their friend any more than Lore was my friend those times they were messaging me after this whole saga of mine began. I remain still, though I'm tempted to phase out of this bookstore as Lore asks their attendees to go around in a circle and tell everyone what their dream power would be.

"I wish I could shift. It would allow me to play with my gender expression some more," Lore says.

A girl raises her hand but doesn't wait to be called on. "Shift like Ness? Was he nice?"

"Ness seems like a solid person. I think the media has the wrong idea about him."

"Maybe he can help you become a specter," someone else says.

Lore shakes their head. "I agree with Emil that specters shouldn't exist. To steal the powers of creatures so we can experience gleam ourselves is wrong." They hold up the book, adding, "The novel does a beautiful job illustrating how it's not easy and why a celestial would willingly walk into a hole in the sky to exist in a world where they can be treated equally. . . ."

I can't believe how brainwashed Lore is. I thought they were smarter than this.

This is why you should never meet your heroes.

This is why I have become my own.

Mercifully, the book club discussion ends, and Lore takes selfies with attendees as a bookseller and barista put away chairs. Once everyone is out the door, Lore thanks the employees and leaves the store. I could say hello now, but I decide to follow them instead. It's possible they're returning to whatever base the Spell Walkers are using as a haven. Then I could sneak in and get an idea of what they're up to next.

The streets are empty as Lore lugs their camera bag and tripod, passing some celestial gym called Mele's Melee, the Night Elk Bar, a residential building, and an ice cream shop. I'm keeping my distance behind them, but when they suddenly turn around after consulting the map on their phone, I'm quick to camo against a wall that is graffitied with anti-Iron sentiments. I don't think it's my best job blending in against these neon sprays, but Lore has no reason to question the distortions as they come back down this street, so close to me that I could reach out and pull them into this wall and phase them into the ground, where they won't have internet to upload videos that make me out to be the unreasonable one.

Lore travels through the neighborhood and after twenty minutes finally comes to a stop. They walk into a tiny house, and from the outside I watch a light turn on in one of the rooms. I make a mental note about the address. I now know where Lore lives, and it's time I let them know.

I knock on the window, and as soon as Lore turns, I phase through the wall and into their bedroom. "Lore, it's so great to finally meet you," I say, taking a seat on their bed. They're staring at me in shock. It's a powerful feeling to have someone I once idolized suddenly scared of me. I know I won't hurt them, but they don't.

"What are you doing here, Brighton?"

Hearing my name out of their mouth like we know each other is special too.

"I thought we should talk."

"Is this about the interview?"

"What do you think?" I ask as I look around their room. I know all of this so well. It's as if I've walked onto the set of a TV show I've watched for years. It's so immersive being this close to their backdrop, the ring lights, bookshelves, the autographed Polaroid with Wesley. There's a new framed picture with Sunstar from the Friday Dreamers Festival on their desk. Boxes of unopened merchandise from various companies are stacked on the floor for what I assume are sponsored posts. "If you're so interested in bringing a balance to these political discussions, why not reach out to me?"

Lore stands tall, as if that's the least bit intimidating. "The public has been hearing your voice loud and clear. I welcomed Emil's and Ness's perspectives. Do you plan on invading the homes of anyone else who gives them a platform?"

"You've got the wrong idea. We somewhat know each other, Lore. More than you can say for Emil, who you brought onto your channel."

"Emil contacted me."

My blood is boiling. This was intentional. "Emil played you. He knows how much I respect you and your work. Out of everyone on the internet, he targeted you to attack me. You gave him the platform to do so."

Lore looks over their shoulder at the door. They know my powers; they can't possibly be thinking they're going to run away. "You understand this isn't a good look, Brighton."

"Do you suddenly care about my perception? That's awesome. Here's what we're going to do. Let's go live right now and have our own discussion so I can share my side of the story."

Their eyes narrow. "Or what? You'll kill me? This Infinity Reaper persona is getting to your head."

I get up from Lore's bed and walk toward them, backing them into a wall. "I've killed before, Lore. Recently. Do you know Stanton? The Blood Caster with basilisk blood? He's dead, at my hands." I hover my fingers over Lore's chest. "I reached into his chest and ripped out his heart. I did that before he could kill Emil or brutalize me again. I will always take a life if it means protecting my own." I back away from Lore, giving them space. "If you are not with me, you are against me. Do you understand?"

Lore nods because their survival instincts have arrived.

"So you'll go online with me?"

"Yes."

"Epic. I appreciate your fairness."

In minutes, Lore has set up a filming station in their room. I imagine they have this routine down at this point. This is probably the first time they've been trembling throughout however. There's no point killing Lore, but it's great that they think they're in danger. I can exploit that. All I want is for Lore to help me even the scales and then leave this all alone afterward. They can go open one of those merch boxes and express enthusiasm over that for a nice check instead of involving themselves in my family affairs.

We sit side by side, lit up by their ring light. They reach for their phone to go live.

"Lore?"

They stop. "What?"

"Your life is not worth seizing this live moment to persecute me as a villain."

My eyes drop to Lore's chest, right around their heart.

Lore is shaking, but as that three-second timer counts us down into the live, they put on a brave face for the thousands of followers that immediately join. The comments section is already alive with shocked emojis and people asking what is going on. "Hello, my beauteous friends, welcome to tonight's live, where I'm joined here with my special guest, Brighton Rey."

It must be eating Lore inside to introduce me as such.

"Thanks for having me on, and welcoming me into your home," I say.

Lore smiles, the performance of a lifetime. "Happy to have you here."

I wave at the camera. "Hello to everyone watching. I'm really grateful that Lore invited me over to follow up on their most recent video featuring Emil and Ness. It's true that Senator Iron is a criminal. I personally endorse Congresswoman Sunstar for the presidency, if that matters to anyone. She will elevate gleamcraft, but here's where I really disagree with Emil. Specters should be able to hold on to their powers, especially when they're willing to do the work that would otherwise be expected to fall upon the shoulders of celestials. I respect Emil's choice to bind his powers because he is not interested in heroism as I am." I turn to Lore, staring them in the eyes. "Before we came on, you were telling me about a discussion at your book club earlier tonight about how specters shouldn't exist." I watch as they realize that I was there, unseen. "Do you agree that I can put all my powers to good use as long as I'm committed to our common cause?"

Lore nods. "As long as you're committed to the common cause."

"So you would support me keeping my powers under those conditions?"

"Absolutely, Brighton."

"Thanks, Lore. That means a lot coming from someone I admire so much." I turn back to the camera. "I'm happy to answer any questions you all might have."

I spend the next thirty minutes speaking to Lore's followers about everything: the challenges of living in Emil's shadow when he wasn't up to the task and how badly I wanted to do the job of protecting the public myself but didn't have powers to do so; how I've given up my dreams of becoming the host of a TV show in favor of saving lives; and how I'm still rattled by Emil's betrayal but grateful for everyone's support, including Lore, who has given me this stage to tell my side of the story.

"Don't forget to follow me on my accounts to stay up to date," I tell Lore's followers.

"Good night, my beauteous friends."

Lore ends the live session and releases a deep breath.

I pat them on the back, and they flinch. "You did a great job."

"You were at the bookstore? I didn't see you."

I won't explain my power to them. "All you need to understand is that I know where you live and have no problem letting myself in if you ever cross my path again." I get up, moving toward the wall. "Don't give me a reason to come find you, Lore. You won't see your death coming."

I phase out of Lore's home, and while they're likely panicking and looking into witness protection, I'm on social media, where my follower count has grown on every platform. Emil tried to expose me as some power-hungry specter, and my counterattack has shown the world the truth about me.

I'm the hero they never saw coming.

FOURTEEN
SCAVENGERS

MARIBELLE

It's been a long day, beginning with recovering Atlas's ashes.

There has been so much going on lately that I'd almost forgotten where I had parked Atlas's car. At one point it was close to the Alpha Church of New Life, where we had our big showdown on the last night of the Crowned Dreamer. Then it was parked by the Aldebaran Center when the Blood Casters arrived to kill Brighton. I was ready to return there when I remembered I'd parked the car here at the loft, the day before I introduced Tala to Brighton, Emil, and Prudencia. It feels like I've lived so many lives since then, and I felt like a whole other person when I went into the closet of the loft's owner, got dressed in a thick hoodie of hers, and became unrecognizable to any of the other tenants as I passed them in the hallways and rode the elevator down to the garage. I ran straight to Atlas's car and was relieved when I found his ashes still inside the bottle that once contained star-touched wine, which was my eighteenth birthday gift from Atlas. Thank all the unseen forces in the sky that protected this car from being impounded or stolen because if I'd done all this work to discover how to resurrect my boyfriend only to have his ashes tossed away in some recycling bin, I might've become the biggest threat this planet has ever faced.

"I'll see you soon," I had told Atlas's ashes, smiling as I held the bottle to my chest, my heart practically soaring at the idea of bringing his body back to this world.

The rest of the afternoon was spent strategizing. It was too risky to ride Roxana to the New Ember Sanctuary since the phoenix would draw attention to us by casting storms wherever she goes, so Tala sent Roxana ahead. I got more than enough sleep through the morning, which I especially needed after retrocycling last night, and was good to drive. Tala tied Luna down to the front passenger seat with a rope knot that was so impressive it looked like Luna wouldn't have been able to phase through even if she'd managed to get her reaper powers. But Tala wasn't as confident, still having chosen to sit behind Luna with a dagger at the ready if she tried anything funny. Luna didn't.

The trip to the New Ember Sanctuary was slower in Atlas's car, especially with all the traffic. Multiple radio stations were claiming that people are eager to get out of New York, fearing for their lives given all the action the city has seen as of late. I kept wondering how many of them dropped off their ballot for Senator Iron before ditching, trusting that he will put an end to this war. I didn't like being sandwiched between drivers, not knowing if they would've ratted me out if given the chance or actually helped me if I was being attacked. When we finally broke through the traffic, I was still wishing we'd taken our chances on Roxana, traveling through the clear skies. That's how it was the first time I flew to the Sanctuary with Tala, shortly before discovering my retrocycling ability. I'd never ridden a phoenix before, and it was much smoother than flying on my own, though I did need to keep close to Tala, my arms wrapped around her even though she was still a stranger to me. There's a lot I still don't know about her because we've been driven by our vengeance, and now we're forced to keep our enemy alive because no one will help us.

The GPS predicts we'll be approaching the Sanctuary soon enough, so I wake up Luna, who has been sleeping so soundly she could've been dead.

"My freedom was not a dream," Luna says.

"You're stuck with us."

"Better than the Bounds, I suppose."

She's not wrong, especially as we begin driving through a forest. I'm tempted to get out and hike the rest by foot just for the experience. But there's work to be done and, no matter how rested Luna is, she's not strong enough for that walk.

"Tell me about June," I say.

"What of her?" Luna asks.

"Who was she before you did what you did to her."

"Before I brought her back to life? June was nobody. She along with many other children were stolen from places where they wouldn't be missed. The streets, orphanages, hospitals, wherever my acolytes could snatch candidates who were young enough for my experiments and faceless to the world so they could operate stealthily in any and all assassinations."

I grip the wheel tightly. "You stole children to practice resurrections?"

"Are you so naive that you believed me to be experimenting on mice? Of course I used children, with the promises of offering them better lives than the ones they were living. Not that I asked for permission, but in my soul I knew this to be true. June had no family. My favorite underground vault has my records, but I remember June being subject number ninety-eight. There was something so poetic about the number, the way nine goes back into eight, like the progression of time spent dead was being reversed."

I honestly feel sick to my stomach. "Ninety-eight children died?"

"I did experiment on some adults, but mostly children, yes."

"Did they just die?" Tala asks. "Or were they killed?"

"Some died of illnesses, but most were killed," Luna says as if sharing the forecast for the day.

"You're a monster," Tala says.

"She's the one who wants to know all about how I turned the ham back into a pig."

This is dark gleamwork that we're tapping into to bring back the dead, but I didn't know how many people have died to bring us to this moment. If Luna hadn't done all these experiments and resurrected June, I wouldn't even know resurrection is possible. Atlas would be dead, forever. It's just sickening to think of how many innocent lives have been lost to pave this road, and how they deserve to be brought back just as much as anyone else for their sacrifice. But if Luna did everything in the Phoenix Pit ritual, then there would be no ashes to distinguish from the various body parts at the end of it all. I feel guilty benefitting from this, but I also won't have let them die in vain either.

"When did you bring back June?" I ask.

"December."

That was one month before the Blackout.

Before I lost my parents and Iris lost her parents.

Before the next generation had to take up the mantle as Spell Walkers.

"When June was born—reborn—how did it happen? Did she walk out of the fire?" I ask, needing as many details as possible for when I retrocycle to that critical intersection between Luna's life and June's rebirth.

"Ashes turned to fire turned to girl," Luna says. "A reverse cremation."

"How did she react?"

"Like a wild beast, a caged phoenix. It was as if a newborn suddenly woke up in the body of a teen girl and did not know how to operate any of her muscles. She ran for me and it was unclear if she wanted help or remembered me slitting her throat, so I struck her with a dagger's handle between her eyes. I studied her for a few nights, but it was clear that she was alive but unable to live. June appeared to be soulless, and that's when I imbued her with the ghost blood in the hopes of restoring some humanity."

So June wasn't reborn with ghost powers. That came later. Which means Atlas won't be reborn as a specter either. He'll be a celestial and will still have his soul if I do the ritual right.

It's dark out, so I drive extra carefully around a mountain, using my headlights to follow the tire tracks like they've become my new road map. Then we turn and stop at the drawbridge, and even though we knew there was an attack, there is still nothing like seeing the damage in person. The Sanctuary looks as if it's been bombed. Tala sucks in a gasp. Just because she knew the Sanctuary was attacked doesn't mean she was prepared to see it in this state. She immediately gets out of the car and begins crossing the bridge, and I untie Luna so we can follow. The river is flowing beneath us, and there are phoenixes crying in the night sky as if lamenting the crimes that have happened here. I feel even more like a vulture given why we've come here. At the entrance, there are blackened husks of cars and torched crates. The door that once had that brass knocker has been blown open, and Tala steps through that hole into the courtyard. A wall has been demolished. There's blood in the pond. Piles of ashes and feathers and phoenixes dead on the ground.

Tala falls to her knees, cradling a tiny yellow phoenix that's been killed, its head swinging and wings stiff. "No one buried them," she says lifelessly. She looks around at this courtyard that's been touched by Death. "The human bodies have been collected, but the phoenixes have been left behind. . . ."

"Not all humans," Luna says, pointing at two men coming out of the Sanctuary.

"Halo Knights, I assume."

Then one pulls out a camera, laughing as he records the other picking up a dead phoenix and dropping it into a bag.

"Scavengers," Tala says.

This is the price to be paid when the public discovered resurrection is possible with phoenix blood. They can never discover that it's also possible with body parts from five different breeds of phoenixes; all of phoenixkind would be extinct within a year.

Tala gently lays down the young phoenix and runs across the courtyard. This is going to be bad. The scavengers are startled when they see Tala approaching, and they're stupid not to be more afraid. She tackles one scavenger and immediately rolls onto her feet, kicking the camera out of the other's hand and punching him in the throat.

As the taller one is gasping for air, Tala pounces back onto the other, swinging both her fists into his face repeatedly.

I should make sure Tala doesn't murder these idiots.

"Don't go anywhere," I tell Luna.

"I wouldn't make it very far if I tried."

I jump into a glide, landing behind the tall scavenger. He's recovered enough that he's about to kick Tala when I sweep my leg into his ankle, forcing him onto his back.

"Stay down," I warn.

"You're Maribelle Lucero!" he says.

"And you're a lowlife."

Tala is crying as she's destroying the scavenger's face, and I have to wrench her away before she kills him. She's fighting against me, desperate to end this poor bastard as if she caught him roasting Roxana on a stick. I lock my arms around her, squeezing as hard as possible because Tala would happily kick my ass too if it means finishing off these scavengers.

Luna is crossing the courtyard, and I don't want them to recognize her.

"Take your friend and go before I have to bury you in the woods," I tell the tall scavenger. He reaches for the bag. "Leave the phoenixes." I would call him a creep, but I'm technically here to scavenge myself. The young man grabs his camera and helps the other scavenger up, and they both limp away as quickly as possible. "Breathe, Tala."

Tala breaks out of my grip. "I need to bury these phoenixes."

"I can help you, but first . . ."

Luna chuckles. "First you must steal from their corpses."

Tala is panting and wipes away her tears.

"I can do this part," I say.

"You don't know phoenixes like I do," Tala says.

"Luna does. She can help me—"

"I will find the phoenixes. You can do the dirty work."

Luna and I sit in the courtyard while Tala explores the grounds, collecting the phoenix corpses I will need for the ritual. It's hard watching her do this, and I'm hating myself for how badly I am turning her against her own values all so she can help me disturb the natural flow of life and death. Tala has become my very own vulture for dead phoenixes, and I don't know how I will make it up to her one day, but I will. I will owe her the world for everything she's done for me.

Within the hour, Tala waves me over, her hands slick with different colors, as if she's been painting instead of picking up phoenixes who bleed in different shades. There are four feathery corpses in front of me, some that look burned as if they were shot or tried resurrecting but didn't have the muscle memory to do so yet since they were so young. Tala points at each one. "Breath spawn. Gray sun. Century. Obsidian. I'll find the eggshells for the crowned elder up in the nest."

Tala turns to walk away, but I grab her hand.

"Don't thank me for this, Maribelle."

"I wasn't going to. I wanted to say I'm sorry."

On the first day Tala brought me to the Sanctuary, she told me a story of how her family didn't grow up with a lot of money and how her parents always encouraged her to make something great out of something ordinary. She'd made an origami bird out of some random piece of paper, throwing it through the air and into my hands. I wish I'd kept it. More than anything, I wish I never used Tala to help me make something great out of something so tragic.

Tala doesn't say anything else. She walks off into the sanctuary.

I'm left alone with the phoenixes, and I bloody my own hands as I desecrate their corpses, getting everything I need to turn ashes into Atlas.

FIFTEEN
CLIPPED

EMIL

I'm in the gym, exercising my powers in the middle of the night because it's clear Brighton isn't going to go down without a fight.

We all watched his live with Lore, which was so damn scary because there's just no way Lore reached out to Brighton so soon after chilling with us to give him his own spotlight. Brighton would pull something like this to exploit the online traffic, and his dreams are only growing bigger by the day. Did he intimidate Lore into doing that interview? Did he hurt them? I hit up Lore over email, but they didn't respond. Wesley dashed over to their home, but Lore wasn't there. I only know they're alive because they reposted some things on their Instagram Story like Sunstar art from Himalia Lim and a link on how to find your local voting site for Election Day.

I'm throwing gold and gray fire-orbs at target boards that are moving at their highest speed, improving my aim for this inevitable brawl against Brighton. Between his bursts of swift-speed and ability to phase through my fire, I got to make sure I don't miss the chance to land a hit on him when I get it. It's exhausting, and the few times I miss, I think about how that could be the moment in battle when Brighton is clear to deliver a killing blow. I tighten my focus as another fire-orb bursts in my palm, hurling it at a target that I'm pretending is my dangerous brother; I don't feel great after watching the orb explode against the board. After thirty minutes, the target boards are craned back against the wall and my success rate for this session appears on a screen: 87%.

"Not bad," Ness says.

I turn. "I didn't know you were watching."

"I couldn't sleep. Thought I'd come up and get in a workout now that everything is clear."

Between living in the basement, preparing for the showdowns ahead of us, and Brighton being so frustrating, we've all got a lot of pent-up energy that we've been eager to spend up here in the gym while it's closed. Ruth and her clones were fighting against all the punching bags, and it was wild watching someone so sweet get so battle-ready like that. Prudencia got some exhausting one-on-one training with Mele for a couple hours, learning new techniques to improve her telekinetic grips as well as mindfulness exercises to become more in tune with her power. Iris deadlifted almost a thousand pounds of weights, which was unreal to watch. Eva honors her pacifism, but she was with us in spirit as she sat in the boxing ring and meditated. Wesley ran on a treadmill that moved at frightening speeds, looking like a glowing blur. They're all back downstairs, knocked out.

Ness and I are the last ones standing.

I'm drenched in sweat, so I start toweling off. "The gym is all yours," I say, walking off.

"Going to bed?"

I stop. "I'm going to shower and try to pass out."

"You're not going to get any sleep, though, are you?"

"Doubt it."

"Then let's train."

"On what?"

"Physical combat," Ness says, sliding into the boxing ring.

"I don't need to throw punches when I can throw fire."

Ness leans on the ropes. "You can't only rely on your powers. What if you get wounded again by an infinity-ender dagger that dampens your abilities? What if Brighton figures out how to possess people and forces you to drink a Starstifler?"

"Then it sounds like I've already lost."

Ness holds down the bottom rope with his heel. "Not if you know how to fight back."

I reluctantly go into the ring. If Brighton does get up and close to me, I could grab him, preventing him from phasing away. But then what? Shooting a fire-orb in close proximity is only going to blast him out of my possession and free him to phase again. Maybe even possess me as Ness said, which is a top-tier haunting thought. But if I got my hands on Brighton and he can't go anywhere, then I need to be able to back that up with my fists.

"Who taught you how to fight?" I ask.

"I got a lot of practice growing up. People knew better than to hit me back. But my time with the Blood Casters made me deadly. Kill or be killed."

Ness begins circling me. I'm expecting some instruction when he just lunges at me without warning. I'm about to throw fire-darts into his chest, when I stop myself. No powers allowed. That split-second decision leaves me open for attack, and Ness punches me in the face. I drop to the mat, massaging my jaw. It hurts so much I'm expecting him to apologize, like he didn't mean to actually hit me because he swore I'd duck out of the way or something, but all I hear are his footsteps as he treads back.

"Hold up, I thought you were going to teach me."

"I am. First lesson: don't let someone hit you."

I get up, fists ready. "I'm rating your class one-star."

Ness lunges again, but this time I dodge. Lesson learned. He swings and swings, backing me into the turnbuckle. I can't get cornered like this—I jump and tackle him to the mat. He groans as he is slammed down. I raise my fist, but I can't bring it down on his face. Ness is not shy about flipping me over him and climbing on top of me.

"Do not show mercy," Ness says. "It's kill or be killed in the streets."

"But not in this ring. I know I'm safe with you."

Ness doesn't roll off of me. He keeps hovering, lit up by the ceiling's spotlight. "I don't understand how you can trust me after everything I've done to you."

"You've always saved me, Ness. Even when it looked like you were going to kill me."

My heart is running wild, and it's not because of the combat training.

Ness leans in closer, like this boxing ring is our own little island where there are no rules, especially no rules about how I'm not allowed to find happiness or discover love. "I may not always be around to save your life. If you know how to fight, then you can survive. And I need you to survive, fire—"

My nickname is killed when my full name is called out by someone I swore was dead.

I'm still underneath Ness, when I turn my head to find Wyatt in the doorway alongside another Halo Knight I don't recognize.

"Pardon the interruption," Wyatt says. "Or were you seeking an audience under that spotlight?"

Ness gets off me, and I slide out of the ring, rushing to Wyatt. I go in for a hug, and Wyatt picks me off my feet and spins me around. I breathe in the smells of pine and wet grass from his black jacket with the feathered sleeves courtesy of Nox. When Wyatt puts me down, our bodies are still super close, but I don't let our lips get any closer, especially knowing Ness can perfectly see us. Still, I want to comfort Wyatt and take care of him like he's taken care of me. His blue eyes look red like he hasn't rested in days, his cheeks are smudged with dirt, his brown hair is sticking to his sweaty forehead, and he holds my hand like he doesn't want to let me go.

"Are you good? Where have you been?" I ask.

"Nox was harmed by the helicopter's turret, but we were able to evade capture and fatalities by diving into a mountain's cave. I'm sorry if you were worried, but Nox recovering was of utmost importance."

The Halo Knight creed is to serve their phoenixes; Wyatt is honorable that way.

"Nox is all good now?"

"He has healed beautifully. I was on my way here when I was summoned by Crest," Wyatt says, gesturing at the Halo Knight who is standing a few feet away. "We were knocking outside, but shimmied our way in after assuming everyone was asleep . . . I guess they all are but you two."

Wyatt and Ness lock eyes.

I'm not getting into all that right now.

"Can we get an intro?" I ask.

Wyatt waves Crest over. "Emil Rey, Crest Calder. Crest Calder, Emil Rey."

The night Wyatt took me flying on Nox for the first time, he told me about Crest. He's the Halo Knight who recently became commander of the Bronze Wings—the biggest division of Haloes, representing those who have served the organization for less than twenty-five years, like Wyatt and Tala. This promotion was born out of the deaths of the Halo Knights at the museum, catching Crest off guard since he still had so much to learn, but now he's thirty-three and taking charge. He's white with dark brown eyes, his blond tapered hair allows me to see his dagger-shaped earring easily, and he's so muscular that I would definitely duck if he swung at me, no second-guessing. What stands out most about Crest is his Halo Knight jacket, which is not black like Wyatt's or Tala's, but instead bronze with feathered sleeves that are so bright yellow I bet they belong to a breath spawn phoenix, the breed that some people call kamikazes because of how they dive into battle and explode upon impact, destroying their enemies, only to respawn within moments.

I reach out for a handshake. "Nice to finally meet you."

Crest stares at my hand like I'm a breath spawn phoenix that will blow him up. "Duties have delayed this moment," he says in an effeminate French accent. He crosses his arms. "The volume of activity has only soared since your brother's damning announcement."

"I'm sorry about everything. The Halo losses, Brighton's nonsense—"

"The invasion and desecration of the New Ember Sanctuary and annihilation of our phoenixes."

Wyatt stares at his commander but doesn't say anything.

Ness steps up, though. "Don't talk to Emil like he shot those phoenixes himself."

"He may as well have," Crest says. "He is Keon Máximo, after all."

"If you want me to feel like the blood of those phoenixes and Haloes is on my hands, then no problem, we're set," I say, standing tall instead of hanging my head low out of shame. It's pretty clear that my dreams of becoming a Halo Knight aren't going to come true, especially if Crest would be my commander, but right now, in this very moment, I don't serve that organization. I'm leading my own team, and I got to act like it. "We have a united goal to save phoenixkind, but if you think you're going to swoop in here and treat me like I'm the enemy, then you got to get back on your phoenix and hit the skies."

Everyone is surprised.

Crest is stunned silent.

Wyatt smiles out of Crest's eyeline and sneaks a thumbs-up.

Ness claps twice. "Bravo."

I'm not trying to fight with Crest; we all got to be in this together.

"Let's start over," I propose. "My past life was Keon Máximo, but that's not me. He may have been the first specter, who created this mess, but I'm hoping the power-binding potion I've discovered through retrocycling can be used to make sure we disempower every last specter in this lifetime."

"An ambitious undertaking," Crest says.

"An important one for phoenixkind. We have all failed big-time if we let creatures known for resurrecting become a dying species."

Crest nods like he's sizing me up. "I understand you're not the enemy, but you do recognize your brother is a threat. Correct?"

"I'm working on it. We tried disempowering him already."

"That went horribly," Crest says, glaring at Ness, who thankfully doesn't bite back.

"Once I know where he is, we'll try again. Maybe Nox can track him?"

Wyatt nods. "If any phoenix can, it's Nox."

"Awesome."

Crest holds up a finger. "You speak of our united goal to save phoenixkind, Emil, so I would actually like to shift your focus to another mission. It's a direct request from the Council of Phoenixlight."

I'm definitely adding this to the running list of surreal things I've heard since discovering I'm a specter. I can't believe the Council of Phoenixlight, the highest order of Halo Knights, is actually counting on me for something.

"Did they really?" Wyatt asks. "Why didn't you tell me?"

"It is information I'm only authorized to release after a judgment of character," Crest says, then turns back to me. "I trust your heart, Emil. It is my understanding you have aspirations of becoming a Halo Knight. While we wouldn't normally accept a specter in our ranks, the council will accept that you did not choose to become one. We will offer you a full pardon and invite you into the fold if you bind your powers upon completing your mission."

I damn near jump, no, fly, no, just jump with joy because these powers are going to get bound and I can serve phoenixkind in a way that's more me. Working with my heart instead of my fists. This is unbelievable, I can't believe that the other Halo Knights will start seeing me as innocent as only Wyatt has.

"That's bloody skybreaking," Wyatt says.

The future is looking up, but it's also crashing too.

Ness is quiet. There's no way he'll want to see my face again if I become a Halo Knight.

"What's the mission?" I ask, trying to ground myself.

Crest lays a hand on my shoulder, finally treating me like I'm not a threat. "You are the only soul alive who can perform this task."

"Retrocycling," I say. That's why I still need my power.

"Exactly. When Wyatt shared your success retrocycling into Bautista de León's life, the council recognized a golden opportunity to part the clouds on a mystery that has long needed a light to shine upon an answer. Its urgency has never been more important since Brighton exposed the secrets of resurrection, tempting alchemists and hunters and others to pursue phoenix blood to turn themselves and high-paying clients into specters. Only an hour ago Tala Castillo alerted me to scavengers at New Ember, trying to steal phoenix corpses to source their powers. If we do not douse these flames now, then phoenixkind will inevitably be annihilated so immortals can walk this world."

I hate how much we're at risk of living out Luna's ultimate plan, but it's Brighton who is causing it. "What do you need me to do? Pop back into Bautista's life for something?"

Crest tilts his head. "Further back."

My heart pounds. "You want me to relive Keon's life?"

"His death," Crest says.

First I had to die as Bautista and now I have to die as Keon.

My bright future as a Halo Knight depends on me going back into my past life so I can be killed by Halo Knights.

I'm really getting a taste for what it's like to resurrect and remember the deaths.

"Why? What happens at Keon's death?"

"Some veteran Halo Knights, now Gold Wings who serve on the council, were present for Keon's death, including the very Halo who fired the arrow that killed him. But before his death, Keon spoke of another creation. A weapon he forged."

"What kind of weapon?"

"A scythe that could kill the unkillable."

What kind of dark alchemy did Keon perform to create something like that? And why? But there's another more pressing question I need answered. "What's your battle plan with this scythe?"

Crest clenches his hand into a fist. "We must demonstrate force in this critical moment. No one will pursue blood alchemy for immortality if they know they can be slayed by this scythe. That begins with conquering the greatest of threats."

I feel like I'm being stabbed by the infinity-ender, or slashed with this scythe that the Halo Knights want unearthed for a devastating reason.

My eyes burn like eclipses as I get up in Crest's face. "I will die before I help you kill my brother."

No one moves.

"Brighton is anticipating the potion," Crest says tensely, careful not to flinch. "But he doesn't know about the scythe."

"Then I guess it sucks that you have no clue where it is."

"I suppose you don't have the heart to become a Halo Knight."

"And you don't have a heart at all."

"This is about the greater good of phoenixkind—"

"Which I'm all about, but not like this. I can win without killing."

Crest shakes his head. "You're awfully defensive of someone who has threatened your life."

"And I will be until the day he actually kills me," I say. I've seen enough terrible things to last a lifetime, but I won't add Brighton being killed by a weapon I uncover to the list.

"If Brighton had the opportunity to procure the scythe to vanquish you, I suspect he would jump at the opportunity."

"Then let's thank the stars that he has no link to Keon's life."

We stare at each other until Crest turns to Wyatt. "It's clear we will find no allegiance here. Let's go."

Wyatt stands still. "I'm afraid that I will be remaining here."

"You serve phoenixkind, not a specter," Crest says.

"I do serve phoenixkind," Wyatt says. Then his blue eyes gaze at me. "I will also follow Emil's leadership through the stormiest of skies to save phoenixes, his way."

He grabs my hand, and I squeeze his, grateful that he's got my back like this.

I feel extraordinary and powerful in this moment.

Ness rushes past us without a word.

Damn it.

"Hold up, hold up," I say, chasing after Ness and catching him in the hallway, right before he can head down into the basement. "That wasn't some romantic hand-holding thing."

"Does he know that, Emil?"

"I obviously haven't had the chance to have that talk yet, but I'm going to. It just means a lot that he would stand up to his commander for me."

Ness stares down the shadowy staircase, like he wants to get lost in that darkness. "He's a good person. I don't foresee myself ever liking him, but he wouldn't be a bad choice for you."

"That's not where my head is at, Ness."

"Your heart will make that call for you, Emil."

Ness kisses my forehead and descends into the shadows.

My face is warm from his lips, but my soul aches from his words. Ness sounded so defeated. He's the one that's great at reading people, and it's like he knows what I'm going to do even before I do. I'm tempted to follow him and keep talking, but I got to give him space.

Right as I'm headed back into the gym, Crest is coming out.

"I hope you're worth it," Crest says.

"Worth what?"

He leaves, and I bolt the doors closed behind him.

Wyatt is standing in the center of the gym, glowing under the bright lights, which are harsh on my tired eyes. "I'm sorry for the trouble I caused," he says.

"Back at you, but also thanks?"

"My absolute delight. I can't think of anyone more worthy of getting my wings clipped for."

"Is that some sort of English expression?"

"Yes, it's English for 'I should probably save the world before I become a disgrace to my parents after they discover I have been booted out of the Halo Knights,' something like that."

I now realize what Crest was talking about. He hopes I'm worth his organization losing one of their best Halo Knights.

"Wait, Wyatt, that's not what I want. That's been your whole life."

Wyatt looks me in the eyes, like I haven't just cost him everything he has been training for since he was a kid. "Perhaps it's time for me to be reborn as someone new, then. What say you and I take on those stormy skies together, sweet Emil?"

SIXTEEN

FAR FROM ORDINARY

BRIGHTON

The Brightsiders are becoming more than a fan base. They're a legion.

I lie awake in bed, tallying up my follower count across all my online platforms. I have hit ten million followers since my Instagram Live with Lore six hours ago; I would send a gift basket to their house, but I hung around long enough after leaving to watch them get into a taxi minutes later with a suitcase. If Lore does pull anything, my Brightsiders across the city, across the country, across the world will help me find them. I set my phone down on my chest, trading in the screen's glow for the twinkling stars through the skylight. Living out all my dreams makes me question if I'm actually sleeping after all, and will wake up any moment now in a California dorm room, living a painfully ordinary life.

Silver and sapphire flames snake around my fingers, born out of a single thought.

I am so far from ordinary.

I am also alone.

Instead of focusing on the empty side of the bed or scrolling through my phone for Prudencia pictures, I return to Instagram, where I'm flooded with notifications every minute. They're mostly supportive, but negative comments do appear across my posts. I could set filters to prevent this or delete them altogether, but there is more power in letting my followers destroy these trolls, defending me so fiercely that my opposers either lock or deactivate their accounts. If you don't want to be fully run off the internet, then don't come trashing me in my spaces.

There's a knock at the door.

"Who is it?"

"Us," Zelda says from the other side.

"Come in."

Zelda and Samuel enter my bedroom, still dressed in the same cozy sweatpants they were wearing when they drove me into the city to have my talk with Lore. While Samuel seems as relaxed as ever, which seems to be his default when he's not scaring people, Zelda seems even more energized. "There's trouble in the city," she singsongs.

I sit up in bed. "What kind of trouble?" There's a large part of me that is concerned that enforcers are attacking Emil and Prudencia again as well as Ma getting caught in that cross fire. But then there's the voice that reminds me that Emil wanted to have things his way and now has to pay the price.

"There's this group of gleamcrafters causing trouble," Zelda says, bringing me her phone. There's a local trending topic on Twitter devoted to these celestials and specters attacking citizens with their powers. A ten-second video filmed in Central Park shows a celestial's eyes glowing before he strangles someone with tree roots. "They've been identified as fugitives who were in the Bounds. The biggest threat to your image is the specter leading the charge. An article I found says Genesis St. James was arrested last month after she attacked her own family."

I sympathize with this specter if she attacked her family in self-defense.

There's a video of the woman, Genesis, fighting an enforcer. The enforcer draws his wand, but white fire shaped like a phoenix flies into his chest, setting him ablaze before he can attack. She turns in the direction of the camera, fury in her eyes. There's something familiar about her. I pause the video on her face, and it all comes back to me. "I recognize her. She's a specter who was defeated by Maribelle and Atlas on the first night of the Crowned Dreamer. Emil and I were at some block party where we witnessed the brawl firsthand; I got it on film. Enforcers then arrested her."

Zelda scrolls through her phone. "The article didn't mention anything about the Spell Walkers."

"Why would it? The media wants to paint the enforcers as the great defenders."

"They're doing a terrible job, as per usual, because Genesis is burning the city with phoenix fire."

"I think she has more than phoenix powers. Luna was doing test runs on her Reaper's Blood formula to see how the convergence of essences would impact a specter. Many were dying because they weren't given pure blood."

The day after our run-in with Genesis, there was a news story about a specter with the same white phoenix fire who had been flying when his arm suddenly snapped off midflight. His arm began regrowing before he died minutes later. At the time we didn't know that was because he also had hydra blood in his system. The same for that specter Orton, who showed signs of having powers from a phoenix, hydra, and ghost. Before he could kill me, he overheated, consumed from head to toe in his own phoenix fire. Maybe Genesis not being able to use her powers in the Bounds is what has saved her life so far.

"All that matters is you stop her and the others," Zelda says. "The best way to prove that specters can be deserving of their powers is to stop another who is abusing them."

No one has to tell me twice to go be the hero.

Especially if that means stopping someone with my powers—I'm the only Infinity Reaper.

But I won't be going alone. I will show up to this fight with my army.

We waste no time waking up the other celestials in the house, recruiting them for this mission.

The world will see that our powers aren't only for entertainment, but also enforcement.

These fugitives won't stand a chance against our pack, especially with the range of powers between the seven of us: Alpha's water-casting can put out that specter's phoenix flames; Zelda can turn our opponents into blocks of ice; Samuel can sneak up on them with his camouflage; Reed Tyler can put his clones to use for something other than choreographed dances; Millie will prove she's more than a walking ring light and charging station with her electric powers; and Bull's stories about his powerhouse strength will make him a foe to be reckoned with as he stampedes into enemies, earning the name he's rebranded with since Alpha said no one will take a Barry seriously.

As we drive down the highway into the city, I go live on Instagram from the front passenger seat. "My epic friends, I'm cautioning you to be very careful if you're in Midtown Manhattan. There are dangerous fugitives from the Bounds who are causing trouble, even killing enforcers. Go home if you're out and stay there if you are. I'm on my way to put an end to this madness along with some familiar faces." I turn the phone's camera on Alpha, who is driving, and then flip to everyone else in the backseat. "We will protect our city. I promise. Spread the word."

There's a grave error Maribelle and Atlas made when they fought that phoenix specter.

They let her live.

That night, after Emil and I successfully fled the scene, we got into a tense conversation on the ride home. I was defending Maribelle and her right to kill that specter, trusting the judgment of the Spell Walkers on which are the necessary lives to take. Emil believed that heroes shouldn't have body counts. I was wishing I had powers so I could have gotten involved in that fight and Emil was relieved we didn't.

Times have changed, but my heart hasn't.

For the sake of the world, I will add that specter to my body count.

SEVENTEEN

STORMY SKIES AND SCATTERED STARS

EMIL

Why can't someone be in my life without burning?

Wyatt is the latest victim whose life is going down in flames. It's not right that he's no longer a Halo Knight just for having my back, but now that he's asking me to take on all the stormy skies ahead of us together, I sense he's wanting to weather this war as my boyfriend. But I can't be anything more than a friend, and more important, a leader while our lives are still being spent hiding in havens because we're being hunted down.

I set this dream of his on fire.

Wyatt is sitting on the edge of the boxing ring as I finish catching him up on the same convo I had with Ness. "You're shelving matters of your heart like some terrible book?"

"It's not forever. It's just until I'm not the Infinity Son."

"If that sky-forsaken scythe slashed you in this moment, would you fall and die without any regrets?"

Not loving the visual, but I've imagined my own death countless times already.

"I'd have a million," I say.

"Then do not wait for the stars to align like some perfect

constellation. Be the Skybreaker you are and embrace the scattered stars in their disarray."

That's poetic and all that, but it's also easier said than done. "Look, I know dying with a million regrets would super suck, but it's better than dying with a million and one regrets. I don't know what goes into love. I could completely screw that up."

"You're not well versed in leadership either, and yet here you are, trying your best." Wyatt hops down from the ring, holding my hands in his. "Your heart is your strength. It is what attracted me to you in the first place when I should have downright despised you for possessing phoenix powers. But you care unlike anyone I know, and those feelings should not be buried away as if they're some, oh, I don't know, deadly ancient scythe that can only bring doom." Wyatt then rests his forehead on mine, right where Ness just kissed me minutes ago. "You must follow your heart, Emil, even if that does not bring you to me."

I want to keep pushing back, but I don't want to push him away.

"I'll think it over," I say.

"I do not envy your position, Emil. Frankly, you would be drama-free if I had died instead of coming back. Something for me to consider the next time I'm facing an epic death."

"You better not die. I'll be so pissed."

"Some of us are not immortal, but fear not, if I die, I will return as a glorious phoenix that you can ride through the night." Wyatt notes my grimace. "Get your mind out of the gutter. I'll be a bird for sky's sake! However, that offer stands and can be redeemed while I am still a nearly perfect human."

"Nearly perfect?" I ask with a smile.

"My bones ache when it rains. It is most unfortunate. A true Achilles' heel."

"Then maybe you should stay away from stormy skies."

Wyatt gives me a sad smile. "Perhaps I should, sweet Emil."

I want to apologize for not having my life together, when I hear someone running up the stairs from the basement. I'm scared it's Ness, so I take a step back so he doesn't get worked up over Wyatt any more than he is. But it's not Ness; it's Prudencia with a frantic look in her eyes.

"We have a lead on Brighton," Prudencia says, holding up her phone. "He's teaming up with some influencers to take on Bounds escapees." She turns to Wyatt. "You're back."

"I am. Just in time to watch influencers request selfies with fugitives apparently."

"Are they gleamcrafters?" I ask.

"I have never seen any of those people before," Prudencia says.

That's often been my experience when I stumble on someone's account who has tens of millions of followers and I've somehow managed to go through life not knowing they exist. But now I'm concerned for how many of these strangers Brighton is about to get killed because he's convinced them to play hero.

We rush downstairs and wake everyone up. They're all groggy at first—Wesley swears he's still dreaming when he sees Wyatt—but they get it together because they're used to jumping into action. Ness is the only one who is up and alert. That energy he was going to release in the ring with me can now go straight to his fellow escapees on the streets. In a welcomed twist, Ruth decides she's tagging along, leaving Esther behind with Ma and Eva. We need all hands on deck to stop Brighton, and no one has more hands than Ruth. I just hope four celestials, three Starstifler potions, two specters, and one clipped Halo Knight is enough to bring home the win.

Armed with the Starstiflers in my feathered bag, I go say bye to Ma.

"Bring Brighton home, my Emilio," Ma says while hugging me tightly.

Of course we don't have a home anymore, but I get what she means.

Bring Brighton back to us.

Then we all head out, exiting the gym's back door into the alley.

"Where were the fugitives last spotted?" Iris asks.

Prudencia consults her phone. "They've made their way down to Alphabet City."

"And we destroyed the car," Iris says.

"*You* destroyed the car, technically," Wesley says.

Iris looks ready to destroy Wesley next. "Then what?"

Wesley shrugs. "Subway? Nassau Ave.? It should be empty this late."

"I wouldn't trust the train to get me anywhere on time, especially a battle."

Wyatt raises his hand. "As charming as it would be for my tourist heart to wait an eternity underground for a train that may never come, I suggest flying. I can seat three of us on Nox."

Time is definitely of the essence.

When we got back to the Sanctuary after breaking Ness out of the Bounds, Brighton made it clear that he wanted to hold on to his powers so he could play judge, jury, and executioner on the escapees.

If he goes around killing the fugitives, especially while his influencer buddies are filming the whole thing, then his crime will be caught on camera and he'll be locked away next. Or worse, everyone will lift up Brighton for killing, pushing our country into an even darker corner.

"I'm going," Prudencia says.

"Flying on a phoenix sounds fun," Wesley says.

"But you can run, and probably beat us there," I say.

"I most certainly can. It just won't be as fun."

"Just get a taxi. The worst someone can do is tell people where we are, which is going to be pretty obvious with influencers livestreaming. I can fly alongside Nox and . . ." I turn to Ness and ask a stupid question. "Who do you want to go with?"

Ness makes a swift decision. "I'll go on the phoenix. You'll need the element of surprise."

Wow, that's really mature of him, I didn't see that coming. Plays to his point.

I hand one Starstifler to Ness and the other to Wesley. "You two have the best shot of sneaking up on Brighton. Don't forget. The potion needs his bloody flesh before he ingests it to work."

One potion. Three shots.

We can do this.

It's time to bounce.

Iris, Ruth, and Wesley run down the block, getting some distance from the gym so they can't be traced back here.

I follow Wyatt down another street and up a fire escape to an apartment building's rooftop, Ness and Prudencia directly behind us. Hidden in the shadows of a water tank is Nox, cuddled up in his own feathers, looking like an enormous nest. Nox awakens at the sound of our footsteps and rises to nuzzle Wyatt and then me. I quickly scratch the top of his head, honored that I've earned his trust. Nox leans forward as Wyatt, Prudencia, and Ness climb onto his back.

I leap off the rooftop, my gold and gray wings of fire carrying me high into the night sky, alongside a phoenix as black as darkness, and as we prepare for a showdown against my brother, I'm filled with dread like we're flying into the heart of a storm.

EIGHTEEN
THE BODY COUNT

BRIGHTON

White and orange flames are rampaging through the streets, but the specter is nowhere to be found.

Our search begins through midtown. We're ready to leap out the car at the first sign of destroyed shops and burning cars, but there is no one to fight. Genesis and the other fugitives seem to have moved on, so we keep following the trail of fire. Along the way, I see a pharmacy has been blown wide open, a gallery's entire collection is turning to ash, and a flower shop's supply has been killed by phoenix fire before they could die in some customer's home. I can't identify the pattern. I think that's because there isn't one. Now that these fugitives are free from their cells, I think they want to watch the world burn.

"Maybe they went home," Bull says, leaning against the window like he's bored.

"There's still activity being reported online," Zelda says, her face lit up by her phone's glowing screen. "It's beginning to trend under 'specter spectacle.' Two things I hate: One, cute wordplay that's not cute. And two, getting canceled for something that isn't your fault.

This not-cute specter spectacle is going to land you under number two, Brighton."

I won't have my reputation damaged by rogue specters.

"Keep tracking the hashtag, Z." I turn to Alpha. "Drive faster."

"We don't know where we're going yet, man," Alpha says.

"Follow. The. Flames."

I can't believe an adult who is almost twice my age needs direction for something so obvious.

Alpha begins speeding through the streets.

We drive past police officers who are securing yellow tape around a crime scene. I glimpse a dead enforcer on the ground. His sea-green power-proof vest has been burned black; it sure seems like they should call that vest something else if it's not actually power proof. This death and every other action unfolding tonight will make the news. My presence needs to become so undeniable that the media won't be able to erase my victory from the narrative.

Zelda has been alerted to Genesis's location from a mutual who's on the scene. Bull bounces in his seat excitedly, shaking the van. We speed toward Avenue B in Alphabet City, ignoring every red light. If we're at risk of getting hit by another car, I can phase through it all; I'd do my best to save the others too, preferably Zelda and Samuel, but even I can only do so much.

When we round the corner, all hell is breaking loose—and the perpetrators are here.

Genesis is hovering above the street, lifted by wings of white fire.

I can't even fly yet.

But I will learn soon enough.

"Make sure you're filming," I say. I will need to prove my case.

"I think this battle will be more than covered," Zelda says, pointing at a dozen civilians who are aiming their phones at Genesis and her two celestial companions.

Are they fans?

Whoever they are, they're in for a show.

I lead the charge as I dash toward Genesis. She's about to hurl more fire. "Stop!"

Genesis spins in the air. Her head cocks as she assesses me. "You."

Being recognized by this particular specter feels like a wonderful full-circle moment. "Good. You know who I am. Surrender now or . . ."

"Or what, Infinity Reaper?"

"You know what."

I'm now flanked by my team, fists and power at the ready.

Genesis unleashes two streams of white fire. I'm ready to call for Prudencia to deflect them back when I remember she's not here. Thankfully, Zelda doesn't need instruction. She freezes the fire midair, and it shatters against the ground. This is when we attract the attention of the other celestials. We know the one who strangled someone with tree roots has elemental abilities, but it's unclear how far they range. The other celestial's powers are completely unknown, but he seems fully unbothered by us as he leans against a car and lights a cigarette. More fire flies our way, and this time Alpha eagerly jumps in line, casting water from his palms, but the pressure isn't enough to overcome the blast. He runs around on fire before falling to the ground, dead. Millie screams in horror, and in her outrage, she charges Genesis while producing electricity from her own core and building on that by drawing energy from the streetlamps. The lights around us flicker as Millie fashions a bolt of pure electricity, as bright as lightning, and hurls it at Genesis, only for it to phase right through her like she's nothing but air.

I'm not the only Infinity Reaper.

But I will be.

I dash toward Genesis in dizzying circles, dodging all her fiery attacks. I run up a wall and onto a fire escape where I get a clear shot. I hurl a fire-bolt and blast Genesis out of the air. She lands flat on a car's windshield, rolls off the hood, and slams face-first into the ground.

Is she dead?

Meanwhile, Millie cries out for Alpha's revenge because he did so much good for so many people—the giving-free-water stunt?—and hurls another bolt of energy, this time at the celestial who's smoking. His eyes glow, and one portal appears before Millie and another opens behind her. The energy bolt shoots through the first and comes out the other, striking her through the back. Her body convulses as she lies on her side, foam spilling out of her mouth until she stops moving, her eyes frozen open.

In a rage, Bull wrenches a mailbox from out of the ground and throws it at the portal celestial . . . who doesn't even pull his portal trick because Bull's aim is so bad that it wasn't at risk of hitting him. This is so embarrassing; I thought I had an Iris on my side, and instead I have someone whose powerhouse strength is so wasted. Bull stampedes toward the root-strangling celestial, ready to earn his name, when he begins floating in the air, his momentum killed. It appears the celestial was never elemental but a terrifying telekinetic all along.

Bull screams in agony as his bones pierce through his flesh, blood spraying the streets, and when he goes quiet, he remains suspended in the air a long time, like a warning that this will be us next. Then Bull's—Barry's—corpse falls to the ground.

It has become very clear that these influencers should have stuck to their day jobs.

"I'm getting out of here," Reed says, turning to leave.

I grab his wrist. "No. We can still outnumber them with your clones."

"I'm not going to die eight times for anyone," Reed says.

Zelda and Samuel are absolutely horrified too, staring at the wreckage of their friends. Though were they actually friends? Zelda mocked Alpha, and it's not as if she ever said anything nice about Millie that wasn't about the lighting she provided for filming or how Bull. . . . Actually, she never complimented Bull for anything. But I guess you don't need to be friends with someone to not be terrified that you will meet the same nightmarish fate that they have. These aren't my first dead bodies, and watching someone so powerful being killed by their bones isn't the worst thing I've ever seen. That honor will always go to watching Dad choke on his own blood.

We take cover behind our van so we can plot our next move.

"This has been a rough start," I say.

Reed is aghast. "Rough start? A rough start is when my clone is lagging behind and won't sync up with my video's audio. This is a bloodbath. We're in over our heads and—"

"Shut up," I command, shocking everyone. There is no time for niceties, and they'll understand my urgency if we get out of this alive. "That celestial could cast a portal out from under our feet any second now, and we'll die as divided as we appear to be. We're lacking coordination, strategy. Here's what we're going to do. Reed, send out your clones. Distract them for as long as you can. Zelda, we'll go on the offensive, but stay close so I can phase you away from danger. Samuel, you have to sneak up on the celestials and kill them."

Samuel, who normally seems so sleepy, has never looked more awake in his life. "Say what?"

I scoop up shards of glass from another's car wreckage. "Creep up and kill them."

"I'm not a killer."

"You have an assassin's power!"

"Which I use to pop out and scare people!"

"This is the same thing except you're going to kill them," I say, thrusting the shards of glass into his hands. "I would do it myself if they weren't watching me. Now don't let them watch you."

Samuel shakes his head, staring at the glass. "This isn't me."

"The you that you were died when you arrived on this battlefield. There is no turning back and returning to a life of pranking people without your followers questioning in every single post why you didn't put your power to good use when your friends were murdered in front of you. But they will worship you in a way you didn't know was possible if you step up as a hero now."

Everything sinks in. His life as he knows it is over. "This is the only time," Samuel says.

"One and done," I say, and then: "Two and done, really."

Zelda kisses Samuel. "Be careful. I'll see you soon."

No one better see Samuel until those celestials have had their throats slit.

Samuel fades into near invisibility, the faintest of outlines walking away from us.

Reed's seven clones manifest in purple glows and charge forward before they begin spacing out like multiple arrows released from the same crossbow.

Zelda and I run down the middle of the street, blasting ice and fire toward our enemies. The portal celestial repeats his trick, but I'm quick to grab Zelda and our elements phase through us. When we corporealize, Zelda is still trembling in fear. She crystallizes a shield of ice as quickly as she casts the sculptures she sells for thousands of dollars. Zelda peeks around the frozen wall, shooting icicles as sharp as needles, but most of them fall short and the few that reach are waved away by the telekinetic as if they were nothing but annoying flies.

"I'm going to run up on them," I say.

Zelda shakes her head. "Do not leave me."

"You have your barrier. I'll be back."

This is my opportunity to strike. I dash backward away from Zelda before she can grab me, then sideways, zigzagging around Reed's clones. I hurl a fire-bolt, which the telekinetic deflects into a clone, causing the real Reed to scream in pain, exposing his location. My eyes widen as the portal celestial drops through a ring beneath his feet. The next thing I see is all seven clones reach for their throats like they're choking on something, struggling, and then their heads are jerked from left to right like whiplash before vanishing in a purple light; Reed's neck has been snapped.

Alpha, Millie, Bull, Reed.

All dead.

I never thought to give an everyone-won't-make-it-out-alive

speech because I didn't anticipate this would go so wrong. Celestials have been thrown into the Bounds for unjust reasons, but it's clear that these fugitives were served the appropriate justice. Inappropriate, come to think of it. These gleamcrafters should never have been allowed to live in the first place. They deserved execution.

The telekinetic is helping Genesis to her feet, when he flinches at the sound of something, but his reflexes are too slow as he's stabbed in the neck with a shard of glass.

"Yes!" Zelda cheers. "Get him! Get him!"

The glass becomes exposed the bloodier it gets, as if Samuel is losing his focus on camouflaging and only focused on killing.

The telekinetic chokes on his blood as he crumples to the ground, unmoving.

"Good job, baby! Yes!" Zelda shouts.

Samuel swings down on Genesis with another shard of glass, when he vanishes through a portal in the ground, like someone who has fallen down a manhole. Zelda is crying out his name, but I don't see where he's coming from. Then I hear him. I look up high into the sky where he falls out of one portal and into another and another, the momentum increasing between each one. I concentrate, trying to fly, but it's too late. A portal opens, and Samuel's screams are cut short as he lands directly onto Zelda's spiky ice wall, dying as he made his living—popping out of nowhere.

Zelda's screams could wake the dead as she watches Samuel's blood stain the ice.

I'm wrong. Her screams cannot wake the dead.

I look around, trying to find the portal celestial. He's not near the van or the spot I first saw him smoking his cigarette. I might have been foolish enough to have stayed here as long as I have, but I'm not stupid enough to think he has left. He can appear any moment now or even bring us to him. But I shouldn't make that easy for him. He seems to only have that one power, whereas I have an arsenal. I dash down the street to create the illusion that I've left, but I creep back while in camo mode, keeping a close watch on Zelda. I will honor Samuel by protecting his girlfriend with this stealthy power he taught me. My heart is pounding as if the enemy celestial will appear behind me and snap my neck, but a portal opens behind Zelda instead. As the celestial steps one foot out, I move forward too, dashing and dashing, racing him. He grabs Zelda's neck right as I skid into place, phasing his heart out of his chest and throwing it through the portal before it closes. Somewhere, the heart of a dead man thuds at the same time as his body.

"I did it, I did it," I say, falling to my knees and catching my breath.

Zelda continues crying, and she's alive to do so because of me.

She won't be another body—

I'm blasted by burning hot white fire and roll across the street, stopping when I bump into Alpha's corpse.

Zelda enters survival mode, shooting icicles at Genesis, who is so close it's impossible to miss her except that she is phasing through each and every one. "Please, no, please!"

Genesis burns Zelda alive in white flames, and her screams last seconds.

Alpha, Millie, Bull, Reed, Samuel, Zelda.

They're all gone.

They sold me on this idea that they wanted to be heroes, to help out the world. But that's not true. They only wanted to live in it. I can't fault that instinct. That's what we all want. But the kind of world they wanted to live in requires some fighting, and they should have spent more time nurturing those abilities and less time bragging about how extraordinary their lives were and making ordinary people feel inferior for not having powers. I don't know how aware they all were that all that flashiness I've seen from gleamcrafters online over the years created such a craving to be among them that I created Celestials of New York just to get as close as possible. It didn't stop there. Like any other product, watching them made me want what they had. They influenced me to power, so I went and got some. And now as I look around at all these bodies—broken bones, burnt flesh, so much blood—it looks as if the influencers have done an ad for Death.

I will not be following their footsteps just as they should have never followed mine.

I rise, standing alone with no army.

The few spectators have wisely vanished.

Genesis and I are the last ones standing.

Infinity Reaper versus Infinity Reaper.

There will be one more body added to tonight's count.

Silver and sapphire flames snake around my arms as white fire roars in her palms.

We attack at the same time, like we're twins, and phase through each other's offenses. Genesis and I may both have all the powers that come from Reaper's Blood, but that doesn't mean they came from the same essences. I won't be able to conquer her with my ghostly abilities since mine aren't as pure as they could be because they came from Luna's family line. The golden-strand hydra allows me to camouflage to great effect, but who's to say Genesis can't do the same thing? What I can be confident about is that we have powers from different phoenixes. Emil said that century phoenixes—like Gravesend, whose blood is running through my veins—are war-hungry fighters with heightened survival instincts because they don't want to be away from the world for another one hundred years. Meanwhile, Genesis gets her powers from a breed known as common ivories and I don't know if they can do anything special but the name certainly doesn't strike fear in my heart.

But I do strike her.

Fire-bolt after fire-bolt, the silver and sapphire flames shooting through her wall of white fire. I dash closer and closer every chance I get, aiming to get my hands on her so she won't be able to phase away. Sweat is getting in my eyes as I overpower Genesis. She's already wearing down, still weak from the first fire-bolt I landed on her at the start of this brawl, but when the next connects right above her heart, wounding her so painfully that her defenses drop, I dash over and slam her to the ground. My hand wraps around her throat. She won't be going anywhere now, and the fear in her eyes screams for her.

I'm a little emotional thinking about how far I've come. "I was there the night you got arrested. I was powerless and unable to help the Spell Walkers stop you, but now here we are. I get to protect the world from all your chaos."

"I only . . ." Genesis chokes. I loosen my grip. Maybe she will concede. "I only did it to draw you out. We knew you would save the world."

I look over at the heartless celestial and the throatless celestial. "I have. They're dead, and you're about to join them."

"You can't possibly believe that we couldn't have defeated you in seconds. Cillian could have fed you your own bones, and Edgar could have buried you alive in the earth's core. But we were told not to kill you."

My heart is pounding like never before, like I'm hungry for the kill. But I need to know more. "You're working for someone."

"It's a trap, all to find Luna. But I don't care about her well-being. I want revenge. She gave me these powers and promised I would become a Blood Caster, that I would become family after being thrown out by my own. Then she abandoned me in the Bounds like I was no one. I had a chance to kill her in her cell, but that Spell Walker, Maribelle, threatened my life. I want to live in a world where Luna is gone. Don't you? We can team up. There are no other specters like us."

My heart rate is accelerating. It's so loud I can hear it in my ears, pummeling my own thoughts. "Luna has no power over me and no powers to overpower me." I stare down at Genesis. Someone like her on my side could be effective or disastrous. "As for an alliance . . . there can only be one Infinity Reaper."

I give in to the war-hungry cries, phasing into her chest to steal her heart, adding her to the pile of bodies that have died under the stars tonight. My fingers brush her heart, when a bright blast rockets into me and I go flying down the street. The air is knocked out of me. This must be the work of whoever lured me here for Luna's whereabouts. I do not know and I do not care as I've gotten everything I could ever possibly need from her. While catching my breath, I look up to find Nox descending onto the street with Wyatt, Prudencia, and Ness on the phoenix's back. If they're here, that means . . .

Emil is hovering in the air with burning wings, and a fresh target on his heart.

NINETEEN

GOLD VERSUS SILVER

EMIL

We're just in time, but also too late.

As I'm descending, I look around the streets at what a horror show everything is. I count eight dead bodies, but who knows, there could be more burning in one of the many fires surrounding us. It doesn't look like anyone died easily. Some look as if they may have been torn apart by a wild hydra or burned alive by a raging phoenix, but I don't think this was the work of any creature. Everyone has been killed by my monstrous brother, and if I didn't get here when I did, another specter would have had her heart ripped out, just like Brighton did to Stanton back at the Bounds.

Would he have smiled again after his kill?

Brighton isn't smiling as he rises. There's murder, more murder in his eyes.

I touch down on the battlefield.

"You saving killers now, Emil?"

"I'm stopping them, Bright."

"Then you're too late."

"Looks that way."

Brighton begins laughing. "You think I'm responsible for this carnage?"

"I just had to stop you from ripping out someone's heart, so yeah."

Silver and sapphire flames begin sparking around his wrists. I don't think he's even about to start swinging with fire; it seems more brought on by how pissed he is. "You don't get to fly in and act all high and mighty. You're not superior to me. You wouldn't even be standing if you just had to watch your friends annihilated."

"You should've never involved them."

"No one forced them. They chose to fight for better lives."

I don't know; I'm not buying it. Brighton is probably telling himself this story to ease his conscience, but it's all good; I'm only hearing him out anyway because I need to keep him talking while we wait for backup. If Brighton comes at us, Ness and Wyatt don't have the power to fight back like Prudencia and I can. And unlike Brighton, I'm all about protecting my people. I won't force anyone into a battle unless there's a chance they can get out alive.

"This isn't a good look. Look, let's calm down and go home."

Brighton stares at me like I'm a hydra who's grown extra heads. "We don't have a home because of specters like her," he says, pointing at Genesis, who is weak on the ground, maybe even dying. "I will kill her for all she's done tonight. Don't bother trying to save her."

"You're the one I'm trying to save, Bright. If you don't bind your powers, you're going to hit a point of no return. Is living forever worth it if you've ruined your life?"

Brighton takes deep breaths, like he's actually cooling down and thinking this over. There's a world where we can bounce back from this. No one knows that he killed Stanton, and I'll take that to the grave since that was all in self-defense anyway, even if Brighton seemed to get a gleeful high out of overpowering the man who tortured him. And if he's not responsible for all these dead bodies, then that's a bright star in his constellation of innocence. But the moment anyone catches him in the act of killing like he's some vigilante executioner, then it's lights out.

I approach Brighton cautiously, holding out my fist for our childhood handshake.

"Fist bump and whistle?" I ask, calling a truce.

Brighton smiles as he holds out his fist—and shoots a fire-bolt directly into my chest.

I'm sent flipping backward, and right before I can collide with that wall of ice with a body impaled on it, Prudencia's telekinesis carries me over to her and gently sets me down. But that doesn't mean I'm not still in a world of pain. This is the first time I've felt the effect of Brighton's power, and it feels like blazing fire lighting me up from inside, attacking all my senses, making me even want to give up. But I have to keep fighting. I've overpowered Brighton before and I can do it again—I just can't let him get another hit on me; if only I could phase through his attacks like he can mine.

Ness and Wyatt help me up as Prudencia stands guard.

"It would seem Brighton is as mad as ever," Wyatt says.

"He's going to be even more pissed in a second," I say.

"Why is that?"

"We're going to disempower Genesis with the Starstifler and prove that the potion will bind a specter's powers. This is the real solution the world needs to see, not executing specters at our will just because we have the power to do so."

"Not to mention the bloodthirst."

Fire-bolts are launched our way and Prudencia deflects them, but Brighton walks through them, untouchable.

"He's coming," Ness says.

"And going," Prudencia says, waving her hand and sending Brighton flying backward through a storefront. The window's glass rains down as Brighton bangs against the front counter.

That should buy us a minute. "Ness, get Genesis to drink the potion. Wyatt, stay close on Nox and get him out of there if Brighton breaks through our defenses." They both look at me like this is up for discussion. This is a battlefield, not some high school lunch period where we get to choose who we sit with. "Go now!"

Ness seems resistant, but he grabs the Starstifler and leads the way with Wyatt hopping onto Nox and gliding after him.

"Are you okay?" Prudencia asks.

I dig my knuckles into my aching chest where that fire-bolt hit. "I'll survive."

I hope.

Brighton comes out of the store, furious. "You're traitors. Everyone knows it."

"We don't care if people worship us like you do," Prudencia says. "There's nothing special about you to worship."

Just like the night of our first fight, Brighton tries insulting

Prudencia, but she lets the words bounce off her as if she's telekinetically waving them away. But she's spot-on about Brighton. He cares for the public's admiration for his powers whereas we're fighting for acceptance. No one is asking for a shrine on our end, just the chance to live in peace.

Brighton looks around and finds Ness and Wyatt approaching Genesis. "What are you . . . ?" He shakes his head. "You better not touch—" He dashes toward them, moving in swift bursts of speed, and I catch on to his pattern so fast that I hurl a fire-orb just north of where he's going next, and Brighton runs straight into it; that target training paid off.

My brother is torn on what fight he wants to fight, and he chooses ours. Fire-bolts fly my way as he stalks toward me. I blast through each and every one with a fire-orb. Prudencia telekinetically suspends the explosions mid-eruption, creating a sun made up of gold and silver flames that is growing and growing. It's radiant until Brighton strikes this bomb with a fire-bolt, setting off a seismic blast that blows all of us off our feet and flying in different directions. I crash onto a van's windshield, glass piercing my skin—my face, my arms, with the sharpest pain coming from my hip. I sit up and find Prudencia beside a corpse with a charred face, and she's struggling to get up. I roll off the hood and land on the ground, a few feet away from a boy whose neck has been snapped. There's so much death on these streets, but we have to keep moving, keep living. I pick out the glass that's piercing my skin, and a gentle phoenix song plays within as my body begins healing itself, a power I hope Brighton hasn't tapped into yet. It seems like he hasn't. He's laid out, maybe down for the count.

This is my time to disempower him.

I reach for the Starstifler in my pocket, and that's when I realize the sharp pain in my hip wasn't from the broken windshield; it's from the shattered vial that pierced my flesh. The potion stains my hand. I don't have another Starstifler on me, but Wesley does. Hopefully he rolls up any second now with Ruth and Iris. In the meantime, I just got to keep Brighton down.

I head his way, my limp turning to a walk and then a run as my power keeps healing me. Brighton moves, sitting up and banging on his ear like he's lost hearing. He's weak, probably ready to tap out and pick this up when he's in better shape, but I can't let him go. I got to get my hands on Brighton before he phases away. I jump, my wings bursting to life, and I glide over. He gets to his feet, turning in time for me to tackle him into a brick wall, pinning him back.

"Get off me!"

"No, Bright, just give up!"

Brighton headbutts me.

This is where my other training session kicks in—I punch Brighton with a flaming fist.

Brighton echoes my move, but he one-ups me, hitting me rapidly. He may not be able to escape with his ghost power, but this phoenix-hydra combo of fiery, hyper-fast punches rocks my chin so hard that I can't hold my grip on him. But Brighton doesn't flee; he's got me dizzy, and he knows it. Silver and sapphire flames flow out of his hands, and I fight back with streams of gold and gray. I'm losing my balance, it's touch and go, but I focus on this battle, knowing that if I can win this one, then I can knock him out, and when he wakes up, he will be powerless. I fly a few feet in the air, applying more pressure. My fire eats away at his, the silver losing to my gold, the sapphire losing to my gray. I don't take this for granted; Brighton can pull a fast one any second now, like dash under me and attack or phase away completely to regroup. I'm going to win this; I've had more time with my powers, and I'm stronger because gray sun phoenixes strengthen with every life cycle. Brighton's teeth are clenching as he begins crashing under the weight of my flames. Then the eclipses in his eyes burn brighter than before, and Brighton screams as his fire roars. The silver and sapphire surge through until they've devoured the gold and gray, and I'm suddenly blasted out of the air, my wings gone as if clipped, and then my breath gone as if dead.

TWENTY
GRAY GLOW

NESS

Looks can always be deceiving, but I find it's easier to fool someone when they're nearing unconsciousness.

I've shifted into a gleamcraft practitioner, modeled after one I observed saving an alchemist during a spy mission on Luna's behalf; the practitioner was lovely, but the alchemist absolutely deserved death after killing the practitioner to protect his secrets. The Alchemist *was* killed, but that's not one of the faces that haunts me at night. The practitioner's does, and at least I can honor her memory right now as I try saving someone else who doesn't necessarily deserve it. I don't know how necessary it is that I even hide my face in the first place since I don't know if Genesis knows who I am or even cares. But since there isn't an actual practitioner in the vicinity in case the specter harms me, I'm playing it safe.

I lure Genesis into a false sense of security, assuring her I am here to help. She must be feeling really awful because she doesn't resist.

Until I start carving into her forearm with a pocketknife.

"You're doing great," I coo, stealing the piece of flesh I need for the potion.

"I'm blacking out. Everything is getting darker," Genesis breathes.

No, it's not. It's already been dark. She just can't tell that there's an obsidian phoenix casting his shadow on us because he blends in so efficiently with the night.

I drop the bloody flesh into the Starstifler vial and give it a good shake, thinking about how I was tasked with studying Genesis's powers when she was last on these streets. Now I'm here to bind them. Like I will my own one day. The same for Emil and Brighton, who will be just as powerless as they were on the first night of the Crowned Dreamer. It was the first time I laid eyes on Emil. He saw me too, but not really. I was still in disguise, hiding, letting the world believe I was dead. Now I've let him see me, and Emil is choosing to close his eyes.

The battle between Emil and Brighton is heating up, even more than when a giant ball of fire blew up. Emil has an advantage on him, and I'm about to administer the Starstifler, when Brighton screams, stealing back my attention. Silver and sapphire flames explode against Emil's chest, and he's flying so high that it will be impossible to survive the fall.

"Wyatt!" I shout.

"On it!"

Wyatt steers Nox toward Emil. The phoenix zooms and fans out its wings, suspended in the air. Emil crashes down on Nox's back, rolling off until Wyatt catches him and lifts him up.

Thank the stars.

And Wyatt, I suppose.

"I need the medicine," Genesis cries out.

She actually bought that lie for why I needed that flesh. I uncork the Starstifler, pressing the vial to her lips.

"Here you go."

Genesis struggles swallowing the potion, but she drinks it all. "It's burning," she says as she shakes violently, pounding at her chest like she's choking on fire.

I am not looking forward to experiencing this myself. Especially when Genesis begins screaming so loudly that she draws Brighton's attention. Of course Wyatt has flown off with Emil, out of sight and leaving me for dead.

If I'm going to die, I'm going to go down fighting.

Gray glow.

TWENTY-ONE
SAPPHIRE VERSUS GRAY

BRIGHTON

I hit the target on Emil's heart, and will rip out Genesis's next.

I run toward the rubble of demolished concrete and twisted metal from the car. I step over the corpse of the telekinetic Samuel, ignoring how it feels, like his frozen eyes are watching me. Genesis runs out from the other side of the car, choking, and then turns in fear when she sees me. I dash in front of her, grabbing her by the shoulder.

"Who do you think you're fooling, Ness?"

Ness-as-Genesis feigns confusion. "Who's Ness?"

"I'm done playing games."

"I don't feel good. The practitioner's medicine is making me weak." Ness's head—Genesis's head—bobs up and down. He then pounds on his—her—chest. "It's burning. Please kill me."

I grab Ness's throat. "Don't you want to die as yourself?"

A sharp pain runs through my back as I'm stabbed from behind.

"That's the plan," someone with Ness's voice says in my ear.

But that can't be him because Ness is currently posing as Genesis in front of me. Except he's not. This was always Genesis. He has outsmarted me again. I release my grip on Genesis as Ness stabs me again and again with what feels like a small knife. I try phasing away, but his arm is wrapped around my throat, holding me close. I try elbowing him, but it's not effective. I feel faint, my head dipping. My back is so wet. It's thicker than sweat. I reach around, and through a dizzy spell I see my hand gloved in blood.

Ness and his clones are standing in front of me, but there's only one hand on me.

But Ness doesn't have clones.

He's a shifter.

How does Ness have clones?

I'm so dizzy.

There is only one Ness, and he is carving my arm.

Does Emil know Ness is trying to kill me?

I am not going to die. I cannot die. I am the Infinity Reaper. I am invincible. I am unkillable. I will outlive every single person in this world, even if that means being reborn and reborn on an empty planet. But this all feels like a lie right now, like I am near death. Everything is going dark and I'm so out of it that I begin hearing an anguished phoenix, like the ones in videos Emil would show me of phoenixes rattling around in cages and desperate for freedom. Do all phoenixes hear squawking before they die? Is that their version of seeing a light at the end of a tunnel, calling them in? The darkness begins fading and color returns to my world and the wounds in my back begin burning as they close like cauterization and blood flows through my body. I have healed, for the first time. I am not going to die. I cannot die. I am the Infinity Reaper. I am invincible. I am unkillable. I will outlive every single person in this world, and it feels truer than ever.

My vision has corrected itself, and there is only one Ness before me. He's holding a piece of my flesh in one hand and a pocketknife in the other. Which means he's not touching me. I dash toward and through him, snatching the knife and flesh with a swiftness he can't escape. I'm about to stab him in the back, a death worthy of a traitor, when someone is dashing toward me in a blur. Wesley has arrived because of course—

I am tackled to the ground, the knife flying out of my hand.

But it's not Wesley on top of me. It's Dione Henri, the Blood Caster with hydra blood. Her curly red hair is singed and plastered to her sweaty face. Her muscular, tattooed arm is flexed as she hovers a punch over me. "You took the bait," Dione says. Her pale cheeks are flushed as she pants, as if she's run across the entire city to come get me. She surveys the dead bodies. "You turned this neighborhood into a graveyard. You could've been a great Blood Caster."

"I know for a fact that you have an opening, but I'm not interested."

"We've long given up on Ness."

"Not Ness." Though he has surely escaped by now.

Dione glares. "Stanton . . ."

"I killed him in the Bounds," I say fearlessly.

She unleashes a flurry of punches, breaking my nose. "Did you kill Luna too?"

"No," I say, laughing. My broken nose hurts, but it will mend itself back together shortly.

"This isn't funny."

"It is. You used to be a threat, but you can't kill me."

Two extra arms punch out of Dione's sides, and she pummels me some more. When I recover from this, I should take an afternoon to learn and master that hydra trick too. I'm weak after this assault. That won't stick. I spit blood on Dione's face just to piss her off. She has been a terror, but now that Stanton is dead and Ness has quit the Blood Casters, the gang is only made up of Dione and June. Once I get Dione off me, I will rip out her heart, and the ghost girl will be the last living Blood Caster.

"You can't kill me," I say as I feel all wounds closing and all swelling going down.

"Think again." One of Dione's arms reaches behind her and withdraws a dagger with a black bone handle and yellow serrated blade. It's the infinity-ender, the weapon used to kill phoenixes—and specters with phoenix blood. Bautista died this way, and now I might too. It's possible my hydra and ghost essences might allow me to survive, but it's the phoenix powers that are healing me and it's the phoenix powers that will resurrect me if I'm destroyed. When Emil was stabbed by the infinity-ender, it dampened his powers for ages, and this is too critical a time to be weakened.

Dione swings down with the infinity-ender, my fate to be discovered in moments. . . .

The blow on my heart is heavy, but nothing pierces through me.

"Looking for this?" Wesley asks, appearing out of nowhere, the infinity-ender in his hand.

He dashes away, and Dione chases after him.

I get up while I can and find Prudencia, Ruth, and Iris approaching.

I really don't want to hurt Ruth. She's only ever been sweet and nurturing. But it's no holds barred for Iris, who couldn't care less if I live or die, and Prudencia, who broke my . . . and Prudencia who betrayed me too. I hurl fire-bolts, which Iris punches back my way with her power-proof skin. It does seem to have affected her, but not as much as anyone else tonight. Ruth casts out six clones, and they move more confidently than Reed's did. It's almost as if Ruth's clones are their own people, which I've seen in action with how they have helped her around past havens. But this time she's not doing housework or tending to Esther or looking after me like when I was poisoned. Ruth and her clones are teaming up with the enemies to take me down. They circle me, and I've lost track of which is the original. If I hurt the real one, the clones will suffer too.

"Don't make me hurt you," I warn.

"This is the last time you'll be able to," Prudencia says.

"Close in!" Iris shouts.

Everyone is running at me from different angles.

My fiery fists are ready. "Have it your way."

The first Ruth gets punched in the face, and the next gets phased through and elbowed in the back of her head. Iris is a moment away from hitting me when I dodge out of the way, and her fist connects with a clone. The real one still hasn't been hit. A Ruth grabs me from behind, and I throw my head back, breaking her nose. Still, the others aren't affected. Iris and I keep swinging, but I'm the only one landing hits. Her powerhouse strength only matters if she can actually touch me, and between phasing in and out and running circles around her, I'm untouchable. The clones are becoming a nuisance, but I know how to draw out the real one. I dash behind Prudencia, blasting her in the back with a fire-bolt; it hurts me to do so but not as much as her screams indicate it hurts her. As expected, a Ruth—the one and true—runs to Prudencia's aid, and that's when she gets struck with a fire-bolt too. The clones vanish in purple lights except one.

The lone clone notices this. "Oops." The clone swings, glowing gray mid-punch, and Ness manages to knock me right between the eyes.

Iris grabs me from behind, and it's like being bound by steel. "Where's your potion?"

"I used it on the other specter," Ness says. "She's powerless."

"Does Emil have his?"

"Ask him yourself." Ness points at the sky where Emil and Wyatt are descending on Nox. "Give us your Starstifler. Let's end this."

I'm doing everything I can to break out. I throw my head back to collide with Iris's, but she's too short. I stomp on her foot, but she's unfazed. I ignite, but Iris's skin is protecting her from being burned. Emil watches me trying to wrestle my way out with this sad look, like I'm one of those pathetic phoenixes that went and got itself locked away in a cage.

"My potion broke," Emil says.

I'm laughing. "You all got me, and you can't even do anything about it."

"One punch and Iris can knock you out," Ness says. "Shut up."

Ruth wipes away the tears in her eyes. "I can't believe you attacked me, Brighton. I tended to you in my home."

"And then you conspired against me."

"To help you. This is essentially an intervention."

"I didn't ask you all to intervene."

Wyatt chuckles while petting Nox. "This is typically how interventions unfold."

Ruth looks around. "Wesley should still have our last potion. . . . Wesley!"

I have to get out of here. I try dashing forward, but I only manage to drag Iris a few feet before she stabilizes. Phasing still won't work. Iris is unbothered by the flames. I might be able to blast a fire-bolt at something, but there is nothing close enough that's explosive. Then Wesley arrives, skidding to a halt with that infinity-ender, and I just know it's about to be game over for me.

"Dione took off," Wesley says.

"Tomorrow's problem," Emil says. "You got the Starstifler?"

"Sure do, boss." He hands it over.

The Starstifler is in perfect condition. I can't angle my hand high enough to blast it apart.

"I'm sorry it had to go down like this, Bright," Emil says.

Ness takes the infinity-ender, ready to carve into me again like a butcher. "This will hurt."

I see an opportunity and take it. I blast a fire-bolt at Nox's talon, and the obsidian phoenix screeches in pain. He barrels through the group, his massive wings stretching and knocking everyone down, including me and Iris. The steel-like grip is released just long enough for me to dash forward and break free. I trip over Emil, who tries grabbing me, but I kick him in the face. Everyone else is recovering as Wyatt tries calling Nox back down from the sky.

Emil hurls a fire-orb, but I blast it apart with a fire-bolt.

The tables have turned.

I have overpowered him before, and if I wasn't so outnumbered, I would do it again.

There is a golden opportunity, as bright as the stars.

I dash into a shoulder roll, grab the intact Starstifler, and wave the vial at Emil. He can see his future as I phase through the ground and drop into the sewer.

The next time Emil and I meet on the battlefield, his reign of infinity is coming to an end.

TWENTY-TWO

ROLE-PLAYING

NESS

Everyone is on edge, waiting for the Infinity Reaper to return and kill us. But I saw the look on Brighton's face as he waved at Emil and vanished into the street. He was fleeing for now, but there was a plan in his eyes for when he comes back. . . .

"We're in the clear," I say.

No one seems to trust me on this. Fists are raised, and gold and gray flames are burning. They're all pacing around and watching the ground as if Brighton will drag them into the earth. The most active person is Wyatt, who is trying to call Nox down from the sky, but if it weren't for that, I'd imagine he'd be high above on his phoenix, awaiting Brighton's sudden reappearance. Minutes pass before fists are lowered and flames are extinguished.

"We almost had him," Emil says.

"Next time," I say.

"He'll be ready for us."

"So we'll have to outsmart him."

Emil sinks onto the curb. "He has a Starstifler now."

The others didn't seem to witness this.

"Really?" Prudencia asks.

Emil wipes the sweat from his face. "Brighton is going to use the potion on me. I guess it doesn't matter. I was only keeping the powers to take him down, and he overpowered me." He looks as if he's about to cry. "I'm sorry I keep failing you all."

I'm about to go comfort him, when I detect movement from the corner of my eye. For a moment, I think I'm wrong and Brighton has returned already. But it's a young woman, crawling behind a bus stop's shelter to hide. Genesis—the specter who should no longer be a specter. Did the Starstifler bind her powers? Emil saw it work in Bautista's past life, but we have no proof that the potion was brewed correctly in this one.

"Maybe you didn't fail us," I say, taking off down the street.

Many footsteps follow me.

I stop around the corner of the bus shelter, surprising Genesis. She holds up her hands to blast me with fire, and someone tackles me to the ground. It's Emil, panting, using his body as a shield to save my life. Except my life wasn't actually threatened. Genesis's hands are not blazing with fire, and she looks like every single person who randomly waves their hands around as if they're about to tap into some long-buried gleam.

"My powers . . ." Genesis says.

"They're gone," I say, smiling up at Emil. "You did it."

"It worked," Emil says, releasing a breath so deep that it feels like he might fully lay his entire body weight on me, turning this sidewalk into our bed. But instead he picks himself off of me and kneels besides Genesis. "Are you okay?"

This moment is one of many that sets Emil apart from everyone else I know.

How many people check in on someone who was destroying the world?

Genesis keeps flicking her fingers, ready to hurt Emil, but she can't even summon a single spark to light a candle let alone blaze us. She backs into the bus shelter's plastic wall, against a clothing ad for celestial half capes. Genesis's confusion has turned to fear.

"We're not going to hurt you," Emil says.

She breaks into tears as she stares at her powerless hands. "What did that practitioner give me?"

"A potion to make sure you can never hurt anyone again," I say.

Police sirens can be heard a couple blocks away, so I gather everyone in front of one of the many destroyed stores while I keep an eye on Genesis. She seems too hurt to get very far, especially without any phoenix powers to heal her, but everyone else needs to get away from here. Where there are police officers, there will be enforcers. The sun will be rising soon, casting the brightest of lights on this neighborhood that was transformed into a war zone overnight, as if it shifted.

"It's time for you all to leave," I say.

"Agreed," Iris says.

Emil pauses. "What do you mean *you all*? You're coming too."

"The world needs to know that the Starstifler works. If you hang around, the authorities aren't going to hear you out. But I can make them listen to me."

"No, the last time you went up against enforcers by yourself you got held hostage. You're coming with us," Emil says, reaching out for me.

I step back.

My life did change for the worse that time I posed as Emil so he could go find Brighton in the abandoned school that had been infiltrated by enforcers. That sacrifice separated us and created space for someone like Wyatt to fall out of the sky like a Halo Knight in shining armor. Who knows what our relationship would look like if I never left Emil's side? Who knows if we would have survived if I stayed and fought alongside him? We're both alive, but people have died and will continue dying because of all the dark pictures the Senator forced me to paint about the gleamcraft community.

"My role in the revolution is to play many roles," I say. I step out of Genesis's eyeline. Gray light washes over me, and I shift into a random civilian—a mid-twenties white male with a conventionally handsome face that people are primed to trust. "I'll act like a witness and tell them that the Spell Walkers saved the day."

"We have to go," Iris says as the sirens get closer.

Emil hugs me. "Please come back."

"I will." As my head rests on his shoulder, I see Wyatt hailing everyone over. "It looks like your help is needed elsewhere anyway."

Nox is perched on the ledge of a neighboring building, refusing to come down. Emil is the only one who can get up there, and he springs into action, fiery wings carrying him toward the obsidian phoenix so he can climb on top and steer him down to the street. I watch as Wyatt hops onto Nox, wrapping his arms around Emil; I go warm, flushing the cheeks of this white man's face I'm wearing. The two take off alone, leaving Wesley, Ruth, Iris, and Prudencia to find their own way back to Brooklyn.

The cop cars arrive with an enforcer tank not far behind. I lean against a wall while holding my stomach, using my real exhaustion to present myself as someone who has been running for his life. I'm not surprised when an officer aims his wand at me, but I tell him that I'm not a gleamcrafter. She's still on edge, especially when I can't present any ID, but she buys into my story about how I lost my wallet during all this chaos. It helps that camera crews begin arriving; no officer wants their face on the news for killing an ordinary civilian. There's always a chance that I could die between morphs, unrecognizable like a previous shifter Blood Caster did, but considering the last time I took a spell to the chest, I reverted back into myself and the world discovered I was alive all along. If this officer killed me, the Senator would probably see to it that she's promoted to director for achieving what no other assassin has.

"Name?" Officer Painter asks.

"Chad Sales," I say, which sounds as fake as her name. I point at Genesis before she can investigate my fabricated life any further. "She's the one who started all of this. But I saw the Spell Walkers bind her powers. She can't fight back."

"What do you mean they bound her powers? With gauntlets?"

"A potion. The one they've been talking about online."

Officer Painter seems suspicious but tells me to stay put as she speaks into her radio, alerting the squad of the situation. Enforcers are called to the scene, and they approach Genesis with wands aimed at her head. She lies face down on the street as an enforcer shackles her with the gauntlets that would render her temporarily powerless if I hadn't already done the job with the Starstifler. This is why we need to get the word out—why I need to.

I'm not waiting around for Officer Painter to return. I go straight to the news reporter behind the police barricade and groan until I catch her attention.

"Excuse me, sir? Were you here during the battle?" the reporter asks.

"I was," I say.

"What's your name? Do you live in the area?"

"Chad Sales. Yes, I do."

The reporter waves over her camera crew, and after a quick run-through on how this will work and a countdown from her network, she holds the mic up and says, "This is Shanyn Morgan from Channel Two news, reporting on our developing story of the power brawl in Alphabet City. I'm here with Chad Sales, who lives in the neighborhood. Chad, can you tell us what happened tonight?"

I weave my lie, making it sound real enough that no one will question why I was coming home late from a date and found myself in the cross fire of a battle that I was certain would end in my demise. "That boy from social media, Brighton Rey, got his gang killed. I couldn't believe how many people died, just like that. . . ." I snap my fingers, as if I can actually testify to the swiftness of the kills even though I wasn't here yet. I notice out the corner of my eye that I'm being watched by a man behind yellow tape. He seems injured with cuts across his cheek, and he's holding his shoulder as if it's been dislocated. He'll get his chance to tell his story, but it's important I tell mine. "Right before Brighton was about to kill another specter, the Spell Walkers stepped in. They were teaming up with Senator Iron's son, Eduardo Iron, I mean Ness Arroyo." I pinch my nose, like I made the mistake accidentally and now Chad Sales is embarrassed. "I saw Ness Arroyo give the specter that potion, the one he was talking about on that interview he did . . . the Star-something?"

"The Starstifler?" Shanyn Morgan asks.

Good, she's paying attention to the world.

Thumbs-up. "That's it. It worked! She doesn't have powers anymore. Emil Rey and Ness Arroyo and the Spell Walkers are telling the truth about clearing the street of specters."

That injured man comes out from behind the yellow tape. "I don't buy it."

Shanyn Morgan seems confused at first on who to interview, but she turns to the man. "Who are you, sir?"

"R-Red," he stammers. "Red Rollins."

"You appear hurt. Was this from tonight's events?"

"Indeed it is. I live a couple buildings that away." He points behind us.

"You're neighbors," Shanyn Morgan says.

Red Rollins looks me up and down with his dark brown eyes. My heart is pounding as if I might get exposed on live TV all over again. "Yes," he says, thankfully confusing me for some other white person in this neighborhood. "At least we were neighbors until my home was blown up. My ceiling caved down on me. I'm lucky I made it out alive." He turns to me. "Don't go acting like the Spell Walkers are doing right by us when they cost a man his home."

The microphone is back over to me. "I'm sorry, but the Spell Walkers didn't start this fight."

"They sure as hell pissed off that whiny specter. This is all their fault too."

"The Spell Walkers are cleaning up their mess with a potion that will make sure no specter can destroy your home ever again."

Red Rollins waves me away. "You're naive if you believe those same criminals who just broke into the Bounds to break out that other criminal who lied about his death." He stares directly into the camera, his cheeks flushed in anger. "We'll only see change if we have President Iron leading us."

Of course he's an Iron supporter. I'm suddenly not upset over the idea of tacky pro-Iron magnets and caps being buried under the rubble of Red Rollins's destroyed home. I want to snap at him that I didn't fake my own death, but I'm not Ness Arroyo right now, I am Chad Sales. That doesn't mean Chad Sales can't have political allegiances. "Senator Iron is dangerous and will only use brute force to stop specters. The Spell Walkers have a humane way to disempower these people who should have never had powers in the first place."

I feel like I'm on the debate stage again except this time I'm not tanking it as Sunstar, I'm telling the truth as an imaginary person.

There's something off about Red Rollins's hazel eyes as he glares at me. Maybe it's because of his murderous look that it feels like no normal person should ever express, especially on live TV. His lip twitches, like all his dark thoughts are about to fight their way out of his mouth, but instead, Red Rollins says, "I'm done here," in a voice that has dropped an octave and he keeps his head down as he walks away, past the yellow tape and the media truck.

Shanyn Morgan asks me, "Do you still believe Congresswoman Sunstar would be a fair president for all people after her many pro-celestial declarations at the third debate?"

I want to say, *Yes, of course, because that wasn't her. It was actually me, Ness Arroyo, forced to take Congresswoman Sunstar's form and lie about her intentions to cast doubt on her campaign and persuade her supporters to vote for Senator Iron instead*, but I'm speechless as I piece together what has been happening here.

Red Rollins had dark brown eyes at the start of the interview, not hazel.

Red Rollins's mouth was twitching, and it wasn't because he was holding back threats.

Red Rollins didn't confuse me as his neighbor since he never actually lived here.

Red Rollins doesn't exist.

I'm completely sure of this when he walks into the back of a black car where a certain campaign manager can be found waiting for him, and right as the door is closing, a gray glow emanates from within.

The man who called himself Red Rollins was none other than the Senator.

TWENTY-THREE

JUNE IN DECEMBER

MARIBELLE

Last night, I dreamed the Sanctuary was still a place of peace. The castle was pristine and whole. There were no scorch marks or ponds running red with blood or demolished walls. The courtyard looked more like a garden with flowers blossoming instead of a stone graveyard for phoenixes. Tala was standing on the terrace, singing that song Sera sang to me when I was a baby about the girl who made a crown out of branches, all while Tala was throwing paper birds through the air. Then it became a nightmare when zombified phoenixes flew out of the garden, looking skeletal with patches of feathers. They breathed fire, burning all the paper birds before ganging up on Tala, torching her until she was nothing but ashes. I woke up before they could kill me too.

I tried talking to Tala about my nightmare this morning, but she was as distant as she was last night. She's been grieving all the phoenixes that died—that were killed. The fire in her belly seems to be going out, like I'm extinguishing everything that has made Tala . . . Tala.

I'm in the dining hall with Luna, learning more about June's resurrection, when Tala finds us.

"Just got off the phone with Crest," Tala says.

That's her commander. "What did he want?"

"To inform me that Wyatt's wings were clipped."

"His wings?"

"He was fired," Luna says before slurping the last of her soup.

"Why?" I ask.

"For going against code," Tala says. She folds her arms as she's shaking a little. "For choosing the life of a human over the lives of phoenixes."

This is exactly what Tala is doing for me. She had me swear that I would never tell anyone that she brought me to the Sanctuary so I can scavenge everything I need for the resurrection ritual. That risk feels more alive than ever now that Wyatt's wings have been clipped.

"So he chose Emil over phoenixes?"

"I don't fully understand why. I'm not high enough within the Bronze Wings to receive that information."

"The Halo Knight—pardon—former Halo Knight chose love over duty, girl," Luna says.

Tala tenses. "Crest says the Halo Knights will be flying to the city soon in search of something. I might know more then. I told Crest I'm holding down the fort here to bury the dead before more scavengers can exploit the phoenixes. But we do need to get a move on. If Crest pops in for a surprise visit and finds us here with her"—she glares at Luna—"I might get clipped too."

"Then let's do this."

"What exactly are we doing?" Luna asks.

"I'm retrocycling through your life."

Discovering Luna is my grandmother after my first retrocycle was painful, but now I can use this bloodline to help me find peace. It still feels bizarre that she's family, especially as I sit in the Sanctuary's meditation room, where I was when I retrocycled into Sera's life. Now I'm here with the woman who killed her so I can witness the rebirth of the assassin who killed my boyfriend.

I'm on a mat, under the vaulted ceiling.

Luna is sitting with her back against the banner of a sun swallower.

Tala stands by the rack of candles, holding the oblivion dagger. She once said this room is a sacred space, but she has no problem spilling Luna's blood if necessary.

"Don't piss off Tala while I'm gone," I warn Luna.

"Oh, I won't. I want to live long enough to perform a true resurrection."

She may be a brilliant alchemist, but she's an idiot if she thinks I'm letting her touch a single speck of Atlas's ashes. I'm going to study everything she does in this ritual and bring him back myself. I'm only keeping her alive in case there's anything else I need to know, especially since it's still unclear if I can retrocycle back to the same moment after once visiting it.

"Here I go," I say.

Dark yellow flames consume me.

Unlike Sera and Fabian, I know who Luna is.

I've seen her, I know her voice, I have felt her.

I don't have to imagine Luna the way I did Sera and Fabian.

Instead of resisting Luna as my grandmother, I have to welcome this bond to strengthen the connection between our lifelines. In the darkness, I hear Luna calling me *granddaughter* and think about how my life could have been different if I'd known that's who I was to her since the beginning. If she'd known too. If Sera hadn't hidden me from Luna because I would have been exploited for my power the way Sera was for hers. The tables are turned. It's Luna who is helping me, the way some grandparents spoil their grandchildren with spiced sunrock candies and glow-in-the-dark toys, but instead, she's gifting me with a play-by-play on how to safely resurrect the love of my life. Luna resurrected June in December, when it was freezing the entire month. It's like my entire body has been frostbitten, freezing my bones and blood, only for everything to be defrosted by the hottest of flames. I push through the darkness, following not just the sound of a whimpering heartbeat, but the feel of it—it's like someone tapping my chest—until it becomes more intense, pulverizing until I'm nothing but the fire that resurrected June and kept Luna alive in the wintry weather. There are phoenixes screeching, their cries cut off abruptly, all killed for another's rebirth. I now know what it's like to pluck out eyes and feathers, to rip out bones and a heart, but I picture Luna's hands doing these things instead of my own. I feel the age in her fingers, how her knuckles crack differently than mine, how much more strength she had to find to do the unthinkable.

Then Luna appears in this void, and the darkness melts away, revealing her in December as she stands outside a Phoenix Pit, moments before she resurrects June.

Luna is in a snowy cemetery around unmarked graves, walking around a pit. She fastens her bloodred robe even tighter to battle the chilly winds, but it does little to guard her from the cold. She's shivering, and I feel it as though it's my own body. I hate how retrocycling forces me to feel everything that my relatives do, but thankfully this is the first time I've traveled back to a time period that won't end in death, as lovely as it would—and will—be to watch Luna die. I just won't have to feel it.

I walk closer to the Phoenix Pit, discovering the corpse of a sun swallower. I can see the stab mark in its belly, likely from an infinity-ender dagger. Then I hear it screech, which makes no sense, especially since its mouth didn't move. It screeches again, and I realize the sound is coming from behind me, where another phoenix, this one a common ivory whose white feathers blend in with the snow, is chained to a nearby tree. I'm confused until I remember that Luna will need the phoenix's flames to light up the Pit when it's ready.

Luna walks over to a tank that's sitting on the back of a truck. She switches on a dial and grabs the hose, filling the Phoenix Pit with boiling hot water and cooking the sun swallower's corpse. Not removing the phoenix was the grave error that cost June from returning with her soul; maybe if she had hers, she would have never killed Atlas and none of this would've been necessary. It's possible I wouldn't have ever discovered that I was a celestial-specter hybrid and could have gone the rest of my life never knowing that I was related to Sera, Bautista, and Luna. But June was soulless because of human error.

Once the Pit is filled to the edges with the corpse floating, Luna reaches into a velvet drawstring bag and tosses in bones. "May you respawn with the strongest of breaths like the breath spawn phoenixes." She drops in a heart the size of a rock, which splashes. "May you come back stronger like gray sun phoenixes." She releases the feathers, which float atop the boiling water. "May you fight for your life so as to never lose it again as century phoenixes would." In go the eyes next. "May your eyes see through the darkness of death as obsidian phoenixes do." She crushes the eggshells, which swim around all the other body parts. "May you carry the learnings of your life like crowned elder phoenixes."

There was nothing in Fabian's tome about these incantations Luna is reciting, but I take note of them anyway, memorizing them as I am all her movements.

Luna grabs an urn from the trunk with a name written on it—June Holloway, Subject #98. There is no ceremony as Luna pours June's ashes into the Pit, underneath the stars as instructed.

"Fire," Luna commands the common ivory.

White flames set the Phoenix Pit alight.

"Undo a death, renew a life," Luna repeats over and over, as if the fire is under her command.

Hope is building within her, within us, even though I know she will be successful. But I still can't believe my eyes when the flames rise higher and higher and become a fiery silhouette. This is the reverse cremation Luna told me and Tala about. The cycle completes when the ashes that became fire become the girl who will kill my family within weeks and my boyfriend months later. But for now June is only a girl with dark silver hair and moon-white skin and fear in her big eyes and a scream that is trying to wake the dead around her. While she's shivering in the nude and panicking at the sight of the charred phoenix at her bare feet, Luna's elation runs through me.

"A miracle," Luna breathes.

June keeps screaming like she doesn't remember how to speak.

"Take a breath, my child," Luna says soothingly.

But it's as if June doesn't remember how to breathe either. Her teeth are chattering and her head is shaking and her legs are wobbly and her arms swing around as if she has no bones. It's unbelievable that she will become Luna's personal assassin. Her screams are becoming raspier, as if she's calling for help. Luna just watches, curious. I can practically feel her heartlessness, a hollowness that does not care about June being scared or cold because, while Luna may have addressed June as her child, there is nothing maternal in her heart.

When June finds her footing and runs for Luna, the alchemist is quick to flip open her robe and unsheathe the infinity-ender dagger from her belt and bang the hilt between June's eyes, just as Luna recounted. Which leads me to understand that everything Luna has said has been true. She was not simply buying time for her life after we almost killed her in the Bounds. But I also hate how Luna's honesty still doesn't mark her as a good person. She continues staring at June unconscious in the snow like she's not human, but only a creation. I want to believe that I'm fully above Luna, that there's no way I share genetics with this monster, but maybe her influence has flowed into me, like blood. I'm ashamed at how I've been treating Tala, like she's not a person in her own right, like she can be as easily discarded as every last soul who died in Luna's experiments. That's not how I feel about Tala at all—I want the world for her.

I've seen everything I need to see from this moment, so I concentrate on returning to my time. It's lovely that I won't have to experience a death to get home. I focus on cycling forward, all the sensations of my own body, how returning my soul to my flesh will feel like getting under the covers of the bed that I shared with Atlas, how soon enough we'll be able to breathe together again.

Darkness takes over, and I welcome it, like lights going off so I can sleep.

My dark yellow flames vanish and I'm back in the Sanctuary's meditation room, but I'm confused because June is in front of me. It's almost like her memory has followed me like sunspots, but this isn't a memory. This June is stable and armed with the oblivion dagger. She swipes down at me, and my psychic sense is warning me of this very obvious danger. I lean back and then elbow June's wrist, breaking her hold on the dagger and catching it with my other hand. I swing up at June, but she fades away.

What the hell happened while I was retrocycling?

Tala is on the floor, breathing shallowly in the debris of the candle rack as if she was thrown through it.

Luna is standing in the corner, grinning. "Exquisite timing, wouldn't you say? Miraculous, even."

I jump to my feet, both hands clutching the dagger's hilt. All sympathy I held for June is remaining in the past. June reappears beside Luna and I hurl the oblivion dagger at her, but June and Luna phase through the floor, unlikely to return. I rush to Tala's side, checking her body for any open wounds.

"What happened?"

"June appeared a couple minutes ago. . . . I fought her off as long as I could."

I don't know how long I was gone. Time moves differently when retrocycling. But if I had taken even another ten seconds to return,

I would be dead. Would my soul have stayed in the past? Been vanquished? It's a question I don't need answered right now.

I help Tala to her feet. "How did June find us?"

"Even if that specter spoke, I doubt she would have told me," Tala says, dusting herself off. "Maybe she tracked Roxana's storms or those scavengers ratted us out online or she thought it could be worthwhile to check the Sanctuary. All that really matters, Maribelle, is that Luna got away with her life when she should be dead."

"I'm sorry."

"Your apologies aren't undoing anything."

I'm so drained right now, and my spirit is being killed. "Maybe not, but I am sorry that I've dragged you into all of this. It's clear you hate me, and I understand if you want to fly away and never see me again."

Tala is quiet as she stares at me. She sighs. "I don't hate you. I just feel like I've been losing myself for weeks and I was so close to finding some closure in killing Luna and now she's gone. You're on the way to having Atlas back, and I predict that I'm going to be alone all over again."

"No, you're not, Tala. We are forever bonded by our grief."

"Will you even keep fighting once you no longer have reason to grieve? Once the life you're seeking to avenge is no longer gone?"

"I will because I promised you that we would end Luna forevermore. I no longer need her to resurrect Atlas, and she's a greater threat now that she knows about true resurrections. Luna must die, and I promise you that I will be by your side when that day comes. Okay?"

Tala considers me. "This is your final chance to do right by our promise."

"I won't let you down. Atlas won't either. You're going to love him."

Tala's eyes fall on the messy meditation room. "We shouldn't stay here."

"Definitely not."

"Where should we go?"

The world can feel small when you're being hunted, but I know of one place that has not only managed to stay off the radars of everyone who hates us, but will also be a wonderful place to welcome Atlas home.

TWENTY-FOUR

MOMENTS OF SILENCE

BRIGHTON

I'm the only person who was able to come home to the influencer house.

The lights are on in every room as if someone is still living here, but it's quiet. Alpha isn't lecturing anyone about reinvention and calling them *man* every other sentence. I can't hear Bull's grunting from another room as he flexes for one of his many empty-calorie videos that are viewed far too many times considering nothing happens. Millie isn't asking everyone how she can help them, desperate for their approval as if everyone will realize they don't need a walking ring light. Reed isn't cursing at his clones for not being in sync for a TikTok dance. Samuel definitely isn't popping out of nowhere and scaring anyone or guiding me through camouflage training just like Zelda isn't here to praise me for being above every single person in the house and trying to help me be loved across the world.

They are all dead, abandoned in the streets for everyone to see one last time.

I grant them a moment of silence.

Moment done.

I'm too tired to wash off all the blood and dirt or change out of my clothes, which stink from the sewers and the long run home. I go into the fridge and grab bottles of Alpha Aqua, chugging one after the other even though these are probably collector's items now. But I don't have any sentimental connection to Alpha or any interest in riches. It wouldn't be very hard for me to walk into any bank and steal whatever cash isn't locked away in some vault that would trap even the likes of me.

What I do want is justice.

I collapse on the couch to see how the attacks are being reported. There are various videos of the attack from all angles, including things I didn't get to witness personally, such as Genesis and her celestials terrorizing the streets before I arrived with the influencers. Someone got an amazing video of me blasting Genesis out of the air with a firebolt, but nothing is more epic than the clip of me overpowering Emil and sending him flying without wings. I'm having an out-of-body experience rewatching that moment over and over, proud of myself. Unfortunately, everyone who was on the ground seems to have fled or not uploaded anything by the time I was being ganged up on by the Spell Walkers and their allies. The only video I'm able to find that shows me being restrained by Iris was filmed from high up in someone's bedroom; it is pretty cool how Nox can be seen flying past their window after I attacked him so I could make my escape.

But what matters most is how people are reacting to the footage.

And there isn't enough discussion about me.

The point of interest is the death of the influencers. There's regret for not spending ten grand on one of Zelda's ice sculptures when they had the chance. Highlights of Samuel's best jump scares being circulated. Inspiration striking for those who want to finally learn one of Reed's dances to do so in his honor. Fan art of Millie replacing the sun and being the new reason the sky lights up. Videos of Alpha's followers "pouring one out for the man" using his water. By far the most bizarre reaction is coming from those who are using Bull's death as a wake-up call to hit the gym, as if that's where his strength came from, and regardless that didn't save his life anyway! If anything, his life was wasted going to the gym for aesthetics when he should have been training!

They could have all been alive if only they'd known what they were doing.

The top trending video about the brawl comes from none other than Russell Robbins, a conversative YouTuber who calls himself the Silver Star Slayer because of his hatred toward gleamcrafters, especially the Spell Walkers. He's pathetic for giving himself a nickname that makes him sound more impressive than he is when he doesn't have any powers of his own. Normally I wouldn't pay him any mind because he's full of conspiracy theories, such as love affairs between past Spell Walkers and the Blood Casters stealing souls to keep Luna alive. But I am curious about how the Silver Star Slayer feels about me, and if he maybe even supports my mission since I don't walk the lines of a Spell Walker or a Blood Caster.

The video opens with Russell behind a desk, his back to a green screen showing a city on fire that doesn't fit the entire frame because he's such a hack. He's wearing an orange shirt that is so neon that I have to lower the brightness because it's hurting my tired eyes. Russell holds up a white board that has the number one on it and erases it. "It has been zero days since our city has suffered more violence because of gleamcrafters!" Russell shouts, his pale cheeks going red. He's in his thirties but must have the high blood pressure of someone much older. "Enforcers were murdered like they're nothing more than vermin on the streets, all because of vigilantes and criminals; one and the same if you ask me. You know why the real guardians of our city are dead? Because specters and celestials are having another pissing match! This time popular social media personalities got involved, and they were wiped out in minutes. This is because the real protecting should come from trained professionals, not little girls making ice sculptures or a boy dancing with his clones because he has no real friends!" Russell leans forward on his desk, almost knocking over his *STRONG AS IRON!* mug. "You know who else doesn't have friends? That boy who calls himself the Infinity Reaper. He only became popular in the first place because he was throwing himself in the Infinity Son's spotlight. Brighton Rey had to fight Spell Walkers—including his own brother, who he threatened to kill!—and a Blood Caster. This clown wants to be a hero? Everyone hates him!"

Does the Silver Star Slayer know that I can see this? Is he trying to provoke me?

I could kill him in his sleep.

I shrink the video, minimizing Russell as he keeps ranting, and I study the stats of his video. It was uploaded half an hour ago and already has two million views, as the East Coasters are waking up to this news. This will easily climb to four million, maybe five as the day goes on. Especially since Election Day is around the corner and all of Senator Iron's supporters are continuing to boost his campaign's messaging as if their lives depend on it. Of course they think it does, since they fear Congresswoman Sunstar's politics after Ness posed as her during the last debate, sabotaging all the hard work she has been putting in to prove that the country is ready for its first celestial president. There are over two thousand comments on Russell's video, and if they are anything to go by, then I am nothing but a clown who everyone hates. I close out completely.

Fine.

The time for convincing this delusional crowd that I am the best person to unite this nation isn't now. But that doesn't mean everyone hates me like Russell's comments section would suggest.

I hold out my phone as I go live. I look like hell because I have been through hell. Let everyone see the real me and everything I have survived. My Brightsiders begin filing in by the thousands and thousands. This is the hit of serotonin I need. I don't welcome anyone to the chat. I'm taking deep breaths and reading some of the comments and questions as they come in.

I'm so happy you're okay!

Dude I was scared you died!

Omg r u ok????

Daddy Brighton wat happened last night, I was ZZZ

I thought Infinity Reaper was going to kill bad guys not friends

u got ur ass kicked lol, serves u right

RIP Zelda RIP Samuel I miss them so much

Did u set up ur frriends 2 die?

thx for leading bull to his death he was so annoying lmao

You look so sad! Please don't give up, Infinity Reaper! We need you!

Fan bases are so much like countries. Large populations, lifestyles, connections . . . and divisions. This country is divided by two parties: the Hearts and the Heartless. The Hearts are relieved that I am alive, and the Heartless are wishing I was dead. How can they be my followers and not support me as their leader when I am doing what's best for all of them? How can they call themselves fans if they're willing to turn their backs on me so easily?

Once one million followers join the live, I address them all. "Maybe I'm not a hero. That's what other people are saying, at least. It's hard to disagree with them. Heroes save people, and I didn't save anyone last night. I lost people. . . . They were strangers when they took me in after my loved ones and allies betrayed me, but they were becoming my best of friends, each and every one of them." This is not true. I was never going to get close with Alpha, Bull, Millie, and Reed. But no one wants to hear that I only valued the lives of the only two people in that group I actually liked. "I wish I could have saved them, but I'm only one person." I wish I could cry on cue, I would be winning everyone over. I take a deep breath and stare off into the distance, as if I'm reliving all the murders I witnessed hours ago. "I'm so alone. But I will tell you all this. . . ." I turn back to the camera, wanting my viewers to feel like I am speaking directly to them. "I will never stop trying to be the hero you all deserve, even if it kills me."

I end the live.

I'm exhausted. I can't even find the strength to go back to my bedroom. My new healing power may have closed my wounds, but it's not doing anything for my muscles, which are sore between all the beatings and dashing across boroughs. I stretch out across the couch, sinking into the cushions that Alpha bragged were stuffed with phoenix feathers. It's not comfortable, but it's better than moving. I close my eyes to sleep, but I can't survive a single moment of silence without thinking about my next action step. Do I look into more recruits? Maybe there are other gleamcrafters in the country who have been fighting in other vigilante factions but are frustrated with how they're supposed to behave? I could use more competent teammates who wouldn't be killed so instantly. I don't know.

I go back on my phone, hoping to scroll through Instagram until I pass out. Himalia Lim's latest Sunstar art is getting a lot of hate by the Heartless. Lore has announced that their book club won't be meeting next month in person, but will be held virtually instead for reasons they haven't disclosed; I know the truth behind this switch, and it's a nice jolt of power across my exhausted body. There is a video clip from some French Halo Knight named Crest begging specter aspirants to not harm phoenixes, and I unfollow the news page. I know it's time to tap out of the feed when I'm mostly seeing tribute posts to the influencers who died.

I check out my DMs, and I double-tap heart reactions on messages from the supportive Brightsiders and I leave the others on read because they don't get the satisfaction of trying to gain clout if I block them. I scroll down but come to a stop when I see a message from someone named Darren Bowes. Why does that sound so familiar? I open the message:

IDK if you know me but my mother was your doctor a couple weeks ago. Billie Bowes.

She got her neck snapped by that Blood Caster Stanton. I blame your FAKE brother Emil for not taking care of her the way she was taking care of all of you. I worshipped Emil, I was even going to dress up as him for Halloween. But now my life is ruined because Emil is the one who dresses up like a hero but isn't. If he doesn't want to use his powers he should get rid of them. I bet my mother would still be alive if you had your powers. Then me and my dad wouldn't be hiding in some haven with so many celestials who suck. Anyway, I see people hating on you. Don't give up. We need people who actually want to save us and not just themselves. If I was dressing up as anyone for Halloween, it would be you. You're the kind of hero I want to be when I'm older.

Darren Bowes, the son of Dr. Billie Bowes.

Dr. Bowes was taking care of me the night of the Crowned Dreamer, when I needed immediate assistance after the consumption of Reaper's Blood was killing me. I was in critical care, and she managed to slow down my death. Then we were hunted by the Blood Casters and Emil's powers were still too dampened by the infinity-ender to fight back against Stanton in any meaningful way. But if Emil dug deeper, Darren might still have a mother today and plans to dress up as Emil for Halloween. Instead, Darren has aspirations to be more like me, and it's exactly what I needed to hear after everything that's happened since I've gone my own way.

If I remember right, Darren could project illusions, just as Dr. Bowes could. I wasn't with Emil when he went to go visit Darren to apologize in person for failing to save his mother, but he'd said that Darren was so furious that he cast an illusion of a ghostly Dr. Bowes to haunt Emil. Of course Emil was shaken up, but he also said he understood why Darren was no longer a fan.

Now he seems to be a fan of mine.

A fan with a really impressive power he dreams of using to save the city one day.

I write back:

Hey Darren. I'm sorry for your loss. I wouldn't be anything without Dr. Bowes. Not the Infinity Reaper or the Infinity Savior. Certainly not alive. But if I could rewind time, I would die so you would still have a mother. That's more important. I lost my father earlier this year, but it's one thing to lose a parent to a sickness and another to have them stolen from you. I hate that you never got to say goodbye to her but had to say goodbye to your normal life. I'm also sorry that things at your haven haven't been going well. I've been hidden from the world a few times too, and it's not how life is supposed to be lived.

You said you want to be a hero when you're older.

Why wait?

TWENTY-FIVE

THE UN-FACE

NESS

I don't trust anyone around me.

On the train back to Brooklyn, I remain suspicious of every passenger. That pregnant woman who asked for my seat? Was that the Senator? Maybe it was the businessman who refused to give up his seat. That entitlement could be a crack in the Senator's disguise. I don't know. I rule out certain people like the identical triplets with backpacks or the tired parent since the Senator can only shift into one person. But everyone else could be a threat. The security guard on his phone. The man in rags asking for change. The teen who shouts "Showtime!" or any other person who groans because they're not in the mood for a performance this early in the morning. Anyone here can be the Senator, waiting to pounce. But there's no way he could know I'm me. I've shifted nine times since leaving Alphabet City, and I'm now disguised as a young woman with cotton-candy-pink hair and impeccable style. Sometimes the best way to blend in is to draw so much attention to yourself that no one could possibly suspect you as someone trying to hide.

Once I arrive in Brooklyn, I keep shifting into random people when I don't have eyes on me, just in case I'm being followed back to the gym, where everyone would pay the price for my mistake. When I'm as certain as I can be, I transform into a girl who has been taking her bulking seriously, and I enter Mele's Melee. My guise is so convincing that I catch Mele's attention. She asks if she can help me out with anything, but I know she isn't just thinking about spotting me as I lift weights. I cough my name, and while she seems disappointed, she's a good enough sport that she applauds my presentation; at least I know her type if I manage to survive long enough to set her up. I head into the back and down to the basement, where Emil, Wyatt, Prudencia, Carolina, and the other Spell Walkers turn to me as if I've caught them in the act of doing something illegal.

"It's just me," I say as a gray light washes away Gym Girl.

Emil comes rushing into a hug. "I'm glad you're back."

I'm surprised I am.

"You good?" Emil asks.

"No. You need to start brewing more Starstiflers. Fast."

"I'm going to, but what's up? What happened?"

"The Senator was there," I say. I can't believe how close I was. I tell everyone how I was getting the word out about binding Genesis's powers with the Starstifler and celebrating this victory for the Spell Walkers, when a stranger claiming to be a neighbor began arguing with me. "I didn't realize it until it was too late, but he escaped in a car with his campaign manager, Roslyn Fox."

Iris looks up from Brighton's laptop, where she's been typing away. "Did you see anyone else from Iron's team?"

"No, but Roslyn was in the backseat with the Senator. I'm guessing his bodyguards were up front. Jax usually drives while Zenon uses his vision-hopping to make sure they're not being targeted."

"Did they know you were there?" Emil asks.

I shake my head. "If they did, I wouldn't have made it back."

"You sure you weren't followed, dude?" Wesley asks, picking up Esther like he might have to run out of this building a millisecond from now.

"I covered my tracks." I'm drained from all the shifting and fighting, so I sit at the table where Bautista de León's journal is open to the Starstifler recipe. Seeing Emil's handwriting decoding Bautista's secret ingredients really highlights how many generations have lived and died for this war. We can't screw it up now. "Let's assume the Senator's core team knows about his power. They've been in on everything from the Blackout to my assassination attempts and the propaganda. But he still doesn't have control over his power yet, and he doesn't have me or Luna to teach him how to use it."

"Sounds like he's figuring it out," Emil says.

"Looks like it too," Iris says, bringing the laptop my way. "Shine just sent these."

Everyone gathers around to view Shine's email. There are two links, and I click the first. It's a video that's been up for forty-two minutes and has over two hundred thousand views. It's only fifteen seconds long, but I can't bring myself to press play. I'm frozen staring at this first frame because it's my face. It would be like looking into a mirror except it doesn't count as a reflection when it's not you on the other side of it.

The Senator is posing as me.

"Bastard," I say as I press play on the video to find out why.

This Un-Ness is somewhere outside, staring into the camera with a mean mug as he punches his own palm. "Come get this, Emil," he says to some cameraperson who definitely isn't Emil. The Senator's impression sounds just like me. Luna always said vocal impersonations are much easier when you're familiar with the subject's voice, and the Senator knows mine good and well, even if it often felt like he wasn't listening to me. The Un-Ness stops in front of a poster of the Senator, getting up in his one-dimensional face. "I'm coming for you, Dad," the Un-Ness threatens before spitting on the poster, where I notice three other spots of discoloration on the Senator's face. The Un-Ness covers the camera with his hand and everything goes dark as the video ends.

"That was creepy," Wesley says.

Of all the moves the Senator has, why this one? Something else is clear to me. "This video wasn't recorded today."

"How do you figure?" Emil asks.

"He didn't mention anything about the recent brawl. He didn't mimic my appearance. And if you look at these splotches . . ." I rewind a few seconds and pause at the poster, pointing out the discolorations. "That's spit that was drying up. I'm guessing this video was the fourth take. Also, why is the video so short? He was able to maintain his glamour as a random civilian longer today, for a few minutes. It's like I said, the Senator is still figuring out how to use the power and must be experiencing some glitches."

This all makes sense given his errors as Red Rollins. The brown eyes turning hazel. The mouth that was about to break form. The voice dropping an octave. It was only a few nights ago when I was being delivered to the Bounds and the Senator shifted into my dead mother, but within moments his true nose and jaw were breaking through his disguise.

"Then why is he posting this now?" Emil asks.

Everything the Senator does is strategic. Some chess moves are bigger than others, such as the Blackout, the propaganda videos, the debate, having me shot on live television after anticipating I would betray him, banishing me to the Bounds to prove his allegiance to the country, and becoming a specter himself. But that doesn't mean the pawns don't advance across the board to aid a bigger plan. "Political gain. He just saw a stranger—me—telling the public what heroes the Spell Walkers are. He would've been especially pissed to hear me painted as good since I disempowered a specter with a potion that now threatens his own power. What better time to remind everyone that I'm a criminal who wants to kill him?"

No one contests this as a sound strategy. Time will tell if the Senator's strategy is enough to counter what we're promising as a solution against specters, but there's still the second link. I click the link, dreading what it will show us. It's a news article that transcribes the Senator's statement on the Alphabet City brawl, but I watch the video that was posted minutes ago because I have to track his every movement, to keep studying every last mannerism knowing what will be asked of me.

In the video, the Senator is looking rough. My fists tighten when I realize he's speaking with the exact reporter we both spoke to before. This must've been done shortly after we were standing side by side. "Pardon my appearance," the Senator apologizes. "I'm afraid it's been another sleepless night with our city in distress." This is a brilliant lie to mask the fact that he looks this way because he's been drained of energy from posing as Red Rollins. It's rare for anyone his age to become an effective specter. He only didn't die during the alchemical process because Luna oversaw everything. She should've poisoned him, just like she'd wished when we were being escorted to the Bounds. "I'm exhausted by how eventful our country has become," the Senator continues. "We only know war and never peace. You're all forced to hide in your homes, and even then you're not safe. My son, Eduardo, and Emil Rey have claimed they possess a potion to bind a specter's power. It's even been said to have been used against a specter hours ago, and we will report our findings after an examination. But if this Starstifler is true, I await the formula so our enforcers can utilize it against every last specter who brings chaos where we deserve calm." He turns, but only for a moment, and I don't buy that he was ever intending to walk away. "If Emil and Eduardo really care for this country, they would drink the potion themselves and banish those powers. Maybe then our streets will be safer and we won't have to worry about any more interference in our very critical election . . . or death threats."

The video ends.

"We already said we want to get rid of our powers," Emil says.

"He knows that. He also knows we won't do it yet."

"Then what's our battle plan?" Emil asks. He might be leading, but this is my area of expertise.

If I want to beat the Senator, I have to play like him to win our own political gain.

There are many players on the board, but some haven't been used yet:

Senator Shine, our hopeful vice president.

Ash Hyperion, Sunstar's husband.

Proxima, their daughter.

Not only do we need Sunstar's closest circle to aid us in finding her, but the country needs to hear from her during what is indeed a critical election, as the Senator said.

Our battle plan?

"I'm going to become Congresswoman Sunstar."

This time, I'm going to do the role justice.

TWENTY-SIX

THE PROBLEM CHILDREN

BRIGHTON

The influencer house will have new guests soon.

I spent the morning trading messages with Darren Bowes over DM, learning more about his life—the life he had to leave behind. He's fourteen years old and started high school last month, acing all his homework. He was days away from his first date before he was forced to relocate. He was going to get a weekend job at a theater, casting illusions for stage effects. Darren was more than happy to accept a payday so he could buy more Spell Walker merch, but he was more interested in strengthening his powers so he would be worthy enough to become a Spell Walker himself. Until their war got his mother killed, like she was nothing more than some faceless civilian caught in the cross fire of a war that began with Spell Walkers—began with Emil's past lives.

By noon, I was on the phone with Mr. Bowes, inviting him and Darren to come stay at the house since there are many vacancies.

He seemed very hesitant, but with Darren feeling more trapped at the haven than protected, it sounds like Darren was willing to leave without his father if he didn't come along. Mr. Bowes doesn't have any power of his own, so he's at his son's mercy—and now mine. He had many concerns, but one was major.

"What if that Blood Caster comes back?" Mr. Bowes had asked.

I earned trust with his son's life when I said, "I killed Stanton."

Now here they are, pulling into the garage with their rental car after journeying from Salem, Massachusetts. I greet them at the door. Mr. Bowes is bald with a beard that is in desperate need of some cleaning up, but he gets a pass since his wife was murdered. Darren is slouching with shaggy black hair that he has to sweep away from his face. He's in a shirt that seems a size too small for him, like he was borrowing someone else's clothes at the haven; he can go through everyone's closets here for a new wardrobe.

"Nice to meet you," I say with maybe more energy than they're expecting. I managed to sleep through the entire afternoon while they've been on the road.

Mr. Bowes nods as he enters the house. "You too."

Darren shakes my hand and looks me in the eye. "You're saving me already. Thanks for getting me out of that school's basement."

I chuckle. "It was a school?"

"Yeah. Why is that funny?"

"My first haven was a school too. It was for celestials and shut down by the government." I pat his shoulder. "This place is much better."

"Emptier too," Darren says.

"Darren," Mr. Bowes says. He's tired. "Be respectful."

"I just made an observation. When did that become a crime?"

Mr. Bowes rubs his eyes as he ignores his son. "Do you have any food, Brighton?"

We all go into the kitchen. The fridge is stocked with Alpha Aqua bottles, boring veggies, Millie's overnight oats, and all of Bull's meal preps for the week. We all take a container and sit down at the table, eating the bland chicken, diced tomatoes, zucchini, and cheese cubes. It all tastes joyless, but at least I'm not in this alone. Darren is very vocal about how much he hates this, and he goes into the cabinet to find some salt and pepper. Mr. Bowes fights back yawns as he tells me about how hard it was to find one radio station in the car that wasn't talking about last night's massacre, the election, phoenixes being hunted, or the Spell Walkers.

"Everything seems to be happening here in the city. I considered driving us to the other side of the country," Mr. Bowes says. "Are you positive we're safe here?"

"Staten Island is the last place anyone is looking for me," I joke. But that doesn't comfort him. They definitely don't need to know that Dione was luring me out before and may be trying to track me down now for revenge. Hopefully she leaves me alone since I don't know where Luna is. "We're as safe as we can be, Team Bowes. If anything happens, I can get us out of here."

"Then why did everyone get slaughtered?" Darren asks.

Mr. Bowes drops his fork out of shock. "Darren," he says again in that scolding tone.

"It's fine." I actually like that Darren is direct. "The others died because they only knew how to use their powers to entertain others, but not defend themselves." Attacking is important too, but I don't get the sense that Mr. Bowes is nurturing Darren's dream of becoming a hero. His son is too special to sit on the sidelines, and he shouldn't have to. "I wish I could have done more for them."

"Do you think their ghosts will come find you?"

I wouldn't be surprised if their ghosts appear, especially Samuel's and Reed's since they were desperate to leave the battlefield and I convinced them to stay and fight as heroes. If they were to bother me, I'd get my hands on an oblivion dagger and vanquish them for my own peace. "I don't think so."

"Why not? They died violently. That's how ghosts are born."

"Yeah, but there's more to it, otherwise we'd be overrun with ghosts."

"Do you think having your neck snapped counts as violent enough?"

It's a shocking question, clearly about his mother. The memory returns. Dr. Bowes had created illusions of herself, Emil, Prudencia, and me. They all swarmed around Stanton to distract him since illusions can't physically attack. They all vanished when Stanton lunged at Dr. Bowes and snapped her neck. I was weak and dying, but survival mode kicked in and I stabbed Stanton with glass before he could kill me as easily as he did Dr. Bowes. But I don't need to share that nightmare with Darren. "I don't think you'll see your mother's ghost."

"I think I will. She's dead because of me."

"No, she's not. She's dead because of me and Emil and everyone else—"

Darren begins tearing up. "But if I hadn't told my friends she was taking care of you all . . ."

I scoot closer to Darren. "No ghost needs to haunt you when you do it to yourself. Don't torture yourself with what-if questions. I did that all the time when I lost my dad. What if we hadn't encouraged him to go through the trial that gave him blood poisoning? What if I used my platform to raise money so we could find the best practitioners and alchemists who could have saved him? What if I did something more when he was choking on his own blood in front of me? I am haunted by all of this, but I can't change that. All you can do now is focus on your future and stop blaming yourself for the past."

Darren dries his eyes. "It's hard."

"It is. Time will make that easier. But repeat after me. 'I didn't kill my mother.'"

Darren takes a deep breath. "I didn't kill . . . I didn't kill my mother."

"Again."

"I didn't kill my mother."

"One more time," I say, giving him the coaching he needs.

"I didn't kill my mother . . . and you killed the monster who did."

There's silence in the kitchen except for the fridge humming. I wasn't aware that Mr. Bowes told Darren that I killed Stanton, but this can only be a good thing. Now I'm even more of a hero in his eyes for killing the man—the monster—who took his mother away from him. I want to tell Darren so badly how I ripped out Stanton's heart, but that might be too graphic.

We finish eating and move into the living room to get more comfortable. Darren still seems unimpressed with the house. Maybe he would have been more into it if he could have seen everyone using their powers for every last convenience, something that could have gotten him crucified out in the real world. Mr. Bowes on the other hand makes himself at home. He kicks off his shoes, rests his feet on the coffee table, and folds his arms over his chest as he leans his head back, claiming that he is just going to close his eyes for a moment. This whole act reminds me of Dad. Darren and I talk about the influencers until a low snore escapes from Mr. Bowes.

I nod at Darren to follow me outside, where the moon is reflecting in the pool. Darren is shivering as he wraps himself up in an Alpha-branded towel. I experience my own chills seeing Alpha's face on some low-thread count staring back at me. I touch the wood in the firepit and silver and sapphire flames roar to life, keeping us warm under the starlit sky.

"How long did it take you to master your powers?" Darren asks.

"I wouldn't say I've mastered them. My strengths so far are fire-casting, dashing, and phasing, but I'm still picking up new abilities. I only learned camouflaging yesterday and then began self-healing hours ago. Flying would be nice," I say, remembering the first time I saw Emil fly the night we were at the cemetery stealing the urn with Luna's ghosts. I wanted that to be me so badly, and soon it will be. "There's retrocycling and—"

"Retro-what?"

"It's a phoenix power. It allows you to travel through your past lives and bloodlines. I tried tapping into that before, but it didn't work. It might be because the Reaper's Blood was brewed with Luna's DNA in mind, so I may never be able to access the full package."

Darren looks fascinated. "What else?"

There's one that's the darkest of them all. "Possession."

"That's real?"

"That's how Atlas Haas got killed. A Blood Caster with ghost blood possessed Maribelle and forced her to kill him. . . . I was there for that."

Darren sits back in his chair and sighs. "That's so messed up. Was he a cool Spell Walker?"

"He was. He didn't deserve to die so young." Age shouldn't matter when it comes to death. Unexpected death is brutal no matter how old you are. This seems clear given the way Darren is staring at the stars, as if he'll find his mother up there. "How about you? What's going on with your power? Were you training at the haven?"

"Unofficially," Darren says.

"What does that mean?"

"I was having some outbursts in the middle of the night. My nightmares kept becoming real. Stuff like my mom as a ghost and the Blood Caster hunting me down. The illusions were scaring other people in the middle of the night."

If Ness wasn't such a two-faced traitor, then he could share his own experiences with Darren about how his trauma forces him into shifting into other people throughout the night. But Darren won't be befriending anyone siding with the Spell Walkers.

"Then . . ." Darren takes a deep breath and eyes me like I'm about to judge him. ". . . these twin brothers kept calling me a freak, so I . . . I made them start fighting each other."

I sit up and lean in like Darren is telling an epic campfire story. "How did you make them fight?"

"I cast illusions over the twins and made them think they were enemies."

That is some impressive gleamcraft. "How long do your illusions last?"

"Not long enough. A couple minutes?"

A lot of damage can be done in a minute. Spells can be cast; hearts can be ripped out.

Brothers can fight.

This power will be really useful against Emil's army. I can already trump his power, but it's everyone else that is getting the upper hand on me, like Ness's deceptive shifting and Ruth's clones. With Darren's power, he can cast illusions so I can trick Ness for a change or even give me the appearance of having my own clones to distract everyone long enough for me to attack. With Darren shadowing me as my sidekick, I will have all the protection I need to never find myself at the risk of losing my powers ever again. But going up against everyone will require more training.

"Does your dad know you want to be training?"

"No. I lied to get here. He thinks I only wanted to get away from that haven, where I won't be treated like a problem child anymore. He would freak out if he knew I wanted to be outside fighting, but he can't stop me."

"As a fellow problem child, I get it. My family tried stopping me, clearly."

"But you have to keep fighting," Darren says.

"So do you. You were born with a gift."

"And you stole yours, but finders keepers. It's not like you can give back the powers anyway."

I like his spirit. "Emil is not going to rest until my powers are gone. But . . ." I stare at my silver and sapphire flames that are devouring the wood faster than ordinary fire. ". . . but with your help I can stop him. I have a potion that can bind a specter's powers."

Darren's fists clench as he smiles. "I'd love to help. Let's go do it."

His eagerness is so welcome. Unlike the influencers who were riding along for the fame, Darren doesn't care about boosting his social media status. He hasn't posted anything on Instagram since the Friday Dreamers Festival in early September, the same event I attended with Emil and Prudencia right before Emil's powers manifested. Little did I know how much my life would change from that moment on and how there was someone else in the audience that day who would come into my life to help me protect mine.

"I only have one potion, which means we only have one shot to do this right. Let's strategize and train before we take on Emil's Spell Walkers."

"I'm already learning so much from you," Darren says. "Thanks for treating me like I can be a hero too. It means so much."

I want to reach out for a fist bump and freeze. This is what I would do with Emil, followed up with a whistle, just like we have for years. But handshakes are so personal; they suggest a closeness between both parties. My brother betrayed me. It's hard to trust anyone properly ever again. But Darren is a good start. I see so much of myself in him. Together, we can not only save the world, but change it for the better.

I hold out my fist and Darren bumps it with his.

"We're going to show the world who the real heroes are."

That's not exactly true.

Darren will become known to the world as a hero, but first, he's going to be my secret weapon that helps me win my greatest war.

TWENTY-SEVEN

BLOOD OF SUN AND STAR

NESS

I last saw the Sunstar family at Doherty University, the pro-celestial college campus that hosted the final debate. That was also the last time anyone has seen Nicolette Sunstar.

I don't know if she's even alive.

The Senator has already said that if he does lose the election, he will simply shift into Sunstar and control the presidency, a trick he will extend to anyone else who is voted into office too. That'll only work if he sustains shifts, but I won't count that out. What's terrifying about the Senator is that he only seeks power, unlike Brighton, who needs the fame too. The Senator doesn't care who people see when they look at him as long as he has the dominion to shape the world.

Personally, I believe Sunstar is dead.

Still, I will do everything in my power to find out the truth so her family can not only grieve, but so we can prepare Senator Shine Lu to step up as president if her party wins the election.

I have never formally met Shine in either of my lives, but back when I was living as Eduardo Iron, we certainly found ourselves at various political conventions. The Senator always told me to keep an eye on her and let him know if she vanished from sight. I should've suspected that the Senator's dealings were all shady given how nervous he was that Shine could be using her invisibility power to listen in on his operations; not even Zenon's vision-hopping would have been able to detect Shine if her eyes were closed. I really didn't like her back then because she was always urging the younger generations to not pay me any mind. Calling me brainwashed just because she didn't agree with our views felt lazy. But now I know she was right. I'll be thanking her in person soon enough.

While most of us were sleeping, Iris managed to set up the meeting with Shine. She was direct about how much convincing it took to get Ash and Proxima on board because she wanted me to know what I'm up against. I understand their hesitation. I not only played a role in Sunstar's abduction, but I also told the world lies while wearing her face. I may have damaged Sunstar's reputation out of my own self-preservation, but now I'll be the one who restores it.

I've been awake for the past hour, mapping out different strategies for all things related to Sunstar. Everything from public presentations to search and rescue missions. The latter requires help. I walk over to Emil and Wyatt, who are hovering over the ingredients for the next batch of Starstiflers.

"We're missing—"

"I need to talk to you," I say, interrupting Emil as he reads through Bautista's journal.

"Yeah, sure, what's up?"

"Not you," I say.

Wyatt is stunned. "I'm all ears. Well, I'm more than ears. I'm dazzling blue eyes and—"

I glare, and he mercifully runs an imaginary zipper across his lips. "When your boss was here, you guys talked about how if any phoenix can track someone down, it's Nox. Is that one of Nox's specialties, or do all phoenixes have that capability? If so, how many Halo Knights with phoenixes would you estimate are in the city? We can use as much help as possible to track down Sunstar."

Wyatt whistles. "I'm afraid I have some bad news for you. Loads of it."

I'm bracing myself for the backup plan, which is far riskier. "What?"

"For starters, someone cannot be called your boss once they fire you."

This is news to me, but doesn't appear to be for Emil. He seems sad, guilty, and grieving. His own future as a Halo Knight has likely been compromised by this, and even if he was invited into the fold, Emil's character wouldn't accept any position unless Wyatt was reinstated. There's a part of me that should probably be relieved that Emil won't be forced into closer proximities with Wyatt, but I just can't get there. Not when dreams are killed.

"You got fired for taking Emil's side?"

"Phoenixes before humans in our line of work. It's no matter. We will prove to the Council of Phoenixlight that our hearts are in the right place," Wyatt says, patting Emil's shoulder and gesturing at the Starstifler ingredients.

Hearts in the right place. . . .

It says a lot that Wyatt and Emil still seem as close as ever, maybe even closer.

"More bad news," Wyatt says cheerfully. "An unfortunate side effect of my termination is I won't be able to call upon the support of the Halo Knights to aid you in your mission."

"Fantastic," I say dryly, and walk away. "Backup plan it is."

"Before you rely on what sounds to be your inferior plan, may I offer a spot of good news? Despite no longer being on the payroll—the pay was quite crap anyhow, it was hardly affording me a luxurious life of books and crop tops, which, to be frank, are barely shirts and yet!—I may still be of some assistance to you. Nox is my forever companion, and not even the Halo Knights have the power to sever that."

This is useful. I'm about to sit at their table as if we're going to be strategizing, but I can't help but feel like I would be a third wheel, so I remain standing. "Nox can track Sunstar?"

Wyatt stares at the ceiling as he nods, shakes his head, nods, shakes. "I make no guarantees."

"I don't get it. Nox is a tracker who can't track?"

"Obsidians are naturally gifted trackers, but Nox soars above the rest thanks to centuries of experience," Wyatt says defensively. "Together, Nox and I have rescued many lives from humans to creatures over the years, but we have failed too. Things get in the way, such as scent trails that fade due to weather interference or outright end because the person was gleamed away."

"You mean because of powers like teleportation?"

"Precisely."

Emil can sense my distress. "How was Sunstar abducted?"

I think back to Sunstar's greenroom at Doherty University, where she was praying with Ash and Proxima and opened her eyes to find me in disguise with Dione and June. Then we threatened her family's lives if they wouldn't cooperate, right before we took her. "June teleported away with Sunstar."

Wyatt cringes. "Locating Sunstar is much more complicated, but doable."

"She can be anywhere in the world," I say.

"What is it your deranged brother always says, Emil?"

"Just because something is unlikely doesn't mean it's impossible," Emil says. He rests his head on the wall, staring at nothing. "I should've come up with this plan sooner."

"We've been stretched pretty thin since that debate."

"Starting with saving your mother," I say.

"And then you," Emil says. "No regrets, obviously, but . . ."

"War forces us to make choices."

If Emil had chosen to pursue Sunstar instead, there's a chance they could have tracked her down by now. But in that alternate universe it's possible Carolina and Eva would still be hostages and I'd be dead in the Bounds. There's a world where we set this right, but we all have to work together. That means we need Wyatt and his phoenix to get it done.

"What does Nox need to locate Sunstar?"

"The strongest link would be blood."

"I don't exactly have Sunstar's blood."

"You don't. But her daughter does."

TWENTY-EIGHT

REMORSE AND REVENGE

NESS

Ask me to look like anyone and I can do it, but transforming this gym basement into an inviting atmosphere isn't as easy. No matter how many times we replace the bulbs, it's still impossible to get good lighting in here. The stench of sweaty laundry persists despite heavily scented candles. We don't even have enough chairs to form a proper sitting circle for everyone once Shine, Ash, and Proxima arrive, but we do have doughnuts from Mele's favorite spot in Williamsburg and a pot of coffee because no one is sleeping through the night anyway. Win some, lose some.

"They're running late," Iris says, reading a text from her phone.

Wesley comes out of the bathroom, wiping sweat off his forehead. "No way. I've been rushing to keep a clean home, and I want my work appreciated ASAP."

Ruth is changing Esther and eyes Wesley suspiciously. "Is that true?" she calls out.

Ruth's clone peeks her head out of the bathroom. "He should be grateful for more time."

Wesley glares at the clone. "Snitch." He turns back to us. "Come on, it's not as if Shine is going to take a shower or that she even needs to. She's invisible!"

"Not all of the time," Iris says.

"But she can be. That's all I'm saying."

"Not your best defense," Eva says.

"One of his creepiest, though," Ruth says.

Wesley drags his feet toward the bathroom. "Fine. Back to the dungeons I go."

I observe the lightness between these four, envying the relationship that the Spell Walkers have versus the one I had with the Blood Casters. Obviously I don't want to spend my life befriending murderers, but there was this hope when joining the Blood Casters that they could become my new family. I was wrong. Stanton was homicidal. June was lifeless. Dione had potential, but she was too eager to assert her power on anyone who crossed her path after once finding herself in a powerless position. We may have creature blood in us, but that doesn't mean we have to be monsters; I wish they could have been more human.

"If they're running late, I'm going to go work out," I say.

"The gym is still open," Emil says. "We can't be seen."

"Not a problem." A gray light washes over me, and I transform into a white guy with a man bun.

I'm walking toward the stairs, when I hear a gasp off to my right—but no one is there. I confirm that everyone is behind me. Emil, Prudencia, Carolina, Wyatt, Iris, Eva, Ruth, Wesley. I stare at the wall where there's a crate of sanitizer wipes that has been here since our arrival. For a second I wonder if there's a shifter who's been watching us, but for those shifters who can turn into inanimate objects, it's unhealthy and unwise to stay that way for too long. Then I remember that Brighton's hydra breed can camouflage, something Luna was very interested in when she hoped to possess the reaper powers herself, which could've relieved me of my spying duties, but if this was Brighton, he would've attacked by now. Also, the gasp didn't come from someone standing at full height, so either they're crouching or they're shorter. Not to mention younger and scared.

"I know you're there," I say, staring at no one.

In seconds, three people appear out of nowhere when actually they have been here for quite some time. Who knows how long. Senator Shine Lu is pale with shoulder-length hair that's inky black with a gold streak that brings out the light brown in her eyes. Whether she's on national television or out speaking to the public, Shine is always dressed to the nines and our dingy basement is no exception. She's dressed in a silver sequined blazer with black leather pants and a big gold belt that makes her look like a wrestling champion. To Shine's left is Ash Hyperion, a handsome man with kind eyes and dark hair that's beginning to gray. Ash is wearing a polo and khakis as if he's about to go play a round of golf. Having studied Sunstar's history, I have a deep understanding of Ash's love for his wife and how he will do anything to save her. Even team up with the person who helped abduct her. And then there's Proxima, a twelve-year-old girl who has her mother's brown skin and her father's brown eyes, but whose power does she have? In all my research, I know Proxima makes blueberry pancakes in the morning with her mother and she's a voracious reader whose big backpack is probably stuffed with books. But there was no info on if Proxima can create burning, dazzling lights like Sunstar or manipulate consciousness like Ash. It's possible Proxima hasn't tapped into her powers yet, because judging by the fear in her eyes, she likely would've used them on me by now.

I glow gray, dropping my Gym Bro disguise, but Proxima only gasps again. It's understandable that she would react this way. I may think of myself as a human with creature blood, but Proxima only sees the monster who came back from the dead and impersonated her mother.

"I'm Ness," I say, kneeling.

Proxima hides behind her father, probably wishing Shine would make her invisible again. She's a sensitive kid; I don't even need to have researched the family to know this for myself.

"You're safe, Proxy," Ash says.

If I had Ash's power, I would probably use it on Proxima to lower her heart rate so she can calm down, but thanks to the wealth of knowledge I have from studying them, I know that Ash only uses his power to help settle situations that can become violent, such as when we arrived for the abduction; I would've passed out if June hadn't intervened.

"Shine!" Iris calls out, which gets everyone's attention. She waves her over. "You just said you were running late."

Shine offers me the slightest of nods before moving deeper into the basement, where she warmly embraces Iris. "I'm sorry to sneak up on you, but I wanted to observe the situation before revealing Proxima and Ash, given everything."

That's clearly about me.

"We would've closed down the gym as an extra precaution," Iris says.

"Life must go on as usual, otherwise people begin to ask why it's changing," Shine says.

Wesley comes out of the bathroom. "Just curious, how long have you been standing here?"

"Long enough to assure you that I shower regularly," Shine says with a smile.

Shine introduces herself to everyone, shaking their hands as if they're all her constituents. It sure feels like she's not interested in my vote. Ash and Proxima sneak past me, like I'm lethal. They're welcomed into the fold, and I'm left standing on the other side of the basement, alone. It's like I'm the one who's invisible, until Emil sees me.

"You good?"

"I'm being treated like I killed Sunstar. Proxima is so scared of me."

"I know we're young, but she's younger. You weren't around when this doctor who was treating Brighton got killed by Stanton. Dr. Bowes was such a champion, and I hated how this all went down. I apologized to her son, Darren, before he got relocated to a haven, but he wasn't having that. He blamed me, and I couldn't even get mad at him."

"But that wasn't your fault."

"Just like Sunstar's disappearance isn't really yours." Emil stands at my side, watching everyone pal around. "But you can relate to losing your mother because of the same person who is actually responsible for this. And out of everyone here, you're the only other person who was a child of a politician. Don't let them treat you like a killer. Show them who you really are, Ness."

This is one of those moments where I wish I was Emil's boyfriend.

But that's not who I am.

Who I actually am has to be proven to Proxima, Ash, and Shine.

Emil and I join the group. "Did you get a chance to say what's up to Ness?" he asks, playing down the tension even though he knows no one said hello to me. "He's got a strategy to help find Sunstar."

Proxima peeks out from behind Ash. "He's the reason Mama is missing."

How do you tell a child that it's far more complicated than that? That I had a choice but it didn't feel like I did. That she could have been killed if I made the wrong one. I don't think you do. "I'm sorry," I say. An apology is a truth that I can tell. "I don't need your forgiveness. I'll never even forgive myself. But I'm going to do everything I can to bring back your mother, and once I do, you'll never have to see my face again."

Ash slowly nods while Proxima looks up at her father. "We'll hear you out. Won't we?"

"Okay," Proxima says.

They all gather around, grabbing coffee and doughnuts, and everyone takes a seat in the foldout chairs except Emil, Wyatt, and myself.

"What's your plan?" Shine asks.

"So, Wyatt has a phoenix who can track—"

"We have recruited celestial trackers already," Shine interrupts. "They're still active on the field, but we haven't had any luck yet."

"No offense to your humans," Wyatt says, clearly about to offend them, "but they don't hold a flame to my phoenix companion, Nox. If your celestials haven't achieved the task, then perhaps it is best to give us a swing at it."

Ash raises a finger as if this is a classroom where he has to be called on. "What would you need?"

Wyatt seems hesitant to answer. "Might we discuss this privately?"

"I'm not a baby," Proxima says with doughnut icing around her mouth.

"Of course you're not," Wyatt says.

Ash gestures for us to proceed.

"We would need blood from Sunstar's closest relative," I say.

"Not a lot of blood," Wyatt says as Proxima's eyes widen. "A cup's worth would be marvelous so Nox can really sink his nose, well, olfactory senses into it to improve his hunt, but if you're averse to this, we can use your mum's clothes instead. It's just . . . well, to not beat around the bush, Proxima, you are our best chance at finding your mother given not just your blood, but how her smell will be traced all over you from every last hug and cuddle you've shared with her. Your essence is worth more than my phoenix rummaging through her wardrobe. Your mum would come home to find that Nox made a nest out of all her dresses and jackets in her absence, which is not a cheap dry cleaning bill, let me tell you."

Proxima grins. "Okay. I'll do it."

Wyatt claps. "See, donating blood doesn't have to sound so scary."

Ash nudges his daughter. "I bet it helps that he sounds like Firenip, right?"

Emil laughs. "You're watching *The Flying Kingdom*? That was my favorite cartoon. I thought the same thing the first time I heard Wyatt's voice."

Wyatt seems playfully appalled. "Is this the show with the talking

British phoenix? He was voiced by an American, I'll have you know. Offensive!"

I'm not familiar with this show. It's not like the Senator was exposing me to any media that painted gleamcraft as anything other than dangerous. As unfortunate as that is, nothing aches more than learning how Wyatt reminds Emil about a show that he cherished. His first impression of me was a dangerous Blood Caster. This is why I have to undo everyone's image of me.

"Thanks for being so brave, Proxima," I say.

"I'll be sure to heal you right up," Eva says.

She doesn't react to me, but she does smile at Eva. I have a ways to go with her.

Shine brings everyone's attention back to other important matters. "Out of fear of retaliation from Iron's collaborators, we have been quiet about Nicolette's disappearance. But the public's last impression of her is everything you said during the final debate. Among many issues this has caused, we have had campaign staff quit and donors withdraw their money because they believe we've shown our true colors as celestial supremacists instead of the party for all."

Proxima raises her hand; it must run in the family. "Why can't you look like your dad and say every bad thing he's ever said?"

"We're trying to live honestly," Shine says.

"But he's a bad man! It's not lying."

Ash squeezes his daughter's hand. "You're not wrong, Proxy, but using our powers against him can do more harm."

"Not to mention, I think he's counting on it," I say. I give them the context behind the Senator's impersonation of me in that video from this morning. "When I was held captive, I filmed so many propaganda videos. I'm sure the Senator now has an archive of his own that he will use. Counters to the truth, alibis. We have to be really smart about how we expose him."

"Then what do you propose?" Shine asks.

"I need to step into Sunstar's shoes again."

Shine, Ash, and Proxima look around the circle, as if they're waiting for someone else to call out what a ridiculous idea this is, unaware that everyone has already signed off on this plan. Shine swallows a deep breath before squeezing her hands together, like she's about to plead. "Please tell me why on earth we would ever trust you to parade around as Nicolette. How do we know you won't do more damage?"

"If you won't believe my remorse, then trust my revenge." I'm so angry thinking about how much the Senator used me that I could cry or punch a hole in a wall. "The Senator has fed me lies my entire life. That a celestial killed my mother when he was the one who had her killed. That he loved me and would protect me at all costs when instead he plotted to have me sacrificed so the world would believe our country's greatest defenders were nothing more than terrorists." Turns out I am angry enough to cry. The Senator has not only put me through hell; he's made me drag others through it too. "When he found out I was alive, he didn't even have me killed on the spot to protect his secret. He turned me into a liar, just like he had my entire life, except this time I knew I was telling lies and couldn't do anything about it. Not if I wanted to protect good people . . . and someone I care about." I glance at Emil, whose teary cheeks are now also blushing. "Everything is different now. Trust me when I say that I will be my father's downfall or be killed for standing in his way. But

I will never be his accomplice again."

I'm breathing heavily as I wipe away my tears.

Emil's arms wrap around me, and he whispers, "Great job."

I hold him close, not caring about anyone else. If the Senator wins the election, then time will be limited to live as I am. But if Sunstar wins, there will be so many years ahead. It might finally be safe to experience true freedom. To be a teenager with teenager problems.

Wyatt shudders dramatically loud. "Goose bumps. You've got my vote."

"You can't vote," I say, releasing Emil. "And I'm not running for president."

Shine turns to Ash and Proxima. "He's not running for president, but how do we feel about him assuming the role of the woman who is?"

These are the votes I actually need. "I won't do anything without your sign-off. We can film videos that the campaign staff exclusively distributes. That way you don't have to worry about me going rogue. Though if you put me on a stage as Sunstar, I promise I won't disappoint. I will let the country know loud and clear what she actually stands for, and regain their support."

Ash chuckles. "Campaigning hard for the job like a true politician. Like father, like son."

"Nothing like my father," I say through gritted teeth. "I don't have to be a liar like him when I can tell the truth like your wife." I turn to Proxima, who is listening intently. "Like your mother."

The father and daughter seem to have a conversation without words. But Proxima speaks to me aloud. "If you lie as my mother, then Firenip's phoenix will claw your eyes out."

"That he will. Pluck, pluck, pluck," Wyatt singsongs, playing along.

"Understood," I say.

I have created a world of hurt by posing as Sunstar.

Now I'm being given a chance to remake it all to end the Senator's reign.

TWENTY-NINE
RESURRECTION EVE

MARIBELLE

The love of my life returns tomorrow.

I'm preparing to welcome Atlas home in Wesley and Ruth's once-secret cottage on Long Island. We obviously have never had a home of our own, always bouncing between havens, but this cottage is not only safe and beautiful, it's also meaningful to Atlas. Months ago, Atlas and Wesley rescued a celestial who was having domestic issues. She'd needed protection when confronting her husband with divorce papers and the news that she was leaving him and taking the kids. Even though she had some telekinetic abilities, her range was limited and hadn't stopped her from being overpowered by her powerless husband. She reached out to Atlas on Instagram among many other celestials, but didn't expect him to respond and show up. After all, aren't the Spell Walkers busy fighting a war? But Atlas cared about everyone living in peace and sometimes the enemy wasn't another celestial or specter or enforcer. Sometimes it was family. The husband threatened everyone, but Atlas made it clear that he could trap him in a twister and he left. The woman was going to put the cottage on the market and start over elsewhere, and Wesley offered to buy it from her to raise his own family in peace. Atlas and I won't stay here forever, but it will be good for his first night back.

The journey to New Suffolk was quiet since I drove alone. Tala stayed behind to tend to the fallen phoenixes, praying for their souls to be reincarnated as well as ceremonially setting their corpses on fire. It was a good thing I arrived alone since I had my own business to tend to that Tala didn't need to witness. While I already had all the phoenix parts, I still needed a whole phoenix to consecrate the Pit. I chose a sun swallower's corpse while back at the Sanctuary, especially after seeing that work for June. I spent the afternoon digging a grave and burying the sun swallower, already daydreaming about how Atlas would emerge from flames in that spot tomorrow night. I wish I could do it tonight, but the phoenix's grave wax needs time to ferment the soil, otherwise all those regenerative properties that trigger the resurrection won't be ready.

I'm back inside, cooking for the first time in ages. Wesley and Ruth's pantries are stocked with rice, beans, canned fruits and vegetables, protein bars, soups, nuts, and bow-tie pasta. The seasonings and sauces had my stomach growling and mouth salivating because I feel like I've been mostly living off of dry cereals and breads. Atlas always said I had trouble taking care of myself, which was definitely true when I was grieving my parents. When he's back, he's going to see that I stayed alive, that I'm able to cook him some rice and beans with steamed vegetables like he loves.

But I'm not cooking for Atlas tonight.

Tonight is for Tala.

I'm beginning to fear this dinner for two will only be for one, when rain patters on the roof, shortly followed by the thud outside the window as Roxana lands outside the cottage. I finish mixing the sauce before rushing for the door, opening it right as Tala is about to knock.

"Hi." Tala's dark hair is frizzy from the flight, and her arms are dirty from the burying. "I'm sorry it took me so long. The ceremonies were hard, and I flew over the ocean so it will be harder to track Roxana's rainstorms."

"It's okay. I'm glad you're here."

Tala steps inside, sitting on the floor as she unties her dirty boots. She sniffs the air. "Are you cooking?"

"It's just some pasta."

"It smells delicious."

"No promises that it will taste delicious, but I'm trying," I say, heading back into the kitchen to monitor the food. "It's a small thank-you for putting up with me."

Tala snickers. "Is spaghetti supposed to make us even?"

"It's actually bow-tie pasta." I wait for her to laugh, but all I hear is the water boiling. "No, this doesn't make us even, Tala, and it's not supposed to. I just thought we deserved some normalcy after everything."

"Before you raise the dead tomorrow."

"Before I raise the dead tomorrow."

Tala looks around the cottage. "Only because it's cozy in here."

I lead Tala to the guest room that's opposite of mine. I set her up with clean clothes and a towel and leave her to shower while I finish cooking the dinner. I plate our pasta and vegetables and grab the bottle of whistle wine that was hidden behind the rice. The wooden dining table is broken, split in half. At first I wondered if an altercation had occurred here, but the fist-sized dent tells me that Iris needed to assert her dominance on the table as she has everywhere else. I set the food and wine in the center of the living room floor, taking pillows from both couches to make it more comfortable. I almost look for a candle, but that seems a touch too far.

The bathroom door opens, and steam from the shower spills into the hallway. Tala comes out wearing one of Ruth's *Every Body Is Super* shirts, which she's knotted into a crop top, and a baggy pair of basketball shorts that keep slipping down her waist. A towel is crowned around her hair, like she's the queen of casual. She sits on a cushion and sighs. "All Halo Knights should stay away from this cliché, but I would be lying if I didn't say that I feel absolutely *reborn* after that shower."

"You smell reborn too," I say, breathing in the cucumber bodywash.

"You weren't exactly smelling like dandelions yourself." Tala grabs her fork, stabbing at the pasta and taking a bite. "I got in trouble as a kid for calling these butterflies instead of bow ties. My mother didn't want me to think it was okay to eat any living being. I obviously didn't think I was eating butterflies just like how she didn't think she was eating bow ties. It's a stupid memory that I haven't thought about in so long. . . . I wish I could argue with my mother over this again." It's as if a shadow has been cast over the room. "Can I tell you a secret? If you repeat it, I will kill you and spread your ashes into the ocean before they can ever find their way into a Phoenix Pit."

"Your threat has been noted," I say, pouring myself a glass of wine.

Tala grabs the bottle and drinks straight from it. "I wish I was a specter like you."

A Halo Knight confessing to specter ambitions is definitely a secret to take to the grave.

"Why?"

"If I could retrocycle, I would be able to see my parents as I've always known them. I could revisit that stupid fight about the butterfly pasta or go back to my father giving me private flying lessons or any other moment where we're all together." Tala takes another swig of the wine. "That power you have is stolen, but it's also the most beautiful ability any grieving soul could have."

"Only if it works in your favor. If I want to see Mama and Papa, I have to travel through Sera's and Bautista's lives. But they died before my real parents could raise me, so I can't replay my childhood with them."

"There's only one thing we can do, then."

"What's that?"

"We can remember them," Tala says.

While finishing up one bottle of whistle wine and starting on another, Tala and I talk about our families. How her father was scared of fireworks but would light them up to see Tala smile. How Papa quit smoking when I asked if he wanted to live long enough to walk me down the aisle at my wedding. How her mother would take her dancing in the rain, and how they would cuddle in bed with tomato soup afterward. How Mama would pet every dog she passed in the street, and how she would wish them long and happy lives as they walked away. How Tala's favorite days with her parents were spent sitting around campfires while their phoenix companions played together. How my favorite days with my parents were the family dinners we could have out in public, back when the world loved us.

Tala peers into the second empty bottle of whistle wine like it's a telescope.

"What do you—what do you s-see?" I ask, slightly tipsy but only slightly.

"I see a girl."

"She sounds beautiful."

"She's average."

"The girl thinks you need glasses."

Tala taps the bottle. "This is glasses—glass."

"Make the whistle wine whistle."

"There is no more wine."

"Just the bottle."

Tala blows over the top of the bottle, creating music. Then she gets bored and grabs a newspaper from weeks ago and tears out pages. She begins making one of her origami birds. It's not going well.

I army crawl to her side. "That wing would never fly."

"Yes, it will." Tala throws the bird, and it sails one inch through the air before falling. "No, it won't," she says through laughter. She grabs another page and begins folding. "I'm not normally so bad at this. I'm really good at this. I once made a paper bird for this girl I thought was cute. She was another Halo. She was the fastest Bronze Wing and was so graceful on her sky swimmer. I would just watch as she rode her phoenix in and out of the ocean. I got a piece of paper and wrote a message, asking her out—"

"Were you nine years old?"

"I was fifteen! And shy!"

"The girl who is always threatening to kill someone for speaking out was shy?"

"I still am when it comes to my feelings!" Tala throws another failed paper bird at me.

"So what happened between you and the fastest, bestest, gracefulest Halo Knight?"

"She was flattered, but—"

"Don't say it!"

"—she was not into girls!"

"No!" I shake my fists at the sky—the roof—I mean ceiling. Ceiling. "I'm sorry."

Tala begins folding another paper bird. "It wasn't meant to be, even though my parents were really rooting for us."

That familiar feeling makes me smile. "I have a similar story with the first person I ever, ever dated. I was fourteen, and this girl Aquila was a celestial who could literally burn you to death with her eyes. Actually literally. Heat vision eyes. It was cool. Not cool, it was hot—you know what I mean! Anyway, Aquila's mother was awesome and Aquila loved Mama too and Aquila really liked Papa but Aquila was more suspicious of fathers because Aquila's father was a nightmare. But Mama and Papa thought Aquila was really nice and funny and nice."

"Then what happened?"

"It didn't work out."

"Because she was a girl?"

"Hell no. I was hot for her, but she just didn't have the same fire in her heart as I did for the fight." I'll always regret not handling things better with Aquila since I really came down on her for not using that heat vision to fight crime, but that wasn't the only thing that drove us apart.

Tala is still working on her paper birds. Just working, working, working. "Then Atlas came around."

"Years later. My parents loved Atlas, but I do think Mama liked Aquila a little bit more. But don't tell Atlas that. . . ." I sigh happily over this little request because it means Atlas is coming back. It's as if Atlas's death was never going to be forever. He's basically just been on vacation with no way to reach me, but tomorrow night he will come home and we'll be reunited and never separated again. "I can't believe you'll actually get to meet Atlas."

She accidentally rips the wing of her paper bird. "Me either." Tala focuses on a new paper bird, each fold more deliberate, more patient, more slowly . . . very slowly. "If the ritual doesn't work, do you think there's a chance you might be able to love someone again?"

"The ritual will work. I've seen it work." It would be a bad idea, a very bad idea to try and bring Atlas back tonight since I'm slightly tipsy but still only slightly. I'd probably butcher his resurrection like Luna did June's, and then he would have no soul and he would have to be put down before he could become someone's weapon. But that's not going to happen. "It will work," I singsong.

"If Atlas doesn't come back to life, can your heart be reborn?" Tala asks, finally folding the wings on her paper bird evenly.

"Atlas will come back to life. But if he wasn't going to, I'd hope I find someone else. Right now it feels like he's my whole heart, but I would defy biology and grow a new heart for someone new out of sheer will. That way I could still love Atlas forever and love someone else forever too. I just don't want to ever be without love, and that's why I'm resurrecting him."

Tala smiles, but it's one of those tired smiles. I get it. That whistle wine must be making her sleepy too. I'm about to tell her she can go to bed, when she holds up her newest paper bird. That is the healthiest paper bird I've seen all night. It's black and white with some newspaper headline wrapped around its paper belly and many words around its little paper feet. "Here, Mari," Tala says. My heart squeezes as the paper bird flies into my hands and I catch it like I'm clapping and accidentally flatten it. "You killed it."

"It'll come back to life. It's a phoenix, right?"

"No, but maybe you can burn it and toss its ashes into a Paper Phoenix Pit."

I point out all the dead paper birds. "There's enough paper corpses to do so." I stare at the flattened bird, its wings gone in an instant, like Atlas was. "I'm sorry, I just . . . You called me Mari, and only Atlas calls me that."

"I'm sorry."

"No, it's nice. Coming from you, it's nice." I gaze into her amber eyes as my head feels foggy and my heart is pounding. "I never thought I'd say this to someone who commanded her phoenix to blow me apart with lightning when we met, but I'm really happy I met you. You really live up to your name, bright star."

Tala inches closer, grabbing my hand. "You've been a bright star yourself, Mari. This grief has been so dark and it was so lonely, but then you were there too. It's like I wasn't alone in the sky anymore." Her head hangs low. "I will be alone in the sky again when Atlas returns, but I thank you for shining with me for as long as you did."

My heart is pounding harder and harder. It's like I won't have to grow a new heart because this heart is expanding and expanding, getting stronger and stronger, screaming louder and louder.

"Maybe we can shine a little longer," I say, pulling her closer.

Tala's eyes seem to glow, right up until the moment when she closes them as her lips press against mine, slowly, then hungrily. I lean back toward the floor, bringing her with me. My legs wrap around her hips as she keeps kissing me, as we keep shining.

Tomorrow I get Atlas back.

But tonight I have Tala.

THIRTY
THE SUN AT NIGHT

EMIL

All paths lead back to blood, like an infinity loop.

Proxima's love for her mother runs deep and she's lucky she's able to aid in her search. When Ma was kidnapped by the Blood Casters, Brighton and I would've given up gallons of blood if it meant Nox being able to track her down. But between Brighton's newly tainted specter blood and my not being her biological son, we couldn't help. Proxima holds her father's hand as Eva injects her with a butterfly needle, drawing enough glistening blood to fill a glass vial, and it looks like stars reflecting onto a crimson river. There's no need for a Band-Aid when Eva shines her colorful lights over where the needle pricked her, healing her immediately.

"Thank you," Proxima says.

"My pleasure." Eva smiles, probably wishing all recoveries were as smooth as that. "As your doctor this evening, I'm prescribing another doughnut."

"Ooh. Stab me next," Wyatt says.

"Grab one for the road along with this," Eva says, handing him the vial of blood.

"I've suddenly lost my appetite."

I roll my eyes. "I'm sure you've seen worse than beautiful blood."

"Naturally, but I'm not hungry after those things either."

Ness is deep in conversation with Shine, which I'm happy to see. I know that trusting a reformed Blood Caster isn't easy, especially when he's hurt you, but Ness is worth fighting past every complication. He has stabbed me with an infinity-ender dagger, and I still trust my life in his hands above damn near everyone else. He excuses himself and comes over to us. "Okay, I've been talking through the rescue mission with Shine. We're not going to send our whole party at the risk of alerting anyone that we're coming."

"But what if she's being guarded by a million enforcers?" I ask.

"Eh, that's quite dramatic, sweet Emil," Wyatt says, biting his lip before turning to Ness. "What, say, if Sunstar is being guarded by a reasonable but still effective number of enforcers? Like . . . twenty-two? How will we beat them?"

"Do not engage. This is for scouting only," Ness says.

"So it's not a rescue mission," I say. "Is this Shine's idea? I can talk to her."

Ness shakes his head. "This is my plan. Phase one is for Nox to locate Sunstar. Once we know what we're working with, we plan a raid. This isn't like barging into the Senator's house and retrieving your mother and Eva. Her captors understand Sunstar's life is valued more for this country, which could be the only reason she's alive. If we rush in and wing it, they might kill her."

"It's a sound plan, if I do say so myself on your behalf," Wyatt says.

"I've often had to track down farms to rescue caged phoenixes, but I couldn't go running in all willy-nilly without getting myself killed. My corpse would be a gorgeous spectacle for the phoenixes to look at, but useless at saving them."

Ness has this face that seems to be asking, *Really? This guy?*

"Okay, I'll follow your lead," I tell him.

"Follow your own. You and Wyatt should be the ones who go."

"Wait. What? We need you."

"If you can't find Sunstar, that means I need to become her. That requires deep dives into her life with Ash, Proxima, and Shine to make sure I'm so convincing that the Senator fears Sunstar did escape whatever prison he's holding her in." Ness looks back at them. "Besides, I think there's more trust to build with the family." He takes a deep breath and gives me this resigned smile. "You two go. Wyatt, you handle Nox. Emil, fight back if necessary. But don't let it get there. Fly away at the first sign of trouble."

I'm all good with Ness shifting into team leader, especially in this territory, but I can't wait until we've won our lives back.

∞

Under the stars and in the dead of night, Wyatt holds the open vial of Proxima's blood out toward Nox, familiarizing the phoenix with the scent. Nox's beak opens, his tongue tasting the air. Wyatt climbs on top of Nox's back, and I do the same, locking my fingers around his stomach. The phoenix's massive wings spread as he kicks off the rooftop and shoots into the sky. The flight isn't some joyride like when we were sailing across the Sanctuary's fields and grazing the river.

This time Nox is on the hunt, first dipping down toward the gym before gliding through the streets and casting shadows over the few cars that are out tonight. We're flying at intense speeds, but there's still something beautiful as we zoom through the Brooklyn Bridge and into Manhattan.

The winds are too loud to talk with Wyatt, which is all good; I'm beat. It's only been three days since that jam-packed night where we broke into Iron's manor and the Bounds and battled Brighton for the first time. Things haven't exactly calmed down since then with fighting enforcers at the Sanctuary and going at it again with Brighton. Honestly, if Brighton is no longer set on killing me and only wants to force the Starstifler down my throat, then maybe I won't even fight him off. Look, I'm honestly not going to let him do that, but a guy can dream about some sleep.

Nox dives back through the streets, and he turns a corner, almost crashing straight into an enforcer tank that is patrolling Alphabet City. Wyatt steers us through an alley and back up toward the sky, where we blend in with the night. Why are the enforcers out? Do they think we're all coming back for round two in Alphabet City? I bet there's nothing happening, and I'd bet even more that people aren't actually feeling safer as that tank creeps past their homes. But the enforcers aren't trying to make citizens feel safe—they're trying to make themselves look like guardians.

Meanwhile, we're out hunting for the person who will create real change.

Sunstar's plans for the Luminary Union have the potential to make our world safer. She wants to unite heroes across the country, tasking them with handling rogue gleamcrafters and calling upon everyone's unique powers to serve the public. I'm not trying to get involved, but maybe I won't have a choice since Wyatt isn't in league with the Halo Knights anymore to put in a good word for me.

We fly past the Light Sky Tower before Nox circles back, spiraling the city's biggest building from top to bottom before shooting all the way up into the sky.

This is not going well.

Nox darts through the sky, and we find ourselves over Older Cemetery, where I fought alongside the Spell Walkers against the Blood Casters and met Luna for the first time. It was freezing that night like winter's worst because Luna had summoned the ghosts of her parents for the Reaper's Blood ritual. I caused a lot of trouble when I stole that urn and got away.

"This is where I flew for the first time," I say into Wyatt's ear.

"Huh?"

"Never mind."

Wyatt steers Nox down into the cemetery, his heavy clawed feet just missing someone's plot. "What's that you said, love?" he asks as he hops off Nox, holding the vial of blood before the phoenix again to refresh the scent.

"Just that I tapped into my flying power here for the first time," I say.

"What was that like?"

"I mean, the moment leading up to everything was terrifying because Blood Casters had me cornered and the sky was my only escape. There was phoenix song screeching from within, like a voice telling me to run away and then my fiery wings burst to life. Then I started flying, and look, I was not made to fly and it was hard as hell, but these powers I've cursed so much have also saved my life. A lot."

Wyatt screws the cork back into the vial while smiling. "You'll miss them, won't you?"

"One day," I say. I'm shivering from the chills, but I'm able to handle that easily by casting one fire-orb and absorbing its warmth. "I'll miss being able to do this when I'm cold or heal automatically when I'm hurt."

"Put your fire out," Wyatt says.

I do it quickly and look around, my heart pounding. Does someone know we're here? "Do you see someone?" I ask. I'm ready to fight, but first sign of trouble, we're supposed to hop on Nox and fly away.

"No, no. Settle down," Wyatt says as he removes his jacket, wrapping it around me. "I'm simply helping reintegrate you into a normal life where you can't create your own fire when you're cold. As for all the wounds, maybe kisses will help."

Wyatt is a breath away, so close that if he leaned in, we would be kissing in this cemetery. He's not closing this space between us because I've drawn a line, but there's this hunger in his gaze that's begging me to cross it.

I back away, focusing on the weight of his Halo Knight jacket. It's made up of cactus leather and sleeved with obsidian feathers that Nox shed, a custom Haloes have to honor their phoenix companions. It's especially heavy on the padded shoulders, but instead of coming down on my body for being too weak to easily withstand this, I'm priding myself of the strength I have that keeps me standing tall under all this weight.

"You wear it well," Wyatt says.

"Are you going to get in trouble for keeping yours?"

"If the council doesn't want me wearing it at the risk of being confused as an active Halo Knight—they would only be so lucky for the world to believe we are not only good-hearted but hot—then I will simply fashion my jacket into a vest and sew Nox's feathers down the back. It would be nice for my arms to breathe more anyway."

For someone who carries himself so confidently, he's also so guarded.

"You can be real with me, Wy. Your whole life has revolved around being a Halo, and now they've clipped your wings."

"That doesn't mean I won't fly again."

"As a Halo Knight?"

"Perhaps but possibly not. It's as I said before, sweet Emil, I will simply have to be reborn as someone else." Wyatt folds his arms and chuckles. "Quite a thing speaking of one's own resurrection while among the dead. Should I make this even more poetic and dig up a grave to bury my dreams?"

I sink to the ground, sitting beside a headstone. "Then what's next for you?"

Wyatt shrugs. "Maybe I'll become a librarian, but at a library for phoenixes."

"Phoenix fire and paper sounds like a bad combo."

"Ah, there we go! I shall invent fire-proof paper instead and charm all bookmakers to make their books with my paper, and soon enough there will be enough fire-proof books to open the world's first phoenix-friendly library. And then I shall lounge in the sun, reading all day. Hopefully one of those books will be the riveting memoir of your life as the Infinity Son."

I fight back a laugh. "I'm not Brighton. Once this is behind me, the last thing I'm going to want to do is cast a spotlight on myself ever again."

Wyatt leans against a tree with folded arms. "Then I hope I will have other ways of knowing what your life looks like."

"You're not going anywhere."

"Our future is unclear, love, but if we do find ourselves together, I promise it'll be a life of adventure—the good kind. We can retreat to a wondrous rainforest where phoenixes thrive. Tend to them, take up shelter in a tree house even. Then wherever else you're burning to visit. If you're worried about being recognized, we can stay somewhere long enough that people will have to wonder if they ever saw you at all or if you were some dashing ghost. But try as we might, evil forces always rise again, and with that, attentions will shift on to the next hero who is fighting their damnedest to prove themselves worthy." Wyatt crouches before me and holds my hands. They're freezing cold, like mine, but we're warmer together. "By then, the world will have forgotten about you, Emil Rey, but I never will."

I can't face Wyatt; I just can't. I stare up at the moon and at the stars, hoping the night sky will begin dancing with a constellation that tells me my future. Or at least tells me how I'm supposed to respond to these declarations and this invitation to a world that sounds so damn epic and amazing.

"Wyatt . . ."

"If you are about to ask if I even know how to build a tree house, the answer is no, but I will figure it out for us."

"A tree house in a rainforest sounds dope and somewhat dangerous, but—"

"Ooh, the one word that is a dagger to the heart." Wyatt releases my hand to dramatically plunge himself in the chest.

I smile a little, feeling guilty having this conversation. We came out here to work; Ness is trusting us to get the job done. Not stop in a cemetery and talk about our future. I don't know if Ness has given up on me, and that's why he doesn't care about sending me out into the night, alone with Wyatt; I can't blame him if he has. But this moment feels like kissing Wyatt in the middle of a battlefield, stealing time from winning the war. "Look, what I do as the Infinity Son will likely go down in history whether I like it or not. My face is going to pop up next to Keon's and Bautista's in the phoenix exhibit at the Museum of Natural Creatures. But I don't want my life defined by this chapter. I want to stop being famous and go back to being a stranger. I want to be a kid who does stupid kid stuff and deals with stupid kid drama that feels like the end of the world but definitely isn't. I'm not there yet. I can fight for my future, but I can't start planning it until I've honored my vow to save the world. I'm sorry."

Wyatt gently nods. "Well, wherever you land, I hope you'll never become a stranger to me."

"Back at you, Wy."

We hug, but in a way that feels like burying another dream in the cemetery, before we hop back on the obsidian phoenix and return to the sky.

THIRTY-ONE
SHINE A LIGHT

NESS

Ask me anything about Congresswoman Sunstar's campaign staff.

I'd done some research before based on the materials the Senator's team fed me, but her work wasn't as thorough as the four-hour conversation and profile presentations that Shine gave last night. This is only the start and we hope it ultimately won't be necessary, but in the event I need to assume the role of Sunstar longer than any of us would like, I'm ready to walk in her shoes to rebuild hope for her voters. For instance, when I arrive at the office at nine a.m. today, I know that their—now my, just for the sake of getting into character—campaign manager will be overly familiar with me since she graduated in the same year as Sunstar and they have been friends ever since. Then there's our communications director, who isn't a celestial herself but her wife and children are, so now more than ever she's trying to create a better life for them by countering all the bad press Sunstar has been receiving since the debate. I've been warned that our speech writer is distant and comes off as antisocial, but they're simply a quiet genius who is very deliberate in everything they say.

Other random facts I've committed to memory include the pollster having a sweet tooth for gummy basilisks, the treasurer being a film buff who hates CGI, and the social media director being inspired by online activism after following Brighton's Celestials of New York accounts. That last one was an important reminder that people can be shaped for the good even if their role models turn out to suck.

What's most important is that no one must know that I am not Sunstar.

For this, I was given a refreshed, more intimate history from her husband and daughter. I learned things that I would never know from all the thirty-plus hours of footage I watched to study all her mannerisms and absorb her worldviews. Things that won't be found in her biography, *Our Country, Our Universe*. On vacations, Sunstar likes to curl up by the fireplace with a Twinkling Spritz and thousand-piece Lego sets. If she could only eat one food for the rest of her life, it would be gnocchi. My favorite detail is that Sunstar once wrote a novel under a pen name that sold very well, but she thinks it's far too steamy to reveal to the public; I know the title and I'm sworn to secrecy, but I will definitely be checking it out.

In acting workshops, my instructors always taught us to really dig into the roles of our characters, to make them as real as possible. This meant that if the script didn't reveal something about them to make it up ourselves. Do I need to know about Sunstar moonlighting as a romance author to portray her accurately? Yes, because even though she has no problem shouting into a megaphone for equality, or standing on a stage before thousands, I know she has bashful energy too. It may seem unnecessary to some, but this work is what allows me to fool Brighton when I posed as Emil, or the nation even as I told lies as

Sunstar. This time around, I'll be an authentic Sunstar.

And I think I will have to.

It's a quarter to seven when Emil and Wyatt finally return. They come down the stairs, slowly, as if they're sore from another brawl. I study their gait as they approach, and I'm almost certain they haven't been fighting. They're just tired. Their expressions of defeat are even more revealing. But what I can't help but notice is Emil in Wyatt's jacket. Instead of freaking out over what that means, I refocus on the mission.

"No luck?" I ask, though it's barely a question.

"Nope." Emil goes straight to Carolina's cot, resting his head on his mother's shoulder. She didn't get any sleep last night. Even I managed about thirty minutes, but I'm also not the parent of two sons on opposite sides of a war. Carolina kept refreshing the news on her phone, praying to the stars that there wouldn't be any updates about Emil or Brighton.

Wyatt pours himself a cup of cold coffee while telling us everywhere they ended up last night. Manhattan, Brooklyn, the Light Sky Tower, the cemetery, Sunstar's house, Shine's apartment building, the closed campaign offices, and even as far out as Doherty University in Boston, where she was last seen. But Nox was never pulled toward the Senator's manor or offices.

"Why the cemetery?" Prudencia asks.

"She can't be dead," Iris says.

"The cemetery was a quick break to chat and reset," Wyatt says.

I'm not going to obsess over what they were talking about. That's their business.

"I'll update Shine," Iris says, pulling out her phone.

"Phase one of the plan was a bust," Wyatt says, turning to me.

"What do we do now?"

I glow gray as I shift—skin darkening, hair growing, shrinking and inflating where necessary, and I top it all off with the solar orange suit from Sunstar's nomination acceptance speech at the Democratic National Convention, an outfit she has recycled a handful of times already.

"Now I go to work."

I'm going to Sunstar's campaign headquarters through a method that feels foreign.

Walking.

Since being reunited with Emil, our modes of transport have included a phoenix, enforcer quad bikes, and a stolen car. I've even been carried about by Wesley, which he kindly offered this morning too, but I really wanted to stretch my own legs. Between being held hostage in my own childhood home, then banished to a prison, and now living in a gym basement, this hour-long walk to Brooklyn Heights is giving me a chance to think about whatever I want. It's a shame that I'm going down these streets disguised as some white businessman who won't draw any attention to myself, but if this is what it takes to live without eyes on me, it's a price I'm willing to pay. I'm soaking it up while I can because once I drink the Starstifler I won't be able to live a life of anonymity anymore. There will be harassment, death threats, maybe even more assassination attempts. But for now, I get to be a stranger on his way to work, someone with ordinary problems on the brain, like if he's going to be able to squeeze in a workout before dinner tonight, or which match on a dating app he's going to pursue first. Maybe this stranger even has loose plans to vote in the election but won't feel the strain despite the outcome.

A low-stakes, ordinary life sounds nice. But that's not what I'm signed up for today.

I go into One Pyx Plaza, our base of operations, and head straight into the lobby restroom as a stranger to the campaign and step right back out as the source of it. I ride the elevator to the third floor, remembering the blueprint Shine shared with me. Before the doors even open, I'm already playing the role of Sunstar for the camera in the corner; just so soon after being carefree in the streets, I'm back to being watched.

As I enter the campaign office, there's a wall that's stamped with colorful Post-its, all containing messages about hope and change by staff members and visitors, serving as reminders of everything they're working for when they come through these double doors. I'm greeted by a team of secretaries, all welcoming me back and saying that they're glad I'm feeling better; Shine writing off my absence as nothing more than a sickness is smarter than the truth. Who would feel safe coming to work knowing that if the presidential candidate they're backing was abducted, what about those who could vanish with virtually no one noticing? Thankfully, dozens and dozens of people are here, doing the unsung work. The space is really welcoming with *Shine Like a Star* banners and pictures of Sunstar and Shine palling around with their staff, government officials, and constituents.

What's striking to me is how familiar this feels from all the time I've spent in the Senator's headquarters. No, there weren't beanbag chairs and gummy basilisks, but there were assemblies of hardworking staff members who believed in the Senator's vision. There was nothing about that environment that made me believe I was on the wrong side. It wasn't some dimly lit cave with poison brewing for our enemies or casting ranges so people can shoot at targets with Sunstar's face with wands. Instead, it was volunteers phone-banking and working together to bring the Senator's vision to life. He even managed to make it look warm with the most photogenic of photographs of himself with his (highest-paying) donors. I wonder if he still has the pictures of us together or he's now installed an actual casting range so people can blow up one-dimensional me.

Having had my foot in both political worlds, I must remember that the lines between good and evil are always a matter of perspective. Someone is always right and someone is always wrong. All that matters at the end of the day is who is better at telling their story.

I am walking sunshine as I move through the office, lighting up some faces of the staff members who have seen dark times lately, but others don't appear as happy to see me and aren't shy about hiding it. Shine warned me to expect this. Morale has been down since the polls have fallen dramatically after the last debate. Once I'm done filming promotional videos, Shine thinks it would be a great idea to call a meeting and have a heart-to-heart about where Sunstar's head was at during the debate. I of course can't tell them that Sunstar's head along with the rest of her body is nowhere to be found. But I can lie about the lies I told as Sunstar to try and make things right. I'll put a spin on that night, pretending I made those claims to win over the celestials who are on the fence for supporting me since my stance has never been strong enough in prioritizing them over the powerless, but admit that was a failure on my behalf, one that I hope won't have cost me the presidency. If I can earn back the confidence of the staff and volunteers, then that will spread out to the public too; people can tell when someone's heart isn't in something.

"Welcome back, ma'am," the campaign manager says while walking with me to my office. She lowers her voice. "We have a thirty at twelve to go over some disruptions we've been experiencing among the staff because of low morale and open criticisms in the workplace about you, but first—" Sarah opens my door where a cleaning lady is hovering over my desk, straightening a stack of papers. "Hi, Lucia. May the congresswoman have her office?"

Lucia looks at me in surprise, like she's going to get in trouble for cleaning. "Of course."

Sarah continues. "Traffic is delaying Shine a few extra minutes, but she called ahead and said last night you both discussed taking some time to film this morning. I have you set up in the media room. And, ma'am, don't forget you can call me at any hour. You and the Senator don't have to strategize in the late hours alone."

"Absolutely. I appreciate your commitment."

I thank Sarah and Lucia on their way out, closing the door behind them.

Sunstar's desk has stacks of paper—freshly neatened—and framed family pictures. I pick up the one of Sunstar, Ash, and Proxima posing in front of the Golden Gate Bridge, which is an annual trip Ash told me they take around the time of his birthday in March. By the window there's a poster of the Dazzling Compass, the constellation that Sunstar was born under at its zenith, resulting in her tremendous power. If only Sunstar had been quicker the night of the abduction, burning out all of our eyes before June had the chance to possess Ash, forcing Sunstar to accept defeat or watch something terrible happen to her husband—or even watch her husband do something terrible. Above the door is that famous celestial quote: *The Strongest Power*

Above All Is a Living Heart. See, this is who Sunstar is. She isn't some celestial supremacist who could choose to value her literal powers over an internal one that we all have within us. I'm going to hold this message tight as I do the recordings.

I exit the office and find my way to the media room, passing Lucia again.

"Good to see you," Lucia says, smiling as she pushes a mop bucket down a hall.

"You too, Lucia."

She's a lot less nervous when not around Sarah Noon, who is an excellent campaign manager but does come off a little intense. I do appreciate Sarah's commitment with leading Sunstar's team and beating the Senator's, but she shouldn't feel self-conscious over Sunstar and Shine having private meetings about the campaign when they're the faces of it at the end of the day.

I arrive in the media room, where the camera is already set up and there's a green screen behind the chair where I'm going to sit.

The social media director puts down one of her phones to mic me, and she seems pleasant enough until "Our accounts have been pretty, pretty, pretty busy since your last debate," Charline says. Her tone is sharper than I'd expect, but Ash did say that Sunstar often encourages the team to treat her as an equal. Some people can't break their habits, like the campaign manager who also calls Sunstar *ma'am* even though they've been friends since college, but Sunstar wants honest collaboration and will often drag the truth out of the staff if she can tell they're pulling back. This is what sets this headquarters apart from the Senator's, where everyone must address him as *sir* and not challenge his ideas.

"The public is turning on us," I say.

"To put it lightly. We built a lot of support with debate one and locked a lot of people in with debate two, but debate three . . . it was very, very, very different. The public feels betrayed, lied to."

They were.

"I wasn't myself," I say. "But I will own my mistakes. Hopefully make your job easier."

"Yours too, Madam President," Charline says with fingers crossed.

There's a knock on the door, and Shine enters. Her outfit is toned down, just a navy pantsuit with no jewelry. She's still stylish, but her office outfit isn't as special as what she wears when she's out and about in the city or even training me to be Sunstar. She comes in and hugs me, which is a nice performance for Charline since Shine definitely walked past me last night and only went so far as to shake my hand when she was done coaching me.

"I'm sorry I'm late. Traffic was a nightmare," Shine says, squeezing my shoulder. She looks around the room and purses her lips. "I don't think the green screen is the way to go."

"You said you wanted us to show coverage of—"

"I know," Shine interrupts Charline. "But we want this to feel real. There's enough reason to doubt media these days without having another green screen behind us."

I nod, agreeing. I spent hours in the Senator's attic doing propaganda in front of green screens, telling lies as people who don't even exist. "How about we use campaign materials as my backdrop? There's the poster in my office about the strongest power being the human heart? That could counter the supremacist perceptions."

Shine claps. "I love it."

Thank the stars. I feel like I'm helping besides just being the face of this operation. I'm using my head too.

"I'll go get the poster," Charline says.

"Round up other fitting materials," Shine says.

Charline grabs her second phone and steps out.

"Nice job," Shine says.

I sigh. "I'm trying. It seems like I'm going to have to do it for a while. Emil and Wyatt tracked all night, but there was no trace of . . ." I mouth Sunstar's name because I'm suddenly self-conscious that there's a hidden camera in here or that this mic might be hacked and fed into some public account. But neither me nor Sunstar are conspiracy theorists, so I need to get it together.

"We should operate as if she's dead," Shine says sadly, with a hand to her heart.

It's a dark thought. "Does that mean telling the world? Or me continuing on as her?"

Shine stops to think, concentrating. It's a big question.

"We don't have to figure it out now," I say.

"We should talk it out with Emil and the others. This involves them too."

"They trust you. So do I. If Sunstar can't lead the country, we're ready to back you."

Shine smiles, but it doesn't last long. I might be slowly winning her over. "I think it's best if we all consult together."

"Do you want to bring Ash and Proxima to Mele's tonight, or should I send out Wesley and Iris to accompany them?"

Shine paces. "I'll bring them."

I look at my mic, almost wishing that it was hacked so this

conversation would get leaked. That seems like an easier path to Ash and Proxima discovering that we have absolutely no idea where Sunstar is than telling them to their faces. But they both deserve better than that, and I can't turn away. "When my mother died, I was so broken and angry," I say, and Shine stops pacing. "No one consoled me. If Sunstar is dead, maybe it will be different for Proxima because she has Ash. He's not the kind of father who will encourage her to take out any aggression on other people like mine did. The Senator thought he was making me strong, but I was weaker for his parenting."

Shine's disdain is practically glowing. It's like every time I badmouth the Senator, it further humanizes me in her eyes. "I'm sorry you went through that," she says, clearing her throat. "I'm going to go see what's taking so long with those posters." She leaves, the door slamming closed.

I sit on the chair opposite of the camera, tired before we've begun filming any of these videos. I wish I'd gotten more rest, but just like when I filmed the propaganda videos for the Senator, I can channel my low energy levels in making my performances more believable. If people truly believe Sunstar has been sick, then I can lean into that while also showing strength, resilience, and, most important, being powered by the heart to best serve the American people.

Charline reenters the room with the poster under one arm and the *Shine Like a Star* banner draped over her other shoulder. She's impressively still on both of her phones like some poster child for ambidexterity and multitasking. "Got everything," she says while scrolling through one note on her phone and firing off a tweet with the other.

"Shine just went out looking for you."

"Oh. I'm sorry for the wait. Sarah had notes on my social language before teasing out your statements."

"Fine by me. Thanks for all your work."

"Always and forever."

Charline is taking down the green screen when Shine comes back.

"So sorry I'm late," Shine says, then immediately hits the brakes. "What are you doing, Charline?"

"Resetting, like you said."

Shine didn't say that. I know this even before she says, "When I said what?"

I know this because Shine is now wearing a cotton-candy-pink blazer with waist-high, double-pleated black pants and rings on every finger. Thought was put into this outfit by someone with an actual eye for details in fashion.

My heart is racing as I pop out of my seat. "Charline, please excuse us."

Charline looks at us so confused, like we're hydra specters who have grown extra heads. "Okay," she says, leaving.

Once the door closes, I study Shine. Everything about her feels so right . . . but apart from the previous outfit, everything about her before felt so right too. There was the clearing of the throat that felt normal but could have been masking a tell. What else? Those moments when she was deep in concentration. I figured she was considering the heaviness of our dilemma, but it was probably to maintain the identity. No eyes switched colors this time. And then there was Shine's hug. It wasn't just a performance for Charline . . . it was a performance for me too. And I fell for it.

"Why doesn't Wesley think you have to shower?" I ask, ripping out my mic.

Shine looks confused. "What is happening here this morning?"

"Tell me now."

I really hope she's wrong. That would mean I have a chance to stop him.

"Because I can become invisible," Shine says. Then her eyes widen, the light brown practically glowing because of the ring light. "Wait. Was that not Charline?"

It's far worse. "He's here. . . . He was posing as you."

Shine looks creeped out, violated. Like she wants to turn invisible. "Iron? Why was he here? How long has he been here? What does he know?" She's shivering as she looks around as if the Senator is still somehow in the room, unseen.

"I don't know, but . . . Sarah said that morale has been down and she's heard staff members speaking ill of me—of Sunstar. What if the Senator has been spreading the poison himself?"

It's brilliant. This is the perfect place to not only strengthen his gleam, but put his shifting to good use on people who are unaware of his power. No one is going to second-guess that this would be an impostor among their ranks, especially if they're venting about how unfortunate it is that the candidate they've been donating hours of their life to support isn't the woman they believed her to be.

The Senator has always been this manipulative, but now he can be so as anyone.

"How do we know who's who?" Shine asks, looking at the door like anyone out in our campaign office could be the very person we're running against.

Then I remember the cleaning lady. Or who I originally thought was Lucia in my office. That's why she was so surprised to see me. The Senator is the only person in this building who actually knows Sunstar's fate. Whether she's a prisoner somewhere or dead. Either way would be shocking unless Sunstar broke free or resurrected. That means the real Lucia is the one who was more relaxed around me in the hall. "He's definitely posing as others," I say. "He was in my office."

"Why? There's nothing in there but campaign plans. Most which are dated."

"Maybe he wants to see how we're fighting against him."

"Then he's going home with nothing. What did you both talk about?"

I go through everything, backward. "I was bad-mouthing his parenting, which I have happily said to his face, but he definitely kept his snide remarks to himself. We talked about breaking the news to Ash and Proxima together about not being able to find Sunstar, later on at . . ."

I'm speechless.

Everything would be fine if I never said a single word.

"What? Later on at what?" Shine asks.

"Later tonight at Mele's."

"Did you actually—"

I can't believe how badly I've ruined this.

I've shone a light on where we've been hiding in the shadows.

"We have to warn the others," I say.

The Senator will be coming for us with full force.

THIRTY-TWO
ILLUSIONS

BRIGHTON

Darren's illusions are impressive.

Before bed last night, Darren and I were still sitting outside by the firepit that was roaring with silver and sapphire flames, when I saw a shooting star. I was this close to making a wish, just like Ma and Dad would tell me and Emil to do as kids. But then the shooting star faded before it could finish streaking across the sky, like I'd been seeing things. And I had. That was the first time Darren cast an illusion around me, and he's gone on to create others at my request. While it was cool seeing a shark in the pool and clones of myself having a push-up contest, on closer look, they all lacked depth and realism.

Darren and I are working on his illusions this morning, but we're making it seem like a game so Mr. Bowes doesn't realize we're actually training for battle.

There are three objects in front of me on the kitchen island: a cooking timer, a compact ring light, and a glass of ice.

Only one is real.

Let's see. The glass is freezing over too much when it should actually look sweatier, so that's out. The compact ring light is really bright on the eyes despite it being as artificial as it gets, but it doesn't have that familiar warmth I know from standing before ring lights. I'm also never really using compact ones like this, so that would make sense for why it's different. I study the cooking timer. Its knob is unwinding second by second, each tick loud and clear as it approaches its one-minute mark. Then the timer goes off, obnoxiously real and making me feel like I need to check the oven for cookies.

"Time to guess," Darren says with a smile. He likes the game.

"The glass of ice is fake. . . ."

The glass vanishes like it was never there. "That wasn't my best."

"Neither is the cooking timer."

Darren's smile vanishes. "How did you know?"

I reach for the timer, and my hand goes right through it. "Just because something isn't a solid object doesn't mean it shouldn't give off the illusion that it is. In this case, the timer wasn't vibrating against the counter."

"Damn it," Darren says.

"Language," Mr. Bowes says from the dining table, where he's reading the news on a tablet.

"Sorry," he says.

I laugh because I can't believe he's getting in trouble over level-one swearing. "My mom used to get so upset whenever she heard me cursing. I knew better than to say it around her, but I'd casually swear while filming a YouTube video. Later she'd be watching with my dad and he wouldn't notice but my mom would. It was too late for her to do anything about it."

"Would you get in trouble?" Darren asks.

"She'd threaten to take away my camera every now and again, but she gave in. It wasn't the end of the world if I said something that wasn't really hurting anyone."

Mr. Bowes looks up. "What does she think about you threatening to kill your brother?"

That question is loaded, casting a shadow over what's been an otherwise good morning. Just because Mr. Bowes is Darren's father doesn't mean that he's an authority over me. For all intents and purposes, this house is currently mine and I invited them into it. I could throw them out, or maybe just him. I believe Darren would stay with me if given the choice.

"I can't imagine my mother is happy, but she also knows I have no filter when I'm upset. A couple weeks ago, we were arguing on the phone. It's when I was at the hospital with . . ." They both realize that I'm talking about Dr. Bowes, and it's like the shadow in the room has grown larger. "I told my mom that I was dying from blood poisoning, just like my dad had. She wasn't soft with me. She called me high and mighty and stupid and selfish. I told her Dad was the better parent. That was almost the last thing I said to her before she was abducted by the Blood Casters and held prisoner at Senator Iron's house."

"And now?" Mr. Bowes asks.

"Now what?"

"What's the last thing you've told your mother?"

We last spoke back at the Sanctuary, the night everyone betrayed me. I had said something about how I was a survivor unlike Dad. It's true, but I regret letting the heat of the moment get to me. Ma told me to not insult Dad's memory, and that if he were himself, he'd be telling me that I don't get to play judge, jury, and executioner with my unnatural powers. The same unnatural powers I used to save her life, by the way. But what I said back was also born out of rage. "I defended how I'm the most gifted gleamcrafter in the world, and how I will decide which enemies get conquered if that means winning the war."

"Including your brother."

"I won't have to kill Emil. I have a potion to stop him."

"Does your mother know this is your plan?"

If that timer was real, I'd set it and tell Mr. Bowes to get to the point. "No, she doesn't."

"Maybe she'd like to know that. Have you reached out to her?"

Ma has tried calling from different numbers and sent texts asking me how I'm doing, but I haven't answered anything. "She chose Emil's side."

"She's your mother, Brighton. She's always on your side. Why don't you invite her over so you can clear the air? I'm sure she'd love to see you."

Darren shifts uncomfortably. "I sometimes cast illusions of my mom. I just miss hearing her ask me about my day or telling me that she'll see me after work. There have been times when I just sit across from her . . . but it's not the same. No matter how much I'll be able to make someone believe that my illusions are the real thing, I can't trick myself into thinking that's actually my mom." Darren wipes away a tear. "Not when she can't hug me, and not when I have to force the illusion to say 'I love you' in her voice. It's just not the same."

I've been more furious than sad lately, but as I think about Ma right now, and how hard this year has been for our family between losing Dad and this saga we've been living out, I do miss her. She hasn't always been on my side, but she's not supposed to be. Anything she's ever said against me has come out of a place of love. Even when Ma yelled at me because I was dying from the Reaper's Blood, she was caught in the heat of her own moment too; like mother, like son. All she's ever wanted is for me to live. Now that I'm immortal, she's getting her wish. But at what cost if my loved ones aren't even a part of my life? Especially the woman who literally brought me to life.

"You're both right," I say. I mean it too. This isn't me trying to manipulate someone. "I'm sure she's going to ask me to play nice with Emil, but we can set up some boundaries."

"Absolutely," Mr. Bowes says, returning his attention to the tablet.

"Does she like illusions?" Darren asks. "I can put on a show for her."

"She prefers normalcy, but she'll appreciate some entertainment too."

If I can have Ma here and not fight about Emil, then we can start closing this chasm between us. I already like the idea of Ma being able to relax in the pool or sit outside and stare at the stars instead of bouncing around from haven to haven. If Emil wants to keep running with his crowd, that's his choice, but it's time Ma stops getting dragged into it. There is always going to be a target on my back as I keep changing the world, but having Darren around to provide backup is going to be so helpful if he needs to hide Ma while I'm away. Also, Ma and Mr. Bowes are both widows who can become their own support unit as we all navigate this new world. This house is the safest, best place for Ma to live.

Mr. Bowes pops up from his chair, like he's just seen a mouse. But he's looking at the tablet. "Brighton, you need to check this out. . . ."

I grab the tablet, already plotting to snap the Silver Star Slayer's neck if he's spreading more lies. But it's a video of the Senator on an emergency broadcast: "For the safety of all in Greenpoint, please stay indoors, as we are pursuing a lead on the location of the Spell Walkers. If you live close to the gym Mele's Melee, we ask that you evacuate and find shelter elsewhere. History has shown that the Spell Walkers will risk innocent lives to save theirs—and even take others down with them."

The broadcast ends.

"Pursuing a lead? Who is?" Darren asks.

"Enforcers," I say. I grab my phone, calling Ma to give her a heads-up but she isn't answering. I send a text: *Tell Emil to get you out of there NOW. Enforcers are coming!* She doesn't respond. Hopefully the Spell Walkers have seen the same broadcast and are already fleeing. "I'm going into the city," I say, springing forward to grab the Starstifler in case Emil tries anything funny when I demand that Ma come home with me.

"I want to go too!" Darren says.

"You are not going anywhere," Mr. Bowes says.

"You'll slow me down, I'm sorry. I'll be back."

I dash out the door, sprinting in bursts, desperate to get to Brooklyn as quickly as possible. I hit the road and I'm faster than these cars, but the stops every few seconds are slowing me down. This is a race against time, and I intend on winning.

THIRTY-THREE
SONG OF HAPPINESS

EMIL

The others are playing a card game, but I'm lying on Ma's cot with my head in her lap as she plays with my curls. As kids, Bright's hair always grew out pretty straight and mine always curled. It took us a minute to understand that being twins didn't mean we had to be identical, but we always thought we'd have more in common. Ma and Dad told us that we took after them in different ways, like how Brighton got Dad's green eyes and I got Ma's hazel. Except I got everything from phoenix fire. "I guess I didn't inherit the curls from Abuelita, after all," I say with a tired chuckle.

"No, but I took care of them," Ma says.

"You did, Ma. And everything else." It's been a minute since we've been able to get into my whole history. "Is all this still weird to you? Me not coming from you?"

"Not at all because you did come from me, my Emilio. You came from me and Leo and Brighton. You have always been my son and will always be my son." Ma's fingers keep twirling my curls. "Is it weird for you?"

"Nothing too serious. It's just . . ." I'm careful with what I'm saying because I want to protect Ma's heart in all of this. "It's just I sometimes have to remind myself that I'm not who I thought I was my entire life, but that I also am? Like how I got my name from Abuelito even though he's not actually my grandfather, but also, yes, he is. Then there's everything about the past lives and how I basically used to be Maribelle's father, but I'm not now? And my brother is threatening my life, but maybe it won't hurt so much if I act like he's not actually my brother. I'm legit living out some telenovela."

Ma's laugh is sad, but it's good to get one out of her. "When you put it like that, it is very dramatic. But you won't be the Infinity Son forever. Soon enough you'll be able to live an ordinary life."

"Yeah, but we're probably not going on any family vacations anytime soon."

"You and Brighton will get through this."

"But it's never going to be the same again."

"It definitely won't, but that doesn't mean it won't grow to be something better."

Look, I'd like to believe our brotherhood can be reborn like some phoenix, and hopefully more like a breath spawn phoenix that resurrects instantly instead of a century phoenix that resurrects, well, after a century. But this isn't like me being reborn without Keon's and Bautista's memories. I know good and well what's gone down with Brighton in this life. He has ripped a heart out of someone's chest, he has threatened my life, he's overpowered me in battle, and he's definitely coming back to finish the job. Even if I manage to disempower

Brighton, there's no way I'm going to be able to act like he's the same brother I grew up sharing a bedroom with, who had my back when things were looking rough in our pre–Infinity Era, and who I was so close with that finding out he wasn't my twin was more shocking than discovering I had phoenix blood coursing through me.

But there's nothing wrong with giving Ma some hope.

"Can't wait until we're all looking back on this," I say, sitting up and tightening the Halo Knight jacket around me. "I'll tell him, 'Hey, Bright, remember when we tried blowing each other up with phoenix fire?' and he'll say, 'Remember it? I watch those fight scenes every night on YouTube before I go to bed,' and we'll fist-bump and whistle while laughing."

Ma touches her hand to her heart. "Nothing will make me happier."

Our friends bust out into laughter. Prudencia cheers as she taunts Wyatt with her hand of cards before slamming it down in the middle of their circle. I've got no idea what game they're playing, I'm just so happy hearing them all have so much fun, it's lifting me up like a really upbeat pop song. It's got me thinking that this is what my post–Infinity Era life could look like if we all stay close. And how can we not after everything we've been through together?

"Do you think Brighton could make things right with Pru?" I ask.

"I hope so. I'd feel so lucky to be her mother-in-law."

"I'm rooting for their comeback too." Since I'm all about hope right now, I don't need to get into how Prudencia is too smart and awesome to give Brighton another chance.

"How about you, my Emilio?" Ma nudges my shoulder with hers. "Have you given more thought about what you want?"

"I want my life to go back to the way it was."

“That’s not happening, and that’s not what I meant.”

“I know . . . and I don’t know.” I lower my voice, not wanting Wyatt to overhear. “I don’t want to break anyone’s heart.”

“That’s not a reason to not nurture yours,” Ma says, holding my hand.

“Yeah, but shouldn’t I just know who I want to be with?”

Ma shakes her head so lovingly, like a no that means good news. “Your father and I had a lot of push and pull in the beginning. We wanted different things. Leonardo wasn’t sure about children, and I have wanted my own since I was a little girl. My friends were dreaming about being brides, and I was always thinking about names for the ten babies I wanted.”

I laugh. “Wow. Imagine ten Infinity Kings flying around.”

“That would’ve been both wonderful and terrible for my heart. We love you both, but your father and I agreed that two was plenty. He didn’t even have to deal with the fighting and hiding and abductions and everything else.” Ma’s deep sigh makes me regret so much about what we’ve done with her life, and has me wishing more than ever that if things were always destined to go down this way, she could’ve at least had Dad by her side. “All this is to say that Leonardo and I were on different paths, but always found our way back to each other. When something went wrong in my life, I wanted his comfort. When something went right, I wanted to celebrate with him.” She squeezes my hand. “You don’t have to know right now. I’d be happy to have either of these boys as my son-in-law, but maybe it’s someone else entirely who becomes the person you want to share your highs and lows with, and you’re there for theirs. But don’t be so scared of having your heart broken that you never fill it.”

Nothing like a Ma talk to make me want to throw out all my rules.

I look down at the Halo Knight jacket, wondering if I should keep it on in honor of Wyatt or take it off out of respect for Ness.

I don't have to know right now, just like Ma said.

"So you really had names picked out for ten kids?"

She nods. "Of course, but thank every last star I outgrew those names, otherwise you and Brighton would've been Noodle and Count."

"Yeah, I would've been pissed if you named me Noodle. Way more than I ever was about the secret-adoption thing. Thanks for a way better name, Ma."

"My pleasure. Though at one point being named Carolina felt like being named Noodle or Count or Pixie. I wanted something that didn't stand out in my world, where girls were all Amy and Stephanie and Laura. My mother always trusted I'd grow out of that attitude, as if she used her little psychic power to sense it, but my father put in the work to make that future a reality. He taught me that my name means 'strong' in Spanish and 'happy' in English. He would ask me, 'Don't you want to spend your life being strong and happy?' and he was right. Who wouldn't want that?"

Strong and happy sounds so impossible, but I'm already living out the impossible as a boy reborn from phoenix fire with two historic past lives. Why can't I be strong and happy too?

"That's really beautiful, Ma."

"On the hard days, I remind myself that I am strong and happy, even when it's only a little bit." Ma turns to the other side of the cot, where no one is sitting. "Take today, for example. I wish Brighton were here with us. But I find strength in having you by my side and happiness in knowing he's alive. That gets me through."

"And you're good even though Brighton is off doing whatever the hell he's got going on?"

"I wish things were different and better, but yes. Even then," Ma says.

Someone's phone is buzzing by the wall where it's been charging; I can't tell whose from a quick glance because we all got identical phones from Wesley's dealer. I get up to see whose it is in case it's Shine or Ness calling with an update. Before I can reach it, someone begins storming down the stairs so fast that I'm scared we're about to be attacked. I almost draw fire, but it's only Mele. She's panting hard like she's been doing one of her major telekinetic workouts, but I get nervous again when I realize I've never seen her look so concerned.

"Enforcers," Mele says. "They've got us surrounded."

Everyone jumps to their feet, including Ma, who gets up too fast. She has a dizzy spell and immediately has to sit back down.

"How did they find us?" Wesley asks.

"Doesn't matter," Prudencia says.

"We have to get Esther out of here," Ruth says.

"How surrounded is surrounded?" Eva asks.

"Very, very surrounded. Dozens by the front and back doors and a tank on the street," Mele says.

"Oh, dear. That certainly qualifies as very, very surrounded," Wyatt says.

"Then we fight," Iris says.

I rush to Ma's side. "Deep breaths, Ma."

She looks as if she might cry or faint, but she's breathing.

If Brighton were here, he could phase everyone out undetected.

But he's not here and we are and we need a plan, fast.

"I can try running out with Esther and come back to help," Wesley says.

"And leave her with who?" Ruth asks. "It's too risky. If you get shot down while escaping, I don't trust these enforcers to not open fire on you both." She's brought to tears just speaking those words out loud. She holds Esther close, and Wesley consoles her with a hug too. "Esther stays here until we've cleared a safe path out."

There's an explosion above us. Glass shatters and people scream.

"We got to move now before we get cornered down here," I say. "Who's going up?"

"I am," Prudencia says, racing up the stairs with Mele close behind.

Iris asks Eva to stay here with Ma, which I appreciate. Ruth is sending clones upstairs to fight, but she only trusts herself to watch Esther in this moment. Iris and Wesley follow Prudencia and Mele.

Then there's one left.

"After you," Wyatt says.

"You don't have powers. Hang back."

"I don't, but Nox does. If you can forge a path for me, I'll ride Nox into battle."

I'm not a fan of this plan, but unless I want to knock out Wyatt with a fire-orb, I don't have the time to win an argument. We run up the stairs with Ruth's six clones marching after us. I instruct three of them to guard the back door while the other three join us.

The gym has already become a battlefield.

Prudencia and Mele are telekinetically hurling weights at enforcers like the world's heaviest Frisbees: a couple enforcers fall to their knees, the air knocked out of them so badly that they're grasping at their throats; another gets hit in his helmet and falls flat on his back like a domino; and the others take aim, blowing them apart with their wands. Wesley dash-tackles enforcers, sprinting away right before they can blast him. Then Iris charges forward and deflects so many rapid spells with her forearms that it begins looking like a laser-light show. But her power-proof skin can only deflect so much. The full might of the tank's wand-turret blasts Iris so hard that she rockets across the gym, like she's nothing but a rag doll. Iris slams through the chalk wall that had clients' personal best records and slams down in the hallway. She's not moving.

"Iris!" Wesley is a millisecond from jumping into a run, when he's shot down by a wand-turret, multiple spells firing through his lower back. He falls face down on the floor.

"Oh no," Wyatt mutters.

Prudencia and Mele tag-team against the tank, rebounding the spells back toward the turret and doing some damage until an enforcer shoots Mele down from the side. I hurl a fire-bolt into his chest before he can knock out Prudencia too, and I dive behind the wrestling ring with Wyatt as more enforcers cast spells our way.

"Get back, Pru!" I shout.

Prudencia stands her ground, putting all her telekinetic training to use to rebound the shower of spells while also working to disassemble the turret that is unrelentingly firing at her from the street. She uppercuts the air even though there's no one in front of her to punch, and she screams as she begins hovering in the air—as she rises and rises with her fist above her, the wand-turret screeches as its wrenches off the tank. Prudencia slams her fist down to the mat and telekinetically slams the turret onto the hood of the tank, folding it in. Brighton would probably tell Prudencia she was born for a moment like that, but she built her way up to that level of power.

Now that the tank has been handled, we can expect more enforcers to roll through.

"Find a weapon," I tell Wyatt. He's not a fighter. He once pierced his mother's shoulder with an arrow. But even a misfire like that could do more to protect his life than his own fists.

"I would've used one of the hundred-pound dumbbells, but those seem to have grown wings," Wyatt says as Prudencia begins telekinetically flinging them at the enforcers.

One of Ruth's clones rushes out to grab Wesley, but she's shot repeatedly in the back, dying and vanishing in purple lights before she can drag him our way.

"Go get Eva," I tell the second Ruth clone.

I rush out to help Prudencia, shoulder-rolling away from a spell, and throwing fire-orbs across the gym and into the chests of enforcers. I'm crouched right beside Mele, who is breathing and conscious, but seems dizzy; I hate how helping us out has threatened her life and literally destroyed her business. "You're going to be okay. We got you." Mele nods weakly. I pop up to my feet and tell Prudencia to get Wesley and Mele out of sight so Eva has privacy to heal them. I provide cover, blasting down four more enforcers like I'm doing target training all over again.

Mele's body slides across the floor like she's pulled by a string, stopping right beside Wyatt, who is wielding what looks like a metallic staff but is just a barbell for bench pressing. But as Wesley's body is pulled toward us, the trail of blood that follows is sickening; he's going to bleed out.

I grab Prudencia's arm, running behind the ring. I check Wesley's pulse, and he's barely breathing. Mele is in better condition, but still not up for a fight. Then there's Iris in the hallway, who still isn't moving. . . . She can't be dead; any other person would've been killed by that blast, but not Iris.

"They know we're hiding here," Prudencia says.

"Good, we're drawing them in. Snatch their wands once they're close enough, and then we take them down before they can retreat."

Prudencia crouches by the other turnbuckle, waiting to make her move. Wyatt stays close to me, holding his barbell at the ready. I call over another of Ruth's clones so she can apply pressure on Wesley's wound, and she's crying while seeing him in this state; the real Ruth must be freaking out downstairs.

How did the enforcers figure out where we are? Did Mele let it slip? Her ex-girlfriend Xyla? It's always someone. We got screwed over at the celestial elementary school because of Luna. Then Dr. Bowes's son, Darren, told some friends we were at the hospital. And we got tracked down at the Sanctuary because of Brighton. Who exposed us this time?

Once the enforcers are close enough on her side, Prudencia rises and telekinetically snatches the wands out of the dozen enforcers' grips, two by two by two by two by two by two. She throws them in a pile behind us. I'm tempted to give one to Wyatt and the others to Ruth's surviving clones, but we can't risk killing anyone today. But that doesn't mean we can't lay them out. I hurl streams of fire at the pile of wands, lighting them all up like a fireplace so the enforcers can't kill us.

I run out with flaming fists, trying to fight off enforcers who are much stronger and bigger than me. This is not going to go down like my training session with Ness. I uppercut one enforcer while another punches me right between my eyes. I'm seeing stars as my head swings. An enforcer holds my arms behind my back while another shouts at him to cuff me; if they bind my powers, who knows what they'll do with me. Lock me up somewhere? Kill me? Can I even resurrect as someone new if my powers are bound? I don't know, but I'm about to find out. . . .

There's a clang, but it's not the gauntlet snapping around my wrist. The hold on me loosens. I break free and find Wyatt swinging the barbell into the enforcer's helmet, which clangs again, and he slams the bar into his ankle. The enforcer falls on one knee, and I clock him with a flaming fist, laying him out.

"Not bad," Wyatt says.

"Thanks."

"I meant my hand in the matter, but you too."

I turn to find Prudencia by the punching bags, telekinetically swinging them into enforcers who are trying to reach her, like a heavy obstacle course. When one enforcer gets through, she flings him onto a treadmill, switches it on, and he goes rolling across the floor, stopping flat before he can be torched by the pile of burning wands.

There's a scream in the hallway, and it's Eva healing Iris, absorbing all her pain. The back door breaks down and enforcers storm in, fighting the Ruth clones. I rush over because if they head down those stairs, they'll kill the real Ruth, Esther, and Ma.

"Ruths, move!"

Once they step out of the way, I blast streams of fire in the doorway, scaring off all enforcers.

Iris sucks in a sharp gasp, like she's been brought back to life. "I love you," she says.

"I . . . love . . . you. . . ." Eva pants.

This is one of those lovely battlefield moments we don't have time for unfortunately. "Iris, we got to block this door! Eva, Wesley is bleeding out!"

I hate to put Eva through more pain, especially so soon, but if she's too late, then there won't be anyone to heal. She runs as fast as she can to Wesley as Iris stacks lockers against the door. I cast fire along the edges, melting the steel into the wall. Even if that only buys us another ten seconds, that's all good—someone can live or die in that time.

Back in the gym, Prudencia is getting worn down, but keeps finding just enough energy to push back anyone who comes near her. Wyatt is in the wrestling ring, swinging the barbell at one enforcer, who ducks but luckily he ends up spinning his new weapon into one who was creeping behind him. Iris charges into action, punching enforcers across the gym. Eva is screaming as the colorful lights wash over Wesley's wounds, but she's staying strong and pushing through.

I'm starting to think we might turn this around until I see an enforcer fling a gem-grenade across the room—and directly into the ring. It's too late to do anything about it. By the time I could move to try and blow it apart or breathe to tell Prudencia to bounce it back, it's just too late. The mat explodes in a bright blue light, caving the enforcers in while Wyatt goes soaring backward over the ropes and crashing into the mirror, shattering the whole wall with his impact. Glass rains down on Wyatt, and tears start forming in my eyes as I run toward him, screaming his name. He's flat on his face, but I can't turn him over because there are shards of glass sticking out of his back.

"HELP!"

I don't know what to do; I don't know what's better. Take out the glass or leave it in?

"I . . ." Wyatt tries craning back his head. "I flew. . . ."

Then he spits blood.

"HELP!" I shout again.

Eva is still healing Wesley, and Prudencia and Iris are holding back the enforcers. There's no one to help.

This can't be happening, after everything I just talked about with Ma, this can't be happening to Wyatt. First he loses his life's work because of me, and now he's going to lose his life. I wish I could do anything, like transfer my powers to Wyatt so he can self-heal. But that's not happening, so I just stay close, holding his hand, even though there's still a battle raging all around us. "Hang on, Wy, we're going to get you healed up."

Wyatt weakly squeezes my hand back. "I . . ."

"You flew, I know, I know. Save your breath."

"I . . ."

"Just chill, okay?"

Wyatt rests his face on the floor, his blue eyes teary. "I lo—"

Eva slides behind Wyatt out of nowhere, ripping out shards of glass. He screams like he's being stabbed all over until the colorful lights bathe his bloody back. Then Eva begins screaming. Her nose begins bleeding, which I've never seen happen before while she's healing someone. Maybe it's because there have been so many people in critical condition. Iris is up and fighting and Wesley dashes into an enforcer and Mele is still down but I'm betting Eva chose to heal Wyatt first since he's so wrecked—he was so wrecked. Life is finding its way back into his blue eyes again, and I feel like my own heart has found life again too.

Was he about to say that he—

"They have a celestial!" Iris shouts.

At first, I think the enforcers have a celestial at wandpoint.

Then I realize the celestial is the enforcer.

It's wild how self-hating celestials like this enforcer must be to team up with the task force that was built to put gleamcrafters in their place. Why not buddy up with any of the vigilante groups across the country if you're dead set on protecting the public? Yeah, there's no pay or insurance, but it's a lot better than being paid and insured to kill your own community. If we can elect Sunstar and Shine into office, they—or just Shine—will replace the Enforcer Program with the Luminary Union so these duties can be handled more responsibly. But until then, this is a Spell Walker problem.

The celestial enforcer is dressed in the sea-green power-proof vest like all the others except his bronze belt sets him apart as a gleamcrafter. His belt has a wand and gem-grenade, but his hands are empty; he is his own weapon. But we have no idea what his power is as he stalks toward us.

"Brace yourselves," Iris says, her fists ready.

The celestial enforcer snatches up a piece of glass before stepping into the shadow of the ring and vanishing. Is he invisible? Then he suddenly reappears behind Wesley, slicing both of his ankles with the glass. As Wesley falls in pain, the enforcer drops through the floor again like he's phasing. There's no way in hell he has ghost blood, right? Then again, if the Senator is now a specter, who's to say he hasn't advised specter recruitment the same way he has celestial bodyguards. The enforcer reappears behind two Ruth clones, snapping both their necks in succession. They vanish in purple lights and only three of the six clones remain. They might not be the real Ruth, but they come from her and are identical to her and it's horrifying watching Ruth die three times this morning. It's about to be a fourth time when the enforcer appears behind another Ruth, but I'm quick enough with a fire-orb that he backs off, falling again through the floor.

"He's traveling through shadows!" Prudencia says. If anyone knows what that looks like, it's Prudencia, whose first boyfriend, Dominic, had this power. "He can't travel through his own!"

I jump, hovering below the ceiling with my gold and gray wings of fire. The enforcer can't sneak up behind me if I'm in the air.

"Should we turn off the lights?" Iris asks.

If we had Sunstar, she could bathe this entire place in so much light that no shadows would exist. My power has the potential to do this, but that would mean burning down this entire gym.

The enforcer falls out of the ceiling where my shadow must have been cast and tackles me out of the air. I slam against the floor, screaming in pain. He's about to twist my neck, when he's flung off across the room, crashing into the target board. I gasp for air as the enforcer vanishes again through the shadows.

Prudencia runs to my side. "Are you okay?"

"You . . ." I catch my breath. "You saved my life."

"Again," Prudencia says, helping me up. Her eyes widen. "Eva, behind you!"

The celestial enforcer grabs Eva in a choke hold, squeezing the life out of her. Iris charges him and is about to get her hands on him right as he sinks into the shadows. Iris catches Eva as she falls, her girlfriend limp in her arms.

"Eva, wake up," Iris pleads. She checks her pulse, and she's relieved for a moment before she panics. No one can heal Eva.

We keep getting attacked like this.

"Everyone get together!" I shout. Some run, some crawl, but once we're all huddled in a circle, we look outward for the enforcer and any other enemy forces. "Pru, build a barrier with my fire." I cast my fire, watching as my gold and gray flames flow around us like burning waves, creating a bright shield that vanquishes all shadows in our immediate perimeter. The celestial enforcer appears several feet away, grinning. He whips out his wand, and we're about to find out how this fiery shield won't protect us from any spells. He aims at us, right when fire strikes him in the chest.

A silver and sapphire fire-bolt.

Brighton is here.

THIRTY-FOUR
A SONG UNSUNG

BRIGHTON

Here I am, saving the day.

Naturally.

A moment ago, after making the exhausting journey from Staten Island by foot, I phased through the gym's walls, out of sight from the enforcers who are lined up on the street with a tank that has a broken turret. Emil and the others are surrounded by a ring of gold and gray fire, which is a surprising new trick of his that I'll have to teach myself. It didn't seem to be scaring off some enforcer who was aiming his wand at them, so I had to strike him with a fire-bolt. I can't tell if Ma is inside that circle with the rest of them, and I'm not going to risk her getting hurt. I dash closer, only finding Emil, Prudencia, Wyatt, Iris, Eva, Wesley, three Ruths, and some muscular woman I don't recognize but am not surprised to find inside a gym. I note that that two-faced bastard Ness isn't present, so it's possible he's posing as that woman or playing dead on the floor as one of these enforcers, but I don't care about him right now. I'll destroy him the next time he gets in my way.

"Where's Ma?!" I shout over the roaring flames. I have no issue taking her and running. This is not my fight.

"Behind you!" Prudencia shouts back.

I turn, surprised that I didn't see Ma when I first looked. Maybe she was in some corner. Not that I needed this attitude from Prudencia after saving her life but—

A spell blasts me before I can finish turning around. I go flying into the turnbuckle of the wrestling ring, which feels too similar to all the entertainment wrestling matches between celestials that Emil and I used to watch. My arm is burning before I begin healing. That enforcer who shot me is looking for the kind of beating he won't be able to recover from. I throw another fire-bolt, but the enforcer's eyes glow like stars as he rolls to his side, phasing through the floor. So he's a celestial. I phase through the floor before he can prepare for me, dropping into a basement. But I don't see him. Only Ma and Ruth and her baby.

"Brighton?" Ma asks.

I'm relieved to see her, but she's still in danger. I look around. "Where's the enforcer?"

"What enforcer?" Ruth asks.

"The one who phased down here." I don't see him. Can he turn invisible too? Camouflage?

"We haven't seen anyone but you." Ruth seems nervous now too.

Ma comes toward me. "When did you get here? Is Emil okay?"

I almost roll my eyes. "He won't be if I don't find this enforcer."

The ceiling is too high for me to jump up, so I dash up the wall, ignoring Ma's calls to wait as she reaches for me, and I phase back up into the gym to take care of her precious son who can't get the job done himself. Emil and the others are still hiding inside his ring of fire. There are so many enforcers on the floor who are unconscious, maybe even dead, though I highly doubt that, and yet the city's greatest heroes are so scared of one enforcer? The celestial enforcer doesn't even have an offensive power; it's essentially limited teleportation. If I were leading the Spell Walkers, I would have Prudencia telekinetically bind the enforcer while Iris pounces with a super punch or even have Emil cast firelight over a shadow while the enforcer is surfacing and maybe we can guillotine him. This enforcer is a traitor to celestials everywhere and a gruesome death like that could serve as a warning to anyone else who wants to play hero for the wrong reasons.

Where is he hiding?

It's possible he's already retreated to the enforcers who are all waiting outside by the street, calling for backup.

"He's gone!" I shout.

Emil won't drop his ring of fire. "What are you doing here?!"

I like that he's cowering behind his power, but he's as stupid as ever if he doesn't recognize that those flames won't stop me. I can phase right through them and hurt them all if I wanted to. I could knock Emil unconscious, snatch him, cut his flesh, and feed him the Starstifler while he's asleep so that he wakes up powerless. But that's not what brought me here.

"I'm here for Ma!"

The gold and gray flames illuminate his confused face. "Ma?!"

"She's coming home with me, where she'll be safe!"

"What?!"

"You can't be trusted with Ma!"

Emil turns, his eyes widening with surprise. I'm ready to phase through whatever sneak attack the enforcer has launched at me this time, but it's not an enemy. It's Ma. She's standing in the doorway. First she's horrified by all the destruction and bodies as she walks deeper into the gym, but then she finds me with one of those quivering expressions where she's sad but proud. This is what her face would have looked like if I'd gone off to college in California at the start of September instead of staying here in New York to support Emil during his Infinity Son journey. Instead, Ma is seeing that I have saved the day as I always said I would and could as my own Infinity hero. I'm ready to dash into Ma's open arms, excited to tell her that we're going to a new home, when the celestial enforcer rises in front of her. I hurl a fire-bolt at lightning speed, and my own eyes widen with surprise when the celestial enforcer vanishes back into the shadow and the fire-bolt strikes Ma.

How can something so horrible happen so quickly?

This is nothing like watching Dad choke to death on his own blood.

Ma flies back, banging into the wall. Then she's on the floor, still, like she's sleeping.

I dash across the gym, passing Emil as he breaks through his ring of fire, and I reach Ma before him. Emil is crying hard. He was just like this a few days ago when he saw Ness shot on national television. It would be really epic if that's what was happening right now. That this isn't Ma at all but instead Ness in disguise. I would welcome that. Except there are no gray glows that break the illusion, so Ness will die as himself. . . . There's just Ma.

"No, no, Ma, please, please, please," Emil cries.

Ma is groggy as she lifts a hand, touching Emil's cheek. "Emil."

No way.

Where the hell is Eva? I turn and find her in Iris's arms, the both of them on the floor next to Wesley, whose legs are bleeding, and that muscular woman I don't know. Wyatt is on his knees, staring at Emil with his hand to his mouth; he's finally shut up. There are three Ruths guarding everyone, but at the end of the day, a clone is just an extra body without any real power to back them up. The only other person who can do some damage is Prudencia, and she's in shock over what's happening.

I look over my shoulder where that enforcer is aiming his wand at Emil's back, and I hurl a fire-bolt so fast that it strikes the enforcer's chest before he can cast a spell. I'm stalking toward him, when Emil calls my name.

"Brighton! Brighton!"

I turn slowly, scared to face the music. There's blood spilling out of Ma's stomach. I was wrong. She isn't still as if she's sleeping. She's convulsing and it's hard to watch, but it's impossible to look away. This is as violent a death as Dad's was, and that scarred me so badly that risking my life for immortality was a no-brainer. There's a tiny voice in my head that says, *Now everyone will understand why you are the way you are*. But I don't want to be proven right, not at the cost of Ma.

I can't lose my last parent.

I also can't be the reason she's lost.

"Ma?"

She struggles to turn her head, so I hover over her. Her eyes widen, but I don't know if she can see me. She could be in shock.

Then I see that recognition in her eyes. She reaches for my face and says, "Brigh—"

Ma's hand falls, the ghost of my name on her lips as she dies.

"MA!" Emil cries. "MAAAAAA!"

I feel hollow inside as I watch my mother lying here with her eyes frozen open and blood spilling. This is the woman who gave birth to me—me and only me. She cannot be dead. This is the woman who still has so much living to do. She cannot be dead. It's too soon for Ma to join Dad in the stars. Emil is holding on to her hands and staring into her lifeless face. I check her pulse as if it's going to tell me something I don't know. I check her heart too. Ma cannot be dead, but she is. She didn't even get to finish saying my name.

I'm no longer hollow inside.

I'm a furnace, raging with fire.

No one, and I mean no one, will be able to put me out.

I stand tall, right when that bastard enforcer is waking up. Good. He's not dead. That means I get to make him pay for tricking me into killing my mother. The enforcer notices that I'm stalking toward him. His eyes glow like stars as he rolls to his side, phasing through the floor. I know better this time than to follow him. He rises through a shadowy corner, holding his wounded chest. That power-proof vest saved him before, but it won't save him again. I move for him when he begins vanishing through another shadow. I know how his power works because Prudencia's piece-of-shit ex-boyfriend who was too good for my Spell Walkers of New York channel had the same shadow-hopping abilities. Every shadow except the celestial's can be used as a doorway, but they have limits. This enforcer can't vanish through one shadow and reappear a mile away, he must surface quickly or he can suffocate in the ether. I watch all the shadowy surfaces, and when I see the enforcer rising out of one, I dash toward him and grab him by the throat in one hand and phase-punch my other fist into his chest and rip out his heart, all before his body can fully emerge from the shadows.

My fire keeps raging as I stand over the enforcer's halved corpse.

I turn to the street, where enforcers are hanging back. Did they think their little mercenary celestial was going to do all their dirty work for them? Do they think they can hide behind their tactical shields? Do they know they've aided in the death of the Infinity Reaper's mother?

Emil and Prudencia are calling my name. Emil is still hovering over Ma's body—her corpse. Prudencia is staring at the top half of the enforcer's corpse, horrified at what's become of this person—of what I've done to him. They begin waving me over, as if I'm about to stop now.

The enforcers came for blood, and now they will bleed.

I dash toward the enforcement unit, phasing through one's tactical shield and attempting to snap his neck. It's not as easy as I thought it would be, but my rage helps me get the job done on the third try. Another reaches for a gem-grenade, and I blast a fire-bolt into it, vanquishing four enforcers with one fiery explosion. Civilians are screaming and fleeing. I count six remaining enforcers. Four are defenseless but one is on top of the tank with a sniper-wand, and before I can strike him, I notice the sixth enforcer has hurled a gem-grenade. I'm prepared to phase right through it when I see that the gem-grenade curls into the air, flying toward the sky as if it has a mind of its own. Prudencia steps out of the gym and telekinetically wrenches the gem-grenade apart, blowing it up where it won't harm anyone; she should have slammed it down on these bastards.

"Brighton, you have to stop," Prudencia pleads.

Then a spell is shot straight through Prudencia's chest, and her scream is clipped dead as she falls to the ground.

My eyes sting with tears as a scream escapes my throat.

How many more people will die this morning?

I know the next.

The sniper isn't given the chance to shoot me as I cast a fire-bolt straight into his head, obliterating his skull.

I dash to Prudencia, hovering over her body within a moment. I'm scared to feel for a pulse as I watch her blood bubble and slide across her breasts. She gasps for air because she's alive but she's fighting for her life. I dash inside quickly, doing everything in my power to avoid looking at Ma's corpse because I don't think I'll even be able to crawl if I see her like that again. I'm only in here to see if Eva is awake to heal Prudencia, but she's still unconscious and useless. I run back out to Prudencia, grabbing her hand.

"Do not die," I say.

The light in Prudencia's eyes is fading as her blood keeps spilling. I'm so furious that I want to keep annihilating every single soul who is responsible for all this devastation. But I'm already surrounded by enforcer corpses.

There is no one left to kill, but there is someone I can save.

I lift Prudencia into my arms and begin running down the street, my eyes blurring with tears and my heart pounding as I desperately try to find any Gleam Care center that can keep Prudencia alive. I'm going to need Prudencia for everything that comes next in my life.

She was there for me when I thought Ma was dead, and now she actually is . . . I don't know how I would have gotten through those dark days without Prudencia and all the ways we opened ourselves up to each other and the amazing power couple we could have been and still can be but only if she lives.

Suddenly, I find myself on fire, the silver and sapphire flames stretching out into sharply curved wings as I begin flying—actually flying—as I carry Prudencia through the air like the hero I am, like the hero I've always told everyone I will be, and like the hero this world needs, even if it means leaving behind a street full of bodies like some villain. I am unable to celebrate my new power, but I do recognize that I am that much more powerful now. This only makes me that much stronger when I must fight the true villain, the one who is the reason my mother is dead and the love of my life is dying.

Senator Iron stands no chance against the Infinity Reaper.

THIRTY-FIVE

THE LAST NIGHT

MARIBELLE

I wake up on the floor, covered by a throw blanket and the towel that smells like Tala.

Tala.

Last night we . . . last night Tala and I did everything. It was euphoric, and I'm not just thinking that because we were absolutely drunk out of our minds. I've always thought she was beautiful, but I'd never felt so connected to her outside our shared vengeance as I was when we were sharing stories about our lives and talking about whether hearts could be reborn. Tala said something about how we're like bright stars in a night sky together, and how she was going to be alone without me. Right now I feel lonely without her, wishing her arms were wrapped around me, but she's not here. Then I remember why Tala said she was going to be alone, and I suddenly feel like a little girl waking up on the morning of my birthday.

Tonight, I am bringing Atlas back to life.

I sit up too quickly in excitement, and I'm dizzy with a headrush.

This hangover is brutal. I tug on my ear, trying to get the low whistling out of my head that the wine is named after. I pinch my nostrils and close my mouth and blow hard until the whistling stops. It's a trick Iris taught me after the first time we drank together, sneaking the wine out of a gift basket someone gave her father. I'll have to show Tala this trick too. I need water and food and . . . underwear. I reach over the broken paper birds and grab all my clothes, slowly putting everything on so I can find Tala.

I go through the cottage to see if Tala is enjoying another shower or asleep in an actual bed, but she's not in any of the rooms. She's probably with Roxana. I step outside, not seeing her. I walk around to the backyard, which is also empty. I look up to the clear sky, as if there's a chance I'll see her flying away by phoenix, but a gleeful screech draws my attention down to the shore, where Roxana is splashing her wings in the ocean while Tala sits on the sand.

The fresh air is good on my hangover as I slowly make my way down the hill, daydreaming about being here tomorrow morning with Atlas. We've never been to a beach together, but it's one of many things that will get a second chance. I plop down next to Tala and dig my feet into the sand.

"If you'd flown away after last night, I was going to hunt you down through every cloud and kill you," I say.

Tala keeps staring ahead like she received bad news. "Do you have any regrets?"

"Plenty. This hairstyle when I was ten, not killing June when I had the chance, when I—"

"About last night," Tala interrupts.

"I regret that second bottle."

"Do you regret me?"

I grab her hand. "I don't regret you, Tala. It's not normally something I would've done, but we were drinking and not thinking clearly—"

"Or were you?" Tala asks, squeezing my hand back.

"I love Atlas, Tala."

"I know you do, Mari. But before you discovered you could resurrect Atlas, could you feel your own heart being reborn for me?"

It's lovely outside, but it feels like there's a storm coming between us. Tala is asking if I was falling for her. There have been many times that I've been charmed by her, like when she tossed me that very first paper bird back at the Sanctuary. I've always been entranced by her graceful movements, even when it was her combat skills as she tried killing me. I've even lusted after her, like when I saw her step out of that hot tub in nothing but her bra and compression shorts as well as last night when she was in a baggy shirt and basketball shorts. She's gorgeous and soulful, but I don't think that I've been falling for her?

"Tala, I love having you around. I wasn't alone in my grief because of you."

"But your grief will no longer exist after tonight."

"Not for Atlas, but isn't that a beautiful thing?"

"For you, but not for me," Tala says, ripping her hand out of mine.

"I'm sorry you feel that way, but we were just allies."

"Is that not how you and Atlas got your start?"

"It is, but he has my heart."

"And you have mine, Maribelle. Though now I understand how unwelcomed that is."

The sun is beating down on my skin and my head is foggier than ever because of these new revelations and I'm so tempted to run into the water and stay there. "In another life, I think I could have welcomed you in, Tala. I'm so lucky I met someone like you, someone who loves so fiercely that they lose themselves when their love is lost. But in this life, my love won't be gone anymore."

Tala stands up, clenching her fists. "You may not have any regrets, but I do. Many of them. I went against everything I stand for by siding with you despite your harboring of phoenix powers. More than that, I guided you through the advancement of those powers. I gave away the jacket my parents gave me, believing we were united by the same goals, but then you went and broke our vow to kill Luna." I try getting a word in, but she screams at the sky. "I know! I know everything changed when Atlas's resurrection was suddenly on the table. Even though it went against my vengeance, even though I had Luna within reach, I spared her because it would help you. I forgave you! I even scavenged through corpses of phoenixes, knowing you would desecrate their bodies in the name of your love. I made all these choices because my fire for you keeps burning hotter and hotter and . . . I even started believing we were soulmates who were brought together by our grief." Tala breaks down in angry tears. "I think you burn for me too. Why else would you make your move on the very last night it was possible for you to do so? We opened ourselves up to each other in ways that I never have with anyone. You're the only girl I've kissed since Zahra . . . and the only girl I've ever given myself fully to. Only you, Maribelle. This morning I hoped that it would mean something. That you would maybe leave the dead alone and live your life with me."

I feel sick to my stomach, and it's not because of the alcohol.

Last night, Tala and I not only did everything, but it was her first time having sex.

I'm not her soulmate. I'm only a stain on her soul.

I stand, reaching for her hand again, but she backs away. "It's beautiful to think that once our vengeance was met and our grief faded that I would've had a clearer head and heart to fall for you. But it doesn't appear that we were written in the stars, Tala. That doesn't mean you can't be part of my constellation. Maybe we can shine as best friends. I'm still in the market for a new one."

Tala wipes her tears. "I would be making that choice for you, and I have done enough of that." She looks to the ocean, where Roxana is bobbing her head into the water. "This is where I take to the sky and we diverge ways."

"Where are you going?"

"I don't know. Maybe back to the Halo Knights to regroup or hunt Luna alone." Tala shrugs and takes a deep breath. "Now that I have nothing to lose with you, I am going to say something and hope you can stop being stubborn enough to actually hear me." Her amber eyes turn to me, narrowing with concern. "One trip to the past isn't enough to tell the story of someone's life. You may have discovered the keys to resurrection, but do you know why Fabian tried burning them? Have you stopped and wondered if he ever tried turning those keys himself and it didn't go as planned? That maybe you're not supposed to disturb the natural flow of life and death?"

I try biting my tongue. "This feels like you trying to scare me away from doing the ritual because you want me for yourself."

"I saw you through your heartbreak once before. I won't be around to see you through it again. Goodbye, Maribelle."

Tala turns away, not looking back once as she walks into the water, hops onto Roxana, and takes off into the sky, a rainstorm following them as they fly toward the horizon.

I'm alone on the beach, but I won't be for long, despite Tala's warnings.

I will disturb the natural flow of life and death, no matter the cost.

THIRTY-SIX

MOURN

EMIL

I'm stuck in an infinity loop, reliving Ma's death over and over.

As I was holding Ma's body, I was thinking about Brighton's fire-bolt striking Ma. As Wyatt was trying to drag me out of the gym, I was thinking about Brighton's fire-bolt striking Ma. As I watched Iris carry Ma out into the alley, I was thinking about Brighton's fire-bolt striking Ma. As we all ran down the street to find safety somewhere, I was thinking about Brighton's fire-bolt striking Ma. As Mele ducked out to go stay with her ex-girlfriend, I was thinking about Brighton's fire-bolt striking Ma. As we started hiding in the basement of a nearby celestial church, I was thinking about Brighton's fire-bolt striking Ma. As everyone keeps asking me how I'm doing, all I can think about is Brighton's fire-bolt striking Ma.

Brighton's fire-bolt struck Ma.

My brother's fire-bolt struck our mother.

My brother killed our mother.

Brighton killed Ma.

Ma is dead.

This world doesn't make sense; it straight-up doesn't make sense. How the hell is the world still spinning? It should stop moving or fall through space or get sucked into a black hole, I don't know, something! But the world spinning like my mother isn't dead, like my mother wasn't killed by her son, by my brother. . . . This doesn't make sense.

Nothing matters anymore.

Brighton killing a bunch of enforcers? Doesn't matter.

Prudencia being shot? Doesn't matter.

This country going up in flames once Iron wins? Doesn't matter.

Nothing matters.

The door opens, and everyone is on edge. If the enforcers have found us already, they're going to win. I have no fight in me. A young woman enters, and I'm sure she's going to rat us out because no one can be trusted these days. That would be her right, anyway. We broke into this basement because we're the kind of people who break into churches because nothing matters and nothing is sacred in a world where a mother can be killed by the one son she actually birthed. The young woman sees Ma's body—Ma's corpse—laid out on the floor, where her shirt is soaked in blood and singed from the fire-bolt. The woman glows in a gray light, and it's Ness who falls to his knees, a hand pressed against his heart as he begins crying. Ness finds me from across the room and just stares at me with his head shaking. I almost get up to comfort him, but I'm too broken to move.

"Carolina . . ." Ness says.

Ma doesn't say anything back.

Ness finds the strength to get up. He walks past Wyatt and the Spell Walkers and joins me on the floor. His hands grip my shoulders and he pulls me toward him and his arms are now wrapped around me and I'm crying so hard that I'm gasping for air. Ness isn't telling me that everything will be okay or that I will be okay or that anything will be okay ever again. Through my teary eyes I see everyone watching us. Wyatt seems heartbroken, and there's no way it's got anything to do with what's going on in all our hearts because that doesn't matter anymore either. But maybe Wyatt wishes he could do more so he can end my heartbreak, but all I need right now is this hug, and I'm getting it from someone who also knows what it's like to lose a mother—and to lose a mother because she was killed by family.

Wow.

My brother is in the same camp as Ness's father.

No, Brighton didn't mean to kill Ma the way Iron had Esmeralda Arroyo killed.

But, no, it doesn't matter.

Ma is still dead, killed at the hands of her son.

Brighton's fire-bolt struck Ma, Brighton's fire-bolt struck Ma, Brighton's fire-bolt struck Ma.

I want to ask Ness when things will start making sense again, but I've forgotten how to speak. I've only ever known Ness as someone without a living mother, but I know so much of the good that's in his heart came from Esmeralda and the rest of it has been discovered on his own because nothing good about who Ness is and who Ness wants to be has come from Iron. I want to thank Ness for taking care of Ma when she was held hostage at his house, but again, I can't get any words out.

Ness leans back and squeezes my hands. "I'm so sorry, Emil. This is my fault."

I'm shaking my head.

"It's not your fault, mate," Wyatt says. "You didn't know we were going to be ambushed."

"It *is* my fault," Ness snaps. "I'm the reason the enforcers knew where you were."

I stare him down through teary eyes because this doesn't make sense.

Did Ness betray us? Betray me? Is this another of his double-crossing, triple-crossing plans?

"I was at Sunstar's office, but so was the Senator. He had shifted into Shine and I spoke openly like an idiot, and by the time I realized what happened, the damage was done." Ness squeezes me even tighter. "I am so sorry, Emil. I understand if you never want to see my face again."

There is nothing but pain and guilt written all over Ness's face. I hate seeing him like this, but I would hate never seeing him again even more.

I relive everything again—the flash of the fire-bolt, the celestial enforcer vanishing into the shadow, Ma being blasted into the wall, her final words. All of that isn't Ness's fault. It's not even Brighton's. "This is my fault. No one else's."

Those are my first words since begging Ma to wake up from the dead didn't work.

"This isn't your fault," Ness says.

"I should've never become a Spell Walker," I say, glaring up at all the actual Spell Walkers around me. "I didn't want to fight. I just wanted to figure out the cure to these powers and save phoenixes and end everything that Keon and Bautista started!" I break out of

Ness's hold and point at Iris and Wesley. "I was never cut out for this, I told you that! And look at everything that's happened since I was guilted into becoming this stupid-ass Infinity Son! Atlas was killed. Dr. Bowes was killed. Sunstar has probably been killed too. And now Ma has been killed by Brighton with powers that he should have never had, that he should have never even been close enough to steal!" I'm standing, running so hot that I want to set fire to the bibles and star-studded banners and this cracked silver altar. "This is all my fault for saying yes to becoming a Spell Walker, and now I'm done."

"What do you mean you're done?" Iris asks.

"I quit. I'm no longer a Spell Walker."

"You said you would lead—"

"And then my mother was killed."

Iris looks like she's about to say more, but Eva grabs her hand.

"We understand," Eva says.

"No one will try to convince you to stay," Ruth says.

Wesley turns to the other Spell Walkers. "Then where do we go from here?"

"I want to go home," Ruth says, holding Esther close to her chest.

"Back to the cabin? It's too risky."

"It's the one place they've never found us, but if they do, at least we'll all be together."

Iris stands on a wooden table so she can see through the tiny window that looks out to the church's backyard. "If we're going to get to the cabin, we should make moves now before anyone tracks us down."

"We should stock up before hunkering down," Wesley says. He brushes Esther's hair. "Hopefully this is the last time we go shopping and traveling with the baby for a while."

"It's pretty sad that it might be," Ruth says.

"Let's go," Iris says. She stops at the doorway when no one follows her.

Wesley and Ruth come up to me.

"You can't convince me to keep being a Spell Walker," I say.

Ruth shakes her head. "We're not trying to. Is there anything we can do for you? Do you want to have a private funeral? Do you need help with a burial or cremation?"

I haven't stopped to think about any of those things. "I'm not cremating Ma. She'll be buried next to Dad."

"Do you want our help, bud?" Wesley asks.

"I got it," I say.

I want to thank them for all the good they've done and hospitality they've shown, but I choke on the words. Nothing outweighs this loss, not even the good. All I can think about right now is how Wesley was always willing to put the mission above my family, like when Brighton was being held hostage and tortured by the Blood Casters and Wesley didn't vote to go save him. That pissed off Brighton so much that he really believed he needed powers to defend himself in a world where the heroes will sacrifice him. And Ruth . . . there's nothing bad about Ruth. But even right now as she hugs me, wishing me well, I can't bring myself to step up for her. We are no longer a team and we're definitely not a family.

Eva kneels before Ma, holding her limp fingers. "I'm sorry I couldn't save you, Carolina. May you rest well in the brightest of stars."

Somewhere, if the universe is good, Ma and Dad are together again . . . and they're watching me give up my heroics and Brighton terrorize everyone unchecked.

The Spell Walkers all pause at the doorway.

"Take care of yourselves," Iris says.

She leaves, and this time they all follow.

I should care more about failing the Spell Walkers, about failing everyone, but I just don't or I can't and I don't have the energy to figure out if it's one or the other or both. I'm just done. I wish I felt freer, the type of euphoria I'm hoping I'll feel once I chug the Star-stifler and bind these powers forever. Once I'm powerless, no one will ever bother me about saving the world because I'll be nothing but a famous nobody who failed to do the job when I had the powers and will be extra useless now that I don't.

I'm left alone in the basement with Ness and Wyatt and Ma's corpse.

"What can we do for you?" Wyatt asks. "Are you hungry? Would you like to rest? We can keep a lookout."

I'm so tired and tempted to lie down next to Ma, just like I would whenever I was sick or sad or even happy. But I don't want to wake up next to Ma even more unnatural as she already is.

"I've got to bury Ma," I say.

"We can help you," Ness says.

"No. I've got to bury Ma with Brighton. She's our mother."

Wyatt and Ness look at each other like I'm saying something in another language.

"Can you trust him to not pull something?" Ness asks.

"Might he not try and disempower you?" Wyatt asks.

"You're talking about losing my powers or life like that's a bad thing," I say.

"Firefly—"

"Don't 'firefly' me. If you guys want to help, then go with my flow. If not, it's not too late to catch up with the Spell Walkers."

Ness and Wyatt don't fight me. They start talking to each other about whatever.

I sit down next to Ma, crying as I hold her hand, wishing it could wipe away my tears one last time. But then that fire-bolt keeps flashing in my head.

Maybe once I bury Ma, I will stop reliving her death.

Maybe I will relive her death for the rest of my life.

THIRTY-SEVEN

THE REAL ENEMY

BRIGHTON

I'm flying toward the Capella Center for Gleam Care with my new burning wings as I carry Prudencia in my arms like a true superhero. I have never felt more heroic than this moment because Prudencia needs true saving. Her pulse is slowing down scarily fast. I don't bother descending to the main entrance and instead fly straight to the building's top level, phasing through the wall so Prudencia can be treated immediately. The gleamcraft practitioners in the hallway are shocked by our sudden appearance, but I snap them into gear with a plead and a threat.

"Save her life or you all will die."

In moments, Prudencia is stretched out across a bed and a team of celestials are hovering over her. A clerk reaches for a phone, fear in his eyes, and I snatch it from his hand and melt it in my own before he can call security. One look ensures he won't try this again. Someone braver begins asking me questions like who Prudencia is and what happened to her and what is our relationship to one another and other data that won't actually stop Prudencia, who is already ghost white, from bleeding out. All I can do is stand here and watch as one practitioner cauterizes Prudencia's wound with a burning touch, allowing the others the time to slowly but steadily heal her. It's unfortunate that more celestials do not have Eva's level of healing, but if she ever decides to wake up, then she can finish the job that these practitioners have started.

No one will be able to heal Ma, though.

For all the powers I have—fire-casting and swift-speed and phasing and self-healing and camouflaging and flying—I cannot bring back the dead.

I also cannot undo the deaths I've caused.

On a nearby TV, the news is reporting the catastrophe that happened at the gym. There's a clip of me annihilating the enforcers, and the footage cuts off right before the sniper's head exploded from my fire-bolt. It's interesting how that is too graphic for viewers, but the reporters couldn't be bothered to show why they all had to die. There was nothing in that programming about Prudencia getting shot or any evidence of that celestial enforcer causing so much chaos and confusion that I killed Ma accidentally. The only thing they are promoting is a picture of my face with the word *WANTED* stamped under it. It goes to show that Senator Iron has many vocal supporters like the Silver Star Slayer, but other stations are still in his pocket, just a lot more discreet about it. I destroy the TV with a fire-bolt, scaring everyone once more.

"Save her!" I shout.

The practitioners wheel Prudencia into a room, closing the door behind them. I phase right through it.

"Allow us some privacy," one says.

"No, I have to make sure—"

"We will do everything we can to help her, but we can't work comfortably with you watching us!"

"Fine."

I am letting them get their way, but I am getting mine too. I will indeed be watching these practitioners to make sure they are caring for Prudencia properly, only they won't realize I'm so close to them that I can rip out their hearts the second Prudencia flatlines. I step outside the room, then phase right back in, camouflaging myself against the wall. Then I am still and working hard to stay so quiet that they won't hear me breathing or fighting back the cry that's building in the back of my throat.

If she dies, then so will the rest of the world.

After waiting and waiting and waiting, I watch the color return to Prudencia's face.

"Have we identified her?" one practitioner asks.

"It's Prudencia Mendez. She's an ally of the Spell Walkers," another says.

"Any family we can contact?"

"Her only living relative is an aunt. We can call her—"

"Absolutely not," they hear me say, still unable to see me. They must think the wall is speaking until I reveal myself. "Her aunt is a gleamphobic nightmare."

The practitioners all seem nervous.

"Anyone else we can contact?" one asks.

I'm ready to put down Ma as Prudencia's emergency contact, when I'm struck with the violent memory of Ma being blasted by my fire-bolt. Then her on the floor, unable to finish saying my name as she died. It's impossible to shut this out, but I keep my voice steady and strong as I tell the practitioners, "I am her point of contact. I assume you all know who I am."

No one asks because I'm famous. Maybe even infamous after this morning.

Prudencia groans, and I push past the practitioners to be at her side.

"Give me time alone with her."

"She should rest—"

"Alone!" I shout, fully waking up Prudencia. The practitioners move for the door when I stop them. "Do not tell anyone she is here. The last time someone revealed our location at a hospital, a doctor was killed by a Blood Caster," I share, thinking about Dr. Bowes getting her neck snapped because Darren couldn't keep his mouth shut. I'm now realizing that Darren and I have both indirectly killed our mothers. That's a terrible thing to have in common. My anger is roaring, and I'm so close to killing everyone in this hospital wing to guarantee our privacy. "If you endanger Prudencia's life, I will claim all of yours." My eyes burn like eclipses as a final warning. "You're all dismissed."

The practitioners leave. I don't need to be able to see the future to know that Prudencia is safe here.

"What's . . . what's going on?" Prudencia weakly asks.

I grab her hand. "I got you to the hospital just in time. We actually flew here—I think my desperation triggered my power to fly." I'm stupid to think Prudencia would be impressed by this when she hasn't genuinely cared for any of my abilities, but given that this new power was born so she could live she could be somewhat appreciative.

Instead she says nothing and stares into space. "How are you feeling? The practitioners did the best they could, but we can get Eva to heal—"

"Carolina?"

Hearing Ma's name is like getting hit by a surprise spell.

"Dead."

I can't believe that's how I have to talk about Ma now. For the better part of this year, whenever someone checked in about Ma it's because they wanted to know how she's been doing since we all lost Dad. They cared about me and Emil too obviously, but we lost our father whereas Ma lost the love of her life. We couldn't understand what she was going through. I'd let people know which days were better and harder for Ma, and that would be that. But now I have to tell people that she doesn't have any feelings because she's dead.

Prudencia tries sitting up on her own, but needs help. She stares into my eyes. "I'm sorry, Brighton."

"It's not your fault. Emil shouldn't have had Ma with him."

"This isn't Emil's fault."

"It certainly isn't mine."

She's quiet.

"It's not!"

"I know you didn't mean to, but your power—"

"My power, my powers do good! I was tricked."

Prudencia takes a deep breath, which brings her some discomfort. She begins crying and squeezes my hand. "Brighton, I know you're hurting here and I don't blame you, but . . . don't you think you should bind your powers now? Carolina got caught in the cross fire of your pointless war against Emil, and now she's gone. Let's end this now so no one has to get hurt again."

I shake my head. "No. I will not rest until the real enemy is taken down."

"Emil isn't your enemy."

"I'm not talking about him."

"Then who?"

"I will crush Senator Iron for what he has taken from me—for what he made me do."

Prudencia pulls her hand out of mine. "You're going to assassinate a presidential candidate?"

"I am going to assassinate a man whose abuse of power killed my mother."

"Your killing spree has already taken things too far, but do you think anyone could ever possibly see you as a hero again if you kill Iron?"

"My killing spree?"

"Did I hallucinate you ripping out a heart and snapping a neck and bombing enforcers?"

Those were all fast, merciful kills. I should have kept the celestial enforcer alive and tortured him for all of infinity. "You're not actually defending the people who were sent there to kill you? The one who would've killed you if I hadn't been there to save you?" She's doing all this judging without knowing that I obliterated her would-be killer's skull with a fire-bolt. I'm sure she'd really see me as a monster if she knew that. "You lost your parents to wand violence and almost got killed the same way. Can't you see that I'm doing good?"

Prudencia's head hangs low. Did I go too far by bringing up her dead parents? She certainly doesn't seem to have an issue accusing me of killing my mother. How about I go ahead and blame her for not interfering with their deaths, for not using her power to save her parents?

"Do you remember the promise you made on your birthday?" Prudencia asks.

That was only a month and a half ago, but I don't remember. Maybe with a clearer head I could find the memory, but unfortunately my mom is dead and I'm being given shit for killing enforcers who were out for blood. "I don't."

She sighs. "I was upset with you and Emil for being reckless on the first night of the Crowned Dreamer. You were so annoyed that your video didn't go viral, but all I could think about was how easily I could've lost you two as quickly as I lost my parents. I told you both that I didn't want you in my life if you couldn't promise to run away the next time there was chaos, and not only do you keep running toward chaos, you keep creating it, Brighton. You get to be furious at the world for what's happened to Carolina, but you can't keep pretending that you're doing good by committing crimes." Prudencia wipes the tears from her cheeks and glares. "Thank you for saving my life, but if the cost to do so is over other lives, then promise you'll let me die and keep that one."

That's such a ludicrous thing to think, let alone say. "Do you really value your life so little that you'd rather lose it than have it stolen by people who only see you as the enemy, even when you're innocent?"

"As far as the world is concerned, I will never be innocent, even when I'm just existing and not bothering anyone. I hid my powers to live a normal life and you've just made that so much more impossible for me after you've proven how easy it is to snap and murder anyone with your gleam. I am always going to be seen as a threat because of real abusers of power like you, and that's especially true if you go and kill Iron."

"*When* I kill Iron," I say.

If no one wants me to be the Infinity Savior, then I will settle into being the Infinity Reaper.

Prudencia's phone begins ringing. She pulls it out of her pocket, and it's different from the one she had last. "It's Emil."

"Let me talk to him."

She seems reluctant at first but hands me the phone.

I answer the call. "Emil?"

"Bright?" Emil asks, crying. "Where are you? Where's Pru?"

"She's safe. I got her healed up."

"Okay. . . . Can we have a, I don't know, time-out on everything?"

"Why?"

"Ma is dead, Brighton. Before you keep trying to kill me, maybe we should bury her together."

First I will bury Ma. Then I will kill Iron.

THIRTY-EIGHT

THE PHOENIX PIT

MARIBELLE

I'm standing before the Phoenix Pit, about to pass the point of no return.

Tala's parting words haven't left my head. She's trying to warn me away from resurrecting Atlas because surely there's a reason Fabian never chose to resurrect anyone himself. I don't have any proof that Fabian didn't. It's not as if retrocycling allows me to download that person's memories while I'm walking through a specific moment in their lives. What I do know is that Fabian never brought back his family and they haunted him for it, driving Fabian to suicide. And what I know even more, deep in my heart, is that after spending the day meditating on whether or not I should be tapping into this dark gleam, Atlas deserves another shot at life, no matter the risk.

Atlas was a hero to all, and he will be again.

This resurrection is as much for the world as it is for me.

Even if Atlas never wanted to save another life, he still deserves his.

And I still want him back more than anything.

I kneel before the grave, about to start digging when I think about

Tala. Everything that happened between us last night was not only because of the whistle wine we drank. That was just the spark to our flame. But that fire is being put out because Atlas is coming back to life. My bond with Tala will never grow beyond allies, and we're not even that anymore. If this resurrection doesn't work, then I will be as lonely as I was feeling before Tala flew into my life. She's already gone, so what do I have to lose by trying? The worst that can happen is Atlas returning as some soulless killer. Then it's kill or be killed. Maybe being killed will save me from a life of more pain.

The bottle with Atlas's ashes is sitting at the head of the grave, almost like it's his headstone.

It's not as cold as when Luna was resurrecting June in December, but this evening October air is even chillier because of the proximity to the ocean. I work up a sweat by digging through the grave, clawing the soil by hand, just like I did yesterday when making this hole. I unearth the phoenix, but unlike yesterday when I was laying the sun swallower to rest, I carry its stiff corpse out of the grave, which will hopefully allow Atlas to keep his soul, and lay it down under a tree. I pray to the shining stars that the sun swallower's essences have had enough time to seep into the earth so this all goes according to plan.

I don't have a water tank and can't find any garden hose, so I make trips back and forth between the house and the Pit, sweating as I carry buckets of water to fill up the grave. Once it's filled to the edges, I hold dark yellow flames over the grave until the water begins boiling like a cauldron, its many bubbles spawning and popping.

I open the feathered drawstring bag from the Sanctuary that holds all the phoenix parts. I don't want to think about how bloody and nauseating that experience was, I only want to be on the other side of those dark memories and hugging Atlas already. I'm not reciting Luna's little incantations since they had nothing to do with Fabian's notes. I drop in the breath spawn's bones, the gray sun's heart, the century's feathers, the obsidian's eyes, and the crowned elder's egg hatchings.

Then it's time for Atlas's ashes.

I couldn't have known that by cremating Atlas with my phoenix fire and saving his ashes that it would have ever led to this moment. I'd only ever intended to one day summon his ghost and send him to rest in peace, which only the person responsible for the other's death can do. I never thought I'd be able to bring him back.

I open the bottle and pause.

This is my only shot. Am I sure the conditions are right? The stars are above, but should the phoenix fire come from an actual phoenix or will my fire work? My powers have allowed me to retrocycle and fly like phoenixes, so why wouldn't this work too? I've already made the Phoenix Pit. If I turn back now, I will have to go find the necessary body parts all over, and unless I can find one of Luna's vaults of ingredients or stumble onto another gravesite for phoenixes, that could take more time. Time spent alone and—

I spill Atlas's ashes into the Phoenix Pit.

There is no turning back now.

I cast dark yellow flames onto the grave.

The same fire that cremated Atlas will now also return him to flesh.

"Undo a death, renew a life," I whisper, I beg.

The dark yellow flames roar as they rise higher and higher. I knew when retrocycling to June's resurrection that it was always going to work, but I don't carry that same confidence now. Maybe I should have waited for a real phoenix to cast their fire into the Pit instead of trusting my own. Fabian's notes didn't say anything about a specter's gleam being effective in this ritual. It couldn't have hurt to use Luna's incantations either; maybe she knew something that I didn't. I could have wasted these ashes, forbidding me from ever seeing Atlas again, not even his ghost to apologize for the role I played in his death, or maybe I've done something far worse and am creating a monster. I'm trying to stay in tune with my body as if my psychic sense is about to warn me of some great danger, but all I feel is my body shaking and my heart pounding.

The stars will never align to help me out.

The flames turn into a fiery silhouette.

Ashes turned to fire and now fire turns to flesh.

A naked boy with blond hair and surprise in his gray eyes stands before me.

Atlas Haas is alive.

THIRTY-NINE

UNDONE, RENEWED

MARIBELLE

Atlas's first breath is sharp, like he's been underwater and coming up for air, and not dead for weeks. For a moment it seems like he's choking, but he breathes and finds life—the new life I gave him.

The life I found for him.

I still can't believe he's here. I actually did it.

"Mari?" Atlas croaks, and then clears his throat. "Mari?"

I would have happily lived the rest of my life never hearing Atlas say my nickname or any other word ever again as long as he was alive by my side, but this is music to my ears.

"Atlas," I breathe. I don't bother wiping my tears as I run straight into his arms. He's real and solid and his skin is warm even though it's chilly outside. It's as if he's still being reborn in phoenix fire. I stroke his face and run my fingers through his blond hair and squeeze his arms and press my palm against his chest to feel his heartbeat. I'm nervous that his heart might be still, as if he's dead inside despite standing upright and breathing, but his heart is beating strong and fast. I break down and cry even more. "I missed you so much."

He holds me close. "Shh, shh. It's okay."

I feel like I've traveled back in time to the many nights following the Blackout when Atlas became the only person who could comfort me. It's as if we're in one of the many beds we've shared and he's holding me as I fall asleep. I've missed touching him and being touched by him so much, and I don't have to miss this ever again.

"Maribelle?"

I look him in the eyes.

"Why am I naked?" Atlas looks around. "Where are we? What's going on?"

I don't want to let go, but I break our hug to give him the clothes I laid out. "What's the last thing you remember?"

Atlas steps into Wesley's sweatpants, drawing the string in and tying a knot. "I was . . . I was in the air. . . ." He puts on his shirt, and his eyebrows narrow like when he's confused. "We were fighting the Blood Casters at the museum and . . ." He looks around and spots the cabin. "Now we're at Wesley's secret house?"

"You don't remember anything else?"

"No. Am I blacking out?"

For a moment, I've wondered if I did the ritual wrong. Maybe I cost him his memories. Back when we were discovering our abilities to retrocycle, Wyatt dragged on with this story about how phoenixes sometimes lose memories between rebirths and that's why they mentally travel back in the past to recall what they've forgotten. I could've screwed something up here. I was too impatient with the ritual and instead of using the fire from a phoenix I used my own power thinking that would be enough. But Atlas remembers who I am and where he was last. He doesn't remember dying because the spell shot through his heart so fast that he never realized he was even being killed.

"You were dead, Atlas."

He looks at me stone-faced before breaking into laughter. "Weird joke, Mari."

"I'm not joking."

"How did I die?"

"I killed you," I say. Atlas laughs even harder, his abs contracting as he puts on his shirt. "Technically, June killed you, but she did it while possessing my body. You've been dead for almost a month." As his head pops out through his shirt, he's no longer smiling. There have been a lot of things Atlas has found funny about me, like the way my voice cracks when I wake up, but I've never been the comedian or lighthearted one between the two of us. He takes a good look at me as if the moon and stars are now illuminating everything about me—my dirty, bloodstained hands, the shadows under my eyes, some weight loss from grieving too hard to feed myself.

"How?" Atlas whispers.

"June forced me to cast a spell through your heart."

He winces and touches his chest, as if he's also trying to see if his heart is beating. "I meant how am I alive if . . ." He can't seem to bring himself to say he was dead. I didn't want to either.

"I resurrected you."

Atlas looks so confused. He told me that he would pinch himself a lot when he was a kid whenever he heard something so unbelievable, but he hasn't done that since he received the news that his parents were arrested and thrown into the San Diego Bounds for robbing a bank with their powers. That was the moment that forced him to grow up in a life that was already hard for him. I almost expect him to pinch himself all over now, but he just stands there.

"I know this is a lot," I say, holding his hands. He stares down at mine in horror. There really isn't a manual on how to welcome someone back from the dead. The only other example I have is June freaking out upon her resurrection and Luna knocking her out with a dagger's handle. I'm not striking him.

Atlas stares at me like I'm a stranger. "What did you do, Mari?"

It's as if Atlas has now shot me in the heart. I take a step back from him and fold my arms like I have to be guarded against him even though he's the one looking at me like I'm some beast. I've been hardened because of how I've grown up, and sharpened since the Blackout. Atlas has heard me wish painful, torturous deaths on my enemies during my lowest of lows and still never judged me. But he's just discovered that he was dead and I've brought him back to life to a world where resurrection is apparently real and he has no idea what that involves. I'm tempted to take this story to the grave, but I didn't bring Atlas back to life to keep secrets from him.

"So much has changed since you've been dead. I don't even know where to start."

"The beginning, Maribelle. What happened after I died?"

"I freaked out and a new power surfaced."

"A new power?"

Dark yellow flames begin glowing in my cupped hands, burning so bright that it illuminates Atlas's shocked face. Between the two of us, I was always the close combat fighter and he fought from a distance with his winds. Now I have fire that I've used to burn an alchemist alive. "My biological parents are Bautista de León and Sera

Córdova. When you died, it ignited something in me and woke up all these phoenix powers. I can cast fire. I don't just levitate anymore; I can fully fly. I can even transport my consciousness back into the lives of my ancestors. What I wish I could've tapped into more than anything are the visions I have because of Sera. Do you remember how I dreamed about my parents dying before the Blackout? Sera could foresee deaths too. My dream was a vision, and if I'd known that I could've nurtured it and tried to stop them and even foreseen what was going to happen to you and—" I stop myself because Atlas is staring at me like I'm speaking Latin. "You're so lost right now."

He keeps staring. "This is a lot to take in."

"That's only covering the hours after your death."

"Wow."

"We don't have to talk about everything now. We have our whole lives ahead of us again."

Atlas sinks to the ground, inches away from the Phoenix Pit. "No, I want to know everything that's happened since I died."

∞

Atlas and I are still under the stars, and a dark yellow campfire is keeping us warm.

"I don't know if I'm going to get used to that," Atlas had said when I cast the fire so we would beat the cold.

That new power is easier to swallow than everything else I've shared with him tonight: how I quit the Spell Walkers and forged an alliance with Brighton to take on the Blood Casters; how we ultimately failed to protect the century phoenix, Gravesend, but did manage to prevent Luna from becoming immortal; how Brighton stole the Reaper's Blood for himself and has become his own hero, who is now at war with Emil over their differences; how Luna is my grandmother and how I spared her life because she told me that I could resurrect Atlas; how my new ability to retrocycle is what allowed me to travel to the past to discover the secrets of resurrection.

"And that leads us here," I say. "This is the Phoenix Pit where you were reborn."

Atlas stares at the scorched earth. "This doesn't feel real."

"This doesn't feel real to me either," I say. I grab his hands. "But you're real."

"How come my death and even my rebirth don't feel as shocking as everything else? It's like one moment I was flying and fighting in the museum and the next I'm outside Wes's house and being told that everything has changed."

"It's how I felt too when I learned about my family tree and powers and the ritual."

"You've had more time to process it."

"Not a lot."

"But more than me. You're now this superpowered badass who travels through time and brings back the dead. The original founders of the Spell Walkers are your parents. Our biggest enemy is your grandmother. Imagine if I told you right now that I'm actually an eight-hundred-year-old celestial with control over every weather element. Oh, and I'm also the only specter in the world with dragon blood and I can breathe fire and hatch eggs and—"

"I get it."

He takes a deep breath. "I believe you, but this is also too much to believe."

Ever since my secrets have come to light, I'm always on edge for whatever big thing will turn my life upside down next. Discovering Bautista and Sera were my biological parents was one thing, but learning Luna is my grandmother was another. "It's shocking to wake up to all of this, but I wasn't exactly charmed to live through this either," I snap, and instantly regret it. "I'm sorry, but I've had to go through all of these unbelievable things and make them make sense."

Atlas closes his eyes and hangs his head. "I'm an idiot. You had it far worse." I still feel like I'm speaking to a ghost until Atlas pulls me toward him, reminding me how real he is. I rest my head in his lap and look up at his gray eyes as if they are the shiniest stars in the night sky above us. "I'm sorry that you were so alone, Mari. I can't imagine grieving you by myself."

Out of everything I've told Atlas, there are some things I haven't gotten to yet. "I wasn't totally alone. I made an . . . ally. This Halo Knight named Tala whose parents were killed at the museum by the Blood Casters. Tala also wanted her revenge on Luna, but when we were ready to execute her, she backed off because of Luna's promise to bring you back, even though there was nothing in it for her."

"Luna couldn't bring her parents back?"

"Their ashes were already gone."

"That's bad luck. Where is Tala now?"

It's a great question. "Probably hunting Luna."

"Well, I'd like to thank Tala for looking after you while I was gone."

Will he feel that way once he discovers her feelings for me? I think so. Atlas has never been the jealous type. I've also never given him any reason to be. My heart has only ever been his since he entered my life, and I would've never thought I'd be sharing an intimate night with anyone but him. If it had to be anyone, I'm happy it was Tala.

"Maybe we'll cross paths with Tala again," I say, and hope.

Watching Tala fly away on Roxana can't be the last time that I ever see her.

Atlas brushes my hair. "Thank you for resurrecting me."

"I didn't want to live without you."

"I'm sorry you had to."

"So you're not mad?"

"Mad? I'm confused, but I could never be mad. I get to be alive again with the love of my life." Our fingers lock together as Atlas smiles down at me. "Does this mean you're stuck with me forever? Or would Maribelle 2.0 have it in her heart to resurrect someone and break up with them?"

I straddle his lap and run my fingers through his blond hair. "You're mine for life, Atlas. Nothing will get between us ever again. Not even death."

"My superpowered hero," Atlas says while pulling me in closer. "I love you."

"I love you too," I say with a tear in my eye. I haven't been this happy in forever. Between losing my parents and then Atlas, this has been my most heartbreaking year, but my grief is quieter now.

I kiss my resurrected boyfriend on his lips, which are no longer ashes because of me. Atlas and I are becoming one, rolling around in the burnt soil of the Phoenix Pit as if we're in a field of flowers, and we make love under the stars that helped undo his death and renew his life.

I feel reborn too.

When you lose someone, you lose every chance to do anything with them ever again. Kiss, fight, love. I never thought it would be possible to be this close to Atlas again—to kiss him, to make love to him, to laugh at how dirty our naked bodies are after having sex on the ground. My campfire helps us find the clothes that we launched across the darkness while undressing.

"That's really why you brought me back, right?" Atlas jokes.

"Absolutely. You can go die again."

Atlas shakes my hand. "Pleasure doing business with you."

"And you."

He pulls me closer and kisses me again. "Should we go inside and lie down on a real bed?"

"Only because I don't want you moaning about a rock trying to kill you."

"It really hurt!"

I grab the buckets I was using to fill the Phoenix Pit. "I should go inside and get water for this fire anyway before we burn the cabin down."

"Allow me," Atlas says. His eyes glow like countless stars being sucked into a black hole. A gust of wind funnels out of his palm and extinguishes the fire. Everything happens so quickly that I can barely form my thoughts as I begin smiling at the steam. "What?"

"You still have your powers. I wasn't sure if you would. You really are . . . you."

"I'm me."

I didn't botch the resurrection. Atlas Haas is Atlas Haas. It's almost too good to be true.

We walk inside the cabin, the living room still a mess. Atlas is used to cleaning up after me, especially from when I was so consumed from grieving my parents and trying to uncover June's identity, but it's sickening to watch him pick up pillows from the floor that Tala and I were using after having sex.

"This is nice and cozy," Atlas says, fluffing the pillow on the couch. "If you're really done being a Spell Walker, maybe we should get our own home in the middle of nowhere."

That was always a dream for the future, one that lives again because Atlas does too. But I have to be honest with him about Tala. It's not as if I cheated on him because he wasn't even alive, but it still feels that way. I feel stupid and weak, as if my love for Atlas wasn't strong enough to hold out for one more night of not being intimate with someone, even if that someone is special in my eyes and heart. If anything, I've betrayed Tala more than I betrayed Atlas. He gets to be with me whereas Tala's only company is her phoenix. Still, I feel guilty and need to come clean.

"Believe it or not, there's more to talk about."

"I believe it," Atlas says, sitting on the couch and patting the cushion next to him.

I'm about to join him, when I hear a car passing by—a car pulling in. I'm not sensing any danger, but I can only trust this power so much since I still don't know if I've reached its full potential. I peek out the window to see Wesley in the driver's seat before the beaming headlights are switched off, shrouding the passengers in the car.

"Wesley is here," I say.

Atlas's eyes widen, and he rushes for the door.

"Hold on. Let me prepare him."

"He doesn't know?"

I shake my head. "Only Tala knows I was attempting this tonight."

"I can't wait to see the look on his face," Atlas says, bouncing.

"I'll knock on the door when it's time for you to come out."

I leave the cabin just as Wesley has parked the car. His jaw drops when he sees me coming out of his house. If he's this surprised at the sight of me, his jaw will fall off his face when Atlas shows his. The rest of the car doors open and Ruth comes out the back with Esther cradled in her arms and Eva comes out the other side. I'm surprised my psychic sense isn't blaring when Iris steps out from the front passenger's seat, staring at me with daggers in her eyes. Our friendship has degraded so much, and I don't know that we'll ever greet each other with warmth again. The Spell Walkers all look like they've been through the wringer—dried blood on shredded clothes, bruises, exhaustion.

"What happened?" I ask.

"Hell of a way to say hello," Iris says.

"That wasn't much better," Eva says.

Ruth looks at me with concern. "Are you okay, Maribelle?"

"I'm fine," I say. "What about you?"

"Are you not watching the news?" Iris asks.

"I've been busy."

"Doing what exactly?"

Wesley shushes Iris. "Give it a break. Please. It's been a long day." He turns to me. "I'm happy to see you, Maribelle, but you're also the last person I'd expect to find here. What's going on?"

In his world, finding me outside his home is the most unexpected. But the world has been undone and renewed, and we can all dream bigger now.

"I'm sorry to crash at your place, but I needed somewhere safe to stay. I've been really busy since the Bounds. I went there to kill Luna, but I ended up sparing her life because she told me she could help me do the unimaginable." I can see Iris about to fire off some snarky comment, so I hold my hand up. "Yes, I believed her, and I'm happy I did because it's changed my life. It's changed life and death as we all know it."

Iris folds her arms. "Are you going to keep being cryptic?"

"This coming from the girl who kept my family tree a secret?"

Wesley looks like he might implode. Whatever they've all been through today, it's cast a shadow over the joy he tends to emanate, even in difficult situations. "As someone who has never kept anything from you, I'm asking you what is going on."

I knock on the door so Atlas can answer the question himself.

The Spell Walkers all eye the door, bracing themselves for some threat because that's how we've always had to live. It's rare that a door opens and it's not someone who wants us dead. But then the door opens and the loved one who steps out is someone who has fought to keep us alive.

Atlas waves. "Hi."

They're all staring at him like he's a ghost.

Wesley shakes his head. "No way."

"Yes way," Atlas says.

"It's really him," I say.

Wesley turns to me. "What is this? Is this Iron shape-shifting?"

"Iron can shape-shift now?" Atlas asks.

The Spell Walkers are still confused.

Wesley is tearing up. "Why are you pranking us like this? This can't be Atlas. Atlas is dead."

"Was dead," Atlas says. He grabs my hand. "I'm alive again thanks to her."

Everyone is still in shock, which is understandable. Everything we've known about resurrection has only ever been about phoenixes or Emil being reincarnated as a completely different person with past lives he doesn't remember living. Atlas is who he was before he died.

"I don't believe it," Wesley says.

"Ask me something only I would know," Atlas says with a challenging grin.

Wesley wipes a tear as he thinks. "What did I do on the first morning of the Crowned Dreamer?"

"You told Iris you were going to help a celestial with errands, but you really took a nap inside a movie theater because you were exhausted from making the trip out here to see your girls."

Wesley bites his bottom lip because he's been exposed for lying, but then snaps back to reality. "Atlas?"

"Atlas!" Atlas shouts.

Wesley is shaking as he walks toward Atlas. This is the slowest I've ever seen him move. He's so slow that Atlas runs into his best friend's arms, and they begin sobbing together. It's not long before Iris and Eva and Ruth are hugging Atlas too.

I've never been prouder of anything in my life.

It's as if we really are the constellation that the Spell Walkers are named for, and I personally plucked a fallen star out of the shadows and set it back into the sky.

Now I have to tell everyone how I saved Atlas from the darkness.

It's late and the Spell Walkers should be exhausted, but they're more energized than when they first arrived because of Atlas's resurrection and my story of everything that led to it. We're all gathered together in the living room, all three couples sitting together, and Wesley is close enough to us that he keeps poking Atlas to make sure he's real. Atlas jokingly threatens to punch Wesley in the face if that'll help him believe it sooner before he bruises his arm.

"It's a good thing you didn't spread my ashes," Atlas tells me.

"If it weren't for me wanting to summon your ghost after I avenged you to apologize, I would've."

"I was there for your cremation," Wesley says. He loses the light in his eyes as he remembers. "I really wish we would've just buried you."

"I never wanted a burial," Atlas says. "Those corpses always look unnatural. I wanted to be remembered as I was."

"Unfortunately I remember you as a pile of ashes. But I guess we have the chance to create better memories now."

I turn to Iris. "I only wish I had the ashes of our parents to resurrect them too."

We didn't get to bury my parents or her parents or anyone who died during the Blackout because of the pure destruction that June caused with those gem-grenades. Bodies were decimated into ashes, and if I could've, I would've tried bringing everyone back to life. I can only imagine the horrors of what would be reborn with all those ashes spread together.

Iris sighs. "I have to be honest. I'm struggling here. Atlas, I'm obviously happy you're alive again. But have we thought about what this means for the country?"

I squeeze Atlas's hand hard like it's a stress ball. "I don't care about this country that doesn't care about me."

"Maybe you don't, but Atlas does. Don't you?"

Atlas nods. "Of course. But isn't my resurrection good for the country? I can get back to saving people."

Iris leans forward. "Did you not tell Atlas about Iron's whole campaign?"

I have had my boyfriend back for a couple of hours, and it's been impossible to fill him in on everything he has missed in that time. Admittedly, this election hasn't exactly been high up on the list since I'm no longer in the business of saving people who want me dead. "That's not a weight Atlas needs to carry."

"It is. Ever since Brighton exposed Emil's past lives, Iron has been casting fear on the public that gleamcrafters are so powerful that we're willing to break the laws of life and death. It was another lie, but now it's true. Atlas, you deserve to be alive and we're not going to reverse what has happened here, but you can't be seen if we're going to keep this a secret. You can't appear on any battlefield—"

"Fantastic because I don't want us fighting anyway," I snap.

"Fine, then stay out of every park and coffee shop and anywhere in the public. Once Atlas is seen, then celestials everywhere will pay the price."

"I can hide until after Sunstar has won the election," Atlas says.

"If we find her," Iris says.

"What?"

"Long story short, Sunstar was kidnapped by Iron's people. We have no idea if she's even alive, but if she is and she's lucky enough to be voted into office, you can't just pop out after she's begun her presidency without pissing off everyone and proving Iron right. That can lead to a revolt."

I'm so angry I could burn this place to the ground. Why can't I have one good thing in my life? Between Iris telling him that he can't show his face anywhere and Atlas wanting to keep fighting, this isn't what I imagined when I performed the ritual. I did all of this so Atlas and I could restart our lives together, not risk them again and again or keep hiding from those who hate us.

"I'm so tired of living in havens instead of homes," I say.

Iris lets out a deep breath. "We all are, Maribelle. This is what we've been fighting for. This is the fight you walked away from, but you can't really have thought you could resurrect your boyfriend and then grab dinner at a fancy restaurant with no consequences."

"I'll settle for a hole-in-the-wall," I say.

"We can't let more people die because I'm alive," Atlas says.

"Then we bring them back!"

Iris sucks her teeth and rises in frustration. "This is insane. Am I the only one who thinks we shouldn't do the exact thing that Iron is accusing us of?"

Eva squeezes her girlfriend's shoulder. "I agree, but this could have waited until the morning."

Ruth sheepishly raises her hand. "Are we planning on keeping this ritual a secret?"

"Only if you don't want another speech from Iris," I say.

Ruth begins crying. "In that case—"

"We shouldn't," Iris interrupts.

"Shouldn't what?" I ask.

A shadow seems to be cast over the Spell Walkers.

"As a mother, I have to put this out there," Ruth says. "Carolina was killed tonight."

"By Brighton," Wesley adds. "It was a mistake. We were ambushed by enforcers, and he was tricked into killing her."

"He was reckless," Iris says.

"An innocent woman was killed nonetheless," Eva says.

This is why the Spell Walkers arrived so beat down. They've been grieving. But I can only imagine what Brighton is going through. Emil too. He's nowhere near my favorite person, but now that Atlas is alive again, I don't have to hold the grudge against him for not letting me kill June before she had the chance to ruin my life. My heart is especially with Brighton since he's the one who actually killed Carolina. I sympathize because I didn't act on my vision-dream that resulted in the Blackout.

"We need to explore the consequences by sharing this ritual with Brighton," Iris says.

If I had the chance to undo my wrongs, then others should be able to as well.

The secret to resurrection should not die with me.

FORTY

INFINITY KINGS: PART ONE

EMIL

I'm standing in the cemetery, thinking about rebirth.

No, this isn't about bringing Ma back from the dead. Senator Iron can run his mouth all he wants about how we're able to perform actual physical resurrections, but that's just another lie he's telling. It's also not about my phoenix powers, which won't even allow me to be reborn as Emil Rey, just as Bautista de León didn't come back as Bautista de León and Keon Máximo didn't come back as Keon Máximo. I get that Ma is dead and I will never be able to bring her back to life. But that's exactly why I've got rebirth on the brain because I'm currently living through my own, just as every single soul does when they're going through big life changes—when they're grieving someone who is gone way too soon.

Who am I now? Who is the new Emil Rey?

The new Emil Rey is an orphan with no one to look up to.

The new Emil Rey is no longer a Spell Walker, just like he never wanted to be.

The new Emil Rey is getting rid of these powers forever.

The new Emil Rey needs his brother back more than ever.

And the new Emil Rey keeps missing an old life that has burned to ashes.

I am being reborn as someone who will always be grieving and unhappy and hated.

Whenever I pictured what life would look like after breaking the infinity cycle, I always imagined having my mother and my brother at my side. Life wouldn't ever be normal again, but we'd be able to find the moments that trick us into thinking it could be. The family dinners where we don't talk about the war we would've all survived. The birthdays that seemed impossible to reach because we'd spent so much time being hunted and captured and tortured. The ways we would all be able to turn to one another, even as we naturally drift apart into our new lives. But Ma is gone and Brighton is a terrorist.

The cemetery is cold tonight, and if life were different, I'd be hugging up against Ness or Wyatt for warmth but they're both here and unless we're all about to huddle together, I'm going to keep freezing my ass off. I could summon some phoenix fire, but to hell with these powers.

I kneel before Dad's headstone, tracing each letter of his name: L-E-O-N-A-R-D-O. I almost whisper that I miss him; then I realize I might actually be reunited with him soon enough. I really wouldn't put it past Brighton to try and kill me on the graves of our parents.

I wonder how Brighton is doing, now that the world is turning against him.

I spent the day in the basement of that celestial church with Ness and Wyatt. I was ready to rush out to the cemetery, but there were helicopters still trying to find all of us. I was sure that Nox could fly past all of them and lose the helicopters, just as Wyatt did with that one after the invasion of the Sanctuary, but Wyatt cautioned that if we were spotted and followed, then we'd be bringing enforcers along with us and I wouldn't get the chance to bury Ma in peace. That was enough to get me to chill out and not rush this. Ness kept checking in with Shine and letting us know what Senator Iron was saying to the media. It's not exactly news that Brighton is being painted as a violent criminal because that's exactly how he acted when he decided to murder an enforcement unit. There's no way Sunstar and Shine could win an election when Iron is playing the game so masterfully. The Spell Walkers are smart to go home and spend time with each other while they can because I bet anything that they will get caught and they'd be lucky to only be thrown into the Bounds.

We've lost; that's it.

Everything is over.

"What on earth—" Wyatt points up.

Streaking across the sky are two sharp wings, glowing in silver and sapphire flames.

Brighton can fly. Another power. He's carrying Prudencia in his arms as he descends, his feet planting onto the ground where we will bury Ma, flanked by the two shovels we stole from the church's basement. Prudencia wastes no time jumping out of Brighton's arms and running straight into mine to hold me close and tell me she's so sorry for my loss. Brighton glares at Ness and Wyatt.

"I thought we would be alone," Brighton says.

"I never said that."

Brighton looks around, uneasy. "You better not be using Ma as bait to trick me. Where the hell is everyone else?"

"They're all gone. I'm no longer a Spell Walker."

"Did you piss them off?"

"No, I quit."

"Good. You've come to your senses."

"Bright, drop this act. Just for tonight, you're not the Infinity Reaper and I'm not the Infinity Son. We're not even in this together as the Infinity Kings." I can see how wounded he is. He's not trying to take directions from me as if it's just another command from someone who was treated more special than he was by the Spell Walkers. "Right now, we're here as brothers who have to bury our mother."

I point at Ma's corpse by Dad's headstone, trying so hard to not think about who killed her in the first place. Brighton braves a look at Ma, and I can see the guilt in his eyes. He looks away quickly.

Wyatt steps forward. "I'm sorry for your loss."

"Same here," Ness says.

The last thing that needs to happen right now is Brighton discovering that Ness played any role in exposing our location.

"Brighton and I need to do this alone," I say.

Ness nods. "We'll give you some space, but we're staying close."

"And we shall keep watch," Wyatt adds.

I don't respond; I just let them back up a couple rows of headstones and chill by Nox.

Prudencia folds her arms. "Am I part of alone? I loved Carolina too."

"No," Brighton says. "Just us brothers."

She tears up. "You might be pissed off at me, Brighton, but I will get to say goodbye to your mother before we bury her." Prudencia walks off to join Ness and Wyatt.

If it were only up to me, I'd be fine with Prudencia helping. Ma always loved her like a daughter. But at the end of the day, Brighton was actually Ma's son and gets to have a say in this.

"How are you feeling?" I ask Brighton.

"This doesn't feel real. It's as if I'm living a nightmare."

That's how I've felt since discovering my true origins. I've always known it could come to this, but Brighton always had his eyes to the stars and head in the clouds. Now he's come crashing down back to earth, face-planting in a cemetery.

"Do you think Ma will become a ghost?" Brighton asks.

I think the real question he wants to ask is, *Will Ma come back to haunt me?*

If ghosts are born because of violent deaths, then there's a real chance that Ma could come back as a ghost. But because I'm protective of my brother and don't want him to live with this guilt, I just lie. "I don't think so. Her death was fast."

Brighton's head hangs low. "It was an accident."

I'm surprised he's bringing this up. "I know, but—"

"I'm not the villain here, Emil. Iron is. He made me kill our mother. I will end him."

"Can you just . . . ?" I take a deep breath, so aware that we're not that far away from Ness as Brighton talks about wanting to kill his father. "Ma wouldn't want you talking like that."

"Ma isn't around to shut me down because of what Iron made me do."

"If Ma and Dad are watching us together, how do you think they would feel if you're out here, on their graves, talking about how you're going to go kill to get revenge?"

Brighton is shaking. "I know they wouldn't be happy. But neither am I."

"I'm not either, Bright. But unless you're trying to join them, chill out."

"I can't be killed," Brighton says like a threatening reminder.

I'm remembering that Brighton has no idea that the Halo Knights are pursuing a scythe that can kill the unkillable—that can kill Brighton. He also doesn't know that I'm the key to finding this weapon. I don't want to go into the past to do this, and I don't want to fight my brother. All I can hope for now is a life where people see that I've quit and won't be a problem anymore. Then maybe I can live. But Brighton is only going to complicate that for me, dragging me into any mess he creates, simply because he's my brother. This is one of those times when I actually wish I could quit our brotherhood as easily as I quit being a Spell Walker.

"Listen, I don't want to fight you."

"Good. We should kill Iron together." Brighton looks over his shoulder at Ness. "I bet Pretty Boy would help."

"Ness is tired of being on the run. Killing his father doesn't set him free."

"I don't care what Ness's life will look like. I only care about what mine looks like now." Brighton stares at our mother's body. "I will never be able to live with myself for what Iron made me do."

Every time Brighton says that Iron made him do this, it's sounding more and more like a story he's telling himself, like he's completely innocent in this. "There are other ways to beat Iron. You have a whole platform of followers—"

"Followers who now believe I'm a cold-blooded killer because of Iron's lies."

I shake my head. "You did kill a bunch of people."

"I killed enforcers who were trying to kill all of you. I saved you all. They fired first and I fired back. This was self-defense."

"You could've disarmed them."

"Absolutely not. I was outnumbered and won by being the last one standing."

There's a voice in my head, almost like a phoenix screeching, screaming at me to draw fire on Brighton now, to hit him so good that he is knocked out and I can bind his powers. But my grief is overpowering all those senses.

I almost drop to my knees, out of exhaustion and to beg. "Can we please, please, please bury our mother in peace?"

Brighton turns to the reserved grave beside Dad's. His eyes burn like eclipses as silver and sapphire flames snake around his wrists.

"Without gleam," I say, getting in the way. "Those powers took away Ma. They won't be used to bury her."

Brighton's face glows from his fire until the silver and sapphire flames vanish.

We grab the shovels and start digging, working up a sweat to combat the cold within the first few minutes. Brighton and I don't really have the muscle for this, but that doesn't stop us. After everything Ma has done for us, everything Ma has sacrificed for us, we can dig deep in what strength we do have to dig deep into this earth so she can rest in peace, close to Dad like she always wanted. I keep wanting to ask Brighton something or reflect on stories about Ma, but all of this is too hard—fighting with the ground, fighting for that next breath to keep moving, fighting to not curl up inside this shallow hole to cry. At some point, Prudencia, Ness, and Wyatt approach us, asking if we want a break, but Brighton snaps, telling them to back off, which they do. He's really doing a solid job pissing everyone off at a time when we can really use the support. I want to believe that Brighton and I can be there for each other and that will be enough, but it's clear we are still charting different courses through the sky. It's as if Brighton and I are going to be on different ends of the planet, never sharing the sun and moon at the same time again.

After the first hour of digging, I'm tempted to use our powers to blow a hole into the ground, but we keep digging and digging into the second hour, and then the third, and until the fourth when we've dug a hole so deep that Brighton gives me a boost to hop out and I reach down to help him up.

"We did it," I say. I'm bone-tired and filthy.

"Let's get Ma in."

As someone who has been helping carry Ma and place her onto the back of a phoenix and praying to the stars that she wouldn't fall off during flight, I'm not about to watch her roll ungracefully into her grave. "Hey!" I shout, waving everyone over.

"What are you doing?"

"We need to say goodbye, and then Pru can safely get Ma into her grave."

"I thought we were doing this without powers."

"We're doing this without the powers that took Ma's life."

Prudencia, Wyatt, and Ness are all shivering and look as exhausted as we feel. Wyatt peeks into the hole and seems impressed.

Together, the five of us walk over to Ma's body and carry it over to the grave like pallbearers without a coffin. We rest her gently on the ground, and I look up at the stars, thinking how Ma must be looking down at us.

"Does anyone want to say anything?" I ask.

"I'll go last," Brighton says.

"And I can't start," I say.

Wyatt clears his throat. "I haven't had the pleasure of knowing Carolina for very long, but I knew she was going to be amazing when I saw the lengths her children went through to save her. She lived up to those expectations, and it was just as clear she would have walked through fire for her sons. May Carolina Rey return again in another life, this one even fuller."

I'm crying as I thank Wyatt with a nod. He bows his head.

Ness steps up. "I have many regrets and impersonating Carolina is high up on that long list. I may have done the job of convincing people that I was Carolina, but the world never actually got to see her. The time I spent with her wasn't enough, and I truly hoped we would have so many more opportunities to get to know each other. She was the closest thing I'd had to a mother since my mom died." Ness walks over to me and grabs my hand. "She was so proud of your heart, Emil. She told me all about how in sixth grade you spent your recesses comforting a girl who'd lost her sister." He looks up at Brighton. "Carolina knew that it only made you closer as brothers because Emil was scared of losing you." His teary eyes are back on me. His hand is shaking as he fights shivers. "She called you her hero, Emil, because of the way you held on to your warmth while grieving your father. I know what it's like to lose your mother suddenly, and it's impossible to not be changed by this, but do not lose yourself in your grief. Especially the parts about you that your mother loved the most."

This story he's just told me has me wanting to lunge into Ness's arms so hard that we might fall into Ma's grave. It's like having a conversation with Ma in the afterlife, hearing what she loved about me. All day I've been wanting to rip my heart out of my chest so I can't ever be hurt again, but here's Ness, someone else whose mother was killed, begging me to keep my heart. This is what Ma would want more than anything. It's what Ma was saying this morning when we were talking about Ness and Wyatt and how I shouldn't be so afraid of having my heart broken or breaking someone else's heart that I don't nurture the love I have in me.

I feel a fire in my heart, flickering back to life. Things are beginning to matter again. I will fight to keep my light, to keep my warmth, like Ma would want. Like I want.

The new Emil Rey is being reborn, but that doesn't mean old-school Emil Rey has to die.

I'm crying even harder, thinking about how I'm Ma's hero, and I want Ness to hold me again as much as I want him to hold me when I'm not crying too. This feeling is one of many that's coming back to me, like my world isn't some ice-cold planet anymore. "Infinite thanks, Ness."

He holds my hand to his heart. "Anytime, Emil."

Then he lets go, but he gives me this look that feels like an invitation to grab his hand again. *Anytime, Emil*, I practically hear him say again.

But not now.

Just because I'm scared of not breaking a heart doesn't mean I can't try to be careful.

Prudencia tries suppressing her own cries long enough to speak. She stares at Ma. "Carolina, I'm going to miss you so much. I would hate to think of the person I would've become if I'd only had my aunt as a role model for the type of woman I could be. I'm so grateful to have known you at a time when I was starting to find myself. At a time when I thought I couldn't be powerful unless I was using my powers. You've shown me that living a powerless life doesn't mean not having strength or that I can't make a difference." She sucks in a deep breath. "I hope you and Leo are meeting my parents and becoming lifelong friends and that they're spoiling you for taking care of me." Prudencia blows a kiss at Ma.

It's sweet to think about all our parents hanging in the afterlife, but horrible too. They should all be here, alive, with their children. Same deal with Ness's mother.

I'm still not sure where to start my eulogy, but it's my turn to speak from the heart. "Ma, you and Dad saved my life. I don't even want to imagine what my life would have looked like in any other home, and I won't ever have to because you brought me into yours the same day you brought home the only son you were planning to. You loved me so much that it was my life's biggest plot twist to learn that you hadn't grown me yourself. But that doesn't matter. You raised me as your own, and I got to grow up so normal and happy. . . ." I choke on my words, crying so hard because, unlike Ness and Prudencia, I did get to grow up in a happy home where both my parents loved me with their whole hearts. "I'm so lucky that you were my mom, Ma. I'll love you in every lifetime."

FORTY-ONE
INFINITY KINGS: PART TWO

BRIGHTON

Having to say goodbye to Ma is like phasing my hand through my own chest to rip out my heart, just as I've done my enemies. But I don't deserve a death like that because I'm innocent and Senator Iron isn't and that's why his heart will be the one I'm holding and torching. Once Ma has been laid to rest, I will avenge her.

I stare at Ma's corpse, wishing she'd drunk Reaper's Blood. Everyone wants to give Luna a hard time, myself included, since her people seem to have their target sights locked on me for all eternity, but she was right that humanity has a death problem. We are vulnerable when we don't have to be, and if everyone was immortal, I wouldn't have to say goodbye to my mother tonight. Then I wouldn't have been the one who killed her—accidentally.

I'm the last eulogy by choice. I'm her firstborn . . . her only born. I am the main event in this funereal space, but now that the spotlight is on me, it's as if I have stage fright or have forgotten my speech.

Everyone else has said such wonderful things about Ma, even Emil's little side pieces, who are basically strangers. I'm not a fan of how much emphasis Ness placed on Ma's love for Emil over her love for me, but I'll just take that aggression out on his father. It was hard watching Prudencia cry and there is still a small part of me that wishes I'd gone up to her while she was crying and comforted her, but there's no ignoring the terrible way she spoke to me after I saved her life. And Emil's eulogy really leaned into what a golden boy he is, what a hero he is . . . a hero who has hung up his cape because he doesn't want to do the actual work, but he lives in the same optimistic reality as Prudencia, where you don't need powers to save the world. Give me a break.

"Ma . . ."

If this were an Instagram Live, I wouldn't be speechless. I would find the words.

"Just speak from your heart, Bright," Emil says.

"I know that," I snap. The problem isn't that I don't know what to say. It's that I do. "I'm sorry, Ma. I'm sorry for delivering the blow that . . . I'm sorry for being the one who . . ." My fists tighten as I turn to Emil. "Let's just bury her."

"What? Come on, I know it's hard, but you got to let it out."

"She's dead, Emil! She can't hear me!" I'm shaking, and he's crying even harder. "Great. I guess I'm the bad guy all over again."

Prudencia steps toward me. "Just because you're hurting doesn't mean you can take it out on other people."

"You're scared of another killing spree?"

Her eyes glow like stars. "Do not try me."

"Stop!" Emil shouts. His eyes are closed and his fists are clenched.

"Fine. Brighton, if you're done, it's done. But we are not turning the graves of our parents into a battlefield."

Prudencia's eyes stop shining. "I'm sorry, Emil."

I don't apologize. "Let's get this over with."

Emil seems annoyed that I'm talking about burying our ma as if it's one of the many chores we've begrudgingly done at her orders, like taking out the trash or doing the dishes, but Emil doesn't carry the same weight of staring at her dead body like I do. He gets to say his nice words without having to own up to the fact that she's gone because of him.

"Do you mind lowering her in, Pru?" Emil asks.

Prudencia places a hand on her heart like she's centering herself before she telekinetically lifts Ma off the ground and gently lowers her down into the grave as if she's as light as a feather.

"The dirt too," I say.

"We can do that," Emil says.

"It's late, and I don't want to throw dirt on our mother."

Emil and I stand together at the foot of the grave as Prudencia telekinetically buries Ma. It's when her face is completely covered in dirt that Emil falls to his knees, crying out for Ma as if there's any chance she will claw her way out and give him a hug. I should be the one to hug my brother, but I can't stop watching all the dirt that we dug up together get poured right back in within a couple of minutes. Prudencia even does her best to tidy the top of this mound. It's done. Ma is now buried six feet under, and I'll never see her again.

There's a cry that's been building in me all day, and it's too familiar after losing Dad this year. I never expected I would feel a loss like this so soon. It doesn't feel fair. If the universe is going to take both of your parents, that should be decades apart. I don't want to give in to this pain. The last time I did, I felt broken and the Reaper's Blood has made me unbreakable. Cut off my arm, hell, even my head and I will grow a new one. Destroy my body completely and I will be reborn in phoenix fire just as I am now unlike Emil's inferior power. Kill me and I will live anyway. But this grief feels like it has the power to destroy me, and I would rather channel this anger into destroying others.

"We're done here," I say. I'm about to take off into the sky to find Iron, when Emil hops up from the ground and grabs my wrist.

"Wait. How can you just leave like that? Our mother is dead. We're straight-up orphans now who only have each other."

"We're too old to be orphans." It's technical, but true. "You also have enough support," I add, glaring at the love of my life and the loves of his.

"You're my family, Bright. The Reys of Light."

"The Last Reys."

Emil and I being the last Reys of Light is a dark thought. Our family seems cursed.

Someone's phone begins ringing—Prudencia's. She answers the call. "Hey, Iris . . . Oh . . ." She then looks at me. "He's here."

This must be a warning. I'm now even more wanted than Emil after defending myself against those enforcers. They better be ready to summon every last enforcer from across the globe to try and stop me because that's what it's going to take once I kill Iron.

Prudencia hands me the phone. "It's Maribelle."

Hearing her name is like a jolt to my chest. It's almost as shocking as being told that Ma is on the other line. I really thought she was going to be my partner-in-crime, so to speak, and the friend I could have relied on to stand at my side at my mother's burial as Emil has his people. But after drinking the Reaper's Blood thanks to her help, our roads diverged with her going down one path with Tala and me going down another with Emil, Ma, Prudencia, and the Spell Walkers. Even though we worked together to break into the Bounds, we were there on different missions. We were rescuing Ness, and she was going to kill Luna. I haven't heard from her since.

"Maribelle?" I ask into the phone.

"I just heard about your mother," Maribelle says.

"The news got it all wrong."

"The Spell Walkers told me. They're here at Wesley's cabin."

So that's where they ran off to. But I'm confused. "Why are you there?"

"Ruth said you were going to bury your mother. Is that true?"

She's not answering my question. "We just did."

"Good. Do not cremate her. Not yet."

"Not yet? We're not going to. She's resting with Dad."

"Not forever. This is going to be nothing more than a nap, okay? Just wait for me."

I'm starting to get annoyed. "Maribelle, what the hell are you talking about?"

"I can bring Carolina back to life," Maribelle says.

Is she drunk? Her speech isn't slurring, but she must be wasted.

Disbelief begins turning into hope.

The life I'm living today isn't one that I've been living my entire life. This is now a world where Emil has famous past lives and people are traveling back through time because of phoenix powers and I'm immortal because of a potion that I stole from a dangerous alchemist who was trying to live long enough to find a cure for death. Maybe Maribelle has found that cure.

"You can bring Ma back to life?" I ask.

Emil, Prudencia, Wyatt, and Ness look as if they're frozen in time.

"As long as I have her ashes, I should be able to," Maribelle says.

"So you don't know that you can actually resurrect someone?"

"I do," Maribelle says with a happy sigh. "Hold on."

The line goes quiet.

"What's going on?" Emil asks. "What's Maribelle saying?"

I hold up a finger because someone else comes on the phone. It's a man—a boy. It's not Wesley. It's a voice that I recognize, but it can't be possible because the dead can't speak.

"Hi, Brighton," someone says. It sounds like Atlas Haas.

"Atlas?"

"In the flesh. Again."

I must look as confused as everyone else does around me. "How? When?"

"Tonight," Atlas says. "Maribelle is how."

This doesn't seem real. I stare at Ness. The day that Emil discovered his powers, we were back at our apartment when Atlas knocked on the door. Except it wasn't Atlas at all. It was Ness disguised as Atlas so he could lure Emil to the Blood Casters. But Ness is here and can't be in two places at once.

"This is unbelievable," I say.

"Believe it because it's the reason I'm not offering you any condolences. It might be a waste of breath, and I've got mine back."

My favorite Spell Walker has returned from the dead. "Can I talk to Maribelle again?"

"Absolutely. See you soon, Brighton."

"See you soon, Atlas," I mutter.

Maribelle is back on the phone. "Like I said, I know I can resurrect someone."

I begin pacing the cemetery, back and forth between Dad's and Ma's graves. "How is this possible?"

"I spared Luna's life at the Bounds because she knew of an ancestor who could speak to ghosts, so I retrocycled back to that time when I discovered a phoenix ritual for humans that requires the ashes of the dead to bring them back to life. Most importantly, it brings them back as they are, if done right. It turns out June was dead before and Luna botched her resurrection." Maribelle takes a deep breath. "All of this must sound bizarre, but none of that matters because Luna guided me through this ritual and I've done it successfully. The Spell Walkers are happy to have Atlas back too, but we're obviously ripping apart the fabrics of the known universe with this ritual. It has to stay a secret, but I had to let you know after hearing about Carolina. I can't bring my parents back, but there's no reason you can't have yours."

This is what I have always loved about working with Maribelle. She gets the work done.

"This is the best news ever," I say.

"I have to go argue with Iris again because that's all we do, but I'll see you soon."

"That you will," I say, hanging up.

I smile at Ma's and Dad's graves before turning to Emil. "We can resurrect them—both of them."

"I'm going to need you to rewind a bit," Emil says.

"Were you talking to Atlas? The fallen Spell Walker?" Wyatt asks.

"You could say that Maribelle picked him up. He's alive."

"How?" Emil asks.

"This phoenix ritual that Maribelle discovered in the past."

Wyatt tenses. "Pardon me?"

I snicker. "Are you really going to act surprised like you Halo Knights have no idea?"

"First off, Reaper, I am no longer a Halo Knight. Secondly, no, this is the first I am hearing of a phoenix ritual that is being cast on humans to bring them back to life. How does one even do this?"

I shrug. "All I know is that we need the ashes of the dead, which we can easily get. Who cares about the rest."

Wyatt raises his hand. "I care about the rest if this involves phoenixes in any shape or form."

I turn to Emil. "Tell your boy that we have an opportunity to bring our parents back to life and that nothing will get in our way to do that."

Emil is speechless. It's understandable. Resurrection is real.

Ness sighs. "You're aware that the Senator's campaign ever since your stunt against Emil's past lives is that we hold the keys to resurrection. Emil and I told the public that they have a misunderstanding of how resurrection works. You're going to make liars out of us."

"Everything you said was true then, but the truth has now changed."

"The truth doesn't matter to these people!" Ness shouts. He looks as if he might try and choke me. "We are working hard to make meaningful change in this world that you're insisting on screwing with at every possible step and making us look like the bad guys! If you perform a resurrection, then you are playing right into the

Senator's hand, guaranteeing him the presidency to keep twisting this world."

I get in Ness's face. "Don't worry about Iron's hand when it's his heart I'll be ripping out."

Ness shoves me so hard I fall to the ground. "I would kill the Senator if given the chance, but that only screws over the rest of the country. This is so much bigger than you."

I rise with fire snaking around my wrists. I'm about to hurl the fire-bolt straight into Ness's chest, when Emil jumps in the way. I pull back.

Emil's eyes are tearing as he releases a defeated breath. "Just do it. Kill me. It won't matter anyway. You can just resurrect me."

I recall my fire. "You can't seriously be on the other side of this."

"It's tricky, Bright. I want Ma and Dad back—"

"You can have them!"

"But at what cost? We started fighting alongside the Spell Walkers to prevent Luna's master plan to become immortal so she can live long enough to figure out resurrection. You're living out her dreams right now."

"I won't pretend that having my family back is a nightmare. We can resurrect them and make them become specters so they won't ever be so vulnerable again. Ma would've been stronger if she had powers, and if Dad gets sick again, then maybe his body will be refreshed through a phoenix resurrection. I know they're older, but if Luna could do it for Iron, she can do it for our parents."

"She's still alive?"

"Maribelle spared her because of this ritual. We can change the world."

Emil steps toward me. "Do you really not see how you're walking in Luna's footsteps?"

"And the Senator's," Ness adds. "You're so consumed by power."

I must be living in some upside-down world where wanting my parents alive makes me the bad guy. "I am neither of those monsters. I see opportunities to make life better, and I'm seizing them."

"So you're going to share this ritual with the rest of the world?" Prudencia asks.

Maribelle said this was a secret for now, but I imagine it won't stop with us. "Yes."

Wyatt steps forward as if that's threatening. "No, you will not. Enough phoenixes have been sacrificed because of foolhardy specters such as yourself, and you will not provide proof that their lives are worth taking so deaths can be reversed." He gestures at the cemetery. "What will you do, dig up every last decayed skeleton and kill a phoenix to resurrect them? What will you do on the very dark day when someone dies and they are unable to be resurrected because phoenixes have gone extinct bringing humans back to life?"

"Then breed more. It's not that hard."

Wyatt claps. "You're a genius! Why hadn't we thought of just getting some phoenixes together, lighting a candle, setting a mood, and let them have at it with each other?" He waves at Nox, who is blending in with the night. "Hey, buddy, go fly away and bang one out to prevent your own extinction. Oh, wait! Obsidians only seek out mates when winter is at its coldest. Sun swallowers only reproduce during the height of summer. Crossing species has had its own benefits and downfalls, but surely you know that because you're a genius."

"Every phoenix isn't going to die for my parents," I say.

"No, but they will die for everyone else, simply because your parents live again."

"I can't control other people's actions."

"Then control your own. Do not inspire a world to trade a life for a life."

I feel a heat building within me, like I might set this entire cemetery on fire, reducing everyone to ashes so they can all be brought back to life.

"This is a bad idea," Prudencia says.

"We can resurrect your parents too! They were stolen from you!"

"Believe me, I know . . . but this isn't a power we can wield. What's to stop the Blood Casters from resurrecting Stanton?"

"I'm not scared of someone I've killed before."

"This isn't only about you, Brighton! Anyone anywhere will be able to bring someone back to life. The worst of people. Unless one of your powers is to be everywhere at once, you won't be able to save the innocent. We can't have the dead walking the earth."

Ness nods. "Luna's vision for a life where death is no longer an obstacle might sound nice on the surface, but that's only the lie she has been feeding people to make it sound more appetizing. Her intent has always been selfish. She just wants her sister back."

"And I want my parents back!" I shout, ready to ignite.

Emil wipes away his tears. "There might be other consequences."

"What are they going to do? Die again? I'm willing to take that risk."

"I'm not! I don't want to keep reopening these wounds anytime they die!"

I finally explode, blasting three successive fire-bolts into the sky.

"What about my wounds?! I'm the one who actually watched Dad choke to death on his blood; I'm the one who killed Ma!" I burst into tears as I own my tragic mistake, but I will make this right. "Those won't have to be my last memories of Ma and Dad if I resurrect them." I'm shaking as I remember Ma's final moment. "My name was her last word, and she didn't even finish saying it. Not like she did with yours. . . . Ma can come back and say my name, Emil. She can forgive me." Everyone is staring at me in sympathy. I might be winning them over. "Dad's death traumatized me so much that I drank the Reaper's Blood. What if bringing Dad and Ma back helps me heal?"

Emil looks at me like I'm a ghost. "You'll stop being the Infinity Reaper if we resurrect Ma and Dad? Will you trade your powers for their lives?"

I stand still and silent.

"That's what I thought," he says.

"I don't have to choose. I can, and will, have it all."

"They wouldn't want this."

"Yes, they would!"

"No, they wouldn't!"

"We can ask them after I bring them back to life."

"I'm not letting you do this, Brighton."

I'm about to detonate, an explosion of phoenix fire that wipes everyone out. "You're so full of shit, Emil! You were just standing at Ma's and Dad's graves crying over how they saved your life, and now you won't return the favor?! Maybe you would care more about seeing our parents again if you were actually their son! Maybe you would help me if you were actually my brother!"

Emil holds his hand over his heart, like I'm going to reach into his chest and grab it—like I already have.

I've said a lot of cruel things to Emil over the years, as brothers do. I've called him stupid and useless and weak. I've even threatened his life and called on an army of strangers to help me defeat him. But nothing is killing him like this. Prudencia has never looked more furious. Ness and Wyatt are judging, but I don't care about them. Still, these aren't words I can take back.

Emil is crying the hardest he has all night. "I am your brother. Your real brother. Ma and Dad were my real parents. I would love for our family to be whole again, and I get why you want to fix this since you're the one who broke us apart, but the dead have to stay dead."

"You didn't stay dead."

"I will after this life. And so will you."

"I can't stay dead when I can never die in the first place."

"There is a way for you to die, Brighton. And I know what it is."

I stare at Emil like he's some strange specimen. No one else seems confused about this. "What are you talking about?"

"Keon Máximo not only created the specters, but he also built a scythe that can kill the unkillable in case a major threat rolled through. Someone like Luna. She couldn't find the scythe, so she had him killed by the Halo Knights, and the Haloes are legit looking for the scythe now so they can kill you. It's been lost to time, but if you're dead set on going down this path, I will find it."

Retrocycling.

Emil can retrocycle to Keon's life to find a scythe that can kill me.

"You would kill your own brother for trying to bring our parents back to life?"

"I thought I wasn't your brother," Emil says with a sad edge.

"For someone who was moaning about us being the last Reys, you don't seem to care about giving this family the chance to live forever."

"That's not real life, Brighton."

"How is it that you come from an innovative soul like Keon and not want change? This system of life and death doesn't work, and we can start fixing it."

Emil's head hangs low, but his tired eyes look up at me. "You're not the Infinity Savior or the Infinity Reaper or the Infinity King acting like this world is your kingdom. If you're going to use your powers to resurrect Ma and Dad and assassinate Iron and kill anyone who gets in your way, then you need to be stopped now." He straightens up. "This is all my fault. I dragged you into this mess, so it's on me to . . ." He chokes on his words.

"Say it, Emil. Tell me you'll kill me."

"It's on me to end your infinity," Emil declares.

I laugh. "Come on. You don't have a killer's bone in your body."

"I never wanted to be a hero, and I did that. I can become a killer too."

My fists tighten. "Not only will you die trying, I will leave you dead."

"It's all good as long as the next person wielding the scythe gets the job done."

I study Emil, trying to sense if he will actually go back in time to find the weapon that can kill me. He's been so righteous about being the type of hero with no blood on his hands, and now he's threatening to swing a scythe into me. I have no doubt that I can take him in a fight, but he's right that I've made many enemies who can benefit with the single weapon that can kill me. It could be a Blood Caster or a Spell Walker or a Halo Knight or an enforcer or Iron, but I don't think it can be Emil. He will never have the heart to kill me. The only way to ensure my own immortality is by possessing the scythe that can kill the unkillable.

"Lives are mine to save and take," I say. "Do not cross me."

"I'm sorry about what comes next." Emil sounds so sad delivering this threat. "I love you, Brighton."

I cast one last look at everyone, locking on Emil last, before silver and sapphire wings of fire carry me high above the cemetery and across the city. Hearing Emil say he loves me after all of this stings, but it's not enough to protect him from being slain.

I will bring Ma and Dad back from the dead, and Emil can take their place underground.

FORTY-TWO
FIRST LIFE

EMIL

I watch Brighton fly away, thinking about how I will have to put him in the ground.

Once Brighton's silver and sapphire wings of fire have vanished, I sink to my knees. This has been the most exhausting, heartbreaking day of my life. I don't carry the full memories of Keon's and Bautista's lives, but I'm betting this is the most heartbreaking day of any of my lifetimes. My mother has been killed by the brother I've now sworn to kill to save the world. I don't know how I'm going to find that strength in me. But I have to find that will.

Wyatt kneels before me. "Are you okay, sweet—"

"I'm not okay," I snap.

"Of course not. That was foolish."

"What do you need from us, Emil?" Prudencia asks.

"Nothing. I'm the one who has to handle Brighton."

I stare up at the night sky, wishing on the stars that Brighton would reverse course and tell me that he's come to his senses and understands that we can't go resurrecting our parents without the rest of the world wanting to do the same thing and how tragic and chaotic that would be. But there are no silver and sapphire flames in the sky. No brother on the ground.

"I have to go back in time and find the scythe," I say.

Prudencia's head hangs low, her dark hair covering her eyes as she asks, "Do you really think you'll . . . that you'll kill . . . that you'll do it?"

"I have to try."

"Okay," she says, her voice cracking.

"I don't want to, but we suck at trying to get him to bind his powers. If this is our only shot at taking him down, I'm the best bet at ending him and I have to do it before he binds my powers or kills me first. If I'm powerless or dead, you're all screwed."

I'm starting to freak out that the Starstifler won't be strong enough anyway. We were able to bind Genesis's powers during the Alphabet City brawl, but her Reaper's Blood wasn't as powerful as Brighton's. What if Brighton has to drink three potions to bind each power set? What if that doesn't stick anyway? All I saw when I retrocycled to Bautista's life was that he bound a specter's power, but I have no idea if that lasted forever or came undone. All I know is that death is rumored to be permanent with this scythe.

"Should we call Maribelle?" Prudencia asks.

"Why?"

"Tell her to not teach Brighton how to resurrect anyone."

"She hates me," I say.

"Me too," Ness says.

"Same here," Wyatt says.

"She doesn't hate me, but she likes Brighton more," Prudencia says.

"Yeah, she's not holding off for us. Especially if she just did this herself," I say.

Wyatt claps and rubs his palms together to keep warm. "That settles that. Where shall we go for you to retrocycle?"

"Nowhere is safe," Ness says.

"Perhaps that loft Tala was using. I presume Bella Quinones is still away on her expedition, and if Tala and Maribelle are at the cabin, then it will be an empty house."

"We won't be spotted on your phoenix?" Ness asks.

"Nox blends in with the night. We will have to squeeze together really close since Emil's golden wings will expose him."

"He isn't in any condition to be flying anyway. Let's go rest at the loft. Emil can retrocycle in the morning." Ness extends his hand to help me up, but I don't take it.

"No," I say, sitting cross-legged. "I will retrocycle right here, right now."

I know they all want to try and stop me, but I close my eyes, ready to start moving into the past. I'm shivering from the cold and shaking from my nerves, but soon enough I will be entombed in phoenix fire and focusing less on how I feel and more on how Keon felt the day he died. Tears are squeezing out the corners of my eyes and down my cheeks as I try concentrating. What do I know about Keon? He was the first specter, he was an alchemist, his next life was Bautista. Was he an orphan? Did his mother die naturally, or was she killed by her son? Did Keon have a brother? A brother who was such a threat that he had to create an unkillable weapon as a precaution? I try breathing, but I can't focus. I'm not ready to ignite, but I'm desperate to hide in the past and maybe stay there too, where I won't have to return to my life and have to deal with everything.

Suddenly someone is touching my face, wiping away my tears. Before I open my eyes, I know these are Ness's hands. He hasn't lost the tenderness I first experienced when he was cleaning the wounds he'd inflicted with the infinity-ender dagger, back when I wouldn't let him look at my body. Now he's seen me and has kissed me and is tending to me like we're alone in a room instead of out in a cemetery with Prudencia and Wyatt watching us.

Ness begins rubbing his hands against mine, warming me up. "You lost your mother this morning and buried her tonight. Now you're trying to stop your brother when what you really need to be doing is taking care of yourself."

"I don't get to go take a nap and save the world when I wake up."

"Fine, don't rest. But don't let your grief drive you the way I let mine drive me. I wish I had taken more time to grieve my mother instead of spending all my waking moments wanting to avenge her."

"I'm not trying to avenge her. I'm . . ." I sit there thinking about how I'm doing the opposite. How I'm actually about to go back in time to find a scythe that will kill my brother so he can't bring our mother back to life. "Am I wrong? Should I get out of Brighton's way?"

Ness looks at Ma's grave. "I can't decide your mother's fate."

"What would you do? Would you resurrect your mother?"

"Her life was stolen, and it's tempting to want to steal it back. Unfortunately, I've done enough to help the Senator hurt this world. I will never be able to live with myself if another one of my actions fully rips the world apart."

Everything I have set out to do since becoming the Infinity Son has been to right the wrongs of my past. To put an end to the death and the destruction Keon started when he created the specters for whatever reason. To finish the power-binding potion that Bautista perfected the day he died. To save phoenixkind and all creatures from being hunted and killed for their powers. This has been my mission so I can get back to being a normal kid again, but that's never happening. My home is gone. My parents are dead. My brother is a stranger. My old life is over and needs to stay buried. Maybe in the far, far, far future there will come a time when resurrections can be done responsibly, but that can't be decided between two brothers who are missing their dead mother—and definitely not by the brother who killed her. My last act as the Infinity Son will be to restore this world for the better so everyone can live their lives as they were before Keon sent us all down this path.

I have to stick to what feels right in my heart, even though it's breaking.

Ma and Dad must stay dead.

And I have to kill Brighton.

"I'm ready," I whisper, my breath frosting between me and Ness. I squeeze his hands. "Thank you."

"Good luck," Ness says, joining Prudencia and Wyatt, who are both shivering.

"Take your time going through time," Wyatt says, his teeth chattering. "Nox's fire can keep us warm."

I feel bad that they're stuck out here with me, but I know they're not going anywhere. "Pru, if Brighton comes back for Ma's and Dad's bodies while I'm in the past, you're the only one who can stop him."

Prudencia nods. "I will."

"I'll try to be fast," I say, but that's an empty promise.

Time moves differently when I'm retrocycling. Minutes in the past can be hours in real life. And I don't know how it plays out when I'm going back decades, but I'm about to find out.

I close my eyes, about to travel into my first life to end the one I've been living.

FORTY-THREE
THE MASTER PLAN

BRIGHTON

I fly back to Staten Island, landing in front of the influencer house and barging through the front door.

My life has changed so much since this morning. For starters, when I first left, I had to run because I didn't have wings yet. I was on a mission to pull Ma away from the insanity and found her in the exact danger I was trying to save her from. Then I was tricked into killing her and had to bury her. If it weren't for Maribelle's call, I would've been coming home wishing I had never left because if Ma died the blood could've been on Emil's hands instead. But none of that matters anymore because Maribelle will teach me how to resurrect not only Ma, but Dad too. That's only if I live long enough to do so.

I dash up the stairs to Darren's bedroom and slam open his door, but he's not here. I immediately rush out into the hallway and shout his name. Mr. Bowes comes out of his room, sleepy and frightened. "Where's Darren?" I ask.

"In here!" Darren's voice calls from behind me.

I return to Darren's bedroom and find him on his bed. "I was just in here."

"I was hiding behind an illusion," Darren says. "I got scared when the door opened."

He has good instincts.

"Is it true?" Mr. Bowes asks. "The news said your mother—"

"It's true, but it doesn't matter."

Mr. Bowes stares like I'm some monster. "Of course it matters."

"No, it doesn't because she's not going to be dead forever. Come with me."

They follow me downstairs and out into the backyard. I'm freezing after this flight, and I ignite the campfire, watching the silver and sapphire flames fan in the winds.

"What do you mean your mom isn't staying dead forever?" Darren asks.

"Spiritually," Mr. Bowes says. "Reincarnation is a lovely idea."

"Not reincarnation. Resurrection." They're both quiet and confused, like I haven't actually woken them up from their sleep and they're still in bed dreaming away. "Resurrection is possible. A friend brought someone back to life tonight, someone who I watched die. I heard his voice, and soon enough I'll be able to hear my mother's again. You will be able to as well."

Darren sucks back a breath. "How do you know it's not a trick?"

"It just isn't. Ever since Emil and I have entered this scene, life as we all know it keeps changing. I've watched ghosts bleed and people time-travel and I have become immortal. Why wouldn't resurrection be real too?"

His eyes water. "So I can have my mom back?"

"What's the cost?" Mr. Bowes asks.

"Does it matter? I'll pay anything to have my parents back," I say.

"So you don't know how it works?"

This man is so annoying.

"Not yet. I won't be able to pursue the ritual in peace because of Emil. He doesn't want me to resurrect our parents—my parents! He's stuck in the old ways, and he's even threatened to kill me with some hidden weapon that was built specifically to kill immortals forever. I have to find it first."

"Then what?" Mr. Bowes asks.

"Then I'll be safe. It's the only one of its kind."

"What will you do with it? Kill your brother? That's not what your mother would want."

As the last living Rey—a true, biological Rey—I will not let anyone weigh in on what happens to my family. "I will either use the scythe to defend myself, or bury it so no one can use it against me."

"So it's a scythe? How are you going to find it?" Darren asks.

"Retrocycling. There are still a few powers I haven't tapped into yet, and I couldn't access it the last time I tried. Things are different now. I've gained so many new powers since then. I even flew today, which means my phoenix abilities are strengthening. I studied all of Emil's and Maribelle's training when they did it. Emil traveled back into his past life, and Maribelle traveled through her bloodline. Emil is going to find the scythe by traveling back to the day his first past life died . . . and I'm going to get there too."

Darren looks like he's counting stars. "But you're not related."

"I'm not traveling back to Keon Máximo's life. I'm traveling through Luna Marnette's."

"But you're not related to her either . . . right?"

"No, but when I drank the Reaper's Blood, Luna's blood was mixed in. If I can retrocycle, I should be able to transport through her life too." There have been so many questions that we have needed answered when it comes to humans retrocycling since it's still a new concept in this age of specters. As far as we are concerned, Emil and Maribelle are the only ones who have ever done this. Back when I was trying to tap into my power to see if Ma was alive or dead, we didn't know if my inability to reach her was because she was still alive or my power wasn't strong enough yet. If Luna really guided Maribelle to travel through her history, then that means it's possible to retrocycle through someone else's life while they are still alive. This exciting development opens new doors. "I don't know that it will work, but if I don't try, Emil could track me down and kill me before I get the chance to resurrect our loved ones."

Mr. Bowes sits by the campfire. "I won't pretend I understand much of what you're saying, but you're a smart kid. You're also just that—a kid. You're being too impulsive and need to slow down. What if bringing someone back to life isn't the dream you think it is?"

It's disturbing how someone who has been on the run because his wife was murdered by a Blood Caster—who I've killed, you're welcome!—isn't more enthusiastic at the prospect of his wife being brought back to life. It's not as if I've seen him really crying and grieving her. It's possible he didn't love her as much as I assumed he did. In no world would Dad not ache for Ma every hour of every day. Darren on the other hand has that fire and pain in his heart. This is all I have to play into.

"With all due respect," I say, not meaning a single word, "you do not understand what your son and I are going through. You are not indirectly responsible for your wife's death, but Darren is. If he hadn't told his friends that Dr. Bowes was helping out Emil and the Spell Walkers, then the Blood Casters would have never found us and her neck wouldn't have been snapped by Stanton." They both flinch, and I regret hurting Darren in this moment, but it's important. "I didn't mean to kill my mother. I meant to hurt the celestial enforcer that was endangering everyone, my mother included. Unfortunately, Darren and I have blood on our hands. We also have the opportunity to wipe them clean."

It's no surprise that Mr. Bowes doesn't fight back when told that his son can be freed from all his guilt. That this violent imagining of Stanton snapping Dr. Bowes's neck can be replaced with new, beautiful moments they create together as a family. That if they choose to stay on the run until I kill all the Blood Casters, at least they will all be together.

"This is your call, buddy," Mr. Bowes tells Darren.

"I want Mom back," Darren says. "What do you need from me, Brighton?"

"Protect me. If Emil finds us, hide me. If I manage to go back in time, I'll be left vulnerable while I'm retrocycling."

"No one will hurt you," Darren promises.

I settle onto the ground, praying to every star in every galaxy that my theory about traveling through Luna's bloodline will be right. This is my only chance at finding the scythe before Emil. If I miss it, then I'll be looking over my shoulder for the rest of my immortal life knowing someone could strike me down at any moment. I haven't worked this hard to be a survivor only for someone to now cheat me out of my life with some deus ex machina weapon.

Silver and sapphire flames wrap around my entire body as I concentrate on Luna Marnette's final intersection with Keon Máximo.

This moment in time will decide the fate of my future.

FORTY-FOUR
KEON MÁXIMO

EMIL

When you have phoenix blood in your veins, dying is as much a part of rebirth as living.

Still, I don't want to die again.

Bautista's death was brutal enough. And unfortunately I have spoilers for what goes down with Keon. Not only does he not live a long life where he dies in his sleep, but he's violently executed by the Halo Knights for his crimes against phoenixkind. Maybe in this next retrocycle episode I can exit before Keon is killed, but I'm not holding my breath. I will die as Keon Máximo as I've died as Bautista de León and as I will die as Emil Rey if I can't find this scythe to stop Brighton before he assassinates Iron.

The gold and gray flames have been burning around me for a while as I try retrocycling into Keon's last day alive. My eyes are closed, and I stare into the void, visualizing Keon's death as a door and our connection as the key that unlocks it. In life, Keon only ever showed signs of golden flames, whereas Bautista only had gray, culminating into me having both. As I picture myself walking through the door and into a dark hallway, I light the way with a torch of golden fire. I'm feeling closer to Keon already, as if I'm walking with his feet, gripping the torch with his hand, staring into the illuminated spaces with his eyes. I can feel the surprise in his core when he cast phoenix fire for the first time because it's also what I felt. That may have been his goal, but I had my own dreams too that I wasn't sure would ever be possible, like watching a phoenix be born, and that wasn't any less shocking when witnessing Gravesend's birth. Keon and I were both ordinary people who became extraordinary because of an alchemic formula that he created—because he made us ghosts of ourselves, specters.

I am Keon and Keon is me.

Emil is Keon and Keon is Emil.

Keon Máximo, Emil Rey.

Keon Rey, Emil Máximo.

Emil, Keon. Keon, Emil.

We are the start of specters and the end too.

Then the golden flames are extinguished and the torch vanishes and all the light gets sucked out of this space until I'm standing in—on—darkness. Just as quickly, I'm no longer alone. I'm joined by a man wearing a black cloak that blends in with our pitch-black surrounding, only allowing me to see his face, which has been tanned like he's been living under the sun. He drops his hood, and his long ashy-blond hair spills out, resting on his shoulder. He turns, his slate eyes peering in my direction, but he can't see me any more than I can tell what he's even looking at since the darkness hasn't melted away and revealed his world just yet. Even if I didn't recognize this man from his museum profile or the countless historical photographs that

I've stumbled across throughout life, I would still know this is Keon Máximo in the same way I know that the reflection in a mirror is me.

I can't believe I'm staring at the alchemist who turned himself into the first specter because he wanted power, as the stories have always claimed.

How is Keon my past life and not Brighton's?

I dreamed of being a celestial, especially when I was a kid and fantasizing about being superheroes with Brighton, but I was smart enough to snap out of that dream because I saw how bad people with powers had it. And I was right. I've never had so many people hate me before and that's all because of the messes that Keon created. If Keon hadn't developed that alchemy, there would be no specters, which means no Blood Casters, which means no Blackout, which means no Reaper's Blood, which means no Infinity Reaper, which means no dead mother.

It also means no Infinity Son.

No me.

If I couldn't be reborn, I would've never been born at all.

I would trade my entire existence to undo Keon's messes, but since I can't, I have to justify my life by making everyone else's better.

The darkness of this oblivion space shrinks, revealing a misty forest under a beautiful night sky. Keon's cloak trails behind him as he steps through the mud, and his shoulders shake water out of bushes as he clears his path toward a field of scorched earth. In the dead center, there's a mossy rock with a yellow line painted across it. Is this where Keon has hidden the scythe? I can't read his mind, but I can feel his feelings and there's dread burning through his heart. I look around, trying to make sense of where the hell we are because if he uncovers this scythe and immediately gets jumped by the Halo Knights, this isn't going to help me find it in my time, and I still have no idea if I can retrocycle to the same moment multiple times. Keon stands over the rock and begins chanting in a language I don't know, but I recognize it from when the alchemist Anklin Prince was summoning the ghosts of Luna's parents.

So Keon is summoning the dead, but who?

There's so much I don't know about his life, but as he's chanting, sadness and hope and guilt begin cycling through him, all up until the moment when a shadow of black light appears out of thin air, forming into the lifelike ghost of a young man who looks like he's in his late twenties, early thirties. The lore behind summoning ghosts is that only the living person who killed them violently can do so, but if a supreme alchemist like Anklin Prince was able to do it for Luna, who murdered her parents, then maybe Keon is versed in that same alchemy too. Or it's as simple as Keon killed this person, whoever they are. It wouldn't be surprising given how much death he's caused. Keon's guilt grows stronger and stronger as he stares into the ghost's dead eyes. Maybe this is a specter who died for the cause, kind of like how Luna was running her own experiments on mixing essences from multiple creatures before locking down the official formula for Reaper's Blood.

The ghost howls, sending shivers down Keon's spine and mine and hopelessness into our souls. He stops when he sees how much distress he's causing Keon.

Then the ghost smiles, and Keon smiles back.

"Hi, Astin," Keon says, wiping the tears from his cheeks. Out of everything I have felt from Keon, nothing is stronger than this euphoria. "I hope you can understand me, my love, because my time here may be coming to an end. I will either be reborn or find you in the afterlife."

This ghost, Astin, is Keon's lover—*was*.

I guess villains have hearts too.

Keon looks to the sky before returning his gaze to Astin. "In the event our souls aren't reunited, I wanted to apologize for everything. Your family may not have accepted me for being born without powers, but you had. You were right that my stubbornness made me an effective alchemist, but it also made me a terrible lover. I couldn't believe that I could ever be worthy of someone as extraordinary as you unless I was extraordinary myself." He's ashamed of himself, so embarrassed that it sits in his stomach like a rock. "I remade the world in the hopes you and I can live in it openly, proudly, fiercely. There were many costs along the way. The humans and creatures who died for my trials, especially our beloved gray sun, who was more than a pet phoenix, but practically our child. I still hear Bion's cries whenever I cast fire. . . ." He chokes on a cry as remorse washes over him. "What kills me the most, Astin, is how I should have appreciated the life I had with you instead of obsessing over formulas for eternities we will never get to live. Instead, I gave all my time to Luna thinking that we would create true immortals, that we would conquer death. Now she will be the death of me because I have threatened her future." Keon offers a sad smile. "If there's anything I did right, it was keeping you a secret so she could never poison you."

I never thought that I would feel so much sorrow for Keon, the man I used to be in another life, who I've spent my life thinking the worst of because of how much pain he's caused. But I absolutely do. I don't know his full story, and I never will unless I retrocycle to every day of his life to witness everything, but I do know that he regrets not loving Astin as much as he could have. It's got me thinking about how I keep putting my life on hold to make the world a better place instead of finding time to live in it too.

Keon reaches inside his robe and pulls out a pair of laced gloves that look familiar. "I created something for this moment, all on my own," he says as he's putting the gloves on. "I hope they work." He extends his hand out to Astin, who does the same, and then I remember where I've last seen these gloves. It was at Older Cemetery on the night I met Luna. She was wearing these gloves to grab the ghosts of her parents. Just like then, the gloves glow as Keon's fingers touch Astin's as if they're also flesh. Keon begins swelling with pride in his alchemical invention, but mostly, he's filled with undeniable love. Their hands lock, and it's the happiest high I have ever felt in any life.

I can't believe my soul has been so lucky to have loves like Keon's for Astin and Bautista's for Sera.

My own heart is growing, and answering its greatest question.

These generations of love are so pure and powerful that I know whose hand I want to hold in life and again in death.

Keon loved Astin.

Bautista loved Sera.

And I love—

There's a bolt of shock that destroys Keon's intimate moment with the ghost of his lover.

He looks around, dread twisting his soul as his eyes land on a woman in a cloak, holding a torch as she breaks through the mist.

"I hope our souls will hold each other in the afterlife," Keon says.

"If not, thank you for loving me in this one."

Astin howls so piercingly loud that it slows down the woman too.

Keon chants through tears, and Astin's ghost disperses, and the forest goes quiet.

The woman rushes over and drops the hood of her cloak. She's also in her late twenties, maybe early thirties. Her torch illuminates her green eyes, like burning emeralds. Dark brown hair fans out across her shoulders. She waves with an infinity-ender dagger. "Hello, Keon."

"Hello, Luna."

It's strange looking at Luna this young, decades before she became the queenpin. "Who was the ghost?"

"A victim," Keon says. In one way it feels like a lie, but in another it's also the truth. "I stitched these gloves together to see if I could touch a ghost."

"Always creating and re-creating," Luna says.

"The life of an alchemist," Keon says.

She twirls the dagger between her fingers. "Admittedly, I am far less concerned with disturbing the dead than I am living a long, long life. Your scythe threatens that. Why did you have to go and create such a weapon of destruction?"

"No one should live forever, and the scythe will see to that."

"It is a shame to see you abandon the ingenuity that drew me to you like a moth to fire."

"I didn't lure you to me, Luna. You sought me out because of my reputation."

Luna begins circling Keon like a predator. "I possess no ego that prevents me from admitting that you are the superior alchemist. Every impossibility that I will make possible began with you, but it will not end because of you."

I know that Keon will be killed by the Halo Knights, but I'm still fearing for his life. I've been attacked by Luna when she wasn't in her prime and that took me by surprise. I can only imagine what she's capable of as a younger woman, and I may not have to imagine it. Keon is nervous too, but there's also some acceptance. It reminds me of how Bautista knew he was about to be killed by Luna because of Sera's vision. There was still a fight in him, but he knew he was fated to lose.

"I can kill you now," Keon says.

"You would break your vow to never kill again for me? I'm touched."

"That vow was penance for all the lives I sacrificed to become who I am. I can make an exception for the woman who manipulated me into thinking this was all for the greater good."

Luna freezes. "This wasn't manipulation. I have always been honest about wanting to do all of this so I can be reunited with my sister, whereas you have never been open as to why you so desperately wanted power. It didn't matter to me as long as our goals were aligned like stars in a constellation, and they have been, shining so bright that we have made our mark on the world. You may be done since you're unable to reckon with the powers we have bestowed upon those who were as desperate as you, but this world will never fully turn to its truest potential until we can unearth those who have been buried within it."

"You will never succeed in resurrecting your sister."

"I will, Keon. What I'm asking of you now is whether or not you hope to live long enough to witness that miracle. Tell me where you have hidden the scythe and I will have your life spared."

Keon laughs. "Why are you so scared of a weapon that you don't even know works?"

"I would never doubt a creation of yours," Luna says earnestly. "When the time comes for me to become immortal, I do not want to be struck down by some man-made weapon. I want to live forever and live the life of an alchemist—creating, re-creating." She lowers the infinity-ender, but she's not fooling me or Keon into thinking she's any less dangerous. "Specters will continue growing in numbers, and as they do, so will their powers and our understanding of their capabilities and limitations. You have created this scythe to combat the likes of them."

"The likes of you," Keon snaps. "Your pursuit for immortality was my truest inspiration."

"Says the man who drank his dead phoenix's blood to live forever."

"A mistake in many ways."

"Well, that phoenix has hatched, so to speak, and there is no putting it back in now."

"Actually, by nature, some breeds of phoenixes do find their way back into eggs."

Luna glares. "I will miss your wit terribly. I have reinforcements on the way, and handing over the scythe is the only way I can have your life spared."

"Unfortunately, Luna, I'm going to have to call your bluff. My alchemic achievements have exposed me to some very powerful contacts, including a set of brothers dealing with their own deathly ailments. They sought me out for help, and one foresaw my demise this evening. Time will tell if my death sticks, but I know it is coming." Keon reaches into his robe and pulls out a folded parchment paper. "If you will excuse me, I have to get going so I can pass on these instructions on where to find the scythe to someone worthy of handling great threats, as I imagine you will grow to be."

That's it—that's a map to the scythe.

After all the happiness and love I've been feeling in this slice of Keon's life, I'm now burdened by my own pain as to what comes next. I'm close to discovering where this scythe is, and once I have it, I'm going to have to use it on my brother to end him once and for all.

Then my heart races, as if the Halo Knights are already storming down from the skies to kill Keon, but the night sky is still empty except for the moon and stars.

Someone has arrived, though, out of thin air.

This is impossible.

How the hell is Brighton in the past?

FORTY-FIVE

THE MAP

BRIGHTON

I have made it to the past, just in time.

The only drug I've ever done was Brew, the potion that produces powerful hallucinations for the drinker so they can imagine what it's like to have abilities, but retrocycling felt like an acid trip through time and space where I experienced senses and memories for a life I never lived. It was difficult to get into the headspace, and it was starting to seem as if it wasn't going to happen. The way Emil and Maribelle talked about retrocycling, they were able to tune in sooner to their past links because of their soul and blood connections. I don't have either with Luna, but I started thinking about how much we are alike. Our desires to live forever and resurrect the ones we love. That's when I began hearing my thoughts in Luna's voice and my bones creaking as if they were as old as hers.

To find Luna, I had to admit to myself that I am like Luna.

Afterward, it was a matter of tracking down this moment in history. It felt like I was trying to eavesdrop on a conversation between Luna and Keon behind a closed door, waiting for them to speak of this scythe that was created to destroy threats like Luna—threats like me. My soul was being shredded apart, as if the scythe was slicing through me. I found myself shaping around Luna's life like a sweater that's hanging too loose. Then I was standing in some black void alone with Luna except she looked to be only a decade older than me. As the void became a dark forest and sound became clearer, I couldn't believe that not only had I traveled back in time, but that I was also staring at the first alchemist whose formula made all of this possible, and how he was now talking about directions to find the scythe that can end these miracles.

Somehow, seeing Emil is here too is the most surprising thing. He's actually tracking down this scythe so he can kill me. Unbelievable.

Emil keeps blinking. "How are you here?"

"I have phoenix powers too," I say, but only Emil can hear me.

"You're not related to Keon or Luna."

"No, but I have Luna's blood. That was enough to do the trick."

At least, I think it is. I'm getting strange flashes of dizziness, as if gravity isn't working and I might drift away, back into my own timeline. A soul-shredding pain comes in waves too, which is not something Emil or Maribelle ever described during their retrocycle episodes. Maybe it's because Luna isn't my family or my past and that's why I don't feel like I belong here. Meanwhile Emil is standing all high and mighty because life always finds a way to make sure he belongs, even when it comes to my real, flesh-and-blood family. I groan as I try holding myself upright.

"What's wrong?" Emil asks as he comes near me.

Can he touch me? I hold out my hand, but no fire-bolt blasts into Emil. I'm powerless in this realm. "Stay away from me."

Emil stops.

"Hand it over," Luna says, calling our attention.

Her emotions are whispering into my senses. There's a touch of relief and desperation, two things that I'm already feeling. We're both on track to find this scythe except I know she won't succeed and I must.

Keon smiles as wings of gold fire bloom behind him, and he waves with that map as he begins floating into the air. The desperation in Luna and myself becomes more charged as we both run toward him, our movements mirrored as if we really are the same person. Emil is sucked up into the air with Keon, and even though it's pointless, I jump into the air as if there's a chance I will be able to get a physical hold on Keon. I fall flat on my face as Keon and Emil become so lost in the night sky that all I can make out are the burning gold wings.

"No!" Luna screams, hurling the infinity-ender dagger into a tree out of anger.

Once again, our feelings are identical. Confusion.

Where do we go from here?

Can I retrocycle back to this moment in time? Could there be another day in the past where Luna had a chance to discover the whereabouts of the scythe? Or should I just remain in the present and get ready for battle against Emil? I'll absolutely need Darren to ensure my safety. Emil may discover where the scythe is, but I still have Darren as a wild card. Darren's illusions will disturb Emil's reality long enough for me to steal the scythe and—

A scream from above has me and Luna turning to the sky, just in time to watch Keon and Emil fall out of the darkness and crash to the ground. They're both in agony, holding their stomachs, even though

Keon is the only one who has an arrow sticking out of him. Emil is writhing in pain, but all I can do is smile because there's still hope for me to discover the scythe's whereabouts. I turn to find Luna as she looks up again, this time to witness the descent of three phoenixes with Halo Knights on their backs.

Luna skids across the muddy grounds and searches Keon's cloak for the map. She finds a pair of gloves that she throws over her shoulder. She pats him down but only gets bloodstained hands for her efforts. Frustration rockets through Luna. "Where is it? Where are the instructions?"

Keon groans in pain.

Luna smacks him, leaving a bloody handprint across his cheek. "Where is it?!"

The phoenixes land on the ground, forming a triangle around Luna and Keon. If I'm remembering the breeds right, the yellow phoenix is a light howler like Tala's, the crimson phoenix is a sun swallower, and the midnight-blue phoenix is a century like Gravesend if Gravesend had lived long enough to grow up. The Halo Knights dismount. One is carrying a pair of sickles, another has an ax, and the third is wielding the crossbow that was used to shoot Keon out of the sky.

"Do not kill him yet," Luna says.

"Why not?" asks the sun swallower's Halo Knight.

"You will not get the scythe you're seeking to kill specters everywhere," Luna says.

I feel the lie in her words, but the Halo Knights do not. They seem to actually believe her.

Keon is staring up at the darkness, and at first I think it's because his eyes are rolling back as his life fades, but he's looking at something.

It's a piece of paper that is swaying slowly through the air, like a lone snowflake.

The map!

I skip over Emil's and Keon's bodies, waiting for the piece of paper to fall already so I can see it.

"She wants the scythe for herself," Keon says. "Do not trust her."

The Halo Knight with the century cocks his head. "Why would we trust you? You are responsible for the deaths of the universe's most sacred creatures. If it weren't for Luna, we wouldn't be aware of your plans for further destruction with this weapon you've created."

"I have regrets. I'm also working on a binding potion to—"

"Lies," Luna interrupts. "I've been in his labs. He's only cooking up more weapons."

"Where is the scythe?" the third Halo Knight asks.

Keon sees the piece of paper, right as it's reaching everyone's eye level, but Luna and the Halo Knights are too busy watching him. How does this scythe get lost in time? Does it fall through the mist and into the mud and get buried into the earth? I want to shout at Luna to turn around, but it doesn't matter. I don't need to see through her eyes what is almost in front of me.

Emil gets up, holding his stomach as if an arrow has been fired through him. He sees the swaying paper too. "I can't let you live as you are, Brighton."

"Then you better hope you get this scythe before me, Emil."

The map falls between us, and we both lean over it, reading the single line that is written under a sketch of the scythe: *The All-Killer is in the Sunny tomb at the Antú Mausoleum.*

The moment I've read the last word, the map is incinerated by a gold fire-orb. Keon's eyes are burning like an eclipse as Luna witnesses the paper turning to ashes. She's devastated and furious, the first time our emotions have diverged because I'm feeling triumphant.

The All-Killer will be mine.

FORTY-SIX
FIRST DEATH

EMIL

I have to race Brighton to the All-Killer.

The name for that scythe breaks my heart. Its purpose is spelled out like a prophecy.

The scythe can kill all, even the unkillable.

Even Brighton.

Even me.

There's no way to know if the scythe can actually kill an immortal because everything was still so unknown around this time. Even Keon wasn't sure if he would actually resurrect or not, so how could he know that this scythe will actually be effective? I guess me and Brighton are about to race to this Antú Mausoleum to unearth the scythe from the Sunny tomb and give it a trial run. Then time will tell if it kills us for good or if we'll be reborn to live out the same nightmarish experience I've had since becoming the Infinity Son, destined to repeat this over and over.

"Kill him now," Luna commands, as if the Halo Knights are her Blood Casters.

Acceptance washes over Keon as he knows he is about to die, but fear charges through me because I do not want to die however the Halo Knights are about to kill him. I'm still reeling from the pain of the arrow that pierced Keon and being dragged down from the sky and crashing into the ground. I'm desperate to escape, to return back into my body, but that's not something I've mastered. I try to kill my connection with Keon, thinking about myself as me and only me. I was never an alchemist; I was an employee at a museum's gift shop. I have never had a boyfriend or husband; I've only opened my heart to two boys, and there's one who I hope becomes more. I am not a killer, but I will be if I can get back to my life and reach the scythe before my brother.

I am not Keon and Keon is not me.

Emil is not Keon and Keon is not Emil.

Keon Máximo and Emil Rey are two separate people.

We are not one soul.

There's a lightness, like I'm about to fly, but I'm grounded when I hear a Halo Knight tell Keon, "You have been sentenced to die for your crimes against phoenixkind."

Keon doesn't beg for his life. "May my soul go where it must," he whispers.

I know where it goes, and where it goes again, and where it may soon end.

Luna backs away, standing beside the tree, awaiting Keon's execution.

Brighton is watching too. I'm betting he doesn't know how to get out of here either, and since he can't be ejected out by a death like I will be, maybe that will buy me some time to get to the scythe before him.

The Halo Knight with crimson feathered sleeves says, "May you be a stranger to breath forevermore."

I'm bracing for Keon to be sliced up by sickles, or beheaded by the ax, or shot in the heart with an arrow, but the Halo Knights drop their weapons to their sides as they stand behind their phoenix companions. That's when I realize I've got this all wrong, that history has gotten this all wrong when we all just believed Keon being killed by the Halo Knights meant the Haloes did the dirty work themselves. This may be an appropriate punishment for Keon, but this death by a firing squad made up of phoenixes is one that I desperately do not want to live.

I go through everything again, telling myself that I am not Keon and Keon is not me, that we're two different people, I lie to myself that we're not even the same soul, but it's not sending me back into my own body and I'm going to be forced to live through my soul's first death.

This isn't acceptance; this is defeat.

"Fire!" all three Halo Knights shout.

The sun swallower roars with red-orange-yellow flames.

The century breathes sapphire fire.

The light swallower blasts a lightning bolt.

Keon is burned alive, and I am too.

The phoenixes are unrelenting with their power, destroying Keon with a vengeance, as if they know he is responsible for the deaths of their kind, and it's strange to think that Keon would've needed to create a scythe like the All-Killer when you can execute someone with phoenix force alone.

It's a miracle that our soul survives after a death this brutal.

FORTY-SEVEN
THE ALL-KILLER

BRIGHTON

This is what it's like to watch Emil die.

The phoenixes are roasting Keon alive, his skin bubbling under the streams of fire and shredding from the bolts of lightning. Emil has fallen to the ground, his body still intact, but he's writhing in pain. It's horrific watching him being tortured like this. I'm hit with memories of Dad choking on his blood and Ma being blasted by my fire-bolt, but watching Emil screaming for his life even though he isn't about to die is so disturbing that I know I don't have what it takes to kill him. I wish I could do something to save him, but as I rush to be by his side, Emil fades away like he's a ghost. The phoenixes end their attack as Keon's blackened corpse continues burning.

"It is done," a Halo Knight says.

"Is it?" Luna asks.

Luna and the Halo Knights watch Keon's corpse as if it is about to come back to life. I know the answer, but I can feel Luna's hope and curiosity building. If Keon resurrects, that means she must confront the enemy she's had killed, but it also means resurrection is real. However, if Keon stays dead, then her ultimate plans with phoenix blood have been derailed. She won't get her answer tonight. But what I'm not feeling from Luna is any remorse for what she's done. She can't be so heartless given how driven she is to resurrect the sister she loves, but she holds no love for Keon.

Meanwhile, I'm still trying to get Emil's screams out of my head.

I watched Emil die.

I did and I didn't.

I know he's alive back home in our timeline, but I'm still unsettled.

Keon's corpse turns to ash, but I'm the only one who sees his ashes snaking out of the flames and slithering into the mist before flying into the night, ready to be reborn somewhere else, and as someone else.

"It is done," the Halo Knight says again. Then he turns to Luna. "As is our alliance. If you are seen committing any crimes against phoenixkind, then—"

Luna holds up a hand. "Save your threats for someone who wasn't audience to this spectacle of your power."

"Very well. Let us know if you locate the scythe. There is still work to be done."

"I will," Luna lies.

The Halo Knights mount the phoenixes and kick off, flying into the night right as it begins drizzling.

Luna watches the raging fire, eyeing it as if Keon might step out of the flames. The drizzle turns to rain and washes out the fire. She's shivering from the cold, but she doesn't bother fastening her cloak tighter or running for shelter. She kneels before where Keon's corpse was and finds nothing. No blood, no bones. He is gone. She scoops up the dirt, inspecting it as if to find a single speck of ash, unaware that his ashes have already fled the scene. Luna sighs as she picks up the muddy gloves, pocketing them inside her cloak like it's some consolation prize since she didn't get the All-Killer. A threat continues to exist that can thwart her, and it keeps a hollowness within her. I'm familiar with this feeling. It's the same beast that can't be fed that's in me too. Everyone tries to weaponize my ambition against me as I've imagined Luna's had her ambitions used against her. There is always another objective, another mission to win, another target to defeat. The beast will eat until I die, and I need to make sure that the beast and I live forever.

I'm going back to my time.

If I had to connect myself to Luna, I now have to unplug.

It's true that Luna and I have a lot in common. Our ambitions for eternal life, the beasts that live within, our willingness to kill for the right reasons. But our hearts are different. That much is clear given how little she cares after watching her partner in crime Keon obliterated by phoenixes. For everything that I have said about being willing to kill Emil, my imagination was never powerful enough to conjure a vision as traumatic as what I just watched. What did I think would happen if I swung the All-Killer into Emil? That he would die painlessly? That everything would go dark instantly instead of Emil watching me hold the bloody scythe as he bleeds out? That I would feel nothing once he's dead?

If Emil dies, I will grieve him across my immortal life.

If I kill him, I may not be able to live with myself.

On the other hand, Luna is not grieving Keon, and when she had the opportunity to kill him, she did the dirty work herself by killing Bautista, and even tried to end Keon's line of infinity once and for all with Emil.

I will not kill Emil once, let alone three times.

Then there's the matter of Luna murdering her parents and killing their ghosts to become more powerful. I hated watching Dad die and I hate myself for killing Ma, but I will be bringing them back to life because I love them.

Luna and I are not one in the same.

I'm Brighton Rey.

I am the Infinity Reaper.

I am the creator of Spell Walkers of New York.

I am the son of Carolina and Leonardo Rey.

I am the brother of Emil Rey.

Darkness swallows the forest, and I'm back in that pitch-black landscape with nothing and no one except Luna. She's drenched and standing tall, still looking as determined as ever to make sense of what her future holds. I know what must be done to secure mine. Luna fades away, and I return into my body. My eyes and ears adjust to the silver and sapphire flames roaring around me. I recall the fire and inhale a deep breath. The sky is still dark, but the sun is beginning to rise. Darren and Mr. Bowes watch me as I orient myself.

"I did it," I say. It's strange using my voice again from my throat and not as some spectral visitor in a memory that wasn't mine.

"You found the weapon?" Darren asks.

"The All-Killer."

"Cool name."

"Not cool," Mr. Bowes says. "How are you feeling?"

I get up and shake out my legs, which fell asleep. "Good. I have to go."

"Slow down. You were just gone for almost two hours," Mr. Bowes says.

Two hours. That felt like ten minutes. Emil has a head start. "Where is the Antú Mausoleum? The All-Killer was buried inside a tomb."

Darren pulls out his phone and does a search online. "It's in the Bronx."

I can't believe it. I was nervous that the mausoleum was going to be somewhere across the country, maybe even across the world. But the scythe that can kill the unkillable has been hidden in my home borough all this time. "We have to go now. Emil knows where the scythe is too."

Mr. Bowes rests a hand on my shoulder. "Take a breath. This is all happening very quickly."

"If I don't get the scythe, Emil is going to kill me."

"Am I supposed to believe you won't kill him if you get the chance?"

I shrug his hand off of me. "I don't need your support."

"You're right, Brighton. It might be best if Darren and I take off and leave you to this."

Darren sucks his teeth. "Dad, I'm not going anywhere. I'm going to help bring Mom back to life."

"You're not thinking clearly, Darren. You haven't slept enough."

"Stop talking to me like I'm some child! I'm fourteen!"

"You are still a child and—" Mr. Bowes begins looking around. "Darren? Darren! Brighton! Where are you guys?"

I don't understand the confusion. I wave. "We're right here."

"He can't see us," Darren says. His eyes are glowing like stars. He's cast an illusion, concealing us like he did himself earlier tonight when I returned from the cemetery. "I don't need his permission. I need to make sure you survive so you can bring my mom back."

Once the scythe is within my possession and my parents have been resurrected, I am going to build my own team of heroes, and Darren will be my first recruit. Someone willing to turn his back on his father is someone I want on my side.

I glare at Mr. Bowes, glad to be leaving him behind.

Silver and sapphire wings bloom behind me, ready to fly to the mausoleum.

Flying across New York while the sun is coming up is an unforgettable experience.

A new day is truly beginning.

It's been almost twenty-four hours since I was dashing across Long Island to reach Brooklyn and rescue Ma from the stresses of hiding in havens. In that time, I accidentally killed her and buried her and discovered I can resurrect her. I've grown stronger with my new abilities to fly and retrocycle. And now I'm en route to unearth a scythe that my brother and Halo Knights want to use to kill me. But I will prevail and hold the world in the palm of my hand, spinning it as I see fit.

The Antú Mausoleum is in Kingsbridge, several train stops north from where Emil and I grew up. It's a small complex of seven buildings, and I descend from the sky into the center of it. Darren practically jumps out of my arms after holding on to me for dear life. He's scared of heights and kept his eyes closed the entire time; no illusion of his own was going to convince him that he was safe on the ground when he knew that he could fall hundreds of feet at any moment. It's unfortunate that we couldn't hitch a ride or steal a car, but we had to be fast. For all I know, Emil is already here and ready to swing the All-Killer into me. If I try phasing through the scythe, will I be okay? Maribelle had mentioned that she was able to cut through June with the oblivion dagger while she was incorporeal, so I shouldn't take any chances against the All-Killer.

This complex is beautiful with its beds of flowers and small fields of grass and open-air buildings that allow for all tombstones to be touched by sunlight, moonlight, and starlight. Maybe in a thousand years when I'm brave enough to die, I will create my own mausoleum to my liking and rest there forever.

"I'm walking home later," Darren says, getting his hair out of his eyes.

I shush him. "Lower your voice. They can be here already."

"Sorry," Darren whispers.

The first time Emil retrocycled, he was exhausted. I'm really tired too, but adrenaline is getting me through this. I'm hoping the horrible death Emil lived through was so taxing that it slows him down.

"How do we know which building?" Darren asks.

"The All-Killer is in the Sunny tomb."

"So it'll be exposed under the sun or something?"

"Sunny is the last name."

"Is that some relative of Keon's?"

"Your guess is as good as mine."

I'm not expecting this person to be related to Keon. If I were Luna and looking for a scythe that I knew could kill me, I would have spent decades exploring every option, including desecrating every family member's tomb in the event Keon hid it there. It's not impossible that this is exactly what happened and that Luna has already found the All-Killer and never told the Halo Knights. Maybe she even found a way to destroy the scythe. If she hasn't, it might be smart for me to do so.

"Let's spread out," I say.

"What? Isn't that the last thing we should do?"

"Stop thinking about horror movies. This is real life, and you're one of the most powerful celestials I know." This isn't a lie either. His illusions could probably trick me into believing the unbelievable. I can tell Darren is trying to steel his nerves, but he's still shaky. "Emil is hunting me, but he's not expecting you at all. He would also never do anything to harm you."

He nods, and I begin walking away. "Brighton?"

"Yeah?"

"I want to be there when you kill Emil," Darren says.

It's chilling how serious he is. I've just told him that Emil would never hurt him, and Darren still wants to watch Emil get gutted. "This mission is no longer about killing Emil. This is about protecting my life from the All-Killer. Once I've dealt with the scythe, then we resurrect your mother and my parents and everyone gets to live happily ever after. Got it?"

"Got it," Darren says. That revenge in his heart will die once his mother is alive again.

I go to the first tiny building that's close to the iron-fenced entrance so I can work my way around clockwise. There is no Sunny tomb, but I do think about my dreams of making resurrections a worldwide accessibility. No one should have to bury their loved ones before they're ready to go. Emil, Prudencia, and Ness all believe everything different is wrong. If it weren't for Keon Máximo creating specters—which has scared generations and continues to—then Maribelle wouldn't have the knowledge to bring back the dead. Maybe this is what it will take to show the world that specters are good for humankind.

There is no Sunny tomb in the second building either, but the third time is the charm.

The headstone reads *ASTIN SUNNY* with his birth and death dates and a gold icon of a sun emblazoned into the granite.

I do not know who Astin Sunny is or who he was in relation to Keon Máximo. It's possible he is no one. If I had to hide something as powerful as the All-Killer and didn't want anyone to track it down, I wouldn't hide it anywhere personally connected to me. I'd bury it under a haunted playground in Arkansas or in some grave of a stranger in Ohio or some cave in Brazil. But for whatever reason Keon chose to hide the scythe in Astin Sunny's tomb, and it's still intact. That means I got here before Emil and that I'm going to be okay.

I phase my hand into the Sunny tomb. Goose bumps spread all over my body because I'm anticipating brittle bones that crack at the slightest touch or mummified skin, but instead my hand grabs something that is as solid and strong as a rock. My heart is pounding as I pull the object out of the tomb.

I have it. . . . It's mine.

The scythe to kill all has been hidden with the dead.

The All-Killer.

I expected the All-Killer to be a standard scythe with a wooden or metal staff and a curved steel blade, but of course it's far more extraordinary. The scythe appears to be fashioned completely out of bone with the staff running about five feet long and the bone-blade curved like a crescent moon. There are veins of black and silver running across the entire thing that shine under the sunlight. Nothing feels more destined for me, the Infinity Reaper, to wield this scythe than the two grips that have been carved out like infinity loops. Maybe I should rebrand the All-Killer as the Infinity Killer. My fingers tighten around the handles, and I never want to let go. The last thing I should do is bury this scythe that was born to kill.

I walk away from the tomb, feeling more invincible than ever.

I look up from the All-Killer to discover I have visitors. I've been so nervous about Emil and his group getting here before me that I forgot the Halo Knights were hunting me too. The triad of Halo Knights are hovering aboveground on their phoenixes. I don't recognize the young man or woman in the back who are riding the sun swallowers, but the one in the bronze jacket is that French Halo Knight who I saw online begging people to not hurt phoenixes just so they can become specters. I believe his name was Chris—no, Crest. I begin piecing everything together. Emil isn't here because he doesn't have the guts to kill me, but he still wants me dead, so he's sent the Halo Knights to do his dirty work. If I'd done this, I would've been villainized. I'm sure Prudencia is comforting Emil right now, assuring him that this is for the best. I grip the scythe tighter.

"The All-Killer is mine," I say.

"It has a name?" Crest asks, dismounting his phoenix, which is bright yellow like his feathered sleeves.

"Emil didn't tell you?"

Crest tilts his head. "I haven't been in touch with him since our first meeting, when he refused to help us in our efforts to destroy you. I'd hoped he'd remain neutral, but naturally he retrocycled and then led you to the scythe."

"I didn't need him," I snap. I'm so tired of people thinking that I've only gotten where I am because of Emil. I'm also surprised that Emil didn't snitch. "How did you find me?"

Crest gestures at the woman. "Jazmin saw a child flying with blue-and-gray wings of fire."

"Silver and sapphire," I correct. He won't dull my shine. "And I'm not a child."

"Technically not. You're old enough to fight your own battles, but you're too young to wage war responsibly."

"Are you here to give me a handbook on how to do so or here to try and kill me?"

"We won't just try," the other man says.

Crest whirls around. "Shut it, Blaise."

"Yeah, shut it, Blaise," I taunt.

"You are guilty, Brighton, of causing lasting damage against phoenixkind with your lies about resurrection." Crest unsheathes an infinity-ender dagger. "We will make you a stranger to breath forevermore."

Fireworks explode into the sky, scaring the phoenixes so much that Jazmin and Blaise are thrown off their backs and slammed onto the ground. Why are there fireworks? What's the occasion at seven in the morning? There is no smoke in the sky after the fireworks vanish because they're not real and they were never there. Darren comes running out from behind a building where he safely cast this illusion; it's good to know that his power can trick phoenixes too. If the Halo Knights try flying away once they've realized what a mistake they've made by challenging me, Darren can cast an illusion to make the phoenixes think they're about to crash into a wall, or even trapped in a box.

"Fire!" Blaise shouts.

"No!" Crest exclaims.

The sun swallower breathes fire at Darren. He freezes. No illusion can save him now, but I can. I dash across the lot and shove Darren so hard that he bangs into a tomb. He groans in pain, but at least he wasn't burned alive.

"My back hurts," Darren says.

"You'll be okay," I say. If he's going to become a hero who's out on the field, he better get used to being thrown around. "Conceal yourself. I'm going to handle them."

"I want to help."

"They're no match for me or the All-Killer," I say, waving the scythe like a flag. "But good job distracting them with those fireworks."

Darren nods with glowing eyes and makes me believe he's invisible.

I run back into the new battlefield, raising the All-Killer high. "You tried to burn a fourteen-year-old alive?"

"No, no! Just wait!" Crest shouts. "Blaise acted outside of my orders—"

I dash past Crest and swing the scythe across Blaise's neck. His head rolls to the underbelly of his phoenix, which cries in lament.

I've claimed my first soul with the All-Killer.

Crest can't believe he's watching Blaise's headless corpse fall to its knees and then flat. He looks at me like I'm a monster when they're the ones who have come to kill me. Typical. The narratives people create in their heads to justify their actions will never surprise me. If he's supposed to be their commander, he is doing a terrible job by standing as still as he is. Maybe he's making peace with the fact that he's about to die too.

Jazmin mounts her phoenix, and the sun swallower breathes burning hot flames in my direction, unrelentingly, but I enter my void so the fire phases through me and only scorches the ground. I hear her battle cry as if she's succeeded in burning me alive, and then her gasp when she realizes I've survived, unscathed. I fly toward the sun swallower, decapitating it with the scythe, and the phoenix's body explodes in fire, consuming Jazmin too, giving her the death she aimed to give me.

Blood drips from the All-Killer as ashes rain down.

"You forced my hand," I say, pointing the scythe at Crest.

"You brought this on yourself when you consumed phoenix blood," Crest says.

"All I've brought to myself is immortality and a weapon to kill the unkillable."

Blaise's sun swallower screeches at the sky before setting its eyes on me. The phoenix runs at me, but instead of using its power, it's trying to attack me with brute force. The phoenix tries grabbing me with its talons and smacking me with its wings, but I keep phasing through all its efforts while keeping an eye on Crest to make sure he doesn't pull a fast one with his infinity-ender. If Crest were smart, he would hop on his phoenix and fly away, but he's a Halo Knight and that means he's willing to lay down his life to save a phoenix that will resurrect when it dies. Technically, this sun swallower won't once it's killed by my scythe, but I still think the Halo Knights are ridiculous as a whole. The phoenix corners me against the gate, and fire begins glowing within its beak. As the sun swallower cranes its head back, I slice its head off, and the phoenix blows up in a fiery fashion.

I wipe the sweat from my brow and march toward Crest. "When you threaten my life, death follows."

"I will die for my cause," Crest says, defeated. "I hope it's clear you will be hunted by Halo Knights until we've put you down."

"Then you will *all* die for your cause."

"Soleil, attack!"

I brace myself for this yellow phoenix, Soleil, to strike with a bolt of lightning just like Tala's light howler, but instead it glides toward me. I'm going to drive my scythe across its underbelly as soon as it's close enough. My moment almost comes when the phoenix screeches and combusts like it's been carrying a bomb. I have no time to wonder what the hell happened to it when the explosion blasts me into the air and I slam into a headstone. I inhale the deepest breath as the nerves in my back scream in pain. Who attacked us? Is it a Brightsider who's come to help me? I realize I'm empty-handed. Where is the All-Killer? My vision is blurry as I look around for the scythe, spotting it a few feet away from me. A swarm of ashes begins coalescing from the ground and forms the same phoenix, good as new. Did I hallucinate this? Did Darren cast an illusion? I suddenly remember Emil geeking out about a breed of phoenixes that combust as an attack, like kamikazes, and are reborn moments later. They're named breath spawns because that's how long they're essentially gone from the world before returning. These breeds are effective weapons, and I should look into getting a few of these phoenixes for myself once I survive this battle against Soleil. Until then, I have to kill this phoenix once and for all before it keeps killing itself to try and kill me.

I cast fire-bolts at Soleil, blowing holes through its wings. The phoenix screeches as it nosedives toward me, but this time I'm fast enough to reenter my void as Soleil explodes.

This buys me a few moments.

I scoop up my scythe and yell at Crest, "You will watch your phoenix die forever!"

Crest runs at me with the infinity-ender dagger, and I charge him with the All-Killer.

There is a slight admiration for Crest because it takes courage to try and assassinate an immortal, but courage can be downright suicidal. Is Crest aware how painfully mortal he is? There are infinite ways for me to kill him. A fire-bolt. Dash-drag him into traffic. Fly him into the sky and drop him into the ocean. I haven't tapped into my ghostly possession powers yet, but phasing into Crest's chest and ripping out his heart is a classic. But those are only deaths, whereas I'm seeking pure demise against those who want me dead. The All-Killer is how I can destroy someone's soul so they will never be reincarnated and can never be resurrected.

Crest swipes at me with the infinity-ender, and I phase through his wide arc, grateful that he doesn't have an oblivion dagger. I sweep up with the All-Killer and slice his hand off, watching as his fist remains tight around the infinity-ender. Crest screams in agony as he falls to the ground. He stares at his phoenix's swarming ashes.

"May I see you in another life, Soleil."

"You won't have one."

Sunlight illuminates Crest as he stares into the sky, his eyes widening as I swing the All-Killer down into his heart.

I dash toward the field of ash, right as Soleil is resurrecting, and hold the All-Killer in the center of the swarming ashes as they come together. The phoenix is reborn with the scythe already inside it, and I stare into Soleil's large eyes as I rip it open. I phase through the phoenix's final explosion, which is so grand it obliterates two buildings in the mausoleum. Tombs are burning as the garden blackens.

I am victorious against the Halo Knights and their phoenixes.

I am admiring the blood on the scythe, when someone shouts my name. I turn to find Emil hovering in the sky with his fiery wings and Wyatt, Prudencia, and Ness riding Nox. They're far too late. There was a chance for them to all stop me if they'd worked together with the Halo Knights, but now I'm too skilled with this scythe. I will spare my brother's life, maybe Prudencia's if she begs, but I will not hesitate to slaughter the others.

The All-Killer has turned me into the ultimate Infinity Reaper.

When I kill someone, they will stay dead forever.

FORTY-EIGHT
FIRST KILL

EMIL

I died as Keon for nothing.

The whole point of retrocycling was to get the All-Killer before Brighton, but there he is, wielding it like an absolute psychopath after I've just watched him use the scythe to murder Crest and slice open a breath spawn phoenix in a matter of seconds.

This is my fault, I took too long to recover after returning into my body, but my first death really took a toll on me. Ness, Wyatt, and Prudencia were begging me to calm down and chill, but after seeing Brighton retrocycle due to his connection with Luna, I knew we needed to move fast. There wasn't time to get into everything I experienced in the past, like how Keon's love for Astin really shone a light on my own heart, or how Keon spoke of having his own death predicted. All I could really breathe out was that Brighton had retrocycled too and that I felt the fury of three phoenixes until Keon's final, choked breath. I tried to take flight to get here before Brighton, but I was too weak to sustain the wings until I rested a bit. Wyatt convinced me to hang back and rest for a few minutes because Brighton would likely be stuck in the past anyway without Luna's death to force him out, and that he would be wiped when he returned, but he was wrong and now this mausoleum is on fire and lives have been taken.

I descend onto the ground and hear Nox land down behind me.

"What did you do?" I ask.

"The Halo Knights threatened my life, so I took theirs," Brighton says.

"Knights? P-p-plural?" Wyatt asks shakily.

"Three Knights, three phoenixes."

"You bastard!" Wyatt cries. He snaps around at Prudencia and Ness. "Off of Nox. Now!" They listen, and Wyatt leans against Nox's head, like a rider mounting their racehorse. "Nox, charge—"

I step in front of Nox, risking major injuries, maybe even my life, before Wyatt can attack. "Wait! Just wait!"

"He killed phoenixes and their protectors!"

Brighton laughs. "You villainize me for killing as if the Halo Knights don't have blood on their own hands. Emil, did you tell your new boyfriend how they brutally murdered you in the past?"

Wyatt is shaking even more as he stares at me with teary eyes. "If you think I will give Brighton a chance to kill Nox, you are sorely mistaken. I am sorry, but I will kill him myself."

I've always believed heroes shouldn't have body counts, but as Wyatt once told me after sharing the story of his own first kill, I will never feel alive if I have the chance to save those I love by killing and I don't take it. The difference is Wyatt killed strangers, and I have to kill my brother. I have known Brighton my entire life. Still, if

Wyatt or Ness or Prudencia get killed because I had the chance to kill Brighton and I didn't take it, I will never be able to live with myself.

I step out toward Brighton. "Last chance."

Brighton shakes his head. "No, this is your last chance to get your people out of here. I hated watching you die and I'm hoping to spare you from a final death. Turn around and never get in my way again."

I'm so exhausted in my bones and muscle and soul that I would be ready to welcome death instead of living in a world under my brother's reign. But I don't get to die until Brighton does.

"If you won't hand over the scythe, then— Pru!"

Prudencia is quick, telekinetically snatching the scythe from Brighton before he can phase away.

The All-Killer flies toward me, and I'm quick to catch it. It's made of bone and heavy like a log. I wrap my fingers around the infinity loop handles, wishing I had greater physical strength to wield this easily. I'm lucky that out of Brighton's many powers none of them are telekinesis. If he's going to make a move for the All-Killer, he's going to have to come close enough for me to kill him. I'm nervous because he can dash at me or phase around or fight me with fire while I'm holding on to the scythe. What I'm not expecting is for Brighton to go invisible.

"He's camouflaging," Ness says.

I start swinging the scythe at the air, both hoping and scared that I'll hit him.

No matter how clear it is that Brighton needs to be stopped, it doesn't make it any easier. For eighteen years we were twin brothers without the world on our shoulders. We grew up playing games of pretend where we imagined ourselves having powers, though nothing has come as close to the real life we've been living out. We have known each other's dreams, and I really thought I was going to get to watch Brighton launch his own talk show one day where he would share the stage with other notable people. But Brighton doesn't want to share the stage; he only wants the spotlight for himself. He hasn't cared about highlighting any other person's story now that he's decided his is the most fascinating and worthwhile. If someone tries to stop him from claiming the world as his own, he will end them. It doesn't matter if they're a dangerous Blood Caster or an enforcer or a Halo Knight or a phoenix. It definitely won't matter if it's his own brother.

There is no coming back from all the damage Brighton has done.

There is only ending him before he can do more.

I keep swinging the scythe, when I spot him by a dead garden.

"Over there!" I shout.

Brighton vanishes.

I'm trying to listen for his footsteps.

"By the gate!" Prudencia shouts.

Brighton is there for a moment before camouflaging.

"Behind you, Wyatt!" Ness shouts.

Brighton vanishes again before Nox can attack.

"The fire!" Wyatt shouts.

Brighton is standing on a burning tomb before vanishing.

How the hell is he moving around so quickly? Is he just dashing while camouflaging? Is he phasing underground and popping up? He's really figuring out effective combos with his powers. Everything gets really chaotic as we all keep seeing Brighton pop in and out of different places, seconds apart. Maybe he's teleporting like June does.

If Brighton can fly and retrocycle, I bet he's unlocked a teleportation power by now too.

"I think he's teleporting!"

"A sound guess!" Wyatt says.

"Then why are there two of him?!" Prudencia asks.

Brighton can be found at the gate and in the garden at the same time before vanishing.

"Is he working with a shifter?" Wyatt asks.

"Shifters can't teleport," Ness says.

"Then I don't know!"

Brighton appears a few feet away from me but doesn't vanish this time. Another Brighton appears. Then a third. Another. A fifth, a sixth, a seventh. The seven Brightons surround us.

"Is cloning one of his powers?" Wyatt asks. "A hydra one, perhaps?"

When we were all studying golden-strand hydras, we never found anything about that breed being able to clone themselves. Only abilities like speed and body regeneration and camouflage. Maybe it's a ghost power? We've never seen June clone herself, but maybe Brighton has some extension because he has the blood of multiple ghosts in him? I don't know, nothing is making sense, and I got to wonder if it has nothing to do with Brighton and everything to do with another player on the battlefield.

"Does he have backup?" I ask, looking around and finding no one.

"Maybe . . ." Ness says, scanning too. "Hold on to that scythe, Emil."

I grip the All-Killer tighter, knowing that Brighton might be waiting for the perfect chance to snatch it out of my hands.

"Over there!" Ness shouts.

Brighton has surfaced again, but this time he hurls a series of fire-bolts directly into Nox, causing the obsidian phoenix to take flight chaotically, and I'm scared Wyatt is about to be flung off. Wyatt yells at Nox to settle, but they're rising higher and higher. Brighton is unrelenting as he continues shooting fire-bolts, and I charge toward him as fast as I can with the heavy scythe to chop off his arm so he can stop the suffering. Nox screeches from above before combusting in bright orange flames and—

And . . .

No . . .

The fire consumes Wyatt too.

The sky begins raining ashes, and Wyatt's burning body slams down onto the fiery tomb.

There's no way he survived this, but please, please, please, I hope he did; I can't live without him. I race toward Wyatt's body—his living, breathing, alive body. I'm about to run through the fire when Prudencia screams like I've never heard her before.

"Behind you!" she shouts.

I swing around with the All-Killer, but Brighton isn't there.

He's behind someone else.

The world freezes as Brighton punches his fist through Ness's back. Ness looks at me for the longest moment before Brighton's fist emerges out of his chest, holding his burning heart.

Brighton throws down Ness's corpse like he was no one.

"NESS!"

I can't breathe.

This is no way to live.

Has the universe charged me with life sentences that span every single life I live because of crimes in past lives?

My soul isn't worth this much heartbreak.

I fly toward Brighton, but he grins as he vanishes, too scared to fight me. I brake in the air, hovering over Ness's corpse. My eyes are stinging with tears as I watch him so lifeless. He should've taken his chance to run away and restart his life across the world. Everything was supposed to be different for him; I was fighting for Ness's freedom so he could live outside the shadows of Iron and Luna and all the terrible things they made him do. Now he's been killed before he can discover who he wants to be.

"Emil!" Brighton shouts.

I turn to find Brighton with his hands wrapped around Prudencia's throat. He won't kill her. She's so outside the realm of someone like Ness, who he's never liked, or Wyatt, who just threatened his life. Not only is Prudencia our best friend, Brighton has loved Prudencia for years—

He snaps her neck.

"You forced my hand," Brighton says, not bothering to even look at Prudencia's corpse. "But nobody has to stay dead."

That's what this massacre has been about.

Brighton is killing the people I love to prove the resurrection ritual is a necessary part of life.

All it's done is made me want to drive this scythe into his heartless chest.

I hold up the All-Killer.

"You can't kill me, Emil," Brighton says as he walks toward me, stopping in my face.

I'm holding the weapon that can end Brighton, but I feel so powerless. Once I kill Brighton, I will be alone because he's killed everyone I love. What does my life look like after he's dead? All I can do now is make sure that no one else in this world has to grieve a loved one who was slain by Brighton.

I swing the scythe down on my brother.

The blade goes right through him, like he's a living ghost.

"You can't kill me," Brighton echoes. "But I will kill you."

Suddenly, Brighton transforms into a younger boy—Darren Bowes. That was never Brighton. It was an illusion. What else was an illusion? The deaths of my friends? Brighton killing Crest and the phoenix? Is Brighton even here? He must be, and he's got to be working with Darren because there's no way Darren would've known that I would come to this mausoleum.

I'm still trying to figure out what was real and what was an illusion.

What about the infinity-ender Darren plunges into my heart?

I live long enough to know this death is real.

FORTY-NINE
THE REY OF DARKNESS

BRIGHTON

My brother has been killed.

Is this an illusion? Did I really witness that?

Darren twists the infinity-ender inside Emil's heart.

The All-Killer falls out of Emil's hands, and then he falls too.

Darren stands over Emil, eyeing the bloody dagger.

This is real.

This wasn't the plan.

After Emil got his hands on the All-Killer, Darren concealed me before I could be killed. I instructed Darren to distract everyone long enough for me to sneak up on Emil to snatch the scythe. I'd been chasing Emil around the mausoleum as he kept flying away with the All-Killer, but I'm realizing that wasn't real. Darren distracted me too so he could get close enough to get his revenge on Emil. It doesn't matter that I'm going to be able to resurrect Darren's mother; he still wanted Emil dead anyway, and he succeeded.

The others haven't noticed: Prudencia keeps swiping the air, screaming about how her powers aren't working; Ness is dodging punches from someone who isn't there; and Wyatt is on Nox, chasing no one. But Darren's illusion for me has broken. It was bound to since he can only juggle so many and mine alone felt complex. What did he make Emil see?

I dash toward Darren, just like earlier to save his life, but this time I shove him out of anger. Darren rolls across the ground, collecting scratches as the infinity-ender clatters on concrete. "WHAT DID YOU DO?!"

Everyone's illusions vanish as Darren groans in pain. "He got my mother killed!"

"EMIL!" Prudencia shouts as she runs toward him. "NO!"

Ness is frozen.

Wyatt dives down on Nox, jumping off the first chance he gets.

I kneel before Emil as his blood continues pooling out of his chest. I press down on his wound because maybe if he has enough blood inside of him, then his power will activate and he will begin self-healing. "Don't die, bro, don't die," I beg, even though his heart isn't beating. Watching Emil die as Keon was enough to prove that I don't actually want my brother dead no matter how pissed off I am at him and no matter how many fights we still have ahead of us as I pursue resurrecting our parents. Except we won't be fighting anymore about anything. An infinity-ender to the heart may be enough to end him forever, but even if he is somehow reborn, it won't be as himself. It will be some stranger wandering the world with no memory of ever being my brother.

Prudencia drops to her knees and feels Emil's pulse. "You killed him!"

"I didn't do this!"

She telekinetically throws me across the ground so that I go rolling toward the burning tomb. I'm dizzy as I look up to see her crying over Emil and Wyatt holding Emil's hand. Ness hasn't moved. He just keeps staring at my brother's corpse from afar.

I set my sights on Darren. I dash toward him as he's gotten to his feet and choke him against the gate. "I didn't order you to kill him!" Darren tries fighting—fighting for air, fighting to speak, fighting for freedom. But I squeeze tighter and watch his face go from red to purple. I am not even going to use my powers to kill him. I want to watch the light fade from his eyes. This disobedience and betrayal cost me my brother. I dig my nails deeper into his throat as Darren loses the energy to resist. "If you obeyed me, you could have had your mother back. Now you can join her." Darren's bloodshot eyes are bulging as his head begins dropping. He is a moment away from death, when I feel something so sharp that it's as if I've been killed myself.

"Got you," Ness says in my ear as he twists the infinity-ender in my back.

Pain ignites throughout my entire body and I try phasing away, but Ness keeps a tight hold on me. He slides the dagger out of my back and blood oozes out of my wound. I need to heal, but then Ness stabs me again and again and again. He's going to kill me. Darren is blue in the face and looks scared out of his mind. I cough, splattering blood on Darren. This is what Dad must've been feeling like when he was dying. Darren gets up and runs away. I try shouting for help, but every time I open my mouth, I can't find the air. I try casting fire to burn Ness and flying so I can drop him out of the sky, but the infinity-ender's effects are preventing me from tapping into my powers.

Ness forces me to my knees and holds my sinking chin up to stare at my brother's corpse. "This is for Emil," he says as he strikes my heart with the infinity-ender.

Everything goes dark because infinity isn't as long as I thought it would be.

FIFTY
DEATH TO INFINITY

NESS

I was once forced to cut Emil with the infinity-ender, but Brighton? I chose to stab him.

My killing days are supposed to be behind me, but that was before Brighton ripped my heart out of my chest by killing Emil. The sun still being up doesn't make sense when the world already feels darker without Emil. Brighton is responsible for this blackout, and that's why I grabbed the infinity-ender that he used to kill Emil and struck him over and over until I could feel his immortal life draining. I should have grabbed the scythe, but the dagger was closer and all I cared about was killing Brighton. If he somehow resurrects, I have no problem killing him again and again for the rest of my life.

I rip the infinity-ender out of Brighton's heart. His body slams against the ground. Blood pools around him as his frozen eyes stare at nothing. Now that Brighton is so still, I can't believe he was the Big Bad with reaper powers who was going to reign supreme. He just looks like any other ordinary teenage boy.

Mortal.

Time moves slowly as I approach Emil.

I still don't fully understand how Brighton tricked us. The way he was moving around had us wondering if he was teleporting and then he began cloning himself? I tried fighting the different Brightons, but I couldn't land a hit on any of them. It was like he was phasing through every punch without throwing any himself. That boy who Brighton was strangling had to be some sort of illusionist. Why Brighton was attacking him is beyond me, but if he's one of those stupid Brightsiders who aligned themselves with Brighton, then screw him too. Especially because his illusions prevented me from seeing what was really happening: Brighton killing Emil.

Maybe I should consider not witnessing Emil's death a small mercy.

"Is he dead?" Prudencia asks.

At first I think she's asking about Emil. "Brighton is dead."

She sucks in a gasp and rushes to Brighton's side.

I fall to my knees and hold Emil's limp hand, ignoring how Wyatt is holding Emil's other hand. His hazel eyes are closed. Blood is still flowing out of the wound in his chest; I'm able to glimpse the tear in his still heart, and it breaks me apart. I haven't cried this hard since my mother was killed. That loss was painful, but I can look back on my life and remember what it was like being my mother's son. I don't have that luxury with Emil. I hoped that we would become partners throughout life the way we were in war, but I will never know what it's like to wake up next to Emil or go on a date with Emil or marry Emil or start a family with Emil or even die old with Emil, all because he's already dead.

But he doesn't have to stay that way.

"Resurrection," I say.

Wyatt wipes his tears. "What?"

"We can bring Emil back."

"We mustn't. You said as much yourself."

"I said I wouldn't bring my mother back because everyone already knows she's dead. No one knows Emil is dead. We can get away with this."

"At what cost?"

"I don't care! If you actually have feelings for him, then you shouldn't either."

"You are aware that this was Brighton's argument too, yeah?"

I hate to relate to Brighton in any way, but I now understand his desperation to bring back his parents. If resurrection rituals become public knowledge like specter alchemy, then the politics of humankind are going to become even more divisive. There will be those who settle in with their grief and those who don't want to hurt in a world that is painful enough. Minds and hearts will be changing as losses of life happen.

"We have to try," I whisper.

"You know nothing about this ritual, Ness."

"I know his ashes will bring Emil back good as new."

"What if his soul has already passed on for reincarnation?"

"What if his soul can't move on? Luna suspected Bautista was able to reincarnate as Emil because she didn't stab him in the heart with the infinity-ender. Brighton didn't make her mistake."

"There are too many uncertainties, among them if Emil would approve of us doing this. He was willing to kill Brighton to make sure he wouldn't disturb the natural cycle of life."

"There's nothing natural about getting killed."

"There's also nothing natural about humans resurrecting." Wyatt looks down at Emil with teary eyes and brushes his dark curls. "I hope you find everything you didn't receive in this life in your next, sweet Emil, and on and on."

Emil shouldn't have to wait until his next life to find everything he deserves. Who is he even going to be? He won't be Emil anymore. Bautista may have retained some of Keon's memories, but Emil didn't have any of theirs. Emil was only Emil. I may not have personally known him during that time, but it's clear that his heart shone brighter than any of his phoenix flames. He was a marvel, and this life he lived should be the one he gets to finish.

"I won't say goodbye to you," I say to Emil, hoping he can somehow hear me.

My hand gets sweaty and then warm and then hot and then on fire; Wyatt's too. We both pat ourselves down until we put our fires out, but we can't do the same for Emil. His corpse begins burning in gold and gray flames and rapidly disintegrating. This gives me hope. If his powers were completely gone, then this shouldn't be happening. He would be like one of those phoenixes who got killed at the Sanctuary and couldn't come back to life. Maybe Luna's theory about the infinity-ender to the heart is wrong. There has been so much speculation as to what rules apply to specters in different circumstances, but not as many discoveries. Maybe specters can't be truly killed by the dagger the way phoenixes can. But what scares me now is that I can't be sure what's going to happen here. The only thing I can trust is the resurrection ritual, but I can't collect Emil's ashes to bring him back because they're flying away. I chase his ashes until they take to the sky, flying high to the clouds.

Maybe I should say goodbye to Emil's ashes, his last physical form. But I still can't stomach the idea that Emil is about to become someone else's past life.

"Come back, firefly."

It's my little prayer to the universe, but I can't imagine it will be answered.

"Ow!" Prudencia screams.

Brighton's corpse is blazing in silver and sapphire flames. Prudencia is holding her burnt hand as that son of a bitch melts away. Everyone in Emil's life had spoken highly of him before he became the Infinity Son, but the same can't be said for Brighton before he became the Infinity Reaper. Prudencia is sobbing. I can't believe she's actually grieving him. I'm not close to her, but my read on her has always been that she's a good-hearted person who deserves someone who isn't a self-absorbed power addict.

Good riddance.

Brighton's ashes swarm together, spinning like a twister, but they aren't flying away. The ashes continue twisting until they create a human silhouette that explodes in silver and sapphire flames. The fiery silhouette glows so bright, and when it dims, Brighton is standing there, alive and well. He gasps and pats down his naked body, which doesn't have any of the scars I inflicted with the infinity-ender. The Reaper's Blood has played out exactly as Luna once dreamed.

"You should've used the scythe," Brighton says.

I run for the All-Killer, but Brighton is faster. He picks up the scythe and swings it at me. I'm a moment away from being a corpse on the ground when the scythe freezes at my neck, but it's not Brighton who has chosen mercy. Prudencia's telekinetic grip is a lifesaver.

"Grab the scythe!" I shout.

Brighton sinks into the ground with the All-Killer.

I tense up, not knowing where Brighton will resurface and attack. He could drag me through the ground and bury me alive. He could be camouflaged somewhere nearby and slice me in half with the scythe. The options are endless because of his powers—powers that I helped make a reality. If I hadn't done so many of Luna's biddings, then the Reaper's Blood wouldn't have ever been brewed. Brighton would've never turned himself into the Infinity Reaper and stolen so many lives or become terrifyingly immortal . . . and Emil would still be alive.

"We must go!" Wyatt shouts, running for Nox.

I run toward the phoenix, looking over my shoulder in case Brighton pops up. Wyatt hops on Nox first, with Prudencia right behind him. I'm climbing on Nox when Brighton surfaces a few feet away, his eyes narrowing as he finds us trying to escape. "There!" I shout right as Brighton blasts fire-bolts our way. Prudencia telekinetically deflects each fire-bolt, even as Nox begins carrying us toward the sky. We're soaring away quickly as Brighton flies high into the air too. If he follows and strikes us down, we're all dead. But Brighton isn't following us. He is hovering in the sky with his fiery wings and the scythe that I should have used to kill him.

If I ever get another chance, I will kill the Infinity Reaper. Forever this time.

FIFTY-ONE

RESURRECTION

BRIGHTON

My infinity almost ended, but I live on now and I will forever.

Everyone thought I was boasting whenever I spoke of being the most powerful gleamcrafter, but here I am, back from the dead, and still the same person I was in life. I seem to remember everything too. My name is Brighton Rey. I'm the Infinity Reaper. I'm the sole survivor of my family. I was killed, and I have come back to life within moments. No specter has ever done what I have done. Not Keon, not Bautista, and not even Emil, who has just been killed.

Only me.

I continue hovering in the sky, staring down at the burning mausoleum and around the city. I go higher and higher and higher into the air and admire this world that I will turn into mine. I was stabbed multiple times with an infinity-ender dagger, the same weapon that killed Bautista with one stab to the stomach, and I still couldn't be destroyed for good. My fingers tighten around the All-Killer. This is the only weapon that is rumored to be able to obliterate my soul forever. I will use this scythe to annihilate my enemies so that my loved ones can never be killed again.

My enemies:

Ness for killing me.

Darren for killing Emil.

Iron for killing my mother.

And anyone else who stands in the way of resurrecting my parents.

I decide who lives and who dies.

This is the life of the one and only Infinity Reaper.

FIFTY-TWO
FORESIGHT

MARIBELLE

"Good morning, Mari."

Atlas's voice feels like a dream.

This time yesterday morning Atlas was nothing but ashes in a bottle, and now he's a real, resurrected boy. I've missed his breath and kisses on my neck, the way he squeezes us closer like we're one body, his fingers gently brushing my arms, and how I wake up with our hands locked together. I'll never have to miss this again. Atlas is already playing all these greatest, sweetest hits, and it makes me feel like we haven't missed a night of sleep together. In Atlas's eyes, we haven't. But I not only lived the truth, I survived it. I slept alone for weeks except two nights ago, when I had Tala and her soft lips all over my body and her fingers in my hair and her breasts against mine as we fell asleep together. Sweaty, gorgeous messes.

Tala may be gone, but Atlas is here.

"Good morning," I tell him.

"How'd you sleep?"

"Amazing. You?"

"A bit like I woke up from the dead."

"I wonder why."

"I wonder why," Atlas croons. He begins kissing my neck. "What do you . . ." Another kiss. ". . . want to do . . ." A deeper kiss. ". . . today?"

I flip over to face him, and I'm entranced by his prankster smile and how the sunlight from the window is turning his blond hair gold and how alive his heart and every other part of his body is. "I want to stay in bed with you today."

"Tomorrow too."

"And the day after."

"Why don't we just block out the whole month?"

"Year."

"Infinity, Mari, but after that we have to go somewhere else. Surfing, flying, anything."

"After infinity," I whisper before kissing him.

I love how hungry we are for each other, even after having sex last night on the very grounds where I resurrected him. If it weren't for how exhausted I was after all the hours spent with the Spell Walkers, debating if the resurrection ritual should be shared or buried, I would've made love again with Atlas in the comfort of this bed instead of just falling asleep together naked. I also need to come clean about having sex with Tala. Especially because I don't believe Tala was just scratching an itch. She was my light in an impenetrable darkness, a light that would have only grown brighter and brighter if Atlas wasn't alive. But Atlas is alive, so Tala's light has to fade.

I trail my fingers from his collarbone to his pecs to his abs and his—

The door knocks and I jump.

"Yo!" Wesley shouts from the other side of the door. "I'm going to run and pick up groceries. Want anything?"

I sigh. "To be left alone!"

"I'll see if they have that in stock. How about you, Zombie Atlas?"

"Same thing as Maribelle . . . and waffles!"

"Got it. I'll be back in a few!"

Atlas pulls me onto his chest. "Did you miss those interruptions?"

"I missed having something to interrupt."

"We have a few minutes before he's back."

"What happened to infinity?"

"We made that rule before waffles were on the table."

"Then I guess we better make the most of our time together."

I sit on top of Atlas, my hands clutching on to his shoulders. He gazes at me intensely. I can always tell by this look that he wants me as badly as I want him. His fingers are finding their way inside me when I look outside the window. The horizon is blue and beautiful except for one patch that's storming; it looks like a dark bruise in the sky. Then I see the massive bird—the light howler phoenix—flying toward the cottage, and I know who's riding her. I gasp and my body clenches as Atlas's fingers enter me.

"You good?" Atlas asks.

"Tala," I breathe. He's confused. I point outside the window. "She's here."

"Oh," he says as he pulls his fingers out. "Were you expecting her?"

"No."

"Rain check?" Atlas asks.

"Rain check."

There have been a couple times where the Spell Walkers interrupted

Atlas and me in the middle of sex, but that was always because we were needed for a rescue mission. I have no idea why Tala is here. Maybe she found Luna and is bringing her head as proof that she will never hurt us again. Or she's here because she wants to profess a love that I can't return. A love that I could've returned in another life.

I throw on clothes and rush through the living room without saying anything to Ruth, Eva, and Iris, and I bump straight into Wesley right as he dashes to the front door with his bags of groceries. Cartons of milk splash and fruit rolls, but I don't bother with the cleanup. I stare up at the sprinkling sky as Roxana descends. I finally get a good look at Tala riding her phoenix. Her dark hair is flowing down her back. Her glittering eye shadow is orange, yellow, and red as if one look can burn you. Her body is tight inside this black jumpsuit as if she's going diving into an ocean instead of flying through the sky. Her crossbow is strung across her back and dagger handles are peeking out from the insides of her boots. She's as beautiful and deadly as the first time I ever saw her.

"That's an entrance," Wesley says before calling into the house. "Ladies, come check this out!"

Everything has been a whirlwind since last night, including how that was the first time we've had our entire Spell Walker family under one roof in seven months. We had all last gathered for Eva's birthday, including Ruth and Esther, who normally spend their days in this cottage, and Iris and I weren't snapping at each other daily yet. It had felt like our war was frozen, that the world didn't hate us as Iris and Eva danced to classical Persian music blasting from a portable speaker while everyone else played cards and ate cake and fawned over baby Esther as she cooed and slept. Even I managed to let minutes go by without crying over my parents or obsessing over June. Last night felt like time freezing over again. I wasn't crying. I didn't care about hunting June. We celebrated life and rebirth (before arguing about the ritual). It was a reminder of simpler times, but Tala wasn't part of that era. Tala and I were forged by a different fire, and we burned differently.

"Maribelle," Tala says as she dismounts Roxana. The way she says my name like it's a curse is enough to stop me from running into her arms for a hug. Tala scans the grounds and finds the scorched earth from the Phoenix Pit. "You performed the resurrection."

"I . . ."

"Hello," Atlas says as he walks out of the house, followed by everyone else. He approaches Tala as friendly as ever with his hand out, but she stares at him like he's an abomination. He stops. "I'm sorry. I'll stay out of your space. I just wanted to thank you."

Tala's gaze becomes as sharp as her daggers. "I am fully aware of the precious lives lost so you can have yours again. Do not thank me for the role I played in your resurrection."

"I'm not. I'm thanking you for caring for Maribelle while I was dead." Atlas curls his fingers with mine, and I blush as Tala stares at our interlocked hands. "I've seen Maribelle grieve before. We all have," he adds, gesturing at everyone else. "You kept her alive, and I'm forever indebted to you."

I wish I could read Tala's mind. Atlas can be an absolute soldier in the streets, especially when trying to save innocent lives, but he's always been an amazing human who means well and does his best. Does Tala understand why I love Atlas so much and how I couldn't live without him? Does she regret helping me use dead phoenixes to bring him back to life? Her body language reveals nothing because she's so guarded when it comes to any feeling that isn't anger. But I've seen Tala be vulnerable as she exposes herself fully, and when our bodies say everything.

"If you want to repay that debt, I have a mission for you—all of you," Tala says.

Iris steps up. "I can't speak for Atlas and Maribelle, but our crew has been through a lot lately and we're taking time for ourselves. No missions."

"Not even to rescue Nicolette Sunstar?" Tala asks.

This gets everyone's attention.

"She's alive?" I ask.

Tala nods. "I've been in the city hunting Luna. Mostly on foot so Roxana wouldn't draw attention to us. There's a lot you see and hear on the ground that you do not in the sky. It seems the Blood Casters are hoping to rebuild after Brighton killed Stanton in the Bounds. Acolytes were on the streets, seeking new recruits, and I followed a gang of them back to the Light Sky Tower."

That's where Tala and I met. Luna and the Blood Casters were operating at the top floor, but by the time Tala and I had arrived, it had been cleared out. Then we destroyed it before fleeing together on Roxana. It would be really stupid or really calculating for Luna to return there knowing her whereabouts were exposed.

"No sign of Luna?" I ask.

"No, but I saw Dione Henri accompanying Roslyn Fox into the building."

"Who's that?" I ask.

"Iron's campaign manager," Iris says quickly. "But how do you know Sunstar is at Light Sky?"

Tala tilts her head. "I followed them inside."

"With no backup?" I snap.

"With no backup," Tala says.

I want to yell at Tala for being so reckless, but I understand her. Some people get so buried under their grief that they can't move, and then there are others who can't stop because they're not ready to sit in this world without the person they lost. I've been on both sides of that coin.

When I lost my parents, I had Atlas.

When Tala lost her parents, she had me.

When I lost Atlas, I had her.

But when Tala lost me, she had no one.

I wish I could have been by her side. We have stormed through the Bounds together, so driven by revenge that we were willing to fight some of the most dangerous celestials and specters just so we could get our hands on Luna. Of course Tala charged into the Light Sky Tower by herself if she thought it meant finding peace in her soul. "I'm glad you got out okay."

"I'm a survivor," Tala says. "There were too many acolytes patrolling the halls with wands to stay too close to Dione and Roslyn, but I managed to follow them underground and overheard Dione interrogating Roslyn on why they haven't just killed Sunstar yet. Apparently, Iron wants to keep her alive until he's voted into office. I don't know what he's planning, but my guess is Sunstar is being held in that vault that Luna told us about."

The vault where she had extra phoenix body parts. "They're cutting off Sunstar's connection to the stars."

"To weaken her power," Iris says. Her fingers curl into fists. "We have to break her out."

The Spell Walkers look among each other. Despite how exhausted they are, everyone nods.

"Brief retirement," Wesley says.

"If we save Sunstar, we're creating a world where we can rest," Iris says.

Atlas squeezes my hand. "I'm ready, Mari, but only if you are too."

I don't want to risk Atlas's life, but I don't want to grieve Tala's either.

"We're in," I say to Atlas and Tala.

Tala mounts Roxana. "I'll inform our commander, Crest, that you're all in. The Halo Knights are willing to cooperate in a recovery mission, as we trust Sunstar will be outspoken against the phoenix hunting and support all efforts to bind the powers of specters. I expect we will strike tonight."

We will need a tight plan to break in undetected with the added stakes of not exposing Atlas. Wesley will need to do a sweep and eliminate any cameras, which might not exist since I'm sure that Iron won't want any record of his campaign manager consorting with a Blood Caster. I imagine Ruth and Eva will stay behind as usual, but between me and Atlas and Wesley and Iris, we have more than enough power to take down armed acolytes. If the other Halo Knights can kick ass like Tala, then we'll really be in good shape for a successful recovery mission.

Suddenly, I feel a warning in my body.

Danger.

My psychic sense is picking up on something, and the warning is intensifying. It's so strong that I'm positive it's about to shape into a vision forecasting someone's death, just like Sera's power. Goose bumps pop up all over my skin, and my bones feel like they're rattling and might collapse. My head is spinning and I'm hyperventilating. I'm reliving the vision-dream I had of my parents dying and now wondering if this is what it feels like to have a vision while awake. There's this certainty in my soul that death is very nearby, that it's going to strike any moment now.

Is someone about to die? Am *I* about to die?

I scan everyone, trying to identify the threat. I'm always safe from Atlas. The same goes for Wesley and Ruth. Eva is a pacifist who wouldn't hurt anyone, let alone me. Baby Esther is obviously innocent. There have been many times that Iris has wanted to rip me apart, but we're actually on the same page with rescuing Sunstar. That leaves Tala. Is she lying about this mission and luring us into a trap? Does she want me dead because I didn't honor our vow to kill Luna? Is it because I rejected her heart? I brace myself, as if Tala is about to command Roxana to blast me with lightning bolts. Tala slides off Roxana, running toward me as if she wants to have my blood on her hands. Except the sense of danger isn't escalating as she charges me. And when she grabs my shoulders and looks me in the eyes with concern, I feel just as safe with Tala as I do Atlas.

"What's wrong?" Tala asks.

"Mari, talk to us," Atlas says.

I walk around the area, toward a pull, as if psychic frequencies are guiding me toward the danger. I stop at the Phoenix Pit. Does this have to do with Atlas's resurrection? Did I disturb some dark, unnatural forces by performing the ritual? The warning is buzzing in my body and screaming in my soul as I reach out at the air, toward some invisible force. I grab hold of something solid—someone solid.

The air shimmers and reveals Brighton with his eyes burning like eclipses. Everything about him is shocking. Brighton now being able to camouflage is the least confusing thing. He's wearing tight pants and a Halo Knight jacket with yellow feathered sleeves, similar to the one Tala traded in to that merchant so we could make the Star-stifler, except this jacket is bronze and bloodied with a hole where the breast pocket was. This was stolen from someone Brighton likely killed. Possibly with this scythe that he's wielding that looks like it was carved out of bone.

"Is this how you did it?" Brighton asks, staring at the Phoenix Pit.

"Brighton . . . What's going on?"

"Is it?" he asks again more firmly.

Brighton's eyes are no longer burning, but there's still a deep darkness in his gaze. He's become so powerful and dangerous that my power continues screaming at me. I'm used to detecting immediate threats that could kill me, but this is different. Brighton is a lasting threat. It's as if he could be sleeping and my psychic sense would still warn me about him like some unending siren.

"Hey, Brighton," Atlas says, walking over.

"Stay back!" I shout.

Tala points at Brighton. "Where did you get that jacket?"

Brighton grins. "I stole it off a corpse. I needed something to wear after my resurrection."

"Crest is dead?" Tala asks as I ask, "You died?"

"Yes," Brighton says to both of us.

Tala flips her crossbow over her shoulder in the blink of an eye.

Brighton holds up a finger. "I was killed by an infinity-ender, and I came back to life. What do you think that's going to do?"

"Let's see," Tala says as she fires an arrow.

I expect it to phase through Brighton, but it strikes him in the chest. He flinches and growls as he rips out the bloody arrow and drops it into the Phoenix Pit. I watch as his wound heals.

"My turn," Brighton says. He's winding up a fire-bolt to throw at Tala, when I jump in the path.

"Don't!"

He freezes. "If someone comes for my life, I take theirs. This was true for those Halo Knights and those phoenixes."

"You killed them all," Tala says, her voice cracking and furious.

"Not all Halo Knights. Just a few. But if the others come for me, I will be forced to kill them too."

I can't believe I helped Brighton get these powers. He's a threat to everyone here, but maybe I can lure him away to protect them. "Why don't we go somewhere to talk? Just the two of us?"

"The only thing I need from you are the ritual instructions."

If only my power could have warned me sooner how deadly Brighton is, then I would've never helped him.

"Don't do it," Atlas says.

Brighton glares. "So you can come back to life but my mother can't?"

"I'm sorry about Carolina, but you're not thinking straight right now. You sound like a different person."

"I am different! Killing your mother changes you! Watching

your brother die changes you!"

Everyone is confused, asking if Emil is dead and how he died. I'm no fan of Emil. Even his connection to my biological father hasn't created any emotional link. But I wouldn't wish death on him. He's a good person. He was a good person.

"Did you kill Emil?" I ask.

Brighton's eyes are darkening. "No, but I will avenge him."

"Who killed him?"

"The son of that doctor Stanton killed."

"You're going to kill a kid?"

"If he's old enough to kill, he's old enough to be killed."

He's a monster who needs to be slain, but he's far too dangerous to take on. I think about what Brighton has always gone on about, that something being unlikely doesn't mean it's impossible. There's truth to it, but I'm not risking everyone's lives trying to kill Brighton. Atlas, Tala. The Spell Walkers. The phoenix. Even the baby. My power is warning me that no one is safe from him. I might not be powerful enough to kill him, but I know how to defeat him.

"No one can tell you what to do, Brighton, and there's no point trying to fight you. You're clearly the superior specter. If you promise to leave everyone alone, then I will tell you everything about the ritual." I note the flicker of pride in Brighton's eyes as I play into his ego. "You deserve to have your loved ones alive too."

Brighton looks like he still wants blood, but he nods. "I promise."

I don't have a pen or paper out here, but Brighton hands me his phone and I begin typing the instructions for the Phoenix Pit into his notes app. I feel guilty after putting down each bullet point, knowing that Brighton will personally kill phoenixes himself to get what he needs, but if I don't give him what he needs, then everyone I love will be killed. Brighton doesn't even have to threaten this for me to know it's true. I won't endanger Atlas or Tala or anyone else, especially against someone who would destroy them so fiercely that I wouldn't be able to resurrect them.

"Good luck," I tell Brighton.

Everything seems to freeze as Brighton reads about the Phoenix Pit with his phone in one hand and a scythe in the other. I really feel like I'm looking at the Infinity Savior and Infinity Reaper at the same time, but I'm sure that he won't be doing much good with the resurrection ritual beyond bringing back his parents. I can already see Brighton flaunting resurrections to appear more powerful and using the ritual to gain favors with influential people and followers. But as silver and sapphire flames carry Brighton into the sky, far away from us, my psychic sense cools down because the most dangerous person I've ever been around is gone.

I don't know what this means for the rest of the world, but I just saved mine.

FIFTY-THREE

THE FUTURE EMIL

NESS

When you're studying someone for impersonation, you study absolutely everything they do. If you're not careful, you could get exposed because you chewed your food differently than how your subject would, or you didn't leave the top two buttons of your shirt unbuttoned as they would, or you breathed out of your mouth instead of your nose. Even though I'm not trying to take either of their forms, I can't help but pay close attention to the ways Prudencia and Wyatt are crying.

The ways they're mourning.

Prudencia cries with her whole body, rocking back and forth on this park bench in Sunnyside, Queens. Her dark hair is plastered to her sweaty face. Her eyes are bloodshot red. In twenty-four hours, she has lost the closest person she's had to a mother since losing her own, and now her best friend too. Then that psychopath she's in love with has also gone full dark side. Who does she have now? Me? Wyatt? The Spell Walkers? I don't know her plans, but she seems to be grieving simpler times, just as Emil did.

Wyatt is a loud crier. That surprises me. He obviously talks too much, but I still assumed he would be more stoic when it came to grief. That's probably just my own conditioning from the Senator. I may have grown up in a home where emotions like sadness are only useful for exploiting the public, even your own family, but Wyatt's upbringing as a Halo Knight means sensitivity is a strength. That's clear from how much Halo Knights openly grieve phoenixes even when they will come back to life. But as Wyatt cries so hard against Nox, hugging the phoenix's neck like a pillow, it's clear he isn't crying as if he is saying goodbye to someone who is leaving town—or life—for a little while.

I'm trying to hold it together. I've always preferred crying privately. I'm also not ready to believe that Emil Rey's soul is gone forever.

"He vanished in fire," I say. Prudencia and Wyatt look at me, confused. "Emil vanished in fire."

"We saw," Wyatt says.

"Luna taught us that an infinity-ender could kill a phoenix with even a simple cut, but if you wanted to permanently end a specter with phoenix blood, you had to drive the dagger into their heart. That's what Brighton did, but Emil still vanished in fire anyway."

"Your point being?"

"Maybe Luna was wrong. If the phoenixes who were killed by infinity-enders didn't go off in flames, then maybe that means Emil's gleam hadn't been fully terminated."

"That's not limited to infinity-enders. Phoenixes could be prevented from resurrections if they're killed without having regained the muscle to trigger their rebirths and—"

"I'm speaking about the infinity-enders. Does it make sense that Emil went up in flames if his power should have been killed?"

"Hard to say. The biology of specters is different than that of pure phoenixes."

Prudencia hops to her feet, her face flushed. "It doesn't change anything! Emil is still gone."

This truly doesn't feel real, no matter what I saw with my own eyes or anytime his death is spoken about. "It changes one thing. Emil Rey might be gone forever, but if his soul is still out there, that gives me a reason to keep fighting. Maybe we can create the world that he was fighting to live in."

Wyatt's blue eyes are fixed on me. "You would do all of that for Emil, even though he will not be reborn as Emil?"

I was raised by a monster in my own home, but outside those walls were people of all moralities. The ones who I was taught were bad were actually good, and the good guys were actually bad. More important, Emil was out there all along, being a sensitive soul who cared about people and creatures because it was the right thing to do. He didn't do that as a performance or to gain any political favors. If even one percent of Emil's heart and soul goes into his next incarnation, that's someone who deserves a long, happy, easy life.

"If Emil can't live in this world, the best thing I can do is make sure the new Emil can."

If I survive this fight, I like the idea of trying to find Emil's soul in any person I pass. The infant in a stroller, adored by their parents just as Emil was. The child on a subway playing with a plush phoenix. The shirtless teenager taking a selfie on the beach because they've grown up loving their body, whatever it looks like. The adult getting married to that lucky someone who loves them so much that they fantasize about their happiness, even if they aren't in the picture—like I am doing now.

"Your beliefs in supporting Emil's reincarnation would pair well with Halo Knight customs," Wyatt says.

That was his dream. Not mine. "I'm no Emil."

"But you're living for him even though he's dead. I will too." Wyatt takes a deep breath, composing himself. "Does this mean we are going to keep fighting in Emil's name?"

"Fighting so we can live," Prudencia says, wiping her tears. "Where do we start?"

This isn't how I've envisioned my next act. I have no issues with Prudencia, but teaming up with Wyatt is too hard to stomach. Emil and I didn't get to pursue anything romantic because his heart was torn between us. "You should regroup with the Halo Knights."

"I was sacked," Wyatt says. "Remember?"

"Over not wanting to push Emil into pursuing the All-Killer. That's done. Your commander just got killed by Brighton. The Halo Knights are going to need some leadership. That should be you."

"I'm ill-prepared for such duties."

"No one trained you to fight gangs, the government, and superpowered killers either."

"What about me?" Prudencia asks.

"Reunite with the Spell Walkers. That's where you'll be safest against the Blood Casters and Brighton."

I hope I'm right. If Brighton could kill Emil, then it's true that he won't be shy about hurting the girl who broke his heart. But she stands a better chance among the likes of Iris, who can fight Brighton, or Wesley, who can help her escape danger, than she is with me.

"Brighton is going to hunt you down for killing him, or trying to," Prudencia says. "We all need to stick together and get our hands on the All-Killer."

"That's not our only path to defeating him," Wyatt says. "There's still the Starstifler. Emil defied time and space to uncover that formula. Perhaps we fool Brighton into thinking we want the All-Killer so badly that he will instead bury it away. Then we will have an opportunity to disempower him with the potion while not having our souls vanquished."

I would love the chance to swing that scythe into Brighton, but Wyatt is right that we stand a better chance at conquering Brighton if the All-Killer is off the battlefield. "Do you have any more potions?"

"Our stock was at the gym."

We shouldn't count on the Starstiflers still being there. "Can you make more?"

"I could gather supplies and brew."

"Great. Make enough so I can use potions against the Senator too."

If I can disempower the Senator, that would be great. But after the mess he pulled that resulted in Carolina getting killed and everything that followed, I am not opposed to drawing blood. I'm already picturing how satisfying it would be to punch his face, the skin of my knuckles splitting as I make the Senator unrecognizable.

"What's your plan?" Prudencia asks.

"Infiltrate his circles as he did ours, and expose him for the two-faced bastard he is."

"What if you get captured by his forces again?" Wyatt asks.

No one will lead a charge to save me as Emil would. If the Senator gets his hands on me again, I will live out the rest of my days as a hostage, or be executed immediately. That'll be curtains for me.

"How much time do you need to make the Starstiflers?" I ask.

"If I can gather everything, I can have some ready tonight."

The beginning of the end begins with those potions.

We'll all split up, fighting for the new Emil's future as well as our own.

I probably won't survive, but if I die, then I hope Wyatt is right about everyone being reincarnated. It's the only way I'll discover if Emil and I were soulmates all this time.

FIFTY-FOUR
THREE HEARTS

MARIBELLE

The threat is gone, but no one has been at peace since Brighton left.

For a few hours everyone was nervous that Brighton was still around, camouflaging and watching us in every room. Even though I assured everyone that my power would sense his presence, the Spell Walkers continued speaking in code. Ruth communicated to Wesley to get Esther out of here, and he dashed away with their daughter to hide her with a trusted companion; even I don't know who that is or where they are. This means Ruth is available to join us tonight at the Light Sky Tower. Eva is tagging along too. There have been too many deaths happening for a powerful healer to not be on the battlefield, and the only reason Iris isn't protesting is because she can't trust that Eva will be safe here at the cottage while we're all away. We'll have the whole gang together for this rescue mission—and our plus one.

Tala is down by the shore as Roxana bathes in the ocean. The sun is up, but the winds are blowing and the sand is cold as I go down the hill to join Tala. A couple hours ago, she asked to be alone to pray for the fallen Halo Knights and the phoenixes as well as to speak with the

Council of Phoenixlight about Brighton's crime, but I've been checking on her every few minutes and she's no longer kneeling in the sand while staring up at the sky or on the phone.

"How are you feeling?" I ask.

Tala continues watching the waves. "He killed them forevermore." She snaps around with teary eyes. "That scythe he had . . . the council told me they'd been searching for it for decades. It was forged with the ability to annihilate someone's soul forever. Those phoenixes and Halo Knights will never be reincarnated."

I didn't know a weapon like that existed. Maybe that's why I sensed Brighton as a greater threat than usual. He has a scythe that can kill someone forever. Even with my ritual I wouldn't be able to call their souls from the afterlife.

"I'm so sorry," I say, pulling Tala into a hug as she breaks down and cries. She was praying for souls that can never return. "We won't let him get away with this."

Tala pulls back and looks me in the eyes; then her gaze falls to my lips, and she sucks in a deep breath as she breaks our hug and steps away. "I don't need your help killing him."

"Yes, you do. You have no power—"

"I have Roxana!"

"Brighton will kill you both!" I shout with an ache in my chest.

"Then we die together. She's all I have anyway."

"You have me," I say.

"No, I don't. You have Atlas, and that's all you've ever wanted."

"I'm capable of caring for more than one person."

Tala's amber eyes are fixed on me, and her shoulders sink as if she's exhausted. "I don't want you caring for me, Maribelle. I want you loving me the way you love Atlas. You didn't let death stand between you two. But if Atlas wasn't alive, would you choose me?"

This is hard. I've been attracted to Tala ever since the night we met, when we were kicking each other's asses and I knocked her mask off and saw how beautiful she is. She became an ember of hope in my dying, dark world, and her flame grew and grew the more time we spent together. I would have gotten myself killed without Tala, and now I hate the idea of her getting killed because she doesn't have me. But now Atlas is back.

"In another life, I would have chosen you, Tala."

She straightens her shoulders and lets out a deep sigh. "I thought it would help to hear that, but it doesn't. Now I have to go through the rest of this life without your heart."

I stare at her lips, remembering how soft they were as she pressed them against mine. My face warms reliving this. "There are so many girls in this world who would love to be with you."

"None of them are you."

"Doesn't it give you hope that if it weren't for Atlas's resurrection, I would have found myself moving on and falling for you? And he's my actual boyfriend."

"You don't have to date someone to love them," Tala says, wounded, as if I'm trying to downplay her emotions.

I nod because she's not wrong. "It's still different when both hearts are in the same place."

Tala looks as if I've fired an arrow into her heart. "I thought professing my love was worth one last shot, but I will have to accept that you're not the target."

"I'm sorry. I really am."

Tala points over my shoulder. "Your true heart is coming." We watch Atlas as he's walking down the sandy hill. "I'm going to go for a ride to clear my head before tonight."

"Please don't go."

"Maribelle, I will fight alongside you, but I cannot be your friend."

Tala heads into the ocean, hopping on top of Roxana. The phoenix splashes her way out of the water and into the air, a rainstorm following them as they fly toward the woods.

Atlas wraps his arms around my waist. "How's she doing?"

I keep watching Tala as she puts more and more distance between us, like I'm poison. "Not well."

"That's to be expected, right? She keeps losing people."

I haven't died, but in Tala's eyes, she has lost me too.

"There's something else you should know," I say, my heart racing as I turn to face Atlas and hold his hands. "Tala fell in love with me."

"Oh."

"I only found out about her feelings for me a couple nights ago."

"What about you?"

"I love you."

"I know, Mari, but do you have any feelings for her? It's okay if you do."

The way Atlas always treats me with compassion is one of the many reasons I love him. I feel even safer opening up to him. "I do have feelings for Tala. I'm not in love with her, but there's another life where I see myself falling for her too. Everything would be so different if Tala and I killed Luna at first sight at the Bounds before she could tease me with the resurrection ritual. We would've found some peace in avenging her parents and mine and . . . you." I run my hands up and down his smooth, strong arms, and I'm still surprised that he's standing here before me. "I'm so happy that you're back in my life. I just wanted to be honest that I could've seen myself being happy with Tala too."

Atlas leans in and kisses me. "That's the best thing you could've said to me."

"Really?"

"I want to be with you forever, but if I can't be, I want you opening your heart again."

This is what Tala and I discussed too. She hoped that I would allow my heart to be reborn, and I echoed that sentiment. I remember that conversation led to our first kiss and our amazing night together. "There's one last thing you should know."

"Do you have another secret superpower?" he asks.

"Tala and I had sex," I say, just getting it out.

Atlas is quiet for a moment and then nods. "That's it?"

"Okay?"

"I was dead, Maribelle."

"But I had sex with her the night before I resurrected you."

Atlas looks me in the eyes. "There's no way you knew that I would come back as me. Listen, anything you and Tala did while I was dead doesn't break my heart. It's okay if things have changed for you now that I'm alive again. Maybe you need space to explore a relationship with Tala, and I can step to the side. If we're meant to be, then we'll be together again."

"I didn't bring you back from the dead to break up with you."

"You also love me enough that you would've resurrected me so I could have my life back . . . even if we weren't together."

"I want to be with you, Atlas."

Atlas smiles and pulls me closer. "Awesome. I really want to be with you too."

"Thank you for being you."

"Thanks for bringing me back as me."

Atlas kisses me so lovingly, but I can't help wondering how long it's going to take before my hunger to kiss Tala fades away.

FIFTY-FIVE

BACK TO SCHOOL

NESS

We're hiding in one of the last places anyone would expect us to go.

This morning, before Wyatt set off on his journey to acquire the Starstifler ingredients, we realized we were going to need to relocate to a new haven because brewing potions in the park wasn't discreet. I considered bringing Prudencia and Wyatt to my family's upstate house, but I wouldn't put it past the Senator to have eyes watching the place. Then we started coming up with places where we could go. Prudencia's aunt's apartment was out of the question because she would rat us out if it meant getting a handshake and picture with the Senator. Wyatt warned us away from the loft that Tala was staying in because we have no idea if she's been spotted going back and forth there, especially since her phoenix carries storms wherever she goes. Then I came up with the perfect place.

Nova Grace Elementary.

Some might think it's stupid to return to the school where we were ambushed by enforcers, leading to my capture, but we're actually counting on everyone thinking it's stupid for us to come back. I conducted my own inspection of the building while I had shifted like an enforcer and found the whole place vacated.

It's been bizarre being back, especially since that night marked a crossroad for me. My choices were run away and start a new life or fight alongside the Spell Walkers. Had I honored my goodbye to Emil, I would've never been held hostage and forced to do all the terrible things I had to do. I would still be in the dark about the Senator being the mastermind behind the Blackout. But I ran back into the building to help Emil, the boy who was so kind to me when I was locked inside a closet because the Spell Walkers didn't trust me.

Emil and I had a cycle of saving each other until I failed to save him.

I get up from the cot in the music room, stretching my legs after sleeping the past few hours. I was too restless to sleep once Wyatt flew away on Nox to collect the Starstifler ingredients. I just researched everything about the Senator's happenings. He has been very vocal against Brighton, especially after his massacre of the enforcers, and while he acknowledged how unfortunate Carolina's death was, he withholds sympathies because he doubts she will be dead for long since Brighton and Emil will resurrect her. There's truth to the Senator's fearmongering, but he still doesn't know there is actually a ritual that can resurrect Carolina just like he doesn't know Emil is dead. Apart from that, the only thing useful was finding out that the Senator will be interviewed by the Silver Star Slayer tomorrow morning. My plan is already forming.

Around noon, Wyatt returned with the Starstifler ingredients and even managed to sneak into Mele's gym to collect the potions Emil had already brewed, narrowly avoiding detection from lingering enforcers. But when Wyatt began sharing memories of working on the first Starstiflers with Emil, I just couldn't stomach it. That's when I retired to the music room so I could cry in private.

I tired myself out and began to dream of Emil. I was in a cemetery, paying respect to Emil's headstone when he began busting out of the grave. I tried digging him out, but he suddenly burst through like a fiery comet that was returning to space. Then time skipped and Emil was watching me in the sky, just like when I last saw Brighton. I jumped into the air and began flying toward him. I was about to hug him, when he exploded into a cloud of fire. Then, when the fire cleared, Emil was covered in gray and gold feathers with eyes like black pearls. He opened his mouth to speak, but there was nothing but screeching, and that's when I snapped awake. I would rather not dream of Emil if it means only seeing him as a nightmare.

I go upstairs. It's a shame that this school wasn't given the funding that it needed to nurture celestials. There will be more cases like this if I can't stop the Senator from being elected. He used to always talk about how these facilities were more about training celestials to use their powers against the powerless than actually receiving a proper education. It's one of many lies I believed. As I go down the hallway, I'm nauseous looking at all the scorch marks on the walls and shattered glass on the floor from the enforcer invasion. There were kids inside this haven, but that didn't stop the enforcers from attacking them as if schools should be war zones. If the Senator becomes president, I'm sure he'll be campaigning for this building to be turned into a private school that forbids celestials. Piece of shit.

I reach the supply closet that I lived in during my stay. I wasn't ready to face the memories early. I am now. I turn the doorknob and step inside. Nothing has been disturbed in here. There are cleaning supplies, a plate left over from my last meal, chains that I got out of easily, and my air mattress. It still reeks of dirty mop. This definitely wasn't a home, but it was my personal haven from the Blood Casters. More important, it's where Emil and I began getting to know each other.

If I ever fall for someone again, I won't waste time.

Someone is coming down the hall. I'm on edge, wondering if we have been discovered by some enemy force. I peek out, and it's just Wyatt.

"There you go," Wyatt says. "You looking to sweep the halls?"

"This was my cage when I got myself captured by the Spell Walkers."

"Cozy."

"Felt that way whenever Emil was around."

"That's our boy." Wyatt clears his throat. "Is it terribly awkward for us to talk about him? Specifically our affections for him?"

"Yes."

"Very well, then. I'll have you know that he spoke highly of you. I believe it was one of his biggest regrets that you two never got to explore your full potential."

"It's one of my biggest regrets too. My biggest, even."

"That's saying a lot."

I turn to him, glaring. "Meaning?"

Wyatt blushes. "Well, you have quite a history, I understand. It speaks volumes to your feelings for Emil that this loss rises above your many unfortunate acts."

I can't tell if this is a compliment or a dig at every life I've harmed or taken. "I would've never done those things of my own will. I was manipulated and—"

"Apologies, of course, I understand that. I haven't known Emil for very long, and I suppose you haven't either, but we both know that he would have never fallen for you if you were some immoral thug who sought pleasure in violence. I'm not innocent either. I have blood on my hands."

That's more surprising than what a loud crier he is. "Really? You seem like you haven't won a fight in your life."

"I've killed before . . . accidentally, but that didn't make a difference to the corpses." Wyatt sees my eyes widen. "They were terrible people who tried hurting Nox. I would do it all again."

"But Emil would never kill anyone," I say.

"There's mercy in Emil dying without being forced to."

These thoughts feel so heavy, so I sit down on my air mattress.

"May I?" Wyatt asks.

I nod, and he joins me. Air slowly creeps out of the mattress, and we'll be brought down to the floor within minutes. "It's funny how safe I felt with Emil even though he wasn't willing to kill anyone in this war."

"It's very American to presume safety must be in conversation with violence. Emil would have given any partner of his emotional security." Wyatt takes a deep breath. "I had my doubts about him killing Brighton."

"Same. I would have done it myself if it weren't for me being scared that Emil would never be able to look at me again." The way I stabbed Brighton over and over with that infinity-ender would have ruined my image for Emil. There's no way he would have thanked me for killing his brother and then kissed me and started a life with me. It would've been too personal compared to everything else I've done. "I sometimes change form when I'm asleep. It's always triggered by nightmares of people I've hurt and killed. One time I woke up as Emil, and I'm sure I'm going to do it for the rest of my life."

"You didn't kill Emil."

"I didn't save him either."

Wyatt looks as if he wants to pat my shoulder but thinks twice. "Perhaps instead of feeling guilty, in this moment, at least, we can celebrate the boy we lost? Back when we were strengthening Emil's retrocycle muscles, he'd asked me if there was a particular moment that I would travel through time to revisit. I for one would go back to the first time I took Emil for a ride on Nox. He'd never ridden a phoenix before, but I'd wanted to show him what his life could look like as a Halo Knight once he was done being the Infinity Son. It was after midnight and enchanting and . . ."

"And what?"

"And we kissed for the first time."

That was Emil's first kiss. It's definitely a lot more romantic than ours. But Emil and I didn't need stars and phoenixes. We had each other, and that's what mattered most.

"I get why you'd retrocycle to that memory," I say.

"How about you? Where would you go if it meant seeing Emil again?"

That's a hell of a question. There are so many contenders. When I first saw him at the start of the Crowned Dreamer, I was disguised as some nobody, but I thought he was so attractive. That reminds me of how cute Emil was when he complimented me by saying my face was solid because he was too shy to call me beautiful, and how he later called me beautiful the night he broke me out of the Bounds. Or how I told him why I chose my new name and how I hoped that we would morph into something together before we finally kissed. There's a lot of good to choose from, but I also can't forgive myself for the bad I've done. I still can't scrub that memory of cutting into him with the infinity-ender dagger and how he was in so much pain he wanted to die. That had a happy enough ending, at least.

"You've probably seen Emil's scars, right?" I ask, feeling a lump in my throat.

"I have," Wyatt says quietly.

"You know I'm responsible for them?"

"I understand it was for the greater good, and you saved Emil."

That time I did. "It didn't feel like saving him, but I got the chance to take care of him after we were safe. I was so concerned that his wounds hadn't been cleaned yet, but Emil was spiraling over the idea of me seeing him shirtless. So we compromised. I got to help clean him, but my eyes had to be closed. I should probably choose a time when I could see him, but we felt so much closer in the dark. I could feel his pulse and the sweat on his lower back and his curls on mine. That's all I wanted to do since hanging out together in this closet. I wanted to hold Emil."

I'm fighting back tears.

"That's a lovely memory," he says. "I think we're all doing him proud."

"I hope so."

"Care for good news? The Starstiflers are ready." Wyatt gets up. "Come."

I get up from the air mattress, where I've only ever slept alone and never in peace.

I hate how I'll never know what it's like to wake up as myself while holding Emil.

The Starstiflers were prepared in a chemistry lab.

Prudencia is bottling the potions as she updates us on her conversation with the Spell Walkers. They're all assembling tonight to try and rescue Nicolette Sunstar, who they believe is being held captive at the Light Sky Tower. If I didn't have to make moves on the Silver Star Slayer, I would join in an instant, especially after all the damage I did while posing as Sunstar. Saving her is the least I can do, but all I can provide is stealth, and something tells me that the fight at the Tower isn't going to stay discreet for very long. The same goes for Wyatt staying on track to recruit more Halo Knights if we're going to win this war.

"Brighton was at the cottage this morning," Prudencia says as she corks the final vial. "That's why he didn't follow us. He wanted the ritual even more."

"Is everyone okay?" Wyatt asks.

"Thankfully. Maribelle's power kept freaking out over what a threat he is. Once we secure Sunstar, it could be a good idea to camp out by Carolina's and Leo's graves to ambush him."

"Assuming Brighton hasn't already stolen their corpses. Truly, is anything sacred to that child?"

"Gravedigging is nothing compared to sending his brother and mother to their graves," I say.

"Metaphorically since Emil . . ." Wyatt shuts up.

While I was asleep, Prudencia collected some abandoned backpacks from lockers and gave us some medical supplies from the nurse's office. I put three Starstiflers into mine. One for Iron and one for Brighton and one for myself once those bastards are powerless.

"So this is it," I say, slinging my backpack over my shoulder.

"It's still so surreal," Wyatt says.

"Emil brought us all together," Prudencia says.

"And we're parting ways to finish his fight," I say.

Prudencia runs into my arms, hugging me tight. "Be careful."

I squeeze her. "You too. Don't hold back against Brighton."

"I won't."

When she lets go, Wyatt and I stare at each other. What's the appropriate way to say goodbye to the person who also caught the eye of the person you wanted to be with? He reaches out his hand, and I pull him into a hug. Now more than ever Wyatt is not the enemy.

"Do not return to the battlefield without an army," I say.

"Do not let your father become president," he says.

Everyone packs their bags, and we leave Nova together. Wyatt flies off on Nox, blending in with the night instantly. Prudencia gives me a little salute as she goes down one street. I glow gray and become a stranger as I go down the other street.

I'm expecting the worst, but if any of us die trying to create a better world, then so be it.

That's what Emil would do.

That's what Emil did.

FIFTY-SIX

THE LIGHT SKY TOWER

MARIBELLE

Tonight is our first mission where we have all Spell Walkers assembled.

It will also be our last.

I quit the group after Atlas's death, but being a Spell Walker will forever be in my blood and bones since it was founded by my biological parents and led by Mama and Papa. But I'm not under any illusion that we're going to spend the next few years fighting alongside each other again. Atlas and I are going to restart our lives, and it sounds like the others are burned out too. Wesley wants to be home with Ruth and watch Esther grow up. Iris and Eva want to focus on their love, but Iris is only going to be ready to step away in peace if Sunstar is elected president and creates the Luminary Union. We would make all our predecessors proud if we fought our way to a victory like that and then chose to live happily in the world we helped create.

I don't know what the future holds for Tala. She's not slowing down anytime soon.

Since speaking with Tala and Atlas at the beach, everyone has been preparing for the rescue mission. Eva managed to find a recent blueprint of the Light Sky Tower online for us to begin mapping out how far underground the vault may be. All of us with powers have been training on the beach, practicing new combos that we could use with my specter abilities; there are deadly moves that Atlas and I came up with that can take down gangs of enemies if we're getting desperate. Meanwhile, Tala was teaching Ruth and her clones how to throw stronger punches, and even though Eva is a pacifist, Tala insisted on showing her how to defend herself if she's going to be on the battlefield.

Once our plan is in place, we begin making our way from Long Island to Manhattan.

I watch Iris, Eva, Ruth, and Wesley get in their car and take off, and then I'm left alone with Atlas and Tala.

"Should we all fly together?" I ask.

"No," Tala says immediately. She blushes. "Roxana's rainstorms will only draw attention to the sky, and your wings of fire aren't exactly discreet," she adds, unaware that Atlas knows about her feelings for me.

"Good point," Atlas says. "How would you like to proceed, Tala?"

"I'll fly alone," Tala says, walking off toward Roxana without another word.

"That felt personal," Atlas says once Tala is fully out of earshot.

"I'm the problem. Not you."

"At least we get to do something that we always dreamed about doing together."

"What's that?"

"Flying together."

Back before I knew I was a celestial-specter hybrid, Atlas and I fantasized about my power of levitation advancing into flight so we could travel through the skies together, just like my parents could. It's a dream come true jumping into the air, my golden wings of fire flapping toward the stars as Atlas's winds carry him up high. We could fly directly toward the city with laser focus, but instead we're doing loops around one another, laughing into the night because we're both alive to have this much fun. I tell myself that life is short before remembering that life can be as long as I want it to be now that I know how to defy death.

Atlas mouths *I love you* over his loud, whistling winds.

I do the same over my roaring flames.

Our fingertips brush before we focus, flying directly into Manhattan, doing our best to stay out of sight so no one sees a girl with burning wings or a dead boy flying. In case someone has seen us, we land a few blocks away from our meeting spot, walking a few blocks in the shadows of skyscrapers until we spot everyone in the alleyway behind an old opera house. Mostly everyone. The Spell Walkers are here with Prudencia, but no sign of Tala.

"Where's Tala?" I ask.

"Wasn't she with you?" Iris asks.

"She went her own way."

"I'm sure she'll be here any moment," Ruth says.

Atlas walks up to Prudencia and hugs her. "Good to see you."

"Welcome back," Prudencia says. She stares at him like he's a ten-headed basilisk. "How are you feeling?"

"Alive." Atlas blushes. "I'm sorry for your losses. Emil and

Carolina were amazing people."

Prudencia nods. "Thank you. I . . . I still don't think it's real. But I'm ready to fight for them."

It can't be easy to mourn the brother and mother of the boy she loves, but Prudencia is still standing. I admire her spirit. Her resilience reminds me of my own, and Tala's too. . . .

I can't stop worrying about Tala. Did someone spot her phoenix? Are enforcers tracing the rainstorms back to Roxana on this cloudless night? Is Brighton hunting her down because of her attack? I close my eyes, trying to tap into my psychic senses. If Tala's life is at stake, maybe I can concentrate long enough to cast a vision. I shut out everyone's voices and peer into the darkness, picturing Tala.

"Hi," Tala's voice calls to me.

My heart is pounding. I've somehow found her wherever she is. "Tala," I whisper.

"Yes?"

"Where are you?" I breathe.

"Open your eyes."

I do, and Tala is standing before me, right next to the Spell Walkers. This wasn't my power at all.

"What are you doing?" she asks.

"I was trying to sense if you were okay," I say.

"That's not your power."

"You were taking too long to get here, and I got worried. I thought I'd give this a shot."

Tala's gaze is soft before hardening again. "I was settling Roxana near an old sewage tunnel." She flips her crossbow over her shoulder. "Shall we proceed with our mission?"

The warmth that was in the air when Atlas and Prudencia were welcoming each other has now gotten cold. The others are picking up on it too, even without being told about my intimate connection with Tala. I can't change her mind, and I have to focus on what's brought us all here.

"Ready when you are," I tell everyone.

Wesley leads the way, dashing back and forth every minute to let us know that the coast is clear as we make our way to the Light Sky Tower. We're traveling through alleyways and a parking garage and even through an empty hotel kitchen that clearly doesn't offer twenty-four-hour dining. We get to the city's biggest skyscraper, and I can't believe Sunstar has been underneath this building all this time. Iron is a criminal, and I plan on making his mug shot my phone background once we've beat him.

"Two guards, back entrance," Wesley says, returning from scouting.

"Cameras?" Iris asks.

"Above the door."

"Disable and disarm."

Wesley salutes and is back within the minute. "Disabled and disarmed."

Everyone runs for the entrance, and Prudencia telekinetically hides the unconscious guards underneath a big truck in an unlit corner. That should buy us some time.

I enter the Light Sky Tower, leading the way.

The bright stark-white hallway is clear, and while everyone else is moving slowly and quietly, I'm barging ahead. Iris tries getting me to slow down, but I remind her that if a threat is popping up, I'm going to sense it first. Tala reminds me that I'm only going to sense fatal threats. This means that I can walk straight into a group of enforcers who don't have what it takes to take me down, and I don't see what's wrong with storming through those idiots too. I head down the staircase, going down two flights below the garage before coming across the door that Eva marked on the blueprint.

"This is as far as I got last time," Tala says.

It's not very far, but I'm glad she didn't risk her life trying to push through.

There's an old-school emergency alarm, and Prudencia telekinetically suspends the dial from ringing, long enough for everyone to get through the door as if we never came through here. It would've been nice to have Brighton by our side so we could phase all the way down, grab Sunstar, and then fly and phase our way back to the streets, but there would've been no convincing him to save the woman who will build her presidential legacy on stopping powerful specters like himself.

This next hallway isn't as polished as the one upstairs. The walls are concrete, the ground is filthy with muddy footprints, and it's so hot that I want to strip down to my underwear. There's murmuring up ahead, and a chill runs through my spine. I peek around the corner to find a pair of acolytes with wands. These are Luna's people, protecting her vault; I wonder if they're aware that Sunstar is in there or if they think Luna is really protective of whatever treasures she has. I hold up two fingers behind me so everyone knows how many enemies are up ahead, and then I add another and another and another as more acolytes file out.

"We've lost contact with the guards on the west side," an acolyte says.

"I'm sure it's nothing," another says before letting out a yawn.

"Always assume the worst," a third says. "Sound the alarm."

I turn back, eyes widening. "They're about to pull the alarm."

I step out to the center of the hallway, hoping that I can take them down before they can alert the whole building. I throw a fire-arrow, but it strikes Wesley, who dashed ahead without warning, and he rolls through the hallway toward the acolytes. They gasp when they see him and draw their wands and another pulls the alarm. Red lights flash through the hallway, and the ringing reverberates through the concrete walls. It's so loud that I can't concentrate. I can't even hear the bangs of spellwork, and I only see the lights of spells flying toward us. My psychic sense goes off, but Atlas manages to tackle me out of the way before a spell can take me away from him. An acolyte aims at Wesley, but Tala fires her arrow straight into the acolyte's neck, killing her. Iris and Eva run through, and Iris ricochets all spells off her forearms, shielding Eva as she heals Wesley.

"Rough start," Atlas says as he helps me up.

It's going to be a rougher end for everyone trying to cross us.

Prudencia telekinetically steals their wands, and the acolytes are immediately scared for their lives. They're doing all this work to suck up to Luna so she can one day imbue them with the levels of power she has for other specters, and anoint them as Blood Casters, but right now they are so painfully powerless. If this alarm wasn't making me feel like my head might explode, I might play with these acolytes, but I'm burning hot and I have a headache, so I charge through the hallway and knock out the remaining three with one-two punches to the throat and head.

"Are you okay?!" Ruth shouts to Wesley over the alarm.

"I am now," Wesley says, giving Eva a high five.

I keep it moving because I don't know what forces will come storming at us now. There's a steel door that's sealed shut, and Iris breaks through with three punches. It's upsetting how I can already predict all the news stories about how celestials are too powerful to exist with everyone else when we use our powers to knock down steel doors and freeze alarms from going off and knock out guards as if we're trying to break into a bank when we're actually rescuing a woman from her abduction and imprisonment.

We go down a few concrete steps, and while the lights aren't flashing down here, the alarm is still echoing down this dark tunnel that smells like rotten animal carcasses. I swat at the flies buzzing around me. I'm about to light the way with a fire-orb, when my psychic sense warns me of danger. There's a loud hiss, and at first I'm scared it's a gas leak and I'm about to blow us all up just so we can see, when I'm struck in the stomach by something slimy and heavy and scaly. I fly backward, knocking down a few people with me as I gasp for breath.

"Basilisk!" Tala shouts between the ringing of the alarm bells.

We did not come prepared for a basilisk guarding the vault.

Tala screams.

I hold up a fire-orb and use its glow to trace the basilisk from its boulder-sized head with pitch-black eyes and down through its ivy-green scales and long yellow belly and its tail that is wrapped around Tala, squeezing the life out of her.

"Tala!"

I throw the fire-orb, and it explodes against the basilisk's belly. The basilisk screeches, and its grip on Tala tightens as it coils around her a second time. I don't know what to do here. My battles have rarely been against actual creatures, mostly just people who have stolen their blood for powers. I have to figure this out fast because Tala's arms are fully constricted, so she can't even reach for one of her daggers.

I provide fire so everyone can see.

"Avoid the basilisk's gaze!" Prudencia shouts.

I know enough that if a basilisk stares at us, we can be petrified.

I don't want to throw fire again at the risk of making it squeeze Tala so hard that it pops, but I have to save her somehow. I need to call on the help of our allies.

"Iris and Prudencia, force the basilisk to loosen its grip!"

Prudencia is doing her best to telekinetically uncurl the basilisk, but its viselike grip is resisting her power. Iris charges and punches the basilisk's belly before grabbing the end of its tail and unwrapping it from Tala long enough for her to breathe and slip out.

Tala is weakly punching her chest, like she's choking.

"She can't breathe!" I shout.

I'm scared of losing Tala. Just because I know how to resurrect someone doesn't mean a million things can't go wrong before then. The basilisk could eat her corpse or an explosion can happen that blows apart her body and ashes. I run toward Tala to help, but Atlas is faster. His eyes glow as he gently blows wind into Tala's mouth, feeding her oxygen. I watch the life return to Tala's eyes and the way her sinking shoulders and trembling knees straighten as she can hold herself up again.

I begin turning until my psychic sense warns me, and I halt. I would have been turned to stone.

"I can't hold it back by myself!" Prudencia shouts.

"I got you!" Atlas yells. Winds whistle over the basilisk's distorted screeches.

I peek, finding that Prudencia and Atlas are holding the basilisk's head at bay and forcing its gaze skyward. I snatch Tala's daggers from her belt and boot, and I float up to the basilisk and drive the steel into its eyes. It writhes and screams in pain as it tries slithering away, but Iris still has a hold on its tail.

"How do we kill it?" Wesley asks.

"Fire to the brain." Tala picks up her crossbow from the ground and notches a new arrow. "Light it up." I poke the tip of the arrow, and dark yellow flames begin burning from the head down. Tala gets in position, takes aim, and fires. The burning arrow shoots through the winds and pierces the basilisk's head. It slams to the ground, dead.

"Everyone okay?" Eva asks.

Tala nods. "Thank you, Atlas."

That's even more surprising than the basilisk ambush.

"Of course," Atlas says.

Wesley hops over the dead basilisk. "I hope that was the final boss battle."

We continue through the dark tunnel all the way until we reach a well-lit lab that smells like flowers and death with a vault sitting between shelves of potion ingredients. This is it. Sunstar is behind that door. Iris wastes no time hammering at the door with her fists, but when it's only making a dent, I place my fiery palms against the steel until it burns orange and weakens it. Iris winds up a powerful punch and her fist connects in the dead center of the door and it slams down onto the floor.

Light floods into the dark room, immediately illuminating Sunstar.

She's been blindfolded with a black rag that's decorated with white symbols that I can't make out from the door. Her back is against the wall, flinching as if she's expecting to be hurt any moment now. Her wrists are bound in power-binding gauntlets that have surely blown through their charge by now, but her captives have kept her restrained anyway as if she's known for her physical prowess like me. Her ankle is chained to an iron hook, and the chain looks long enough for Sunstar to reach this hole in the ground that seems to serve as her toilet. I walk into the room and find a warning graffitied in white that sends chills down my spine before a fire begins burning in my heart: *LIGHTS OUT, CELESTIALS.* I freeze when I realize that this isn't some room that's only being used for Sunstar but instead one of many underground cells that have been designed to sever a celestial's connection from the stars in the hopes they will lose their powers forever. Mama and Papa told me stories about rescuing some celestials from these underground camps across the country, and how all the captives slowly regained use of their powers over time. I've never seen these cells in person, and witnessing Sunstar as a victim has me so furious that I'm surprised I haven't found myself on fire. I kneel before Sunstar and see that the white symbols on her blindfold are actually crude illustrations of scratched-out eyes, a common hate sign from those who fear the power that makes our eyes glow.

"Please don't hurt me," Sunstar whimpers. Her voice is strained as if she's been screaming for help, or screaming in pain. I'm nervous that if I remove the blindfold I won't find her eyes in their sockets as terrorists have done to celestials in other countries. I never thought I would see someone who was poised to become the leader of the free world so vulnerable, but as I stare at her malnourished cheeks as if she's been starved of water and the hand-shaped bruises on her arms and the blood on her dark green pantsuit, it's clear she has lived through some terrors. "Please don't, please don't," she cries some more.

"You're safe," I say.

Sunstar freezes. "Is that . . . ? No, you're not Maribelle. It's another trick."

I reach for the blindfold, but Sunstar flinches. "It's Maribelle."

"I'm not falling for more of your mind games, Edward! Maribelle hates me!"

It's true that I'm not the biggest fan of Sunstar, and I made this clear a couple weeks ago when she had the nerve to ask for our support for the Luminary Union despite never being vocal enough about siding with the Spell Walkers at the risk of losing votes. But none of that matters in this moment. This isn't even about her being the key to a better world for celestials if she's elected as president. Sunstar is a mother, a wife, a woman in her own right who doesn't deserve this abuse.

"I'm not Iron," I say.

"None of us are," Iris adds.

"I hope not," Wesley says, looking around suspiciously.

Iris kneels in front of Sunstar too. "It's me, Iris Simone-Chambers. I'm here with Maribelle Lucero and the rest of the Spell Walkers and friends. We're here to rescue you and get you back to your family."

Sunstar is shaking. "I'm not falling for this again, you son of a bitch."

Iris is tearing up. "I promise it's us. Iron may be able to impersonate us all he wants, but he can't imitate our powers. I'm going to remove your blindfold so you can see that it's us with your own eyes. Okay?"

Sunstar still seems uncertain and flinches when Iris begins sliding off the blindfold, but as she blinks multiple times and sees all of us, she begins crying. Even without showing off our powers, she already has enough common sense to know that Iron can't be eight people at once. But Sunstar really believes her own eyes when Wesley dashes in dizzying circles and Iris breaks the gauntlet and chain with simple squeezes and I cast an orb of fire that breaks the darkness in this room so she can see more clearly.

"It's you," Sunstar cries, but this time it's tears of joy and relief. "Is my family okay?"

"They're safe," Iris answers. "We're going to get you home to them."

Eva gently massages Sunstar's shoulder and offers a smile. "Let's get you better first." The colorful lights emanate from her palms as she begins absorbing Sunstar's physical pains, biting down on her lip to keep in her screams, and the bruises and cuts vanish as if they were never there. But Eva can't heal someone's trauma and it's clear that Iron and others have done a number on Sunstar.

"Thank you," Sunstar breathes.

"It's what we do," Iris says. "I'm sorry it took us so long."

"You have Tala to thank for tracking you down," I say.

Sunstar squints. "A Halo Knight? Thank you for all your services."

"We're counting on you to put an end to all specters," Tala says.

"After seeing what Iron can do, I am more motivated than ever. Are you aware of his power? How long has he been a specter?"

"He became one during the night of the Cloaked Phantom," Prudencia says. "Did he tell you about how he had Ness pose as you during the final debate?"

"Edward bragged about this after showing off his power for the first time. He posed as my husband and . . ." There's a fire in Sunstar's eyes. "Edward wants me to hurt him as retribution for how he's tortured me like some caged monster. I felt myself cracking too, especially as he kept staging rescues as many of you and talking to me as my husband and daughter. Their faces were shifting and their voices kept breaking, but it only made me want to burn him alive so I wouldn't die remembering Ash and Proxima wrong. . . . Thankfully I have no power here."

I shake my head. "He would've never let you attack him here."

"No?"

"He would want the world to see the monster come out of the cage."

If Sunstar publicly attacked Iron, that would only show the world that celestials can't be trusted to be president because of that time that the only celestial candidate used her powers to attack her opponent. That would ensure that our country will only ever be run by those who hate us. That the real monsters are the ones banishing us to cells like this.

"An act like that would not only secure Edward the win, but he would collect the political support he needs to accelerate every law that will make our lives even more difficult," Sunstar says, shaking her head. "Most politicians are two-faced, but Edward Iron's powers have taken that to new heights. How do we expose him?"

"His son is working on taking him down," Prudencia says.

"I still can't believe that boy is alive," Sunstar says. Her eyes land on Atlas. She squints even harder than before. "Is that you, Eduardo?"

Atlas steps forward. "His name is longer Eduardo. It's Ness. But that's not me."

"It's actually Atlas," I say.

"You were killed," Sunstar says, and turns to me. "You were grieving him."

"I resurrected him."

If Iris weren't holding Sunstar up, I think she would faint. "Edward mentioned that Emil Rey can resurrect. He spoke of past lives and I assumed it was nonsense he was spewing to fool his followers into thinking we are far more powerful than we are, but it's true?"

"It's complicated, but you have to keep Atlas's resurrection a secret."

Sunstar stares at Atlas as if this is some trick Iron is playing on her, but one look into my eyes is all she needs to see to believe me. "If anyone finds out this will cause a nationwide—a global panic."

"Then you better hope no one finds out that we actually possess the power to raise the dead or you will not be elected president."

"It would be disastrous for all of Edward's lies to be validated simply because one happened to be true." Sunstar's exhausted eyes glance at Atlas before returning to me. "But we will have to figure out some reassimilation without alarming the public. Maybe we can say we faked his death, but no one must know that he was resurrected or we will have much bigger problems than Iron shifting around as whoever he pleases."

"You have bigger problems now," a voice calls from behind us.

FIFTY-SEVEN

THE TIES THAT BIND

MARIBELLE

I sense different waves of danger washing over me, some stronger than others, but all deadly.

Standing at the door is Dione Henri, ready for a fight with a total of six muscular arms. If she's here, that means June can't be too far since they're the only ones remaining of Luna's Blood Casters. Flanking Dione are two other people, their eyes all burning like eclipses, but neither of these specters are June. The young woman is holding crimson fire. The young man has scales running down half his face and scattered across the rest of his exposed skin like scabs. So we're up against a specter with hydra blood, another with phoenix blood, and the third with basilisk blood . . . and the dozen acolytes who are charging down the tunnel with flashlights and wands.

"Breaking and entering?" Dione asks, stepping in.

Iris steps in front of Sunstar and Eva. "I'll break your arms off next if you come any closer."

Dione waves at Eva. "Your girlfriend let you come out and play after your own abduction? Bold."

"I chose to be here," Eva says.

"You're nothing but a butterfly on a battlefield. Pretty to look at, but useless."

"I keep my friends alive."

"I guess that doesn't apply to me anymore."

"Not when you chose to steal powers to keep yourself alive."

"So preservation is okay for others, but not for ourselves?"

"Our powers are natural. Yours are not."

"You celestials don't even know where your powers originated from! You wax all this poetic nonsense about the sky and the stars and the universe, but those are nothing but stories and theories. I at least know that a hydra died so I could live, that my life couldn't be so easily threatened ever again." Dione's extra arms point to the specters at her side. "Olympia here was blessed with phoenix powers by Luna in Texas after being helpless in a closet as she watched her family get murdered by some bastard celestial. Maynard was bestowed his basilisk powers after a gang of celestials bullied him with their powers for an hour and left him for dead in the streets of New Orleans. Now we have our own powers."

"To hurt others," Eva says.

"I will choose being the predator over the prey any day."

"So there's no hope that my old friend is still somewhere in your heart?"

"Don't try to heal me with sentiments."

"I'm not. I just don't want to feel bad when my girlfriend is kicking your ass."

The dark room begins flashing with spellwork as the fight officially breaks out. Iris charges forward, but Dione dashes behind her, attacking her with speed and a fury of punches. Wesley tries keeping up, but the space is too small to build any effective momentum, and Dione is quick enough to bounce between both fights. Ruth's clone shields Sunstar, prepared for this great sacrifice to protect the woman we need to reshape this country. The acolytes continue firing spells from the doorway, and there's nothing for anyone to hide behind, so Prudencia and Atlas are doing their best to protect everyone, but Prudencia is sniped in the leg with an electric spell that has her convulsing on the ground. Atlas's winds grow stronger, slowing everyone down, even our team. Olympia throws a fire-arrow at me, and when I glide-flip out of the way, I'm blown back by the winds and left exposed for a second fire-arrow to blast into my stomach. I slam against the wall with the threatening graffiti and bang against the floor. It distracts Atlas long enough for Maynard to spit acid on his shoulder, and he groans through the pain as he does his best to lift Maynard in the air and keep him suspended.

"I'm coming!" Eva shouts as she runs to Prudencia, and she's taken by surprise when Dione dash-tackles her to the ground and begins wrapping the chain from Sunstar's ankle around her neck.

"This is what helplessness feels like," Dione says, strangling Eva with the chain to the point that her legs dangle.

Suddenly, the steel door goes flying into Dione, pinning her against the wall. At first I think Prudencia has recovered, but it's Iris who has thrown the door across the room. She's unbothered as spells bounce off her skin because these acolytes are too stupid to realize she's impervious to their attacks. Iris screams as she smacks the door away like she's swatting a fly, and she grabs Dione's arms one by one and rips them off like they're nothing but insect wings. Dione's screams are cut short when Iris punches her so hard that her neck twists, and she falls onto her chest with her head facing the ceiling.

Iris wastes no time tending to Eva, shielding her body with her own as spells continue exploding against her back, all so Eva can get the chance to find her breath after her former best friend tried killing her.

One of Ruth's clones is looking after Prudencia as the others fight acolytes, wrestling their wands away from them. Wesley runs along the wall and leaps into Maynard and choke-slams him onto the ground. Acidic blood spills out from the back of his head, shocking Wesley. I wouldn't have the same remorse in my eyes for killing a Blood Caster in self-defense, but he does. Ruth—the original—consoles Wesley as he stares at Maynard's corpse.

I recover from my blow to find Tala fighting Olympia like a dutiful Halo Knight, but if she fails at dodging any of these fiery attacks, she'll be the next dead body. I levitate to my feet and fly straight into Olympia. She bangs her elbow into my shoulder, dropping me to my knees, but I'm quick to sweep my leg into her ankles and she slams onto her back. I'm about to beat her unconscious, when Tala flips through the air, landing on top of Olympia as she drives a dagger through her heart.

"May you rest forevermore," Tala says as the burning eclipses in Olympia's eyes flicker before the darkness fades completely and leaves nothing but frozen open blue eyes. Tala is panting as she keeps pushing the dagger into Olympia's heart, the blood getting on her fingers.

"She's dead," I say, wrapping my hands around Tala's.

"I avenged the phoenix," Tala says.

"You can let go now."

Tala stares at my hands over hers. It's like the dagger isn't even there tightly gripped between her fingers that are only getting bloodier by the second. Tala only sees us. The life over death.

"Gem-grenade!" Ruth's clone shouts from the tunnel, running back toward us.

The emerald gem-grenade detonates, and green fire rockets toward us, completely swallowing Ruth's clone along the way. The explosive fire is seconds away from flooding the cell, and my psychic sense is warning me of an obvious danger that I can't do anything to avoid. I stare into Tala's amber eyes, which are illuminated by the bright green firelight, and I squeeze her hands tighter as our deaths approach. Powerful gales blow the fire back out of the cell, and the roaring flames drown out the panicky screams from the acolytes before consuming all of them too. Once the fire dissipates against the end of the tunnel, all I can see are burning corpses.

Atlas falls to his knees, exhausted, as Ruth drops to hers in agony and grief over the death of her clone. If Atlas had stayed dead and Ruth had stayed home like usual, this generation of Spell Walkers and Tala and Prudencia and Sunstar would have been killed by some nameless acolyte's lucky grenade. I let go of Tala's hands to go rush into Atlas's arms, so grateful that he was alive to help save us and so selfishly relieved that he's still alive as I want him to be forever.

"It happened so quickly," Atlas says with that heaviness in his voice. He also doesn't like getting blood on his hands, but he's done it before and he knows this is what happens in wars.

"You saved us," I say.

"Those idiots shouldn't have thrown their lives away for Blood Casters."

"They made their choices." I look around at all the dead bodies, thinking about how this didn't work out for any of them, when I see Dione's body twitching. "Dione is still alive."

Everyone watches as Dione's neck begins turning back into place so violently that we can see her bones poking up against her flesh as they rearrange themselves.

"Do I rip off her head?" Iris asks.

Prudencia works her way up from a crawl to a limp. "We don't have to kill her," she says as she pulls out a potion from her backpack. "I have a Starstifler." She picks up one of Dione's arms from the floor and telekinetically guides the blood into the vial, mixing it around.

"Gross," Wesley says.

"Effective," Iris says. "But also gross."

As Dione's neck almost finishes turning into place, Prudencia rolls her over onto her back and leans over with the potion.

"Can I?" Eva asks. "I want to be the one who makes sure she never fights again."

No one fights the pacifist on claiming this moment for herself.

Eva pours the Starstifler between Dione's lips, right as she's regaining her breath, and Iris is quick to clamp Dione's mouth shut so she can't spit it out. Dione begins shaking around as she realizes what's happening, but none of her arms have regrown to fight her way out of this. Eva and Dione cry together as Dione becomes as helpless as she was at the start of her journey that led to her becoming a deadly Blood Caster. If the ties that once bound them together weren't already broken enough, everything was severed when Dione tried killing Eva and with Eva now disempowering Dione forever.

Dione screams in agony once Iris removes her hand. "HEAL ME!

MY ARMS, THEY'RE . . . AHHH!"

"I can't heal missing limbs," Eva says, as if she would consider this request if she could.

Dione looks dizzy as she fails to get up on her feet as if we're going to let her run away. She shimmies toward the wall, looking as scared as Sunstar when we found her.

"You aided in weakening Sunstar's power," Iris says. "Now we've taken yours."

"Kill me," Dione pleads. "This pain . . . I . . . Please kill me."

"No," Iris says.

"You bitch!"

"Just because I won't kill you doesn't mean I won't knock you out."

Dione's teeth grind as she screams through the pain before her lips break into a grin. "If you won't kill me, that means I get to watch Atlas die again."

I wrap my hand around her throat. "I don't have to kill you to make you wish you were dead even more."

Atlas grabs my shoulder. "Ease up, Mari."

"She's not going to threaten us," I say, shaking him off of me.

"I'm no threat anymore," Dione says. "But Luna is about to create the biggest war this world has ever seen."

"Talk."

Dione groans as she shakes her head.

Heat begins emanating from my palm, against her throat, and I elbow everyone that tries to stop me. I haven't gone through everything to risk losing Atlas again. "What do you mean?" I remove my hand and see my blazing fingerprints marking Dione's neck. She tries finding her breath, but she's taking too long, so I threaten her again.

"Luna is going to pull back the curtain on the resurrection ritual," Dione quickly says. "She upheld the customs of alchemists to keep secrets to themselves, or trade with professionals, but now she's going to resurrect Raine and prove that every sacrifice has paved the way to this new world. Anyone who wants to bring back the dead will be welcomed to do so."

"That's going to cause disorder, riots, mass hysteria," Sunstar says.

"Luna believes this world needs to die for a greater one to be reborn," Dione says. "We know there will be growing pains. The resurrected will be hunted . . . as will their resurrectors."

I am not doing all of this so Atlas and I can spend our lives in havens from people who don't understand how dark the world was when his light was stolen from me.

Tala trails her bloody dagger against Dione's face. "I won't let more phoenixes die for these unholy resurrections. Tell me where Luna is or I will cut you a thousand times."

Sunstar turns away. "I don't condone this."

We ignore her.

Tala delivers the first cut into Dione's cheek. "The eye is next."

Dione is sweating and crying. "You're supposed to be the heroes? Torturing powerless people for information?"

"You may be powerless, but you're far from innocent." Tala raises the dagger.

"Stop! Stop! Luna is at her childhood home in Albany. Some small town, Ravena Hollow."

"You've seen her?"

"Yes! She's there with June. I've been bringing her ingredients she needs for the ritual. Some from her vault, others from trades. Equipment too."

"Equipment for what?" I ask.

"To broadcast the ritual tonight."

My heart races.

Tonight.

Luna is resurrecting Raine tonight.

She needs to perform the ritual under the stars, which means she could have started already. She could have already called her sister back from the dead. All while we were here rescuing Sunstar from this hidden cell.

"I've told you everything," Dione says. "Will you kill me now?"

I move as if I'm about to burn her, but I just rest a hand on her bloody shoulder. "We only kill in self-defense, and you're no threat." I rise to my feet as Dione screams for death. I ignore her and focus on the Spell Walkers and Prudencia. "Handle Dione's imprisonment and get Sunstar home to her family."

"Where are you going?" Iris asks.

"To stop Luna, obviously."

"Then I'm going with you. This isn't your war to fight alone."

"I won't be alone because it's Tala's war too."

Tala cleans her dagger on her pants.

Iris shakes her head. "I should be there when we finally get justice for all our parents."

"Justice comes with Sunstar becoming president, and you have to guard her with your life." I'm not lying to get her to back off. She is the best bet at making sure that Sunstar is safe from any captors or assassins. We've all seen how powerful and deadly she's willing to be if her love and future are at stake. I have to prove what I'm willing to do to protect mine. "Me and Tala and Atlas can handle Luna and June. Once and for all."

Iris folds her arms. "You better get moving, then."

"Where will you be? We'll come find you when we're done," Atlas says.

"The Izar Center in Hunts Point. That's where Shine is hiding Sunstar's family."

He nods. "See you soon."

We turn to race ahead, when Iris calls my name.

"What?"

"Get some hits in for me," Iris says, boxing the air.

"For your parents too," I promise.

I run through the tunnel with Atlas and Tala, around the burning bodies and back up and out of Light Sky Tower.

I will hunt down Luna before the rebirth of her sister can lead to the death of my love.

FIFTY-EIGHT
SLAYER

NESS

The Silver Star Slayer lives alone.

Now I'm just waiting for him to come home.

When I arrived at his one-story house about an hour ago, I looked for signs of life through his windows and found nothing but roaches running around. I had to be quick so I wouldn't draw unwanted attention. Not that anyone would've known it's me because I'm disguised as some white boy who doesn't exist. I stitched this image together with people I observed on the subway: the growing mustache and long torso of the teen who was dribbling their basketball on the platform; the round nose of the woman who was leaving the train; the shaggy blond hair of the surfer on an ad; and the tired eyes of the man who kept snapping awake on the train ride into Queens because he was scared of missing his stop. I didn't even have to break in because the sliding back door was unlocked, and judging by all the cigarette butts littered outside, the Silver Star Slayer probably forgets to lock the door after his many smoke breaks. I maintained my disguise while inside just in case there are any hidden cameras, but this place was so upsetting that it almost killed my concentration and broke my shift.

The Silver Star Slayer's entire house is a shrine to the Senator. It reminds me of the campaign offices, where you couldn't turn in any direction without seeing the Senator's face on a poster, sign, magnet, water bottle, mug, button, notebook, T-shirt, baseball cap, or bumper sticker. Except this is someone's home. I was relieved that there weren't any Senator-branded blankets in the bedroom, but there is an autographed photo on the nightstand of the Silver Star Slayer trying to appear tough beside the Senator. The Silver Star Slayer—Russell—is dressed in that lime-green shirt and navy tie from the day he interviewed me as Eva and Carolina and then kissed the Senator's ass about how he was hosting a watch party for the final debate in this very house.

I hate it here.

I'm so tempted to destroy all the equipment in his office. But it's not as if Russell would stop production without his computer or cameras or tripods or the green screen. He would just film everything on his phone and treat the destruction of his property as some badge of honor that he's on the right track if people are going so far as to break into his house to prevent him from spreading his propaganda.

I flip through the notebook on his desk, studying his sloppy handwriting and reading through his insane conspiracies. The first is about how the night sky can make any celestial invisible so they can commit more crimes. Another is about how specters can shift into the creatures they stole their essences from, which is a belief I was raised on as a kid too. A crew of celestials faking the moon landing with their powers of illusion in an effort to hide the fact that celestials regularly fly to outer space to source more gleam. There's nothing in this notebook about the truth behind my mother's murder or the Blackout because these believers don't care about the truth. I keep flipping through the notebook, stunned that anyone could believe that celestials can use any star in the world like binoculars and that specters with shifter blood often live as house pets because they're too lazy to get real jobs and . . . I stop when I see Emil's name at the top of the next page. Russell is talking about Emil's past lives and has written about how Emil will live forever, and that's unfortunately another lie. I close the notebook.

If I think about Emil for too long, I won't be able to fight in his name.

A car pulls into the driveway. Russell is finally home.

I hide inside the tiny closet where the shelves have wires tangled together, dusty binders, and a hanger of ugly ties that Russell has worn during filming. I'm waiting him out in here because he's a night owl who is very online in the middle of the night, especially this election season, where every minute counts when you're trying to secure votes. The Senator's lead is already strong after the final debate, when even Sunstar's die-hard supporters couldn't believe what they were hearing coming out of her—my—mouth, but the Senator has insisted that no one get too comfortable with his numbers because celestials will try to cheat their way to victory as they have everything else in life.

Sure enough, Russell enters the office with a gallon of orange soda and sits down at his desk. Even if I hadn't been careful in leaving his notebook exactly as he left it, I don't think Russell would've noticed as he puts on noise-canceling headphones and resumes editing a video of himself where he's red-in-the-face angry. I step out of the closet with one of his ugly ties so I can choke him until he's unconscious and then gag and bind him somewhere so I can assume his identity in peace. I'm standing right behind him as I begin raising the tie over his head. Russell's screen goes dark as he's editing a fade-to-black cut, and he sees my reflection. He acts fast, sliding his chair back into me, and his metal armrest bangs into my knee so hard that I fall onto it, like I'm kneeling before him. Russell punches me in the face like it's his first time ever hitting someone, but he begins stomping me out like I'm one of the many roaches running around this place.

"Who the hell are you?!" he shouts.

"You . . . know . . . who . . . I . . . am," I answer between his stomping.

Russell studies my face, unable to recognize me. "I've never seen you before."

I glow gray as I drop my morph. "How about now?"

His eyes widen with fear, and that's when I kick him away from me; I knew my reveal would disarm him. He rolls toward the door and then crawls out into the hallway, running off somewhere. He's not brave at all. He goes into his bedroom and slams the door shut. I knock it down with two kicks, but when I step inside, my life is being threatened.

Russell is wielding a wand that he's grabbed from that nightstand with the Senator's photograph. He's sweating and smiling as I realize something critical about his grip on the wand beyond his shakiness. "Your father is going to be so proud of me."

"You really need a better role model. This man cave is embarrassing."

"There's no one more admirable than soon-to-be President Iron."

"Your brain must be really rotted to believe that."

"You're the one whose brain got poisoned by that creature blood."

That's not what happened, but the truth doesn't matter here. "You're defending a man who had his wife assassinated and tried having his son killed multiple times for his own political gain. Iron doesn't care about people, including you. He only cares about power, and you're helping him gain more by spreading lies to your impressionable followers."

"I'm telling the truth."

"You're telling dangerous stories that have cost lives."

"I have saved lives. . . . I'm a hero."

"Good to know you're telling yourself lies too."

I take a step closer.

"Stay back or I'll shoot," Russell threatens.

"I wouldn't do that if I were you . . . and thank the stars I'm not you."

Russell squeezes the wand, but no spells are cast. He tries again and again. Fear returns to his eyes as he realizes I can strike and kill him. He begins banging the other end of the wand like it's a remote with a busted battery, not realizing he was wielding this deadly weapon the wrong way.

I flinch at the loud bang and flash of red light.

The Silver Star Slayer has slain himself with a spell to the face, dying unrecognizable.

FIFTY-NINE
THE KNIGHTS AT NIGHT

BRIGHTON

For the first time in a long time, I'm scared of what will happen to my life.

I am not fearing for my life. It's clear that no one can kill me. But I am scared of completely unraveling if I stop moving. I'm not ready to face the eternal loss of my brother and I won't be until I've resurrected my parents so we can console each other as a family. I am all-powerful, but there are some battles you shouldn't take on alone and grief is one of them.

Once securing the ritual's instructions from Maribelle, I flew back into the city, where I phased into the empty penthouse suite of a five-star hotel. I was tempted to go straight to Staten Island to see if Darren was there so I could rip out his heart for going against my orders, but he's too smart to betray me and then run back to the home I invited him into. I have all infinity to deal with him, but I need my parents back now. The requirements for the ritual only make me ache for Emil even more. Why couldn't he just get on board with this? Everything would be so much easier with someone as knowledgeable about phoenixes as he is. Where am I supposed to find feathers of a century phoenix or the bones of a breath spawn phoenix or eyes of an obsidian phoenix and everything else? Is this available in some local shop I can break into? Can I order it online? Do I have to go rip apart phoenixes myself?

I go online trying to find answers for my questions, when I remember this is why it's helpful to have legions of followers to outsource this. Some people are trolling my comments section ever since I annihilated those enforcers, but they're not loyal fans. The true Brightsiders will follow me into every corner of the universe, no matter the choices I make for all our betterment. I operate discreetly on Instagram so the Spell Walkers or Darren or anyone else won't interfere with my plans. I message with die-hard Brightsiders, whose minds are all blown to receive a DM from me in the middle of the night; one even says she thinks she's dreaming. I ask them all how I can find phoenix body parts without telling them why. One suggests going to restaurants that specialize in creature cuisines and even finds one that serves bone broth from breath spawns, which is a start. Another lets me know that fashion trends are incorporating more phoenix feathers lately because they're both smooth and strong. I write back, asking this woman to send me addresses to designer studios that might have feathers in stock. It seems like there's no one-stop shop for this until I receive another DM from the girl who thought she was dreaming.

The Council of Phoenixlight has been spotted in NYC, she writes. *Maybe you can ask if they have the supplies you're looking for? IDK if Halo*

Knights would have that but worth a shot!!!

The girl links me to a video of a fleet of phoenixes flying across the city like shooting stars. Storm King State Park is geotagged, which tells me everything I need to know about where the Halo Knights are residing: the New Ember Sanctuary. This girl on Instagram doesn't seem to know that the Halo Knights have spoken out against me and would never willingly hand over body parts, which is why I quickly study the profiles of different phoenixes so I know which ones to kill.

The Sanctuary already faced one massacre.

Tonight will be another.

I arrive at the New Ember Sanctuary within the hour, and the soothing birdsong of phoenixes in the night makes me want to settle down by a tree and close my eyes for some rest, especially after such an exhausting flight, but there will be no sleep until I have reversed the deaths of my parents.

Even if I wanted to be courteous and knock before entering the Sanctuary, the front door has already been blown open along with an entire wall where a helicopter seems to have crashed. I glide over one of the observation towers and hover above the courtyard, where my burning silver and sapphire wings catch the attention of a dozen Halo Knights below. I count just as many phoenixes and like my chances of collecting everything I need for the ritual.

"Who's your leader?" I shout.

A Halo Knight notches an arrow into their bow.

"I wouldn't do that," I warn as I swing my scythe in the air.

The Halo Knight wisely backs down as another runs into the Sanctuary. Within moments more Halo Knights flow out into the courtyard, most of them wearing black leather jackets with feathered sleeves of all colors. I recognize one particular Halo Knight pushing his way to the front of the crowd.

Wyatt hops on Nox and glides up. "I must say, Brighton, you've committed many heinous acts, but showing up to our sacred place while wearing the jacket of the man you killed is just terrible form. Though nothing surprises me after watching you kill your own brother over that bloody scythe."

I wait to see if this is all a joke, but Wyatt is glaring. "I didn't kill Emil."

"Do you truly expect me to believe—"

"I don't care if you believe me or not, but I did not kill my brother. Darren Bowes killed Emil because he wanted revenge."

Wyatt doesn't have any jokes to crack. "If true, I apologize and I am sorry for your loss, but you are still trespassing."

"If you give me what I need, then I'll be on my way."

"You must be the git of gits to think I would negotiate with a killer such as yourself."

"That's exactly why you should entertain my offer. I'm only seeking body parts from five phoenixes and two of their corpses for the resurrection ritual. Give me that and everyone else lives."

"You are not touching a single feather off any phoenix's head."

"Who's going to stop me? You're all powerless."

"We might be, but they're not."

Three sun swallowers dive from the sky, breathing fire. I phase through the flames right before they can burn me alive. The flames are still blinding until I fly through them, and when I emerge, more Halo Knights are mounting their phoenixes.

"Attack!" Wyatt shouts.

His command has sentenced every last person and phoenix in this sanctuary to death.

The Halo Knight with the bow shoots his arrow, and it sails right through me and into the chest of a Halo Knight who was sneaking up to me on his sun swallower. I don't bother watching the man plummet from the phoenix and instead blast the shooter with a rapid fire-bolt. I swing around with the scythe, decapitating the sun swallower. There are two owl-sized phoenixes with emerald wings and brown bellies that don't fit the description of any phoenixes that I need for my ritual except for the fact that phoenixes need to be buried in the Pit, so I kill them too since they'll be easier to transport than any of these bigger phoenixes that the Halo Knights are riding. I combine my dash and flight abilities to fly toward three phoenixes at hyper-speed, slashing each one within seconds, and pausing briefly to watch those Halo Knights explode in flames.

They all brought this chaos on themselves by not surrendering the phoenixes I need.

I continue advancing through their pathetic attempts to stop me while targeting the beautiful midnight-blue century phoenix that looks like an older version of Gravesend. I possess the power from this very breed, but that doesn't stop this phoenix from screeching as it charges my way. I'm not intimidated in the slightest as I fly toward this war-hungry phoenix, even as it begins breathing sapphire and silver flames. I blast my own, and when the fire meets in the middle, an explosion erupts through the air. I'm caught off guard as the phoenix flies through the cloud of fire, barreling into me so hard that the All-Killer flies out of my hand as I spiral onto the ground. I roll across the rocks jutting out of the ground, and my body burns as they rip off my flesh. I'm dizzy as I try sitting up, wishing I could combine my dash and heal abilities to speed up my recovery.

"Grab him!"

Two Halo Knights grab my arms, preventing me from phasing. I don't understand their intention with pinning me to the ground until I see a Halo Knight leap off her phoenix mid-flight. Her hands are held above her head, and a yellow blade glints under the stars until the Halo Knight slams the infinity-ender dagger into my chest. "May you lose your breath forevermore," she says.

Pain surges through me, eating away at my insides.

"You can't kill the reaper," I whisper as I feel my life fading.

I try calling my flames, but it's harder than ever before while the dagger is eating away at my phoenix powers. I think about how that century phoenix didn't let fire get in the way of fighting me, and I push through the pain, screaming as silver and sapphire flames burn the hands of the Halo Knights who are pinning me down. They try holding on, but the heat increases and, once I'm free, I blast them both with fire-bolts before punching the Halo Knight who stabbed me with a flaming fist. I rip the dagger out of my chest and slam it straight into hers.

"You will never breathe again," I say as life fades from her eyes. I push her off of me and taunt my would-be assassin further. "Your soul will never be reincarnated as a phoenix like you've spent your whole life believing. Your time ends . . ." Her head falls to the side, her mouth frozen open. "Now."

I rise, ready to clear the courtyard and skies of everyone.

I grab the infinity-ender and dash-tackle another Halo Knight, slicing his throat.

I cast fire-bolts into more riders and watch as their phoenixes fail to save them.

I hurl the infinity-ender into the air, straight into a breath spawn that screeches one final time before crashing to the ground. I phase my hand into its corpse and pull out a fractured wishbone; I can split this for the ritual. I steal a satchel off a Halo Knight's corpse and put it on, throwing the bone inside.

I fly into the air for what will be my second and final round against the century phoenix. We charge each other, and I phase through all of its fire, only solidifying in passing so I can rip off some feathers before blasting the phoenix from behind with a succession of fire-bolts. The phoenix explodes in sapphire flames, its ashes raining down onto the courtyard as their Halo Knight falls to their knees in tears. I realize I could have just stolen the feathers off the Halo's sleeves, but that's a solution that we could have reached before Wyatt commanded everyone to attack me.

Oh well.

I now possess the breath spawn's bone and the century's feathers. I still need a gray sun's heart, a crowned elder's eggshells, and an obsidian's eyes.

A few Halo Knights have begun flying away with their phoenixes, but from what I can make out in the darkness, they are breeds that mean nothing to my ritual.

Two phoenixes are circling the sky with their yellow wings and long dark tails flowing behind them like banners. They swoop down and the golden crowns on their heads make them appear even more majestic, but it's the gray belly that confirms that they are gray sun phoenixes . . . the very breed that coursed through Emil's veins. It was always such a big deal that gray suns return stronger with every resurrection, but even if they're so powerful because they've lived a thousand lives, that won't stop me from killing both so I can resurrect my parents.

I take flight, and it's harder than usual after the attack from the infinity-ender, but I push past the struggles to reach the phoenixes. The gray suns stare with their pearl-black eyes before breathing gold and gray flames. I counter with silver and sapphire fire, causing another explosion. This time I'm braced for a sneak attack, so when a gray sun charges through the flames, I let it phase through me, and watch as the phoenix sinks through the sky in a blaze of fire because I've stolen its heart out of its chest. The surviving gray sun cries, grieving the other. It's strange for phoenixes to mourn, especially when they will see each other again in their next lives. The gray sun zooms toward me, but I camouflage against the darkness, confusing it. The phoenix's beady eyes expand as I reach through its gray underbelly to steal its heart and watch as the phoenix dies its latest death.

I throw the bloody hearts into my satchel with the bones and feathers.

I descend to the courtyard and empty a duffel bag of its birdseed so I can pack those two dead phoenixes that are no bigger than owls.

"You heartless arsehole!" Wyatt shouts from above.

I look up to find Wyatt on Nox, and he's wielding my All-Killer. I fly up. "That doesn't belong to you."

"You'll see it up close again very soon, worry not."

I laugh. "I'm supposed to be intimidated by someone who orders Halo Knights to kill me and then vanishes from the battlefield?"

"While you were rude to barge in, I thought I would be the bigger man and fix you up a snack like a good host." Wyatt holds up a potion. A Starstifler. "It's nice and fresh for you."

I glare. "You don't have my blood."

"You took quite a tumble after the century phoenix knocked you out of the sky. Squeezing the blood from the flesh that ripped off your body was absolutely disgusting, but we all must get our hands dirty for the greater good."

"What do you think is about to happen here, Wyatt? I'll drink the potion or you'll kill me?"

"Precisely, but it is my greatest wish that we don't have to go there. Be the bigger man—"

My fire-bolt blows apart the vial before Wyatt can finish his sentence. He winces from the explosion of glass that cuts into him. "I will never bind my powers, so if you want to stop me, you will have to kill me."

"Emil believed in you—"

"Do not speak of Emil as if you knew who he was. You were nothing but a stranger."

"A stranger who loved your brother."

"He didn't love you back."

"Maybe not, but I push on in his memory anyway. That's more than you can say."

I am so tired of being villainized by everyone simply because I live outside their moral code. "Did the love of your life ever tell you about our psychic grandmother? I always felt like I was destined to have visions of my own, the strongest in our family. That power unfortunately never came to be, but I can still foresee your future. You will be forced to watch as I rip out your phoenix's eyes for my resurrection ritual. Then I will kill you both."

Wyatt's voice cracks as he says, "Emil would hate you for this."

"Probably. I will have to live with that. You won't."

We fly toward each other like we're jousting, and as Wyatt swings the scythe at me, I blast Nox in his belly. The phoenix recoils in pain, and Wyatt flies off his back without any power or wings of his own. I watch as the Halo Knight falls and falls until he slams on the ground. I descend where I snatch the scythe off his still body, reveling in how he isn't breathing.

I have finally shut up Wyatt Warwick forever.

Nox cries over his owner's death.

I fly up, hoping to take advantage of the phoenix's grief, but Nox catches on and begins soaring away. I chase the phoenix away from the Sanctuary, through the woods, and across the river, but the obsidian begins bleeding into the night, and after one sharp turn around a mountain, I lose sight of Nox. I hover in the air, catching my breath. I know my limits. That phoenix is long gone.

All isn't lost.

In fact, with two more ingredients, lost lives will be found again.

SIXTY
RAVENA HOLLOW

MARIBELLE

It's a beautiful night to kill Luna.

The stars are kissing my skin and strengthening my powers, which is necessary as we all continue this long journey through the skies to upstate New York. I'm leading the way with my burning wings so Atlas can see where he's going as he rides his winds and as Tala steers Roxana through the darkness. We're so high up that even if someone does see dark yellow wings of fire and a light howler phoenix, it's unlikely they'll see Atlas. I can't have anyone knowing he's alive until it's time to reintroduce him to the world with Sunstar's help.

I won't let Luna ruin my life any more than she has.

We arrive in Ravena Hollow, a small town I've never heard of before tonight but would have probably enjoyed growing up in myself. I love the city, but I never got the chance to live in it like other kids did. Ravena Hollow is charming with its cozy storybook houses that look like illustrations brought to life, and I would've loved running across these white cobbled streets. But I didn't get to grow up here because I had to bounce between havens. It pisses me off that I can only experience Ravena Hollow as a child by retrocycling through Luna's past. She would've been happy too with Raine given how far she's gone to bring her back to life. But that won't be happening.

Luna hasn't come home to resurrect her sister.

She's come home to die.

"This way!" Tala shouts, using her phone's map to guide us to Luna's home.

We fly toward a mansion on the top of a hill, which helps me understand the entitlement that has followed Luna throughout her life. Her parents must've come from money because there's no way being professors pays for an estate like this. The mansion is four stories high with an open-sky glass ceiling that looks modern compared to the rest of this house; maybe some wealthy celestials purchased the house years ago and wanted to sleep under the stars. There's a maze garden with large trees obscuring many corners, a barn that's bigger than Wesley's cottage, and miles of land that stretch into a dark forest. We glide over the iron gate, landing on the ground next to stone statues of a phoenix and three-headed hydra coiled together as if they're at war or in love.

"Strategy?" Tala asks.

Atlas holds up a finger as he leans over, casting air into his lungs. "That was a long flight."

"That may also be your last breath if we don't move quickly."

"The strategy is simple." I pull out the oblivion dagger. "Stop Luna at all costs."

Tala prepares her crossbow. "Forevermore."

"Where is Luna?" Atlas asks.

I look around as if I'm going to find the Phoenix Pit blazing somewhere. We would know where Luna is, but we'd also be too late to stop her. "She has to be outside. The ritual needs to be performed under the stars. . . . Tala, go check the barn's perimeter. Atlas, fly through the forest. I can sense my way through the maze."

"We're not splitting up," Atlas says.

"We don't have a choice."

"You always have a choice, Mari. You don't have to live by your first feeling."

"So what are we going to do? Let people hunt you down?"

Atlas holds my waist. "I would rather be alive and hunted instead of killed because we didn't stick together."

Tala looks away. "I'll scout the barn's perimeter," she says, running off with Roxana gliding behind her.

I point at her. "See? This is how we get things done."

"It's different. You're not Tala's girlfriend. You're mine," Atlas says gently. He is not taking a shot at me, but I still flinch over his words anyway. "I love you, and I will happily piss you off if it means saving your life. Any day." Atlas grabs my hand. "I will die before I leave your side again."

I remember the grief and how I'm fighting to never live that again.

"Then let's go."

We run toward the garden. I'm tempted to burn the maze to the ground, when I begin sensing danger. It comes and goes, but it's unnerving, like someone breathing over me. Someone out of sight. I stop to hone in on the source of the danger and feel a pull toward the mansion. Suddenly I feel like I'm being watched from the many windows, but I still don't see anyone. It reminds me of that time that Shine Lu snuck up on me with her invisibility except this is far more threatening. I do have an enemy that can be stealthy.

I steady the oblivion dagger. "June . . ."

Atlas looks around. "Where?"

"The house."

"If she's close, then Luna can't be far. Let's get Tala."

"We've wasted enough time."

I run and jump into a glide toward the house, kicking down the front door. The foyer is decorated with professional photographs of prime constellations, and there are half capes hanging on hooks. This is definitely a home for celestials. There's an oil painting of a family I've never seen before until I find the man and woman on the living room floor with their throats slit, blood glistening onto a moon-white carpet. I hope I don't stumble onto the twin girls. Atlas catches up with me, upset over the bodies, but there's no time for this. I keep sensing my way through the house, following the danger beyond the staircase, through the lavish dining area, past the library, and out into the sunroom, where coloring books and crayons have been abandoned.

"Do you think . . . ?" Atlas doesn't finish his question.

"Luna killed June. Why wouldn't she kill more children?" I'm even more motivated to end her, but I'm no longer sensing the danger that was leading me to them. "The trail has gone cold."

"Maybe they left. Luna wouldn't risk her sister after everything she's been through to get to this moment, right?"

When I last saw Luna and June, they fled before I could kill them. They've run for their lives before, and they'll do it again, especially as I'm wielding the oblivion dagger.

Suddenly, the danger flares up, closer than ever.

I swing around with the dagger, and Tala catches my forearm before I can slice her.

Tala puts a finger to her lips, telling me to be quiet as we sneak down a hall and walk out into a courtyard.

There she is.

Luna is circling a Phoenix Pit, just as I watched her do in the past to resurrect June. There are two phoenixes—one living, one dead—around her. The sun swallower's corpse is lying unceremoniously near the grave, showing that Luna has corrected her mistake, which prevented June from keeping her soul. There's a young cerulean chained to a stone bench, and it's not even screeching; it's like it's already resigned itself to captivity. It should expect death. Once Luna uses that phoenix to set the Pit ablaze, I'm sure she won't be setting it free when its blood can be sourced for power.

I turn to Tala, expecting to find murder in her eyes because of the treatment of these phoenixes, but her gaze is blank, as if her will to live is gone. I've only brought more death and heartbreak into her life, and she won't even let me make it up to her. I can only hope that killing Luna will finally bring her the peace I've been chasing.

"Welcome," Luna says to me, and then turns to Atlas. "And welcome back."

"Thanks," Atlas says dryly. "I haven't missed much judging by the dead bodies out there. Did you kill the kids too?"

"Of course not. I'm no monster." Luna's grin pisses me off. "We spared the children and let them know that goodbye would not be forever after my demonstration tonight."

"There will be no demonstration."

"The world must know that its greatest flaw has been corrected . . . thanks to you."

I already feel some responsibility for Brighton becoming the

Infinity Reaper, but I don't know how I'll be able to live with myself if this world begins weaponizing resurrections.

I look around but don't find any cameras. I still feel like I'm being watched, and I try making sense of the threat my power is warning me away from. "Where's June?"

"Why would she show her face when you possess the weapon that can end her?"

"To protect you from me," I say.

"My darling granddaughter, you will not be killing me."

"I certainly haven't come all this way to bond."

"Well, you'll be doing just that as I introduce you to your great-aunt."

"Screw her. You've killed the only family I care about."

"There is nothing to be done about that, so it's best you move on, girl."

Dark yellow flames glow around my fist. "Or I can just end you."

"Why you think you will succeed now when you have always failed is beyond me."

"You have nothing to offer me this time."

"Maybe not, but that doesn't mean I'm ill-prepared for your childish threats."

Danger intensifies as bare knuckles connect with my chin out of nowhere. I flip back around, expecting to find June, but it's Tala who's punched me . . . Tala who knees me in the stomach . . . Tala who springboards off my back and tackles Atlas to the floor.

Is this some trap? Has Tala snapped because I didn't choose her?

No, this isn't like her.

That's because this isn't her.

Tala has been possessed by June.

SIXTY-ONE
THE ARMOR

MARIBELLE

The most brilliant armor June can wear is hiding within someone I care about.

Even if I wanted to hurt June, I'm more concerned for how Tala is doing inside her own body. When June possessed me, I was screaming and suffocating and freezing like I was naked in an ocean. I couldn't blink my own eyes or move a single muscle. It's terrifying to be that powerless.

This is my fault. If we'd all stayed together, I could have prevented this or at least known it was happening. But everything makes so much sense now for why I couldn't detect June and when I only did again as Tala reappeared. June played it smart by gesturing for me and Atlas to stay quiet to hide the fact that she herself can't talk.

Just because I can't kill June doesn't mean I can't fight back.

When June flies at me again, I restrain myself from stabbing her with the oblivion dagger because killing June would mean killing Tala—and her soul—too. I've already glimpsed what it's like to not have her in my life, and I hate it. I won't be the reason it happens forever. Thankfully, June doesn't have Tala's combat skills. The first time I brawled with Tala, I assumed she must have had some supernatural powers in her blood with the way she moved, and while June is deadly, that's only because of her powers. I levitate into a backflip, kicking Tala's chin so hard that June goes stumbling back, and I torpedo toward her, but I end up phasing right through and crashing into the ground; I scream as my shoulder dislocates. June runs for the oblivion dagger, but winds carry it straight into Atlas's hand.

"Payback!" Atlas charges at the girl who cast a spell straight into his heart, ready to rip her apart.

I fly off my back and tackle Atlas before he can stab Tala. The dagger clatters as Atlas groans.

"Don't kill her," I say.

"I wasn't going to," Atlas groans. "I just want to scare June out of Tala's body."

That's a great plan. I snatch up the dagger with my good arm and swing at June like I'm feral. I can see the fear in Tala's amber eyes. June can't phase through the dagger without getting hurt, so I get closer and closer, trying to press her. I have to commit—I lunge at Tala's chest with the dagger. June dives out of Tala's body, and I pull back the dagger a moment before it can plunge into Tala's heart.

Tala sucks in a deep breath as she falls to her knees.

"You're free," I say.

Tala looks up with teary eyes. Then she points behind me. "But he's not."

Atlas is staring at us with a haunted look in his eyes. It wasn't enough for June to kill him; now she's possessing his body that I worked so hard to resurrect. Dark yellow flames trail my arms in fury.

"I wouldn't do that!" Luna shouts. "You may not be able to collect his ashes this time around, and he will be lost to you forever."

"That doesn't mean I can't hurt you instead."

Right as I turn to hurl flames at Luna, June punches me with Atlas's fist; this is a first. Unlike Tala, I have never engaged in true, no-holds-barred physical combat with Atlas. We've trained together, but he always pulled his punches even though I asked him not to. This is what the full force of his knuckles feels like. Then his knee into my rib cage. His elbow into my neck. His forehead against mine.

"I'm sorry," I say to Atlas, hoping that he can hear me over his own screams. I double-punch his beautiful gray eyes to blind June before slamming my knee into his groin so June can be shocked with a pain she's never known before. Then I let loose as if Atlas isn't stuck in his own body. This is the only way I can bully June into leaving his body. But I stop when I see his beautiful smile paired with that haunted gaze. June wants me beating on him. It's going to take more than strong blows to scare June away. I apologize again with tears in my eyes as I grab Atlas's wrists and begin burning him alive to save his life. June tries fighting out of my grip, unable to phase away until I let go.

June vacates his body, and Atlas falls forward into my arms.

"I'm so sorry," I say.

Atlas is groaning in misery as he summons winds to cool his burning hot wrists. "You did what you had to do," he says. "Always do what you have to do to survive, Mari."

I'm not interested in surviving right now. I'm interested in avenging.

June and I run for the oblivion dagger, but Tala leaps into a shoulder roll and grabs it first.

"We've got you now," I say. I hurl streams of dark yellow fire, but they phase right through June. She runs at me, and I realize she's about to try and possess me next. "Throw the dagger!"

"I—"

"THROW IT!"

Tala hurls the oblivion dagger.

The bone blade flies straight through June's back and out her chest.

And directly into mine.

June and I fall to the floor, face-to-face, the both of us bleeding out of our new wounds. Her eyes begin burning like eclipses, and I fight through the pain to grab her hand so she can't escape. She stares at me as she coughs up gray-and-red blood. She keeps trying to fight out of my grip, but she's too weak. I'm fading too, but I have to hold on long enough.

"I did not want to hurt you," Tala says as she crouches beside me.

"Kill her," I breathe.

Tala looks at June, who can't breathe. "She's dying."

"Finish her."

I hate that Luna killed this girl and rebirthed her as a soulless assassin, but I have to accept that there will be no good that comes from June in her second life. If June escapes and survives, we will never be able to live in peace. She could hunt and possess us in our sleep and make us kill each other and then leap off the Light Sky Tower in the sole survivor's body so they plummet to their death. The ways she can hurt us are infinite, and we have to end her now.

I scream as I rip the oblivion dagger out of my chest, already feeling my gleam slowly work to heal me. "Do it!"

Tala watches the blood drip off the dagger before turning to a panicking June. Her amber eyes tear up as she hovers over the murderer who possessed her father only to trick her mother into killing him. Luna may be behind this operation, but June got her hands dirty. "I sentence you to oblivion for your crimes against my parents, against the Spell Walkers, against peace. May you be a stranger to breath forevermore."

June opens her mouth as if she wants to scream for help, scream for mercy, or just scream, but nothing comes out as Tala plunges the oblivion dagger into her heart, ending her soulless life.

The girl who caused the Blackout is dead.

I want to cry thinking about all those sleepless nights grieving my parents, the investigations I led trying to figure out June's identity, the night she possessed me and made me kill Atlas.

We are all safe from June.

Tala is shaking as she removes her bloody fingers off the dagger, leaving it implanted inside June's corpse. She turns to me with a sad smile. "It is done. We have avenged—"

I sense danger as a spell explodes against Tala's chest, blasting her backward.

Then another warning as a spell strikes Atlas.

And one more as Luna casts a spell at me.

SIXTY-TWO
BURNING WINDS

MARIBELLE

How am I alive?

I'm lying on the floor, entangled with Tala and Atlas, both of whom are unconscious. I groan in pain as I check their weak pulses. Better weak than nothing. We were already so weak and tired from our fights against acolytes, a basilisk, and Dione at the Light Sky Tower and then our final battle against June that our bodies stood no chance against those spells. I hadn't even finished healing from the oblivion dagger in my chest, and now Luna's spell has ripped through my core, making my gleam work extra hard to patch up my insides.

I feel near death, but my heart is trying to speed up when I see blood soaking Atlas's chest.

"No . . . Atlas, wake up. . . ."

I relive the trauma of his first—and only—death. I will not go through this again.

I climb on top of Atlas, pressing down on his wound.

"You brought this on yourself, granddaughter," Luna says with her back to the Phoenix Pit. "You whine as if death follows you wherever you go when instead it is you constantly running toward it."

"Someone has to stop monsters like you!"

"That may be how you choose to see this, but understand that when you hunt a monster, it will always defend itself. Even if that means killing family."

"I'm not dead."

"With good reason. Bringing Raine back to life is just the beginning of our eternal lives, but only possible once a woman of my age can survive the specter transition from mortal to immortal without the power of the Crowned Dreamer constellation."

"What does that have to do with me?"

"I need to further utilize your retrocycling talents. My darling Sera ran in alchemic circles that were working on treating older bodies with essences from creatures, but only you can take those voyages through time to unearth such a ritual."

"I will never help you."

"You already have, my dear. I would not have my sister back without you." Luna opens a jeweled box that's caked in dirt and pulls out a steel urn that's painted with golden raindrops. "It is time the world discovers its potential."

I'm fading in and out as Luna pulls a small clicker out of her robe and aims it at a bush where I can now see a camera light blinking green.

"Hello, world. My name is Luna Marnette, and you do not truly know who I am. I am aware that stories of my nature have been passed around, that my reputation seems unsavory, and that the very people who speak ill of me publicly also worship my name in the shadows because of what I can do. Whether you praise or fear me, I want you to understand that everything I have done has always been in service of you. We live in a broken universe where there have been far too many deaths, all unstoppable even by the likes of supreme alchemists such as myself. I come to you now not with a method by which you can prevent death, but instead to offer guidance on how to undo it. I possess the wisdom of resurrection and will share it with you all after this demonstration in which I will bring my dear sister, Raine Marnette, back to life ever since losing her as a teenager."

Luna begins spreading Raine's ashes into the Phoenix Pit.

I have to stop her, but I'm so weak. I'm trying to throw a fire-arrow, but my projectile dissipates before it can reach her. I'm failing to protect Atlas, who doesn't seem to stand a chance anyway. He's going to die and Tala will be killed and I'll be held captive by Luna until she finally becomes immortal.

"I'm sorry, Atlas," I say as I lean down and kiss his lips, possibly for the last time. Atlas chokes. He tries speaking but spits up blood. I fight through all the pain to drag him into my lap and elevate my head. "You've been shot."

Atlas is shivering. Color is leaving his face as glistening blood stains his teeth and lips. His gray eyes turn away from me.

Luna finishes spreading the ashes into the Phoenix Pit and commands the tethered cerulean to ignite. The phoenix breathes blue fire onto the Phoenix Pit, setting it alight. "Undo a death, renew a life!" Luna shouts to the stars.

Atlas weakly lifts his finger as if telling me to stop her.

"I can't. . . . I'm not strong enough." I'm not strong enough to do it alone. I squeeze Atlas's hand. "I need your power too. Can you cast?"

Atlas's finger curls back into his fists as his gray eyes begin glowing.

Two things begin happening at once.

A gentle breeze builds around us.

Blue flames rise high from the Pit.

The breeze turns into a wind.

Luna watches her ritual with a smile on her face.

Atlas sweats as he concentrates on casting.

The flames turn into a fiery silhouette of a girl.

The wind spins into a furious twister, and I cast a fire-arrow into its center.

The fiery girl is turning to flesh.

The burning twister flies toward the silhouette, setting the bush with the camera on fire along the way, before blowing Raine apart moments before she can become whole.

Luna screams as if she's cursed with the guilt of every life she's stolen. She falls to her knees as her sister's ashes rain down upon her, too scattered to ever collect again.

My body is not the only thing healing at this sight—my soul is too. Between June's corpse lying a few feet away and disrupting Luna's reason for living, I feel as if I'm being reborn. Mama and Papa have been avenged . . . almost. I can't take to the skies for a victory lap yet, because as long as Luna can breathe, then she will be able to hurt us.

It's finally time for Luna to join Raine in the afterlife.

"Are you going to be okay?" I ask Atlas.

He wipes the blood from his lips as he pants. "I think so."

I'm so relieved this spell wasn't a fatal shot to the heart.

Luna eyes me as I stalk toward her. "I have spent all my life trying to bring my sister back, only for you to steal her away forever."

"As you did with my parents—and Tala's."

"But not your love. I gave that back to you. I should reap the benefits too!"

"You won't, and this is the price you pay for all the heartbreak you've caused."

Luna glares, and I sense danger as the wand slides out of her cloak's sleeve and into her hand. She is about to cast a spell, when an arrow strikes Luna in her chest. She stares in disbelief at me and then Tala, who is weakly sitting on one knee with her crossbow still leveled from the shot she took. "Not like this," Luna mutters as she falls on her back.

Tala limps over, finding force to kick Luna's foot out of her way as she goes to untether the cerulean phoenix from the stone bench. She gently pets the smooth blue feathers before watching the phoenix screech in delight as it flies out toward the stars, free. Then Tala's eyes lock on Luna. "You have lost everything. Your Blood Casters. Your sister. And now—"

"My life." Luna rips the arrow out of her chest. "I have heard it all before, but it appears to be true now." She groans in pain, and I could listen to her agony the way others bask in birdsong. She coughs up blood and slides her hand inside her cloak to grab a handkerchief, but she freezes as if she realizes how pointless it is. The blood around her lips is nothing compared to the blood staining her blouse. She's paler already. "I only sought to defy death."

"If only you could have done that without killing countless people."

"If only," Luna says tenderly.

Footsteps shuffle behind me as Atlas slowly makes his way over. He wraps his arm around my shoulders and holds himself up.

"Do you think it will hurt?" Luna asks.

"The hard part is done," I say, looking at Tala's bloody arrow.

Luna spits up more blood. "I am talking about the explosion," she says as she pulls a ruby gem-grenade out from her cloak. My psychic sense screams at me to get far, far away. This is the same kind of gem-grenade that obliterated Mama, Papa, Iris's parents, and everyone else at the Nightlocke Conservatory on the day of the Blackout. "If we cannot live forever, then let us die forever."

Her last breath is cut short when the gem-grenade detonates, blowing apart her body beyond recognition, beyond recovery, as it did for my parents and as it will for us now too.

Electric red light races toward us.

I brace myself for eternal death, squeezing Atlas with one arm and grabbing Tala's hand with the other, trying to find comfort that I got to love in this life and kill my greatest enemy. The house is already crumbling as I find myself spinning rapidly in a burning hot twister. I cling on to Atlas's waist and am about to break the bones in Tala's hand as I hold on. I can make out Atlas's glowing eyes in the darkness, knowing that he is saving us from the full impact of this explosion, but it's not enough, and the fire breaks through and blasts us out of the twister. I lose my grip on Atlas and Tala, and I spin and spin and spin through the air until I crash onto the floor.

The house has been destroyed, and the heat of the many fires is baking me alive.

I have to find the others and get out of here.

I'm dizzy, bleeding, and choking on smoke.

I get to my feet but crumble right back down. I'm so weak.

"Atlas! Tala! Atlas! Tala! Say something!"

No one is responding.

I fly toward the sky, where I can breathe. All I see below are raging fires and black smoke. How am I supposed to find Atlas and Tala through all this mess?

"ROXANA!"

The light howler flies toward me, and I have her follow me in a circle so her rain can put out the fires. Her storm isn't enough to put out a massive fire that's only growing and growing, but it's clearing a path for me to descend and try to find Atlas and Tala.

"Tala! Atlas!"

I cast dark yellow flames to break through the smoke, and I find Tala's body. She's slumped against a wall with her arm twisted behind her back and blood running from her nose, ears, and lips. I scream her name as I approach, but she doesn't wake up. My hand is shaky as I reach for her neck, but I'm relieved to find a faint pulse. She's alive, but I don't know for how long.

I now desperately wish the other Spell Walkers had tagged along: Eva could be saving Tala's life; Iris could be carrying her easily instead of me struggling to balance Tala over my shoulder as I light the way through the smoke; Ruth could be fanning out with her clones to find Atlas; and Wesley could have helped us avoid this completely by snatching that gem-grenade before Luna could blow everything up. But none of them are here and I'm alone and the smoke is getting heavier and the fire is raging on despite Roxana's rainstorm.

"Maribelle!"

"Atlas!"

I follow my name through the darkness, falling to my knee under Tala's weight, but I get up and keep going and going through the smoke until I find Atlas on the floor. "Get up. We have to go," I say.

Atlas smiles. "Mari . . ."

"Come on, I need your help with Tala."

"Mari . . ."

"What?" Dark yellow flames illuminate the sadness in his gray eyes. "What, Atlas? We have to go."

Atlas looks down at his stomach, and that's when I see that a bar from the phoenix's cell is nailing him to the floor. "I'm not going anywhere, Maribelle."

I set Tala down and rush to Atlas's side. I grab the bar, and he grabs my wrist.

"Don't take it out."

"I have to."

"I'll die."

"You'll die here if I don't."

"Not before I get to tell you how much I love you, Maribelle Lucero."

It was hard enough to see from the smoke, but hot tears are clouding and stinging my eyes. "You're not going to die, Atlas, and if you do, I'm going to bring you back."

Atlas weakly shakes his head. "This house is coming down. If you stay here trying to save me, then you'll die too."

"Then I die too!"

"What about Tala? You can't sacrifice her for me."

I look at Tala, who's still unconscious. I want to smack her awake, but then what? She's severely injured. The impact when she was thrown out of the protective twister could have done so much internal damage. I have to help her, but I also have to save Atlas now so I can resurrect him later.

Do I choose my boyfriend, who is destined to die so I can bring him back to life, or do I choose the girl who is alive and still has her whole life ahead of her?

I can't do both.

"No, I have to . . . I can . . ."

"You have to survive," Atlas says.

"Not without you."

"You did it before, and you will do it again."

I shake my head. "No, no. You can't die again. This wasn't enough time. We were supposed to have forever."

Atlas grabs my hand. "No one gets forever, Maribelle. But we got more time together thanks to you. I got to fight and win with you. I got to save you. I got to kiss you. I got to tell you how much I love you again." He begins sobbing and squeezes me. "I didn't waste this new life, but now you have to find yours without me. . . ."

Everything about this feels so final. It's almost as if I'm having a vision warning me of Atlas's death and preparing me for a future without him. Again. This time I get to brace myself. This time I get to say goodbye. I just can't believe I have to say it.

"I want to love you forever, Atlas."

He brushes my tearstained, bloody cheek. "I will die in peace knowing that. But you know what you can do for me?"

"What?"

"Live and love, Maribelle."

"I can't—"

"You can! You're a survivor and you're a lover." Atlas nods at Tala with a fondness. "But you can only focus on your future if you keep the past buried."

"If I keep you buried."

Atlas is doing his best to hold back his tears. "Leave me dead and live your life."

Beams from the ceiling begin crashing around us, growing the fire. I sense the danger, but I don't want to go. I'm so scared of facing life without him again. I can turn to Tala, but that doesn't mean my heart won't still be broken again. My psychic sense is warning me of graver danger the longer I wait, like I'm condemning all of us to die here. If I didn't owe Tala my life for all the times she has saved me, then maybe I would stay, curled up inside Atlas's arms so we can begin our journey through the heavens in the stars together. But I have to survive for Atlas even if I don't want to survive for myself.

I kiss Atlas and run my fingers through his hair and press my palm against his racing heart. I try to back away, but it's like I'm frozen inside this burning landscape. "I can't leave you."

Atlas smiles, and the pain in his eyes becomes hidden behind glowing stars. "I love you, Maribelle."

Winds blow me away from Atlas and up into the air. I scream for Atlas to stop, to let me go, but I'm flying higher and higher toward the sky and watching as he shrinks like a distant star. A silhouette rises, and it's Tala's body swirling around me. Atlas must be using every last ounce of his strength to save our lives. I begin flying with my dark yellow flames to grab Tala and carry her in my arms, staring down through the tunnel of wind that Atlas has conjured for our clear journey out of the burning house. Then the winds carrying us vanish, and Atlas waves one last time before the dark smoke obscures the fire journeying toward him, about to turn him into ashes I can never—and will never—use to resurrect him.

I fly Tala to Roxana, setting us down onto the phoenix's back.

I watch the fire eat away at the house.

I scream at the stars when I feel death in my heart; Atlas is dead.

But Tala isn't.

If I don't save her, then there will be no one to live for, and living is what survivors do.

"I love you, Atlas," I say again, and a wind brushes my cheek where his fingers were, and then the phoenix takes off through the night.

SIXTY-THREE
A LIAR'S DEATH

NESS

I have to cover my tracks even though I didn't kill the Silver Star Slayer.

There is something ironic about Russell preaching everything the Senator says, including how every household should carry wands for self-defense, only for Russell to silence himself forever when trying to kill someone without any offensive powers. It's a nightmare in here. Bloody bed. Bloody wall. Bloody nightstand. I freeze at the bloody streaks running down the photograph of Russell and the Senator smiling. This man died serving someone who will not mourn him, but will use his death as a tool to further his own agenda as he did with my mother's and with mine.

I refuse to go down for this crime.

I'm about to drag Russell into the backyard to bury him when I stop myself.

The stage has already been set for Russell's death. It just needs a story, and Russell needs to be the one who tells it in front of the camera that made him famous enough.

Gray light.

I shift into Russell as he was before he killed himself—orange soda on his lips, auburn hair, brown eyes, and a lemon-yellow shirt with a bright red silky tie that might have some class to it around any other neck. I consider grabbing the wand, but it would be too easy for forensics to suspect foul play if I rinsed the wand for the video and then rolled it around in more blood to re-create what happened.

I step over Russell's corpse and go into his office. I consider sitting in front of his green screen, but this isn't a news report or some conspiracy I'm going to be sharing; it's a suicide note. I sit at his desk, where he does his editing, molding my body into his chair and leaning forward like he always does, as if he's going to reach through the screen and grab you by the throat.

Once I'm in character, I tell the Silver Star Slayer's final story.

"Attention, viewers. This is the final episode of my program because it is also the final night of my life." I'm tempted to blame this decision on Russell's fear of celestials coming to get him, which I've seen firsthand when he had his interview with Eva, who also doesn't possess an offensive power to hurt him with, but I can't have this video be used to scare the idiots who already hang on to his every word. I do have to speak from his heart, though. "I *hate* this country!" I blush my cheeks so they get as red as Russell's do whenever he's angry, which is most of the time he's in front of a camera. "I hate what this country is becoming, and I have played a big role in this. I lied for views, for clicks, for follows. I have said many things I don't believe because I hated celestials so much that I would do and say anything to make sure their lives are miserable. I even knowingly interviewed Senator Iron's son, Eduardo, as he shifted into other people and pretended to be them, all to make the Spell Walkers look bad. . . ." I cry as Russell once did in a video—scrunched face, hyperventilating, and head bobbing like whenever a guest shared a new conspiracy. "This has gone too far! I'm scared of getting caught and going to jail or being hunted by the Spell Walkers and tortured! I can't keep living like this, so I am going to go grab my wand and end it all."

I stare at Russell's reflection in the camera before switching it off.

I'm being honest about his death even if I lied about what drove him to it.

He spent all his life lying. He can lie in death too.

SIXTY-FOUR
REDEATH

MARIBELLE

Tala must be near death for my screams to not wake her up.

We're flying as fast as we can on Roxana, but the journey to Shine's hideout in Hunts Point is miserable. Every second that passes, I can't believe Atlas is dead and I keep turning around as if he's going to be soaring behind us and I scream in agony every time I don't see him because this means he is dead and that he burned to death and that he was alone and that I wasn't there to die with him and he knows I would've died with him and that's why he saved me one last time and cast me into the air with Tala so we could live. It's not looking good for her, though. I keep steering Roxana toward the Izar Center, which is an urgent care facility for celestials, and I don't know why Shine's hideout is so public, but I'm not going to question an invisible woman about hiding in plain sight when all I care about is getting Tala the medical attention she desperately needs.

I can't lose anyone else.

Especially not Tala.

I find a billboard that's advertising the Izar Center's services, and I pay attention to the address instead of the horrific graffiti of the celestial model's glowing eyes scratched out. In minutes, Roxana descends in front of the center.

"HELP!" I scream as I carry Tala through the entrance. "EVA!"

Out of nowhere, the Spell Walkers appear as if they've been invisible. They've been hiding behind an illusion, just like Sunstar and Shine arranged for everyone at the Clayton Center for Recovery during Brighton's stay.

I set down Tala on the lobby floor.

"What happened?" Eva asks.

"Explosion," I say. "Luna died while trying to take us out with a gem-grenade."

Iris's mouth hangs open, likely reliving the Blackout footage we're very familiar with.

Eva feels Tala's pulse, and there's panic in her eyes before they begin glowing. Rainbow lights emanate from her palms and shower Tala's wounds. I'm shaking as I watch, and the louder Eva screams as she transfers the pain from Tala's body into her own, the more scared I am that it's going to be too much and that Eva will quit and Tala will die and I will lose my last reason to live. But Eva is strong and powerful and pushes through to save Tala's life, giving extra attention to the back of Tala's head. Sunstar and Shine come out of a room the longer Eva screams, but Ruth blocks their path to give us some more breathing room.

"You've got this," Iris encourages as Eva looks fatigued.

Eva squints as she pushes, her lights growing brighter as her scream gets louder, until finally she collapses back into Iris's arms. "She almost died," she whispers as she wipes the tears and sweat from her face. "You saved her life."

"You did," I say.

"Only because you got her here in time." Eva is fading. "She needs to rest. . . . I do too."

I'm too choked up to thank her.

Iris helps Eva to her feet.

Ruth rushes over with a rolling bed and clones herself to help get Tala onto it.

Wesley is standing in the center's doorway, staring up at the sky. "Where's Atlas?"

My cry answers the question.

Life.

Death.

Rebirth.

Redeath.

Wesley shakes his head. "But . . . but . . . you can bring him back again, right?"

I can't stop crying long enough to tell how I don't have Atlas's ashes or how he didn't want to be resurrected or how he wants me to focus on the future. All I can do is hug my knees to my chest and cry and cry and cry, hating how Atlas Haas is dead forever.

SIXTY-FIVE
THE SHED

BRIGHTON

A Brightsider has clued me in on where I might be able to find the last ingredients for my ritual.

I arrive in Saffron Square in Brooklyn, which I've always avoided because of its high crime rates, but there isn't a single mugger alive who could scare me now. I descend into a train station where construction was abandoned after basilisks kept devouring the workers. The news coverage of that incident gave me nightmares when I was younger until I watched the interviews of the celestials who went underground and killed the basilisks. This Saffron Square train stop never came to be, but a market called the Shed was born in its place.

As I enter the Shed, I admire the graffiti along the walls of its tunnel. My favorite is of a telekinetic celestial who uses her power to strangle a basilisk with a train track. At least it was my favorite until it reminds me of Prudencia and how she would like to do the same thing to me.

I'd like to see her try.

I walk through the market, which is barely illuminated by lanterns.

I cast my own orb of fire to light my path, announcing my presence since everyone will be familiar with my silver and sapphire flames. I can see the fear in people's eyes as I walk down the aisles, and I wonder what they must be thinking. Here I am, the Infinity Reaper, wielding fire in one hand and a scythe in the other while wearing a Halo Knight's jacket and carrying two blood-soaked bags. No one seems interested in finding out what's inside.

As I pass each vendor, they almost seem relieved that I haven't stopped at their booth. Except one. "Nice jacket," an older woman says. She's wearing a Halo Knight jacket too except hers is black leather with yellow feathered sleeves. "That bronze is to die for. I take it someone did from that glorious scythe?"

I appreciate her boldness. "Someone did. He certainly wasn't the last Halo Knight to try me if you're thinking about taking your shot next."

"No, no. I am not a Halo Knight. I got this in a trade with some Halo girl and a Spell Walker, but the jacket isn't as sought after as I had hoped—"

"Do you mean Tala and Maribelle?"

"I didn't get the girl's name, but she was with Maribelle Lucero. They were collecting soil from a high mountain. I assume it was for that Starstifler potion your brother spoke of online."

It's strange to think about this place having roots for the potion everyone wants me drinking. "It was."

"Good on you for not relinquishing your power. I won't be parting with my hydra powers either."

"Specter to specter, maybe you can help me out. I'm looking for the eyes of an obsidian phoenix and the eggshells from a crowned elder's hatching."

"Cooking up another potion?" she asks, but I remain silent. "So many secrets. I can help you out for a price."

"I've paid enough prices."

"Condolences," she says. This woman is up to date on Ma too. "But there are no handouts in the Shed. I'll trade you information for that jacket. A Bronze Wing commander's jacket will hold far more value than what's-her-face's. I'll even throw in this cloak, which will really complete your whole Death look."

The cloak is black with some rips in the sleeve. I can spray-paint an infinity symbol onto the back. "Deal," I say, trading Crest's jacket for the cloak I put on immediately. I somehow feel more powerful in this.

"Walk with me," the woman says. We go down a few booths, and there's a vendor with labeled jugs of phoenix parts such as gray sun toes, evergreen blazer feathers, and sun swallower air sacs.

"Hey, Gemma," the vendor says, eyeing me nervously before bowing his head. "Brighton."

I can get used to this.

"No need for pleasantries, Dell. The boy needs obsidian eyes."

"Two pairs," I say.

Dell opens a cabinet where there are many eyes floating around jars. He retrieves two pairs of pitch-black eyes with his bare hands and bottles them up for me. "That will cost . . ." Dell forces a smile. "This one is on the house."

I thank him and walk off.

"So much for no handouts in the Shed," Gemma says, sighing. "For the eggshells, you'll have to head into Manhattan—"

"Wait. You were trading the eyes and eggshells for the jacket."

"I was trading *information*," Gemma says. "There are no crowned elder shells down here, but you can find them on display at the Museum of Natural Creatures. I trust you don't need to wait until morning to buy a ticket and get inside."

I'd be surprised if the museum is even open after the brawl between the Spell Walkers and the Blood Casters and the Halo Knights the night we first retrieved Gravesend's egg.

"So that's the real thing on display and not a replica?" I ask.

"Mm-hmm."

Returning to the Museum of Natural Creatures to collect eggshells so I can resurrect my parents really shows how far I've come since not having any powers of my own.

It feels like destiny.

"Thank you for your help," I say, turning to leave.

"Brighton?"

"Yeah?"

Gemma grins. "How much for the scythe?"

"Over my dead body," I say with a smile.

SIXTY-SIX
ALL THE INFINITIES

UNKNOWN

I was ashes, then fire, then flesh, then bones, then blood, and I'm now alive.

The first breath hurts, just like last time.

What, wait, no, I have never been through this before.

Yes, I have.

No, I haven't.

Yes, I have, but never like this.

I am naked on a street, just like when I was born in fire.

No, my mother gave birth to me in a hospital.

No, no, I was born in fire, but it was in a park. I burned a bush. That's how someone found me.

What the hell, no, Dad found me on a street, a few blocks from where Bautista died, I mean where I died . . .

Who is Bautista?

The first breath hurt, but the next ones hurt even more as I hyperventilate.

Who am *I*?

I am Keon Máximo.

I am Bautista de León.

I am Emil Rey.

My mind is scrambled with memories of lives I lived and memories of lives I don't remember living. I am Keon Máximo, but I was also Bautista de León and Emil Rey? That's who I became? No, I am Bautista de León and I began having flashes of Keon Máximo's life when I was young, but I have never seen Emil Rey before. He's a stranger. There's no way I could have become him because I was killed by the infinity-ender dagger. Apparently not if I can think. I somehow got another shot at life. I want to scream to the stars that I am Emil Rey. I've known so much about Keon Máximo and Bautista de León because of history but the only actual memories I had were from retrocycling through their lives. In a split second, retrocycling feels like a foreign concept and then becomes instantly familiar.

More and more memories keep appearing, like stars are abandoning their original constellations to tell the story of three lives in one mega-constellation that will stretch across the entire night sky.

Different stars blink, different memories appear, melding us together: how I—how Keon—was given a homework assignment where he was asked which supernatural creature he would like to be, the first of many daydreams about flying like a phoenix; how I—how Bautista—got his ass kicked during his first fight as a kid and how he trained to become a better fighter before he had powers to rely on; how I—how Emil—couldn't stand the heat of my abuelita's kitchen whenever we baked flan and later found myself casting fire way hotter; how delighted Keon was the first time Astin walked into his life in a market, carrying books and a bouquet of flowers he had bought for himself because it was a gloomy day that needed some beauty; how hard Bautista would laugh whenever he'd pop out from a hiding place to scare Sera, making fun of her for being able to predict a death but not foresee this; how Emil couldn't believe that a shape-shifter like Ness didn't have to use his powers to be so beautiful, and how he could have spent his entire life looking at him; and how Emil believed he could spend every morning and every evening listening to Wyatt say absolutely anything in that glorious English accent.

But everything hasn't been flowers and laughs and beauty and music.

Everything hasn't been love.

There have been deaths, too many deaths for one life, let alone three.

For starters, Keon lost his best friend in a random act of violence. Then his father to a boating accident when a frenzied hydra attacked the ship. Then his mother to a sickness that accelerated too quickly. Then there were all the humans and phoenixes that died for Keon's specter trials, including his own gray sun, Bion, whose blood successfully fused with Keon's, but it pained Keon to hear Bion's screeches every time he cast fire. Nothing was more heartbreaking than discovering Astin, his sweet, amazing Astin Sunny, had been killed because of some gleamphobic bastard who took his hate for celestials out on Astin. Of all the deaths Keon was responsible for, he never regretted slowly torturing Astin's killer in a hidden cave before claiming his life and soul with the All-Killer, the first victim to be reaped by the scythe.

Bautista was no stranger to loss, even before founding the Spell Walkers. He didn't luck into loving parents who gave him a home like

Emil, and instead found himself bouncing between foster families. The hardest was when he was five years old and starting school and living with his favorite foster parents, who loved him so much that he felt like their own kid. Until six months later when he was returned to the shelter for reasons no one tried explaining to him apart from parenting was harder than they thought it would be. Everyone said he would understand when he was older, but understand what? Years later, when Bautista and Sera conceived the first of what they had hoped would be many children, he was already so defensive of his daughter. From the day Maribelle was born to the day that he died in the hopes his daughter would live, Bautista was the father he never got to have—and he never did learn what was so hard about parenting that his life wasn't worth sacrificing for his child's.

And most recently, there was Emil, whose father died from illness and mother was killed by his brother.

Brighton killed Emil—he killed me.

No, the Halo Knights killed me.

No, Luna killed me.

No, it was Brighton.

Wait, no, it wasn't Brighton, it was Darren. Darren killed me because his mother died protecting me. This kid used to be my superfan, and then he stabbed me in the heart with an infinity-ender.

I should be dead.

I should be dead forever.

Why didn't that kill me?

I look down at my body, which I know very well, but it looks like it did before I became the Infinity Son. I don't have the scars that Ness inflicted with the infinity-ender or a wound over my heart from where Darren killed me. But this is impossible. I run up to a store's window and find Emil Rey's reflection staring back at me.

This can't be real.

This has to be some afterlife because specters with phoenix blood don't ever resurrect as themselves, and definitely not in eighteen-year-old bodies. I was a newborn as Bautista and a newborn as Emil. Then Keon's years of research begin flowing through me, all arriving at the same point that I've always known—when gray sun phoenixes are reborn, they are stronger than their previous lives. I was always stronger, wielding both Keon's golden flames and Bautista's gray flames, but I'm already sensing they knew things about our powers—about my powers—that I never did. Things I can use now.

This is all real.

I used to be Keon Máximo.

I used to be Bautista de León.

I am Emil Rey with their memories woven into mine, but this is my life.

This is my life again.

SIXTY-SEVEN
FALLEN HALO

EMIL

I can't believe I was dead, that I was killed, but nothing is more shocking than being alive again.

Everything happened so quickly, and if there's an afterlife, I don't remember a damn thing about it.

One thing I do know: I'm very naked.

I spent so much of my life struggling with my body, even hiding from mirrors after showers or when changing from one outfit to the next. I finally started finding beauty in my body for no other reason that it was mine, that it was strong, that it survived horrible things that I will forever remember even if the physical scars are gone, and now it was miraculously reborn out of fire, but that doesn't mean I want to show it off to the entire world. No one is out right now, but there is a residential building up ahead and anyone can turn the corner any second. I've managed to avoid detainment from enforcers as the Infinity Son, but getting locked up by the cops for indecent exposure would really suck.

I don't recognize these cross streets, but I'm getting a Bronx vibe.

That doesn't help me figure out where I'm supposed to find clothes in the middle of the night. I start freaking out and begin remembering when I—I mean Bautista—needed to scavenge for clothes during the times he was living on the streets; it's going to take a second getting used to Keon's and Bautista's memories fighting to the surface as if I lived through those events myself. I recall Bautista stealing clothes from laundry lines in backyards, public pools when people were off swimming, hospitals, offices, and coat hangers in restaurants.

I'm running through the streets in search of a hospital, which isn't ideal because I don't want to be recognized, but it'll be open. Then I spot a lit-up laundromat a couple blocks away, and I'm so lucky to live in the city that never sleeps. There's only one guy in there, listening to music as he sketches with his back to the door, and I feel guilty jacking him for his white T-shirt and black jeans, but I use Bautista's later-in-life justifications that these small thefts are in service of saving everyone's lives.

I get dressed and the shirt is really baggy, which I always loved because it hid my body, but I tuck it into my jeans, embracing myself.

I'm still barefoot as I walk through the streets before remembering I don't have to walk at all.

Gray and gold wings of fire burst to life, glowing brighter and expanding bigger than ever before. I fly into the air and overshoot my ascent because I'm so used to my power weighing me down. For the first time ever, I feel like I'm coasting through the air, like I have never been this free in any of my lives. I feel so in tune with my abilities that I begin recalling Keon's memories of Bion, whose blood has surged through all of our powers: how Keon stumbled upon Bion in a forest, as small as a chick, and as alone as he was; catching Bion whenever he fell during his first attempts to fly; and how proud he was to watch Bion soar through the air, and how touched he was that Bion actually came home when he had a whole world to explore.

I have a whole world to explore too.

But first, I have to return to my life.

I hover in the air, trying to figure out my next move.

I have no idea how long I've been dead, or any way to connect with anyone I know. I don't have a phone, but that doesn't mean I don't have another way to communicate. I was able to sense Gravesend's feelings even though she wasn't a gray sun phoenix. Keon and Bautista each had their own experiences where they felt ties to other phoenixes, but Keon was the only one who tried exercising that ability. He had some success, but not a lot. I'm also two lives stronger than he was; three technically now that I've died. The only other phoenixes I know are Nox and Roxana. My best bet is sensing Nox since we've had such a connection. I close my eyes, trying to shut out the world around me. I only feel blowing winds. I've got to be an idiot to think I can connect with Nox as if he's within reach as Gravesend was when I felt her emotions, but I concentrate even harder. I picture Nox's thick black feathers rustling while in flight, his eyeline as he flew around the Sanctuary the first time I rode him, how his wings splashed water on me and Wyatt the night of my first kiss, and how Nox took years to trust Wyatt and only Wyatt after he experienced abuse from his former companion, and how when Nox was reborn, he flew onto his shoulder and—

I sense Nox's fear, and it chills me to the bone. I can't get a clear read on what he's feeling. Is he panicking about a loss on the horizon or scared of how to move on after a death?

Is Wyatt dying, or is he dead?

I fly without another thought, so fast that I must look like a comet streaking across the sky.

Keon hoped to one day understand a phoenix's feelings so clearly that it would be just like speaking their language. That would be really helpful because I have no idea where I'm going, only that I'm following Nox's emotions like a trail. As I get out of the city and begin making my way upstate, I begin realizing that Wyatt must have returned to the Sanctuary. But why? Is he living there now? Rebuilding? Dealing with the dead? I don't know, but the only question I really care about is if Wyatt is okay.

I fly over the Sanctuary and brake in the air, wondering if anyone is alive. There are so many corpses scattered around the courtyard with fires still burning. This was recent, a different battle than the one where we all fought against enforcers. There are more dead Halo Knights this time and only one living phoenix . . . Nox. I descend, tears in my eyes as I hope that Wyatt is only in critical condition. Nox screeches when he sees me, nudging his head against my body so forcefully that I stumble back, rocks pinching into my feet. Then Nox sinks to the ground, his beak gently nudging Wyatt.

"Wy? Wyatt?"

I sink to my knees and reach to feel his heartbeat.

"I'm dead," Wyatt whispers. His beautiful blue eyes blink rapidly, like he's seeing stars.

"No, you're not," I say, crying in relief.

"I must be dead because you are too, love."

"Nope, I'm alive too."

Wyatt focuses his gaze on me, like he doesn't believe his eyes. "I saw your body vanish in fire and ashes."

"I resurrected."

His fingers brush my face. "As yourself . . ."

"And then some," I say, and it just confuses him even more. "Don't worry. I'm so glad you're okay, I sensed Nox's distress and—"

Wyatt groans as he sits up, pulling me into a deep kiss. I feel so at ease with his lips against mine. He sinks back to the ground with a smile on his face. "That hurt, but it was worth it. I missed you so much, sweet Emil."

"How long was I dead?"

"Almost a day, but it felt like much longer."

When I was originally reborn after Bautista, that was days after he died. The window of resurrection is shrinking with every death. I really am stronger.

"What the hell happened here?"

"Your deranged brother was born eighteen years ago and then reborn more pissed than ever."

"Reborn?"

"Yes, Ness gave him a rather good stabbing with an infinity-ender, but the death did not stick, unfortunately."

"Ness killed Brighton," I say aloud. It's a statement and a question. I don't like the weight of those words on my tongue. Things got bad after I died. "Was it self-defense?"

"It was revenge. We believed Brighton had killed you. I only just found out it was the illusionist. I must confess, I did try killing Brighton too with his ancient death-stick, but that was only after he invaded our grounds and annihilated a cycle of phoenixes and a squadron of Halo Knights in pursuit of his resurrection ritual."

"And he let you live?" I ask.

"He assumed I died after I fell off Nox mid-flight. Then Nox . . ." Wyatt pets the phoenix. ". . . lured Brighton away before he could realize I was still alive. My brilliant boy."

As I look around the Sanctuary, I experience the variety of feelings Keon experienced throughout his life after creating the specters: awe in the alchemy itself; sorrow for Bion; happiness as he discovered more and more about his powers; shame when early day specters used their powers for crimes; guilt when a specter killed for the first time; anger at Luna for creating the Blood Casters; and pride for creating a weapon that can kill absolutely anyone to ensure that no one can become immortal while working off his original formula. Keon would've hated the sight of this courtyard as I do, but he didn't count on the immortal specter also wielding the scythe that was designed to kill the likes of him.

"I'm sorry," I say.

"Brighton isn't your fault."

"I haven't stopped him either and he could have killed you too and—" I stop because there's a question I'm terrified to ask. "If Brighton is on a killing spree, does that mean he got anyone else?"

Wyatt picks up on what I'm asking immediately. "Ness is fine, last I saw him." Then he adds, "Prudencia too."

It's almost like Wyatt thinks I only care about Ness. That's not true; I shot across the skies to come be here with him. I just don't think Brighton could ever bring himself to kill Prudencia, just like I don't think he would ever kill me, no matter how big a game he talks. But I know he'd kill Ness in a second, so I'm just really happy Ness is still alive.

"Where did you see him? Them, I mean?"

"An abandoned school . . . the one where you met Ness."

I can't believe they all went back to Nova. "Why there? That's so risky."

"It was Ness's call. He thought it would be safe, but if you want my two cents, it seemed he was wanting to feel closer to you. . . . I felt the same way returning here."

There's so much that I have to get into with Wyatt and Ness, but just like before, this is not the place or time. "Why did you split up?"

"We wanted to keep the fight going in your honor. Prudencia is helping the Spell Walkers rescue Sunstar, Ness is infiltrating his father's circles, and I was convincing the Halo Knights to help us against Brighton. Let us hope the others are having better luck than I did."

The dead deserve to be buried, but Brighton is the Big Bad I got to handle. "Do we need to get you to a hospital?"

"I'm very sore, but it's not my first time falling off of Nox."

"Hopefully your last."

"Statistically unlikely given how often we fly together, but a lovely thought nonetheless."

"You good to come with me?"

"If we're going to fight your brother, I will be needing a weapon, preferably a scythe that can, oh, let's say kill any living soul, or at the very least, pepper-spray to buy me time to fly away."

"I sort of have a different weapon in mind."

"And what's that?"

"The boy who killed me."

SIXTY-EIGHT

THE MUSEUM

BRIGHTON

I hated coming to the Museum of Natural Creatures on our thirteenth birthday.

Growing up as twins—I mean being raised as twins—Emil and I got used to splitting up our actual birthday with activities that we had to do together. That day I really wanted to go play laser-wand tag at this new court that opened up, but first Ma brought us to the phoenix exhibit at the museum because of Emil's obsession. I was bored out of my mind, especially because Emil took forever reading each and every display sign around the Sunroom. Looking back, it's hard for me to get mad because he at least stayed interested in phoenixes enough to get a job here, even if it was just at the gift shop.

I should have visited him at work more.

I phase through a wall of the museum and find myself in the Hydra House exhibit. I turn to find that I've just walked through a massive oil painting of a seven-headed hydra chomping at phoenixes in the sky. I'm sure Emil hated this, but he doesn't understand creature nature any more than he understands true human nature.

Instead of taking the stairs, I fly up different levels until I find myself outside the Sunroom's entrance. Above the locked door is a stained-glass window of an egg and phoenix connected by a ring of orange flames. I phase inside the exhibit and search through their displays. If I ever needed to get in good with Gemma, I could steal these old-school Halo Knight masks that are made of clay with dangerous sharp beaks that must have doubled as weapons too. I walk past the candlesticks, flutes, and fans made from blue, green, and black feathers, but I do stop to admire the iron crossbows with the limbs shaped like wings and an assembly of infinity-enders with charred black hilts and yellow serrated blades. If I didn't have the All-Killer or Reaper's Blood, I would add these weapons to my collection.

I find a glass case with eggs and eggshells, all of them different colors and sizes. Some are smooth, and others look solid as rocks. My heart races as I read through the different note cards to identify the one I need, knowing I'm one step closer to completing everything I need for this ritual. For the crowned elder, the museum reconstructed its actual egg that is gray like a storm cloud with patches of white fuzz. I reach through the display and pull out the egg, hugging it to my chest before cracking it apart; I don't have space in my bag for an egg the size of a basketball, and it's only useful to me fractured anyway. I drop the shells into my satchel with the feathers, eyes, hearts, and bones.

I turn to leave, when I notice the blinking camera.

Even if someone was watching, there is nothing they—or anyone—can do to stop me.

I smile at the camera before I phase out of the museum and fly toward the cemetery where I will resurrect my parents.

SIXTY-NINE

THE OTHER SIDE OF INFINITY

EMIL

Wyatt and I are flying together on Nox, but this time, he's holding on to me as I lead the way.

Feeling this close to Wyatt, especially while riding a phoenix under the stars, reminds me so much of the night of our first kiss, and how great it was cuddling together in the Sanctuary's library. It brings up memories of lives I once lived. Bautista was a fighter, but he was also fighting for his love, something that must be genetic because that's alive and well in Maribelle too. The years before he died were mostly spent living the life of a Spell Walker, but he always made space for Sera because their future together was his north star. Keon struggled with physical affection, but he thrived on romantic adoration, always spoiling Astin with little gifts that he'd stumble upon while out on an errand that proved he was listening to every word Astin said, even if Keon's mind was always in the clouds, even just a bit.

I'm learning so much about myself while recalling Bautista's and Keon's lives.

"You're a natural," Wyatt says into my ear as I steer Nox. "I still think there's a Halo Knight in you. I suspect there are many openings after your brother's killing spree."

"Yeah, that's why I should stay far away from them, so I don't attract more trouble. Besides, I'm not becoming a Halo Knight without you there too."

"You can't bear the idea of living without me?" he asks, squeezing his arms around me tighter. I don't respond, so he adds, "That silence can't be good."

"I'm just focused on our mission," I say as we swiftly journey through Manhattan with Brighton's influencer house in Staten Island as our destination. Of course the address was easy to find online because enough of the influencers had boasted about it.

"There is nothing to be done until we find Darren—if we even do. I didn't want to be rude before because I will follow you wherever you go, but it would be downright daft for Darren to hide in the home of the man who wants to kill him."

"Yeah, and anyone could've said it was stupid for Ness to willingly walk back into the school where he was kidnapped, but sometimes those places are really the last place anyone would look for you. It's also our only real lead," I say. I have no idea at what point Darren left his haven to join Brighton, but I'm betting it would've been at that fancy house. "Darren could be our key to victory—"

"Yes, you said all that back at the Sanctuary, but if we win this fight, you will have to figure out who you are and what you will make with your second chance at life. Fourth chance at life? How are you counting your lifetimes? Nonetheless!" Wyatt rests his chin on my shoulder, his hair brushing against my bare neck. "Who will you be on the other side of infinity, Emil?"

There was something so exciting and promising the first time Wyatt brought up this idea of who I will be on the other side of infinity. It was on the night we kissed, but before we had, when we were just friends. He believed in me and swore that I would make a great Halo Knight after hanging up my cape as a Spell Walker. Then he brought it up again after we saved Ness from the Bounds. Now? It's too big to answer. I stay quiet because I can't get into this right now.

"I fear that we are flying toward our death, so you must know something," Wyatt says.

"We're not going to die."

"Maybe you're not, and if you do, you will just have another cute resurrection."

"It wasn't cute. I was freaking out and naked in the streets—"

"Naked! How did you leave that out before?"

"Did you think I was reborn with jeans?"

"I hadn't given it much thought. I was just happy to see you, jeans and all."

"What do you want me to know?"

"I've just gone and said it after you dragged it out of me. How I was so happy to see you, love." Wyatt gently kisses my neck, and I close my eyes, enjoying his touch. "I haven't known a happiness like that since Nox resurrected and chose me as his companion. . . . I suppose I'm wondering if coming back from the dead has made you want to choose me too."

I'm not only being asked who I will be once I'm done being the Infinity Son, but who I will be with: Wyatt or Ness?

My heart is racing. "Wy, can we talk this out another time?"

"I'd like to know now, even if it's you telling me I'm not the one for you. I could never hate you for your choice, but it would be a great deal of mercy if you tell me not to hold my breath anymore since Ness is back in the picture. But if you do choose me, then I will continue following you across the world, even if that means family holidays with your mad brother where I'm fighting him and his scythe off with cutlery. I will risk my life for you, sweet Emil, knowing that if I died, it was for someone who loved me too."

"Too?" I ask, spinning around on Nox to look Wyatt in his blue eyes.

"Too," Wyatt repeats, grabbing my hands. "Your death cast a storm that I thought I would have to weather forever, but of course your rebirth parts the clouds, of course you are the sun in the sky, and of course I love you."

This is the first time a guy has told me he loves me.

A memory surfaces of Keon and Astin. Keon was pacing their bedroom, cursing a vendor for not having the proper ingredients that he needed to brew an elixir for Astin that would relieve him of a fever that had begun overnight.

Between coughs, Astin was laughing at Keon's rant and said, "I love you for so much, but I love you most for always trying."

Then Keon stopped pacing and asked, "You love me?"

Astin said, "Yes."

And Keon leapt into the bed like a phoenix in flight to kiss Astin, the man he loved.

Another memory, this time as Bautista stumbled out of a burning building, falling to his knees as he choked on the dark smoke obscuring the doorway. There was blood dripping from the corner of his left eye, like he was crying blood. He turned and tried to say something, but he kept choking until he finally shouted, "Sera!" He looked up to the windows, which were glowing from flames, right as an explosion obliterated them. There was shock and heartbreak in his eyes, but he shook it off as he ran for the door, right as Sera exited with a young woman limping beside her. Bautista couldn't get his eyes off of Sera as he helped get the innocent to safety down the block. Then he swept Sera up and hugged her like it was going to be his last chance to do so.

"I thought you were dead," Bautista said.

"I would've had a vision," Sera said. "But I had to save that woman—"

"I'm in love with you," Bautista interrupted, wiping ash off Sera's cheek. "I'm sorry to spit it out like this. I can't see the future, but I did just imagine my life without you and I hate it so much. I just need you to know that I love you."

Sera smiled with tears in her eyes. "I didn't see that coming."

"You never see anything good . . . and this is good, right? It's okay?"

"This is really good. I love you too, my sunray."

I feel all the love that Keon and Bautista have given their partners. How Keon cared for Astin and how Bautista couldn't risk bottling up his feelings for Sera any longer.

I think about everything I want.

I stare into Wyatt's beautiful blue eyes and smile. "I've been learning a lot about my heart since retrocycling, and even more since resurrecting. I've gotten to feel Keon's love for Astin and Bautista's for Sera, and I needed my past lives to shine this light for me since they also know what it's like to fall for someone while also fighting for your life. And now that I've legit died, I can't ignore my heart anymore. Even if it gets me killed."

"And what does your heart say, sweet Emil?"

"That I love you, Wyatt. But not the way you'd like."

Wyatt lets go of my hands. "Hmm. Somehow this doesn't feel as merciful as I waxed on about. It feels a lot more like falling off of Nox again." He peers down at the city below. "Though more like if I'd fallen from these heights."

"Are you going to push me off?"

"No, but I might start charging you for these rides." He begins looking everywhere else but at me. The stars, the moon, Nox's feathers. "I lost you and found you and am losing you again."

"You're not losing me. You're never losing me."

"I'm losing the life that was exciting me most."

"But we'll be reborn, right?"

Wyatt's gaze finds mine again. "I trust that we will. There is beauty in reincarnation, but it may take some time. You will not be easy to get over, Skybreaker. Or should I say Heartbreaker?"

Now I'm the one who looks away, staring down at my hands. "I'm sorry. I would've been so lucky to date you and—"

"It's not too late to change your mind. I will happily pardon this faux pas." His fingertip lifts my chin so that I can see his smile. "I'm kidding. Besides, as grueling as it will be to not share a bed and skies and more with you, this does mean I won't have to put up with Brighton at the family functions. Good luck with adding a shape-shifting evil politician to that mix." Then it's quiet, like Wyatt's brave face has been unmasked and there's nothing but a heartbroken boy underneath. "I am too bruised to give Ness all of his flowers tonight, but I will say that he has great character. I, however, I am the prettier one, and don't you forget it— Oh, oh, oh! Damn it, he can turn into me! Wow, you have really gotten yourself the complete package, yeah?"

"Breathe," I say. I laugh as Wyatt takes some exaggerated breaths. "Look, I don't know what the deal is with Ness, but I don't want him shifting into you. There's only one you."

"That's very, very sweet, sweet Emil, but how do you mean you don't know the deal between you and Ness?"

"There's just stuff we got to figure out. Like if we're even meant to be a thing."

"Perhaps you and I should have had our talk after your talk with Ness, then."

"We still would've ended up here, Wyatt."

"Rude!"

"You're too good to be anyone's runner-up. You need to be with someone who is choosing you out of everyone else in the world."

"Well, it appears I'm in the market for such a person. If you happen to know anyone with stunning hazel eyes, silky curls, the biggest heart, let me know. Preferably someone who won't crush my dreams when they return from the dead, but I'm not picky."

I reach for his hands, and I'm so relieved when he doesn't pull away. I hold on to him. "For real, Wyatt, I do love you. You have been such an amazing friend who has seen me through some serious highs and lows. No matter who I'm with, I'm only able to be who I am in that space because of who you were for me during this whole Infinity Son era. If all goes well I won't be able to retrocycle anymore, so I won't be able to relive that magical night where you kissed me under the stars, but I'll never forget it. That's one of my all-time favorite memories."

"Mine too, sweet Emil. Perhaps we can re-create that kiss one last time—"

My heart races as I pull Wyatt in, pressing his lips against mine.

In another life, Wyatt and I could have been happy, but he's not who I see myself being with on the other side of infinity. My heart wants Ness the same way Keon's wanted Astin and Bautista's wanted Sera. I've got to see that through in this life, especially since I've got a second chance at it. Until then, I'm present with Wyatt, the boy who brought me into the world of Halo Knights, who has held me as I've grieved, and who encouraged me to find love in times of war.

We pull back, tears in our eyes and smiles on our faces.

Our first and last kiss will live in the sky.

SEVENTY
DISILLUSIONED

EMIL

Nox lands in the shadow of the woods with the influencer house up ahead.

"So we're good, yeah?" Wyatt asks as we make our way to the house. "Should the Insanity Reaper attempt to slay me again, you won't leave me for dead since I'm not your lover?"

"Infinity," I correct.

"I said what I said."

If Brighton is here, then I'm ready to fight, but I'm betting that he's going to be out hunting for the other ingredients he still needs for his ritual; it hurts my heart thinking about how Brighton targeted Nox to rip out his eyes. I would've never been able to look at Wyatt again until Nox was reborn in his next life with new eyes, and even then. And I won't be able to live in peace if my brother kills my newest best friend.

"I'm not letting Brighton hurt you or Nox ever again."

Wyatt clicks his tongue. "That's not a promise I will hold you to given how extreme your brother can be. I should say, sweet Emil, that should some terrible fate befall me—whether by the Insanity Reaper's hand or another's—I ask that you don't resurrect me. I understand that it will be depressing for all of you to not have this body to gaze upon, but it's my deepest wish for my soul to move on to its next life."

I stop by a cluster of bushes, right before we're about to cross the front yard to the house. "I respect that, Wy."

"Even after your own miracle?"

"My life isn't any more valuable than anyone else's, and I'm going to make sure this never happens again. My soul will continue on naturally after my life."

"Perhaps our souls will find each other in the next life, in the way I had hoped they would in this one."

"Maybe," I say with a smile.

We sneak up to the front door of this house that is so fancy compared to where we grew up. I melt the handle and push the door open. I cast a fire-orb, holding it steady in case Brighton or any other enemies pop up and surprise us. I've glimpsed the house from YouTube videos, but this place is definitely more gorgeous in person. Brighton must've had a blast living here with all of his new friends.

"I suppose your brother is off torturing some phoenixes," Wyatt whispers. He peeks out the sliding glass doors, where there's a pool and firepit. "He probably would have ripped out my heart by now otherwise."

"Let's check upstairs," I whisper.

If we can find anything of Darren's, then we can track him down. Just because he can cast illusions doesn't mean that Nox won't be able to pick up on his scent.

My heart is racing with every step and with every bedroom door

I push open. Then I walk into a bedroom with Brighton's clothes in the corner; I immediately recognize his outfit from the night he outed me on social media. It's weird being in a bedroom that is only his. He wanted his own spot in college so bad, but he seemed fine sharing a dorm with someone else; it really felt like he didn't want it to be me anymore. It's like I was always in his face all the time, and unless I was helping him film some content, he wasn't about it. Maybe we would've been closer if we actually had the chance to have some space growing up.

"Hello?"

I hear a woman's voice.

An impossible voice.

Someone who can't speak—who shouldn't be able to speak because they're dead.

"Ma?"

I can't believe she's alive. "He did it. . . . Brighton did the ritual. . . ."

"Oh my . . ." Wyatt says from the doorway.

I rush out into the hallway with Wyatt stepping back, not getting in my way. I follow Ma's voice as she calls again, this time for Brighton, but when I find her in a bedroom, standing by an open window, her eyes widen when she sees me.

"Emil," Ma breathes.

"Ma?"

"It's me, my boy."

My heart sinks. "Where's Brighton?"

"He went to find food."

"Where's Dad?"

"He went with him. He's alive too."

"Wow, it's like Brighton always says: 'The impossible always finds a way.' Right?"

"Exactly."

Ma opens her arms for a hug, but I hurl a fire-orb at her, thinking that this is how Brighton must've felt as his fire-bolt blasted Ma except mine goes through her because she's not real. The fire-orb sails out the window and into the darkness.

"How did you know?" Not-Ma asks.

"For starters, she calls—called me her son or her Emilio. Never her boy." I would love to hear Ma—the real Ma—lovingly call me her Emilio right now as she pulls me into a hug. "And then Brighton always says that something being unlikely doesn't mean it's impossible." My heart breaks that this isn't real, but this impostor illusion needs to go away. "You can drop the act, Darren."

Not-Ma's hands lock behind her back as she paces the room. "What's wrong with appearing as your mother? Don't you miss her?"

"I miss my real mom. Not this twisted version of her."

"At least your mom's neck wasn't twisted," Not-Ma says.

I flinch at the memory of Dr. Bowes having her neck snapped. "I know it solves nothing, but I will regret that death for the rest of my life."

Not-Ma's eyes darken. "You shouldn't be alive to regret anything. I killed you."

It's so strange hearing those words in Ma's voice when I was given a good life because of her and Dad; Darren must only know Ma's voice from the interview where Ness posed as her. "I resurrected because of my phoenix gleam. I should be dead, but I'm going to make the most out of this new life. I promise." I turn, remembering Wyatt and his hopes for my second shot at life, but he's not there. Darren must have him hidden from me. "Can we talk face-to-face, Darren?"

"Why? So you can kill me back?"

"People like your mother have died because of me, but I would never kill anyone directly."

"Your brother would. . . . Your brother tried killing me."

"I'm not Brighton, and you're not Brighton either. You're Darren Bowes, the son of Billie Bowes. Your mother was a hero, but she shouldn't have sacrificed herself for me. I wish I had died instead of her."

"You're saying what Brighton said."

"Except I mean it. I love my brother, but he would not have traded your mother's life for his own. Brighton is too scared to die to be that noble. That's why he fought to become the Infinity Reaper, that's why he fought to get the one weapon in the world that can kill him, and that's why he's fighting for the resurrection ritual, so he doesn't have to live without those who've died before. Brighton is on a rampage and has to be stopped before more people die because he's acting like a god."

The illusion of Not-Ma vanishes.

"You're going to kill Brighton?"

I turn to find Darren standing in the corner. He could have killed me again if he wanted to, but this means I'm getting through to him. "I'm not going to kill him."

"But you said he has to be stopped!"

"I have a plan, but I'll need some help."

"You want me to help you? But I killed you. You should be sending me to the Bounds."

"No one is going to charge you for murder when I'm still alive."

"Fine, attempted murder."

"I won't tell if you won't." I sit at the edge of the bed, wanting to look as relaxed as possible so I don't scare Darren, who is already backed into a corner. "I don't deserve your help in fighting Brighton, and if you say no, I'll go away forever. I just want you to be able to live openly and without fear. If I can win you back your freedom by stopping Brighton, then that's how I honor Dr. Bowes's sacrifice."

Darren stares. "Brighton wanted me to be a hero too."

"I don't want you to be a hero. I want you to be a kid again."

I'm working to get my life back too, but I can only make peace with that if Darren is able to live out his first.

Darren vanishes, and I realize that was just an illusion. I'm nervous that I've said something wrong and it's all about to be over, when Darren appears directly across from me with his hand extended. "You trust me?"

I rise and shake his hand—it's solid, sweaty, real. "I trust you."

"So you really are a hero and Brighton is the villain?"

"Honestly, with your help, it won't matter who's who. No one else will get hurt because of the Infinity Kings ever again."

It's time to take the crowns off our heads.

SEVENTY-ONE
THE PHOENIX PITS

BRIGHTON

Just because something is unlikely doesn't mean it's impossible, and that includes resurrecting my parents from their ashes.

I land in the cemetery, directly between Dad's and Ma's graves.

"I'm bringing you home," I say.

There's a smile on my face until I remember I will have to deliver the news that Emil is dead, and unlike them, I won't be able to resurrect him. But we will be there for each other as we mourn him.

It's still dark out, but the stars will be leaving the sky soon, so I have to move fast. First I set down the gallons of water I stole from a bodega that I'll need to boil inside the Phoenix Pits. Then I unpack the eyes, feathers, eggshells, bones, hearts, and the two dead phoenixes. I lay them out at the foot of the graves as if we're about to have a very disturbing picnic. I review the ritual's instructions on my phone. Maribelle wrote something about the phoenixes needing their own graves first so their essences can consecrate the grounds. I'm not fully certain what that means or for how long the phoenixes need to be buried, but

I begin digging up the Pits anyway because that's the next step.

"Brighton."

At first I think it's a ghost, but people can't understand ghosts and ghosts will usually go on to haunt the ones who killed them and I didn't kill Emil.

I look up, and there he is.

My brother . . . except it can't be.

This is the son of a bitch who killed me.

"You're stupid if you think I'm falling for this trick again, Ness."

My war with Emil started when Ness impersonated my brother and tried to force-feed me the Starstifler. It didn't have to be this way, but I blame Ness. I pick up my All-Killer so I can vanquish his soul.

"It's actually me, Bright."

Emil's gold and gray flames burst to life, and he hovers in the air.

Ness can look like anyone he wants, but he can't impersonate their powers.

This is actually Emil?

"I'm alive again."

There is a happiness burning inside me until it's washed away by some jealousy. So we're both unkillable? I'm supposed to be the only one. I'm supposed to be special. Can anyone with phoenix blood be reborn as themselves? Does this mean other specters will also be able to challenge me? Should I be working to eliminate all specters so I'm the one and only? No, Emil can live. We can be the only immortal specters, but I'm still going to have to be the reaper that ends the others.

"I'm sorry about Darren. We were only going to disempower you, but he went too far."

"You're the one who's gone too far. You recruited a kid into a war. You've killed so many Halo Knights and phoenixes."

"To resurrect our parents!"

"Their lives aren't worth all those deaths!"

My fingers tighten around the scythe, but I take a deep breath. "You're either delusional or a hypocrite if you think you can come back from the dead and then lecture me about resurrection."

"I didn't choose to be reborn."

"You also don't get to choose what happens with Ma and Dad."

"And you do?"

"Yes, because I am their real son! Ma gave birth to me; I get more of a say than you do!"

Emil shakes his head. "I know you're hurting, Brighton, but you're going to be in for a hard lesson when you resurrect Ma and Dad and realize how heartbroken they are because they don't recognize their own son."

Of course Dad and Ma are going to recognize me. Emil doesn't know what he's talking about. I'm not pretending as if my parents will enjoy hearing about the lives I've taken so they can have theirs back, but they will one day be proud of me. They will be grateful to not only be alive again, but to be alive again together.

I can't wait to see my parents reunited.

My brother may not get that luxury.

There's a violent fire raging within me, and I need to free myself of it. "Don't make me hurt you," I warn Emil.

"You can't hurt me. Gray sun phoenixes are stronger after every death, and I now have enough power to beat you."

I have the blood of a century phoenix coursing through me. Those phoenixes are the ultimate survivors. I can't be beat. "I have died once before, but I will never die forever."

"I'm not trying to kill you, but I will stop you," Emil says.

"I won't kill you either, but I will beat you to the brink of death for getting in my way. Then, when you come to, our parents will be alive again and you can realize I was the hero all along."

Time to prove Emil wrong. I hurl a fire-bolt, but he glides out of the way. I dash and fire again, but Emil dodges that too. I jump into the air and chase Emil around the cemetery, firing and firing as we fly in dizzying circles. Only a coward claims they can beat someone in a fight and then runs away the entire time. I hover, studying Emil's fleeing pattern; I remember during his training sessions with Wesley that he was being taught to anticipate where someone would be going, not where they are. I charge a fire-bolt and thrust it through the air, timing it perfectly with where Emil is—but the fire-bolt sails right through him. No, Emil can't phase. That's not an ability gray suns or any phoenixes have. You're either a celestial born with that power or you're a specter with ghost blood. Did Emil inherit some ghost powers because he was dead?

Or is Emil not actually alive?

Not actually real.

I descend to the cemetery grounds, furious that I was tricked. That I was led to believe my brother was alive. It wasn't enough for Darren to kill Emil, but he's now playing puppet master with illusions of Emil. I close my eyes because his power only has so much range. I think back to when Maribelle's phoenix powers surfaced and how her anger and grief sparked a spectacular explosion that blasted everyone around her. I concentrate and cast a ring of silver and sapphire fire, exploding rows of headstones—and a boy screams in pain.

The Emil in the sky vanishes.

Darren is groaning, buried under remnants of a headstone.

I dash and grab Darren's throat before he can conceal himself. His eyes begin glowing, and he casts multiple illusions in a panic: a hydra with five heads stampeding toward me, but the ground isn't shaking; a phoenix dives out of the sky, breathing fire with no real heat; a basilisk coiling around me, but not squeezing; and Ma and Dr. Bowes begging me to let Darren go with each other's voices. None of these illusions will fool me again, not even the new one of Emil casting fire at me as I'm about to rip out Darren's heart. There's warmth and screeching and the fire collides into my chest. I fly backward and crash through a headstone. My back hurts from the impact, and my next breath stings. Darren is a quick study, but he's nowhere near being in the league of illusionists who can make someone believe they're in pain when they're actually fine. That can only mean that everything is real.

I'm in real pain after real fire sent me crashing through a real headstone.

Which means Emil is real too.

SEVENTY-TWO
THE REAL SON

EMIL

I've been here the entire time.

Before leaving the house in Staten Island, I had to convince Mr. Bowes to let Darren come along. It took a few minutes, but Mr. Bowes realized that they will never be able to live in peace as long as Brighton has the powers to stalk them with his camouflaging or invade their personal spaces with his phasing or ultimately kill them with his powers. Darren was eager to step up so he can go back to his real life, so he hopped on Nox with Wyatt and we raced to the cemetery. Then I sent Wyatt on his way to find Prudencia and let her know I'm alive, but really I was just trying to protect him too. He made it clear that he was willing to die for me if he had my love, but I can't give him that. As Wyatt and Nox took off into the night, blending in with the darkness, Darren concealed us as if we're invisible, right as Brighton's silver and sapphire wings could be found burning through the sky.

Now Brighton is getting up, wiping headstone dust off his cloak that makes him look like Death.

We stare each other down like a game of chess that's hitting stalemate.

Both kings live, but one must win.

"Our fight ends here, Brighton!" I shout across the cemetery. I've wanted to yell ever since whispering responses to Darren for his illusion of me. My heart hurt so much seeing Brighton in pain, still trying to justify his actions, and how quickly his happiness for my resurrection faded.

"It will end—starting with his death!" Brighton points at Darren.

I shield Darren with my body. "You brought him into this. Now leave him out of it."

"You're protecting your killer over your own brother?"

"He's innocent. You're not."

Brighton spins his scythe like a sword. "I will kill him, Emil."

Another Bowes will not be murdered on my watch. My fists glow gold and gray. "Darren, hide."

Darren creates the illusion that he's invisible, and I hear him walk away.

Brighton paces toward me. "What's the point of siding with your killer? Was your claim that you're strong enough to beat me another lie?"

"Nope, I'm stronger. Darren's here to make sure you don't create the Phoenix Pits."

"How's he going to stop me?"

"You can't bring Ma and Dad back to life if you can't find their graves."

"What are you—" Brighton looks around and sees what I see.

We're in a cemetery with no graves.

Darren has hidden everything—the plots, the phoenix corpses, everything Brighton needs for the ritual. He's overextending himself to cast an illusion this big, but he's buying me time to wear Brighton down for my ultimate plan.

"This is not making me want to kill him any less."

"You got to get through me first."

One way or another, this is my final battle with my brother.

Brighton draws fire, but my reflexes are fast, and our attacks collide in the middle, exploding. I fly toward him, swerving around his fire-bolts, and as I swing at him with a flaming fist, he phases underground. I don't know what he's seeing since Darren's illusions are for the surface, but I can't find him. I fly up into the air so Brighton can't sneak up on me, right as he resurfaces with his own flaming fist. He's confused when he doesn't see me, and I rain down dozens of fire-darts that blast him in succession. Brighton loses his grip on the scythe. I dive down like a raging comet, desperate to get my hands on the weapon. Right as I'm about to grab it, Brighton grins; I've flown right into his trap. He grabs my wrist and unleashes a fury of swift-punches on my face and stomach, dizzying me and knocking out my breath. I try flying backward, but Brighton swings me around and throws me. Even though the cemetery looks like an empty field, the physical objects around us still exist, and I crash into a headstone; not hard enough to break it, but hard enough that it hurts like hell.

Streams of silver and sapphire flames flow out of Brighton's hands, and I match him with my gray and gold fire. He's applying more and more pressure, his fire eating mine, but I focus, reminding myself that I'm stronger in power and mind and heart, and I turn the tide against him. The fire is about to reach him, when he releases his hold, letting everything phase through him as he stares in anger.

Memories flash, one into the other, like a nesting doll. The first is of Bautista casting an attack of gray fire shaped like a phoenix that flies, but it dissipates before reaching the target board, which unlocks the next memory of Keon doing the same thing except his golden-flamed phoenix dies even sooner. I begin remembering Keon's research into channeling the soul of his phoenix, Bion, to strengthen his power, but ultimately coming to the conclusion that Keon wasn't strong enough since he didn't even possess Bion's gray flames. Then Bautista tried, but he didn't have Bion's gold flames. I have the full range of a gray sun phoenix, which will be even stronger in this life.

I think about Bion, a beautiful phoenix I know only in Keon's memories. Pearl eyes as dark as a starless sky. A golden crown on his head, like a true king. A gray belly that loved being brushed. The yellow wings and dark tail that always brought him home. Bion was the rare phoenix that loved flying in the rain, whereas most phoenixes usually conserved their energy and fires. Other birds fear or tolerate cats, but Bion loved playing with the neighborhood cat so much that Keon tried adopting her. He went absolutely feral over coconuts, hammering away with his bronzed beak and drenching his face in milk. And Bion had the most beautiful birdsong, which Keon desperately wanted to hear again in person, as badly as I want to hear Ma call me her Emilio one last time.

I cast fire, crafting a phoenix out of gray and gold flames as if I'm making it out of clay, and instead of a furious screech, there is birdsong—Bion's birdsong—as the phoenix takes flight toward Brighton, doing everything in its power to save my life, and to save our soul. Everything is so melodic and violent as the phoenix-spirit claws at Brighton's face with fiery feet and begins breathing fire. By the time Brighton phases through it, so much damage has been done, and his body can't heal while he's incorporeal.

I grab the All-Killer and fly toward him, holding the scythe above him.

Brighton shakes his head, almost daring me.

"I could kill you right now," I say as the phoenix-spirit circles us in the sky.

Brighton corporealizes. "Then do it. Swing the scythe into my flesh. Kill me forever."

"You know I don't have that in me. You don't either."

"Is that what you think?"

I toss the scythe beside Brighton, fully trusting that he won't kill me, even after I proved that he needs this weapon if he's going to beat me in a fight.

"Face it, Bright. You love Ma and you love Dad, but you don't love them more than you love me. I'm your brother. I have been with you since the beginning of our lives, and if today is where our brotherhood ends, you got to follow me back to our start."

SEVENTY-THREE

THE FIRST REYS

BRIGHTON

Anyone else would have killed me.

I pick up my scythe, which Emil has tossed my way like it's nothing. The All-Killer is a special weapon that was created to kill absolutely anyone, even unkillable immortals like me, and I'm actually still alive when I should be a ghost. Not even a ghost. Just . . . nothing.

Now Emil wants to go somewhere.

"Back to our start?" I ask. "What the hell does that mean?"

"I want to retrocycle to the day you were born . . . the day I was reborn."

"Why?"

"You swear I'm not really your brother. If you still feel that way after going back to the day we became brothers, then I will stop thinking of you as mine too."

"Then what? You think you'll have what it takes to kill me?"

Emil tears up. "I'm done fighting you, Brighton. I'm not wasting my second shot at life by being the Infinity Son until I die again. If you retrocycle with me, I will bind my powers."

This offer feels too good to be true. Emil is the only person who has any chance of conquering me. If I retrocycle, I'll be incapacitated. Someone can harm me. "This is a trap. Darren could kill me with my scythe while I'm retrocycling." I look around, as if I can spot Darren, but he's hidden in this field of illusions like a predator and I refuse to be his prey.

"He's not going to. He's here to help."

"That's what I thought and then he killed you!"

"And that was enough to haunt him. He's never going to kill again."

How weak can Darren be to be bothered by killing someone he hates? I didn't shed a tear over Stanton, but Darren went and whined about Emil? That's weakness.

The only death that haunts me is Ma's, and Emil is the only person standing in my way from undoing that.

"If I retrocycle, then you won't stop me from performing the resurrection ritual."

"You can have Ma and Dad back, but you will lose me forever."

That gives me pause, but Emil is just being emotional. Once Ma and Dad have resurrected, souls and all, begging to see him, then his moral compass will swing the other way.

"Fine," I say, which seems to cut Emil like a knife. "But how are you going to retrocycle to that moment? You can't revisit your own life, and you don't have blood ties to Ma or Dad." He flinches, like I've twisted the knife. "I'm just trying to cooperate with your plan."

"Yeah, sure you are," Emil murmurs before waving me off. "When

I died, I finally unlocked all of Keon's and Bautista's memories, which have taught me so many new things about my powers." He looks up at that fire phoenix that's been circling me like a vulture. The fire phoenix descends and perches itself onto Emil's wrist before Emil recalls the flames into the palm of his hand.

So this wasn't even just Emil overpowering me; it was Keon and Bautista adding weight in his favor. It doesn't matter. Those powers will be gone soon enough, and I can reign on.

"What did their memories teach you?" I ask.

"You remember when Wyatt was teaching us about retrocycling? We found out that the historian Elodie Badeaux was the earliest voice in researching the retrocycle phenomenon centuries ago. Keon studied her work, but he went deeper and darker and found out things I will never tell another soul. But I know so much about retrocycling now. Like how we can go back into our own lives since we've technically died."

I want to know more about Keon's discoveries, but that can wait.

"Then let's go," I say.

We sit down in what still looks like a plotless cemetery, preparing to return to eighteen years into the past. I hold the All-Killer to my chest as I ignite the silver and sapphire flames around my entire body; if that sneaky bastard Darren thinks it's going to be easy to grab this scythe to kill me, he's got another thing coming.

I focus on everything I know about the day I was born: how Ma was in labor for twenty-two hours, something Abuelita always claimed was a prophecy that I would be a difficult child since I was a difficult delivery; how Dad hounded the doctor and nurses with everything he learned from reading the baby books; how Ma hated living off ice and was so excited to eat pegao with hot sauce once we—I—was born; and how Dad called his dead best friend's mother after I was born to tell her that I was named Brighton after her son. Then I remember the story Ma told us and the Spell Walkers on the day Emil first came into his powers. She'd always imagined herself as a new mom, holding her baby in a hospital room with yellow daffodils and balloons; I never found out why, but I can ask her once she's resurrected. The hospital's helium tank wasn't working, and Dad was determined to get her balloons—

I feel a voice; the delirious retrocycle trip is officially underway.

This voice is filling me up like air in a balloon so light that I'm flying through the past. It's a man's voice, and he's speaking in gentle whispers. I can almost make out what he's saying, but as I begin recognizing the voice, I'm disoriented over how much younger he sounds. My soul vibrates because this voice has been around for almost all of life, back when he would sing to me when I was in the womb and years and years of love when I was growing up. This is my dad, and this teaser has only gotten me extra excited to resurrect him. I've never heard him sound so young because my parents were awful at documenting their lives, but that's okay because I'm going to be the Infinity Reaper forever and I'll be able to retrocycle through their histories as their son by blood. I can see what my dad was like as a child and at my age. I can follow his love story with Ma. But I'm not just giving myself the gift of the past, I'm forging a once-impossible future by resurrecting him. Not only will I be able to hear Dad as I've always known him, but I will be able to discover how he sounds as he ages. I cling on to Dad's voice in this dark void, like my eyes are closed and he's standing above me, trying to tell me something.

I think he is.

Dad is just talking to newborn Brighton, who only knows his father's voice.

A baby surfaces in the void, and as light and color breach the darkness, I can see Dad and Ma in the hospital, holding me. They look exactly as I remember from the pictures in our baby albums, but now they're here in the flesh. Ma's smile is tired as she gazes at me, and Dad parts her hair so she can get a better look. Meanwhile I'm staring at Dad because I can only run through him instead of into his arms. I can't believe this is my dad, a few years older than I am now, alive and well with so much life ahead of him.

Love and pride wash over me, coming from Ma and Dad together.

I am the son they created, and the son who will re-create them.

Dad brushes my little baby hairs and kisses my forehead, which only grows my heart.

"Don't grow up too fast, Brighton. I'll only be gone a few minutes," Dad says.

"Stay, Leo, it's okay. I don't actually need the balloons," Ma says.

"Nonsense. This room needs balloons."

I look around the room, finding Dad's jacket slung over a chair, a container with grains of rice in a puddle of hot sauce, empty water bottles, and daffodils by the window.

"I don't want you to go," Ma says.

"Is this because you love me or because you're still scared—"

"Yes, I am scared, I am *terrified* that I will mess up our child if you're gone."

Then, between Dad's amusement and Ma's genuine fear, I feel

something no one else does: heartbreak. Dad did leave Ma alone with me. Not alone-alone since Emil was around too, but he's not my parent. After Dad dying this year and this war breaking out between me and Emil, I hope Ma wasn't blaming herself. Ma may have been siding with Emil, but before I accidentally killed her, I was coming to rescue her and protect her and care for her as she always has with me. On the off chance she died thinking she messed me up, her mind will change after she's resurrected; she'll see that she raised a good, no, *great* son.

"I am not going anywhere except the store," Dad says, brushing her cheek. "And in that time, you will not mess up Brighton . . . unless you drop him."

Ma's face flushes. "Leo!"

"I'm kidding! I'm sorry!" Dad laughs, and I miss hearing this so much. "You have carried our child for nine months already, you will not drop him now."

"That's beautiful and all, but I couldn't drop him before."

Dad tucks baby Brighton deeper against Ma's chest. "There we go."

"What did that do?"

"I just cast a rare form of gleam, protecting Brighton forever as long as he's with you."

Ma rolls her eyes. "I didn't realize I married a celestial."

"A very powerful celestial . . . who needs to go get you balloons."

Dad kisses Ma on the lips, lingering there long enough for their love to keep swelling within me. It's like nothing I've ever felt before. The closest I've come to this is Prudencia, but that was a breath compared to this gale. Will—could—my love for Prudencia grow this strong? Were Dad and Ma always like this? It's definitely what I always saw growing up.

"I love you," Dad says, staring into Ma's eyes.

"I love you too. If you're going to go, be fast. I don't want your gleam to wear off."

"I said it works forever, but even if there is a glitch, I trust you wholeheartedly with our son."

Dad smiles, fully confident in Ma as he rushes out the hospital room.

My initial link was to baby Brighton, but I manage to follow Dad out into the hallway, running to catch up with him instead of being bound to the hospital room with my newborn self. There are many bright sides to being me, and being able to jump between the bloodlines of my family is another. I follow Dad down the staircase and out the building, ready to meet Emil at our crossroads where he was reborn.

I don't know Emil's master plan for this trip down memory lane, but it's already backfired on him. The great benefit of retrocycling means that I haven't only just seen my parents again, but I have felt every feeling that touched their soul. More than ever, I'm so ready to resurrect my family, even if that means it looks different than what I've known my entire life. If Emil doesn't want to be my brother, that's his choice. I'm making mine.

SEVENTY-FOUR

THE LAST REY

EMIL

I retrocycle into the past, right as my resurrection is beginning.

This is the earliest moment I could travel to; any further and I would have been reliving Bautista's death for the second time. My life actually begins here, and while I can sense myself, I don't see myself. I look up at the clear blue sky and blinding sun as if I'm going to find newborn me flying around on fiery phoenix wings. I can't feel the sun's heat, but I do feel myself burning up, echoing my recent resurrection as my body was coming together. That's when I see the trail of ashes swirling through the air before zooming toward the street like shooting stars. The ashes cluster together, forming a tiny silhouette, and they burn hot, hot, hot as gray and gold flames burst to life, creating a baby, creating me.

I just watched myself be born.

Reborn.

I take the deepest breath with baby Emil as he breathes for the first time.

Even with all my new memories, I don't remember this. I only remember what everyone else does, and Keon and Bautista don't remember what it was like being born any more than I do. Until now.

Just like when I was resurrected, the baby is naked, but that's more expected for a newborn versus an eighteen-year-old. I was just reborn standing on my feet in the middle of the night, but as a baby I was on my back, writhing around on a dirty street. The sun isn't as hot as my phoenix fire, but this still sucks for anyone, especially a newborn who doesn't have anyone to care for him yet. The baby opens his mouth, and I feel the distress and discomfort all before that very first cry. I kneel before the baby, wishing I could pick him up—pick myself up.

"Everything is going to be all right," I say, even though baby Emil not only can't understand me, but can't even hear me because I'm not really here. Still, that doesn't stop me from wanting to talk to him. To talk to me. "Listen, Emil, you're going to be okay. Someone is coming to rescue you, and he's going to become your father and he's going to love you for almost eighteen years before he dies. It's going to feel like you won't survive that, but you will. Then everything is going to get wild when you discover you have extraordinary powers. You're not going to want to be a hero, but you'll fight for peace, the same peace you had growing up with a family that treated you as one of their own. You're going to lose your mom. . . ." I choke up, envying this baby who still has my whole life ahead of him, a life where Dad and Ma are alive and Brighton and I were the closest brothers could be. "And it looks like you're going to lose your brother too. But you will be reborn—one time literally—after all your hardships because you're a survivor. Death hasn't stopped you from living, Emil, so make sure you live."

I'm crying, just as hard as baby Emil, the both of us unsure and scared of what comes next.

My heart races when I look up to find Dad—younger, but definitely my dad—turn the corner with his head tilting, like whenever he was confused. He squints at the street and sees baby Emil and breaks into a sprint. Brighton appears, chasing after him, but nowhere near as fast as Dad, who is running to me as if he has swift-speed. I open my arms as if Dad can hug me, but he runs right through me and picks up the baby. I can feel Dad touching the baby, and the baby keeps crying, but his heart rate is slowing down while mine keeps pounding.

Dad looks around for whoever left me here. "Hello?! Hello!" The baby cries louder, startled. "I'm sorry, I'm sorry. I want to find who did this to you." He curses under his breath. "Who left you out in the middle of a street?"

Brighton stares, looking furious.

I stand here, still crying.

"Dad is pissed," Brighton says.

I can see that, but Brighton can actually feel it.

"It's no one's fault," I say.

"Dad doesn't know that."

"And Dad died never knowing that."

"He will soon," Brighton says, which sounds like a threat.

This means my brother has made his choice: our parents over me.

Dad gently rests his palm on the baby's forehead. "You're burning up," he says, looking up at the sun and cursing again. He holds baby Emil to his chest and rushes back to the hospital. Brighton and I chase after Dad, keeping close as he rushes through the emergency room's doors, screaming for help, and confusing the nurses, who just watched him leave without a baby and now returning with one. "I don't know whose baby this is. I just found him abandoned on the street!" There are tears in Dad's eyes as he holds me like I'm a body that's been shot. "Please help him!"

A nurse approaches Dad and tries taking the baby.

"Wait! What's your name?"

"I'm Nurse Alex."

"Please take care of him," Dad says as he hands me over. "I'm Leonardo Rey. My wife, Carolina, is on the fourth floor with our son. Room 401. I want to know that he's okay."

Then Dad watches as Nurse Alex carries me into another room, and he can't stop himself from following to peek in through the window; the nurse pulls the curtain close, but she leaves enough space for Dad to see that they're tending to me. He goes from shoving his knuckles into his mouth to pacing outside the room to just staring through the window.

I both wish I could and am glad I can't feel what Dad is feeling, but I'm happy that Brighton can. "What's Dad feeling?"

"Isn't it clear?" Brighton points at Dad. "He's freaking out. He's scared and protective."

Nurse Alex comes out of the room without me. Dad is so close to her that she's startled at first. "The doctor is going to treat the baby soon. His vitals are all looking good apart from his temperature, but he's cooling down."

"Some bastard left him out in the sun. A baby!" Dad says. He's not a violent man, but I see his fingers twitching like he's ready to punch through the window.

"It's unfortunate and sadly not uncommon, but you did a great thing by bringing him here. You saved his life," Nurse Alex says with a little smile. "Why don't you head up to your wife and son? This baby still needs to be seen by the doctor, and we'll be notifying the police."

"I'm around for any statements, whatever they need."

Nurse Alex nods. "We'll know where to find you."

"Thank you, Ms. Alex."

Dad peeks his head through the doorway, looking at me with all these wires wrapped around me. "Hang tight, big man. I'll come check on you."

It seems to take Dad a great deal of force to finally leave baby Emil, and me too. Something I never really tried to do during previous retrocycle episodes is to get too far away from my link, but even though it's like walking through sand, I'm able to follow Dad as he rides the elevator to the fourth floor. He still doesn't know what my fate is, or how proud I am to be his son. He heads straight into the room, where I see Ma holding baby Brighton, and I want to sink to my knees and cry over how much I miss her and how much I love her and how happy I am to see her again.

Ma is puzzled. "No balloons? You took so long I figured you were blowing up the balloons yourself." She takes another look at Dad. She sits up. "Leo, what is wrong?"

Dad falls back into the bedside chair. "I found a baby."

Ma is even more confused. "You found a baby?"

"I found a baby on the street. Someone left him there. . . ." Dad begins crying and stomps his foot, furious. "What kind of monster would do that? He could have been run over. He was burning under the sun. Did they want him to die?"

Ma starts crying too. She groans as she shifts in bed, clutching Brighton to her chest as she slides her legs out from under the covers and gets to her feet so she can be there for Dad; she's always been the strong and selfless woman I've known. Ma kisses the top of Dad's head, just as she would with us when we were crying. "You did an amazing thing for that boy."

Dad looks up with teary eyes. "The nurse said I saved his life."

"You did. You're a hero, Leo."

I look over at Brighton, wishing I could feel what he was feeling in this moment. Is he thinking that he's a hero just like our father, or is he realizing how different they are?

Dad stares into the distance before snapping out of it. "Carolina, back in bed. You need to rest. Here, here, give me Brighton." He takes the baby and offers his arm to Ma, assisting her as she sits down. He bounces baby Brighton while holding him as close as he held me. "These children, these babies are so innocent. They need us."

"I hope those parents are well," Ma says.

"After what they did?!"

"After what they did."

"If you can't handle a child, fine. But leaving him in the street? Bring him somewhere. A hospital, police station, church, even inside a cat's crate at a bodega! Just not out in the open where he could have been killed!"

Ma told us she'd never seen Dad so angry than that day, but right now she's able to keep her composure. She takes deep breaths and motions for Dad to do the same. "Leo, breathe. I am on your side. I just do not know what could have been going through their hearts and minds when they did such a terrible thing."

Dad takes his deep breath, but he's still shaking. "I just love our son so much already. I don't understand how someone else didn't love that kid enough."

"We will never know the full story, but I hope that boy finds a great family."

Dad is pacing, and I swear I can see the first flicker in his eye that he wants to adopt me. It sucks that we're not mind readers while retrocycling, but I'd bet anything I'm right. Then he stares at baby Brighton. "I will never leave you. Ever."

"Except when it's time for us to pass, of course."

"Not even then. I'm going to live forever for my son."

My heart sinks as Dad says this, whereas Brighton smiles with teary eyes.

"See?" Brighton says. "He wants to be alive for me."

This is backfiring on me. I wish I'd had more time to retrocycle to this day to make sure Dad or Ma wouldn't say anything that would hammer the nails into the coffin, or I guess shovel the dirt out of their graves, but Dad has just gone and done that.

Maybe I was wrong.

Maybe Dad would be happy to be alive again, even on unnatural terms.

Maybe Brighton does know our dad better than me.

"Maybe" is all I say.

"What do you mean? He just said so."

"Yeah, but he's not plotting on how to live forever."

"That's because he doesn't know it's possible, but you and I are living proof of immortality!" Brighton stands between Dad and Ma.

"Are we done? I'd like to resurrect my parents now."

Staring at my family, I feel so guilty. If Dad hadn't found me on the street, this would've been Brighton's life. He would've never been sucked into this war, and while Dad would have still died from his illness, at least Ma would be alive to grieve with Brighton the natural way. No one would've known about the possibility of resurrection and true immortality. If I could change time instead of just traveling through it, I would run downstairs and grab baby Emil and leave him with the Spell Walkers along with instructions on how to create the Starstifler so they can bind my powers. Then no family would have to go through all the chaos I caused by being the Infinity Son.

But I can't change the past. All I can do is use it to win this war, once and for all.

"We're almost done," I say. "We have to skip ahead."

"Skip ahead to when?"

"To when Mom meets me for the first time."

"Why not just wait?"

"That's hours away," I say, recalling Ma's story of how she didn't get to meet me until the evening. "Just concentrate on that moment."

We both stand still, expecting to reappear in our past's future, but instead we watch time rapidly fly by: Ma nurses Brighton; Dad pops in and out of the hospital room, always returning with kisses for Ma and Brighton; Dad looks exhausted and anxious as he watches Ma and Brighton sleep; Brighton wakes up crying for more milk; and Nurse Alex and police officers speak with Dad in the doorway until he follows them out of sight. The sky outside the window has been darkening as hours pass within seconds, and it's gone fully black when Dad returns to the room, carrying a baby. Brighton and I both step back into our past's present at the same moment.

"This is him," Dad says as he carries baby Emil toward Ma, who is already cradling Brighton.

Ma has this sad smile. "He's so beautiful."

"He was crying bloody murder downstairs. The nurses couldn't calm him down, so they let me give it a shot. He calmed down quickly. I think he just wanted to be held."

"He wanted to be held by *you*."

"I guess so," Dad says, swaying with me. "The police said they'd look into it, but were transparent that this wouldn't be a high priority. They got plenty going on with all those specters." Little does Dad know that he's holding the soul responsible for that mess. "The nurses said the maternity ward is pretty busy too, so—"

"Leo . . ."

"—maybe we can help out with this little guy."

Ma sighs. "It hasn't even been a full day with one kid. You want to foster another?"

Dad shakes his head. "I was thinking more that we should adopt him."

"I thought I was the only one on drugs today. We're not ready."

"No one is ever ready, are they? This is no different than if we had twins."

"I have spent the past few months mentally preparing to be a good mother for one son. My heart goes out to this little boy, it truly does, but I was already scared to be left alone with Brighton."

"You won't be alone, and when we pass, they won't be either," Dad says, bringing baby Emil closer to baby Brighton.

"I thought you were going to live forever."

"I won't, just as you won't, and just as they won't, but we can be a family while we can."

Ma stares at baby Emil. "Give him to me," she whispers. Dad settles me into her lap beside Brighton. She just watches us, squirming around while yawning. "Aww, he's not crying with me either." She perks up. "It's not fair that you've sprung this on me while my emotions are already all over the place."

Dad cracks a smile, like he knows he's getting to her. "We always wanted another kid. This is like two for the price of one pregnancy, and you didn't even have to carry both."

"That's a great sales pitch, but you might actually have to become a salesman because one kid is already so expensive and adding another who may have needs we don't know about—"

"We will figure it out."

"That's just the financials, what about physically and mentally? Are we able to do this? Are we able to be the very best parents this child could have?"

Dad is tearing up as he says, "I don't trust anyone to love this kid more than we will."

As a tear slides down his face, I full-out cry. Discovering I was adopted was brutal because I'd always been made to feel like I was part of the family. That's because I got so lucky with parents that loved me in all my forms. They didn't care that I was overly sensitive or that I struggled in school or that I'm gay or anything else that other kids have been weighed down by. Ma didn't even hate me for being the Infinity Son, and Dad wouldn't have either. I love them so much that it hurts that they're dead, but I'm forever grateful for the life they selflessly gave me as if I was their flesh and blood, and watching them choose me has healed the scar of our family secret.

Ma turns to baby Brighton. "I hope you want a brother, because you've got one now."

Dad kisses Ma, and they're crying too, but we're not the only ones.

Brighton—my brother, the Infinity Reaper—is crying too.

"What are they feeling?" I ask.

"Infinite love for their sons," Brighton says, pressing his hand on his heart, like he's overloaded with so many emotions that he might phase into his chest and rip his own heart out for relief.

Dad squeezes into bed with Ma, gazing upon our family. "He'll need a name."

"We don't even know yet that we'll get to keep him."

"He's ours," Dad says as if he's psychic. "We could use Miguel now. It doesn't have to be a middle name."

"It's already on Brighton's birth certificate. What about after my father?"

Dad lights up. "Hi, Emil."

Baby Emil squirms.

"Hi, Dad," I say for the both of us.

"Our boys," Dad says. "Brighton and Emil."

"Emil and Brighton," Ma says. "We have to raise them as equals."

"Twin brothers," Dad says. He looks down at the babies. "No matter what, boys, you must always look out for each other. You are family, you hear me?"

"I hear you," I say to Dad even though he can't hear me.

Brighton remains quiet, wiping away his tears.

This is all I could've hoped for. Retrocycling isn't just about seeing. It's about feeling too.

I go to Ma and Dad, and I kiss both of their heads, even though my lips phase right through them. "Bye, Dad. Bye, Ma. I'll love you forever."

I wave at Brighton before closing my eyes.

I concentrate on my life, thinking about how I am Emil Rey, the son of Leonardo and Carolina Rey, the brother of Brighton Rey, and I'm so sure of all of these things that for the first time ever I am able to end retrocycling without being killed first.

My gray and gold flames vanish from around me, and the sun is now high in the sky; I can't help but think about how far I've come in life since being reborn on that street with nothing but the sun to look at until Dad saved me. Directly across is Brighton, who is still surrounded by his silver and sapphire flames with the All-Killer in his grip. I look around us, seeing that the headstones are now visible again and a few feet away from me is Wyatt's backpack that he gave me with three essentials. This means Darren followed my instructions and got the hell out of here while Brighton wasn't able to chase him down. It also means Darren didn't try killing Brighton while he was vulnerable. It's strange feeling proud of a kid who killed me, but I am.

I get up with my backpack and walk down the cemetery, finding Ma's and Dad's graves easily because of Brighton's bags with the ritual ingredients. Destroying this stuff would only delay Brighton, not stop him forever. I'm also honoring my word. If everything goes down the way I want, then this won't matter and Brighton and I can set up a headstone for Ma. If it doesn't, then Ma won't need one and Dad's headstone can be removed.

"Bye, Dad. Bye, Ma. I'll love you forever," I say again, this time hoping their souls can hear me.

The silver and sapphire flames stop roaring as Brighton's soul returns to his body. He slowly gets up, carrying the scythe at his side as he walks over. He glances at me before staring at Ma's and Dad's graves. "Retrocycling might be my favorite power."

"It's definitely mine after that. Seeing myself be reborn was wild, but watching Ma and Dad choose me is something I'll never forget."

Then Brighton is quiet. His lips twitch, but he keeps biting his tongue until he says, "Did that journey change your mind?"

"No. It actually gave me some closure. You?"

"No—I don't know. You're my brother, Emil, and those are our parents," Brighton says, almost pleading as he points at their graves. "We can have it all, bro."

"No one can have it all, Bright. Not even the Infinity Kings or the Reys of Light. If you go through with this, I'm out of the picture. You won't be resurrecting the family you've known your entire life, but it'll just be you and Ma and Dad back like it could've been all along."

"It's not fair to make me choose between you and them."

"It's also not fair that you get to play god over people's lives and deaths."

Brighton keeps staring at Ma's and Dad's graves. "I watched Dad die and I killed Ma. I deserve to see them alive again."

"You just saw them alive—happy, in love, starting a family, making us brothers. It's my new favorite memory, and I got to experience it with you. No matter how much I miss Ma and Dad, I got to see how they loved us before they even knew us and how I felt that love my entire life."

"You got to feel it your entire life. Ma took your side at the end."

"Before she died, Ma wished you were with us, and while she

wasn't thrilled about how you were using your powers, she was still happy that you're alive. I know you think you have to resurrect them to be forgiven, but all you got to do is be alive and good to make things right." As Brighton starts shaking, I put a hand on his shoulder to steady him. "Not having our parents back doesn't mean you'll be alone. We've got each other, just as Dad wanted."

Brighton begins crying. "This pain is too much."

"You're scarred from Dad's death and from killing Ma, and even with all your powers, those scars will never fully heal, but you can't live your life only thinking about what hurts. You've done a lot of good, and there's still so much more you can do."

"You mean being a hero your way?" Brighton asks, wiping a tear away.

"I can't tell you who to be. You chose to become the Infinity Reaper in ways that I didn't choose to become the Infinity Son. But I'm done fighting you. You get to be the reigning Infinity King. The last Rey of Light."

I open my backpack and pull out a knife. Brighton steps back before realizing this is an ordinary blade that would be useless against him. My body has been through so much during my era as the Infinity Son—thrown around, slashed, stabbed, even killed—but I still flinch as I drag the blade across my palm. The blood pools in my hand as my gleam heals the wound; my heart races as I realize this is the very last time I will use my powers. I pull out the Starstifler from the backpack and squeeze my blood inside the vial, shaking it up with my stained and fully healed hand.

"To the end of infinity," I say, raising the Starstifler.

Then, just as I watched Brighton drink the potion that gave him powers, he watches me consume the one that will bind mine forever. The Starstifler is sludgy and just as disgusting as the night Brighton force-fed me the potion. Instead of trying to spit it out like last time, I swallow it all down, feeling the thick liquid melt down my throat. My insides begin burning, and I sink to my knees, my fingers clawing at the soil and grass. Brighton is at my side, yelling at me to throw up the potion, but I know this will pass after watching Bautista bind the powers of a former Blood Caster. I warn him to back up as I feel myself getting hotter and hotter. Brighton moves away just in time for gold and gray flames to swallow my body whole, burning so fiercely that I bet I'm about to be nothing but ashes again until the fire vanishes and I suck in the first deep breath of my new-old life.

"I'm powerless," I say.

"Are you sure?" Brighton asks.

I try casting a fire-orb, but nothing. Not even a spark.

I smile.

"How do you feel?" Brighton asks.

"Free," I say.

There are still so many unknowns ahead of me, but when I first agreed to become a Spell Walker, my goal was to figure out the potion that could bind the powers of a specter with an eye toward drinking it too so I could return to my normal life. I know better, that my life will never be normal again, not really, but the weight of the world will no longer be on my shoulders and I can figure out how to live in it.

Brighton rests the scythe at the foot of Dad's grave. He knows I'm no longer a threat. "What now?"

I gaze across the cemetery, finding the gate in the distance. "Now I get out of your way."

"To do what?"

"I'm going to go find the guy who chooses me, even when things get rough."

He squints, figuring it out. "Ness? He tried killing me!"

"And you've threatened my life a lot."

Brighton's head hangs, before he straightens up, like he's remembered he still has a crown on his head as the sole Infinity King. "I wouldn't have been able to live with myself if I killed you. It was brutal enough watching you die alongside Keon, and that wasn't even your real death."

"It was once upon a time ago. But this is it for me. The next time I die, it'll be for real."

"You accept that?"

"I'm not freaking out about death. I'm going to live the life I've been fighting for."

"I'm going to do the same," Brighton says, then adds in a whisper, "I have to."

Once again, Brighton chooses himself, but I'm not going to try and force him to be anyone else. All that's done is made him prioritize his only life above anyone else's and gotten tons of people and phoenixes killed. Maybe he'll chill out once he gets his way, but I'm not counting on it.

I have to go, but giving him a throwback fist bump and whistle doesn't feel right.

"Goodbye, Bright," I say, hugging him.

Brighton squeezes me back. "Goodbye, bro."

I stay strong as I break from our hug. I throw on my backpack and begin walking away.

"Emil!"

I stop.

"What am I supposed to tell Ma and Dad about why you won't see them?"

"Tell them I wasn't family enough for you."

Brighton stares with teary eyes, and I turn my back on him so I can cry myself.

I break into a run, past Dad's and Ma's graves, and countless others through the cemetery as I race toward my future.

I don't know who I'm supposed to be if I'm not going to be Emil Rey anymore.

Maybe I'll be Emil Máximo de León in honor of my past lives.

Then one day I can become Emil Arroyo if Ness really wants me for life.

All I know is one thing.

I am no longer the Infinity Son.

SEVENTY-FIVE
DISTURBANCE

NESS

I snap awake when the alarm blares, shutting it off with a light-skinned hand that isn't my own.

Or Russell's.

As I was finally falling asleep in the middle of the night, I was sure that I was going to have nightmares about Russell after his graphic death. But I actually had a dream that was both heart-racing and peaceful. All because Emil's face appeared like a firefly in the night. I dreamed he had been reborn in these beautiful golden flames that shone so brightly that sunspots danced around him once he was standing before me. Then he threw his arms around me and I cried because I was so happy to see him. Time skipped and we found ourselves inside my closet at Nova and we were holding each other on this king-sized bed that would have never fit in that room in real life. I started kissing him as we pulled off my shirt, and as I fully wake up from the dream, I see Emil's reflection in the living room's TV.

This is the first time I've woken up as someone because I was dreaming something good.

Of course Emil still being dead is a nightmare in and of itself, but he's not haunting me from the great beyond.

I hug my body as if it's Emil's actual body I'm getting to hold.

The alarm goes off again along with a text message from Russell's phone.

Be outside in 1 min.

The text has come from Zenon. Morning has come, and he's picking me up for the town hall.

Last night, after I finished tidying Russell's office from our little fight, and poured the Starstifler into a water bottle so no one would be suspicious of "Russell" carrying a power-binding potion, I prepared for today. First I uploaded his suicide note video, scheduling it for this evening in case I'm killed before I get the chance to post it myself. Then I shifted back into Russell to unlock his phone using the face ID function to read up on everything that I could need to know to convince everyone that I am the Silver Star Slayer. I combed through so many emails, text messages, and notes that I even began tricking myself, thinking ahead to the busy week I was going to have between today's rally, tomorrow's dinner with a conservative podcaster, and so many other meetings that I—or Russell—won't actually be going to. I memorized the itinerary that Roslyn Fox sent over and set multiple alarms to be up on time to meet her and Zenon Ramsey, but I clearly overslept, losing myself in the dreamscape with Emil.

Now the Senator's vision-hopping bodyguard is here.

I get up from the couch and quickly morph into Russell, scared that Zenon may have already used his power to peer through my eyes and seen my reflection in the TV where I was Emil one second ago and now I'm Russell. Even an idiot could figure out there's a shifter in the house, and Zenon is no idiot. But he's not a fighter like I am. I've been stuck having to punch my way out of situations whereas Zenon gets to be more strategic with his power to avoid danger.

I grab Russell's phone, his backpack, and the water bottle with the Starstifler potion before leaving the house, locking the front door with his keys. I begin moving as Russell, going so far as to film myself approaching the black car even though it's only ten footsteps away as if I'm going to post this later. I get in the backseat, speaking into the camera, "All of this so I can speak with my hero, Senator Edward Iron. I can't believe my life sometimes," I say, repeating sentiments Russell expressed in other videos.

Zenon's dark blond hair is parted as he stares through the rearview mirror. "Delete that."

I blush and fiddle with the phone. I tap on the screen.

"I'm watching," Zenon says with glowing eyes.

He sees everything that I'm seeing, so I delete the video.

"Sorry about that," I say. This is probably the first time anyone has seen the Silver Star Slayer utter an apology. Someone like Zenon may not know Russell's nuances, but I still have to be careful. I realize I'm the only one in the backseat. "Hey, wasn't Ms. Fox supposed to be here too?"

Zenon begins driving off. "She is meeting us at the site. She's been dealing with a disturbance the Spell Walkers created at the Light Sky Tower last night."

There were no mentions of any attacks on the Light Sky Tower when I searched the news last night, but it's possible the media has suppressed it on the Senator's orders, especially if he thinks this can be traced back to him so close to the election. I heard nothing from Prudencia before my phone's battery died on if their mission to rescue Sunstar was a success. I'm beginning to think it was, which means the tide is going to change in our favor once she goes on national television and announces her abduction before Election Day. Unlike Russell's death, I am willing to go down for that crime against Sunstar if it means the Senator is thrown in jail too. But Russell wouldn't be happy about this, so I have to hide my smile and keep up this facade.

I let out an angry sigh. "What did those damn terrorists do this time?"

"Roslyn will update you."

"Looking forward to it. Iron couldn't have chosen a smarter campaign manager. I thought she only got the job because of her looks, but she's pretty smart too," I say, and add Russell's deep chuckle, which always follows his many misogynistic statements. "It must be amazing working for Senator Iron. He's always been such a role model of mine and it's a privilege to help him out on his path to presidency and—"

Zenon glares through the rearview mirror as the partition rises, cutting us off. He's no more a fan of listening to Russell being a kiss-ass than I am having to do the kissing. There are no illusions that I'm not still being watched, but it's nice to not have to engage with Zenon. Fewer chances of slipping up. I want to reach out to the Spell Walkers through social media to find out about Sunstar, but I have to keep playing the role of Russell in case Zenon watches my activity out of my eyes. I scroll through Russell's feeds hoping to find some truth about the Light Sky Tower, but I'm only met with propaganda and conspiracy theories that are eating my brain cells by the word.

Thankfully, Zenon can't read minds because that's where I actually get to be myself in peace.

If the Senator's team thinks the campaign is at risk because of the Spell Walkers, then they've got their eye on the wrong enemy.

I am their fatal disturbance.

SEVENTY-SIX

IRON, BISHOP, AND FOX

NESS

The town hall has attracted legions of the Senator's supporters.

Growing up, I was always so proud to find the crowds squeezing together so they could cheer on the Senator as he made promise after promise. As nerve-racking as it was whenever I had to take the stage, I felt safe with the oceans of faceless people who believed in me as much as they did the Senator. But as Zenon fails to find a clear path through Midtown Manhattan to get us to the St. Duval Theater, I'm so disturbed by every last person flooding these streets in their Iron-Bishop hats and shirts with signs that outright speak to their hate of celestials. Most of these people may not have powers, but they are still dangerous in my eyes; somewhere here might even be the reason I'm killed once I do what I'm setting out to do today.

Zenon finally breaks through the traffic and parks the car in the theater's garage. We walk through the corridor, which is lined with dozens of enforcers. I'm really lucky that no one has invented any sensors to detect shifters, otherwise the bang of spellwork would echo through these halls before my body could hit the floor. I know we're about to walk into the belly of the beast when I see Jax Jann standing outside the door. He's wearing a power-proof vest over his sharp suit, and his red ponytail gives him a pop of color.

The closer we get to the greenroom, the more I can hear shouting from inside. There's only one person in this building who can yell at someone and get away with it.

"I am tired of your incompetence!" the Senator shouts. "I will handle this my way, just as I have everything else around here!"

I chuckle. "Sounds like Senator Iron might be hiring soon, huh?"

Zenon parts his blond hair to glare. "Wait here."

I watch as Zenon and Jax exchange glances.

"Good luck," Jax says.

Zenon knocks and lets himself in.

"Where have you been?!" the Senator shouts right before the door closes behind Zenon.

On the ride over, I was thinking about how surprising it was that the Senator charged Zenon with picking Russell up in the first place considering Zenon is tasked with making sure that no one is targeting the Senator. Then again, the public doesn't know that the Senator can now appear as anyone he wants. He could stand right next to his would-be assassin, and they would have no idea their target is one foot away. The only thing that makes sense is that Russell is considered important enough—and easily manipulated—that his life isn't to be trusted with anyone outside the Senator's elite circle. Formerly elite, by the sounds of yelling.

Jax pays me no mind, which is nice. It means he believes I'm Russell.

The door opens, and Zenon waves me in.

I enter the greenroom, which is decked out with leather couches, a big-screen TV, mini fridges, and a hair and makeup station for those who can't change their appearance at will. It's one of the many lavish perks for headlining events, but no one in this room seems happy. I should say truly happy since Roslyn Fox is trying to hide behind her smile, but I see right through her embarrassment of being put in her place. I make a note to get under her skin even more by grossly complimenting how good she looks in her white blouse and pencil skirt, and how she could be prettier if she freed her black hair from its bun. Barrett Bishop, the oldest in the room, doesn't regard me with his icy-blue eyes. He's wearing a red-and-black checkered suit that makes him look like the king on a playing card; even a tacky dresser like Russell would not carry this catastrophe in his closet. But Bishop is more interested in designing prison cells for celestials at the Bounds, where he's the chief architect, than he is dressing himself up to look like someone who is campaigning to become vice president. Then there's the Senator, who isn't parading around as anyone else and instead looking presidential in his crisp black suit. He's doing a better job at masking his disappointment and frustrations with his team, but I still recognize what a two-faced bastard he is. It's too bad I can't treat him as such. I have to admire him like he's my hero.

"Great to see you again, Senator," I say.

The Senator approaches me and shakes my hand. "You too, Russell." He shakes his head slightly. "Forgive me for anything you may have overheard while outside. These campaigns are stressful."

His tone is so manipulative, and someone as impressionable as Russell would have fallen for the Senator's attempt to twist his outburst into a moment of bonding, as if Russell has been treated to a true behind-the-scenes moment of an election.

"I can only imagine," I say, waving it away. "You only want what's best for our country."

The Senator clicks his tongue and grins. "See? You get it."

I smile proudly. Playing the role of Russell is truly humiliating, but it's also my most impressive performance to date. Instead of killing the Senator for manipulating me into giving him the location of our hideout at the gym, which got Carolina killed, I'm standing here and idolizing him as if I actually believe everything he's doing is what's best for our country.

"Is everything okay? Your driver mentioned there was a disturbance last night."

Zenon takes offense to being labeled as the driver, but it's the dark glimmer in the Senator's eyes that I pay attention to as he shoots Zenon a look before turning back to me. "Everything is not okay and never will be as long as the Spell Walkers are an active force against us. Roslyn will update you with new talking points so we can bring this latest act of terrorism to light during our discussion." He pats my shoulder like we're friends. "I have to tend to another matter, but I'll see you onstage shortly."

"Looking forward to it," I say. It's the most honest thing I've said today.

"With me," the Senator says to Zenon on his way out, the door closing behind them.

Roslyn seems to exhale for the first time once the Senator leaves.

Bishop lets out a low whistle as he sits on the couch.

I love seeing them so tense. "Rough morning?"

"No one likes waking up to terrorism," Roslyn says as she grabs some pages out of a binder. "Here are the revised questions you'll be asking Edward—Senator Iron." She blushes. I'm very familiar with her affections for the Senator and her dreams of becoming his first lady, but Russell wouldn't be. Roslyn is usually more careful and discreet, but this scolding must really be throwing her off. "This attack from the Spell Walkers resulted in many deaths, inspiring us to push up a special announcement."

"Special announcement?" I ask.

"That's for the Senator to reveal when the time is right."

"Just tell the boy," Bishop says.

"That is not our call."

"I thought you were campaign manager."

"I am, and I have a boss."

"A boss that just chewed you out," Bishop says. He has no respect for her.

Roslyn composes herself. "I am not going against the instructions that Iron has signed off on, especially not in the minutes leading up to—"

Bishop holds up a finger, silencing her. "My least favorite part about politics is when you people say so much and nothing at the same time." This conversation should never be held in front of an outsider, but Bishop really doesn't care about his appearance. He has said horrific things about celestials that should be enough for people to not want someone so hateful in office, but he's only ever rewarded with cheers by the Iron-Bishop supporters. Bishop turns to me. "Our wonderful news is that despite the mass breakout of the Bounds, we have completed reconstruction. Just in time to throw every last celestial and specter into a cell, along with any and all accomplices and accessories to their crimes."

I flinch for a moment before I twist that reaction into awe. "Whoa. That was fast."

"I'm the chief architect," Bishop says. "I get things done."

The Bounds were only destroyed in the first place because of the Senator's strategy to further paint the Spell Walkers as criminals by breaking me out. Now it's up and running again with a new twist. "By accomplices and accessories, do you mean normal people too?"

Bishop grins. "We will have to go through the formal proceedings to get the laws changed, but this is our intention. If people want to aid gleamcrafters in their devastating crimes on our nation, I see no reason why we wouldn't lock them up in the same cells. Our supporters will be excited to hear about this."

"And you get to set the stage," Roslyn says, tapping the page she's given me.

Roslyn Fox can feed me all the lies she wants, but I have no intention of telling any of them.

Once I'm onstage with the Senator, I will expose him for the shape-shifting fraud he is.

Even though it will get me killed.

SEVENTY-SEVEN
THE RISING SUN

NESS

My dreams of being a professional actor will never come true, but as I'm behind this curtain, ready to go onstage, I'm about to put on one hell of a show for this audience of Iron-Bishop fans. I hope I can make them see that the Senator and Bishop have been putting on an act all along.

My name—Russell's name—is announced over the speakers, and I step onto the stage, holding the new talking points in one hand and waving with the microphone in the other. The real Russell would have loved to have all these strangers adoring him, feeding his ego of how valuable he is to this regime. I salute the cameras for everyone watching at home.

I keep the energy going by shouting, "Strong as Iron! Strong as Iron!"

The audience chants with me.

I stare into the sea of darkness, unable to clearly make out the faces of any of these supporters, but wishing I could see these monsters showing who they really are. It wasn't until I could shape-shift that I learned this lesson, but I'll never forget it now: anyone can be anyone, even without the power to change their appearance at will; your neighbor who tells you to your face they believe you should have equal rights and then casts a vote against you; your friends who say they will never betray you and then hurt you; your lover who chooses you and then breaks your heart because they've chosen someone else; and even your parent who can try taking you out of this world as quickly as you were brought into it. These supporters might be living in the dark now, but if the Senator wins, their monstrous faces will find the light and raise hell for all.

I settle everyone down, quieting their sickening chant.

"Our city has been through a lot," I say, remembering my lines. "But we have always had Senator Iron to protect us. Imagine the good he will do for our country once he is President Iron!" I lock a smile as everyone cheers, thinking about how my moment is coming, when I will never have to pretend again. "There have been unsettling reports about the latest act of terrorism from the Spell Walkers, and here to clear up everything is none other than Senator Edward Iron!"

The crowd goes so wild that the stage is vibrating.

I watch the curtain, waiting for the Senator to emerge, but he doesn't show his face. The applause begins dying down. I call out for him again, wondering if there's some issue backstage, but still nothing.

"I'm sure the great Senator will be with us any moment now," I say, going off script.

What the hell is happening?

The curtain parts, and Congresswoman Sunstar steps onto the stage. First I'm relieved she's alive, even if I have to mask that with a look of fear and disgust as everyone in the audience boos her. Then I study her, as I would anyone. She looks strong—stronger than I would expect anyone unless they were held captive in a comfortable environment. Sunstar is wearing a black military jacket with buttons shaped like the phases of the moon from top to bottom, as many celestial soldiers wore after returning from war before realizing it painted a target on their backs. Sunstar has never dressed like she's ready for battle, and while people can change, I'm positive the only change that has happened here is the Senator's appearance.

"Quiet, or I will blind you all!" the Senator warns in Sunstar's voice, raising what looks like her palm as if he's about to cast her light into all their eyes. The threat is effective. The audience is quiet except for doors swinging open as the supporters in the back flee. "If anyone else moves, I will burn this building to the ground." There are panicked whispers, but everyone remains seated. "That's better."

Everyone is terrified of Sunstar, but this is the greatest gift the Senator has ever given me.

I have to bide my time before I open it.

The Senator walks over to the empty chair. "I know this was reserved for someone else, but I deserve a chance to speak to this corner of the country."

What would Russell do in this situation? How would he react? The first question on his mind would be the same as anyone else's who has come to this town hall. "Where is Senator Iron?"

"He's alive," the Senator says. "If that's what you're asking."

"I asked where he is."

"He's been thrown into a cell, where he belongs."

There are gasps and cries, and while it's not true, it should be.

It will be if the Senator slips up.

"Terrorists," I say, going so far to actually spit on the Senator's face. "All of you."

The Senator looks up at me with Sunstar's dark eyes; I recognize he's done a good job with this morph, but this won't last. He wipes the spit with his sleeve. "You will regret that."

Except I won't because the Senator would never punish Russell for spitting on Sunstar. "You don't scare me," I say, even though Russell would absolutely be shaking if the real Sunstar threatened him. I'll never forget how scared he was of Eva, who doesn't even have an offensive power. Sunstar can actually do damage but has always chosen not to wield her power like a weapon. "However you want to hurt me, do it in front of the world!"

The Senator leans forward. "I will make you pay on my own terms."

That's because he can't hurt me with Sunstar's light. He's already using his only power. I cower anyway because every second that passes will work in my favor.

"Now, I have not been as face-forward on the campaign trail lately because instead of making empty promises, I've chosen to work very hard behind the scenes to create a safer country. I feel especially supported by this decision after an assassination last night." The Senator takes a deep breath, ready to spin the narrative of the Light Sky Tower in his favor instead of how he abducted Sunstar, and now all I can do is worry about whether she's alive or not. If she's dead, then why was he freaking out on his team? Did someone get evidence that ties him to everything? "As many of you will have seen, in the middle of the night, the alchemist Luna Marnette was going to share a resurrection ritual, until her feed was cut short, presumably because of the gem-grenade explosion that claimed her life."

I freeze.

Luna is dead?

Is this another lie?

No, she—he—is saying that the public is already aware of this. There must be some proof.

Luna is dead . . . ?

I almost can't trust this until I see her corpse, but those blasts pulverize bodies to ash and blood.

Luna is dead.

I wouldn't be alive without her, but I still won't grieve her. I will never grieve her.

"That's great news," I say.

"We have lost an enemy and gained a valuable ritual, one that will not be used on the likes of her—or anyone else without natural power. Instead, the resurrection ritual will be used on the fallen celestials whose lives have been stolen, and we will welcome them into a world where we run supreme, where they will never be threatened with death again!" The Senator raises both arms, as if Sunstar is about to open the sky for celestials to return from the dead. "For those of you who oppose this, you will have to take that up with the strongest army this world has ever seen, comprised of the fiercest celestials, who couldn't be held by the Bounds. If you do not help elect me into office, my army will not serve you, and don't think we won't know which way you vote. Shine Lu's network of invisible celestials will be watching you all at the polling booths and keeping record of those who wish to serve the superior species and those who foolishly believe this country can be strong as Iron."

This is all insane. The Senator has never fed the public such bizarre, outlandish threats. This is the kind of overreaching fearmongering that the Silver Star Slayer did. Are these people so brainwashed they really believe that Shine has thousands of invisible celestials at her disposal to spy on them during the election? That Sunstar would sentence Iron's supporters to death instead of being a president for all? Probably.

What I'm trying to figure out is the Senator's objective. How will he emerge as the winner against Sunstar if he's just laid out a fake plan that will scare people into voting for her?

Unless Sunstar is executed before Election Day.

Does the Senator know where she is? Has he already killed her? Will he announce this soon as a demonstration of his power?

"If you will join me, rise like the sun!" the Senator shouts.

There's confusion in the crowd as to what to do, and as some begin standing, others booing, the Senator says, "You're all being lied to."

Except it's not the Senator speaking as Sunstar because he's standing there as her looking perplexed.

Is it . . . ?

In the blink of an eye, the real Nicolette Sunstar appears. She looks malnourished, bruised, and weak, the opposite of the Senator's impression of her. Everyone in the audience is shocked by the appearance of two Sunstars, but I'm smiling on the inside because of how much the Senator must be freaking out right now.

I back into my seat as if I'm terrified. "There's two of you!"

"I am the real Sunstar," she says into a mic.

No one knows how to react.

"Then who is that?" I ask, pointing at the Senator, right as his glamour begins cracking: the hair grows a quarter of an inch; one eyebrow shrinks, unnoticeable to anyone not on this stage; the dark skin on the right hand lightens before shading itself in again; and the confidence of someone who planned on cheating his way to victory is fading.

"I'm the real Sunstar," the Senator says. "Why are you impersonating me?"

"It's bad enough that you lie to the world, but you're going to lie to me using my own face?"

The Senator shakes his head. "You—you must be a shifter! Eduardo Iron! Are you working for your father again?"

It's time to open the gift the Senator has given me.

I rise, glowing gray as I become myself. "My name is Ness Arroyo," I say, staring down the Senator. "And I will never serve you again."

Everyone, including the Senator and Sunstar, is shocked at my reveal.

I step toward him, right as Jax and Zenon run onto the stage. I have to be fast. This might be my last chance to get the truth out before Jax telekinetically snaps my neck.

"That impostor is Edward Iron with shifter's blood!"

Jax raises his hand, but he goes flying back through the curtain.

"I have some guests," Sunstar says.

Then, just as quickly as Sunstar appeared out of nowhere, so does Shine alongside Prudencia, Iris, Eva, Wesley, Ruth, and Wyatt. Who knows how long they've been here, but judging by how Shine is taking a knee as if she's carrying a boulder on her back, masking everyone with her invisibility took a toll on her; I didn't even know she could turn others invisible, but this reveal is a brilliant way to expose that range. What breaks my heart, though, is that Emil isn't standing alongside them and never will again. I have to hold those shattered pieces, no matter how much they hurt, and then sit in that pain when this is all done.

"I stand with the Spell Walkers," Sunstar says. "They are honest heroes, unlike you."

"I—" the Senator stammers. "I am the real—"

"You are nothing but a liar, and everyone can see that," I say. "Or they will any moment now." The Senator's eyes flicker as he tries maintaining his shift. "You warned all your followers that I would pretend to be you, but the truth is, I hate you so much that I never want to twist my body into yours ever again. Especially not after you had me shot in front of our home." Some of his supporters have begun running away, but most have stayed, and the cameras are still rolling. I'm getting everything I've ever wanted. All I need is the reveal and a confession. "You've made an art out of lying, but you haven't mastered shifting. You're doing your best holding on to that disguise, but the real Sunstar can do something that you can't—cast light."

Sunstar's eyes glow as golden light emanates from her palm, washing over the Senator and everyone else onstage. This should break the last threads of his concentration so that everyone watching will see him for the monster he is—the monster he's been all along while posing as their hero. I shield my eyes from the light that's burning so bright it's as if I've been staring into the sun. Once the light fades and I'm able to see again, I only count one Sunstar onstage, but there's no sign of the Senator.

"Run!" a pale woman shouts down from the orchestra as she runs up the aisle. Her hand glows gray for a moment before she shakes it off and keeps rushing for an emergency exit.

"That's him!" I shout.

"Which one?" Wesley asks.

I'm about to identify the Senator's disguise by clothes, but there are now multiple women in Iron-Bishop shirts fleeing for their lives.

I can't single him out, but I can go get him myself.

I leap off the stage, locking onto the Senator as I run through the crowd.

"Ness, wait!" Wyatt shouts after me. "I have to tell you something—"

But I can't stop.

If I lose the Senator, who knows what damage he can do, especially now that we're this close to exposing him for the fraud he is.

I have to make sure the sun finally sets on the Senator.

SEVENTY-EIGHT

LUMINESCENT

NESS

The Senator can be anyone.

I followed him into a hallway alongside dozens of his supporters and watched as his hand glowed gray again before the rest of his body glowed too as he transformed from a woman in an Iron-Bishop shirt into a security guard who continued down the hall as dozens of supporters filed out of an emergency exit. I keep running, noticing that there are many other doors in which he could have escaped through. This is bad. We never got proof that it was actually him posing as Sunstar, and now he can go do it again where we won't be able to track him. He can shift into her or me and claim this whole act was staged to make him look guilty, or even post a video of himself battered in a cell, as if he's verifying the lie about him being held hostage somewhere.

The Senator can not only be anyone; he can say anything to repair his image.

If I'm going to have any chance of catching him, I have to get to his team.

I read the signs and reverse course, charging back toward the greenroom in the hopes of finding Roslyn or Bishop. My rib cage hurts and I'm almost out of breath, but I push through because this is my last chance to catch the Senator in the act. He won't be stupid enough to make another public appearance while using his power, not without risking everything he stands for.

Up ahead there's a boy with curly dark hair, and when he turns, my heart freezes.

Emil.

I begin shaking, speechless.

This is rich. The Senator has no idea he's posing as a ghost. I'm furious that he's abusing Emil's image, but this mistake means I'll get to stop the Senator once and for all, just as I wanted to do in Emil's name when his death inspired me to keep fighting.

"F-firefly!" I shout, the nickname catching in my throat.

Then the Senator turns, widening Emil's eyes, which probably won't even look anything like his. "NESS!"

He runs toward me with his arms wide open and I'm running at him, and as we're closing in, I tackle him to the floor and begin punching the Senator so hard it's like I'm trying to beat Emil's face off of his.

"How . . . dare . . . you . . . pretend . . . to . . . be . . . him!"

I punctuate every word with a punch, even though it breaks my heart again to inflict pain on Emil's face.

"Ness . . . stop . . . it's . . . me. . . ."

The Senator tries shielding himself, but I pin his arms under my knees and keep beating him bloody.

"You . . . evil . . . asshole!"

If the Senator hadn't tricked me into giving him the location of our hideout, then Brighton wouldn't have killed Carolina and gone so berserk that he killed Emil too. There would've been justice in watching the Senator thrown in jail, but I'll settle for killing him myself for this offense.

"I'm . . . alive. . . . I resurrected!"

I stop punching, blood dripping off my knuckles and onto the swelling face. This can't actually be Emil. Right? The infinity-ender was driven into his heart . . . but I did see his ashes fly away. I thought that was a good sign, but . . . no, this can't be Emil. This is another trick of the Senator's, one that would've been smart to use against me if Emil was actually alive. The Senator's head is rocking side to side, dizzy. He should've dropped his disguise by now. I lean forward, trying to see if the eyes are actually hazel, but he's only squinting after my beating.

That's it.

The Senator can only know so much about Emil's appearance. Emil never posted his beautiful body online because of his dysmorphia, but he shared it with me. I lift his shirt, finding a lean chest that's clear of all scars—the scars I inflicted on Emil. It's a beautiful sight, but another lie.

"You forgot his scars," I say, grabbing his throat with both hands so he can't keep lying to me. I am going to strangle the Senator until he reverses back into himself and watch the light fade from his own eyes.

He struggles to breathe out his next words as his face goes red:

"I'm . . . safe . . . with . . . you."

I stop, releasing my grip that was so tight my fingermarks are imprinted on his neck.

The night I was trying to train Emil to be a better fighter, he said he trusted me. That he was safe with me. Our entire relationship has always revolved around saving each other, and despite the pain I've inflicted on him, he still found security in me.

"Firefly?" I ask.

"I keep . . . popping up . . . like a firefly at night. . . ."

That was my description of Emil; he remembered it, word for word.

This is him.

Emil is alive again—and I almost just killed him.

"Firefly!"

I roll off of him and rest his head in my lap as he spits out blood.

"Hi," he says weakly.

"How—how did you—how are you still you—"

Emil catches his breath instead of answering anything. I can't believe this is him. I keep wondering if this is some weird trick that someone is playing on me, like another illusion. But I can feel Emil—wiping the blood off his cheek, pushing the curls from his sweaty forehead, pressing his chest where his beating heart tells me that he will be okay after all of this.

"I'm so sorry, I swore you were the Senator. I had no idea you were alive."

"I know," Emil says, tapping my elbow.

His shirt is still lifted, and I lower it down, knowing that's what he would do for himself if I hadn't just beat him an inch from his death. He must've been reborn without the scars I inflicted on him. Of course I have to ruin this clean slate by attacking him again. "You're going to be okay, Emil, you'll heal any second now—"

"No powers," Emil breathes. "I drank the Starstifler."

He's actually done it. He bound his powers. "I'm proud of you, firefly."

"Can I still be a firefly without fire?"

"Fireflies don't actually start fires. Their light is heatless." I suddenly remember a childhood myth that I was raised on. "My mom once told me this Dominican superstition about how all fireflies—the Nimitas—are actually souls of the dead who are checking in on the living . . . on their loved ones." I stare at Emil's face—bruising and bloody, but here—and whisper, "You actually came back and found me."

"I always will," Emil says, reaching up to brush my bottom lip.

My heart is racing. "Firefly, I missed you so much and—"

I'm thrown backward with incredible force, the wind knocked out of me as I bang against one wall as Emil is launched into the other. We're both falling to the floor, when we're suspended in the air and spun around so quickly that I get whiplash. Jax and Zenon are the first ones I see, their eyes glowing.

Then there's the Senator, showing his true face.

"Bring them inside," he says.

We're telekinetically pushed into the empty greenroom, the door slamming behind us.

"Found you, Eduardo," he says.

"I thought you left."

"I can't risk you hiding from me and pulling another stunt like that," the Senator says, and I hate that we both shared the same thought. He approaches me, glaring as I'm still suspended in the air and unable to move a single muscle. It gives him a chance to punch me without getting hit back.

"Don't touch him!" Emil shouts.

Jax telekinetically slams Emil into the wall again, so hard that he cries out in pain.

"Leave him alone!" I shout.

The Senator looks between us. "I'm surprised you care so much for him considering Zenon says you were beating him to death."

"Only because I thought he was you," I say.

"I wouldn't look like that after a fight with you."

"Bold words from someone who has me restrained."

"You don't deserve fairness after the trick you just pulled."

"Don't get mad at me when your security detail failed you," I say, glancing at Zenon.

"I'll have to agree with you there, son," the Senator says, looking over his shoulder at Zenon. "His slowness with detecting our invisible guests could have cost us, but I'm still very much in this race. Besides, his ingenuity allowed me to be found quickly amid the pandemonium." His hand glows gray, revealing a tattoo that spells *Find Me*. That is genius for Zenon to track down the Senator easily. The tattoo fades away. "Give yourself some credit too, Eduardo. You utilized your power expertly with fooling everyone into believing you were the real Russell. Where is he?"

The graphic memory of Russell's accidental suicide flashes. "He killed himself with a wand when trying to kill me."

The Senator's creeping smile turns into a laugh. "He's dumber than I thought. Still, his death will suit me well as I spin the narrative against you and build back any trust you may have severed with my just-as-dumb, if not dumber, supporters who hang on to my every word." He grabs me by the throat, squeezing as hard as I was choking Emil. I look away from the Senator, gazing at Emil for as long as I can before I'm killed. "Before I kill you, son, I want you to watch me kill the boy you love."

I tear up as I fight against the telekinetic restraints, but it's useless. "Don't touch him!"

The Senator holds out his hand, and Zenon gives him a wand. "Unlike Russell, I know how to defend myself with one of these."

"He can't move! He doesn't even have his powers anymore!"

The Senator puts the tip of the wand to Emil's chin, turning his head to face him. "That's not the story I'll tell when I let the authorities know why I had to kill you."

"Don't do this! Kill me! Let him go!"

"No, kill me," Emil pleads. "Let Ness live. He's your son. Please."

The Senator laughs. "Not many can claim nobility in their deaths, but you two can. Beginning with you, Infinity Son . . ."

I can't believe I'm going to be forced to watch Emil die again. This time, final.

The Senator presses the wand between Emil's eyes and grins.

"Sir . . ." Zenon says, staring at a wall.

"What?"

"We're being watched," he says, pointing at a spot.

This must be Shine operating under her invisibility again. Hopefully with the Spell Walkers again to save the day.

The Senator casts a spell at the wall, blasting a hole through it.

"You missed," Zenon says, turning around. "They moved."

"Where?!"

Then a faceless voice says: "Stay away from my brother."

SEVENTY-NINE

REY IS KING

BRIGHTON

I'm here to save my brother.

After Emil drank the Starstifler and ran away, I sat by my—our—parents' graves. Ma and Dad aren't alive, but I carried their feelings with me back to the present. It's so hard to hate Emil after feeling all their love for him, after hearing their dreams for us as brothers. If I resurrected Ma and Dad, they wouldn't be proud of me. They would be disappointed that I chose them over the brother they saved and brought into our family so I would never be alone once they were gone.

That's when I realized I had to save Emil too, at any cost.

I'd gone online and saw the footage of the town hall of Ness, the two Sunstars, Prudencia, Wyatt, and the Spell Walkers. I didn't see Emil, but I assumed that's where he would be headed next, so I took off into the air, flying as fast as I could to Times Square. People were flooding the streets more than usual as they vacated the theater. I phased right through, dashing around for signs of Emil. Then I heard his screams while in a corridor and phased inside the greenroom while camouflaged, right as Ness was telling his father how he could take him in a fight. When I saw how bruised up Emil was, I was ready to kill everyone on the spot. But that wouldn't solve anything.

Unlike the opportunity I saw and set up expertly.

Now I stop camouflaging with the wall, revealing myself with my scythe.

"Brighton!" Emil shouts.

This is my chance to be the Infinity Savior instead of the Infinity Reaper.

I dash straight into Zenon, colliding into him so hard that he bangs into a TV screen and falls flat on his face. I cast fire-bolts at Jax, but he telekinetically deflects all of them, and I have to keep dash-dodging out of the way. He flings a couch at me, but I phase through, and as I'm winding up another fire-bolt, I'm shot in the chest with a spell.

Then another.

And another.

One more as Iron is killing me.

I sink to the floor, the scythe falling out of my hands.

"BRIGHTON!"

My gleam is trying to heal me, but I'm so weak I feel like my powers are slow.

"Enough with you," Iron says as he tries firing another spell, but the wand is empty.

"You can't kill me," I whisper.

Iron picks up the scythe. "I can cut off your head."

He swings the All-Killer, unaware that this will kill me forever. I try phasing but I still feel solid and the scythe is about to connect with my neck, when the door slams open and Prudencia telekinetically snatches the All-Killer. The scythe hovers before Prudencia as she suspends Iron in the air and binds Jax's arms behind his back as if she's telekinetically arrested him before banging him against the wall repeatedly until he's unconscious. Emil and Ness fall, and Prudencia gently rests them on the floor before they can crash.

She runs past me and hugs Emil. "I'm so happy you're alive."

"Only because of you," Emil says.

My gleam finally heals my chest completely. "You saved me—us."

Prudencia turns. "I did what was right."

"I'm doing the same. Trying to."

She stares like she doesn't know what to make of me. "We'll see."

I'm going to have to earn her trust back—everyone's. "Where are the Spell Walkers?"

"And Wyatt?" Emil adds.

"They're all helping people evacuate," Prudencia says. "It was chaotic as everyone fled."

It shows great character that the Spell Walkers saved anyone in this building considering they're all casting votes against celestialkind in this upcoming election. I can't claim that I would do the same. I know for a fact that I wouldn't. There's a long road ahead to prove I was really the Infinity Savior all along.

"Should I go help?" I ask.

"Depends on what you consider helping," Prudencia says.

"Give me a break. I came through just now."

Emil limps into my arms for a hug. "You really did, Bright. You saved me."

"Anytime," I say. That's a promise.

There's so much more I need to say to Emil that's just for Emil and not the entire world.

"We should get you healed, bro," I say.

Emil pats my shoulder. "I'm good. I need to be here for . . ." His eyes widen.

I turn, shocked to see what he already has, even though I shouldn't be.

Ness possesses the All-Killer, and he's holding the scythe to his father's throat.

EIGHTY

UNLIKE FATHER, UNLIKE SON

NESS

I could kill him now.

One slice across the Senator's throat and he will never be able to lie again.

The Senator is helpless as he's still suspended in the air, but he's smiling anyway. "Do it. Make me proud."

The scythe is shaking in my grip, like it has a mind of its own, but I'm the one who has to swing the All-Killer if I'm going to end the Senator forever. I wonder if he'll still be smiling when his head rolls off his shoulders.

I shake my head. "Unlike you, I don't go around killing my family."

"This is why you will never sit atop this world. Even the Infinity Reaper understood this before he went soft on his brother," the Senator says, disdain in his voice. "This world spins because of the people in control, and if that means sacrificing you and your mother to be a force of good for everyone, then I would do it all over again—and I would guarantee your death this time."

How is it that the Senator seems more monstrous than Luna, who had me spy and kill her enemies? Then the answer becomes really clear.

"You're my father," I say. I have worked so hard to not even think of him this way, instead only trying to refer to him as the Senator or Iron, but I own it now because I can't keep letting this truth scare me. "But I am nothing like you."

The Senator—Iron—my father sneers. "I am aware. I wanted an heir with iron bones who would continue the important work of eliminating celestialkind to save our world, just as I have and the men before me. Instead I got a son with soft bones who bends to those who will break him."

I have spent so much time thinking about how easily my father brainwashes people that I forget that he's been brainwashed too by his own father, a man who invented and manufactured power-proof vests. It's insidious how much hate we're taught as kids, groomed to believe that someone innocent is a threat because they're different. I remember my grandfather telling me that he created those vests to protect himself and his family. I see how my father would have believed that as easily as I did. Except now I understand the truth. Those power-proof vests exist as armor so those who want to kill celestials will stand a fighting chance. This family is despicable, and while I've risen above the manipulation, I'll forever carry the guilt of everyone I took down along the way. The hate speeches. The physical violence. The deaths.

"You hate me for not being more like you when you're not even being true to yourself. Don't you think your father would be ashamed of you for stealing powers and becoming a specter?"

"That was another necessary sacrifice for the greater cause."

"So you can discredit those who see you for who you are."

"And who is that, Eduardo?"

"A criminal who staged the Blackout, killing thousands. A husband and father who went on camera grieving the wife and son he wanted dead to advance his own life. A two-faced man who is lying and cheating to become the president so he can prevent unity."

"Who's lying now? I'm capable of more than two faces." My father's eyes burn like eclipses as he glows gray, transforming into Sunstar. "Such as hers, since you refuse to impersonate her again." He glows gray again, becoming Emil. "And this one that you love so much." He changes into Brighton. "This formidable threat who is so dangerous I can build my entire campaign around stopping him." He begins shifting in quick succession, turning into Prudencia and each individual Spell Walker. "All these terrorists who go around calling themselves heroes. And of course . . ." He shifts into me. ". . . you. I will commit crime after crime with your face, immortalizing you as the infamous son who cannot be trusted." He glows gray, becoming himself again. "Unless you kill me, you cannot stop me."

Going to jail for killing my father would be an important sacrifice for the world, but it would kill my soul as much as it would kill his.

I drop the scythe, the bone clattering at my feet.

"You can't manipulate me anymore. I know you want me to kill you so you can become a martyr to your cause and ruin every gleamcrafter's life. I've done enough to hurt celestials, and I won't cause any more pain."

"You're foolish if you believe you stand any chance of winning peace for your kind—all of you," my father says, glaring at everyone in the room. "These people will always fear you, will always hate you, will always want you dead. Now I'm the face of their salvation."

Brighton clears his throat. "We'll see about that." He begins walking over, but Emil tugs at his arm. "Just trust me." It takes a moment, but Emil lets go and Brighton walks past me and stares into my father's eyes as he puts a hand on his chest. "I was really tempted to rip out your poisonous heart, especially after your enforcers got my mother killed . . . after they tricked me into killing my own mother." I'm not convinced that Brighton won't execute my father right now, martyrizing him. "But I'm going to make my mom and dad proud and be the son and hero they want me to be." He phases into my father, and for a moment I think he's going to possess him, but instead he walks through and grabs something from the corner of the room. "Thankfully I have enough power, one that my parents nurtured and I started abusing. Until now." Brighton comes back around, holding up his phone. "Before I made myself known, I propped this up so everyone could see you for who you really are. Millions and millions have watched you admit to your crimes."

Then, for the first time in my life, I get to watch my father's face as he loses.

"This is a lie," he says. "I'm being held at wandpoint to say all of this."

"Nice try, but everyone saw you empty a wand into me," Brighton says.

I take Brighton's phone and scroll through the comments that are continuing to come in. There's overwhelming disappointment and disbelief in my father and responses from those who will now be casting their votes for Sunstar or sitting out the election entirely. There's a sprinkling of people who don't care about my father's crimes, which is to be expected, but they're being drowned out by a larger base of conservatives who can't excuse this. I smile as I look my father in the face and say, "They hate you. They will always hate those with powers, and that includes you now. You probably could've gotten away with your murder and terrorism, but these people draw the line at you not being one of them anymore." I hold the phone up to his face so everyone can see him as he reads their comments. "They don't want you as their president."

My father's silver tongue has been tied.

We've finally unmasked him.

I end the live chat.

"Why'd you stop it? This is great!" Brighton says.

"No one needs to see what I'm about to do."

"You are going to kill me after all," my father says.

I stare him down. "No, you're going to live. Instead of sitting on top of this world, you'll be buried alive in a prison cell for your crimes. If it were up to me, I'd have you locked up in the Bounds alongside every celestial and specter you've campaigned against, but your partner-in-crime Bishop will only set you free and we'll never find you again. The only way to keep you out of the Bounds is if you don't have powers. . . ." I go into Russell's backpack and grab the water bottle with the Starstifler along with a knife from the snack table. "Your influence and impersonations end here."

My father struggles against the telekinetic restraints, but I still cut his forearm and let his blood drip into the bottle.

"I'll never drink that," he says as I shake the potion. "You can't make me."

"Who says you have to drink it?" I ask.

I turn to Brighton. We have never liked each other, but my father is our common enemy and together we can defeat him. "For Carolina," I say, handing him the Starstifler.

"For Ma," Brighton says.

"For your mom too," Emil says.

I tear up, thrilled I'm also getting justice for her.

Brighton phases the potion inside my father's stomach and pours everything out before retracting his hand with the empty bottle.

My father begins twisting in the air as he glows gray, screaming as he keeps shifting into different body shapes against his will. Then his light fades one last time and he goes quiet.

This is it.

He has no more gleam.

He has no more influence.

My father stares daggers into me, but he can't cut me anymore.

"You're powerless," I say.

Prudencia releases her telekinetic hold and my father falls out of the air, slamming against the floor. "That was for Carolina too," she says.

I watch him squirm on the floor, breathing and sweating.

"Did we do it?" Brighton asks. "Was that enough to beat him?"

I'm nervous to get my hopes up, but I think we've got him. "He has friends in high places, but no one will risk their own necks to save someone who won't be elected president. Anyone associated with him only cares about power, and he doesn't have any—"

My father jumps up, grabbing the All-Killer, and before he can swing the scythe, I punch him between his eyes so hard that he falls back, unconscious.

I knew I would beat him in a fight.

Emil grabs my hands. "Take a breath. You're okay."

My heart is racing, but I breathe with Emil. "You didn't try talking me out of killing him."

"I knew you wouldn't," Emil says, looking me in the eyes. "That's not who you are, Ness."

I'm lucky to have a friend like Emil who has always seen me for who I am and who I am not. Like how I have killed before, but I'm not a killer. I'm a survivor who has only ever found myself under the care of hateful people who manipulated me. But now that my father has no power over me and Luna is dead, I'm going to be able to find my voice.

Find my face.

Someone is running down the hall, and I'm on edge until Wyatt enters the room.

"Bloody well done!" He then takes a couple steps back toward the doorway. "Hold on, Emil, is Brighton as good as he made himself out to be online, or should I be running for my life?"

"I'm not going to kill you," Brighton says.

"Lovely to hear, but you're not Emil."

"He's good," Emil says.

"He did a good thing," Prudencia says. "There's a difference."

Emil nods. "When it mattered most."

"Thanks, bro," Brighton says.

"Well, that move was brilliant. Everyone now knows what a tricky bastard he—" Wyatt stops himself and points at my father's body. "Wait! Did you go on and kill the tricky bastard?"

"Disempowered him," I say.

"Ah, are we not throwing him in the Bounds? I suspect no one will be breaking into that prison to save him as we did you."

It really is a shame that my father won't get to be the target in a game of Hunt the Shifter like I was. He definitely wouldn't survive the night, but forcing him to be powerless in a cell after a life of abusing his power feels more justified than an easy death.

"It's better this way" is all I say back to Wyatt.

"Your call, I believe, unless Sunstar and Shine see otherwise. They should be here any moment now with the Spell Walkers to personally deliver your father to prison."

I wish it would end there, but there's still going to be a trial ahead of us. I don't want to think about how long it will be dragged out, but as long as my father loses the election, then that will be a great start to his ultimate downfall.

Brighton comes up to Emil. "I need to go back to Ma and Dad. I want to spend some time with them before I make my next move."

"What's your next move?" Emil asks.

Brighton glances at Prudencia. "I still have to prove I'm good."

Prudencia crosses her arms, but I see the hope in her eyes.

I also see the determination in his. "Brighton?"

"Yeah?"

"You finally did something right with those powers," I say. That's my thanks.

Brighton nods. He grabs the All-Killer and tells Emil, "I'll come find you soon, bro."

As Brighton flies and phases through the ceiling, the Spell Walkers arrive with Sunstar and Shine. They're all speechless as they see my father and his bodyguards unconscious, but the Spell Walkers step over their bodies so they can hug newly resurrected Emil. There have been so many losses, but at least the best soul I have ever known is back with us. Eva stays strong as she heals Emil's bloody face, undoing the damage I did to him.

Sunstar approaches me, and I'm nervous. "How are you doing?" she asks.

"You don't have to be nice to me. I ruined your image."

"That was never your fault, and even if it was, I believe in showing grace to those who are willing to change."

"Even someone like him?" I ask, nodding at my father.

"Even someone like him," Sunstar says. "But you are not like him. Whether you like it or not, you will be the face for those who not only have changes of heart but act on them."

I don't like that I'm still going to be talked about in political circles, but there are certainly far worse legacies.

"I'm still sorry," I say.

"I accept your apology. I'm sorry for everything you've been through. You were never given a fair chance at life, but if I'm elected president, I promise that you will be pardoned for your crimes so you can go and discover yourself outside your father's shadow."

I'm tearing up as I shake Sunstar's hand, sealing this promise.

Emil hugs me.

"Do I really deserve this?" I ask him.

"I can't think of anyone else who deserves a second chance more than you."

My father molded my heart into hating innocent people and Luna sharpened me into a weapon, but for the first time in my life, I'm going to get to shape my appearance and show everyone who I really am. I don't know what that looks like yet, but I'm free to find out.

EIGHTY-ONE
SAVIOR

BRIGHTON

I'm at the cemetery, scrolling through social media.

In an alternate universe where Emil wasn't my brother, I would have never been on the front lines of this war and I would currently be at home creating Celestials of New York content around Iron's crimes. But Emil is my brother, and I not only followed him into battle, I took charge with my own army and became the deadliest weapon this country has ever seen. I tap in and out of videos where influencers are debating if I've been a hero all along or a villain who performed one heroic act because it was more about saving myself instead of the whole world. It's neither. I did this for my family . . . what's left of it.

I put down my phone, looking back and forth between Ma's and Dad's graves and the ingredients for the resurrection ritual. It's not too late. I proved that I can be responsible when I didn't rip out Iron's heart. Maybe everyone will be forgiving if I choose to resurrect my parents too, just this one time. I've earned this by taking down the greatest threat to our society. There's this voice in the back of my head telling me that I haven't. The voice is telling me that I'm the greatest threat to our society, and it's putting myself above natural and unnatural laws that proves this.

"I can't be trusted," I say, grateful that Ma and Dad can't talk back because if they agreed their words might do the impossible and break me.

There's an inky black shadow in the clear sky, revealing itself to be Nox as it comes closer. As Nox is descending, I see that Emil is riding the phoenix, alone.

"Nice ride," I say.

"The best," Emil says, dismounting the phoenix. "You good?"

"That's the question everyone's asking."

Emil sits across from me. "How are you going to answer them?"

"That's the question I'm asking myself."

"If you were covering your actions for Celestials of New York, what would you say?"

I choke up because I know the answer immediately. "That I abused my power instead of being the hero this world deserved . . . and that I need to give up my powers."

Emil reaches into his backpack, pulling out the knife and Star-stifler, just as he did for himself this morning. "I was hoping you'd say that."

I grab the potion, stunned that something so little and light can disempower me versus the scythe, which is heavy and huge and would vanquish me forever. "I'm going to go online, one last time," I say. "The world deserves an apology." I hold up my phone, opening Instagram, when Emil takes it from me.

"You've got me here to film you," Emil says, grinning.

"You really want to be my cameraman again?"

"Nope, but I'm being your brother. This is a nice full-circle moment."

I could've never imagined when I first started reporting for Celestials of New York that all of this would have happened, but it's nice that I haven't lost my brother after all the chaos.

Emil aims the phone's camera at me. "You're live in three . . . two . . . one."

I stare into the camera, but I don't burst with any of my usual performative energy. I'm owning who I really am, even the ugly parts—especially the ugly parts. I try composing myself, but my knees are shaking because I'm so nervous. I haven't been this scared since I was dying in the hospital before my powers surfaced. If I had made different choices, I wouldn't need to be this scared. I can go back through time, but I unfortunately can't change it. All I can do is own it.

"Hi, everyone. You probably know by now that I'm Brighton Rey, but you don't actually know me. Sometimes we start to believe we know someone because we follow their every move on social media, but no one is ever really honest about who they are. Especially me. I'm going to tell you all the truth before I sign off on the internet, probably forever. I grew up wanting to be a famous hero, like the Spell Walkers. I created Celestials of New York to feel closer to a community that I dreamed of becoming part of, and I got really jealous when I discovered my brother had special powers and famous past lives. And, Emil, I'm sorry for shouting your business to millions of people. You didn't want anyone knowing about your past lives, and I told everyone to hurt you." I stop, looking my brother in the eyes, and he accepts my apology with a nod. "Our parents raised me better than this, but after I watched our dad die this year, I was broken. I became so desperate to never find myself that close to death again that I seized the chance to become an immortal hero. Except I wasn't a hero. Emil believes that heroes shouldn't have body counts, but I have so much blood on my hands." I flinch, thinking about all the lives I've taken. "Killing in self-defense is one thing, but I was pursuing targets." I can't believe I was going to kill Darren; he's just a kid. "I went from being someone who was scared of dying to someone who used his powers to kill others. That's why I don't deserve to possess these abilities anymore." I hold up the Starstifler and the knife, turning my back to the camera so no one has to watch the blade slice my palm. I squeeze my blood into the vial for all to see, feeling like a Starstifler influencer as my wound heals. "I chose to drink the Reaper's Blood, and now I'm choosing to drink the Starstifler."

I look at Ma's and Dad's graves, knowing that one day I will die and find them in the afterlife.

Then at Emil, who is alive, here and now, and wants his brother back in his life.

I drink every last drop of the Starstifler for my family . . . and the world too.

As my insides begin burning up, I try bracing myself with thoughts of what it was like having powers: how victorious I felt when I cast that first fire-bolt into the sky; how safe I felt when I was phasing or camouflaging, like I couldn't be touched or found by Death; how remarkable it was to regrow limbs or heal wounds; how free I felt when I was dashing or flying; how invincible I felt when I resurrected; and how beautiful it was to go back in time and remember that Emil and I were both raised to be kings. Silver and sapphire flames consume me, burning so hot that I wish this wasn't happening, that I wish I could change my mind, but I accept my fate because of all the hell I raised by having powers: how I would rip hearts out of chests; how I spied on people; how I went back in time to find a weapon that could kill my brother; and how I killed my own mother with a fire-bolt. I shout in agony, gesturing for Emil to stay back until the last of my silver and sapphire flames die out.

I'm no longer the Infinity Reaper, but I'm forever Brighton Rey, a king that made his family proud by removing his crown.

EIGHTY-TWO
THE STRONGEST POWER ABOVE ALL

EMIL

We're no longer Infinity Kings.

I thought I would die before I saw this day—I guess I did.

This journey has felt so long even though it's only been about two months since I came into my powers and a month since Brighton stole his powers the night of the Crowned Dreamer. It's wild thinking about how much has happened in that time: fighting alongside the Spell Walkers; battling the Blood Casters and stopping the ritual that would've made Luna immortal; our entire family being abducted and abused at different times; opening up to love during war; too many death scares; losing Ma forever; retrocycling into the past for the Starstifler and the All-Killer and our brotherhood; and getting killed, obviously. But we're not only alive again, we're looking out for each other as brothers instead of facing off as enemies.

I kneel with Brighton, steadying him as he groans and catches his breath.

"I'm proud of you, Bright. Ma and Dad would be too."

Brighton stares at their graves. "I hope so." He flexes his fingers, like he's waiting for fire to burst out of his palm. It's like he's a kid again, playing pretend. "I had it all, and now I have nothing."

"You got me."

"I meant my power."

"You got that too."

"Everything is gone. I can't cast fire. I can't fly. I can't—"

"That stuff doesn't matter. Do you remember that old celestial saying?"

Brighton's confused as hell at first, but I know he's got that memory in him because it's what sparked his idea to launch that Spell Walkers of New York feature. Then he looks up at me and sighs. "I remember."

I get that he would rather be throwing fire-bolts and soaring through the sky, but our battle didn't end because we kicked each other's asses—it ended because we care about each other. "'The strongest power above all is a living heart.' We used our hearts to save the world from a true tyrant."

Brighton nods, but there's still this look in his eye that tells me he wishes he'd killed Iron. "My heart isn't as powerful as yours," he says.

"Is this what we're fighting over next? Who has the biggest heart?"

"No more wars," Brighton says, tearing up. "But you would win that one too."

"I wasn't trying to beat you. I was just trying to get you back."

"You did both, bro," Brighton whispers. I know it must pain him to admit this because he really wanted to be seen as the strongest gleamcrafter on the planet, but he's letting his heart do the talking and thinking. "Anyone else would have killed me if given the chance."

"It's messed up, but I would've died before killing you."

"That's why your heart is stronger than mine."

"Or weaker because I wouldn't take you down after everything you did."

Brighton seems haunted, flinching like he's remembering the devastation he's caused. "I wish I could blame everything on the powers, like having ghost blood in my system made me soulless, but that was all me. I committed all those crimes. . . . I took those lives. I swore I could have mounting body counts and still be worshipped as a hero. A god. I'm just an eighteen-year-old who should've been more like his twin." He grabs my shoulder. "I'm really proud of you, Emil. You had your powers longer than me and never killed a single soul, whereas I vanquished many. I wish I could get away with that, but I have to turn myself in."

My heart squeezes, really not feeling so powerful right now. "Are you for real?"

Brighton stares at the sky. "The world knows I have blood on my hands. I don't get to keep walking free in it."

I hate this thought, but with Iron and Brighton locked up for their crimes, this could shine the way to a Sunstar victory, where she will create her Luminary Union to make this country, this world, a safer place to live.

"So I'm still losing you," I say.

"You'll visit," he says, running his fingers through the grass like it'll be the last time he'll get to do so. "But we were always supposed to go find our own ways. What are you going to do now?"

I just sit still, staring at headstones and wondering what I want mine to say at the end of this life. I was the Infinity Son and a Spell Walker. A son and a brother. Maybe I'll become a Halo Knight. A lover. A father.

"I don't know yet, but I've got this one life to figure it out," I say. "Promise you'll live enough for me too?"

"I promise."

Sitting between our mother's and father's graves, Brighton and I fist-bump and whistle, reborn.

EPILOGUE
CHANGE

NESS

Election Day.

The countdown to this day has been stressful, but ever since the country watched me, Sunstar, and the Spell Walkers turn my father over to the police, opinions began changing for us overnight. That's when I knew I had to hit the campaign trail alongside Sunstar and Shine, so we could change as many minds as possible by clearing up my father's lies. Running those circuits was uncomfortable, but as each day passed, I found more and more peace with taking the stage again because I know I'm on the right side of history this time. There is still—and always will be—hate for people with powers, but the polls are showing that many conservative voters are sitting out this election because they're furious at my father for causing the Blackout or they don't like Bishop enough to vote him into office or they still believe the conspiracy that invisible celestials will be watching them at the polling stations. Then there are those who are voting for Sunstar after admitting they were wrong to believe in my father's propaganda. I've spoken with many of these citizens across the country, sympathizing because I was raised on the same lies.

Returning to New York this morning felt strange because I still don't technically have a home outside the house I grew up in, which has remained empty since my father's imprisonment. I can't go back there—I don't want to go back there. That place will forever haunt me: being taught to hate and fear celestials while enjoying breakfast in the dining room; the office where many devastations were planned; how empty the whole house felt after Mom's murder; and even how my own bedroom became my cage when my power was being exploited. I could have that entire manor demolished and rebuild something new on its grounds, but I don't want generations of poisonous roots invading my home and soul ever again.

For now, Sunstar has arranged for another hotel, just as she has during our campaign visits, but even though it's a couple hours after midnight, I'm not ready to go back yet. I'm staying here in the convention center, currently sitting in one of the suite's bedrooms. Sunstar and her family, Shine, and key members of their staff are in the living area with their special guests: the Spell Walkers, Prudencia, and Emil. Everyone was invited to await the results because we've worked for this moment together. Things are thankfully shaping up in our favor, with promising projections in California, Washington, and Illinois, and we are already securing many states on the East Coast. Our biggest celebration tonight was when we locked down New York, which was home territory for both Sunstar and Iron, but it appears the New Yorkers who were supporting my father shifted against him after we shone a light about the Blackout that threw our city into disarray.

I lean forward on the bed, eyes glued to the TV when it shuts off.

"You need a break," Emil says as he comes in, setting down the remote and closing the door behind him.

"We need to win," I say.

"You've done everything you can."

"I could've done more. We were so close with turning Texas and Florida. Maybe we should have spent an extra day there and—"

"You might be able to look like anyone, but you can't be everywhere."

If only I could clone myself.

Emil sits beside me and grabs my hand. "Instead of being hard on yourself, be proud of who you are."

"Whoever that is."

I stare at our hands, how our fingers are chained together, like we're becoming one fist.

Ever since the day my father and Brighton went to jail, Emil and I haven't had a real chance to sit down together. We were both busy giving statements to officers about everything that went down, making sure that Iron or Brighton weren't eligible to be bailed out. Then, that evening, Sunstar invited me on the campaign trail, but I didn't want to go because Emil was clearly devastated to be losing his brother in a very different way from how he'd just lost his mom. Emil pushed me to travel with Sunstar and Shine because he knew I wouldn't be able to live with myself if Sunstar lost this election. Point proven, because after all the traveling, sometimes a couple states per day with the help of teleporters, I still wish I had done more.

"I don't want to tell you who you are," Emil says. "You've had enough people forcing you to become someone you're not your entire life. But if you're still confused on who you are, maybe start with who you're not?"

"I'm not my father." That's becoming my mantra.

"You're definitely not your father."

"I'm not a Blood Caster."

"You're a hero."

"Isn't that telling me who I am?"

Emil blushes. "Oh. My bad."

I smile. "You're the one person I trust to tell me who I am."

His cheeks grow redder. "Really?"

"Tell me who you see, firefly."

Emil's hazel gaze is burning. "I see a brave guy with a huge heart. I hated being famous, and if I had your power, I would've run away and become someone else instead of the Infinity Son. That pressure was too much, but you never let that get to you. Instead you kept risking your neck to put out the fires your father started. And I really admire how you've always used your voice for what you thought was right, even when you were wrong. It says a lot about your character about how much you care about making a difference instead of settling for how things are. But above everything, I see my hero."

My heart is pounding. "I'm your hero?"

"You're my hero, Ness. That's who you are."

"But I failed to save you," I say, thinking about how I held his corpse.

"And my powers brought me back so I could live my life right," Emil says.

I stare at Emil—the shadows under his hazel eyes, the curly brown hair, the pink lips—and I'm still so happy that he's here, talking to me, holding me, breathing. "I still can't believe it's you."

"And you're you." Emil touches my heart, and then his own. "It's always been you, Ness."

I'm even happier than when Emil came back from the dead because now he's choosing me in this life.

I lean in to kiss Emil, when we hear screaming.

I tense up, nervous, until we hear whistling and clapping. Did we win another battleground state? Two? We rush out of the bedroom and find everyone jumping up and down and hugging and high-fiving each other. Iris is leaning forward on the couch, crying as Eva wraps her arms around her. Wesley and Ruth are dancing with baby Esther. And Prudencia spots us, her hands over her mouth as she nods and nods and nods. I feel like I'm in a trance as I walk through the sea of celebrating staff, getting close up to the screen, where I read the declaration:

NICOLETTE SUNSTAR
FIRST CELESTIAL PRESIDENT

I'm in disbelief as the news anchors talk about the swing states that brought us to victory: Pennsylvania, Alaska, Michigan, Wisconsin, Arizona, and Georgia. Those are all states I visited where I drowned out my father's lies and showed people the truth.

Sunstar is hugging her husband and daughter, then Shine, then campaign staff.

Then she sees me.

I wonder if she also sees a hero like Emil does.

Sunstar walks over with a soft smile.

"Congratulations, President Sunstar," I say, shaking her hand.

"Thank you, Ness. I couldn't have done this without you. Your voice was critical."

"This is probably the only time I wish I could see my father's face right now."

"That would be quite the sight, but because of you, we'll never have to see him inside the White House casting darkness upon us all. I will lead this country to a brighter age."

"You've already won," I say with a smile. "You don't have to keep campaigning."

"No, but I now have to make good on those promises—all of them."

This includes Sunstar pardoning me for my crimes. I'm free.

"I'll let you get back to your people. Congratulations again."

I'm about to walk away when Sunstar invites me in for a hug, and I go straight into her arms. Her embrace makes me miss my mom so bad.

"Join us when we go onstage?" Sunstar asks. "Please?" she adds when I don't answer immediately.

"Yes, Madam President."

I go over to the Spell Walkers, hugging them all one by one, and they congratulate me as if I've been elected president. They've done their part on the campaign trail too, dividing and conquering in different states to repair the image of the Spell Walkers as heroes instead of terrorists and speaking about the future of the Luminary Union, which will protect the country once Sunstar takes office. Then I join Emil and Prudencia, who are holding each other's forearms, crying together.

"I wish they were here," Emil says.

"Who?" I ask.

"My family. Ma, Dad. Brighton."

I'm still surprised that Brighton turned himself in.

"Do you regret not resurrecting your parents?" I ask.

"No, but I would've loved for them to see this moment."

"I would've loved the same for mine," Prudencia says.

"They're all watching from the beyond. Hopefully with my mom."

"And Atlas," Emil adds, glancing at the Spell Walkers.

No one could get Maribelle to be here. She's chosen to be alone since Atlas died again, only telling Iris that she needs to settle into her grief since there's no vengeance to seek out with Luna dead. I'm not very close with her, but I hope she's proud that all the hard work of the Spell Walkers, including Atlas, has paid off in getting this win for celestialkind.

An hour later, Vice President–Elect Shine Lu takes the stage, thanking the American people who turned up in record numbers to make their voices heard, especially after the divisiveness this country has experienced since the Blackout. Then President-Elect Nicolette Sunstar comes out to roaring applause and delivers a victory speech where she echoes her many promises that she will be devoting her life to in order to create a better, united world for everyone—those with powers and those without.

Music is blasting as Sunstar invites her staff, family, and friends to join her and Shine onstage. Just like I've been feeling since the campaign trail, it's surreal to show my own face to the general public. This is even more surreal, though. I originally envisioned this moment with my father being voted into office, but instead I'm celebrating the better person's victory.

Sunstar's eyes glow as she casts bursts of golden light above everyone like fireworks.

Change is coming for our country and for me too.

Soon enough, I will no longer be a specter who can shape-shift. I'm going to drink the Starstifler and discover who I am now that no puppet masters are pulling at my strings. That freedom will be terrifying and liberating, but that's how reinvention should feel. That's how it felt when Eduardo Iron died so I could become Ness Arroyo. Now that I'm shedding the skin of a politician's son and an alchemist's servant, I'm ready to see who I will be.

I'm holding on to who I'm not—my father—and who I am—a hero—as my north stars.

I want so much more and that begins with someone I want in the next phase of my life.

Underneath the glowing lights, I pull Emil into a kiss, my heart pounding for this boy who makes me want to be better even though he's already accepted me for who I am. I can't wait to get to know him better as I'm also getting to know myself.

On this stage, I reflect on all my dreams of acting, of performing for audiences this size, of bowing during standing ovations. Pursuing that is not something I see in my near future.

There will be no more role-playing.

There will only be me.

THE ATLAS OF STARS

MARIBELLE

I'm returning to the world, as if I'm resurrecting.

It's been over two weeks since Atlas died again, and I've been living alone in Wesley and Ruth's cottage while they and the other Spell Walkers traveled the country in advance of the election. The lightness I felt from discovering Sunstar's victory was short-lived because of course I'm happy that Atlas's death wasn't in vain, but the dream was to share a life with him in the world Sunstar and Shine are hoping to create. I sink deeper into the bed, hugging the pillow that still smelled of him, wishing I could somehow track Atlas's scattered ashes and resurrect him so he could be here to hold me back.

I wish Tala were here to hold me too, but I've needed to keep my space from her as I grieve Atlas.

Today I showered.

Braided my hair.

Changed into fresh clothes.

Cooked an easy breakfast and ate most of it.

Accepted an invite over text for a meeting with the Spell Walkers and our president-elect.

And I took to the skies, stopping mid-flight to cry because of how badly I wish Atlas were flying alongside me.

I arrive at Sunstar's campaign headquarters, where there are still deflating balloons and confetti all over the floor. There are boxes all over the workstations and cubicles as staff and volunteers are packing up the office. I get some looks, but I detect no danger—or even hate. I may have been fighting for my life on the streets, but these people are the reason why the public knows about Sunstar's efforts. I offer some quick nods of appreciation on the way to a conference room where all the Spell Walkers are gathered around a long table with Sunstar and Shine at the end.

"Maribelle!" Wesley stops rocking Esther's stroller to give me a tight hug.

"Hey, Wes."

Ruth's hug is more gentle, loving. "I'm so happy you're here."

Eva holds on to my wrists. "Do you need anything?"

"I'm fine," I say.

Anything I need, I want to fend for myself. With Atlas gone and Tala away, I have to learn how to take better care of myself so that I don't always fall apart whenever I lose someone. That could be any day now since I was marked for a life of grief after descending from those brothers with deathlike powers.

Iris approaches. I'm expecting a handshake, when instead she hugs me. "I'm always around if you need to talk."

I thank Iris before taking the seat between her and Wesley. I look down the table at Sunstar and Shine. "Congratulations."

Sunstar smiles. "Thank you, Maribelle. We appreciate you joining us, especially during this difficult time."

"I'm no stranger to grief." I'm not even a stranger to grieving Atlas.

Shine nods. "You're a strong and capable young woman, but should you need grief counseling, we have celestial specialists at the ready. Just say the word."

Accepting guidance from someone I won't get close to isn't the worst idea in the world. "Thank you," I say. I do hate having everyone's eyes on me. "I'm assuming you called us in for the Luminary Union."

Sunstar pulls a folder out of her bag. "That's certainly one of the three reasons, but there's something I wanted to personally show you first," she says, sliding the folder across the table. "We have reconstruction plans for the Nightlocke Conservatory with a wing devoted to all those who were lost in the Blackout. We'd also like to have a special Hall of Heroes for the fallen Spell Walkers."

I open the folder, and Iris leans in, looking at sketches for golden statues of Sera, Bautista, Mama, Papa, and Iris's parents. They all look heroic with their proud postures and smiles, like they had just saved the day.

"This is amazing," Iris says, her voice cracking. "Thank you."

"Our country needs to know the truth about the Spell Walkers," Sunstar says.

"There's another statue on the back," Shine adds.

I flip the page and tear up as I see a sketch of Atlas in gold. I wish it existed right now so I could sit and stare. "He's beautiful," I say.

"The world will never know that he died twice, but we will make sure they know they're alive because of his heroism," Sunstar says.

Celestialkind will truly be shown respect under the Sunstar-Shine administration.

Then Sunstar and Shine get into all the Luminary Union business, reminding us that they want to unite vigilante factions across the country into a single division that will be supported by government resources in order to abolish the Enforcer Program so celestials aren't assaulted and killed by officers that fear them for their powers. A council formed by Sunstar and Shine would carefully evaluate every Luminary to do their best to make sure no one would abuse their authority.

Sunstar gestures at us. "Now we'd like to know who is interested in becoming a Luminary."

Wesley and Ruth turn to each other before he says, "We've been giving this a lot of thought, but after everything that's happened, we'd like to take some time to focus on our family. Esther is getting older, and if something happens to me on the field, I don't want her to only remember me as that guy who was always running in and out of the house."

"Or that she was raised by me and my clones," Ruth adds. She seems nervous as she looks at the rest of us. "We're so sorry if this puts you out."

Eva pats Ruth's back. "You don't have to apologize. Especially not to us because . . ."

"Because we're on the same page," Iris says, grabbing Eva's hand.

"We've been discussing our plans for the future. Travels, marriage, starting a family. It would be an honor to die making this world a better place, but I would rather grow old with Eva and be there for our children and their children. I'd like for our family to have a home."

"We're rooting for a successful term, but if the Luminary Union fails and you're not voted back into office, we're scared that we're going to get sucked into the fight again anyway," Eva says. "It would break our hearts if we didn't get a chance to really live in this world while it was safe to do so."

"If things ever got desperate, you have my fists," Iris says.

"And my healing hands," Eva says.

"And my very fast feet," Wesley says.

"And every me," Ruth says.

"We will always be Spell Walkers," Iris says, touching her heart. "But we need time to live before we find ourselves as statues in the Hall of Heroes."

Sunstar and Shine are nodding, but I don't think this is how they thought this meeting was going to go. Out of every vigilante faction across the country, the Spell Walkers have always been the most famous—and sometimes the most infamous. Having the same celestials who have fought for everyone, even when the public was nothing but awful to us, is a huge selling point in building trust for the Luminary Union. But they're all going to live out my dreams.

"I take it you're not ready yet, Maribelle," Sunstar says.

I kick my legs up on the table. "Count me in."

Sunstar's eyes widen. "Really?"

The others echo her surprise.

"I have no one to start a home or family with," I say. "But I do still have fire in me."

"We're delighted to have you on board," Sunstar says.

"I have conditions, of course," I say.

"We're listening."

"The Spell Walker name lives on within the Luminary Union. I don't want my family's legacy just gone under your group. I will work with your council in determining who becomes a Spell Walker, but I get the final say. And I will not be pressured to bind my phoenix powers. If I drink the Starstifler, I'll only be left with my visions, and I would definitely foresee my own death as I step onto the battlefield. I don't plan on dying before I get my own chance to live like my family here," I say, nodding at the Spell Walkers—retired Spell Walkers. "Lastly, I want them to get severance packages. If you're going to be paying Luminaries, you can take care of the predecessors who helped you get elected."

Sunstar and Shine exchange glances before agreeing to my terms.

I swing my feet back onto the floor and get up. "Looking forward to doing business with you."

Sunstar calls after me.

"What?"

"There was one more item on the agenda," Sunstar says. "Emil Rey is here to see you."

"What for?"

"A personal matter. He's waiting for you in my office."

I wouldn't have gotten out of bed for Emil, but I'm curious enough that I go down the hall and find him sitting in the chair opposite of

Sunstar's desk. I let myself in, and Emil jumps like he's scared, accidentally stepping on some long brown sack. He stutters a hello.

"Why are you so surprised? You requested me," I say, sitting in Sunstar's chair.

"I didn't think you'd actually come."

I cross my arms and lean back. "I'm here. What do you want?"

"Look, I know I'm nowhere near your favorite person, and I'm not trying to be in your space. But I wanted to offer my condolences in person about Atlas. I hope being able to see him again has given you more closure this time." Emil is too intimidated to make eye contact. He'll only be more scared of me if I snap about how his condolences still wouldn't be necessary if he had helped me kill June when we had the chance, but I can't keep pinning the blame on him. He's right that losing Atlas again did come with some closure this time around.

"Thanks. Atlas thought you were a good guy. I do too."

Emil looks up, smiling a little. "I also wanted to pass along an apology from Brighton. He's sorry for threatening you, Atlas, Tala, and everyone else. He was so obsessed with getting that ritual from you—"

"I'm sorry for helping him become the Infinity Reaper," I say. I can't be mad at Emil and not own my faults too. "Your mother would still be alive if Brighton didn't have those powers."

Emil's haunted stare pierces me. "So much would be different, but ultimately, it's on Brighton. He's the one that abused those powers. And now he's going to pay for his crimes."

I saw the footage of Emil and Brighton walking into the police station. Some of it, at least. It was too hard watching their painful, tearful goodbye out on the street. I would ask how Brighton is doing, but I'm still angry that he betrayed my trust. There's a future where I go visit him, but that's not anytime soon.

"Did you come because of condolences and apologies?" I ask.

"There's something I wanted to give you." Emil grabs the long brown sack at his feet and reaches inside. "I don't know what's going down with the Luminary Union, but you're the only person who can be trusted with this." He pulls out that bone scythe that Brighton was wielding when he threatened our lives. "This is the All-Killer. Keon Máximo created it to kill absolutely anyone. Even immortals. I'm sure you're not surprised that I don't have the heart to ever use this. . . ."

"But you know I'll kill someone."

"If it meant saving the world . . . even if it's just your world."

I would have killed Brighton with that scythe if he was still the Infinity Reaper—and I think this is Emil's way of telling me he would have understood.

I take the scythe, admiring how ancient it looks, and how safe I feel with it in my possession.

"I'll wield it well," I say.

"Please do," Emil says. "I'll stop bothering you in a minute, but I wanted to talk about our family link for a sec."

"You're not actually my father," I say.

"I know, I know. But after I died, I resurrected with Keon's and Bautista's memories. They've been fading away ever since I bound my powers, but I still remember a lot. I thought I could tell you some stories of how much Bautista and Sera loved you, and then you can retrocycle to experience all of that yourself. I went back to when I was born, and it's really healed the struggles I've had since discovering the family secret. Maybe going back might heal you too."

There's this part of me that doesn't want to be healed, that wants to live in my grief and be furious at all the injustices. But Atlas didn't sacrifice himself so I could be miserable. He died so I could live.

"Tell me everything you know," I say.

A few days later—four, maybe five—I'm walking out of the Shed with my latest acquisition from the underground market and I continue on through Brooklyn by foot. Lately I've been flying between my latest campsite upstate and the city, but today I'm choosing to go for a stroll to help battle my nerves. Most people wouldn't deal with nerves by walking among those who still think it's acceptable to give me dirty looks even though the Spell Walkers are being cleared of terrorism charges for the Blackout, but let them glare. I refuse to be run out of the city I'm tasked with saving, so anyone who hates me better get used to seeing me enjoying meals in restaurants, exercising at the gym, dancing in nightclubs, and existing everywhere else.

There is one living person whose eyes I do want on me, and I'm finally seeing her soon.

I haven't seen Tala since the night Atlas died—since the night she almost died too. I watched over her as she recovered in the center, but once she was fine, I had to take off. I'd flown to a beach in the middle of the night, unleashing streams of fire into the ocean and screaming until my voice was gone. I'd slept in the sand, woken up by the sun burning me, and then I ran through the beach, the woods, the streets until my lungs and ribs couldn't take it anymore. No one had any means to reach me until I found my way back to the cottage, where Wesley had left behind a new phone, programmed with everyone's numbers, including Tala's. An hour didn't pass where I was so tempted to call her, wanting to be wrapped up in her arms as I cried, but she deserves so much more than to be my caretaker.

Very early this morning, when the sun hadn't finished rising, I walked for miles and miles through the woods, getting lost. Considering I've spent the past few weeks getting worked up over little things like my drinking water being too warm, running out of toothpaste, and my apple spoiling the morning I was finally wanting to eat it, it's a miracle that I didn't have a panic attack in the middle of the woods. Instead I sat in the discomfort, finding my way back by foot instead of flying overhead until I could find my bright yellow tent. Then I heard the birdsong of two young phoenixes, and I followed their music until I found them in a nest, identifying them as evergreen blazers. It made me think of Tala's parents, reincarnated. It made me wish I was lost in the woods with her. I had found my way back to my base and immediately flew toward town until I had a signal so I could text Tala: *It's Mari. Can I see you?*

I hung around in the sky, waiting for a response. I would've understood if she never wanted to see my face again, but that wasn't the case.

Tala texted, *Of course. Are you still in NY?*

Yeah, but I can meet you anywhere. Whatever you want.

I'll come into the city this afternoon, she said. *Meet me at the loft. 5pm.*

It was nice connecting with the Spell Walkers when I returned to the world, but I wasn't bursting with excitement like I was at the idea of reconnecting with Tala. That energy has continued living in me throughout all my errands today, including a meeting with Shine and archivists about the Hall of Heroes where I was given a power-proof vest that once belonged to Mama, lunch with Prudencia to see if she was interested in becoming a Spell Walker, and then finally the Shed to pick up something for Tala.

It's nearing five, so I take off into the air, flying to the loft and landing on the rooftop. I've been appreciating my time out in the wilds, but I'm a city girl and this rooftop garden is giving me the best of both worlds. I sit on a stone bench, holding the bag with Tala's gift in my lap, and wait. I close my eyes, meditating under the sun, reflecting on how strong I am to have survived everything I've been through, when drizzling rain falls onto my skin. I open my eyes to find the sun obscured by the silhouette of a girl on a phoenix. Roxana lands on the rooftop, stepping in a puddle of her own making.

Tala Castillo is hiding her beautiful face behind her beaked mask, which I haven't seen her wearing since my last visit to the Shed. She dismounts Roxana and stands there.

"Hi, Maribelle."

"Hi, Tala."

I get up, wanting to run into her arms, but she doesn't even seem to want to be around me.

"How are you feeling?" Tala asks, leaning back on Roxana's sturdy body.

It's hard for anyone to know which days I have and haven't been punching rock faces since my power keeps healing my broken bones and torn skin. That's why I have to be honest about what I'm feeling. "Some days have felt impossible, but today feels like . . . possibilities." I wish I could see her reaction. "What's with the mask?"

Tala traces a finger along the beak. "The weight of the mask helps me keep a clear head and focused on my cause. Between the two assaults at the New Ember Sanctuary, we lost many Halo Knights. Those tragedies have led to bittersweet promotions. I'm now co-lieutenant commander of the Bronze Wings alongside Wyatt for our work with the Starstifler and defeating Luna and the Blood Casters. This work is how I continue honoring my parents."

"Congratulations, Tala." Between avenging our parents and now continuing the fight in honor of them, it's feeling more and more like Tala and I were always destined to cross paths. "Believe it or not, I'm going to be working directly with the Luminary Union to lead the next wave of Spell Walkers since the others have stepped down to focus on their personal lives."

"Didn't you want the same?"

"That life I wanted is gone, but it's hard to hate the battlefield when that's how I met Atlas . . . and you too."

Again, I want her to take off this mask that's acting like a shield.

"I see," Tala says. "I wish you all the best in your new role."

"You too."

The silence between us is killing me, like we both have words to share but I'm scared of hurting her and she's scared of getting hurt by me again.

"I got you something," I say, grabbing the present and finally closing the distance between us.

Tala stares at the brown package. "For what?"

"As a thank-you for all you've done for me."

Tala squeezes the package and stiffens; she's figured out what it is. She unwraps it slowly as if giving herself time to process what else it can be because getting this wrong would only break her heart, but she's so right. The brown paper falls to her feet. "My jacket," Tala says, holding up the black cactus-leather jacket with yellow-feathered sleeves she traded in at the Shed so we could get a valuable ingredient to brew the Starstifler. Tala begins crying under her mask. "How?"

"I went to the vendor, praying to the stars she still had it. She did, and I got it back for you."

"How? What did you trade?"

"This morning an archivist gave me one of Mama's old power-proof vests. I loved it, but the vest seemed like a fair trade since your parents gave you that jacket."

Tala shakes her head. "But now your mother's vest is gone."

"This jacket was always yours, and needed to be again."

I wanted to hold on to Mama's vest and wear it to battle, but considering the only other undeniably valuable items I own are the scythe and the resurrection ritual, I chose to part with history—with a very serious threat that if this vest is given to anyone who makes a mockery of the Spell Walkers, then the Shed will burn in dark yellow flames.

Tala puts on her jacket, looking just like when I met her. Roxana brushes her face against the sleeve, sniffing the feathers that used to belong to her. "My parents feel close again," she says. "Thank you, Maribelle."

"You're welcome, Lieutenant Castillo."

Tala bounces, almost as if she's thinking her feathered sleeves are wings.

I'm beaming.

"What?" she asks, cocking her head.

"You're different . . . lighter. It's like I'm meeting the girl you were before your parents died."

"I'll never be that girl again," Tala says as she looks up at the sky. "But I do feel like a bird freed from her cage."

"You deserve to fly around this world in peace, Tala."

"As do you, Maribelle."

"Naturally we've both chosen to keep fighting."

"Peace doesn't create itself," Tala says, grabbing the discarded wrapping paper off the ground and tearing off a big piece. She begins folding a paper bird by the looks of the thin wings. "Maybe we can create an alliance between the Halo Knights and Spell Walkers."

My heart is in my throat as I say, "Maybe you and I can be more."

She stops folding. "Such as?"

"More than partners in battle. Partners in life, maybe."

Tala pockets the paper bird and bows her head, the mask's beak pointing down. "I do not mean to be insensitive, but you cannot choose me now that I'm the only choice."

"Once I was on the other side of my grief, I believe I would have chosen you. You're someone I've wanted to explore since the beginning, but when I had the chance to resurrect Atlas, I couldn't leave him dead. Not when he was killed so young."

"Not when you still loved him," Tala adds softly.

"Not when I still loved him," I agree. I walk to the edge of the roof, leaning on the ledge as I stare down at the city. Atlas and I should be able to walk on those streets, but he's gone forever and I'm working to accept that. That means opening myself up to another hand to hold through the world. "You and I talked about my heart being reborn. Rebirth doesn't mean a fresh start. It means I've lived before and I carry that with me. It means believing that I can find someone else who makes me excited about life even though I've lost love to death. In my heart, that someone else is you, Tala."

Tala walks over but still keeps distance between us. "It is hard to trust your heart, even though mine wants you too."

"What can I do to earn your trust?"

Tala is quiet, staring at the sky. "Before trusting you with my heart, I need to watch how you hold yours as you continue grieving the boy you loved. Grief often makes survivors want to fly through life while they still have theirs, but we should have a slow ascent before soaring under the sun, moon, and stars." Tala removes her mask, her amber eyes glowing from the sunlight. "If your heart is truly reborn, then I will share mine with you." She pulls the paper bird out of her pocket, kissing its head before handing it to me; it feels like a piece of her heart that I will hold close. "I hope to see you in the sky soon, Maribelle."

"As soon as you'll have me, Tala."

I watch as this beautiful Halo Knight puts her mask back on before spinning on her heel and climbing atop her phoenix. I walk over to Roxana and kiss her between the eyes, just as Tala did with my paper bird.

"Fly safely," I say.

"We will," Tala says.

That's exactly what Tala and I will be doing—we'll be flying safely through our relationship. As badly as I wish Tala would invite me along for a ride, not rushing into anything will pave the way for clearer skies, where our hearts and minds won't be clouded by the grief that brought us together.

The phoenix kicks off into the air, carrying the Halo Knight away from me—for now.

My visions might prophesize death, but in my heart of hearts I foresee Tala in my life. In the future, my arms link around her waist as we soar under the sun and moon and stars. The blowing winds will always remind me of how we're able to be with each other because of how Atlas lifted us into the sky before accepting his own death.

I will live for him, I will live for her, and I will live for myself.

Forevermore.

THE BRIGHT SIDE

BRIGHTON

In the end I was a hero, but for all infinity I will be a cautionary tale.

After turning myself over to the authorities and confessing all my crimes, I pled guilty to everything because I don't need to be the face of a trial that pointlessly disrupts Emil's and Prudencia's lives. It's a good thing I'm no longer immortal because the judge sentenced me to life in prison; no one needs psychic powers to have seen that ruling coming. It's only been a month behind bars and I've already tried phasing through the wall multiple times, ready to live my life on the run, but I never make it to the other side. I never will again.

My cooperation—and a plea from golden-child Emil to Sunstar—has granted me a single cell until the end of the year, just until things settle. Stories of the Infinity Reaper have traveled far and wide, and there's no telling who wants me dead. Some inmates are furious that I didn't cause a mass breakout like I did at the Bounds. Others worship me for killing so many enforcers. The officers here hate me for the same reason. No one seems to care that I'm no longer the Infinity

Reaper. That I'm just an eighteen-year-old who is scared of dying all over again.

The single cell is a privilege, but I'm beginning to wish I had company. The longer I sit here, the more I realize I don't want a stranger—I want the millions of strangers who proudly called themselves Brightsiders. Not having the internet reminds me of a time I was grounded by Ma and Dad for mocking Emil's low grades. I wasn't allowed to go on the internet all weekend, which felt like an eternity. I'd still had so many freedoms like watching educational programming, reading a book, going to the rooftop, even helping Emil with his homework, but I didn't do any of that. That's all been added to my mounting list of regrets. Not knowing what's being said about me has only made me more anxious, but I'm slowly accepting that I've lost my infinite access to the internet. If I could ultimately use my platform to do good, what's stopping me from using it recklessly again as I did all my powers? Not having the internet, that's what.

"You have a visitor," an officer tells me.

I cooperate with all the officer's security measures so I can go see Emil. He's only been allowed to visit me once, and that was the day after the election. It was hard for the both of us, especially because everything was still so fresh for me and I couldn't stop myself from crying over how happy I was to see him and how sorry I was for everything I did. I desperately wanted to take back my plea and go to trial and pray that a jury would forgive my crimes because I was young and stupid and grieving. But just like everyone else, I have to live by my choices.

I'm brought out to the visitation booth, but Emil is not on the other side of the partition—it's Prudencia. She's wearing a blue beanie over her long dark hair, a pale green trench coat, and gauntlets over her wrists that temporarily bind her powers, which is standard procedure for any celestial visitors. She watches as the officer uncuffs me before we pick up our phones.

"Hi, Pru."

"Hi, Brighton."

"I can't believe you're here."

"Me either, honestly."

When I turned myself in, Prudencia kept her distance. She was crying from across the street, but she refused to come any closer, as if she still viewed me as the most dangerous person alive even though I was already powerless.

"How are you?" I ask.

Prudencia bites her bottom lip. "I don't know how much I want you knowing about me."

There's a voice rising to the surface, one that wants to yell at her for coming here to talk to me but not wanting to answer a simple question. I bury that voice, pushing it into the same unreachable corners where my powers are bound. "Do you think I'm going to hurt you again? I don't have any powers or any internet—"

"You don't need powers or internet to break a heart, Brighton."

This hurts, reminding me of when she called me a dangerous egomaniac. Now that I've sat with it, I know she was being honest. I'm the one who was being hurtful when I told her to keep her love, even though I really wanted it.

"I'm sorry," I say.

"Sorry for what?"

"Breaking your heart. Pushing you away." It's uncomfortable

maintaining eye contact, but this might be the last time she ever shows her face around here. "I was so obsessed with being the best hero that I stopped being a decent person. You didn't trust me with powers, but you still gave me the benefit of the doubt that I would act responsibly. If I listened to you, I wouldn't be serving this sentence. I could be out in the world with everything I ever wanted—the powers, the fame, my brother . . . and you."

Prudencia's eyes tear up, but she shakes it off. "I wish you proved me wrong."

"Me too. I promise I'll never take you for granted again."

She sighs. "You better not or I'll never visit again."

"You're going to come back?"

"Not as often as Emil, but yes . . . I'll check in on you when work isn't busy."

"Work? Did you get a job?"

"I haven't started yet, but I've begun training. You're looking at a new Spell Walker."

My shocked face reflects back on me from the partition. "You're a Spell Walker?"

Prudencia raises a finger. "If you're going to be weird or jealous or treat me like a Celestials of New York profile, I will walk away."

I shake my head. "No, I'm just . . . surprised? You've always concealed your powers so you could have a normal life and now you're becoming a high-profile hero?"

"The world already knows who I am because of you and Emil."

"I'm sorry about that too."

"I chose to follow you all into war. You're my friends."

It means a lot that she's calling me a friend. "What inspired you to join now that Emil and I aren't involved in the war anymore?"

"I want to help move the world in the right direction. Using my voice at protests as an undercover celestial was great, but I'm done hiding. Besides, if the Luminary Union is going to be a trustworthy replacement for enforcers, we're going to need celestials who are responsible with their powers. I trust myself—as does Maribelle."

"Maribelle?"

"Sorry, I guess you wouldn't have heard. Maribelle is the new leader of the Spell Walkers. Everyone else has stepped down to lead normal lives. Maribelle always admired me and my power and trusted me to represent the group. I slept on it before accepting the offer. I'm the first recruit of the new team and will help her find new Spell Walkers."

I try hiding my jealousy. It was hard enough watching Emil become a Spell Walker and then Iris rejecting me to become one when I had powers, but now Prudencia has been formally chosen too? I want to claim that I wouldn't have been pushed to villainy if only I'd been welcomed in as a Spell Walker, but that's a lie. I would've tried taking over the group.

"That's amazing," I say through gritted teeth.

"You're upset."

"I'm—"

"Don't lie."

I stop myself before I do. "I'm upset at myself. It's my fault I'm missing out on this. But you, uh, you're going to be amazing. I mean that."

Prudencia nods, taking this in. "This is also why I didn't want to say anything. You can't be having an easy time being powerless again."

Nothing about this has been easy. I've been in withdrawal, isolated from family and friends, and haunted by all my executions. The cell block isn't quiet, but the other inmates screaming in the middle of the night is nothing compared to the anguished cries I hear in my head from the victims I personally sliced open or set on fire. The nightmares are even worse, especially the ones with Emil's dead body.

"I miss how powerful I was. How intimidating, even. If I were free, I would try and find a reversal to the Starstifler and never part ways with my powers again. That's terrible, I know."

"It is. It's also honest. That means I can trust you."

"Do you hate me?"

Prudencia's eyes tear up, but she allows herself to cry this time. "Some days I hate you so much that I end up hating myself too for not doing enough to stop you sooner." She then presses her palm against the glass. "Today I don't hate you. Today I'm seeing the boy I first became friends with . . . the boy I wanted to be my boyfriend. Today my heart breaks for you and not because of you."

I wish I could phase through this partition to hug her, to kiss her. I press my hand against the glass instead.

"I should go," Prudencia says, wiping her eyes. She's about to hang up, when I stop her.

"Do you think I could've been a good boyfriend to you?"

"No," Prudencia says. That one word is like being stabbed by the infinity-ender again. I should've let her walk away instead of exposing myself to heartbreak like this. She grins slightly and adds, "But just because something is unlikely doesn't mean it's impossible."

I smile as Prudencia hangs up the phone. I wave goodbye before the handcuffs come on.

Once I'm back in my cell, I reflect on everything; that's all there is to do.

Everyone is defined by their choices: Dad and Ma chose to adopt Emil, raising him as my brother; Emil chose to be a hero who never killed, and now he's living his life freely without blood on his hands or a weight on his soul; Prudencia chose to keep her powers a secret and is now becoming a Spell Walker to fight for equality so no one will live in fear as she did; and I chose to drink the elixir that turned me into the Infinity Reaper, where I played judge, jury, and executioner, before choosing to bind my powers and turn myself in for my own crimes.

Now, behind bars, I choose to accept I was the Infinity Savior too.

I saved lives with my powers.

I saved this country by exposing a soulless politician.

I saved the world by not resurrecting my parents.

Those choices were mine to make, marking me as a hero when it mattered most.

One day, I will die in this cell, painfully ordinary, but I got to be extraordinary first.

That's how I'm choosing to look at the bright side.

INFINITY ENDING

EMIL

I'm living on the other side of infinity.

I wish Ma and Brighton were living it with me.

This year was hard enough with losing Dad, but I would've never bet on everything only going more and more downhill as our family found themselves in a war that was generations in the making. What the hell happened to waking up to find Brighton editing his latest YouTube video or Ma's good-morning kisses or Dad cooking up breakfast before we begin our days? How did it get to the point where if I want to see my parents or brother I have to go to the cemetery or prison?

My family might be gone, but I'm not alone.

Like always, Ness has my back.

City life was getting hard because Ness and I couldn't walk down the street without someone stopping to thank us for our services (which is unnecessary but appreciated) or cursing us out for rigging the election (which is really unnecessary and straight-up wrong). I suck at telling who's who when they walk up to us, but Ness is a lot better at figuring that out. Like the grown man last week who threw on a smile that I trusted, and Ness knocked out the man before his knife could reach my stomach; I wouldn't have healed from that. That's when we decided to bounce from the city, relocating from the hotel Sunstar put us in to Ness's family house in Albany, where we're hidden from the world by top-tier illusionists.

The house still legally belongs to his father, but since Iron is in prison as he awaits trial, we're taking it over. Ness doesn't want a damn thing to do with the manor where he grew up, saying that everything about it feels poisonous, unlike this house, which wasn't really lived in because Iron preferred operating directly in the city. It helps that Ness has positive memories of putting on shows for his mother in the barn house as if it were a Broadway theater. He's been promising to put on a show for me all week—and I think tonight is the night.

I'm in the living room, reading Dad's once-favorite book, wanting to feel closer to him and figure out why he stopped loving it, when Ness comes back inside the house.

"I got something to show you," Ness says.

"Showtime?" I ask, setting down the book on the coffee table.

I don't play dumb because Ness has been in the barn the past couple of hours and it's not like we've got animals or creatures we're looking after here.

"Sort of," Ness says. He helps me up from the couch but doesn't let go of my hand.

Today marks one month since Election Day—since Ness and I became boyfriends.

We're committed to each other, but we're taking the relationship slow, especially since we're both going through some really low lows. Sometimes I need to be held when grieving Ma or missing Brighton, and other times I need to sit alone on the porch swing and mourn my old life. Some days Ness is really seeing me as we're hanging out, and other days he's staring right through me as he thinks about how unloved he was by his father. No matter what's what, Ness and I are able to go to bed every night, wrapping ourselves around each other, knowing we're sleeping with the person we want to be with more than anyone else on the planet.

Outside the barn, Ness covers my eyes with his hands and guides me inside.

"You ready?" he asks.

"Ready for what?"

"Your show," he says.

Then Ness lets me see everything he's been working on. This barn was once nothing but a patio table, bales of hay, wooden beams and steel wires for fences that were never made, and rows of bricks Ness had used as a stage, but like the transformer he is, he's done it up. The steel wires have been staked into the ground with string lights woven into them. The projector we used to watch a movie outside a couple nights ago is now sitting on the dining table, casting a light onto the brick stage, which has been leveled out. I'm kind of obsessed with the brown, yellow, and red leaves we were playing in this morning now being swept inside into two lines, creating an aisle that leads me to one of two chairs that face the stage.

"Are we expecting someone else?" I ask.

"We're not," Ness says sadly.

"I can hit up Pru if you want. She can probably use a night out after all her Spell Walker training and—"

"I only want you," Ness interrupts, a smile breaking out.

"I only want you too."

Ness kisses me. "Wish me luck."

"Good luck. You got this. I believe in you."

Ness hops onstage and gestures to the audience—me, only me. "Welcome to my one-man, one-night-only special. This show is dedicated to two people. First, my mother, who should be here tonight," he says, looking at the empty chair beside me. That explains why he sounded so sad. "If it weren't for her, I would've grown up an absolute monster with no respect for anyone who wasn't like me." He puts his hands together, directing them at me. "And it's dedicated to you too. You inspire me to be a hero . . . and I can't think of a better person in this world who I want to be with when I take off my mask forever." He reaches inside his jacket and holds out a vial—a potion. "This show is an anti-performance. No more pretending to be anyone else."

Over the past month, Ness has brought up binding his powers a few times, but he kept getting nervous to actually go through with it. I never pushed him because I get it. This is a choice we all have to make—I made mine; Brighton made his.

I raise my hand.

"It's a show, not a Q and A," he says.

"It's an amazing show! I just . . . This is really big."

"I know. That's why I'm putting on this 'amazing' show."

"I guess I'm just curious why now?"

Ness nods slowly. "I've gotten so used to paying attention to other people that it's time I figure out who I am. It's hard to rediscover myself when I can be anyone." He puts a hand on his heart. "I just want to be me . . . and I only want to be myself around you, firefly."

I smile. "Don't ever let me stop you from being you."

Ness takes a deep breath as he stares at the potion. "Time for curtain," he says as he opens the vial and drinks the Starstifler. His face scrunches up in disgust as he consumes every last drop. Then he braces himself, knowing what's about to come after watching his father go through the same thing. Ness glows gray as his shoulders jerk around and his knees fold in. His body inflates and shrinks. His skin lightens and darkens. His face changes into so many others like mine and his father's and his mother's before all those masks fall away with one final gray glow.

"You good?" I ask, standing at the edge of the stage even though I don't remember standing.

Ness stares at his hands before smiling at me. "I'm good. . . . I'm me."

"You're you," I say, hopping up on the stage. I hold his hands in mine, his hands, which are always going to be his from here on out. The transformations put his body through it, and sweat is glistening on his smooth brown skin, racing down his cheeks to his jaw. I stare at his lips as he catches his breath before gazing into his beautiful amber eyes. "Wow, so . . . this is really just your face. You're just legit this beautiful."

"Did you think I was faking my face?"

"Maybe a little. It seemed too perfect to not have some gleam backing it up."

"That's all me, firefly," Ness says, pulling me in so close that heat rushes to my cheeks.

"It's definitely all you, and I . . . I think I'm ready for you to see all of me."

Ness's eyes widen. "Really? I'm happy to keep waiting until you're ready—"

"I'm ready, I swear. I just trust you with my heart, and I'm ready to trust you with the rest of my body."

Our fingers are locked as we run out the barn, through the garden, and into the house, straight up the stairs into Ness's bedroom—the bedroom we've made our bedroom. His shirt flies off, as he's always been confident in his body, saying himself that he had even shifted into different shapes before recognizing he liked himself best. And I get it because it seems like the whole world is into anyone with a toned chest and smooth abs. But no matter what natural shape Ness takes as life goes on, I'll always be into him, just like I know he'll be into me. I throw off my shirt, which definitely isn't new, especially as we go to bed, but I really let him take me in before we remove any more clothes. Some days I'm still not about my body, as a voice tells me I'm not good enough, but I'm into myself a lot more these days. I remind myself this is a survivor's body and it's on me to keep taking care of it, to love everything about it—even honoring the scars that vanished after I resurrected. Those scars will always be a part of me.

"You're beautiful," Ness whispers as his gaze travels from my bare chest to my eyes.

I take a deep breath, shaking as I drop my pants and reveal everything. There's a part of me that wants to hide, that wishes I could shift into a different body, but those thoughts go up in flames when Ness smiles at me, all of me, at this body whose reflection in a mirror sometimes upsets me. My boyfriend is so into me, and this is going to help out on how I see myself. Ness bares all too. It's unreal how real he is. He lays me down in our bed and explores every inch of my body with his fingers and lips. I'm running hot, like I'm still the Infinity Son and casting fire, but everything I'm feeling is just human. Ness doesn't need any gleamcraft to speed up my breathing or get me moaning. He's just showing me love. The first second I get to pay back the favor, I explore his body too.

And then everything begins happening.

I'm so happy to be alive for this, that my ashes became flesh again so I could feel *this*. If I could still retrocycle, I'd be returning to this moment time and time again because it's so damn euphoric, but I can't, so Ness and I will just have to keep re-creating this.

What I'm loving so much about our relationship is that Ness and I are rediscovering ourselves as individuals while also figuring out who we are as a couple. As former specters of shifter and phoenix blood, Ness and I know a lot about reinvention. The longer we're lucky enough to live, the more changes we're going to face. Everything won't always be for the good. It's only been a month and sometimes I get nervous that Ness is going to change his mind about me as quickly as he was able to change faces. But I'm not going to live my life like it's the end of the world—not anymore.

We're both survivors in a war that killed us, and now that we're alive, it's on us to live.

This is an amazing start.

The sun is high, but that mid-December chill is not joking.

Ness and I are bundled up in coats and winter gear because the cold hits extra hard upstate.

"I miss my powers," I say. A fire-orb would be amazing right now.

"No, you don't. You just hate the cold," he says, removing his scarf and wrapping it over mine.

"I suck at the cold."

"Wait inside. I'll bring your guest in."

"Our guest," I correct.

Ness rolls his eyes. "I guess."

I bump my shoulder into his. "Look, Wyatt is one of my best friends, but you're my one and only boyfriend."

"Well played."

During our first week together, Ness asked if we could have a talk about "the Halo Knight in the room." No matter how much Ness wanted to be my partner, he never hated Wyatt. He seemed more upset at himself for getting abducted by his father's forces, leading me to believe he was dead. Ness had concerns that I might fall for Wyatt again, and I'm not psychic, but I feel it in my bones that Wyatt is someone who I love and was there for me at a time when I missed Ness so much that I never wanted to regret not acting on my feelings again. That plus experiencing all of Keon's love for Astin and Bautista's for Sera just illuminated who had my heart all along.

Still, I love Wyatt and I was so happy to hear that he was back in the country. He returned to London before the election to spend time with his parents, especially after his close call with death, as well as meeting with the senior Halo Knights, who not only reinstated him but promoted him to co-lieutenant of the Bronze Wings with Tala.

I smile as Nox appears in the bright sky, descending in a smooth spiral, the beating of his wings blowing more cool air into my face as his talons sink into the dying garden. Then Wyatt perks his head, waving from phoenixback. He dismounts, looking geared up against the cold too. Underneath his new bronze leather jacket with black feathered sleeves, Wyatt is wearing a dark hoodie and a gray wrap that looks like a scarf but is tied across his chest.

"How is one supposed to wear a crop top in this weather?" Wyatt asks as he walks toward us, holding his jacket close.

"One is not supposed to wear a crop top in this weather," Ness says in a solid English accent.

"A travesty to hide our bodies under so many layers. Shall we run inside?" Wyatt asks, storming past us and into the house.

Ness squints. "Did he just let himself in?"

"That's Wyatt for you."

We go inside, following the sound of Wyatt's heavy boots into the living room to find that he's already taken off his jacket and gray wrap, bundling them together on the couch where I do my reading. I'm honestly surprised he still has the hoodie on and isn't showing off a crop top.

"What's a gent got to do to get a hug around here?" Wyatt asks, arms open.

"You're being weird," Ness says.

"I am being perfectly pleasant. You are projecting, my friend."

Ness squints. "I know how to read people. Emil, tell him he's being weird."

"You're being weird," I say.

Wyatt gasps. "I see you've traded your shape-shifting for mind control."

"Not a real power," Ness says.

"That's what the mind controllers want you to believe," Wyatt says, clicking his tongue. "Well, I reject the premise that I am being weird, but I will admit that I am being a bit dodgy because I have a surprise—"

A sound interrupts him.

"Did your jacket just . . . chirp?" I ask.

Wyatt lets out a deep, exaggerated sigh. "No, sweet Emil—oh, apologies—I mean, plain Emil," he says, holding up his hands as if Ness is going to come at him. "My jacket did not chirp, but my surprise did . . . a surprise that I hoped would still be sleeping until we had a moment to chat." He goes to the wrap and pulls out a phoenix that's small enough to sit comfortably in his cupped hands. "Why must babies always be so needy?"

I rush over, gently petting the phoenix's gray belly and frizzy gold crown. "A gray sun," I say, smiling so big when the phoenix stretches its tiny dark wings.

Wyatt sways with the phoenix. "He loves being rocked. Makes him feel like he's flying, I reckon."

Ness walks up. "Cute."

"Why, thank you," Wyatt says.

"The bird."

Wyatt winks. "Whatever you say."

I take off my coat and hold out my hands. "Can I . . . ? I'll be careful."

"I'm well aware. I've seen you handle newborns before," Wyatt says, passing the phoenix over. The phoenix pecks at my palm, its beak feeling like the tiniest pinch. "Funny story, but Nox and I were out for a morning ride when he suddenly changed course and found this little guy alone in the forest. I tried tracking down the phoenix's family, but the scent led us nowhere. As you very well know, it's tough with gray suns since they respawn away from their deaths."

"He's lucky you found him," I say, thinking about my own shot of luck with Dad. "What's his name?"

"I've taken to calling him 'Little Guy' when he's being cute and fluffy and 'Little Pain in My Arse' when he's behaving as if I exist solely for him. Perhaps you might have an idea what to call him . . . and be interested in looking after him?"

I suck in a breath, stunned. "Like foster him? For how long?"

"A few months, if that's not too much trouble. We obviously lost many Haloes during the battles at the New Ember Sanctuary, and these younger phoenixes could use some looking after. I'll admit there are dozens of families who are more traditionally trained to look after Little Guy, but I couldn't help but think of your parallels. This phoenix might very well be your soulmate." Wyatt flashes a grin at Ness. "His avian soulmate, my single-faced friend. No need to get worked up over a baby bird."

"Good to know," Ness says, looking over my shoulder at the phoenix. "If you want to do this, firefly, I'll help you."

I feel destined to watch over him but scared to go through with it too. "What if I get him killed like Gravesend?"

Wyatt shakes his head. "That happened during the height of a conflict with an alchemist who is long gone. I know you will torture yourself anyway because you're a sensitive soul, but Gravesend's tragic death is not a burden you need to carry for the rest of your life. Trust me here. Even if you and Little Guy do not bond for life, this could still be healing for the both of you."

The gray sun phoenix chirps, looking up at me with its pearl eyes.

I think about how Dad didn't trust anyone to look after me and gave me the best life. I can do the same for this phoenix, however long we have together.

"I'll do it," I say, gently kissing the phoenix on his head.

"Fantastic! You're an absolute hero, Emil. Your willingness to devote yourself to caring for phoenixkind really demonstrates what an excellent Halo Knight you would be. I have said as much to the Council of Phoenixlight. Naturally I was met with resistance, but even more naturally, I can be a tad persistent, especially in my new role, and I reminded them that no one has done more for phoenixkind in years than you. That included them, which should have gotten me sacked, until they reviewed the truth. You're the reason Brighton forfeited his powers before killing more of our phoenixes and people. You secured the Starstifler formula in the past and brought it into the present, where it will be so widely produced that few will bother hunting down phoenixes for powers that we will only quickly bind. You have saved phoenixes from extinction and honored the natural cycle of life and death by making sure the resurrection ritual remains a secret. And as if all that isn't enough, you honored your word by binding your phoenix powers, even after it brought you back from the dead stronger than ever. No one can dispute that you, Emil Rey, were born—reborn!—to be a Halo Knight. What say you?"

My life isn't infinite, but it's still going on and on, and I hope it doesn't end anytime soon.

Every day that passes, I have to remind myself that I died and have come back stronger. Maybe not in power anymore, but definitely in spirit. That's the only way to get through the tough times, like this past holiday season, which was my first—and unfortunately won't be my last—without my brother or parents. But I did get to hang out with my new family at the upstate house: my boyfriend, Ness; my best friend, Prudencia; my new boss, Wyatt; all the throwback Spell Walkers I fought alongside; my sort-of friend Maribelle, and her sort-of girlfriend, Tala; and, of course, my phoenix companion, Gris Rey, whose name translates to "gray king," which fits since I live to serve that little guy who is growing so fast.

It's not a perfect life, but it's a promising one.

At the start of the year, I officially began studying to become a Halo Knight. I'm definitely not a fighter, so I won't be training for field combat like Tala, and my face is too famous to be an undercover investigator like Wyatt, but it turns out I'm a natural at tending to young phoenixes, so I'm going to be stationed at the New Ember Sanctuary once it's rebuilt. The Council of Phoenixlight even suggested that I could travel the country, maybe even the world, to tell my story and speak to the dangers of blood alchemy to further ward off any specter aspirants.

Today is Inauguration Day. It was an honor being in attendance with the Spell Walkers, old and new, and watching Sunstar address the nation with powerful words about history, hope, security, and unity. I couldn't hang long after, even though it would've been great to chat with some of the future Luminaries who were in attendance. I just had to go be with someone else who played a big role in making today possible.

I'm at the prison, sitting across from Brighton, pressing photographs of Gris against the window between us. He's surprised at how big Gris has gotten since the pictures I showed him a couple weeks ago during my first visit of the new year. For someone who ruthlessly killed cycles of phoenixes, he's really invested in Gris living a long life. He checks in on if Gris has made any progress with flying, which he really hasn't, but he's still young. If Gris is still struggling, I trust that he'll retrocycle to relearn that skill.

"Look at you, bro." Brighton has a proud smile. "You're a Halo Knight with a phoenix son."

"Who would've thought."

I received my official Halo Knight jacket when I began my studies, which isn't tradition, but the Council of Phoenixlight is fast-tracking some things since I'm a high-profile recruit. I'm really not about the special treatment, but having the gear made this next phase of my life feel even more real. My sleeves are still mainly just the black cactus leather like the rest of the jacket, but Gris has shed a few dark feathers that I've been able to weave in around one wrist. And my bond with Gris is growing stronger and stronger every day. Sometimes I understand him so well that it's like I still have powers to sense his emotions. It's just all about connection.

Like the one I still have with my brother.

"You really should've been there today," I say. This inauguration was to celebrate Sunstar and her administration, but this ceremony could've looked really different if Brighton hadn't used his platform to expose Iron for the fraud he is.

"Maybe Sunstar will make it up to me with a much-welcomed pardon," Brighton jokes.

"Hey, unlikely doesn't mean impossible, right?"

"It's safe to call this one impossible, bro." Brighton not holding on to a flicker of hope breaks my heart. "I haven't made peace with life behind bars yet, but to pass the time I've been creating visions about the future, as if I got Abuelita's power. It's comforting."

"Visions about what?"

"Everything. Everyone."

"Me?"

"Of course you."

"What do you see?"

Brighton's green eyes tear up. "You live a long life as a Halo Knight, eventually becoming a Gold Wing. You're awarded a medal for your preservation of phoenixkind. You marry Ness, who becomes a politician even though he wanted out of that world. Everyone thinks he should run for president, but he doesn't want that much power and would rather focus on your family. You adopt two kids, who you raise as your own flesh and blood. One boy was abandoned and the other had an abusive father. No one knows how to love those boys more than you and Ness. The boys become brothers who are so close they can't believe they're not blood. They also know none of that matters. Family is family."

I'm crying, praying to every star in the galaxy that Brighton is secretly psychic.

"Where are you in all this?" I ask.

"I'm here . . . and I'm happy that my brother is alive and living the life he deserves."

I wipe my tears, hating that we can be this close and feel like we're in different universes, where time moves on for me but freezes for him.

Brighton press his knuckles against the glass and looks at me knowingly.

We fist-bump through the window and whistle into our own phones.

"I love you, bro."

"I love you too, Bright."

This is one of those times where I have to remind myself that even though I died, I came back strong enough to not have my soul vanquished by the heartbreak of my brother not being in my life anymore. And the beautiful truth is that's a lie. Brighton spending the rest of his life in prison doesn't mean he's dead. He's alive, and there's no way I'm going to go live in the world he helped save and pretend he's buried six feet under.

We're brothers—the Reys of Light for life.

And those lives are limited, so I've got to make sure that everything I do, I do it using the strongest power I have.

I'm on my last life, and I'm dead set on living it right.

ACKNOWLEDGMENTS

Ever since I was a kid, I've dreamed about writing my own fantasy series, and with this conclusion to the Infinity Cycle, that dream has come true. I feel so truly charmed.

I have infinite people to thank, but I don't have infinite pages to thank them because there are paper shortages around the world and this 700+ page book isn't helping that issue, so I'm going to rein it in here as best as I can.

First, thank you to Andrew Eliopulos for helping me open the Infinity Cycle and to Alexandra Cooper for helping me close it. Andrew edited *Infinity Son* and *Infinity Reaper*, and Alex edited *Infinity Kings*, which is basically as long as those first two volumes combined so also twice as hard, but they both worked their magic on this series and I'll be grateful for all of INFINITY. (Does this make sense grammatically? I don't know. I also don't have to care because the series is done so STET for voice, STET for voice, STET for voice!) And truly, a much-needed, much-deserved special shout-out to Alex for her work on *Infinity Kings*, which involved many calls in many time zones as I traveled the world while drafting and her many late nights working on this behemoth that she knew meant such a great deal to me. It's not easy for an editor to dive into a series right at the finale, but she worked with me as if she's been here all along. Thanks for falling out of the sky, superhero-style, to help save the day, Alex!

Jodi Reamer, who always helps me get the time I need to write my books, but also lovingly pushed me to get this done for the patient (and even not-so patient!) readers who had basically waited all of infinity for me to close out this trilogy.

Kaitlin López, for all her assistance across the board, but especially for the editorial backup. She has such a great eagle eye and my favorite catch of hers this time definitely has to be me spelling a character's name wrong for an entire 700+ page book. (I'm sorry, Esther!) (Please note that I just had to double-check the spelling of Esther's name and indeed wrote it wrong the first time because I'm a mess.) (Thank you, Kaitlin.)

My HarperCollins crew + our incredible freelancers: Rosemary Brosnan, Allison Weintraub, Michael D'Angelo, Audrey Diestelkamp, Nellie Kurtzman, Lauren Levite, Jennifer Corcoran, Erin DeSalvatore, Mark Rifkin, Allison Brown, Amy Ryan, Jacqueline Hornberger, Patty Rosati and the school and library team, Kerry Moynagh, Kathy Faber, and the sales team. And thank you to Erin Fitzsimmons and David Curtis for their work on designing some of the most gorgeous covers in existence, and to artist Kevin Tong for my favorite phoenixes ever and artist Meybis Ruiz Cruz for making Emil, Brighton, Ness, and Maribelle look cooler than I ever imagined.

My Writers House crew! Shout-out to Cecilia de La Campa and Alessandra Birch, who are so brilliant at getting my books around the world, and for all the fun I've had with them around the world too.

My mom, Persi Rosa, for having the best heart ever. Well, maybe not literally the best heart ever given all her medical issues, but definitely the best heart when it comes to love. There was a big moment that I was building to in this series that I was scared to write and almost backed out of it, but one call with my mom gave me the blessing to see it through and it made this story so much more powerful—and sadder. I love you, Mom! And my brother, Andrew Silvera, because I couldn't have written this series without knowing about the many shades of brotherhood.

My dog, Tazzito No-Middle-Name Silvera. Having a dog who will whine and huff when it gets too late because he wants to go to bed and cuddle with me has helped me create a better work-life balance where I don't stay up all night writing and instead get much-needed rest to be there for Tazz AND myself. And thank you to Traci and the entire Doggie Goddess family for showing Tazz all the love at daycare whenever I'm traveling and on deadline.

My friends: Luis Rivera, Jordin Rivera, Georgia Rivera, Miles Rivera, ILYTM! Elliot Knight for being Ness in the audiobooks and for being Elliot in life. Arvin Ahmadi, Robbie Couch, Anita Lashey, Jeff Kasanoff, and Tyler Sage Alvarez for getting me out of the house (even out of the country!) when I was writing too much, and an extra shout-out to Arvin for staying in the house with me so I could write even more. David Arnold, Jasmine Warga, Nicola and David Yoon, Sabaa Tahir, Dhonielle Clayton, Mark Oshiro, Patrice Caldwell, Zoraida Córdova, Marie Lu, Tahereh Mafi, Ransom Riggs, Angie Thomas, and Victoria Aveyard, who have cheered me on since the start of this series and all the way up to the end. Alex Aster for hyping me up whenever I was getting down on myself. Ryan La Sala and Aaron Aceves for loving Brighton. Susan Dennard, whose newsletters on craft helped me so much throughout this entire series. Victoria Mele, okay, alright, okay, alright. Amanda Diaz, Michael Diaz, Cecilia Renn, Sandra Gonzalez, and Michael Martinez for all the love, no matter where we are. And huge thanks to Sabaa Tahir, who kindly gave me her blessing to open this book with the perfect quote from *A Torch Against the Night*.

My readers, particularly those who followed me into these Infinity books. This series hasn't found the same success as my They Both Die at the End novels, which made it really hard at times to write the third book for a trilogy it sometimes felt like no one was even waiting for, but that was a lie I had to stop telling myself because the Infinity readers kept finding me—online, book festivals, even just out and about—asking me where the last book was. So thank you for asking, thank you for waiting, thank you for reading. I hope you love this finale as much as I do.

And, lastly, this is a first for me, but I'd like to acknowledge myself. Between the darkness happening in my life while writing *Infinity Reaper* and a deeper, angrier darkness while writing *Infinity Kings*, I'm genuinely surprised that I lived long enough to finish this series. But I'm alive and I'm so proud of that, maybe even more than this entire trilogy, which I wrote for Young Adam as much as I wrote it for Still-Youngish-But-Also-Older Adam. But the work I've done—the work I *had* to do on myself—is paving the way for more Older Adams. Not quite Infinity Adam, but hopefully an Old Adam who will have loved living as long as he has instead of the Past Adams—and even, at the time of this writing, the Now Adam—who have thought that life is sometimes too long. So while the work on this series may be done, the work for Older Adams continues.